# READER'S DIGEST

## CONDENSED BOOKS

# FIRST EDITION

Published by

**THE READER'S DIGEST ASSOCIATION LIMITED**
25 Berkeley Square, London W1X 6AB.

**THE READER'S DIGEST ASSOCIATION SOUTH AFRICA (PTY) LTD.**
Nedbank Centre, Strand Street, Cape Town

Printed in Great Britain by Petty & Sons Ltd., Leeds

Original cover design by Jeffery Matthews A.R.C.A.

For information as to ownership
of copyright in the material in this book see last page

ISBN 0 340 21559 3

# READER'S DIGEST
# CONDENSED BOOKS

## THE PILOT
**Robert P. Davis**

## TOUCH NOT THE CAT
**Mary Stewart**

## VETS MIGHT FLY
**James Herriot**

## HARRY'S GAME
**Gerald Seymour**

COLLECTOR'S LIBRARY
EDITION

# In this volume

## THE PILOT
### by Robert P. Davis (p.9)

Alcohol and flying are a lethal combination. Capt. Mike Hagen, however, believed it something that he could control. After all, he'd been flying all his life and was one of the best pilots Intercontinental Airlines had. His wife certainly didn't help. But there was

always Pat, the woman he loved and planned to marry—one day, when his children were old enough to understand. One day he'd have that frank talk with his wife. One day he'd quit the drink. Except that *one day* might not be soon enough.

## TOUCH NOT THE CAT
### by Mary Stewart (p.129)

It did not worry Bryony Ashley that she would not inherit her ancient family home. The magnificent but dilapidated mansion within its encircling moat was more of a liability than an asset. But when the warning in her father's muddled, dying words was secretly echoed by her "lover", the Ashley motto, *Touch not the Cat*, took on a new and sinister significance. Perhaps her enigmatic cousins would be able to set her mind at rest. . . .

Here, once again, Mary Stewart—master story-teller—weaves an unrivalled tale of mystery, suspense, and romance.

## VETS MIGHT FLY
*by James Herriot* (p.271)

At the beginning of the last war James Herriot—whose recollections of his life as a vet have already delighted countless readers—joined the RAF, leaving his young wife safely back at home in the Yorkshire Dales, while he went off to basic training in London. His ambition was to become a pilot. To fly.

During those early, hilarious weeks as a recruit, however, it is hardly surprising that his thoughts were often to return to the country people he knew and loved. Jim Oakley, the postman, for instance, who knew a trick worth two of the vet's. Or old Mrs. Ainsworth and the Christmas cat. . . .

## HARRY'S GAME
*by Gerald Seymour* (p.385)

As one of television's leading news reporters, the author of this powerful novel has seen for himself the drama and tragedy of Northern Ireland today. He writes vividly of the bitterness, the bravery, the betrayals . . . and the love that can flower even in the war-torn streets of Ardoyne and Andersonstown.

Harry's game? A deadly kind of chess in which—unless you were very careful—there would be no winners, only losers. And Harry Brown, the army's special agent, could lose most of all.

# THE PILOT

A CONDENSATION OF THE BOOK BY

## Robert P. Davis

ILLUSTRATED BY HARRY J. SCHAARE

PUBLISHED BY HAMISH HAMILTON, LONDON

Mike Hagen was one of the safest of men—an experienced airline pilot. With a faultless record and more than twenty-six thousand flying hours to his credit he was now captaining sophisticated DC-8s for Intercontinental Airlines. He was good with the passengers. He was good with the planes.

But Mike Hagen was also one of the most dangerous of men—an experienced drinker. His speech was never slurred. You never saw him falling about. He flew like a dream. Not one of his fellow crew members ever guessed that when he left the flight deck for brief intervals he was taking quick "spookers" of whiskey from the thermos flask he had with him. Like all experienced drinkers, Mike believed that he had his habit strictly under control. He never believed that the time would come when it might cause him to endanger the plane and everyone on it. And if that time ever did come, he told himself he'd quit. Either the drink, or the job, or both.

But things didn't work out that way. Quitting wasn't so easy. And the battle Mike had—with the survival of himself and his crew and his passengers at stake—makes a tension-packed story, impossible to put down.

## ONE

IN WINTER it was always dark when he got up, but Mike Hagen hadn't been asleep very long. He didn't remember whether he had passed out when the late movie started or finished, but the booze had gotten to his head and he woke up at 3:00 a.m. looking straight at a TV test pattern, hearing the buzz from the set. He glanced around the small study on the first floor of his Ridgefield, Connecticut, house as he eased his feet to the cold floor. He always slept downstairs when he was going out early. He brought his stocky frame upright, feeling the stiffness in his neck and the hot dryness in his mouth.

Padding across the scatter rug to the small bathroom off the kitchen, he hit a roller skate and bumped hard against the doorjamb. He stopped to listen for Jean to open her door or for one of his two children to awaken, but the stillness remained, so he continued to the bathroom, where he flicked on the light and looked at himself in the mirror.

He did not look forty-two, he thought. Although his eyes were puffy and there were dark circles under them, his hair was still abundant and amber brown, not dull or streaked with gray. Mike thought he looked a little like a young John Wayne, but there was a bit more of the Irish in his face, and a ruddiness crisscrossed by rivulets of minute blood vessels, the tiny, damning evidences of a man who has drunk too much for too many years.

When Mike awoke prematurely, he had three choices: take sleeping pills; take a drink—but never both—he knew that much; or just go back to bed and toss around for an hour or so until it was time to prepare for his trip. He hated this extra hour.

On mornings like this he would allow himself one drink, and the closer to 7:00 a.m. he could take his "spooker," the better it was. But if he started at 3:00 in the morning, he would need another by 7:00. And if he took a couple of pills to go back to sleep, he would have to drive the sixty-one miles to JFK airport with a barbiturate hangover. He decided to do nothing, and he went back to the study, tried to read for a while; then he put down the book and listened to an all-night radio show.

Finally, after an hour or so, he got up again and made himself coffee and started the bacon. Hot bacon and eggs eased the empty feeling in his stomach, and grease, lots of it, made a large slippery coating. His father, a hearty Irish drinker who had worked as a carpenter in Florida, always told him to "butter up before the sauce." He never forgot that, because his father had escaped liver problems and died at seventy, sitting in the shade of the front porch, still pouring down the Paddys.

After breakfast Mike put on his dark blue pants, white shirt, and a mechanic's jacket marked EL AL. Shortly after 5:00 he gathered the things he'd need for the trip, and then went to the desk in the living room and wrote:

Dear Jean,
    Please see that the bills on the right pile are paid. I think we're behind—there're some dunning letters. See you soon. Kiss the girls for me.                                   Mike

He stepped outside into a slashing, windblown rain. He opened the garage door and put his bags, uniform jacket, and black raincoat into the Nova. Suddenly he remembered his cream. He returned to the house and slipped the half-pint of heavy cream he had bought the night before into the side pocket of his jacket. Then back to the car to start toward Kennedy International Airport.

Driving down the New England Thruway, Mike thought about

his wife, Jean: the way she squandered their money; her room littered with every cosmetic on the market, and expensive dresses tossed aside unworn. Everything that had once been beautiful and gay about this woman was now gone. The love they had shared had evaporated long before they started to use separate bedrooms. Mike often asked himself why he put up with the situation, but he was prone to holding things in, and every time he thought of confronting Jean with those four well-rubbed words, "I want a divorce," he would think of his daughters, Karen and Debbie, and something would stop him.

He felt like hell this morning, but then it was always the same: the first part of the drive was the worst—with the alcoholic fatigue, the dull hangover one gets after years of constant drinking. Then came a feeling of blankness, and finally an out-of-sorts sensation that could lead to a minor panic when, at times, he felt his head was coming off. This didn't happen too often; Mike tried not to drink too much before a working day.

The empty feeling usually returned to his stomach during the last five miles of the drive, when the greasy bacon and eggs finally let the pain through. It was at this time that Mike started counting the minutes to Ellen's Place, a drab, half-hidden bar and grill about nine blocks from JFK. Mike had selected Ellen's carefully. It was far enough away from the airport so the cargo handlers, mechanics, and other airline people wouldn't use it; and most of Ellen's early morning customers were from the milk-distribution plant on the next street.

Mike had been coming to Ellen's for two years. Once he realized that he needed the morning spooker, he had gone on the search for the shabby bar, his launching pad. Finally, one hot summer day after work, he walked into Ellen's and had a drink. He told her he was an El Al mechanic and she laughed at an Irishman working for the Jewish carrier. Now when he walked in there for that first spooker of the morning, he hated himself because he knew he was over the line.

Mike had made up a whole false life for himself for the benefit of Ellen and the customers at the bar who nipped before going to work. The imaginary existence included a wife who taught school and the sons he wished he had. He also talked about how he went to Mass and Communion, which he wanted to be true; how he worked in the Little League and took vacations with his sons out west. Ellen, a buxom, lighthearted widow, listened and never asked too many questions that Mike couldn't answer.

He liked his fantasy life.

The rain seemed to be letting up a bit as he pulled into Ellen's back driveway. Mike stuffed his small thermos into a pocket, drank his half-pint of cream, and moved toward the rear door. The place opened at 6:00 a.m. Mike never got there later than 6:30.

Ellen made him the large cold drink in a special glass with his initials. He looked lovingly at the amber liquid flowing from the bottle of one-hundred-proof Old Grand-Dad over three cubes of ice, and he could already taste the bourbon. The second Mike brought the drink to his parched lips, his world changed. His mind and stomach seemed to ease; the edge was off. He knew there were twenty-three sips to a four-ounce drink the way he took it. One time he had ordered another, but it was too much and he was afraid of the smell, even though he could pack five away by this time without visual effects. Mike had devised a much better way: he gave Ellen the thermos he always carried, which she filled with Old Grand-Dad. Then she put tiny ice cubes in a plastic bag and slid the pouch into the thermos, where it bobbed on a small sea of bourbon.

"Damned smart," she had told him. "They could knock yuh for drinkin' on the job."

Mike had wondered what Ellen would say if she really knew.

Ten minutes later, on this morning of December 10, 1974, Mike reached the Intercontinental Airways building, where he changed into the deep blue jacket with the four gold stripes ringing each sleeve. Over this went the raincoat. He put the thermos in his flight bag. His eyes were slightly glazed, but he had a solution for that also. His captain's hat was one-eighth of a size too large. It slipped down deep on his forehead, so that the visor cast a shadow across his eyes.

As a precaution, Mike took a small pouch from his flight bag—his "survival kit"—which contained a very sharp men's cologne; Sen-Sen, which worked better than the breath sprays or gargles; Visine for his eyes; and a bit of cover-stick makeup that he applied to the

12

side of his left cheek where the blood vessels were beginning to appear like lazy red rivers.

This furtive deception was necessary before he entered Flight Operations—the sterile green-and-white room at JFK which served as a weather-dissemination, flight-plan, and crew-scheduling center. Mike loathed the harshly lit room as much as he loathed the mechanized matter-of-fact quality that characterized modern flying: buttons, numbers, procedures, cockpit challenges and responses, checklists, and rules written by zealous little people in little offices who, according to Mike, neither understood the finer points of aircraft operation nor, more important, human nature.

Mike had started as an agricultural pilot—a crop duster—letting down foul-smelling, eye-blinding fertilizer or pest killers while trying not to hit trees, electric lines, poles, water towers, windmill pumps, all the enemies of low-level precision "row" spraying. Now he thought he could outfly anyone on the IA payroll except, perhaps, for a few of the senior captains who had flown by the seats of their pants in DC-3 days before World War II. But they were rapidly disappearing from the business.

In Mike's mind one needed the sense, the feel of flying, to be really good. He had it. When a guy can twist an "Ag" ship in and out of tree-lined fields, he thought, and not break it up, that's flying—a special perception one learns when the pilot sits in the open and feels the hot clay dust of an Alabama cotton field. That was *his* kind of flying.

Now he had a small, complicated office that went up in the air. The plane could almost fly itself; it all came down to numbers and procedures, not skill, for any fool could read numbers. Judgment was something else. Mike knew he shouldn't be drinking, but he figured his ability wasn't impaired; he still had air instinct, perception of the skies; a copilot; and a big, well-designed plane that flew on an autopilot, which was backed up by another autopilot. At the thought of that, he laughed. It summed up the magnificent sophistication of modern commercial flying: the autopilot that didn't trust its autopilot.

But it wasn't the equipment that was bothering Mike. He had to get in and out of Operations without detection. Intercontinental had the same regulations as most of the other carriers: flight personnel had to sign in one hour before departure. The sheets were constantly monitored to make sure that every flight had a full crew. If a crew member was more than ten minutes late, a reserve pilot or stewardess would be called to cover the trip.

As Mike opened the heavy, unmarked door, he looked at his watch—7:20. He was ten minutes early. To the left, as one entered, were the sign-in counter and a rack where the crews put down their flight kits and overnight bags; to the right, a sagging leather couch and a bulletin board. In the center of the Operations area was a large wraparound counter; inside it were banks of Teletypes, desks, and computer terminals. On one side of the counter were row upon row of terminal and area forecasts for every U.S. and foreign station served by IA and cities used as alternate airports. On the other side were winds aloft charts, the "progs," storm warnings, and other weather data.

After signing in, the flight personnel were supposed to check their mailboxes. Mike went to get the "garbage," as he called it: updates on procedures, Federal Aviation Administration (FAA) safety directives, union notices, junk from IA's executive suites in New York City.

Most of the route planning, overhaul and maintenance, traffic, and other procedures of running the giant carrier were handled from the Third Avenue office, but the airline also maintained offices at La Guardia Airport. These included personnel and payroll records, additional stewardess supervisory and credit union offices, plus the headquarters of the chief pilot, Joe Barnes, and his five check pilots. Joe Barnes reported to Cliff McCullen, vice-president of the Flight Department. And Cliff McCullen reported to the vice-president of Operations, a Mr. Fitzsimmons.

Mike threw the junk from his mailbox into the wastebasket and went over to say hello to the senior stewardess on today's flight, Nancy Halloway, a tall, slim blonde, about thirty-seven. Once, years ago, Mike had gotten Nancy out of a jam and she had never forgotten; she always had a warm smile for Captain Hagen.

They chatted for a few minutes, and Mike had just stepped over to the weather counter when his copilot, Jim Cochran, approached. Jim was a short, wiry man in his early thirties who had flown carrier-based jets in Vietnam. As did Mike, he broke the airline rules and drank during the twenty-four hours before a flight, but he was far from being an alcoholic, limiting himself to one or sometimes two drinks on a layover. Mike and Jim had found out about each other in Houston one night, and it had been a small joke at first, because they said they had to *protect* themselves. Since then they had bid all their flights together. In addition to the drinking problem, Jim knew Mike had a girl friend in San Diego. Their route was woven around Mike's special needs: flight 467, JFK–HOU, with a three-hour, fifteen-minute layover in Houston; then 221, HOU–SAN, with an overnight layover in San Diego; and 602, SAN–JFK nonstop service, the following morning. Mike, having been with the line for fifteen years, could have flown copilot, perhaps captain, on the overseas routes that were operated with 747 equipment. But he had the Houston routine worked out with Jim Cochran and they always received their first-bid preference.

"What's it look like today?" Mike asked Jim.

"Sort of wild. A lot of wind moving up there."

Mike, who always paid special attention to the weather because he had begun in an open-cockpit plane, looked at the Houston terminal and area forecasts of the Flight Advisory Weather Service (FAWS). The terminal forecast was okay. But the real story that December morning was high above thirty thousand feet, and Mike studied the winds aloft chart; as he did, the second officer–flight engineer, a youngish black man, came up and introduced himself. The third occupant of the cockpit was different each trip and he was the one Mike had to guard against, the reason for using the thermos.

There was a deep aggravated low-pressure system that day, just north of Nashville, moving fast, with severe thunderstorms and icing conditions associated with a cold front; another, less aggravated front was pushing off into Pennsylvania.

There were weather advisories out for light aircraft, and special interim warnings (sigmets) for all aircraft operating in the area of potentially hazardous weather conditions. Mike flipped through the pile of storm warnings: company advisory 39 caught his eye; so did Sigmet Charlie 4. Both indicated light to moderate CAT (clear-air turbulence) around Shreveport, Louisiana.

Then he studied the winds aloft charts again, comparing them with the pressure gradients at various altitudes. The wind shear was there. Small arrows showed tangential wind directions along the sharply defined front which, combined with the location of the jet stream, seemed to set up a much stronger genesis for CAT than the advisories indicated.

Mike's route would take him directly into the core of the turbulence over Shreveport, and he thought there must have been an update not yet posted. He walked over to the dispatcher. "Any updates on advisory 39 or Sigmet Charlie 4?"

The dispatcher looked at the printout in the still clicking machine. "No, nothing new."

"Do you have my machine flight plan?" Mike asked.

"Here it is, Captain Hagen," the dispatcher said, handing Mike a printout. The MFP, which came in from the IA operations center in Kansas City via a Detroit-based computer, indicated the best route from JFK to Houston, considering meteorological conditions, load factor, and other data. All routes were designed to keep schedule and conserve fuel within the existing weather pattern.

While the crisp, sterilized exactitude of Flight Operations was first on Mike's list of things obnoxious, the MFP, which took over much of the captain's preflight work, was certainly next. "How dare some machine tell me what to do!" he had said four years earlier when the chief of the Flight Department directed that the plans would henceforth be handled by the IA computer.

In the beginning most of the IA pilots had distrusted the machine flight plans, but as the quasi science improved, they began to rely on the MFPs, which for the most part were quite accurate. Mike was different; he still disliked the MFP. The IA computer, the cockpit autopilot, and the flight director were all chipping away at the pilot's traditional role of flying the plane.

MIKE Hagen had first learned about turbulence in his open-cockpit plane. He respected its power. There have been bizarre accidents in which modern radar-equipped jets, guided by highly qualified pilots with correct turbulence warnings clipped to their dispatch papers, somehow got tangled up with turbulence and were torn apart in midair by the shearing winds.

Mike knew about the accidents that involved turbulence. He

16

often sat at home with his bourbon and read the National Transportation Safety Board accident reports, trying to establish a pattern of what to do, what not to do. The facts were shocking in this day of sophisticated forecasting and highly developed airborne radar. All the reports confirmed his suspicions: don't go near that stuff and it won't get you. But the problem was that although you could see a well-developed thunderstorm on the airborne radar, CAT was different. The radar didn't pick it up. Yet when this turbulence grabbed a plane, it could lead to a structural breakup, with the aircraft disintegrating in flight.

MIKE walked along the jetway to his plane, a DC-8-61, the familiar "Stretch-8," license number N8907C. It was a long-bodied plane configured by IA to seat 29 passengers in first class and 175 in coach. Mike trusted the Stretch-8. He had 4878 hours "in type" of his 26,756 hours overall. For his age, this was "high time," but he'd logged over 9000 of his hours in Ag flying, where a seventy-hour week was usual in the dusting season.

Now, as Mike boarded his plane, he needed a drink. But it wasn't time yet. He went into the cockpit, his office, and sat down at his desk—a vertical board jammed with instruments and switches.

Settled in the cockpit, Captain Hagen could get on with his thermos routine, which he had down to a finely practiced art. The flight engineer would be outside walking around the plane's undercarriage for his visual flight check. And the copilot, Jim Cochran, always made a special effort to look away when Mike opened his black flight bag, slipped out the thermos, and then lifted his heavy frame from the cockpit to move to the lavatory. On the DC-8-61, just aft of the cockpit, there were two forward lavatories, a coat closet, and the forward galley, serving first-class passengers. Mike could hear the clatter of catering equipment being loaded, so he knew that the stewardesses would be busy and would not see him.

In the lavatory, he slid the spooker inside the small flap door marked DISPOSABLES. There he had hunks of an epoxy adhesive that did the job; the spooker never came loose. Mike pressed the adhesive against the stainless steel sheet on the upper side of the bin; then, when he was sure the thermos was fast, he looked at his face in the mirror. He was amazed how well the Visine worked.

The glassy, reddish look of his eyes was almost gone, and when he smiled, his fleshy face seemed to blend evenly into the bags under his eyes. He put Sen-Sen in his mouth, splashed on a small bit of after-shave lotion, and returned to the cockpit, where he took off his coat, hung it up, and slid into the left seat, fastening the belt lightly around his thick stomach. The rain continued to fall, creating small beads that padded against the front windshield.

As Jim, in the right-hand seat, was going through his paperwork, Mike picked up the phone and pressed the stewardess call button. "Nancy, could I see you for a moment?"

"Be right up." A minute later she appeared. "Yes, sir, what can I do for you?"

"Tell the other stewardesses we're going through rough weather this morning. So delay your food service until we find some reasonably smooth air."

ONE of the passengers taking Intercontinental Airways flight 467, DC-8-61 nonstop service to Houston, on this December morning was Peter Hanscom, executive vice-president of IA's marketing division, who was going down to Houston for a meeting with the southwest sales chief. Hanscom had been in the airline business for twenty-two years, but he didn't like flying. He couldn't explain it, nor did he ever tell anyone.

Peter Hanscom arrived at JFK just before 8:00 a.m. and went directly to gate 9. He was allowed to board early, along with an elderly lady in a wheelchair.

At 8:14 the rest of the passengers began to board. The invalid had been taken to seat 29-A in the aft section and Pete Hanscom to 6-D in first class. The aircraft door was closed, and 467 was signed off just before 8:30.

In the cockpit, the crew began their preflight checklist, which, according to the manual, had to be read aloud—the captain, first officer, and second officer–flight engineer each reciting the procedures from a prepared page in IA's DC-8-61 handbook. This never failed to bring a small grimace to Mike's lips, because in the old DC-3 days the checklist was a routine—mostly common sense—lodged in the pilot's head. But now a script had been written for the men in the flight deck. On the left side of the page was the

18

heading, CHALLENGE—THE READOFF; on the right side, the response. Jim Cochran played the challenger. "Windshield heat," he began.

"Warm up," Mike answered.

"Cabin signs," Jim continued, and thus they went down the eighteen items on the list; then Mike began his "engine start." Even this had to be in sequence: number 3 engine was usually first, followed by 4, the outboard turbine; then on the other wing, number 2, and finally, number 1.

Mike waved at the lineman below his window; then he nudged the thrust levers forward and the DC-8-61 rolled away from the gate. He was feeling better; the pains in his stomach had eased, and his head, although slightly light, now felt attached to his neck.

Ground control cleared 467 to runway 31-Left, and Mike taxied out to the active runway. The ceiling at 8:40 was nine hundred feet overcast with two miles' visibility in light freezing rain.

Mike pressed his PA button and began his customary announcement. "Good morning, ladies and gentlemen, this is Captain Hagen. Welcome to Intercontinental's nonstop service to Houston. We're about eighth in line for takeoff. Things are a little slow this morning because of the weather. The rain we're having here is associated with a deep depression down over Nashville. Our flight plan calls for us to divert north of our usual route, but we still might experience some turbulence. I've asked our stewardesses to delay food service until we see how conditions are. In the meantime, sit back and relax. It's a pleasure to have you aboard."

Mike's PAs were about the best in the airline, some said; he had a friendly, convincing voice and often made scenic announcements, which few captains bothered to do. The federal air regulations do not require a pilot to make any announcements unless a safety measure must be initiated, but Mike felt that PAs were good public relations.

As the plane slowly taxied toward 31-Left, Mike silently cursed himself for having let the spookers take him prisoner, making his life into a series of small deceits. He often felt deep regret.

When the plane was near the threshold of the runway, Jim informed the tower that they were ready. The tower acknowledged, and when its turn came, the DC-8-61 turned onto 31-Left, pointed its nose into the wind, and was cleared for takeoff.

19

Mike eased his feet off the brakes, made a slight directional correction, and the plane picked up speed as the four turbines sucked in the damp morning air. At 153 knots he eased the nose up so that the wings would attain their needed lift. Moments later the plane entered the low-flying scud. Everything went black in the cockpit except for the red light illuminating the instruments. At two thousand feet they came out into a broken layer of fast-moving clouds, and five hundred feet higher they entered another, darker layer.

The air was smoother than Mike had figured. They trimmed up the ship at three thousand feet, and after being cleared to the Robbinsville, New Jersey, VORTAC radio beacon, they punched in the automatic flight director, which would take them over the station by homing in on the ground transmitter signal.

Rain pelted the plane as it struggled up through light to moderate turbulence over Pennsylvania. Then, just before they reached their cruising altitude, when they were close to the Harrisburg, Pennsylvania, VORTAC, 467 picked up the severe turbulence. The plane bounced twice and then dropped rapidly. Mike felt his stomach jump into his throat. The autopilot returned the plane to her course, but the air continued to be choppy and the aircraft shook violently.

"We'd better take her off the altitude hold," Mike said.

Jim snapped off one axis of the autopilot and curled his hands around the wheel. Moisture appeared along Mike's brow; it was not fear but what he'd come to know as the "mean reds." He pressed the stewardess call button. "Nancy, this choppiness might continue for a while. Worst air I've seen in a long time. Keep everyone in their seats."

Then Mike made another PA. "Ladies and gentlemen, this is Captain Hagen again. The rough air we're having might give some of you concern. Please understand that these conditions are not unusual and our aircraft is stressed for anything the sky has to offer. It's uncomfortable, but the flight is proceeding routinely. We hope to begin our breakfast service as soon as possible; in the meantime, please remain in your seats with your seat belts securely fastened. Thank you."

The plane was tossed about in the air, but most of the passengers

20

felt no fear; they were comforted by Captain Hagen's deep, reassuring voice; some, however, began to associate the plane's shuddering, racking motion with danger. Peter Hanscom, the marketing executive, for one, sat petrified by the turbulence.

TWO

FLIGHT 467 was handed off to the Cleveland Air Route Traffic Control Center, and Mike asked for another altitude. Cleared to thirty-five thousand feet, where the turbulence was worse, he requested thirty-one thousand—what pilots call flight level 310—and went to it. Mike took the wheel. Even though he felt his spooker wearing off, his touch—the practiced dexterity—seemed to settle the plane down. He had an almost perfect sense of the ship's controls, knowing when to force them, when to nudge them, and when to let the plane take care of itself. Some IA pilots let the autopilots run even in turbulence, but Mike felt that the gyros were slower than a good pilot's reactions. This theory was controversial. And there was only so much even the most skillful pilot could do to smooth a plane's path through disturbed air.

Half an hour later Mike felt the need for his spooker, gave the controls over to Jim, and left the cockpit. He took a paper cup from the dispenser beside the lavatory door, then went inside. The stewardesses were sitting in the jump seat opposite the lavatory. Usually when he went in for his spooker, they were serving.

Mike reached into the disposal unit, felt the thermos, and eased it through the door. He unscrewed the top and poured the bourbon into the paper cup. He wanted to bring a slight dignity to his closet nipping and he thought the tiny paper cup was less degrading than drinking out of the thermos. He lifted the cup to his lips, drank hurriedly, and poured a second drink. The plane took a hard bounce and part of the bourbon sloshed down on the counter. He wiped it up, replaced the thermos, and returned to the cockpit.

At 9:55 a.m. Mike called Cleveland again and requested pilot reports on various flight levels; he was advised that none was reporting smooth air, but that the latest weather prog indicated improvement after 10:00 a.m. Mike's spooker brought a calm to his head; his shoulder and neck pains eased, as if a giant masseur had worked the kinks out. He looked over at Jim and smiled. It was a bold, confident smile that said to the younger man, You're doing fine.

The plane went into a gradual bank and started south, the turbulence at thirty-one thousand feet having subsided. At 10:55 Mike told Jim they could go back on the autopilot. Streaks of fluffy clouds began to slide by the plane as it entered the back, or receded, side of the Tennessee low. The air was now velvety smooth. The passengers felt they had been rewarded for their bravery. Mike instructed Nancy to begin the meal service, then slipped on his headset and called the dispatcher in Chicago.

"Flight 467. Do you have an update on Sigmet Charlie 4?"

"Affirmative, 467. Sigmet Charlie 4 is canceled. Sigmet Charlie 5 indicates light turbulence over northeast Texas and Shreveport."

"Are you sure that says light?"

"Yes, sir. I'm reading it off the Teletype."

Mike clicked off the transmit button.

"Would you say that wind shear and the position of the jet stream on the board this morning indicated light, moderate, or severe turbulence?" he asked Jim.

"More like severe." The copilot had guessed what the captain wanted to hear.

Mike was about to lash out at the company meteorological department, but he checked himself. Every flight deck is equipped with a voice recorder, and nothing can be said in the cockpit without its being taped. "Those creeps," Mike had told Jean when he came home after his first trip in a bugged cockpit. But actually he knew the recorder was installed because federal air regulations required that tapes be submitted in crash situations.

Mike gazed at the crystal skies around them. The fear of hitting the turbulence haunted him. He remembered the statements of one particular airline crew that had entered an area of extreme unforecast turbulence. The captain had told investigators that immediately before it happened, the outside air temperature dropped about ten degrees. Now Mike kept his eyes on the outside temperature gauge, and when it began to slide, he called Little Rock, Arkansas, asking for pilot reports from the Shreveport area.

"IA 467, I have three pilot reports," replied Little Rock. "A Gulfstream II at flight level 210 over Clarkdale, Arkansas, reported light turbulence. An American 727 at flight level 350 near Hot Springs reported light to moderate, and the third, a corporate plane, 280 over Fort Smith, Arkansas, reported light turbulence."

Mike looked at Jim, who shrugged his shoulders.

Mike watched the temperature drop, sure now that something was out there. He slowed the plane down to its turbulence-penetration speed, which on this day was 245 knots. Then he retrimmed the plane and pressed the stewardess call button. Seconds later Nancy Halloway entered the cockpit.

"I believe we're entering an area of severe clear-air turbulence, Nancy. I want the galley secured, all trays off the tables, everyone belted in, including you girls." She left, and Mike started his PA.

"Ladies and gentlemen, this is Captain Hagen again. We might be penetrating an area of turbulence, and as a safety measure I am suspending meal service. I'm also putting on the No Smoking and Fasten Seat Belt signs. No one is to leave his seat under any circumstances. We apologize to those who did not receive our usual good breakfast, but this is a precautionary procedure initiated for your safety. Thank you."

Besides the temperature drop and the apparent indicators on the IA weather map, something else told Mike Hagen they were heading for an upset: his intuition. Some pilots get premonitions about the skies, just as sea captains possess an unexplained sense of their universe. As he looked out into the morning light, Mike was certain they would hit CAT. It was just a matter of when. But they were prepared. The jet was down to her rough-air speed; everyone was securely fastened in.

The flight deck became very still as they waited. But nothing happened.

Forty miles southwest of Shreveport, Mike began his descent into the Houston terminal area. He debated whether to turn off the seat-belt sign or not, give the passengers a chance to go to the lavs; the plane must be past the area of turbulence, or maybe it was never there and Sigmet Charlie 5 was right.

When Mike had made his PA about the possible turbulence, a few well-traveled businessmen remained totally blasé, but others in the cabin had become alarmed in varying degrees. The passengers were very quiet now, as the low whine of the four turbines eased off.

The first jolt snapped everyone's head.

There was an upward acceleration, a buffeting, and then the jet began to shake. In an extremely turbulent situation passengers suffer complete spatial disorientation, thinking they are upside down when they are not, that the plane is diving when, in fact, it is going up. Peter Hanscom believed they were in a steep bank; the jet was actually pitching on the flanks of a violent updraft. As Hanscom looked out of the window, he saw the wings shaking. He dug his fingers into the arms of his seat.

Then there was a crash. It came from the aft galley, but Hanscom thought it was the wings being ripped off. His panic became even more intense. He closed his eyes and started praying, thinking of his wife and children.

A sequence of critical events took place in fragments of seconds. As the shock wave darted through the aircraft, it began to climb, borne upward by violent vertical air currents.

For a few seconds the men in the cockpit had no idea of their attitude, heading, or airspeed. Pencils, papers, charts, and jackets spun crazily in the air, and the instruments vibrated so violently that the numbers and needles became fuzzy white streaks, impossible to read. The trembling young flight engineer sat with his eyes glued to the board in front of him as the racking and the noise intensified.

Mike gently, cautiously removed a little thrust; the climb was arrested and he nudged the wheel forward just a bit. It took eleven seconds to bring the plane under control, but it seemed much longer to its occupants.

The plane had ascended fifteen hundred feet in the climb and was far out of its assigned altitude. Once he had adjusted the speed, Mike regained his proper flight level, which returned them to smooth, velvety air. The cockpit was silent; everyone's heart was thumping wildly.

Jim peered over at Mike; he could not understand how a man who was drinking could have forecast the clear-air turbulence and handled the plane the way he did. The copilot chalked it up to experience. Mike was a high-timer. Jim's own flight time was under five thousand hours, and he had never witnessed anything like what just happened. He knew, though, what the consequences would have been if meal service had been going on when they hit the CAT: hot drinks would have been tossed around; there would have been injuries and, possibly, deaths. Jim's feelings for Mike Hagen were mingled. He felt sorry for the man—his desperately unhappy marriage, his drinking problem. And yet he admired the captain— his air sense was almost uncanny. Or was he extraordinarily lucky? The copilot didn't know.

IT TOOK several minutes for the passengers to get their balance back. The screams that had filled the cabin turned to cries of joy at being alive, but the passengers were still apprehensive. Why hadn't the captain made a PA? Was he injured?

But Mike was busy talking to Fort Worth Center.

"What's happening up there?" the controller asked. "We've just gotten a bunch of pilot reports on extreme turbulence."

"Copy this. IA 467 hit extreme clear-air turbulence at flight level 290, sixty miles north of the Lufkin, Texas, VORTAC. Get it on the machine right away. CAT almost broke us up."

"Roger. You ought to read some of the others."

"Can't wait."

As Mike clicked off the transmit button, the cockpit phone rang. "Wow!" Nancy said. "It's an absolute shambles back here. Nobody's hurt. But someone better check the aft galley. It came apart, and please say something to these poor souls—they're out of their minds."

"Okay, I'm coming back." Under the circumstances, Mike thought it advisable to reassure the passengers personally.

As he passed the first lavatory, Mike wanted to duck in for a big, cold spooker. He felt he deserved it, but when he looked at the chaos of magazines, books, attaché cases, and pillows strewn about the cabin, he decided to talk to his passengers immediately. They were looking up at him wide-eyed and nervous.

He spoke to those in first class. "Everything's all right now, folks. We've just experienced what is called clear-air turbulence, and while this has been extremely uncomfortable for all of us, we never exceeded the limitations of the aircraft. As I said, everything's fine now, and we should land in Houston very soon." Then he moved to the coach section, where he made the same speech.

Finally, he looked at the aft galley and, seeing that nothing was structurally wrong, returned to the cockpit as Jim Cochran was letting down into the Houston terminal area.

NANCY Halloway had been sitting in the forward jump seat when the shock wave hit the plane. She had heard a crash inside the nearest lavatory. After everyone had settled down, she checked the lav. An overhead compartment had come down and towels were piled up on the floor. She bent to pick them up and was struck by the pungent, unmistakable smell of bourbon. Odd, she hadn't noticed anyone going into the lavatory; the passengers had been under seat belts most of the morning. She glanced out at the catering section. The suitcase with its rack of little bottles was still locked; that was for the snacks on the next leg. Maybe someone had brought his own. Sometimes a nervous passenger wanted a nip early in the morning but was too embarrassed to ask for it. Then, realizing that they would be on the ground in a few minutes, she hurried away to complete her prelanding duties.

MIKE'S pilot report, among others, set into motion a string of events. The terminal and area forecasts for Houston were immediately amended. The turbulence messages went on the line to a high-speed computer in Kansas City and were relayed out on the circuits. A new sigmet was prepared.

At the same time, control positions working traffic in the affected area began to divert aircraft. A total of twenty-nine planes slowed to their turbulence-penetration speeds. A few let down to the lower skies; others gradually banked away from the murderous CAT.

Flight 467 touched down in Houston. Many of the deplaning passengers paused on their way out to thank Mike. Peter Hanscom approached the pilot, showing his company ID. "That was some ride, Captain."

"It was," Mike said with a victorious smile.

"Ever happen like this before?"

"Not exactly."

"There's a lesson here," Hanscom said. "If this kind of thing can happen, perhaps there should be a safety rule to keep everyone in his seat as much as possible."

26

"CAT's difficult to forecast precisely. I wasn't even sure we would hit the stuff. I had a strong hunch, that's all. The weather map back at JFK didn't quite agree with the turbulence advisory. Only one chance in a hundred that we'd hit the center of it."

"Well, I'm going to report this to Fitz. The vice-president of Operations ought to know what a fine job you did."

"Thank you, sir."

When Peter Hanscom left the cockpit, Mike went into the lavatory to retrieve his spooker. Luckily, the thermos had not been unleashed by the turbulence. The pilot often wondered what would happen if the thermos came loose and fell to the bottom of the disposal bin. How would he get it when he needed the spooker? He sometimes saw himself clawing away at the bin, ripping it open like a starved animal going after a trapped piece of meat.

MIKE had a layover routine in Houston. Flight 467 normally arrived there at 11:00 a.m., giving him over three hours before the Houston–San Diego leg, which went out at 2:15 p.m. Most of the pilots hung around the pilots' lounge, a gloomy place where a TV set was always blaring away. The captain had picked this flight sequence because it would allow him enough time to check into a room at the airport hotel for a light lunch, a cold drink from his thermos, sometimes a bath, and a nap. The rest helped him to feel relaxed and lifted enough to guide the DC-8-61 over the south end of the Rockies, across the desert to San Diego. A three-hour and five-minute flight, it usually put them on the apron at Lindbergh Field, San Diego, around 3:30 p.m. Pacific time.

Today, however, flight 467 arrived in Houston almost an hour late, and Mike knew his time in the hotel would be limited. He was exhausted. At first he thought of telling Operations he'd had enough—logical, acceptable—but that would be a tacit admission that he had gone too far, and he earnestly believed that the spookers didn't affect his job performance.

Mike realized he had crossed one line—daytime drinking—and he knew there was another line out there someplace. How far away it was, he didn't know; yet he was certain he would not come near it. He had his own guidelines: the first day he called in sick after a night of drinking, if his hands began to shake, if his flying was in any way impaired, he would stop. Up to now, none of these things had happened.

There was another reason why Mike didn't want to deadhead back to JFK: the pilot had a date with his girl friend, Pat Simpson, that evening, and he really wanted to see her. He suddenly decided to delay the flight. Yes, that would be wise, conservative, and pilotlike.

"How are the control surfaces?" Mike asked the young flight engineer as he reentered the cockpit.

"No damage, sir."

Mike then felt the trim tab wheel. He nursed it back and forth. "Don't like the feel," he told his copilot.

Jim felt it and shrugged his shoulders.

"I want this checked," Mike said. "Call Dispatch."

The captain's authority was supreme. All he had to say was, "I don't like it," and the flight would be delayed while mechanics crawled over the equipment. And if the captain said, "I *still* don't like it," new equipment would be pulled in. The inspection would take an hour and a half—enough time for Mike to enjoy his spooker.

When they reached Operations, Mike told the chief airframe mechanic to check everything out and to examine the trim tab cables. Then he picked up his flight bag and moved toward the door. Jim followed him out, and they stood in the bright, warm Texas sun. Jim touched Mike's arm. "There's nothing wrong with those cables, is there?"

"You never know," Mike said, looking at his feet.

"Take it easy, Mike, we still have the West Coast leg."

"I'll be in the hotel room. I need a little sleep, that's all. Bad experience—that damn CAT!"

Mike walked through the main terminal to the International Hotel, where he checked into a small single room. No one—except Jim—knew where the pilot went between flights, not even Nancy Halloway, who, because she had friends in San Diego, turned up on Mike's schedule more often than anyone else.

The DC-8-61 was hauled away from the loading gate with the group mechanic in the right seat and Jim in the left. They taxied the plane to a hangar on the far end of the field, where six airframe mechanics were waiting.

WHEN HE REACHED his room, Mike flung his coat on the bed, dipped into his flight bag for the icy spooker, got a glass from the bathroom, and poured himself a drink. As he gulped the bourbon, his nerves immediately calmed down. Then he dialed room service for a melted cheese on rye and a bowl of thick onion soup.

At the knock on the door he pushed his drink under the bed and jammed the thermos back in the flight bag. He signed for the food, ate, took a hot bath, and crawled into bed.

About one hour later the phone woke him up. "Mike, you okay?" Jim asked.

"Sure, just sleeping."

"Funny thing. There was some sloppiness on one of the trim tab cables. I don't know if it was the dive this morning or not."

"Find anything else?"

"No, we looked over the whole undercarriage, all the control surfaces, spoilers, flaps. The flight's scheduled to go out at 3:30 local time."

"I'll be over."

Mike put in a call to San Diego. Just the sound of Pat's voice made him feel happier. He told her the flight was delayed.

"I'll work late at the office. We're behind anyhow," Pat said.

"I can't wait to see you," Mike said. He dressed, studied his face carefully, and applied just a bit of the cover stick. Then he rinsed the glass with mouthwash, went downstairs, and paid his bill.

MIKE sat in the cockpit and felt the trim tab cable and the tension of the other controls. Next to turbulence, he thought control failure was one of the worst hazards facing heavy aircraft operation. Many times he imagined a cable coming off a pulley, and the feeling the pilot must have with a wheel in his hand connected to nothing while the plane went into a graveyard spiral.

Mike asked the flight engineer to check the position of the trim tab on the tail assembly. As the engineer left the cockpit, Mike slid the thermos into his coat and made his way to the head. Inside, he opened the disposal door and shoved in his spooker, his icy umbilical cord. He returned to the cockpit and asked Nancy to bring him coffee before they were airborne.

Jim handed him a wire from New York Operations.

ADVISED BY HOUSTON OPERATIONS THAT FLIGHT 467, JFK–HOU, EXPERI-
ENCED EXTREME CLEAR-AIR TURBULENCE. FAA REQUESTS COMPLETE PI-
LOT REPORT. PLEASE COPY OPERATIONS NEW YORK. DO NOT SPEAK TO
PRESS ABOUT INCIDENT. FITZSIMMONS RECEIVED WIRE FROM HANSCOM,
VP MARKETING, ABOARD 467. SAID YOU HANDLED SITUATION EXTREMELY
WELL. GOOD WORK, MIKE.

JOE BARNES, CHIEF PILOT

The flight engineer returned, saying all was well. The turbines
were spun up, ignited, and the plane proceeded to the active runway. They were cleared for immediate takeoff. Mike fed in the
power and felt the jet surge ahead as Jim read off the knots. The
DC-8-61 climbed smoothly into the bright, warm Texas afternoon.
The autopilot was activated, and Mike sat back and relaxed.

Around 4:30 the hollow, empty feeling returned to his stomach.
Mike excused himself and left the cockpit. Nancy was preparing
her serving cart and happened to notice him take a paper cup and
enter the lavatory. Ordinarily she would have thought nothing of
this, but she remembered that Mike had done exactly the same
thing on the morning flight, and she couldn't understand why he
didn't simply take a drink of water from the spigot.

Mike entered the lavatory, removed his thermos from its hiding
place, and poured the bourbon into the cup. He leaned against the
bulkhead and felt the liquor running into his stomach, bringing the
nice warm feeling with it. He replaced the thermos, left the lavatory, and used his key to unlock the cockpit door.

He took his seat and leaned back and relaxed. This was the time
of the flight day he waited for; the spooker refreshed him, and the
air west of Tucson was usually tame. He could look into the lower-
ing sun hovering over the southern end of the High Sierras; to the
south, Mexico, with its lemony light and the outline of the Sierra
Madre rising out of the burnt-sienna plains—the beauty of flying.
Mike also liked the last part of the leg because he would be seeing
Pat Simpson within a couple of hours.

Mike's eyes became heavy as the warm rays sifting through the
tinted Plexiglas window bathed his face. He laughed silently to
himself. Six hours earlier this same plane had nearly been shaken
apart. Now he felt drowsy. What a job, Mike thought. Sometimes
he was grossly overpaid for doing nothing—like this afternoon—but

30

this morning, no amount of money could have paid for his expertise. It was worth much more than the $55,000 he received annually. He had saved lives this morning, of that he was sure.

But this did not make Mike any more satisfied with his job. He remembered, as if it were yesterday, flying junior routes in a DC-3 back when the VOR stations were just coming in. The autopilots were cranky, and one had to fly to a great extent by visual landmarks. He had been in touch with the earth he loved; he had watched the seasons change and he knew his way around the clouds because the old bird could not fly much above ten thousand feet. The pilot loved contact flying.

Over Gila Bend, Arizona, they received clearance for San Diego, and less than an hour later they landed at Lindbergh Field.

As they taxied to the gate, Jim looked at Mike's face. He thought the pilot looked drawn and old. He wondered how far this man could go, or where he would go, how it would end. How many times could a pilot drink in the air before he misjudged or misread something and caused hundreds of deaths? Jim suddenly thought about his own family and decided to do what he had wanted to do for a long time.

PAT Simpson sat in her office at a San Diego advertising agency, waiting for Mike's call. At thirty-two, tall, slender, and striking, she had been recovering from a broken marriage when she first met Mike Hagen. Now she thought she had never been happier.

The phone rang, and she smiled in anticipation of Mike's warm voice. "Darling."

"Uh, this is Jim Cochran. Mike's copilot."

"Oh yes, of course." She remembered the amiable sunburned young man. Her heart sank. "Is anything wrong?"

"Everything's all right. We're on the ground here. But I just have to talk to you about Mike."

"What is it?" Pat asked, her voice rising with apprehension.

"Look, I'm awfully sorry to spring this on you, but I was hoping you might say something to him. Mike's a damned fine pilot, but he's been drinking during flights."

"You're crazy." She knew Mike drank illegally, on layovers; she drank with him. But on the job? The hand holding the receiver began to tremble. It couldn't be true, not Mike—he couldn't do such a thing. "How?" she said.

"He hides this thermos filled with bourbon in the lavatory. I saw him going in there all the time and I asked him about it because I thought he was sick."

"How long has this been going on?"

"About a year, and it's getting worse. You can't hide something like this forever; somebody's going to find out. If he gets caught, he'll never fly for anybody again. Don't tell him I called you, but I didn't know what to do."

Pat didn't want to accept what Jim was saying; yet something deep down told her it was true. "When this started, why didn't you say something? You're as guilty as he is."

"I did. We talked, but Mike doesn't believe he's got a problem. He thinks he can stop anytime. Frankly, I think he's lost control and it scares the hell out of me. There'll come a time when the booze affects his flying, and I don't want to be aboard."

"I don't blame you, Jim. I'm glad you called. I'll speak to him right away, do what I can."

Pat put the phone down. The significance of what Jim Cochran had said was tearing through her. She felt helplessness, then a rising panic. She thought back to the first time she ever saw Mike Hagen. She had set up an easel at the end of a pier in Coronado, just south of San Diego, and was finishing a watercolor of the harbor. She had stopped to rest a moment, and happened to look aside. Her gaze fell upon a roundish belly full of freckles. Her eyes slid upward and she saw another mass of sun-bleached freckles all over a big face with a pleasant smile. He was wearing a baseball cap and had a fishing pole in his hand.

"Am I making you nervous?" Mike had asked.

"No more than the painting," she answered.

"I used to sketch a little bit myself—airplanes, two-wing jobs. Teacher said I was pretty good."

"Do you fly?" she asked, putting away her brushes.

"I'm a captain with Intercontinental."

This surprised Pat, because the man standing in the hot sun looked like a farmer, a Texas cattleman.

They sat talking on the end of the pier. She liked Mike Hagen from the start—the outgoing way he spoke, his earthiness and openness. They continued their conversation at a small seaside restaurant where she often went. Mike had some drinks at lunch, but she hadn't thought anything of it.

Later she was too much in love with the pilot to ever think about his drinking. He never seemed to be drunk; he drove her Jaguar with precision; he never stumbled, slurred his words, or forgot things. She thought alcoholics were disturbed, brooding people who sat alone in dark bars. But there was nothing outwardly wrong with Mike Hagen except his marriage, and he told her that it had gone downhill almost from the beginning.

To her, Mike just drank a lot; she didn't know how much was too much. Their love affair had been going on for almost three years, and they had never had a serious argument. She thought Mike Hagen was one of the most dependable, straightforward men she had ever met. The call from Jim scared her. What was she to do? When Mike phoned a short time later, Pat was still at a loss.

HE LOOKED the same to her, a bit tired perhaps. He told her about the day's problem with the clear-air turbulence. All through dinner at their favorite Mexican restaurant, she listened and watched him carefully. His drinking pattern was no different—four bourbons, no trace of intoxication. But she decided she had to say something.

"Mike." She reached across the table and took his hand. "I'm worried. I think you drink an awful lot for someone who has to fly a plane."

He smiled. "You're right. I know I drink too much."

"Why do you do it, Mike? Aren't you jeopardizing your job?"

"Yes, but you know what I think about this kind of flying."

"But what about the passengers?"

He grasped both her hands in his. "Pat, I really don't think my drinking affects my flying. I'm sure I saved some lives today."

"Isn't there an airline rule that you're not supposed to drink twenty-four hours before a flight? You've had several big bourbons tonight and you have to fly in the morning."

"But I've been drinking like this for years. I can handle it. In all the time we've spent together, have you ever seen me soused?"

"Darling, no one can drink as much as you do and not have liver problems or something. I don't want that to happen to you."

"Okay, I'll let up a little if it'll make you feel better."

Despite Mike's response, Pat had to ask the question she'd been dreading. "Mike, I want an absolutely truthful answer. Do you drink on the job?"

Mike Hagen didn't say anything for a minute. "Yes, dammit! I drink on the job!"

They didn't discuss it further until they reached Pat's small, well-furnished beach house in Coronado. She made coffee and he took a brandy with it, as he always did.

"Mike, I wasn't kidding about the drinking. Promise you'll see somebody back east. Please, darling, for your own sake. This thing has got to be cleared up now. If you won't do this for me, then I don't want to see you anymore." She was surprised at her sharpness.

At that moment the phone rang. Pat answered. It was Jim with a message for Mike. He was to call Joe Barnes.

It was almost 2:00 a.m. New York time, and Mike wondered about calling the chief pilot at that hour. But they were close friends, so he went ahead. "Hello, Joe, sorry it's so late."

"That's all right. You certainly did a fine job yesterday. Did you hear about the Inter-Texas flight?"

"No."

"They were around Shreveport same time you were. The CAT caught 'em and they dropped four thousand feet. Half the plane came apart inside. One killed, twenty-two injured. They made an emergency landing in Shreveport."

"Wow! What kind of equipment?"

"Seven twenty-seven. The FAA called. They got the report on your experience. They want to know how you got through without even one injury when Inter-Texas got so messed up."

"Almost twenty-seven thousand good flying hours in my book. That's how."

"I told the FAA that our Captain Hagen knew more about flying than half these clowns in the air today. Anyhow, here's the point. They want to send out a team of experts from the safety board. They're going to interview all the flight personnel, and they want to go over the plane. Fitz says it's a real compliment, and we've got you up for a safety award—maybe a thousand dollars. The first meeting is scheduled for 1:00 Pacific tomorrow. I'm coming out to San Diego for it. Oh, almost forgot, there was a report that you ordered the equipment checked during the Houston layover and that they found some problems in the trim tab cables. FAA wants to know how you figured that one out."

"The wheel felt slightly different," Mike said, telling a convincing lie.

"Well, it was a smart precaution. Nice going, Mike. I wish we had a hundred guys like you."

"Thanks, Joe. I needed a boost tonight."

"Well, you got one. See you tomorrow, Mike."

A broad smile bloomed on Mike's face. He walked over and kissed Pat. "The chief pilot is coming out tomorrow with an FAA team. An Inter-Texas flight hit the same air—one killed, twenty-two injured—and you talk about me not being able to fly. Ask Joe Barnes if I can handle the equipment. Ask him."

She was about to say something, but she remained still and shared the happiness of the moment. He filled their glasses; they took a blanket out to the beach and watched the bright moon sailing in from the sea.


### THREE

THE jurisdiction for the incidents of clear-air turbulence over Louisiana on that December 10 fell within the bounds of several agencies, among them the National Transportation Safety Board—an independent fact-finding group that works closely with the Civil Aeronautics Board—the Federal Aviation Administration, and the aircraft manufacturers. Most critics agree that the NTSB is the best in the world when it comes to finding out what happened after accidents. But some critics feel their procedures for preventing accidents leave much to be desired. The NTSB itself says that prevention is the FAA's job. It has been suggested that too many bureaus control pilots and planes, and that a single superagency should take command.

Pilots' reports were filed indicating that six planes had encountered turbulence on December 10, but only one pilot, Mike Hagen, apparently knew his aircraft would enter the core of extreme air movement. The others, with just as much available weather information, flew into the situation with no sense of what was about to happen. Why? What did one pilot know that the others didn't?

Further, the same plane was grounded in Houston by the captain. The other aircraft were sent on their way *without* control surface or cable inspection. What did the IA pilot suspect? The safety board, among others, wanted facts. They began by grounding every plane that had experienced the identical air disturbance. Then they directed the local FAA branch chiefs to remove flight and voice recorders from the grounded planes.

The flight recorder keeps a log of a plane's direction and inertial forces. In the case of the IA flight, perhaps the most important of the five indications recorded was the G-force indicator, which would tell what negative or positive gravitational forces had been exerted against the aircraft. The recorder also indicated the aircraft's magnetic heading, airspeed, altitude, and recorded time. By feeding this data into a computer, the investigators might be able to piece together an explanation of what had happened.

At 5:00 a.m. on the day after the incident, while Mike was sleeping off seven outsize inputs of Old Grand-Dad, the IA flight recorder was taken to the FAA regional office for readout plotting. The completed plot showed a very interesting pattern. The plane entered the climactic CAT at a reduced airspeed, 245 knots; during turbulence the maximum incremental G forces were about 4.8, going from plus 3 Gs to 1.8 Gs negative. When the investigators compared notes with the Inter-Texas 727, her flight recorder showed a lower exertive G-force pattern; yet there had been a fatality on that plane and three people were on the critical list.

The NTSB wanted the answer to one question: Was there an operational lesson to be learned from the CAT incident? Their sophisticated recording and monitoring equipment would never reveal the most imperative factors in air safety—the strengths, wisdom, and weaknesses of the human being who sits in the left cockpit seat of a giant flying machine. Investigators could not get inside the head of a man like Mike Hagen. And then, if they could, and if they had been able to see this pilot at Ellen's Place, it would have been a bitter paradox.

JOE BARNES, IA's CHIEF pilot, was a vibrant, sturdy Midwesterner. He was a legend around the industry, because he was the only man left on the operational side of the airlines who had actually flown a Ford Tri-Motor on regular service. He was fifty-nine—six months away from retirement—and he planned to return to the Midwest and buy into a small, fixed-base operation. He had grown up in the infant days of barnstorming, and he wanted to live out the rest of his life near a flying field.

Joe Barnes had met Mike on IA's transcontinental service in 1968, when Mike was flying copilot on the senior flights. They had flown together several times before Joe asked the younger pilot how he got into flying.

"Crop-dusting in Florida," said Mike. "Citrus spraying while I was going to the university."

"I used to be a spray devil myself," Joe said.

A fellow crop duster! In the eyes of the older pilot Mike Hagen immediately gained enormous stature. An Ag pilot knew what it was all about: the small, private, closed world of those great half-crazy pilots who sprayed crops, followed the seasons, and saw some poetry and beauty in rural America—the taste of the earth, Joe called it.

"These big jets go too high," Joe had said. "I like the low world."

From that moment in the cockpit, the two former contact flyers shared a fellowship and respect for each other that rarely exists between modern airline pilots. When Joe became chief pilot, he never allowed Mike any special breaks or preferential treatment, but because he shared with the younger pilot something very special, he began teaching Mike everything he knew. And in a way Joe thought of Mike as the son he never had.

When the reports of the December 10 incident reached Joe's office, he had felt a warm, special pride. His student had saved lives and placed the carrier in a favorable light. This meant a lot to Joe, because unlike Mike Hagen he was a company man all the way.

BEFORE the hearing, Mike and Joe met for a quick lunch at the Del Coronado.

"Isn't it strange how things come round," Joe began. "Here we're sitting on the edge of the field where Ryan built the *Spirit*

38

*of St. Louis.* At Lindbergh Field, almost fifty years later, we're talking about something that happened to a giant airplane in the crazy upper air."

"That's right, all those years, and we're still experimenting. Probably we'll keep right on."

"I hope so," Joe said. "But flying is getting so mechanical. You brought the human factor in yesterday. Level with me, how did you know you would hit that stuff?"

Mike hesitated and a smile crept across his red face. "I didn't know. I just played a hunch, took precautions, and it paid off."

"That's what I figured." The chief pilot laughed. "But this afternoon Fitzsimmons wants me to come on strong—act like we always tell our pilots to do more than necessary."

"Am I supposed to say that?"

"No, I'm going to give an opening statement on behalf of the company. Then you tell them how you sensed the CAT and thought safety was more important than serving breakfast. Don't lay it on too much, just enough for believability."

"Joe, you know if we tried to keep passengers under seat belts all the time they'd get pretty annoyed. That's what the marketing VP I had aboard proposes."

"Well, he was certainly impressed. Told Fitz you were a remarkable pilot. Don't play it down too much, Mike. Remember, someone was killed on the other flight; you got everyone through. That's what counts."

"I'll say my piece. Don't worry."

" 'The line always has its captains take every meteorological condition into consideration,' something to that effect."

"Sure, but you and I know every carrier does the same."

"Say it anyway. You could be chief pilot at IA someday."

Mike did not answer.

THE hearing was held in the Federal Aviation Administration building adjacent to Lindbergh Field. The government safety officials sat around the long conference table, waiting to hear what the flight instruments could not tell them.

Joe Barnes gave his opening statement; Jim Cochran praised the work of the captain; the flight engineer echoed the copilot's testimony. Each stewardess told her story. Finally they called Mike.

"What was your clue that severe clear-air turbulence was coming, Captain Hagen?" the official asked.

"At JFK I saw the position of the jet stream yesterday morning. I figured the relationship to the wind shear, and it seemed to me that Sigmet Charlie 4, the light to moderate warning, didn't reflect the situation, if the weather map was right. Frankly, I didn't know which was correct, but then the temperature began dropping, as it does sometimes near turbulence."

"I see. So you sensed that serious clear-air turbulence could be in the region. How did you know the trim tab cable was loose?"

"It felt different."

"You could actually feel it in the trim tab wheel?"

"Sort of," said Mike, repeating his small lie.

"What recommendations do you feel we could introduce, based upon your experience?"

"I think the downgrading of turbulence sigmets should be handled very carefully," he said. "That appeared to be the problem yesterday. If I had been the forecaster, I would have worded the updated sigmet differently. Maybe Charlie 5 was misleading in downgrading the turbulence from 'light to moderate' to just 'light.' "

Weather forecasting, even in this day of advanced monitoring and reporting, is still an infant science. Pilots flying through the Texas–Louisiana area early that morning had reported no problems. Perhaps they were just lucky in not encountering the turbulence, or perhaps the CAT had not yet developed. In any event, the forecaster in the Houston area, seeing their reports, had seen fit to downgrade the sigmet.

To a pilot, light turbulence means small bumps causing slight discomfort; seat belts are not normally required. Moderate turbulence *does* call for fastened seat belts. With light to moderate turbulence, a pilot has some latitude. While one might snap on the seat-belt sign, another may feel it's unnecessary. Clearly, downgraded Sigmet Charlie 5 had not provided an adequate warning.

THE hearing ended at 5:10 p.m. Mike went immediately to his hotel room and took a long drink from the thermos. It was just about time; he could feel that gnawing, familiar urgency coming

40

on. Then he called Pat and told her about the hearing and the congratulations he'd received from NTSB's administrator. She bit hard on her tongue, wishing the incident had never occurred. What irony, she thought.

That night, before dinner at her beach house and after, the pilot drank heavily.

Angry, Pat said, "You've got to straighten yourself out. I'm not going to sit around worrying about you."

"All right. I promise you I'll go to AA when I get back. Don't worry about it. I'm not that guy Ray Milland played. I haven't dropped a weekend yet, baby, and I'm not going to start."

FOUR

THE next morning, flight 602, IA's eastbound SAN–JFK nonstop, took off from Lindbergh Field twenty minutes late. It was the same plane, N8907C; it had been inspected by the FAA, put back together, and signed off. Mike decided to deadhead back, and he was replaced by a captain from the carrier's Los Angeles–based reserve list. Mike told Joe Barnes jokingly that he was going to relax and ride with him in first class on the way back, courtesy of IA.

Joe was pleased, because he wanted to talk company policy. He'd be able to go over the story with Mike again, to make sure that the brass would know what a splendid job the IA New York–based flight department had done. Joe saw the possibility of a bonus coming up for this.

Mike had slipped his refilled spooker into a coat pocket, and after boarding the aircraft, he entered the second forward head, opened the flap door, and attached his lifeline. Thirty-five minutes after takeoff, the stewardesses came by with the drink cart. Joe nudged Mike. "Come on, we'll gas up."

"No, thanks. Never drink during the day. I'll have ginger ale," Mike said.

"Give me a double Scotch and soda," Joe said.

The drinks were served. Mike excused himself and went forward to the lavatory, took a paper cup, and had his third spooker of the day, the first two having gone down in his hotel room.

The old chief pilot talked over the CAT business. Then all the way back east he rambled on about the early days in flying, spreading his joyous life out before Mike Hagen.

When the flight landed at JFK, Mike collected his spooker and said good-by to Joe Barnes. He had agreed to write a memorandum for him on clear-air turbulence and the measures the company could suggest as precautionary policy.

In the parking lot, Mike saw Jim moving toward his car; they waved, and then Jim came over. "That was some job you did the other day. But just as a friend, Mike, I think you ought to cool the booze. I'm sorry to have to say this, but it's getting worse."

"I realize," Mike said solemnly. "I'm going to do something about it. Stick by me for a while, Jim, will you?"

"You know I will. Anything I can do, I'll do. But I want you to know that I have a responsibility here—to the passengers and my family. We're in the same cockpit, right?"

"Sure, Jim, sure. Thanks."

Minutes later Mike waved as his copilot drove by. Then he got into his Nova and put his head between his hands.

"What happened?" he said out loud. "How?"

He would begin by *not* stopping at Ellen's Place.

That was the first step.

It was 8:30 p.m. and the traffic was worse than usual. This provided a good, practical excuse for Ellen's Place, but much as he needed to stop, Mike drove past the turnoff and felt a small victory. Then, as the Nova crawled along the jammed highways, he felt the empty, painful sensation in his stomach and head. He thought about stopping at a gas station, but drinking in a fetid men's room revolted him, so he got off the New England Thruway at Pelham, New York, and pulled into the parking lot of a place called the Candlelight Club. He put on his dark raincoat and ran in. There he sipped the bourbon that a taciturn bartender poured for him and, refueled, set out again for Ridgefield.

He was disgusted with himself.

"I can't even get home," he said aloud. "I can't even get home."

RIDGEFIELD, Connecticut, is one of a string of old pre-Revolutionary towns in Fairfield County. The pleasant, rolling terrain is dotted with magnificent houses dating back to the late 1700s.

Among the various affluent groups living there now is a new generation of pilots. Many captains chose the town because it is just about an hour away from JFK—if one drives at three in the morning in good weather—at the outer limit allowed by the air-for a pilot's residence.

The Hagens had moved to Ridgefield shortly before a heavy influx of business executives drove up real estate prices. They bought a large place, said to have been built in 1781; it had almost three acres, and even the remnants of an old orchard.

But age in a house, Mike found, has its drawbacks. From the beginning things went wrong: plumbing, shingles, wiring, rain gutters, rotten beams. Each year there was a project, and on his copilot's salary, Mike fell behind, even though he did much of the work himself. When he became a captain, it was still difficult to tie all the financial ends together.

JEAN. She was thirty-nine and aging unwillingly. She had met Mike one summer when he was crop-dusting, working the citrus groves around Indian River, Florida. At the time Jean was taking flying, waterskiing, and scuba-diving lessons at a women's junior college in Fort Lauderdale. Her father was a fairly successful real estate dealer in Jacksonville.

Life at the Ag strip was lonely, and to Mike, Jean seemed like a gift from heaven. She was blond and pretty, and before long they were involved in a love affair. A few months later they were married, in a lavish wedding. Jean's father was quite pleased, because he liked the young Ag pilot. Her mother, a snobbish woman, was not. "What's the future for a crop sprayer?" she asked her daughter.

After Mike graduated from the University of Florida at Gainesville with a degree in agriculture, he continued crop-dusting. Jean, who had quite a bit of artistic talent, designed exotic plants for an artificial-flower factory in Fort Lauderdale. She was no happier than her mother had been with Mike's job and urged him to join a commercial airline, which would guarantee steady employment and some respectability. He resisted, but when he realized she'd never be happy as the wife of a crop duster, he gained an Air Transport Rating and flew junior routes as a DC-3 copilot with a

43

national airline. He joined IA in 1957 and was transferred to the carrier's New York base. Jean stated emphatically she would *not* live in Queens, where most of the younger copilots settled; so they moved to Ridgefield, and the pressure was on.

As the bills mounted, Jean said they needed supplementary income. Mike began teaching at the Danbury, Connecticut, airport, some seven miles to the north, but Jean felt that the additional money he earned was inadequate. "We need a steady business that will grow," she said. "We have to put the girls through college, and I mean good schools."

"You can always send them down to your alma mater to learn waterskiing," he said sarcastically. Jean ignored his acid comment.

"I'd like to start an artificial-flower business, mail order. It would cost about fifteen thousand to get going. I've been talking about it to Bill Cousins. He's a chemist and he said he'd invest in it. We can borrow the rest. Bill has a marvelous gimmick, a spray that'll make the flowers smell. Different jungle scents. You have a lot of time off, so you can help me. I'll make the flowers and you run the business."

"For heaven's sake, I'm a pilot, not a florist," Mike said, hating what she was trying to do to him.

But Jean prevailed, as usual. Their synthetically scented artificial flowers were soon in production at a small office in Ridgefield.

WHEN Mike reached home after the San Diego hearing, Jean greeted him with a "We're way behind at the office."

He pushed past her to set his heavy bags down. Karen and Debbie had homework spread out on the dining-room table, and they both jumped up and hugged Mike. "Hi, Dad, where you been?" Karen said. "We were about to send out the Mod Squad."

Jean broke in and told the girls to go upstairs.

Mike threw his coat on a chair and went directly to the bar, poured some bourbon, and then turned to Jean. "My lovely, concerned wife. You didn't even ask me what happened. Not where I've been, or the reason I was delayed. All you're interested in is those stinking flowers!"

Their two daughters looked at each other resignedly and gathered up their books. They knew what was coming.

44

Jean started toward the den. "Well, well! The pilot of all time has come home in a mood. There's a turkey TV dinner in the icebox," she yelled, and slammed the door behind her.

THE following morning Mike went to their office over the local hardware store. It was three rooms jammed with foul-smelling, exotic, outsize flowers, shipping boxes, and piles of orders that overwhelmed Mrs. MacGregor, the elderly retired schoolteacher they employed. Mike spent the morning shuffling orders, and by 11:00 he was ready for the spooker. He went to the small icebox and fixed his drink.

Mrs. MacGregor suspected he nipped now and then, but she didn't particularly think anything of it. The pilot never changed his smile, raised his voice, stumbled downstairs—things she associated with those who drank heavily.

That was Mike's problem. He drank *too well.*

As he brought the cold drink to his lips, the pilot looked out the window at Main Street, at the women with their children and station wagons. For a split second he pictured a crop duster working a field somewhere south of the Indian River. A flick of a strange lens.

Bearing down on him was the promised telephone call to AA, an admission that he was in trouble. Was he? No, Mike thought, he didn't need to hear a bunch of reformed drunks swap horror stories, holier-than-thous commiserating over coffee, telling it like it was when. But he knew Pat would question him, so he might as well get on with it. Where? He couldn't go across to the Presbyterian Church, where a sign announced the AA meeting every Wednesday night; it would only be a matter of days before the IA flight department heard that one of their senior captains was so deep into the sauce that he needed Alcoholics Anonymous. Anonymous? Not in Ridgefield, or any of the towns nearby, for everyone knew everyone else in this part of Connecticut.

Then the idea came to him. He had a biplane at the Danbury airport. Why not fly to AA? The thought of a pilot showing up in his own plane for the weekly "drunk talk" amused him.

Mike studied the sectional chart of airports ringing the area: New Haven's Tweed Airport had landing lights, long, hard-surfaced runways, and radio navigational aids. He would find an AA group that met near New Haven. Perfect strategy.

In the back of his mind he wanted something, anything, to come out of the meeting. He loved to drink and he'd *never* give the bourbon up, but he wanted to throw away the damned thermos, never see Ellen's Place again, and make it through the day without needing a boost to get over the previous night. An obvious solution would be to knock off the nights before, but that he couldn't do, at least not yet.

He knew that Branford was near the New Haven airport. Maybe it was the kind of town that would have his sort of drunk. He dialed the Branford AA.

"Alcoholics Anonymous," a woman said.

"I'd like some information. Where does your group meet?"

"At the firehouse. Tonight at seven thirty. If you need any help before that, I could have someone call you back now."

"I *don't* need any help!" Mike slammed down the phone.

He wanted to fly. Immediately. The meeting wasn't until 7:30, so he had plenty of time. He took another spooker, which cleaned out some of his anger.

He knew the routine and limits of constant, experienced drinking; how far he could go, what he could do and not do. On his way to the Danbury airport, he stopped at a trucking diner and piled into a large order of bacon and eggs, hot and greasy, to counteract the morning bourbon and line his gut for the next spooker. After two cups of coffee his head was clear, and he went on toward the field.

As he drove along, with the windows down and the air hitting him in the face, his thoughts bounced back to his Florida childhood. He had spent every minute he could at the Ag field among the rough-edged flying cowboys, men who worked the crops down through Louisiana and Alabama for the various seasons, always ending up in south Florida for citrus dusting, the last stop before they would binge it, sober up, feel sorry, and fly north to repeat the crop cycle. Sometimes those cowboys would take him up.

By the time he was sixteen Mike had saved enough money for flying lessons, but not in a Piper Cub trainer. He talked a citrus sprayer into letting him learn in a weathered Waco UPF-7.

When Mike went up alone the first time, he was at the stick of that same old, but beautiful, rugged two-winger, one of the wire-and-cloth jobs, with a radial engine in front spitting out over two hundred horses. It was all there: the whistling air, the loneliness, and that great hungry sky he loved.

Years later, in 1971, when Mike bought a plane, it was an antique Waco, the very model in which he had soloed. It took seven months to locate it, for most Wacos had wasted away, rusting in cornfields; a generation of great planes was gone, except for a few sitting it out in air museums, or in the hands of antique plane collectors. Mike had placed an ad in *Trade-A-Plane*, a national weekly newspaper, and finally he tracked down the model he wanted on a Kansas farm. The old, faded UPF-7 needed work, thousands of dollars' worth, but it could be done.

Mike and his older daughter, Karen—she was twelve at the time—drove all the way out to Kansas. Together they disassembled the plane, marking each part. Then they hoisted the old fuselage onto a flatbed trailer and fastened the wings to each side. They came east the slow way, making stops at the National Air and Space Museum and the Edison Museum, enjoying their time together.

When he got home, Mike rented a corner of a hangar at the Danbury airport and installed the Waco on blocks. He worked on his plane whenever he could, removing the old fabric, taking out the rotted wing spars and replacing them with well-seasoned spruce. In his cellar he made a new instrument panel out of rare burled walnut, into which he set modern flight instruments ringed with highly polished, top-quality brass. It was a work of love, an odd kind of pilgrimage back to the Florida of the 1940s. Jean said nothing about the plane and never came to the damp, lonely hangar to see what was going on.

The plane was sprayed with orange lacquer five times and trimmed with a blue-and-white stripe, like the Waco he soloed in many years before. And he named her *Alice* after that first plane. When he finally rolled her out one spring day, it was doubtful that a more perfect Waco had ever emerged from a hangar. People around the airport—the "hangar rats"—gave a beer-and-hot-dog party for Mike that afternoon. His children attended, but not Jean.

The event had been capped off when Mike put on his old flying jacket, climbed into the cockpit, and fed in the power. The plane rolled down the runway, the tail came up, he held the stick forward for a moment, and then his beloved Waco lifted off. It went higher and higher over the green Connecticut hills. He had thought about pulling a few inside loops or Cuban eights, but he wanted to familiarize himself with the plane, so he just flew by the crowd and waved. When the Waco landed, everyone, including Mike Hagen, had been satisfied.

MIKE parked the Nova by the side of the hangar, waved to one of the regulars, and pushed against the hangar door. As it slid back, a shaft of bright afternoon light touched the orange Waco. Mike put on his flying suit, not a mail-order variety but a real one, with a moth-eaten fur collar and cracked, oil-stained leather. He had bought it for two dollars from an old crop duster who was about to stuff it in the ash can.

He climbed in, put on his helmet and goggles, and hit the electric starter, one of his few concessions to progress. The engine choked, sputtered, and finally caught, knocking out a puff of blue-black smoke. He smelled the hot oil and his ear okayed the sounds as the engine warmed up and the tone evened.

He taxied *Alice* into position and fed in the power; the runway blurred under him and he brought the tail up, finally the wheels. The engine thundered and the chrome prop chewed the still air, taking the Waco higher and higher, up through the clouds, into the fresh, free world he loved. Clean air rushed past his face. Mike called it his air therapy; it dampened the flow of a new spooker and flattened out the ache for another.

Higher and higher.

They were eating up the sky. With a close look at the airspeed, he pulled back the stick and the bird curved up into the deep blue of the higher sky; he fed in full power and the Waco set on her tail, going up and over. He cut it on top, hanging blissfully upside down. Then to complete the inside loop he worked the stick again and the Waco came around.

He was laughing.

Mike went again, pulling her up with full power until he hit the top, and he curved off, performing an acrobatic maneuver, the Split-S. As he leveled the plane once more, he searched for a hole in the cloud cover. When he found it, he put the Waco into a spin.

"Don't think I can fly, Jim Cochran? Very few guys can do this, baby, so wherever you are, Jim Cochran, Pat Simpson, Joe Barnes, hope you're watching. This is dedicated to you, kiddies."

The pilot pulled a perfectly executed Cuban eight for them, for himself. Satisfied, he used the omni-frequency radio device to get the magnetic heading to New Haven. Then he banked around and flew off to his Alcoholics Anonymous reconnaissance.

Twenty minutes later he was calling the New Haven tower for landing instructions. When cleared, he slapped down the heavy old Waco on the runway with an acute crop duster's slip.

AFTER he had the Waco parked by the New Haven terminal, he called Pat to tell her he was going to join the Branford, Connecticut, AA chapter. He didn't tell her how he was getting there; that was his delicious secret. Then he called for a cab to the firehouse. Once there, he instructed the driver to return for him in about two hours.

As soon as Mike ambled into the meeting, a balding man with a large smile raced toward him, his eager hand outstretched. "Welcome, good to have you."

Mike wanted this friendly, self-satisfied ex-drinker to disappear. He considered flying back to Danbury at once, but he stayed on.

The meeting was just as Mike had imagined. The first speaker, an elderly retiree, told funny stories of her intoxicated days: stepping on the dog, falling over the mailbox, clipping zigzagged hedges after a few in the kitchen. To Mike her talk was sad, for her former inebriated state seemed to have been the high point of her lonely life.

Next a man told his story. He had been fired from his job at a boat company in Groton; his wife had left him; in the end he found himself strapped to a bed at the state mental hospital. After release he fought a losing battle with booze, in and out of hospitals, with no hope until he met another alcoholic, a once attractive, now ravaged woman. They had joined AA together and were finding new contentment.

The third speaker was a smartly dressed woman in her fifties. "My name is Helen and I'm an alcoholic," she began. "Unlike the other two speakers this evening, I didn't know I was in trouble. Before marrying and moving to Branford, I was having a glorious time in Chicago as an account executive for a well-known advertising agency."

Mike was interested in this speaker. She was obviously sophisticated and she seemed to draw a bead on his own problem. He somehow couldn't identify with the devastated people who had preceded her.

"At the time I joined the advertising agency I didn't drink during the day. In the evenings I had a martini, sometimes two, but there was no dependency, no habit, not even a bare hint of alcoholism. Then I started going out to lunch with clients and I would have a cocktail. Eventually I was drinking two martinis at lunch and three before dinner. Saturdays and Sundays became very difficult, because around noon my body and mind would say it was time for martinis. Saturdays I called up girl friends and we combined two-martini lunches with shopping trips, and on Sundays it would be one of the hotels that served brunch. It's important to understand that I didn't drink any more than two at lunch and three, possibly four, before dinner.

"One evening a date and I were on Lake Shore Drive. A drunken driver swerved and hit us. True irony. I woke up in the emergency ward of a city hospital with a minor concussion. It was about eight o'clock. I had missed my three martinis that night, but it didn't bother me because they gave me a handful of pills and I slept until nine thirty the next morning.

"About five that afternoon I began to feel dizzy and very strange. The intern said it was probably due to my head injury. He prescribed more pills, but by seven the dizziness was much worse. I became disoriented and my hands started to shake. The attending physician was called in. He took one look at me and asked, 'You drink?' I nodded. He wanted to know how much; and when I told him, he said, 'You're suffering withdrawal symptoms.'

"The hospital had a general rule that all alcoholics or suspected alcoholics had to be sequestered in the 'alkie' ward. I protested and screamed, but still I ended up in that foul-smelling ward. They gave me pills, tied me down to the bed, and all that night I sweated, hearing the yells of the poor helpless women around me.

It was a nightmare. When I was able to, I called my lawyer and doctor and was transferred to a small, private drying-out sanitarium. I joined AA and haven't taken a drink since.

"Later I learned that a good many people are borderline alcoholics. Some progress, others don't, but *anyone* whose life has to be adjusted to alcohol, arranged around it, is in trouble. Finding out about myself the way I did was a terrible shock."

The story depressed Mike. How did one know where the border was beyond which one could hit bottom?

He had coffee with the man who had greeted him, then he looked at his watch, put on a small smile, and briskly walked out to the waiting taxi. It was past spooker time. He asked the driver if there was a bar on the way to the airport; the cabbie knew a place. Mike went in and ordered an Old Grand-Dad. He was about to push the glass over for a refill, but he caught himself. At the airport he had his retarder: a bacon cheeseburger with two cups of coffee.

A light rain had begun, and when he dropped out of the black sky at the Danbury airport, he was wet, cold, and tired. The landing was hard, followed by a bounce. He didn't quite understand what had happened. It was probably the restriction of night vision. Of course, that was it.

AA wasn't going to work for him.

Mike knew it as he went to the bar in the Ridgefield house.

THE following week, just before his next San Diego flight, Mike drove over to an AA group in Stamford. Between the two meetings he experimented with his spookers. For five days prior to his trip he cut out the midmorning spooker, timing the rest of his intake precisely to a normal flying day. There were six and a half hours between the Ellen's Place fill-up and the one at the Houston hotel. The first four days were difficult, but by the fifth day he didn't quite feel the nagging emptiness around 10:00 in the morning.

On the day of his flight Mike stopped at Ellen's, but he didn't leave the cockpit all that morning. He wasn't ready for the afternoon withdrawal yet. When they left Operations in San Diego, Jim said softly, "Getting ahold of it, Mike?"

"Damned right. It'll take a while, but I'm in AA now, cutting way back, Jim."

51

That night at dinner Mike had two drinks instead of four, and he told Pat about AA.

"Aren't you supposed to *stop* drinking?" she asked.

"Honey, I don't want to stop entirely, I just want to drink less. I'm not an alcoholic in the real sense."

Pat didn't know what to say, but at least she knew he was easing off. He didn't even take his usual after-dinner brandy.

THE next few flights were routine. Mike skipped the midmorning drink, and on the third trip out to the coast without a problem, he decided to abandon the afternoon spooker. But the craving seized him before they got to San Diego. As soon as he left Operations, he raced for the men's room and unscrewed the thermos. He didn't sip, he gulped.

That evening he and Pat went to a beach party. It was the middle of January, but the weather was fairly warm. Steaks, seafood, corn, and potatoes were cooking, and as the party got into gear, Mike began to drink. By 11:00 he had had four stiff bourbons. He was enjoying himself, but about 12:30 he edged over to Pat, who was a little into it herself, and suggested they cut out.

"In just a minute, darling," she said.

That minute was an important one in Mike Hagen's life. He went back and asked for a bourbon refill, and the salesman tending the bar poured the pilot a stiff one. He finished it off, then asked for another.

Mike went to bed at Pat's at 4:15 a.m. He was not stumbling or wheeling about, but he was drunk. Pat woke at 8:00, looked over at Mike, sound asleep, then made sure that the alarm was set for 9:30.

As she dressed she realized that it had been a mistake to take Mike to the beach party. The buzz in her head told her so, but she had an important client presentation that morning and her mind was on her job, not Mike. She wrote a quick note, put it on the kitchen table, and left for the office.

The alarm went off at 9:30. When Mike finally switched it off and sat up, he had that fuzzy out-of-sorts feeling he had experienced so many times. Still, his hangover wasn't bad, considering the amount of bourbon he had consumed. He leaned back on the bed, thinking. Call in sick? No. As always, Mike rejected that one easy phone call. His recipe for mornings like this was a very cold shower, the heavy breakfast, a bigger than usual spooker, three vitamin B complex pills, and a little oxygen when he reached the cockpit.

Mike entered the kitchen and read Pat's note. Then he put on the bacon, and went to the bathroom to take an icy shower. The cold water cleared his head, his "fat" breakfast calmed the shout in his stomach. He packed some ice in a plastic bag, slid it into the thermos, and poured in Old Grand-Dad. At last it was time for the vital lifeline spooker. He drank thirstily, then called for a cab, telling them to make it fast.

FIFTEEN minutes past sign-in time, Mike walked into Operations after his usual routine with Visine, Sen-Sen, and cover stick. He ambled over to the dispatcher to get his machine flight plan. Then he walked to the weather boards and looked at the prog, the surface charts, and finally at the winds aloft. He was satisfied with the situation, and went out to the DC-8-61.

The pilot climbed the steps to the aircraft, said hello to Nancy, then concealed his spooker in the first head. When he entered the cockpit he told Jim and the flight engineer to double-check some figures in Operations. After they left he locked the cockpit door and slipped an oxygen mask over his mouth. He hit the switch and the cool, rejuvenating oxygen rushed into his lungs. He often did this to ease his head pains, and today, as usual, he felt much better in a matter of minutes. He put down the mask and unlocked the cockpit door so as not to arouse suspicion. Shortly afterward Jim Cochran and the flight engineer returned.

THE Stretch-8 lifted off routinely at 11:38 that morning and climbed to three thousand feet on a course that would take the flight over Blythe, California, then up to northern Arizona. The purity of the morning light magnified the ground colors. Through the front windshield they could see almost a hundred miles—the rugged end of the High Sierras, the rough plateau country beyond, then the burst of yellow desert stretching before them, finally disappearing into the soft horizon. The plane was on autopilot, and Mike sat back, feeling the first hunger of the day. He knew he would need two spookers—one at 12:30, another about 2:00—and he wondered if he could wait until 12:30 without a third, a damned third!

Jim looked over at the pilot. He saw his pouchy, heavy eyes and recognized the signs of a hard night, even through Mike's cosmetics.

At last it was 12:30; Mike lifted himself out of his seat. Both lavatories were in use, and when the second became free, he pretended not to notice. It seemed to take forever for the sign on the first to switch from OCCUPIED to VACANT.

The cold bourbon tasted delicious that day, colder, nippier than usual. He almost saw the tawny liquid trickling down his gullet into his stomach, absorbed into his bloodstream, traveling up to his head to work the nerves. He stood there for a minute, took a refill, replaced the spooker, and shoved Sen-Sen into his mouth.

When Mike returned to the cockpit, Jim had the New York forecast: Ceiling one thousand feet, light rain with two miles visibility.

IT WAS now 3:40 p.m. in New York and the rain had started. A low-pressure center, predicted to sweep through the area around 4:00, had picked up considerable speed and was already over the Atlantic and deepening. As a young IA meteorologist later said, "She was a freaky low, without a constant rate of speed." But the men in the cockpit of the DC-8-61 weren't aware of the change in the weather until they reached their next checkpoint, southwest of Cleveland, just about the time Mike left for his second spooker. The thermos went dry on the second paper cup, and when Mike returned to the cockpit, Jim told him to call Chicago. Mike dialed the company frequency, and the chief dispatcher came on.

"Captain, we notice you're behind on the check-in points."

"Affirmative. There's a bad head wind."

"How many pounds of fuel on board?"

Mike asked the flight engineer, then answered, "Twenty-four thousand, two hundred."

"That's about what we show. Captain, JFK's above minimum visibility for landing, but you can expect thirty to forty minutes of holding pattern near the airport. That'll put you into your reserve. Would you elect Cleveland or Pittsburgh to take on fuel?"

"I'll get back to you on that, Dispatch."

Mike clicked off the button and leaned back in his seat. By the time they landed and took on the fuel, at least another hour and a half would have gone by, and this delay would put Mike close to the "mean reds." He couldn't leave the cockpit in Cleveland or Pittsburgh and shop in uniform for liquor. The pilot felt like hell; he needed a drink and he couldn't wait an extra hour and a half.

Then he made a mistake. He told Dispatch the flight would continue to New York.

This was the first time that Mike's decision making had been affected by the spookers. He knew he was over the line now.

Jim, meanwhile, was doing calculations of his own. He found they might be pinched into a low-fuel situation if fog suddenly closed down JFK. "Mike, I think we should file for Cleveland," he said. "We're playing this too close."

"We're fine," Mike told his copilot. Then he whispered, low enough to outfox the voice recorder, "Get the hell off my back!"

At 6:30 New York time, JFK's ceiling was down to five hundred feet and the incoming traffic runway's visual range was about two thousand feet. Flight 602 was nine minutes late at the next checkpoint, the Philipsburg, Pennsylvania, VORTAC. But they pushed on.

What was about to happen was not entirely Mike Hagen's fault, although Jim Cochran and the flight engineer believed otherwise. The mistake of not taking on fuel along the way was clearly Mike's blunder, but this was compounded by the IA dispatcher working the flight, because he let the plane into the New York area when holding time was erratic. All that day, as the fog drifted in and out, holding time had alternately decreased and increased. Now, as Mike circled and circled, he was indeed cutting it close in his fuel, but he held on, hoping. The dispatcher finally had to say, "Captain, you're going critical."

"That's affirmative," Mike answered with an ease that Jim Cochran couldn't believe.

"Name Philadelphia," the dispatcher ordered, his voice edgy.

There was a pause.

"Philadelphia it is," Mike said mechanically.

He made a PA. "Ladies and gentlemen, we have been diverted to Philadelphia, and we should arrive there in about twenty minutes. We will return to New York as soon as weather conditions improve. We apologize for this inconvenience. Thank you."

Mike knew they'd be over Philadelphia with barely enough fuel. With fatigue creeping up on him, combined with self-disgust for not landing earlier and his belly's futile scream for another spooker, Mike realized he was in trouble. He prayed silently, Get me down on that strip, and I'll do anything! Just get me down!

The cockpit was dark, except for the reddish glow rising from the instrument panel. Still, even in this dimness, Jim noticed Mike's erratic hand movements as he fumbled about, adjusting knobs that didn't need adjustment. The flight was descending routinely and the last of the fuel was being pumped to the slowly revolving turbines. The men in the cockpit understood the perils, but the sleepy passengers behind them were unaware of the problems, mechanical and human, that could affect their lives.

At 7:20 that night, as the DC-8-61 was descending rapidly from fifteen thousand feet, Jim contacted Philadelphia approach control, seventy miles away. He pushed the button on the transponder and the flight was identified on the radar in the tower.

"We have you, IA 602. Descend and maintain eight thousand."

Nancy unlocked the cockpit door. She often sat down in the fourth seat to enjoy a cigarette before tackling her prelanding duties. Ordinarily she found a relaxed, easy atmosphere on the flight deck. Tonight the men appeared tense, their movements jumpy. "Is everything okay?" she asked.

"We have a problem, but we can't go into it now, Nancy," Mike answered. "Please return to the cabin. Everything will be all right."

Mike's skull was pounding. For a second he thought of asking Jim to take over, but Mike was stubborn, and he had decided this was going to be his final landing before running for help.

WHEN a large jet is being landed, everything—speed, horizon angle, sink rate, among other imperatives—must come together, and corrections cannot be made as quickly as they can in a heavy piston aircraft. All the way down the alley Mike was sweating, and when they broke out of the scud, about fifteen hundred feet from the threshold, he was about fifty feet too high and his target speed—which should have been around 140 knots—was reading 157.

56

"High and hot, Mike!" Jim yelled.

"There's plenty of concrete here."

It was *clearly* a go-around situation, but Mike continued, determined to stick it on.

"We're much too hot, Mike!" Jim yelled again as his hands reached out for the thrust levers.

"You touch those and I'll break your butt!"

Some eleven hundred feet later they literally hit the runway. The noise sounded like an explosion. The plane bounced, then they were flying again. But they were fully committed to a landing. It was too late for a go-around.

The runway lights whisked by in a trail of blurs; the needed concrete was slipping away, rushing by under them, and they were still in the air. Mike drove it on again.

This time the big plane stuck. The spoilers went up. Mike flipped back the reverse-thrust levers, pushing down on the brake pedals as he saw the end of the runway appear out of the mist.

We're going off the end! Mike thought in terror.

They started to slow; Mike had the brake pedals just about pushed through the floor. The reverse thrust screamed, and Mike was silently screaming, too. Then they stopped, not forty feet from the fence. They were so close to the end that if the plane had had its proper fuel weight aboard, the momentum might have taken them off the runway.

But they were on. Safe and stopped.

The passengers knew only that it was a hard landing, and most of them didn't realize they had landed twice.

In a matter of seconds, as the big DC-8-61 turned off the last taxiway from runway 9-Right, Mike came on the PA. His voice was steady and he had regained his composure.

"Ladies and gentlemen, this is the captain speaking. We apologize for that rough landing, but we had wind gusts on the way down and, as a safety measure, we kept a little more power on to better control the aircraft. This routinely results in hard landings, fully within the aircraft's operational parameters. The continuation of your trip to New York will be arranged in the airport."

The PA sailed over the passengers' heads, but the men in the cockpit knew the announcement was bull. The DC-8-61 had been

58

too high and too hot. Had the landing occurred on a shorter runway, they would have plowed off the end. It was only the structural integrity of the giant plane that prevented the undercarriage from collapsing and spewing everyone out on the wet runway.

The plane and the passengers had survived the human factor. This time.


MIKE taxied to the gate. Then he went to the head and vomited. When he had washed up, he saw what he never wanted to see again: a bloated face with puffy red eyes. He left the lavatory and went into the galley where Nancy was standing.

"New York's reporting below minimums, Nancy. We'll probably let the flight go here. That was a rough one. You got any of those little babies left?" Mike asked, indicating the liquor locker.

She looked momentarily surprised. "I've already locked it up, but I think I can find a few bottles." Nancy went out of the galley and returned in a few minutes, closing the curtain behind her.

"Here you go. Bourbon, right?" She handed him four of the small bottles and he stuffed them in his pants pocket.

"Thanks. I'll take them to the Belvedere with me."

"You're staying in Philly tonight?"

"Yeah. I'm tired of traveling. I just want to put my feet up."

Mike went back to the head, where he quickly drank two of the bourbons. He was bad off, and he knew it.

At 8:50 that evening the flight was terminated and the passengers were provided with ground transportation to New York. As Mike and his copilot made their way through the corridors of Philadelphia International Airport, Jim said he wanted to have a talk with him.

"I'm going to the Belvedere," Mike said. "We can talk there."

They rode in silence to the hotel, where Mike checked into a room on the fourth floor. He ordered ice and poured himself a drink. Then he slumped wearily into a chair, waiting for the reprimand from Jim.

"All right. Spit it out."

"Mike, until today I went along with you. I respected your flying and I thought you were really trying to lick the booze. But you're not. This morning you looked like hell warmed over. I won't sit in the same cockpit with you again. I feel sorry for you, but you have to pull yourself out. Can't you see what's happened? You have to get a doctor, Mike, real quick!"

There was a long pause.

"Jim, please." Mike got up and crossed to him, put his hand on the younger man's shoulder. The copilot saw Mike's bleary, pleading eyes. "Look at the job I did over Louisiana. My record is perfect. You know that, Jim."

"It's not perfect. Drinking—"

"Don't get sanctimonious!" Mike thundered. "You drink, too."

"Sure, I've taken drinks on layovers, but I've stopped that. And I've never taken a drink in flight. Why didn't we stop at Cleveland for fuel, Mike?"

"Because I couldn't wait another two hours. My spooker was dry. I needed a drink. Don't you understand what it's like? Haven't you ever desperately wanted a drink?"

"No, and I hope I never do. On that landing, couldn't you just have said, 'Take it, Jim'?"

"It was going to be my last landing until I got off the booze."

"*Your* last landing! It could have been my last landing, the last for over two hundred people." Jim walked toward the door, then turned. "Look, do everyone a favor. See Joe Barnes. Take yourself off the line until you've straightened out."

"I'll think about it, Jim. I will."


THE pilot slept fitfully that night. The next morning he had his usual large breakfast, drank the last bourbon, and deadheaded back to JFK.

When he arrived in Ridgefield the house was empty. He sat in the study, trying to decide what to do. Finally he called Dr. John Martinson, the family GP, who agreed to see him at 2:00 p.m.

Mike entered Dr. Martinson's office, and he waited for about twenty minutes until the nurse announced the doctor would see him. Dr Martinson was about sixty-five and he had a thin, wrinkled face. Straight out of a Norman Rockwell painting, Mike thought as he sat across from him.

"What's wrong, Captain Hagen?" the doctor said.

There was a long pause. "Well, I'm a little embarrassed to tell

60

you, but I drink too much," Mike finally said. "I have to have booze during the day."

"How long has this been going on?" the doctor asked calmly.

"About a year or so—I mean, during the day."

"How do you stop when you have to fly?"

"I don't. I guess you could say I'm sort of hooked on it."

"You drink while you're flying?" This time there was consternation in the doctor's voice. "In the cockpit?"

"I've been smuggling a thermos aboard. I put it in the lavatory and, uh, go there a couple of times during the trip."

"Don't you think you should stop flying until you get this cleared up, Captain Hagen?"

"I can't take sick leave without a lot of questions being asked. Besides, I never seem to get drunk like other people. In all the time I've been sneaking drinks, it hadn't reached the point that it affected my ability or judgment—until yesterday."

"Did you have an accident?"

"No, but we came damned close."

The doctor was silent for a moment, and then said, "You need more help than a general practitioner can give you. I think you should see Court Jameson in New Canaan. He's a psychiatrist who specializes in drinking problems. I've referred quite a few patients to him, with success. But you'll have to tell Court the truth, and then do what he says. Agreed?"

Mike nodded.

"All right. He'll want a complete physical. We can start this afternoon. I'll have my nurse call Danbury Hospital and make arrangements for you to have a liver-function test and X rays for an indication of liver shrinkage or enlargement. When you come back here we'll go through other tests."

Mike thanked the doctor and walked out into the bright sunlight. An exultation came over him, for he had made one decision. But he wasn't sure yet whether he could ever leave the spookers behind, or really wanted to. Deep down Mike didn't think he was an alcoholic—he never had blackouts, was abusive, or missed a flight because he couldn't get up in the morning. He characterized his problem as alcoholic addiction, not alcoholism. But he wondered about Dr. Jameson. What would he call it?

LATER THAT AFTERNOON the pilot checked into Danbury Hospital for the liver-function test and X rays. By 4:00 he could hardly wait to get out. It was spooker time. He needed a drink more than ever.

He left the hospital and drove to a liquor store, where he bought a pint of bourbon. Then he picked up a glass at a roadside shop, some ice from a machine, and headed for the Danbury airport.

In the hangar he poured a spooker, then another, and just sat there gazing at his beautiful, shiny orange bird. Finally he rolled *Alice* out, got in, cranked over the engine, and taxied down the field to a place where elm trees bordered the threshold.

He pulled out the mixture knob and the engine died. The pilot felt extremely low, thinking about his life, where it had gone. When the air became chilly, he taxied the Waco back to the hangar and went home.

Mike called Dr. Martinson. "Look, I've had enough hospital stuff for today. Could we let the rest of it go until day after tomorrow?"

The doctor agreed.


FIVE

LIKE many stewardesses, Nancy Halloway lived in the East Sixties of Manhattan. When she arrived back in her apartment that night after the Philadelphia landing, it was late and she was dog-tired.

While she got ready for bed she thought about Mike asking her for that booze. Somebody could have seen him stuffing those bottles into his pocket. That was the one thing the airline was rigid about: no liquor while in uniform.

A couple of days later Nancy trip-traded and went out to San Francisco on IA's flight 365. One of the other stewardesses was a girl who had been aboard flight 467 the day of the clear-air turbulence, and she and Nancy rehashed the trip and talked about how scared they'd been.

On takeoff from New York, they were again in the jump seat of a DC-8-61. Nancy happened to glance toward the lavatory door and the water fountain outside, and something that had been gnawing at her began to take shape. She concentrated, trying to reconstruct that earlier flight. She remembered Mike coming from the cockpit, taking a paper cup, and going into the lavatory. She had wondered about the cup then, because the water inside wasn't for drinking.

She had been the first one up after the turbulence, checking on the damage. She had gone to the lavatory to find out what the crash was all about. There had been a very strong smell of bourbon. No passengers had been in there; the only person to use the lavatory up to that point had been Mike. She was sure of that.

Next, the Philly trip. That was what was really bothering her. She had smelled liquor again in the lavatory. Then her visit to the cockpit, the guys' nervousness, and that awful landing. And the little bottles of bourbon Mike had asked her for.

She was sick with what she was thinking. One minute she was convinced it couldn't possibly be true; she decided to forget it; the next minute, she was sure it was. She knew many pilots who drank discreetly on layovers, and occasionally, on a difficult trip, she had a nip or two herself behind the closed curtain of the galley. If Mike Hagen was sneaking a few on the job, she could almost understand it; she'd heard his homelife was falling apart and he was seeing some girl in San Diego.

Mike was a cautious, skilled pilot—one of the best. She respected him; look at the way he'd handled the CAT incident. On the other hand, she had a responsibility to the people aboard Mike Hagen's flights. If she didn't mention her suspicions and something terrible happened when Mike was drinking and at the controls . . . As a matter of fact, she was scared for herself; she flew with Mike more than anybody. Maybe the best favor she could do him would be to bring things out in the open so he could get professional help. Rationalization. Reporting it would ruin his life for good. She didn't want to be the one to blow the whistle on him.

What she wanted to do was lay the whole burden at somebody else's feet. But whose? In her eighteen years with the airline Nancy had never heard of a stewardess reporting a captain.

Finally she decided that when she got back to New York she'd tell Gloria Esposito. Gloria had been a supervisor of cabin attendants at La Guardia for about five years. They were good friends.

When Nancy called, Gloria told her to come right over.

"What's the matter?" Gloria said, opening her apartment door.

"Offer me a drink, will you? That's what I want to talk about."

Gloria poured them both Scotch, and they sat down. Nancy began to detail the December 10 flight's turbulence, the Philadelphia landing, at last her growing suspicions about Mike Hagen.

"You mean he's drinking during flight?"

"Well, that's what it adds up to. I don't want to think it's true. Mike is the one who saved my hide that time in San Diego when I was dating Paul, the navy pilot, and missed the return flight. Mike covered for me with a story about how desperately ill I was. He put his own job on the line for me. Not only that, the guy is a really good pilot. I just don't know what to do."

"I understand how you feel, but if he is drinking, somebody higher up ought to know. I have an idea. I'll check ride out on 467 next time Hagen's on, and sit up front where I can see everything. We may be worrying for nothing. But if we do catch him doing it, we'll have to report it."

MIKE passed his physical. There was no liver damage, and he set up an appointment with Court Jameson for the following week. Mike had spoken on the phone with Jim Cochran three times after the Philadelphia incident, and had told him about seeing Dr. Martinson. Jim agreed to fly with Mike again. On a cold day in late January they both showed up at JFK Operations for flight 467.

"Morning, Jim," said the pilot. "How's the en route weather?"

"Looks good." Jim handed the captain the MFP, and the terminal and area forecasts for Houston. As Mike walked over to the weather desk, Gloria Esposito came up to him. She didn't think he looked like a lush. But Dr. Martinson had told Mike that he should start by cutting down on his drinking immediately, and the pilot had only taken two drinks the night before and a spooker at Ellen's Place that morning.

"I'm Gloria Esposito, check riding first class," she said.

"Oh, sure. Well, looks like we'll be having a smooth flight."

Nancy, standing on the far side of Operations, never looked up.

Before boarding the DC-8-61, Mike took Jim Cochran aside. "I want to thank you, Jim. I'll still be taking one or two probably. I don't have the cure yet, but it's coming."

"I understand. No problem, Mike. I'm glad you went to the doctor. And relieved that you didn't mind me sounding off."

64

Mike boarded the plane twenty-five minutes before departure and stowed the thermos in the first lavatory. Gloria Esposito was sitting in 1-B, where she could see the forward head and the cockpit door. She was pretending to read *Vogue,* but over the pages she watched the captain enter the lavatory and close the door. After Mike returned to the cockpit, she entered the lavatory and studied everything carefully.

"No sign of booze," she reported to Nancy.

The takeoff was effortless. As soon as the plane reached cruising altitude, the stewardesses started the meal service. About two hours into the flight, Mike Hagen stepped out of the cockpit. He did not notice Gloria Esposito as he reached toward the dispenser, snapped a paper cup down, and entered the lavatory.

Mike looked in the mirror. The red rivers on his left cheek seemed lighter. He wondered how he would look when he stopped the spookers. But it wasn't time. He carefully pulled the cold thermos through the disposal locker door and poured the bourbon into the cup. Then he poured a small amount back into the thermos. He touched the icy liquor to his lips and felt the first bite of the fluid running down to do its work. He loved the feeling. He swallowed the rest, rinsed the cup, and put it in the disposal.

As soon as he came out, Gloria glanced at her watch; he'd been in the lavatory four minutes, ten seconds. She immediately went inside. No smell of liquor. Nothing unusual.

"Nancy, he just took a cup into the lav," Gloria whispered as she stepped into the galley. "But I didn't smell anything."

"I want to check myself." Nancy entered the first lavatory. Gloria was right. No odor.

On the last leg of the flight, when they were over Arizona, the pilot left the cockpit and went to the lavatory again, and that evening, at dinner in San Diego, the women began to discuss the Mike Hagen routine.

"He does the same thing each time," Gloria said, "but I noticed something on the last leg. When he came out to use the lavatory, the first one was occupied; the second lav wasn't, but he waited until the first one was free."

"You think a bottle's hidden in there?" Nancy said.

"Possibly, but I searched that place thoroughly." Gloria sighed.

"Maybe he's just carrying a couple of miniatures around in his pocket. I'll try to look for that tomorrow."

"Perhaps you won't find anything," Nancy said hopefully.

MIKE Hagen sat across from Pat in the small Mexican restaurant; he was unusually silent, only drinking one bourbon. Hurrah for AA, she thought.

"I want to tell you something," he said slowly. "AA wasn't for me. Those people seem to enjoy telling the whole world about their boozing. I just couldn't do it. I'd be embarrassed." He paused. "But," he went on, "something happened last week. I made some mistakes on the flight back to New York."

"I knew it! That party the night before. It was my fault."

"No, it wasn't your fault. I should have decided to land at an alternate to take on fuel, but I didn't." Mike looked down at the red tablecloth. "My bourbon was gone. JFK's weather was marginal. We held too long, fuel ran low, so we put in at Philly. I made a sloppy one-bounce landing. I was scared, Pat, for the first time in twenty-five years of flying."

"Oh, Mike." She grabbed his hand.

"Anyhow, I went to the doctor, had a complete physical, and next week I'm seeing a shrink."

"You're not fooling yourself anymore, are you, Mike?"

"No, I'm in trouble. I know now what I have to do, Pat. For me. And for you."

THE flight back was a long one, with very little push from the westerly winds. Mike went to the head twice, and after his second visit, Gloria Esposito went in to inspect the lavatory. Bourbon!

The supervisor bolted from the compartment and signaled Nancy with her finger. Both women entered the lavatory.

Nancy sniffed. "Bourbon," she said. "Very faint, but it's bourbon."

THEY landed at JFK twenty minutes late. Mike got into his Nova and headed for Ellen's Place. He parked, sat in the car for a minute or two, then drove home. It was one of the few times he'd reached Ridgefield without the kick of a spooker. He felt elated.

During the next two days he was able to cut down a bit more

and he thought he looked better. Then it was time for his appointment with Dr. Jameson. He dressed carefully and applied just a hint of the cover stick.

Court Jameson's office was in his home, a very large, restored eighteenth-century colonial house, with a manicured lawn reaching out in all directions. The doctor must be good if he can afford this, Mike thought, or maybe he's just expensive. For a split second the pilot considered bolting, but he remembered Philadelphia and walked to the door with the polished brass plate, at the side of the house. He pressed the buzzer and a woman appeared.

"Good morning. You must be Captain Hagen." She led him across the waiting room and opened the door of the doctor's office.

Court Jameson was sitting with his feet up on an antique desk. He looked much younger than Mike had imagined. Maybe it was his smooth Ivy League face, the kind that immediately tells you there's been plenty of money in the family for a good long time. Mike was relieved. No beard and no psychiatric couch. The doctor got up immediately and shook Mike's hand.

"Glad to meet you, Captain Hagen. Have a seat." He gestured to a red leather chair. "We're kind of informal around here. If you don't mind using first names, call me Court."

"That's fine. Well, how do we begin?" Mike asked.

"We already have. You're here. Dr. Martinson has filled me in. Now, Mike, let me ask you a question. Are you committed to licking this thing, whatever it takes?"

"Yeah, no choice. I didn't think it was affecting me until the other day, when I messed up a landing in Philadelphia. That's some admission, isn't it?"

"Well, you're here now because you want to work it out. I'm not going to tell you all the horror stories, but the liver can only take so much, and the booze eats away the brain cells, can even cause impotence. It's progressive. You just have to catch it or it'll wreck you. And it's a bad way to go down."

"I know."

"Alcoholism is a treatable disease. I can help you get off the booze, but for a real cure, we have to find out *why* you drink."

"I understand."

"There're three ways we can pull you off the stuff. AA does a great job. Then there's the hospital, where we detoxicate you under medical supervision. It's a real tough five days. Scary. You'll probably have delirium tremens and convulsions, but it will stop your drinking, and it's safe. Also expensive. The third option is to set up your own program of withdrawal, cutting down a little bit at a time. We measure it very carefully."

"Might as well tell you. I'm an AA dropout, and I'd have to borrow for the hospital."

"If you really have willpower, you can wind down yourself."

"I've already cut down some, so I know I can do it."

"I have a little plan that you're going to laugh at, but it works," Dr. Jameson said. From his desk he took out a shot glass ringed with different colored lines.

"You'll have to buy a jigger like this, a four-ouncer, and on it paint five circles: red, four ounces; green, three ounces; blue, two; and pink, one. Yellow, the last circle, is a half ounce. Next, get a small diary with a page for each day and a line for each hour. And a box of stars like the kids have for spelling."

"Okay. What do I do with them?"

"You match colors—if you drank to the red line, paste a red star. You're drinking on board the plane by hiding the thermos in a lavatory, Dr. Martinson said. From now on, you keep the jigger with the thermos and measure how much you drink. Begin by drinking just as much as you normally would. If you have three or four a night— Is that about your level?"

"About."

"Then record that. Write down your exact intake. But measure it. Pour your drink into a glass—or paper cup—then into the jigger, then back into the glass again. Day after tomorrow I want you to cut down the size of your drinks by dropping down one ring on the jigger. If you start on the red, go to the green. Spend three days like that, then we'll move to the blue for three days."

"How far do we go?"

"That depends, Mike, but the only way this is going to work is with total honesty. I want the record to be accurate. If the stars get clumsy, buy colored pencils—anything to keep track. One final unorthodox bit in this little plan of mine—if you feel a withdrawal attack coming on after you've stopped for a period, take two pills that I'll give you a prescription for. They're strong enough to keep you calm. Now, rather than have you come into the office week after week and tell me your life story, which would take a lot of time, I'm going to ask you to write it in three installments: boyhood to teens, teens through early twenties, and adult life. Don't be afraid to express your emotions, and don't try to tell me what you think I want to hear."

"How do I know what's important?"

"What I want are the facts; you choose what's relevant."

"Can I tape it?"

"No. Do you type?"

"Hunt and peck."

"Then type it and deliver installment number one to my secretary the day before your next appointment. Will you be able to take a little time off until we have a handle on this?"

"Yeah, I'm not scheduled out again until February."

The doctor stood up. "Good luck, Mike. Don't cheat. If you do, it's just a waste of my time and your money."

MIKE drove very fast to a stationery store, where he bought the paints, the diary, and the colored stars. Then he went to a phone booth in the rear and called Pat Simpson.

"Hi, it's Mike. Just came back from the psychiatrist's. He's a nice guy, a little Ivy League, but okay."

"I was praying you'd go. What did he say?"

"Well, he said my thing was treatable." Mike went on to tell her about the stars, the jigger with the colored bands, and the three-stage autobiography.

"I'm so proud of you, darling. And please do everything the doctor asks."

"I will, Pat, believe me. I'll call you later tonight."

Pat said good-by and put down the phone. She had not been this happy for a long time.

LATER that afternoon Mike went to five or six stores before he could find a four-ounce jigger. He bought it and then went over to the office, where he painted colored lines around the glass. He felt good, so good he went to the icebox and poured himself a spooker.

He was just about to drink it when he remembered the prescribed routine.

He poured the bourbon into the jigger—three and a half ounces. Mike decided not to split ounces. Should he pour more in or some out? What the hell. He poured a bit of the gleaming liquid back into the Old Grand-Dad bottle, the rest into his ice-filled glass. He was at the green line. He chuckled out loud as he took the box of stars and pasted a little green one next to the 4:00 p.m. line in the diary. He put the whole kit into his desk drawer.

Then he rolled a piece of white typing paper into his old Remington. He stared at the blank paper, and began:

"I was born on January 8, 1933, at Mercy Hospital, Miami, Florida, the second of two children. My brother, Tom, was born four years earlier. My grandfather and grandmother came from Galway, Ireland, in the late nineteenth century, and settled in Washington County, Maine, near the Canadian border. They bought a sixty-acre potato and blueberry farm, where my father was born in 1900. He had four brothers, and they all worked on the farm. My father also worked for a lumber dealer, and in 1925 he began selling lumber for shipment to Florida.

"The hotel-building boom of the 1920s was in full swing and my father moved to Miami as the representative for the Maine lumber dealer. He made quite a lot of money and bought a small citrus farm on the outskirts of Homestead, Florida. He married a girl he met in Miami, whose father ran a restaurant. They started citrus growing and lumber jobbing, turning out doors and other stock items for the hotels.

"When I was born, the Florida building boom was over. We had a difficult time during the early years, and my brother and I both worked. My family was able to get by, since we grew our own food and my father took odd jobs as a carpenter. He was a very religious man. We always attended Mass, and he shoved me into the confessional almost every week.

"Nothing much happened that was too unusual when I was a kid, except that I took up flying, and I was spraying groves at sixteen. Had a lot of friends around Homestead, played on the high school baseball team, but flying was my whole life. I received a

70

partial scholarship to the University of Florida at Gainesville; the other half I paid for by crop-dusting. I started at the university in September 1949, four months before my seventeenth birthday. End of Chapter One."

Mike read over what he had typed. He knew it was inadequate, but he made a few corrections, put it in an envelope, and set it aside, ready to drop off at Jameson's office.

SIX

IRENE Monihan, head supervisor of cabin attendants at IA's La Guardia base, was an obnoxious spinster who took her frustrations out on the girls. In return, they hated her. How such a disagreeable person avoided being fired was a mystery. She had begun as a stewardess long before the jet age, then moved on to a supervisory post. She had been transferred from base to base, and the older she got, the more she bore down on the young, bright-eyed girls fresh from the carrier's training school. Both Gloria Esposito and Nancy Halloway had had run-ins with Irene. There were few who hadn't.

After flight 602 arrived in New York, Nancy and Gloria decided they would have to go through regular channels in reporting their suspicions about Mike. And that meant Irene. They also decided to report the incident together, partly for moral support, and to share the blame for what might happen.

The following morning Gloria called Irene. "Nancy Halloway and I have a very important matter to discuss with you."

"Shoot me a memo, sweetie," Irene said.

"I can't. If you can't see us, we're going to Fitz."

There was a lengthy pause. The head supervisor's tone changed. "That important, huh? Okay, eleven o'clock."

When Nancy and Gloria arrived in Irene's office, they found her looking as if she'd had a bad night, which was going to make matters worse.

They told their story. The head supervisor said nothing, listening without a change of expression. When they finished she said, "Do you realize what it means to wreck a captain's career? If you're wrong, you'll both be out looking for jobs. Joe Barnes is a tough man. But we might as well get this over with. So, come on, ladies."

She got up from her desk, crossed the corridor, and pushed open Joe Barnes's door. Nancy and Gloria followed. "Want to hear a horror story, Captain Barnes? It seems one of your pilots drinks on the job."

Joe stiffened. "What the hell are you talking about?"

"There's a supervisor and a stewardess here with the goodies."

Joe knew Gloria only slightly, but he recognized Nancy Halloway from the hearings in San Diego. "Sit down, girls. It's all right. I'm not half as bad as Irene," he said with a big grin.

They relaxed a little, but no one spoke. Finally, Nancy drew a deep breath and said in a low tone, "It concerns Captain Mike Hagen. I'm afraid he's been drinking on the plane."

Joe Barnes laughed. "He's the best man at this base! Whatever put that in your head?"

"He takes a paper cup and goes into the lavatory during flight. I've smelled liquor in there."

"I can back up Nancy's story. I was check riding one of Captain Hagen's flights and saw the same thing. Here're my notes."

Gloria passed the paper to Joe Barnes. He read it and tossed it back to her.

"All this tells me is that Mike went to the can several times. Later, you went in and smelled bourbon. A lot of passengers bring flasks aboard and nip in the lavs. You know that." He paused, no longer pleasant. "Did either of you ever actually see Captain Hagen drink?"

"No," Nancy said.

Gloria shook her head; she knew Nancy wouldn't tell Joe Barnes about Mike asking for the bottles in Philadelphia.

Irene sat back in her chair. She was enjoying the delicious little drama, one of the few that came to her dull office routine.

"Mike Hagen probably saved your life during that clear-air turbulence, and you march in here with this story!" Joe thundered at Nancy. "Why are you doing a number on Mike? You been going out with him? This a personal grudge?"

"No, no," Nancy cried, jumping to her feet. "I happen to like Mike Hagen very much, but I did see this thing and you have an obligation to check it out."

72

"I didn't mean to imply that I don't believe you; it's just that you're making a very serious charge based on purely circumstantial evidence."

"I realize that," Nancy said. "It was a difficult decision for me."

Joe was thinking. He had sent Cliff McCullen a memo on Mike's handling of the CAT, and in reply the vice-president had called to say that he and Fitz wanted to take Mike to lunch. Cliff had even suggested that Mike might be management potential, and Joe was basking in the reflection of Mike's good work. Now this. What a bad scene!

"Nancy, Gloria, of course you did the right thing by coming here, and I appreciate it. I guess I just got a little upset because I know Mike very well. To tell you the truth, I very much doubt that Mike Hagen's sneaking into the head for bourbon. But we'll sure find out! Until we do, you're not to mention this to *anyone*. That means boy friends, girl friends, the man in the supermarket."

Irene grinned. "Sorry we ruined your day, Joe."

"You did that. Oh, one more thing. Gloria, would you mind leaving me those notes you took."

She hesitated for a moment, then smiled. "Sure, why not? But will you let us know what happens, Captain Barnes?"

"Yes, as long as you promise me this stops right here. That's the deal."

The women trooped out of the office.

For almost ten minutes after the women left, Joe sat in his office looking straight ahead, too stunned to concentrate; he didn't even hear the roar of the jets. Then, forcing himself to think about what the stewardesses had said, he convinced himself that it wasn't true. Mike had just told him on the way back from San Diego that he didn't touch the stuff in the daytime. If it did turn out to be true, it would rock the entire Flight Department.

Slowly he began to sort things out. Who to tell? McCullen? No. Should he call Mike Hagen in and confront him with it? No, not yet. Joe had to be sure. He thought about Mike's copilot, Jim Cochran; Joe was certain Jim wouldn't reveal anything, even if he suspected a problem.

He decided he'd call Larry Zanoff, a check pilot in Los Angeles.

Larry was an old buddy. They had started in DC-3s together and had worn down a lot of seats. Joe would ask him to request a temporary New York assignment. Larry would check Mike out.

After Joe had contacted Cliff McCullen, he called the chief pilot on the West Coast and arranged for Larry's transfer. Then he set to work on the next part of his plan, which involved assigning Zanoff to Hagen's flight sequence. That job would be handled by IA's crew-scheduling department at JFK.

Joe Barnes knew one of the men handling the bid sheets, Gordon Terrell; he had been studying flying for some years, hoping to move into IA's Flight Department, but the going had been slow, and Joe wondered if the young man would ever make it. He called Terrell and asked him to come in that afternoon.

"WANTED to see me, Captain Barnes?" Gordon Terrell said as he stood at Joe's office door later that day.

"Have a seat, Gordon. How's the flight training coming?"

"Pretty good. I'm almost ready for the flight test. That's what the instructor says."

This pleased Joe. "Well, I'm proud of you. I had two reasons for calling you in. First, I'd like to see you in the cockpit one day and I wanted to make sure you were still flying. Second, I need a little confidential favor from you."

"Anything, Captain Barnes."

"You heard that Mike Hagen did a great job on that turbulence last month? Fitz thinks maybe Mike could help update our standard operating procedures. We want to take a closer look at Mike."

"I understand."

"Now, if we just put a check pilot in to watch him in action, Mike would become nervous. So, Mr. McCullen had a very special idea. He picked out a man from our L.A. base, Larry Zanoff. He's a check pilot, but no one knows him at this end. I want him assigned to Hagen's trips as copilot. If anyone asks who the new face is, tell them he's here temporarily because his mother in White Plains is sick. Got that?"

"No problem. The bid sheets are due back in a couple of days. When I get Hagen's, I'll just assign Zanoff to his trips. No one will ever know that you requested it, Captain."

JOE BARNES CALLED Larry Zanoff that evening and told him about the cabin attendants' report on Mike Hagen.

"That's something," Larry said. "Think it's true?"

"No, but I have to find out."

"Well, I'll take a couple of trips with him. If he's putting down a few, Joe, we can sure find out."

The following day Joe Barnes picked up the medical and flight-performance records on Mike, and drove to Newark to meet the arriving Larry Zanoff.

Larry hadn't changed much in the twenty-seven years Joe had known him. He had been prematurely gray, and his pocked, hard face hadn't aged, even though he was now over fifty. With twenty-six thousand hours in his book, Larry was one of the finest captains IA had on the line.

Larry was to stay with the Barneses in Englewood, New Jersey, a kind of family reunion. The job that had brought him, however, was extremely unpleasant. It wasn't discussed during the first part of the drive to the Barneses' house; finally Larry said, "I don't like this sneaking around behind Hagen's back. But I guess it's better than jumping the gun. Could there be any reason for the girls to lie about this?"

"Don't know. Hagen and this stewardess have been flying together a long time. Wouldn't be the first time a guy got rapped by a jealous broad. But he's got such an excellent record. Just look at his file."

Larry picked up a tattered folder from the seat and studied it as they drove. It was the record of an impressive high-timer.

That evening, after a steak dinner, Joe called Mike on the pretense of setting up the lunch date with Fitz and Cliff McCullen. Then he said casually, "There's a Larry Zanoff in here from L.A. One of our senior captains. His mother is quite ill. I arranged a transfer east for a few weeks so that he could be near her. He's supposed to go out on 467 as your copilot. Hope you don't mind. Cochran's assigned to reserve."

Mike Hagen felt an immediate alarm, but he calculated that he was doing so well with his booze wind-down that he would be able to manage, even with a new copilot. "Fine. I'll see him in Operations Tuesday."

Mike called Jim Cochran. "Did Barnes phone you?"

"About an hour ago."

"He mention anything, you know, about—uh—the spookers?"

"No. He just told me there's a West Coast crew member coming in and I'm on reserve. Nothing else." Jim paused, then said, "How are you doing, Mike?"

"I'm seeing a psychiatrist now; no phony baloney, though. Straight guy, and he's already got me drinking less."

"That's the way to do it, Mike. You planning to take the thermos aboard with this new guy?"

"Have to. Might not need it, but it's a security blanket, and I want it there just in case."

<br>

SEVEN

MIKE didn't feel easy about his second visit to Dr. Jameson's office. He felt he had done a poor job with the autobiography, but he had kept the drinking log with him at all times. He had faithfully pasted in the stars. At first they were all green, then he moved down to the blue. He felt pretty much the same, but he was able to sleep a little longer in the mornings. He was delaying his first spooker of the day until just before leaving for the artificial-flower business. But by 11:00 he would desperately need another. Still, the log indicated that he was slowly, successfully coming off the booze. As soon as he entered the office, the doctor looked at the diary.

"Everything accurate?" he asked Mike.

"Down to the ounce," the pilot said proudly.

"How do you feel, Mike?"

"Not too different."

"Good, considering you're drinking less. When are you supposed to fly again?"

"Tomorrow."

Court Jameson took up the paper Mike had written. "I was surprised at this. It's the shortest first chapter I ever received, and you didn't write about yourself. You wrote about your father. I'd like to know more about growing up in Florida during the 1940s. You liked it there, didn't you?"

"It wasn't the Florida of hotels, beaches, pools, all that. South of

Miami it was a really wild place, full of gators, snakes, swamps. The crop dusters would come in for the spraying season. I liked those guys. They were a very close group, they had their own thing going. They flew their own equipment and did what they wanted. I was their mascot. We'd sit under the shade of the wings, drinking Dr. Peppers, eating Moon Pies, swapping stories. It was special, the Florida I remember."

"When did you take your first drink, Mike?"

"At fourteen. But everyone thought I was sixteen. Big for my age. Every night the Ag flyers would get bonkered at the Gator Hole—a bar that had country music on Saturday nights and good chili for twenty cents a bowl. One time they said, 'Let the kid come along.' They were going to get me drunk."

"Did all the flyers drink? I don't mean Dr. Peppers."

"Almost every guy had a flask. They were tough, hard drinkers— that's why they were called flying cowboys."

"So you never saw anything wrong with drinking and flying?"

"Never did, up to a point. You were judged on how well you could drink and fly—not separately—together."

"Did you continue to drink at the Gator Hole?"

"That or others. Each Ag strip had a Gator Hole. Bartenders knew the flying cowboys drank. Do you remember Woody Guthrie? Well, the flying cowboys used to collect his seventy-eights and spin them when there wasn't country music playing. A couple of cowboys had met him along the dusting route. That was a whole other world."

Mike spoke in a nostalgic, affectionate way, as if the old crop dusters were still down on the Ag field and the Woody Guthrie seventy-eights were spinning as always in the Gator Holes of the South. Mike was living in the 1940s, Court Jameson was certain of it. The wistful man in front of him was far away in a place that no longer existed—if, indeed, it ever did exist exactly the way Mike imagined.

The doctor tried to visualize the hard-flying men piloting planes along rows of crops under a hot sun. It was a unique world of flying Mike had talked about—too high and the fertilizer spread in the wind; too low or too near, death. Court realized that Mike Hagen was a cowboy and probably as good a one as they came.

Packed in his words was a love and respect for wide-open spaces, big fields, and big skies.

"Tell me," Court said. "What does it really take to be a good pilot? Does it mean going by the book?"

At the word book Mike shifted in his leather chair, then got up and walked to the end of the room.

"I'll tell you about the book. Half the people who write them don't fly. All they know is numbers, not feelings. When I started in DC-3s, the book told you how to get it going. The rest was in here." He pointed to his heart. "We wrote the book each day while we flew. They issue us a handbook for the DC-8 that's over five hundred pages!"

"But the equipment is more sophisticated."

"You asked me what it takes. It's not in the book, it's judgment—knowing what to do and when. And what *not* to do."

"I find it interesting that you talk about judgment."

"I know. I drink in the air. That's *not* good judgment, but let me tell you about judgment—the way I see it."

"I wish you would," Court Jameson said as he reached for his yellow pad. He was anxious to hear the definition of judgment by an alcoholic airline captain.

"In all the years that I've been drinking and flying, I never thought I was taking a chance. I've always compensated. I've always known exactly how many spookers I could get by with. Early on I realized my reactions in the air were slowed down by the booze. So I wrote away to the FAA for accident reports and studied them. It became my hobby. What did I learn? Two basic things. Sometimes there are accidents that a pilot cannot control—like midair collisions—but looking at the whole spectrum of accidents, I found few with no pilot error. Pilot error very seldom has to do with fast reflexes; I figure it is ninety-five percent judgment. Big equipment does take numbers—book flying—but once in a while numbers don't help. When you're making an instrument-landing approach to a field where the ceiling and visibility are right at the minimums, that's when judgment comes in. What to do? Try to land, or go to your alternate?

"Another thing. Imagine a situation in which all the autopilots are out. The crew has to fly by instruments accurately, hour after

hour. Few guys can do this unless they practice like hell. I can hold a better course and altitude with severe turbulence, on instruments, than any pilot at IA."

"You know, Mike," Court Jameson said, "there's a flaw in all this. The Philadelphia landing . . . what happened there?"

"It's hard to explain. There's a lot to think about when you're putting a heavy plane down. I was nervous, my mind was jammed. We were high and hot over the threshold and the copilot was screaming to go around." Mike shrugged. "But I decided I could put her on. And I did. And I was craving bourbon like a crazy addict."

"Mike, I want to make sure you realize you *cannot* fly while drinking the way you have. It *did* impair judgment and reflexes. You might have killed everybody on board."

"But I didn't. I handled it all right."

Mike was still rationalizing; even as he admitted a potentially catastrophic mistake, he ended up by saying he had pulled it off.

"Do you really want to stop drinking?"

"No, I don't think so. But I want to get it under control," he said forcefully.

"Okay, we had a good session. Remember, one more day on the blue, then go to the pink. Don't get overconfident; you'll slip once in a while. Don't worry about it or feel guilty."

TUESDAY. Mike woke up a little later than usual. He dressed and cooked his eggs. After breakfast, with his diary and the ringed jigger packed in his heavy black flight bag, the pilot began the drive to JFK. He was at the fourteen-ounce level for the last time; tomorrow he would reduce his consumption to twelve ounces, the next plateau.

He decided to have only one ounce at Ellen's that morning while she refueled his thermos. You could barely see that amount of bourbon: a tiny brown puddle circling giant icebergs. He brought it to his lips and in a second it was gone. He hardly felt the bourbon as it disappeared inside him. Another one, he thought. No. There were thirteen ounces left for the rest of the day. He wanted to stretch them out, leaving a good reserve for his night with Pat. He took a page from the back of his diary and charted his last fourteen-ounce day.

6:30 a.m.—1 oz. at Ellen's
10:00 a.m.—2 oz. in flight
1:00 p.m.—2 oz. lunch at hotel
(No drinks on afternoon leg)
Evening—three 3-oz. drinks with Pat

The big change from his old pattern—the one Mike wasn't sure he could handle—was in the afternoon segment over the southwest. He planned to take his meal and two ounces at the hotel as late as he could, pushing the 12:00 Houston spooker to 1:00; that would be just enough time before checking in to Operations at 1:15.

The pilot gave himself a final glance in the car mirror—eyes, cheeks better this morning—and walked across the lot to Operations. At the crew-scheduling counter, Mike signed in and asked the guy behind the desk to point out Larry Zanoff.

"Over there, Captain Hagen."

Mike saw a tall man with a pepper-and-salt crew cut studying the winds aloft chart. He walked over and introduced himself, noting the four stripes on the sleeves and the tiny red wings, IA's thirty-year insignia.

"Nice to meet you," replied Larry Zanoff. "I guess we'll be flying together for a few trips. I'm in the right seat today. Just picking up time while I'm here."

A voice came over the loudspeaker. "Hagen—Captain Hagen, there's a telephone call."

Mike walked to the phone on the far side of the scheduling desk.

"Mike, this is Court Jameson. Sorry to seem to be checking up on you, but I've been thinking—maybe you shouldn't take any flights out at all until we wind this thing down some more."

"Everything's okay. I cooled it last night, slept well, and this morning I only had one ounce. Could hardly see the stuff. I have a new copilot today, a senior captain in here temporarily. So there'll be two senior captains in the cockpit, a flight engineer who flies, and two autopilots."

"All right. You have the pills?"

"Right in my pocket."

"Call me when you get into San Diego. And keep on that schedule, Mike."

As Larry was filing the flight plan, Mike walked over to his bag.

He knelt beside it with his back to the rest of the room and slipped out the thermos, the jigger attached to its side with broad rubber bands. He pushed his raincoat over it, closed the flight kit, and stood waiting in the narrow corridor for Larry.

LARRY Zanoff resented his task. There exists between pilots a rare camaraderie—an allegiance to and an utmost trust in each other. Each man on the flight deck must rely on the rest. For one captain to be spying on another was a sensitive matter in their close world, yet Larry knew it had to be done, distasteful as he considered the assignment. He would find out about Mike Hagen, if, indeed, there was anything going on. He was a professional cockpit investigator, recognizing the small clues that index a pilot. Ironically, what Larry was to observe on that morning's takeoff from JFK would add up to a performance he wished every IA pilot could execute.

Like many longtime drinkers, Mike Hagen was a highly proficient actor. As they walked to gate 7, Mike joked with Larry, who noted the pilot's apparent ease; Mike's cheerful manner was not that of a man under pressure, squeezed between the last drink and the one coming up.

When they stepped into the cockpit, Mike placed his raincoat over the left seat, backhanded the thermos, and was into the first lavatory before Larry knew what was going on. Mike worried that the piggyback spooker with its attached jigger wouldn't fit through the small flap door, but it just did. As a safeguard, the pilot edged it far back into the upper corner of the bin with a hooked five-inch wire that he had stowed up his sleeve. Thirty seconds later he was back in the cockpit.

Meanwhile, Larry had riffled through Mike's flight kit and his raincoat. As the pilot slid into the left seat, Larry brushed against him. He could neither see nor feel the bulge of small bottles and he was sure Mike couldn't have hidden any in the lavatory in such a short time. Larry felt better, for he was hoping not to discover anything.

Mike went through his flight-deck work load with care and efficiency. He studied the dispatch papers and the route they'd take into Houston. Data on the computer printout indicated the flight would be very light that day—well under the JFK and Houston allowable weights.

"That means we'll go with reduced thrust," Mike said.

"Guess so," Larry answered.

Mike noted the outside temperature and scrupulously checked the calculations of the flight engineer. When the paperwork was finished, Mike slid out of his seat and stood at the cockpit door, greeting the last of the oncoming passengers with his big, congenial smile.

In the days when Mike flew DC-3s he had walked slowly up and down the aisle to reassure people. But as jet flying developed, and because of the increased incidence of hijackings, pilots had been ordered to remain on the flight deck and to work behind locked doors. Mike made up for this by chatting with the passengers a few minutes before and after each flight. Larry Zanoff had only seen one or two other pilots do this, and he thought it was a good idea from a company point of view.

THE flight was pushed from the gate, the turbines started, and ground control directed the DC-8-61 to runway 31-Left. When they were cleared for takeoff, Mike took the four throttles forward just enough to give the Pratt & Whitneys the necessary speed and distance—about eight percent under full power.

The purpose of the reduced-thrust takeoff is to increase engine life while conserving fuel. Some pilots argue that it lowers the level of safety to reduce power on takeoff, but the FAA does not object to as much as ten percent reduction when conditions such as weight, runway length, and temperature are met. Mike felt it was safer, as a rule, to employ full power, but when he was flying with a senior captain like Larry Zanoff, he used the reduced-thrust takeoff.

When they reached takeoff speed, Larry called it, but Mike left the bird on the runway a couple of seconds for a touch of extra airspeed. It was an old habit from his biplane days, when a little extra was often the difference between life and death. But this technique has little relevance for big-jet operation.

Mike held his airspeed needle right on $V_2$ plus 10 knots, the takeoff safety speed. They climbed to fifteen hundred, and Mike started his left-hand turn, which brought them over the old Floyd Bennett Field.

They cleared the Long Island coast at three thousand feet to allow inbound traffic to runway 4-Right to slide in under them.

Larry quickly added up the points in his head. On the plus side, Mike looked good; his cockpit procedures were correct and businesslike. His passenger contact was approved, so was his reduced-takeoff decision. His ground handling was expert, his course holding and transitions right on the button. The only minus was Mike's decision to delay the lift-off.

Larry Zanoff was satisfied with Mike Hagen. He knew a professional high-timer was in the left seat and he was almost certain the man wasn't nipping in the lavatory. But there were many miles before them, and Larry continued to observe the pilot closely.

AROUND 10:00 a.m. Nancy saw Mike leave the cockpit. Then something different. The pilot went directly into the head without taking a paper cup.

Inside the lavatory, Mike hooked his baby with the five-inch wire and pulled it toward him. He grabbed the thermos and poured two ounces into the ringed jigger and drank slowly. He would put the star in his notebook later. He rinsed the jigger, refastened it, and pushed his spooker far back into the disposal locker.

Immediately after he went out, Nancy slipped into the lavatory. She sniffed the air. No smell of alcohol.

A few minutes after Mike returned to the flight deck, Larry excused himself. The check pilot was certain Mike wasn't carrying a bottle, so if indeed he had booze aboard, it would have to be hidden someplace in the lavatory. Nancy, who had been briefed about Larry Zanoff, waited for the check pilot to leave the cockpit and then approached him quickly.

"He used the first lavatory," she said, "but there was a change this time."

"What?"

"He didn't take a paper cup."

"I'll go look around anyway."

Larry was methodical; he started on the left side of the counter and pulled up every panel that could be removed, taking out the tissues and small soaps, and dipping his hand into every opening.

He even applied pressure to the bulkhead panels to test their security. Larry was just about to leave when he noticed the disposal flap door. He poked his hand inside as far as it would go; he felt nothing. He came out, shook his head at Nancy, and reentered the cockpit.

They landed at Houston on time. Again, Mike went to the head; he came out a minute later, his black raincoat concealing the thermos. Larry went in and ripped open the disposal locker; there were no bottles buried in the trash. When they reached Operations, Larry suggested they have a bite to eat, but Mike said he had a luncheon date.

Feeling awkward, Larry followed the pilot at a distance. He saw Mike go to the front desk at the International Hotel, take a key, and walk to the elevator. Larry crossed the lobby to the counter.

"A friend of mine, pilot for IA, just registered."

"Oh yes, Captain Hagen, room 409."

Larry went up to the fourth floor, where he passed room 409 and took a position at the far end of the hall. He realized that if Mike Hagen were drinking on the plane, he'd certainly be taking a few in the hotel room, a very private place.

Inside 409, Mike was holding back on his next spooker. After a hot bath, he called room service. He rested on the bed, watching TV until a young waiter delivered his order. When the young man left the pilot's room, Larry approached from down the hall.

"Son, I need a little help. I'm from the airlines," he said, showing his official IA identification card. "What did you just take the man in 409?"

"Swiss on rye and onion soup. He has the same thing all the time."

"Ever see any booze around the room, or bring him some?"

"No, sir."

"What about ice? Ever bring up a bucket of ice?"

"Nope."

"Is there an ice dispenser on the premises?"

"Nope, you got to get it through room service—me. Say, what is this about anyhow?"

"Routine check." Larry pulled out a five and handed it to the waiter. "Have you ever noticed a woman go in there?"

"No, he's always alone—just reading or watching TV."

"Thanks, son. Don't mention our conversation, okay?"

"Sure. Thanks for the bill."

Larry was sure that Mike wasn't sitting around the hotel room drinking warm booze. But why had he said that he had a luncheon date when he didn't? And why did he take a room at these prices?

Larry watched the door from a distance. No one entered Mike's room. A few minutes later the pilot came out and went to the elevator. Larry hastily tried the door of room 409. Locked. He ran down to the maid and persuaded her to unlock the door and let him in.

There was no smell of bourbon and no empty bottle in the trash basket. The check pilot crossed to the bathroom and saw that one of the glasses had been used and he smelled it. It had the unmistakable odor of mouthwash.

Larry returned to the cockpit fourteen minutes later.

"Where were you? I don't like late check-ins," Mike said crisply.

"Oh, I met someone I used to know." Larry Zanoff felt just a trifle dirty.

THE delayed lunchtime spooker helped, and Mike got through the afternoon segment of the flight without leaving the cockpit, although his baby was stored just in case.

He arrived at Pat's office around 4:00 and they left immediately for her house. But as they drove south the pilot felt that lust for the bourbon, as if alarms were going off deep in his belly, in his head. It was not imagination. The signals were real.

LARRY Zanoff rode over to the El Cortez Hotel with the rest of the crew. When they reached there, he called Nancy aside. "He never left the cockpit this afternoon, but if he is drinking, it must be stowed somehow in that first head. I want to try something different tomorrow. I think I know how we can be absolutely sure about this. If he's hiding booze in there and if he's an alcoholic, he'll have to get to that head, won't he?"

"I guess so. It's a long flight back to JFK."

"After Mike comes aboard and goes into the first lav tomorrow, I'm having the mechanic turn off the valves so the toilet won't flush. You put up a sign to seal it off, and if Mike makes a lot of noise about using that head, we'll know he's got something in there and we'll tear it apart when we get into New York. If he merely uses the second one, then I think we can be pretty sure there's nothing to worry about. You agree?"

Nancy nodded her head slowly.

PAT prepared a festive meal that evening and Mike drank his remaining nine ounces; it wasn't enough, but he had promised Jameson, and when he considered the other two choices—standing up in the AA meetings or blowing a wad on a hospital—he decided to stick with the wind-down, if he could. And tomorrow would be rough—his first twelve-ounce day.

After dinner Mike plotted the next twenty-four hours. The flight left at 11:30 a.m. He would take his first three ounces in the morning before departure.

> 9:00 a.m.—3 oz. at Pat's
> 2:00 p.m.—3 oz. in flight
> Ellen's—3 oz.
> Ridgefield—3 oz.

He put the notebook away and went in to call Jameson; the doctor was glad to hear that Mike was holding on. Later that night Mike showed Pat his book with the stars. She smiled; then, catching the earnest look on his face, the small glint of hope, she grabbed his hand.

"I'm proud, very proud of you, Mike."

"You know," he said with a rueful look, "I'm scared of getting to the point where there are no more stars in the book. Then what? Something has to change. Like everyone, I've been drinking to escape. But there will come a day without stars and I'll see it all: Jean. The stinking flower shop. It's so awful. I don't like my life, any of it, except for my daughters and you."

"Darling, I have something to tell you. About two months ago I sent my portfolio to a New York advertising agency."

"I thought you didn't like the big city." She had been in New York years ago as a scared little kid and had told him often she could never live there.

"Things are different now, Mike. I want to be with you."

"Do you really mean it?" he asked, brightening.

"Yes, I'm coming east, Mike."

They embraced, and Pat knew things were going to be different for both of them.

EIGHT

LARRY Zanoff arrived at IA's San Diego maintenance office at 8:00 the following morning. The men there had instructions from Joe Barnes to do anything Captain Zanoff requested.

"Turn off the stop valve! I never heard of such a thing," one of the maintenance men told Larry. "Why screw up a toilet?"

"There's a good reason."

"Yeah, well, okay, the first head on flight 602."

"I'll walk out with you," Larry said. "I also need a roll of steel strapping tape and some heavy scissors."

Before the 11:30 departure Larry headed for Operations, where he looked at the MFP and studied the weather situation. Winds aloft were swift. It would be a fast flight.

Mike was right on time for the 11:30 flight to JFK. When Larry met him in Operations, he noted the captain's smart, straight walk. Larry was certain that the girls were wrong about the booze, and he was glad, because he knew the whole embarrassing matter was just about destroying Joe Barnes.

Mike entered the first head and stowed his spooker. He had already taken three of the allotted twelve ounces. It was going to be a tough day and he patted his pocket to make sure he had the bottle of pills.

At precisely 11:31 a.m., flight 602, San Diego–New York nonstop, was on its way. The flight director would take the plane on autopilot to its first VORTAC station, in Arizona. Mike made his usual cheerful good-morning PA, then settled down. Spooker time was two hours away. Two hours of boredom. He wished he could stick his head out the window and feel the wind, yell. Anything.

Nancy Halloway covered the first lavatory door with strapping tape, enough to hold a tiger gone mad. Then she tacked a sign on the door.

LAVATORY CLOSED. TOILET INOPERATIVE
PLEASE USE OTHER LAVATORY

MIKE began to feel the first hungry sensation—his body's initial cry for the booze—when they were fifty miles west of Tulsa. He asked for some food, which always helped. But past Tulsa the shriek came again. He looked at his expensive chronometer. Ten minutes to spooker time. The ache surged through him, but he stuck to his schedule. Five minutes, three minutes. Time.

Just as Mike left the cockpit, Nancy was coming out of the galley. She stopped, put down a tray, and crossed to the magazine rack. Mike saw the note on the lavatory door and a bolt of fear tore through him. Aware that Nancy was watching him, he managed a smile. "Shouldn't the flight engineer look at the head?" he asked her.

"It's no use. The flush button is out. Can't be fixed in flight."

The pilot smiled again to cover his surprise and fright. He moved to the second head and went inside. When he came out, with the pills in his hand, Nancy was shuffling magazines into the rack. Mike took a paper cup, filled it with water, and stepped into the galley. She followed him.

"You ever have an allergy?" he asked her.

"No. What do you take for it?"

"A prescription. Better than drugstore antihistamines."

He took the tablets and returned to the cockpit, his stomach flip-flopping. He was experiencing the stark panic of withdrawal jitters. The doctor had said the pills would work. What if they didn't? What if he got the shakes? More pills?

The gnawing hunger switched to pain. Then he became slightly light-headed. His vision seemed to be affected; he lost focus. He felt he was floating. "Our next checkpoint?" he asked Larry, hoping to get his mind off the panic.

"We're 140 miles off the Nashville VORTAC."

Twenty minutes later Mike began to feel the shakes. He tried to remember what he knew about the d.t.'s. Would he have hallucinations, see pink elephants, go into convulsions? Maybe he was far enough into the cure not to have full-blown d.t.'s. More pills? No, he would hold out as long as possible. Jameson had said they were strong. Nearing the Nashville radio beacon, Mike began to feel calmer as the pills entered his bloodstream. He wanted to slip off into a long sleep; he ordered coffee and began to talk with Larry just to keep awake.

The drug was worse than the drinks. But what would have happened if the head had broken down before he met Jameson, before he had the pills? In his mind he saw himself rushing to the galley and dumping all the liquor bottles out as the girls looked on petrified. Questions were spinning around in his mind. What would he do now if Larry Zanoff were to slump over the wheel suddenly? What if there were an inbound traffic delay at JFK and they had to circle? Could he get the plane down with a flight engineer whose ability to help with the giant aircraft was limited?

Mike feared the unexpected. Would he fall into a stupor? If he only knew what the pills would or wouldn't do. The coffee seemed to help. He felt more awake, but quite strange—his head seemed to be wobbling loosely on his neck and he was sweating heavily. He asked Larry for the chart.

"Right here," Larry said, pointing to a VORTAC forty miles west of Baltimore.

Where had the minutes gone? Was he losing his sense of time? "We'd better pick up the JFK weather," Mike said. "And you take her in, Larry."

It was a clear night and Mike could see the speckled lights of the farmlands below. Above, the moon was playing with the fast-racing cirrus clouds. He felt all right for a while. Then suddenly, without warning, the anxiety returned. He was going to explode. Mike knotted his fists and prayed, fumbling in his pocket for the pills. He grasped two from the container, picked up the intercom, and asked for a Coke.

The second stewardess brought the drink to the flight deck. Mike washed down the two pills, and soon he felt heavy and lethargic: drugged. The thought that JFK was near helped ease his terror.

Larry landed the plane easily, and Mike said a private prayer of thanks. Almost eight hours without a drink. But Ellen's Place wasn't far away. He would call Dr. Jameson immediately, Ellen's Place or not. Should he try to enter the lavatory? Trying to rescue his liquor when the lavatory was inoperative would be too risky.

He could always buy another thermos. Mike edged off his seat, and things seemed a bit blurry.

He stood at the cockpit door, saying good-by to the passengers. If these people only knew, he thought. If they only knew.

An elderly woman with two children approached. "I've been promising my granddaughters they could shake hands with the captain." Nancy watched Mike laughing with the children. She felt a terrible guilt.

Larry and Mike left the plane, walked across the concourse, and said good-by. Mike found a phone booth in the concourse, took out a handful of quarters, and dialed Jameson's number. The answering service said the doctor would call right back, when Mike told them it was an emergency. The phone rang almost immediately.

"Mike, are you all right?"

"I think so, but I was damned scared. The lavatory broke down on the plane. Haven't had a drink for eight hours. I started to feel it up there and took the pills. First two, then another two."

"That's a lot. Now, Mike, listen carefully. Don't take a drink under any circumstances. Don't drive, either. Take a taxi to Silver Glen—the hospital I told you about. I'll meet you there and put you under observation for tonight and tomorrow. This is a critical time for you. Call your wife and say you're staying in town. I'll have you signed in under another name, Robert Brown." He gave the pilot the address of the private hospital.

Mike called Jean, then caught a cab. He felt so drowsy he dropped off to sleep once or twice. The cab took a long time to find the hospital, once a private estate in the hills outside of Stamford. He paid the driver, placed his uniform coat and hat in his bag, and put on a sweater. He rang the doorbell. A woman answered and took him to a comfortable paneled room, where Dr. Jameson was waiting.

"How do you feel?"

"Drugged, dammit!"

"You *are* drugged. I'm going to give you a quick physical, a light supper, and a shot that'll really make you sleep. In the morning, try not to have a drink, just the pills. When your condition is stabilized and you're awake, we'll have a session here. We'll probably be able to break down the withdrawal symptoms very quickly."

JOE BARNES WAS full of anxiety as he waited for Larry Zanoff to reach his home. He met Zanoff at the door. "Does he or doesn't he?" he asked the check pilot.

"No, *he* doesn't. But *I* do. How about a drink?" Larry was smiling. They went to the sun porch, where Joe fixed drinks.

"I guess you want everything," Larry said. "First of all, Mike's a good pilot, just as you said. His technique was flawless, except that he left the plane on the concrete a little too long in New York."

"I know. It's a carry-over from his DC-3 days."

"Okay, but it isn't good. I don't like guys in the cockpit doing things their way, not ours."

"All right. I agree, but it's not serious. I know he can fly a plane. What else?"

"Mike checks into a hotel on the Houston layover. I thought he might be drinking in the room, but the waiter claims he's never seen liquor or brought him anything from the bar, not even ice. I went over the room after he left, trying to figure out why he was willing to pay so much for such a short stay. There was no woman, no booze. Nothing. But he had ordered some food, so maybe a private meal and a short rest are worth the money to him."

"What about his trips to the head?" Joe asked.

"He went in once during the morning leg yesterday, but Nancy said he *didn't* take the cup. Today we taped the first lav shut. According to Nancy, Hagen just looked at it and entered the second one. He came out in thirty seconds, took a cup, and swallowed two pills—allergy medication, he told her."

"So that's why he's been going to the head," Joe said with a sigh of total relief.

"Could be. I'd say it's all a mistake, a bad one. I'm sure he wasn't taking anything into the head, and I searched the place thoroughly both before takeoff and after we landed. That head was empty. One more thing. Nancy's very upset. I wouldn't take it out on her, Joe. She was only reporting what she saw and smelled."

"He didn't appear to be drunk at any time?" Joe asked, just to make certain the verdict was unequivocal.

"No. But I'd like one more ride with him just to be sure. Could you arrange for Mike to take out flight 15 to Los Angeles next week instead of his regular trip? It would give me a good six hours in the cockpit with him. And if everything is okay, we'll forget this whole business."

"Ordinarily he would be going out again in five days, but—"

"Eight days would be better for me," Larry interrupted.

"Okay, I'll see what I can do."

The next morning Joe Barnes called Nancy and Gloria into his office. A heavy burden had been lifted from the chief pilot's back and he could afford to be magnanimous. "First of all, you did the right thing and I want to thank you. Don't be afraid to come to this office anytime. But it's obvious that Captain Hagen isn't drinking in the lavatory. He was taking some kind of pills for an allergy. None of us will mention this matter again. It's over."

It was 9:30 a.m. when Mike awoke after his night in the hospital. His head was fuzzy. A nurse entered his room with a bright good-morning and lifted the blinds.

"How are you today?" she asked.

"Feel sort of funny—musty."

"You'll get over that. Take these two pills. And here's our breakfast menu and *The New York Times*."

Mike obediently swallowed the capsules.

"Incidentally," the nurse continued, "you have an appointment with Dr. Jameson at eleven. We have a gym with a pool, and I've scheduled you for a massage, if that's all right."

"Yes, thank you." A massage would be great, Mike thought. He checked off bacon and eggs and gave the menu back to the nurse. Then he took a shower and shaved. He felt better, and the events of the previous day seemed like a far-off nightmare.

After breakfast Mike walked out of the manor house toward a new brick building. He felt good. No morning drinks; he was back across the line. Inside the building was a small gym, where several men were exercising. They were obviously wealthy, middle-aged businessmen on the dry-out run. Mike took a swim, then rested as a big, burly masseur worked him over. At 11:00, Mike was back in the main building, meeting with Court Jameson.

"Mike, I made a bad mistake in letting you take that flight out. Coming off the booze is often worse than being on it. Anyhow, you're going to have to drink something today. We can drop it down to six ounces. If you can get by today and tomorrow at that level, we're in good shape."

"Do I fly next week?"

"If I can get you stabilized at six ounces, maybe less, without anything during the day, you can go. If not, then call in sick."

"I think I can do it, I'm sure I can."

"Okay, then. Let's pick up on your autobiography where we left off. You're a licensed pilot now. You're crop-dusting and you have a scholarship to the university."

"I graduated in 1953, when I was twenty. Soon I was married to Jean."

"We haven't talked much about that, have we?"

"She was very pretty, the sexiest woman I ever knew. For a while I loved her very much, but slowly our marriage came apart, until there seemed to be nothing left. She spent money like crazy and criticized me for flying."

"If you wanted to be a crop duster, how did you end up with the airlines?"

"After our marriage, I continued spraying. I had my own plane, a Stearman. Well, Jean would drive from town to town in our cranky old Chevy station wagon and meet me wherever I would land to load up on spray.

"We had an apartment in Fort Lauderdale, but we spent most of the time on the circuit. One night Jean told me a baby was on its way. I was pretty happy; I sort of wanted a son. Then she said that I'd have to settle down. It got to me. Our first blowout. I thought I was settled down. Hell, how many guys of twenty have their own fifteen-thousand-dollar plane, a college degree, thirty-nine hundred hours in their logbook, and a good client list along the crop-spraying route? I was bringing home about five hundred a week after expenses.

"Jean said we couldn't raise a kid in motels and Gator Holes. She was right about that, but I figured she could live in Lauderdale. I'd base the ship there for the long sugarcane and citrus season—just be out for the soybeans and cotton. But she wouldn't listen.

"Instead, she suggested I go to law school or learn a profession. Now what would I do in law school? I didn't care about a fancy profession, I already had what I wanted. I was never anything but a rural kid who loved Florida and planes. I had a thing about dusty roads and big clouds, and I thought crop spraying was the greatest thing in life. Still do.

"Then, Jean says maybe I should fly for an airline. Me in a uniform flying an airliner! Do you know that up to that time I had only flown in a closed cockpit three times? I was an open-cockpit guy. I sat outside with goggles and felt the wind and smelled the oil in that big old radial up front of me, and I'd know every change in the engine. That was my life—sniffing hot oil, seeing the rows drift by, pulling up at the last moment when I came to the end of a row. I'd pull that stick back and feed in the power. Half the clowns would miss plants on the section line. Not me. I knew what I was doing.

"Jean persisted, and finally I gave in. I signed with a factory flight school in Miami to get my Air Transport Rating. I had to sell the Stearman to pay for the course. I didn't just sell an old biplane, I sold myself.

"Anyhow, I went to the flight school. I had more flight time than half the instructors, so I made it out of there in four months. Afterward I went up to Boston, flew a DC-3 as a copilot. It was wild flying—little fields, lousy weather, wings icing up half the time. But I liked it."

"If your whole orientation was crop-dusting, the South, I can't imagine your liking flying in New England."

"I was surprised, too. But the airline was small, informal, and it was beautiful flying. When the spring came, I could see the crops starting to grow. I began to know the routes, the landmarks, the station managers. I thought I was doing something important; the railroads had gone bust, and we provided about the only service for a lot of people.

"When we got to Boston, Jean had a miscarriage. I think she always blamed it on me. Then we bought a house in Needham, Massachusetts, and life was okay. After about two years Jean and I had another talk. She didn't think I was making enough money, wanted me to fly jets for a major carrier. I told her I was with my kind of airline. But Jean was pregnant again so I applied to some larger lines. In 1957, I was hired by IA to fly copilot."

"Were you drinking?"

"Yeah. Couple of drinks a night. But I never flew hung over. Then we moved to Ridgefield and things really began to sour. I made my transition to jets and the money was much better, but the bills were bigger, too. I realized the marriage wasn't going to last. Or if it did, it would only be a front for the children."

"Were you drinking during the day at this time?"

"Yes. I used to have one or two before lunch. I remember the first time I took a drink in the morning. It was at home. I just needed it somehow. Then it became a habit."

"How long ago was this, Mike?"

"A couple of years, I guess."

Court Jameson looked down at his yellow note pad. "Let's backtrack. You liked flying the DC-3s. . . ."

"Yeah, because you couldn't just push a button and let an electronic device take you to the VORTAC station. But our equipment became more and more sophisticated. Autopilots for the autopilot. What the hell was I? No more than a bus driver. I tried to get some of the old feeling back by buying a biplane and restoring her—I call her *Alice*—and by doing some instructing at Danbury."

Court got up and walked over to a big bow window. Mike sensed the next question.

"If you weren't in love with your job or your wife, why didn't you do something about it?"

"I did. About three years ago I met Pat Simpson and fell in love. I also drank."

"If you had all the options in the world—could do anything you wanted, had the money—how would you change things?"

"I'd like to marry Pat. We talked about it, oh, maybe a year ago, and we agreed to wait until my daughters were a little older. They're thirteen and sixteen now. But they know something's wrong. Maybe a divorce would be better than living in the middle of a squabble."

"Assuming you work your personal relationships out satisfactorily, what about your job?"

"I'd like to buy a couple of Ag planes and develop a route through the crop areas, starting in Mississippi with soybeans, moving along to cotton, sugar in central Florida, finally winding up the loop in the deep citrus country. I have this idea of buying into a

96

fertilizer factory and organizing the sprayers into a co-op. In fact, I've talked to a few of 'em. Even without the factory, I could at least set up a distribution point—buy wholesale, make a couple of cents a pound. It wouldn't be bad."

"As soon as we pull you off the booze, Mike, you'll have to come out the other side with something new, something that you really want. Without that, you'll be back on the juice in a month."

"Yeah, I know, but I'll never let it get to me like it did."

"Remember, Mike, most alcoholics can't drink at all. You could, and as we've said, that was part of your problem. Your system handled it very well to a point, but if you'd gone on much longer, we'd have had an even more difficult job on our hands."

The doctor then told the pilot that during the rest of the wind-down period he was to report to the hospital daily on an outpatient basis, and they would continue to talk.

THE week went well. Mike bought another thermos—for safety's sake, he told himself—and painted the rings on a new jigger. He continued to paste in the stars; there weren't too many now. He was down to six ounces and holding. On the third day in a row that he reached 5:00 p.m. without taking a drink, he slid open the door to the hangar that housed *Alice*. He started the old bird and flew her around the pattern one time.

It was his special victory flight.

Dr. Jameson had told Mike that once in a while the spooker need might catch up with him, and he should take a drink if he had to. During the late afternoons of that week, he felt the urgency and wondered if he would ever be able to get by the cocktail hour without a drink. But he had come a long way and he was proud of himself.

The day after he flew *Alice* around Danbury airport, Mike went into New York for the luncheon meeting Joe had arranged with McCullen, Fitzsimmons, and Hanscom. They ate at the Harvard Club, and everyone ordered drinks before lunch. Mike decided on a dry sherry, not to impress the others; he was out to impress himself. When the sherry came, he thought it was much too dry and only took one taste, which Joe Barnes noticed.

As they stood in front of the club after lunch, Fitzsimmons came over to Mike. "Did you ever think of management, Captain Hagen—moving over to Third Avenue?"

"Not really."

"Well, if you ever do, give me a ring. The management team always needs men who can think, who know airline operations."

Mike thanked the vice-president, but running through his head was a small laugh. If they only knew how little he cared about airline management—the books, memos, manuals—a treadmill of trivia from which he was so desperately trying to extricate himself. He shook hands with the immaculately turned-out executives. On the street, they went east and Mike walked west; he didn't know why, but he went the other way.

NINE

MIKE sat in his study contemplating the changes in his life. Day by day, as the craving for a spooker lifted, a new lucidity was coming to him; he saw and smelled more, suddenly discovering details—a few pleasant, but most of them disturbing—that had been hidden in clutter and shadows. The branches on the maple tree in his front yard seemed larger than he remembered. His house seemed sloppier. The office, the stinking, jungle-scented upstairs world of fake exotic flowers, was worse than he imagined. Even things at the Danbury field began to look different: the hangar for old *Alice* seemed smaller, and the brutish Waco's color seemed brighter now.

He knew that it was decision time. If he continued with the same life, he would be right back at Ellen's Place.

It was easy to sit in a psychiatrist's office and jabber on about a rural Florida youth, but to return to those times, a way of life long gone, was a whimsical goal. Mike was intelligent enough to know that his beloved daredevils were no longer sliding glued-up biplanes onto dirt strips. They had been replaced by young, highly trained men flying sophisticated, expensive equipment. The spray business had gone big time, too.

Chucking in the towel on a $55,000-a-year captain's job for a crop-spraying venture appeared more and more frightening. But what were the options? He could report to IA's Third Avenue offices and become an executive, although that new life might

98

evoke the same old problems; or there was instructing, at maybe $10,000 a year. He'd have to develop a plan.

First he had to tell Jean that it was over. Then he and Pat could take an apartment in New York. Perhaps he would call Fitz and say he was interested in the executive job. While he was collecting his checks, he could investigate the crop-spraying business.

THE pilot had his talk with Jean. They sat in the study and she looked bored, as if she knew what was coming.

"Jean, I guess you know our marriage is over."

"Darling, it's been over for some time," she said. "Hadn't you noticed?"

"So how do we do it without hurting the girls?"

"I don't know," she said, getting up and moving to the bar. "We could get lawyers and fight, like everyone else, but I don't think we need that. You, obviously, have someone you want—"

"Yes."

"Maybe I do, too. I want a lot more than you can give me, Mike. I'm enlarging the flower business, moving it to New York; I've obtained new financing and a partner. He's a lawyer. I might marry him. Also, I've spoken to a few real estate dealers about the house. They think we might get a hundred and forty thousand, with the price of land around here as high as it is."

"That much?" Mike felt a burden lifting. Perhaps the house *had* been a prudent investment. They had only paid $65,000 for it and the mortgage had been reduced considerably. They sat talking calmly for a while, and it was the most sympathetic and rational conversation they had had in years.

MIKE called Pat that evening, and the following morning he drove out to JFK to meet her. They put the bags in the car and went to Ellen's Place. Pat understood the significance of the visit. As they entered the squalid, gray-shingled place, she was overcome with pity, but when they slipped into a booth and Mike told Ellen he wanted a Coke, she knew he had won. Pat had a glass of milk, and finally Mike stood, a big smile on his face as he crossed toward Ellen.

"Ellen, I'm being transferred and I want to say good-by."

"Sure, good luck—whatever you do."

Mike walked out of Ellen's Place forever, and they drove north to the Hilton Inn in Rye, where Pat registered. During dinner Mike said that he was just about off the booze, down to four ounces a day. He told her about the talk with Jean, and at last he said, "How would you like to be the wife of an airline executive, or of a crop sprayer or something?"

Pat smiled and leaned over and kissed the big, red-faced pilot. "Anything you want, darling."

They talked about living in New York. She was going for an interview with an advertising agency, and Mike kept thinking about working on Third Avenue. Other people did it, and with Pat there, maybe he could survive.

Early the following morning he took Pat up in *Alice*. They flew over his house, then he pulled an inside loop. Mike felt higher than God. Pat screamed, partly from joy, partly from fright. Everything seemed perfect; the pilot knew he had made it.

THE next morning Joe Barnes called, asking Mike to take out flight 15—the 7:30 p.m. JFK–LAX nonstop—three days later, with Larry Zanoff flying in the right seat. During the period before their departure, Mike wondered whether or not he should carry the spooker aboard. Finally he decided to take it along. It would be a long trip, six or more hours, depending upon the head winds. Every once in a while he still felt the need for a few ounces.

Mike didn't know if he wanted to come off booze all the way, but he knew his limits now. He had his final session with Jameson just before the nonstop to Los Angeles.

"Is this graduation?" Mike asked.

"I think so, but when things begin to go wrong, and they will from time to time, don't reach for the bottle. Come back and let me help you. You've proved that you have self-control, Mike, and that's the most important thing."

Mike left Court's office that day a confident man.

IT BEGAN as a light snowstorm, the morning of Mike's scheduled departure for Los Angeles. Suddenly the storm intensified, and shortly before noon on that February 20, snow covered the JFK taxiways and runways. It had been a difficult week for snow-removal operations at the airport. Two previous storms had left residual accumulations in below-freezing temperatures.

That afternoon heavy winds forced the closing of all but two runways. By 3:50 p.m. the snow had turned to rain, but the temperature had risen only to 32 degrees, so ice formed on both active runways.

The snow committee—airport officials and pilots from various carriers—was watching the situation closely. Continuous aircraft operation and wind often make a runway patchy, so that one part of it may be slick, while another section remains rough; this can affect an aircraft's traction and braking, and the only remedy is constant sanding. All that afternoon and evening they alternated runways, closing one, operating the other.

MIKE had a three-ounce drink at lunch and then went to Pat's room at the Hilton and slept for a few hours. When she woke him at 4:00 p.m., he saw the snow and called IA Operations.

"This is Captain Hagen. I'm taking flight 15 out tonight. Do you have an estimated time of arrival on the inbound equipment?"

"Yes. It left L.A. on time. No delays en route, but we have half-hour inbound delays now."

"What about outbound?"

"No delays yet. I'd say, at the worst, 15 will be away from the gate maybe an hour late."

Flight 15 was a DC-8-61, license number N4962C. The plane was configured exactly like the equipment used on flight 467. The required 180-hour special inspection of the plane had been carried out two weeks earlier. That check had shown no maintenance problems.

MIKE and Pat arrived at JFK at 6:15 p.m., and Mike took Pat in to see Operations. As soon as they entered the impersonal, airless room, she understood why he detested it.

For Mike, entering Operations totally sober was another victory, like drinking a Coke at Ellen's Place. Pat, who would be flying out to the coast with Mike, left for the lounge, and Mike and Larry Zanoff began to discuss the flight.

101

"The front is beyond us," Larry said. "Some turbulence up to nine. After that, it should be relatively easy. Situation's local."

The equipment was on the daily JFK–LAX route, spending each night in Los Angeles; and when flight 14, the inbound service, landed in New York at 6:25 p.m. on that February 20, no maintenance report on N4962C was filed. The trip was thirty minutes late arriving at JFK, and 15 was set up to go out at 8:30 p.m. instead of 7:30 as scheduled.

In addition to Larry and Mike, there were seven others in the crew: the flight engineer and six cabin attendants, five female, one male. Louise Conners, a pretty blonde, came up to Mike and introduced herself as the senior stewardess that evening.

"This weather's local," Mike said. "We shouldn't have too much trouble once we're out of here."

Louise smiled and thanked the captain. She and her cabin attendants left Operations together and walked along the concourse toward gate 6, on the left side of IA's terminal.

MIKE and Larry walked down the loading ramp with that confident air and slight swagger that told everyone these were high-time veterans. The spooker in Mike's left pocket was hidden by the raincoat over his arm. After entering the aircraft, he stored his thermos in the first lavatory and looked at himself in the mirror. Not bad, he thought. His face had lost much of the old puffiness, and the telltale rivulets on his left side seemed lighter, almost blending into the apple-red of his cheek. It had been nearly eight hours since the pilot had downed his three-ouncer and he felt extremely well. He was over the worst of his problems, and most of his self-respect and pride had returned.

When he entered the cockpit, Mike noticed the force with which the hail was hitting the front windshield. "What's the runway visual range?" he asked Larry as he slipped into the left seat.

"Three thousand. Doesn't look it, does it?"

"Sure doesn't," Mike said, peering about. He could hardly see the line of red lights on top of the terminal.

As the two pilots were going through their paperwork, George Gibbons, the flight engineer, was moving around underneath the giant transport. Among his preflight duties was inspection of the exterior of the aircraft. The hail was blasting him in the face as he completed his visual checks of the undercarriage, turbines, and control surfaces. Everything satisfied his cautious eye. George did not linger at each inspection station, but spent just enough time to convince himself that N4962C passed her test.

PAT was now standing just outside the gate area. Mike had told her she could probably board early. She felt deliciously happy. There was no question in her mind that Mike had licked his drinking problem, and since Jean had agreed to a divorce, her own future appeared rosy indeed. Pat studied the clusters of anxious passengers who were bunched up around the check-in counter.

From where she stood she could see the giant tail of the plane through the large wraparound windows. Finally an IA passenger service representative led a group toward her—a small blond girl, clutching a doll as well as her mother; four flashy-looking TV executives, two nuns, and a TV talk-show personality, Brenda Moore—the preboards. The service representative told Pat that Mike had arranged to have her come aboard with this group.

They walked down the loading ramp toward the plane. Inside the first-class cabin they felt a blast of cold air rushing in through the open galley door where the stewardesses, still in their overcoats, were taking in the last of the catering supplies.

The little girl was starting to cry, and Pat smiled sympathetically at the mother. "This is Marsha. It's her first flight," explained the mother. "My sister will be meeting her on the other end. I hope she'll be all right."

"Why don't we make friends?" Pat said to the child. "I know the captain. Would you like to meet him?" Marsha stopped sniffling and a slight smile crossed her lips. Pat took her by the hand and the mother followed as they walked toward the flight deck.

"I'm Pat Simpson, a friend of Captain Hagen's," she told the senior stewardess. "I thought this little passenger would like to meet the pilot."

Louise Conners nodded. "Mike asked me to take special care of you, Miss Simpson." She indicated that they should move forward.

"This is called the cockpit, and there's the man who is going to fly us all the way to California."

Mike, delighted to hear Pat's voice, turned and saw the small girl and motioned her toward him. "Come into my office," he said with a big smile, and took the child on his lap. "See all those instruments? They're going to tell us where we are."

"I hope she won't be too much trouble," the mother said.

"We have children all the time. They settle down very quickly. The stewardess will take good care of her," Mike said, handing the little girl back to the mother, who returned with her to the cabin.

Pat lingered for a minute. "What a night," she said.

"Bad down here, but the upper air is forecast to be fairly smooth. We'll be out of this stuff soon after takeoff."

When the flight engineer entered the cockpit, Pat went back to the cabin. She was in 1-A, the first seat on the left in the first-class section, and the little girl was next to her. The child's mother had left the plane feeling relieved. Two rows behind, Brenda Moore sprawled in a window seat reading *Variety*, and across the aisle the nuns sipped hot chocolate.

The rest of the passengers on the fully booked plane were boarded, and the heavy door of the DC-8-61 was swung closed. Then there was a tug on the plane and the aircraft was backed from the gate. The ground controller advised the aircraft there would be some departure delays because of weather conditions, and he rattled off directions to runway 22-Left.

JFK's runway 22-Left is a hundred and fifty feet wide, eighty-four hundred feet long. Jamaica Bay is on the runway's far side; approach lights mounted on pilings run about a half mile into the bay. Along the edge is a bulkhead that keeps the water from encroaching upon the airport's landfill. At its nearest point, the bulkhead is less than four hundred feet from the runway. The slope from 22-Left to the bay is on an incline of about 4 degrees. On the night of February 20 the runway was under twenty-two inches of snow and ice. The tide was high and waves were breaking against the bulkhead, sending sheets of icy water curling back up the incline toward the runway.

Piles of snow seven feet high had accumulated, but they were far enough from the runway not to interfere with aircraft operations.

The outside noises—wind, sleet, and the powerful Pratt & Whitneys hanging below each wing—completely drowned any cabin conversation. Most of the passengers were quiet; some were tense.

Besides those on the flight deck, there was one other pilot on board, Carl Smith, sitting in the coach section. He flew for another airline and he could relax. He knew that the hail pounding on the DC-8-61 wasn't a problem; the wings had been deiced, and once the plane was airborne, the internal heaters would take over.

When they reached the taxiway adjacent to 22-Left, Mike counted eleven planes in front of his aircraft. He switched over to the tower frequency and told the controller they were ready in sequence. The time was 8:45, and it would be over half an hour before flight 15 could be airborne. Mike knew it would be a long night, and he wondered if he would be visiting the first lavatory. He decided not to think about it. He picked up the PA.

"Good evening, ladies and gentlemen, this is Captain Hagen. The noise you're hearing is, of course, hailstones. While it's annoying, they don't hurt the plane. Our runway visual range is improving, and the weather upstairs—above ten thousand—is forecast to be smooth. There are about eleven planes in front of us, so we'll be delayed up to half an hour. I think we'll open up the bar now, but before we take off, all tray tables must be secured and the seats brought to upright positions. I would also recommend that your seat belts be securely fastened for your comfort and safety. We hope you enjoy your flight with us tonight. Thank you."

The stewardesses shook their heads. The coach passengers wouldn't order too many drinks, since they had to pay for them, but there'd be a lot of action in first class, where the drinks were free. On a night like this, probably everybody would want a couple. One of the girls working coach came forward to help out. She and Louise and a stewardess assisting her moved down the aisle, taking orders.

Brenda Moore and a few of the TV executives were sitting together. "We'll have three vodka martinis, sweetheart, and some nuts if you have 'em," one of the men said to Louise. She ignored his rude manner and told them to fasten their seat belts.

"Did you get the drink order, honey?"

"Yes, sir, I did!" Louise said snappily.

When the DC-8-61 was number two in position, Mike made another PA. "We are next in line for takeoff, folks. We apologize once more for the delay. Please be sure all cigarettes are extinguished, tray tables are up and fastened, and your seats are in full upright position."

The stewardesses quickly secured the galley. Louise and her assistant went through first class, while the four other flight attendants checked the coach section, seeing that everyone was belted in and that all tables were stored. When they were satisfied, they sat down. Billy Joe, the male cabin attendant, and a very young stewardess were on the left side of the galley door, near exit 11; two older stewardesses were on the right side, adjacent to exit 12.

In first class, Louise's assistant belted herself in on the jump seat that unfolded from the forward bulkhead near the main entrance door. Louise sat next to her and took out a Gothic paperback.

The wind was gusting, holding from the southwest and whipping across the field just a bit from the left side. The before-takeoff checklist was read. As the plane ahead started her takeoff run, the control tower notified IA 15 to taxi into position and hold. Mike brought the throttles forward and steered the Stretch-8 onto the runway. He lined her up with the white center stripe; he saw almost all the way down the runway. He called the tower.

"Say wind again."

"Thirty knots, gusting forty, two hundred degrees," came the word back from the tower controller.

"Hurricane," Larry commented.

They remained at the threshold for about twenty seconds. The controller could not see the runway, but he was monitoring the departures via his ground-surveillance radar.

At precisely 9:19:30 the controller said, "IA 15, you're cleared for takeoff."

"IA 15."

Mike took his feet off the brakes and eased the thrust levers slowly up to forward position. The plane directly behind them was a United 747. Its copilot, who was watching the IA takeoff, thought that the jet was *not* gathering speed as quickly as it should have. The turbines roared out their full thrust, seventy-two thousand pounds, and the noise was deafening. But ten seconds into the takeoff run, the plane had covered only four hundred and fifty feet of the iced runway. As the copilot in the waiting 747 saw the tail

106

of the Stretch-8 disappear into the slashing rain, he continued to feel that the acceleration was slow.

Mike had the same thought. He sensed that something was wrong. But what? To the pilot's sensitive ear, the high-pitched roar of the turbines sounded okay.

"George, are those turbines up there?" he snapped loudly.

"Yes, sir! Fine."

The airspeed needle struggled up to 90 knots. Dammit, Mike thought, that needle should be at 120. Innumerable thoughts raced through his mind; they came in microseconds. Then, after thirty-five seconds, the plane entered the final stretch; almost half the runway was behind them.

"Airspeed, Larry?"

"One ten."

Carl Smith, the airline-pilot passenger, pressed his face to the window. He noticed how slowly the runway lights were passing. He listened. No change in the turbines; pitch, whine continuous— one hundred percent output.

They had been into the takeoff run for forty seconds. The strobe lights at the pier end of the runway were coming up like the entrance lights to hell.

Although Louise sat with her eyes fastened on the pages of her novel, she suddenly realized the plane was taking a long time to get off. She had been flying for six years and was aware, unconsciously, of changes in the sound of the plane.

The nuns sat staring out the window. It was their first flight and they had no idea whether the takeoff should last forty-five seconds (the right time for a gross-weight DC-8-61) or five minutes. Others scattered about the plane thought that perhaps the takeoff was lasting longer than it should have.

"I DON'T like it!" Mike screamed. "Abort!"

At that moment the plane was forty-nine hundred feet down the runway; the airspeed needle was vibrating in the 121 range. Mike yanked his four throttles back; his hand flipped on top to four smaller throttles and he pulled them back, reversing the thrust of the turbines. He touched the brakes.

Nothing.

For an instant the roar of the turbines went dead and only the bawling wind could be heard. An eerie stillness. Of the six cabin attendants, only Louise had experienced an aborted takeoff. She threw her book down. She knew what was coming: the extreme high pitch of the turbines in reverse thrust; the accelerated forces pushing people about. She hoped they hadn't missed any seat belts; it was too late now.

The scream of the reversed turbines pushing out thousands and thousands of pounds of hot, compressed air evoked alarm throughout the cabin. Three seconds had gone by. The plane traveled another 528 feet, and the needle encased in the airspeed indicator dropped back into the 110 range.

As soon as Mike realized he had lost directional control, he took out his thrust, putting it back to forward idle. Then he used the only thing he had going for him at that point—the rudder. He jammed his foot in to straighten out the plane, and for a moment she seemed to swerve just a bit toward the center of the runway.

"Dammit! Do something, rudder!" Mike shouted.

"Let me try my side," Larry yelled.

Nothing.

Mike used a touch of reverse thrust asymmetrically, hoping to bring the plane around. The jet was now making a beeline for the ice piles on the side of the runway. Then the DC-8-61 began an insidious side-to-side motion that accelerated, rocking the passengers faster and faster.

Inside the cabin, there were shouts of "What's wrong?" Carl Smith thought he knew; he quickly put his head down on his knees and called to the other passengers to do likewise.

Mike was helpless. He saw the snow pile coming up. After a painful few seconds, the surging, swaying plane's left wing was thirty-seven feet over the side of the runway. There was a seven-foot clearance between the piled snow and the underside of the wing tip.

No problem. But twenty-seven feet in from the wing tip hung the outboard Pratt & Whitney turbine.

A crucial obstruction.

The turbine smashed into the packed icy snow. The collision speed was 78 knots—just enough to rip the turbine from the wing.

108

The engine hung on for a split second before it fell away, belching out kerosene and black smoke. The grinding tear had ruptured the outboard fuel tank, and the distillate spurted up and out, covering the left wing.

Mike felt the plane halt briefly. Everybody did. The seat belts dug into the passengers' stomachs as the decelerating forces took effect. The violent swaying movement, the sickening rolling sensation assaulted the frightened people with one wave after another.

Again Mike fought in vain with the limp rudder pedals. Still no response. Suddenly the plane shifted direction and skidded across the runway toward another snow pile. The jet hit at 73 knots. The controls came back in Mike's hands and his knees were jammed to his stomach. The windshield was blocked by flying ice. The nose gear, fifteen feet in from the front of the plane, hit the wall of snow. The whole underside of the plane began to peel away; the ice opened up the jet as easily as a surgeon's knife cuts into a fleshy stomach.

On impact, the passengers' heads struck the semipadded seats in front of them. Teeth sank into lips, jaws were smashed, and noses gushed blood. There was a moment of stunned silence, then everyone cried out at once. It was a nightmare as the cabin lights flickered and went out, leaving them in blackness.

Louise's head snapped back against the bulkhead; her body went the other way. She felt a pain in her stomach as the seat belt settled farther down into her gut. But it held. Louise's assistant was not so lucky; her seat belt came loose. She was thrown aft, her head hitting the back of the first-class section. The girl crumpled up in the darkness.

The forward galley became a hot pressure chamber. It did not come apart; it disintegrated, more like an explosion of grenades, spitting out trays, bottles, glasses, knives, forks, oven doors, and, finally, splashes of hot coffee. The barrage hit the TV executives. They fell forward, uttering loud, agonizing screams.

As the plane went over the snow wall, two floor beams in the coach section burst, thrusting the jagged, raw aluminum up through the cabin floor. Gallons of volatile fuel gushed out.

Once over the banked ice and snow, the plane began to slide down the incline toward Jamaica Bay. The beautiful DC-8-61 was nothing but a long tube now, one wing partly attached and dragging. The other parts—the turbines, horizontal stabilizers, and the left wing—were scattered about the icy wall. The windshield was clear of ice now; Mike could see the bay in front of him, the waves curling and breaking into long froths in the black night. The nose of the Stretch-8 slid over the bulkhead. The entire plane would have plunged into the frigid waters of the bay had not the longitudinal beams in first class cracked and burst. The shock wave opened the fuselage twenty-six feet aft of the nose. The front part dug into the soft, slimy mud several feet down; the left front windshield popped out, and sewage-filled water burst into the cockpit. What was left of the nose slid along the mud for a few feet, then bounded up from the bottom, breaking the surface once again like a whale coming up for air. The 820-foot slide of the DC-8-61 finally came to an end.

It had been only eleven seconds since the huge airliner had begun her final, uncontrolled swerve.

THE controller monitoring progress of flight 15 on the surface detection equipment could not believe what he was seeing. Not only did the little airplane on his scope begin to slow down, it went crazy, zigzagging across the runway until it left the strip on an erratic route toward the water.

"IA 15 just went off the runway!" he screamed out loud. Instinctively the controller pushed the crash alarm, notified the emergency-equipment units and the New York City Fire Department, and closed down runway 22-Left.

THE pilot never thought it would happen like this. His crash, the only one of his life, taking place before flight. A ground crash! Most appalling of all, it had happened with two high-time captains in the cockpit. What had gone wrong? How did they lose it? Why hadn't the Stretch-8 accelerated in time? George had said the turbines were functioning. What had gone wrong with the brakes and the rudder? Mike's mind was jammed with questions.

He became aware of the icy bay water creeping up around him and released his seat belt. He heard nothing but wind and the slap of waves upon the bulkhead behind them. It was pitch-black. How long had he sat there thinking? Perhaps only a second; he had lost track of time.

"Mike, we're not polar bears," Larry said. "Let's get out and help those passengers."

Both men stood; the water was already up to their waists. George Gibbons sat dazed at his board. He was close to tears. "The turbines were okay," he cried. "*Nothing* was wrong!"

Mike and Larry pulled George from his seat. They could feel his shoulders shaking. Mike groped for the flashlight mounted on the bulkhead wall, found it, and turned it on the engineer's panel. Then he threw the emergency lighting switch; not even a flicker.

The ice had smashed the power packs. The vital light units were gone. Mike cut off the fuel-control levers and pulled the fire-control levers that disconnected fluids to the engines. By now Larry had reached the cockpit door. He jerked on it futilely. In the glare of the flashlight he saw that the bulkhead was twisted.

The three men trapped in the front did not know what was on the other side of the door. All they knew was that water was cascading in, and they thought the cockpit was going down. George tried to pull open the emergency top hatch, while Mike and Larry yanked at the door.

"The axe!" Larry yelled.

Mike took it down and began to hack through the five layers of almost impregnable Formica-clad plywood, of which the door had been designed in order to keep out hijackers.

For some seconds after the plane came to rest, the passengers in the dark cabin experienced the stillness of shock.

Then, amid soft sobs and screams of panic, the water level began to rise in first class, and the stench of kerosene spread through the coach section.

The cries assured the flight-deck crew that the cockpit had not been severed from the rest of the plane. They had feared that they were no longer attached to the main body of the fuselage; that the cockpit alone was sinking into the bay. They chopped furiously at the door, all the while expecting a delayed distillate explosion. That was the worst that could happen—not drowning, but burning to death.

BILLY JOE HAD been with IA only a year and had always wondered how he would react in a crash situation. The young steward had memorized safety procedures and undergone hours of simulation and training. He knew the exact position of the Jetescape doors. They looked like emergency window exits; however, upon pulling the red handle, a whole section of the fuselage came out and a pneumatic slide appeared from under the bottom of each door plate.

When the plane began to swerve and rock violently, Billy Joe knew they weren't going to get off the ground and he immediately started thinking about emergency procedures. Remain calm, of course, wait until the plane came to a complete stop, open galley door, activate the slide, and command the passengers in an orderly evacuation.

It didn't work that way.

In the blackness, just after the jet came to a stop, Billy Joe unstrapped himself, got up, and removed an emergency flashlight from its mounting. In the beam of the powerful light he saw the destruction.

Seats were upside down. Passengers had been flung about; arms and legs were twisted together in the center aisle, along with coats, pillows, blankets, attaché cases, and overhead hat racks. His light beam swung back and forth, and he noted the twisted metal of what had been the right aft galley. He quickly went over and dug the stewardesses out. They were dazed, but didn't seem to be seriously injured.

A stewardess was already wrestling with the left-galley exit. Billy Joe stumbled over coffeepots and debris to help her. As they yanked the door open, a blast of icy wind and rain entered the dark cabin. It was about a seven-foot drop to the ground below. Billy Joe let out the chute; the wind picked it up and flung it around.

Two other stewardesses found flashlights and moved forward to assist in evacuation from the Jetescape doors, exits 9 and 10. The deluge from the galley had completely blocked one of the exits.

The stench of kerosene was strong and someone yelled, "The plane's going to blow up! Explosion. Let's get out!"

This started a stampede. Carl Smith, the pilot passenger, had been sitting close to Jetescape 9; he was uninjured and already had the door open. He shouted, "Take it easy, everyone. This way, don't panic."

The slide was inflated. Carl began pushing the people out, yelling at them to get away from the plane. Meanwhile, the stewardesses were struggling with the other Jetescape door. One of them was shouting, "Don't try to take your personal belongings. Leave everything and get off the plane."

WHEN the flight crew broke through the cockpit door, the first thing Mike saw was Pat's bloody face. She was sitting dazed in a litter of spilled galley trays, still holding Marsha, who was hysterical. Mike pushed through the partly submerged rubble and unbuckled her.

"Are you hurt, darling?"

"No, I'm okay. What happened?" she asked.

"Don't know, we lost directional control somehow."

Mike noticed the water streaming up through the floor. The forward entrance and galley doors were completely useless. Mike made his way to the Jetescape door that the stewardesses couldn't manage. He pulled it open, but saw at once that anyone using this exit would probably slide off the slick ice straight into the water. First-class passengers would have to reach the wing section exits.

"Out over the wings!" Mike yelled. "Use the right side."

He climbed over broken seats and helped Louise get the wing exits open. They threw the windows out and yanked on the nylon ropes. People would need them when they got onto the slippery, tilted wing. One of the passengers helped lift the injured stewardess over the sill. Louise hurried back to get the nuns. Two men dragged out Brenda Moore, who was unconscious. Mike picked up Marsha and led Pat to exit 6, where she and the child stood in line to follow the coughing, petrified passengers onto the wing.

People tried to form a human chain along the wing, but they had to fight just to stand up on the slippery surface. The plane's main fuel tanks had burst, and the wing was coated with the lethal liquid. Pat clutched the little girl and made her way over the wing; several times she slipped in a gushing pool of kerosene. All she could think of was getting the child away from the plane— And Mike! She didn't want to leave him there.

113

As the passengers started clawing their way up the slithery kerosene hill, the crash equipment dispatched by the tower began arriving on the scene. The crews from the rescue vehicles directed the passengers away from the kerosene outflow, bringing them up the far side of the incline. Hoses were unrolled from the 3000-gallons-per-minute pumpers, and a mixture of water and foam was quickly sprayed on the distillate fuel to seal it. Two ambulances arrived, followed by the triage unit, a vehicle into which the passengers were placed to protect them from the weather and evaluate their physical conditions.

It took six frantic minutes for Mike and the rest of the crew to evacuate the plane, but nobody was sure the aircraft would not blow up; when kerosene pours out at high rates, sometimes there are delayed detonations. Satisfied that everyone was out of the wreckage, Mike climbed the hill to find Pat. She was in the triage unit, and had a gash over her left eye; other than that, she appeared to be all right.

"Darling, I have to go back and help," he said to her. Then to the attendant, "Where will she be taken?"

"Jamaica Hospital, Captain."

Mike kissed Pat and climbed back over the snow pile. There were a few stretchers being maneuvered slowly to the top.

The spooker!

Mike suddenly realized he would have to board the plane again. The FAA would tear it apart inch by inch; his spooker would certainly be found. The discovery would have a devastating effect on the whole industry; Mike didn't care very much about IA, but he didn't want to ruin Joe Barnes. He looked over at the nose of the DC-8-61 and saw it was settling lower in the water, while the body of the plane was settling in the mud. The pilot grabbed a flashlight and climbed onto the wing.

Larry struggled up the field with the last of the injured passengers. He looked around for Mike and didn't see him; puzzled, he approached a rescue worker. "Have you seen the captain?"

The man jerked his head toward the dark hulk below. "Went back on board."

"He's on the plane?" Larry said incredulously. "But it's sinking!" He turned and stumbled again toward the DC-8-61.

Far down the aisle of the mutilated plane, Mike was struggling to open the door to the first lavatory, which was wrenched and twisted. The water slapped at his chest; his legs were numb from the cold. But he had to get the door open and remove the spooker. He found the fire axe and began to chop through the barrier. When he had enough of the door open, he wedged his large body inside. The disposal bin was canted back at a 30-degree angle. Mike stuck a numbed hand inside.

The spooker was gone!

It had obviously become loose in the crash and was now somewhere under the water with the litter. He grasped the axe again and began to hack away at the Formica counter. Between his furious smashes he heard a loud, wrenching sound.

It came from behind him. The plane was moving forward!

The water rose another few inches; Mike pounded desperately at the counter. It finally split open and he reached into the rising black water. He found his spooker almost at once.

The water rose again. The added weight of the rising tide was dragging the shattered plane deeper and deeper into the bay. Mike started out, but the door opening was smaller now; the water pressure had built up. At that moment Mike realized he was trapped in the sinking jet. This is the ultimate irony, he thought. He gazed at the spooker in his hand, seeing the dim outline of the thermos that had almost ruined him and now was finally taking his life.

"You little bastard!" he screamed. "You're *not* doing this!"

The front section of the plane lurched sickeningly on the ice. Mike sucked in a deep breath and crashed against the lavatory door. It moved slightly. He hit it again and the door gave a little more. He only had enough strength for one more heave; this time the door cracked just enough to let him through.

Suddenly there was a sharp, crunching sound beneath him; the front part of the DC-8-61 was breaking away, sliding into the bay, and Mike was going with it; he grasped the back of a seat and jerked himself toward the rear. The water was up to his neck; his muscles ached with the strain. He pulled away to safety just as the cockpit disappeared in the bay.

Mike was standing there looking at the black, gaping hole, still clutching his spooker, when Larry found him.

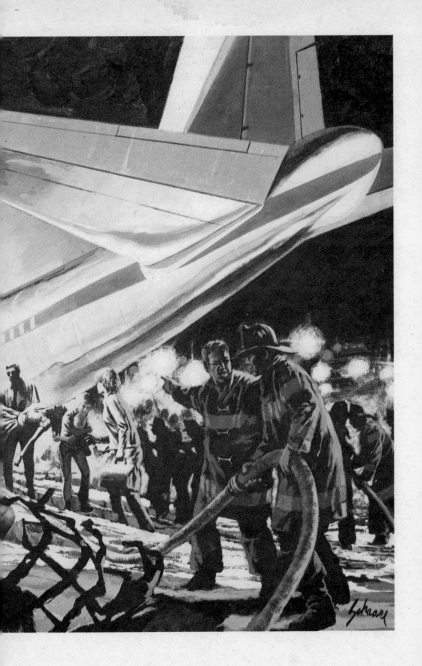

"Are you crazy! What are you doing here!" Larry shouted. Then the check pilot saw the thermos in Mike's hand; he grabbed it, screwed open the top, and sniffed the bourbon.

"Damn you! How the hell did you hide that?"

"It was attached to the disposal bin. Joe Barnes knew something, didn't he?"

"Yeah, a couple of girls got suspicious when they saw you going to the head so much, and Joe asked me to check it out."

"Larry, I was almost off the stuff," Mike cried. "This mess tonight had nothing to do with it. You felt those rudder pedals!"

"I honestly don't know what happened tonight, but one thing's for sure, it's all over for you. Joe Barnes can handle the matter any way he sees fit, but for now I'm chucking this thing in the bay. That's all we need. Someone to spot the pilots running around with booze on 'em."

"It *wasn't* my fault!" Mike was wild.

"Maybe not. Maybe you're just unlucky. Come on, let's get out of here."

They stood at the edge of the bay, and Larry was about to throw the thermos into the churning black water when Mike reached for it. "Let me," he said.

Mike watched his spooker sink below the surface. They paused there for a moment in the wintry air, then made their way up the incline.

TEN

JOE Barnes arrived at the airport by chartered helicopter. After he checked in at Operations, he rushed to the small office where the flight crew were lounging on chairs.

"You guys okay?" he asked.

They nodded.

"The company officials and the FAA are on the way. Let's get the stories straight. They tell me the plane is totaled."

"Very totaled," Mike said.

"We're lucky there weren't many injuries, but enough to make this damned serious. What happened, Mike?"

Mike got up and walked around the room. "Well," he began,

"conditions were bad—not below minimums, but windy, with some freezing rain. We started down the runway, but the plane wasn't coming up to speed. It felt like we were dragging something."

"What about the turbines?" Joe asked the flight engineer.

"Nothing wrong, Captain Barnes. Every engine was up to full takeoff thrust."

"Maybe your brakes locked," Joe said.

"But the frictional heat alone would have melted that," Larry interjected.

Joe motioned Mike to continue.

"Well, I just didn't like it. So, we aborted. We had her in reverse thrust and suddenly she started to weathercock. I had absolutely no steering control. The outboard engine struck an iced-over snow pile. This wrenched us around; we crossed the runway at right angles and hit another ice pile at about seventy-five knots, I guess. The left wing and engines came off and the plane continued down the slope and crashed. The cockpit and part of the first-class section are in Jamaica Bay."

"Why didn't you abort sooner?"

"We still would have lost direction control," Mike said. "We couldn't brake her on that ice. Besides, nothing seemed to be wrong."

"Nothing wrong, except the plane didn't accelerate! Of course there was something wrong—*had* to be," Joe said.

"Joe, can we speak to you alone for a minute?" Larry asked.

"Okay. Gibbons, leave us," Joe said. "And don't say anything to anybody until I tell you."

When the flight engineer had left the room, Larry turned to Mike. "Do you want to tell him, or should I?"

"Go ahead, it doesn't matter anymore. Tell him everything."

"What!" Joe blasted. "Tell me what? Come on, don't play games. The FAA and the execs will be here in a minute."

"Mike went back on board at the last minute," Larry said. "It was a crazy thing to do, he almost got trapped in there. But he had a thermos in the lav, Joe. The booze was there all along. Stuck in with heavy adhesive."

Joe's face was beet red with rage. "Is that true, Mike?"

"Yes, it's true," Mike said, with a kind of marked despair. "I was drinking on the plane a while back, but I was almost off the stuff. Joe, please believe me, I had it under control. I wasn't endangering anyone."

"What did you do with the thermos?" Joe said.

"Threw it in the bay."

The chief pilot sat down and tried to calm himself. It was lucky they had retrieved the thermos; FAA investigators would have found it. Just the appearance of booze hidden in the lavatory would have cast doubt over the accident, no matter what had gone wrong with the equipment.

"Why didn't you tell me before, Mike? I would have understood. I could have helped."

"I'm sorry, Joe. I should have."

"Well, we're going over to the hospital to take some blood tests. I want to know if there's any alcohol in your system."

AT IA, AS at most of the large carriers, it was routine procedure to examine the flight crew following any accident, and Joe Barnes took the two pilots over to Jamaica Hospital. After his blood sample was taken, Mike went down to see Pat. Her head was bandaged, but X rays revealed no skull damage. Marsha had been placed in the pediatrics section, and her mother was already there. Of the 204 passengers aboard flight 15 that night, sixty-one remained at the hospital for treatment.

Just after midnight the lab technician called Joe. "We have the crew's blood and urine analyses, Captain Barnes."

"Give me Hagen first."

"Normal, sir."

Joe's heart was racing, but he gave a deep sigh of relief. He walked into the solarium, where Mike sat dozing. Joe shook him. "Okay, Mike, there was no booze. Let's go over and make out the accident report."

"What happens to me, Joe?"

"I can't think straight tonight. We'll talk tomorrow."

LATER that night, after Joe Barnes had explained the accident to the executives who had come in, he, Fitz, and Cliff McCullen took a company station wagon and drove to the crash site. The rain had let up by this time, but the wind still blew hard from the south-west. As soon as they reached the threshold of 22-Left, Joe noticed something odd. All along the runway, men in storm parkas were laying down small cinder blocks. Joe asked the driver to stop. "Want to see what this is all about," he said.

Joe climbed out and walked over to one of the men. He saw a piece of rubber being held down and protected by a heavy block.

"Don't touch it!" the man said. "FAA said to mark each one."

"What is it?" Joe asked.

"It's worn-down rubber from the Stretch-8," the man said.

"How many pieces are there?" Joe asked.

"Twelve. She blew her tires out long before the abort."

Joe stood rigid, paralyzed. The clues were devastating, and one thing was certain: the plane had proceeded down 22-Left losing rubber all the way—the wheels weren't turning! As Joe looked down again at the shredded tires, he could see that one side of the jagged rubber was black with heat friction.

He returned to the car. "What happened?" Cliff asked.

"Wheels froze," Joe answered. "Maybe the whole gear."

At the next stop on the runway, Joe saw more shredded bits of evidence: blackened pieces of undercarriage rubber. The plane was surrounded by investigating authorities. Joe finally located the FAA district branch chief, who told them that the entire area was being roped off. The chief pilot asked if he could inspect the gear, which was lying about.

"Sorry, NTSB says no. They'll be up from Washington on the first flight tomorrow. But there *is* something you can see."

"The rubber?" Joe asked.

"No. Score marks in the ice. That plane was sliding on her rims."

The branch chief took the IA team down the runway about 1850 feet from the point where the Stretch-8 had hit the snowbank. In the glaze of the work lights Joe could see deep score marks, which had been painted with red dye in case the ice melted before the investigators arrived. Photographers were recording the marks—the trail of N4962C's final moments.

Joe Barnes suddenly felt sick. What if the plane had taken off? What if Mike hadn't grabbed those throttles? If he hadn't decided to abort! Joe saw the whole agonizing scenario. Takeoff would have been normal. With the accelerated head wind, the Stretch-8 would have rotated successfully and become airborne. The gear would have retracted as usual, flight 15 would have moved across country. On their long final into Los Angeles, the gear handle would have been pushed into the down position, and three green lights on the panel would have indicated that the landing gear was down and locked.

Joe saw it all in his mind. Sparks kicked off by the bare, tireless wheels touching the runway surface. Perhaps a swift bump would have been felt in the cockpit. Mike and Larry would have known then that something was wrong, but it would have been too late. At that speed, probably 130 knots or so, there would have been structural failure—wings ripping off, a cascade of volatile A-1 fuel sparks, and the inevitable:

Explosion!

Joe stood there for a long time looking at the score marks.

"What are you thinking, Joe?" Cliff McCullen asked.

"I was saying a prayer."

"That they didn't take off?"

"Yeah, it would have been hell on the other end."

"I know what you mean. They're lucky people," the vice-president of the Flight Department said solemnly.

They were just about to enter the station wagon again when Mike Hagen arrived in an FAA car. He got out and walked over.

"How do you feel, Captain Hagen?" Fitz asked.

"Not too bad. I didn't get hurt. The plane was fairly well decelerated by the time we hit the snowbank."

"Tell 'em what you told me about the accident, Mike."

The pilot related the events leading up to the abort, emphasizing how slowly the plane had accelerated.

"Your whole undercarriage was frozen, Mike," Joe said. "All the tires were blown out. By the time you reached the halfway mark, you were sliding over the ice on your rims. There are chunks of rubber all down the runway—score marks where the rims cut the ice. When you aborted, you lost directional control because there were no tires on the nose wheel!"

Mike, in silence, realized what a complete tragedy would have followed had the flight taken off.

"Something must have gone wrong with the brakes between the gate and the runway," Joe said. "We'll know in the morning. It's an investigator's dream."

Joe realized now that his pilots had done all they could. And more. There were many pilots who, having seen nothing wrong, would have taken off. Mike Hagen wasn't one of them. He turned to Mike and said, "Beautiful work, Captain Hagen."

IN PILOT's language, the abort on 22-Left was a rejected takeoff, but the news media called it a bad crash. The press, and especially TV, quarries this sort of story; it's big, hard local news, always visual.

The newsmen arrived on the scene to find their image of a bad crash realized. The harsh emergency lights, the foam-soaked infield, the shredded ends of the fuselage resting by the bay with the nose submerged in the black water, the stench of kerosene, all of this made the accident appear much worse than it was.

"You mean everyone walked away from that?" a CBS newsman asked.

"There were a few injuries, but no one was killed," an IA public relations man told him.

"How did the pilot save everyone?" The TV reporter knew he had a newsbreak—a serious airline crash where the angle was pilot heroism and skill, not death.

NINETEEN safety board experts arrived at dawn. After they measured the bits of rubber and the score marks, they hauled the remnants of N4962C back to an IA hangar for study. By 10:00 the runway was again open to traffic.

WHAT rattled Joe Barnes's mind was the cluster of approbations surrounding Mike Hagen. The legend of Mike Hagen became even more entrenched when the New York *Daily News* printed a picture of the wreckage on the front page with a thick black headline: PILOT SAVES 213 LIVES IN JFK CRASH.

If they only knew, Joe thought.

He was still trying to put things in perspective when Mike walked into the office the next morning. They had a friendly, candid conversation, and at the end Mike said he was quitting the airline.

"Why did you dislike IA?" Joe finally asked.

"It wasn't IA, the whole business—I'm just not right for the job. But there are a few things I can point to. Take last night. Superspy Zanoff, the perfect IA skipper, sat there like a lump before I rejected the takeoff. He didn't suspect a thing. Whatever else you may think of me, Joe, you better make sure you remember that I saved lives."

Joe agreed with part of Mike's rationalization. It was true the pilot could do things with planes that few, if any, other captains at IA could match. But the days of seat-of-the-pants flying had long been over. Mike's uncanny air sense and his magnificent inventory of contact-flying skills were not enough in an age of computers and specialization. When Mike finally admitted he wasn't right for the airline job, Joe knew that the pilot had come to terms with himself. He was far better off spraying a soybean field.

There remained a large question: Were Mike's twenty-one years in the airline business a total waste?

The answer was no. He was an anachronism; he liked to do things his own way. That was the particular tragedy of Mike Hagen. But Joe realized that perhaps there should be just a touch of Mike Hagen in every airline pilot.

They talked a little while longer, and then said good-by. As Mike walked down the hall, Joe saw a magazine sticking out from his side pocket—*Ag Flyer*, it said.

Joe leaned against the doorjamb. Mike stopped, waved at him, and then disappeared into the stairwell. The clacks of his heavy footsteps on the metal stairs were wiped out by the roar of a jet.

"Mike," Joe said, though there was nobody there to hear him, "good-by and thanks for not taking off last night." He looked down the long corridor. Its emptiness seemed to mirror the hollow created by the departure of Mike Hagen, the last of the contact men. The chief pilot returned to his office and closed the door.

## Robert P. Davis

Robert P. Davis comments on his hero and his story: "Many will ask, 'Even pilots? Could there possibly be an alcoholic airline captain?' Unfortunately, the answer is yes. There have been some.

"Readers might then infer that there are many Mike Hagens sitting in the cockpits of commercial airliners. This is not true. The chances now of finding another Hagen on the flight deck are infinitesimal. All carriers—large and small—have the highest and strictest standards for pilot proficiency and conduct. Every day of his life, on and off the job, the pilot's career is on the line—more so than in most other professions. But pilots, like anyone else, have certain weaknesses and emotions. Mike Hagen's story is not one of defeat, but of an ultimate victory over a devastating problem, because in coming to terms with himself he discovered a new identity, a truer one.

"Although the main incidents in this book are based upon fact, the characters and the airline for which Mike flew are fictitious. This is the story of a pilot, *not* an airline."

Robert P. Davis was born in New York City in 1929, but spent part of his youth in west central Florida, where he saw first-hand the Gator Holes and "flying cowboys" he describes in his novel. He also has vivid memories of being taken for occasional spins in the old biplanes.

Before becoming a novelist, Davis worked in films, first as an art director, and then as a scriptwriter. In 1961 he won an Academy Award for his short film, "The Day of the Painter". He is to write the screen version of *The Pilot*, for which he will also act as co-producer and art director.

Davis has recently moved to Palm Beach, Florida, where he is at work on a new novel entitled *Hurricane*.

# Touch Not
# the Cat

A CONDENSATION OF THE BOOK BY

**MARY STEWART**

ILLUSTRATED BY ROBERT McGINNIS
PUBLISHED BY HODDER AND STOUGHTON, LONDON

For centuries certain members of the aristocratic Ashley family have had a special extrasensory gift enabling them to communicate mind to mind. Lovely young Bryony Ashley has it. Indeed, it is the gift that invades a moonlit Portuguese night to tell her of her father's impending death.

Bryony returns to England and the once magnificent family home, Ashley Court. With her she brings her father's deathbed message—with its enigmatic warning of danger to his beloved only child. As Bryony tries to unravel the mystery behind the message, other deadly forces come into play. And suddenly she is swept into a whirlpool of greed from which there may be no escape.

Mary Stewart, that master of the romantic mystery, has again written a totally engrossing tale—one that shimmers with suspense, authentic background, and human emotion.

# Part One

My LOVER came to me on the last night in April, with a message and a warning that sent me home to him.

Put like that, it sounds strange, though it is exactly what happened. When I try to explain, it will no doubt sound stranger still. Let me put it all down in order.

I was working in Funchal, Madeira. Funchal is the main town of that lovely Atlantic island, and in spite of its having been for centuries a port of call for almost every ship that has crossed the ocean, the town is still small and charming, its steep alleys tumbling down the lava slopes of the island's mountain spine, its streets full of flowers and trees, its very pavements made of patterned mosaic which glistens in the sun. I was working as receptionist and tourist guide at one of the new hotels east of the town. This sounds an easy job, but isn't; in tourist time, which in Madeira is almost the whole year, it is hard indeed. But what had led me to apply for the job was that very few qualifications seemed to be needed by a "young lady of good appearance, willing to work long hours." Whether I was the best for the job I don't know, but it happened that the people who owned the hotel had known my father, so I was hired. The old-boy network, they call it.

It's barely a year since the things happened that I am writing about, but I find that I am already thinking of Daddy as if he were long gone, part of the past, as he is now. But on that warm April night in Madeira when my love told me to go and see my father, he was alive, just.

I was still awake when my lover came, but drowsy. He had not been to me for so long that at first I hardly recognized what was happening. It was just my name, softly, moving and fading through the quiet and airy room, as the shadows of flowers outside the window moved and faded across the bedroom ceiling.

*Bryony. Bryony. Bryony Ashley.*

"Yes?" I had said it aloud, as if words were needed. Then I came fully awake, and knew where I was and who was talking to me. I turned over on my back, staring up at the high ceiling where the moonlit shadows, in a still pause, hung motionless and insubstantial. As insubstantial as the lover who filled the nighttime room with his presence, and my mind with his voice.

*Bryony. At last. Listen. . . . Are you listening?*

This is not how it came through, of course. That is hard to describe, if not downright impossible. It comes through neither in words nor in pictures, but—I can't put it any better—in sudden blocks of intelligence that are thrust into one's mind. They say it comes with practice. Well, he and I had had all our lives to practise; I had known him all my twenty-two years, and he (this much I could tell about him) was not much older.

To begin with it had seemed like sharing dreams, or having, as I believe is common among children, an imaginary companion who shared everything with me. But unlike most children, I never spoke about him. Somehow, imposed over those thought patterns was a censor which wouldn't allow me to share our secret with anyone else, not even my parents. And a censor must have worked with him. Never by the smallest sign did he let me know who he was—though, from our shared memories, I knew he must be someone close, and it was a safe bet that he was one of my three Ashley cousins, who had played with me at Ashley Court daily when I was a child, and who had later on shared almost every holiday. It's a gift that goes in families, and there were records that it ran in ours. Ever since the time of Elizabeth Ashley, who was burned at the stake in 1623, there had been a record, necessarily secret,

130

of strange "seeings", and thought transference between members of the family. By the same token my lover knew I must be someone very close to him, and since I was the only Ashley girl, he could guess who I was, and he addressed me as Bryony. In return I called him Ashley, the title of the heir to Ashley Court, in an attempt to provoke him into identifying himself. He never did, but accepted the name with the same guarded and gentle amusement with which he accepted "boy" and, in unwary moments, "love". All I could get from him was the assurance that when the time was right, he would identify himself and we would know each other openly; but until that time we must be close only in thought.

I know I haven't explained the gift well, but then it is a thing I have known all my life, and that I gather very few people know at all. The gift had never worried me. Indeed, I could hardly imagine life without it. I don't even know when my secret companion became a lover; a change in thought patterns, I suppose, as unmistakable as changes in one's body. With us the minds translated our need for love into vivid patterns which were exchanged and accepted without question, and—since bodily responses were not involved—rather comfortably.

It was probable that when we met and knew one another physically, it would be less simple, but at the moment there seemed no prospect of this. You can't, out of the blue, ask a second cousin, "Are you the Ashley who talks to me privately?" I did once try to probe. I asked Francis, my youngest cousin, if he ever had dreams of people so vivid that he confused them with reality. He shook his head, apparently without interest.

So I summoned up my courage to ask the twins, who were my seniors by almost four years. When I spoke to James, the younger of the two, he gave me a strange look, but said no, and he must have told Emory, his twin, because Emory started probing at me. Full of questions he was, and rather excited, but somehow in the wrong way.

My lover tells me that I have got so used to communicating in thought blocks that I am no good with words. I never get to the point, he says. But I shall have to try, if I am to write the full story of the strange things that happened at Ashley Court a year ago. Write it I must, for reasons which will be made plain later, and to do that I suppose I ought to start by saying something about the family.

The family is as old as Noah, and Ashley Court, our home, is a moated manor—not unlike a waterlogged ark—that was built piecemeal by a series of owners from the Saxons on. But it is very beautiful, and brings in something over two thousand pounds a year from the tourists, God bless them.

The family goes back further even than the oldest bits of the house. There was a Saxon Ashley, Almeric of the Spears, who fled in front of the Danes in the tenth century and established his family in the densely forested land in Herefordshire, near the foot of the Malvern Hills. There had been settlers in that spot before; it was said that when the British, earlier still, had fled the Saxons, they had lived on like ghosts in the fragments of a Roman house built where a curve of the river let the sunlight in. Of this early settlement there was no trace except the remains of some tile kilns half a mile from the house. The Saxons dug a moat and led the river into it, and holed up safely until the Norman Conquest. The Saxon heir to the Ashley name was killed in the fighting, and the incoming Norman took his widow and the land, built a stone keep inside the moat, then took the name as well, and settled down to rear Ashley children, who were all, probably to his fury, fair and pale-skinned and tall, and Saxon to the bone.

The Ashleys have always had a talent for retaining what they wanted, while adapting immediately to the winning side. We were Catholics right up to Henry VIII, when we built a priest hole and kept it tenanted until we saw which side the wafer was buttered. Then somehow there we were, under Elizabeth, staunch Protestants. That's the Ashleys for you. Opportunists. Turncoats. We bend with the wind of change—and we stay at Ashley. Even in the 1970s, with no coat left to turn, and with everything loaded against us, we stayed.

The formal gardens, which had once been beautiful, I had never known as other than neglected. They, along with the lovely, crumbling old house on its moated island, and the wilderness surrounding, were all that was left of an estate which had once been half a county wide, but which by my father's time had shrunk to a strip of land beyond the river, the buildings of the once prosperous farm, and a churchyard. The church stood just beside our big driveway gates, and I think it officially belonged as well, but Jonathan Ashley—my father—didn't insist on this.

In 1950 my father sent most of the family silver to Christie's, in London, to be sold, and we lived on what it brought, and kept Ashley Court up after a fashion until I was seven or eight years old. Then we moved into one wing of the house and opened the rest to the public. A few years later, after my mother died, Daddy and I moved out altogether, to live in the gardener's cottage, a pretty little place at the edge of the apple orchard, with a tiny garden fronting on the lake that drained the moat. Our wing of the Court was put in the hands of Mr. Emerson, our solicitor, to let.

The most recent lessee was an American businessman, who, with his family, had been in residence for six months before the April night when my story starts. We had not met the Underhills because, two months before they moved in, my father had contracted a bad bronchitis, and his doctor urged him to head for a drier climate. We had sold a bit more silver and gone to Bad Tölz, a little spa town in Bavaria. My father had often been there as a young man, visiting a friend of his, Dr. Walther Gothard, who now had a considerable reputation, and who, for old times' sake, took Daddy into his sanatorium cheaply.

I stayed with Daddy for a month, but he mended so rapidly in that air that there was no reason for me not to take the Madeira job. I went off happily to the sun and flowers of Funchal, with no idea in the world that I would never see my father alive again.

*Bryony?*
*Yes. I'm awake. What is it?* But the trouble was there already, a clenching tension of pain and the fear of death. The sweat sprang hot on my skin. I sat up.
*I've got it, I think. It's Daddy. . . . He's been taken ill again.*
*Yes. Something's wrong. You ought to go. Can you read me, Bryony? You're a long way off.*
*Yes. I can read you. I'll go. . . . I'll go straight away.* Then urgently, projecting it with everything I had: *Love?*
It was fading. *Yes?*
*Will you be there?*

Denial printed on the dark; denial, regret, fading. . . . *When?*
I said soundlessly.

Something else came through then, strongly through the fading
death cloud, shouldering it aside; comfort and love, as old-
fashioned as pot-pourri and as sweet and haunting. It was as if the
flower shadows on the ceiling were showering their scent down
into the empty room. Then there was nothing left but the shadows.

I ran to the telephone. As I put a hand on it, it rang.

―――――――――――――――――――――――⋘――*Ashley Court, 1835*

*He stood at the window of the pavilion, looking out
into the darkness. Would she come tonight? Perhaps,
if she had heard the news, she would think he could
not be here, waiting for her; and indeed, for very
decency, he surely ought not to have come. . . .*

*He scowled, chewing his lip. What, after all, was a
little more scandal? And this was their last time—the
last time it would be like this. Tomorrow was for the
world, the angry voices, the cold wind. Tonight was
still their own.*

*He glanced across in the direction of the manor
house. The upper stories showed, above the yew
hedges, as a featureless bulk of shadow against a windy
sky. No lights anywhere. His eye lingered on the south
wing, where the old man lay dead behind a dark
window.*

*Something like a shudder shook him. She must
come. Dear God, she had to come. He could not face
the night without her. He could almost feel the call
going out, to bring her to him.*

IT WAS twenty-seven hours after the telephone call came from
Daddy's friend that my taxi slid up to the sanatorium at Bad Tölz.
Twenty-seven hours is a long time for a man to hold on to life
when he is rising sixty and has been knocked down by a passing

134

car and left there for about four hours. Jon Ashley had not held on. He was dead when I got to Bad Tölz.

I had known when it had happened—while I was on the plane between Funchal and Madrid. Then it was over, and I waited in a curious kind of limbo while the Caravelle took me nearer and nearer his dead body; waited, too, for my lover, but he did not come.

Walther Gothard and his wife were divinely kind. They had done everything that had to be done. They had arranged for the cremation and had telephoned the family lawyer in Worcester. Mr. Emerson would by now have been in touch with Cousin Howard, the father of the twins and Francis.

The police were asking questions, with most of them as yet unanswered. The accident had taken place on the narrow, fairly steep road up from the town, just at dusk. My father had gone down to buy some things he needed and had started to walk back. A car, going fast and clinging to the edge of a bend, had apparently struck him a hard, glancing blow which flung him clear over the edge of the road. There he lay among the bushes, barely visible in the dusk, until some four hours later a cyclist, pushing a flat-tired machine up the hill, saw him. The man took him at first for a drunkard. But the wound on his head was black and crusty with blood, so the cyclist started off down the road until a car overtook him, and he stopped it.

It was Walther Gothard's. He, growing anxious about my father, had set out to look for him. He took Daddy, unconscious, straight up to the sanatorium and telephoned the police.

Dr. Gothard told me about it, sitting in his consulting room. A bowl of blue hyacinths on the desk filled the room with scent. Beside it lay the small pile of objects which had come from Daddy's pockets: keys, a wallet I had given him with the initials J.A. stamped in gold, a silver ball-point pen with the same initials, the letter I had written to him a week ago. The doctor sat quietly, watching me, and then went on with the story.

"He came round towards morning and talked a little, a very little. Not about the accident. He had other things on his mind."

"Yes?"

"You, mainly. I couldn't get it clear, I'm afraid. He said, 'Bryony,

135

tell Bryony.' I reassured him that you were on your way. But that is not what worried him. We got a few more snatches, none of which made much sense. He died at about ten o'clock."

Walther talked on, professionally smooth and calm. I have no recollection of what he was saying, but to this day I can remember every petal of the blue hyacinths on the desk between us.

"And that was all?"

"All? All that Jon said, you mean?"

"Yes. I'm sorry. I wasn't really taking in—"

"Please. I did not imagine you were. You ask me what else Jon said at the end. I have it here." He slid a hand into the desk drawer and brought out a paper.

"The police had a man sit by his bed in case he managed to say anything about the accident which might help them to trace the culprit. The officer spoke very good English, and he took down everything that was intelligible. There was another emergency that morning, so I had to leave your father for a while, but after that I stayed with him until he died. This is all that he said. I'm sorry." He handed me the paper.

*Bryony. Tell Bryony. Tell her. Howard. James. Would have told. The paper, it's in William's brook. In the library. Emerson, the keys. The cat, it's the cat on the pavement. The map. The letter. In the brook.*

It broke off there, and started again on a fresh line.

*Tell Bryony. My little Bryony be careful. Danger. This thing I can feel. Should have told you, but one must be sure. I did tell Bryony's [word indistinguishable]. Perhaps the boy knows. Tell the boy. Trust. Depend. Do what's right. Blessing.*

I read it slowly, then looked at Walther. My face must have been blank.

"Does it make any sense to you?" he asked.

"No. Scraps here and there, but nothing important enough to be so much on his mind then. There's this about a letter. It might all be there. Did he leave a letter?" I knew the answer. If he had, Walther would have given it to me.

136

"I'm afraid not," he said. "Possibly he took something with him to mail from town. In which case it will be on its way to Madeira. No doubt they will forward it to your home."

"I'll find out once I get there." I would of course go home to England now, and it had already been arranged that I would take my father's ashes back to the Court, as he had wished.

"Do you intend to stay on there?"

"I'll have to, I think, until things are settled. I suppose Daddy told you that the estate is entailed to the nearest male heir? That's his cousin, Howard Ashley, who lives in Spain."

Walther nodded. "Your lawyer said he had been unable to get in touch directly with Mr. Howard Ashley. He is ill."

"Yes. Daddy told me he had virus pneumonia. I gather Cousin Howard's been quite ill. His sons Emory and James will have to see to things."

"It seems this was one of the things your father had on his mind. They are twins, are they not, this James and Emory?"

"Yes, identical twins. When they were boys, no one could tell them apart, except the family—and sometimes not even the family. It's not so hard now, but I still wouldn't bet on it if they were trying to fool you. They're twenty-seven. Emory's the elder, half an hour's difference, something like that."

"A big difference when it comes to inheriting an estate," Walther said dryly.

I said, just as dryly, "A crumbling old house that never quite got over the flood ten years back? Some legacy."

"As bad as that? Jon loved it."

"So do I."

"And your cousins?"

"I don't know. They were brought up there, as I was. But whether they want a beautiful old millstone around their necks I've no idea. Beautiful old millstones take money."

"I understood they had plenty of that."

"I suppose they have." The wine shipper's business which Howard Ashley had started some years back had always seemed to prosper. In the early days it had been based in Bristol, and the family had lived near us—in Worcestershire. Then when the twins were about thirteen, and Francis eleven, the boys' mother died.

Their father was in Bristol during the week, and his housekeeping arrangements were so erratic that my mother took my three cousins in. Some five years after his wife's death, Cousin Howard went off to Mexico City to negotiate a deal, and met a Spanish girl and married her. Howard's deal had been with her father, Miguel Pereira, who owned a share of a prosperous wine business in Jerez. Howard and his new wife settled in Spain. Emory took over the Bristol offices, and James more or less commuted between the two.

"Would Howard want to live at Ashley?" asked Walther.

"I've no idea. I doubt if his wife would. She's years younger than Cousin Howard, and she'd hardly want to settle in a remote little place like Ashley. But I suppose one of the boys might."

"The boys . . ." Walther said it half to himself, and I realized he was thinking of the paper I still held in my hand. But he only said, "I understand the two elder ones are in their father's business. What about the youngest?"

"Francis? Oh, he is, too. He's with his father in Jerez. Rather reluctantly. He doesn't have his family's head for business—he's more like our side. But he has to earn a living somehow, and I suppose Spain is as pleasant a place as any. He's a poet."

"Oh. He's not married, is he?"

"No." I took in the implication. "Nor are the twins, Dr. Gothard." I raised my brows. "You've been listening to Daddy, haven't you? That was his plan, too. Get me back to Ashley. But Francis would be no good, obviously. It would have to be the eldest, and that's Emory."

He smiled. "Something of the sort was in my mind, I confess."

"But Daddy didn't say who I was to stay on at Ashley with?" I was looking down at the paper in my hand: *This thing I can feel. . . . Perhaps the boy knows.* And, *I did tell Bryony's*—Bryony's lover? I wondered sharply whether my father had known about my secret love.

Walther nodded towards the paper. "You were studying that. Have you worked it out?"

"Not really. It sounds as if there's some paper, perhaps a letter, where he's written something important to me."

Like a treasure hunt, I was thinking, the mystification of papers and letters and maps. It wasn't like him. Jon Ashley was sane and direct. I added, aloud, "This paper or map or whatever, he says it's '*in William's brook*'. That simply does not make sense. Are you sure the words are right?"

"Those, yes. I thought there might be a stream at Ashley, something with a local name, perhaps."

"Not that I know of. There was a William Ashley, though, early last century. He was a poet, too, and a bit of a Shakespeare scholar. But the only brook in the place, apart from the river, is the overflow channel that helps to control the level of the moat. It's never been called anything but the Overflow." I stopped, struck by an idea. "It might have been made by William, I suppose. There's a maze at Ashley, and he built a pavilion in the middle, where he used to retire to write. The Overflow runs past the maze."

"'*The map*'?" suggested Walther. "A map of the maze?"

"Perhaps. I don't see why it should matter. All my life I've known the way, and so have my cousins." I shrugged. "In any case, it's nonsense. How could a paper—a map—be in a stream?"

"I agree. But the next bit is more sensible. '*In the library*' and '*Emerson, the keys.*' This paper could be in the library. Does Mr. Emerson keep keys to the Court?"

"I suppose he must. One set was handed over to the tenants. They live in the south wing, and normally all the rest of the house is locked up, except when the place is open to the public. The Underhills have to have the keys to the locked rooms because of fire regulations."

He merely nodded, and I didn't elaborate. I assumed that Daddy had told him about our latest tenants. Jeffrey Underhill was president of Sacco International, a construction firm. The family had been living in Los Angeles while the daughter, Cathy, was at school there, but now they had come to England for a year. Mr. Underhill had told Mr. Emerson that it didn't make a bit of difference where he was actually domiciled as long as he got "back home" to Houston, Texas, for board meetings, and that his wife was keen to live for a while in a "real old English house", and that it would do eighteen-year-old Cathy good to have a taste of country peace and quiet.

"The bit about '*the cat on the pavement*'," I said. "Do you think the car might have swerved to avoid a cat, or something, and mounted the pavement and hit him?"

"That's the way the police see it. There is no pavement on that section of the road, but there is a kind of footpath. Jon might have been speaking loosely when he talks of a pavement."

"But this last bit, Dr. Gothard. He wasn't speaking loosely there. He says I have to be careful; there's some danger."

"Indeed." His eyes were troubled. "When he speaks of '*this thing I can feel*,' he seems to mean danger of some kind."

I took a breath. "You're a doctor, so I don't expect you to believe me, but some Ashleys have—well, a kind of telepathy. It's sort of spasmodic, and works only between members of the family, but if someone you love is hurt or in danger, you know."

"Why should I not believe you?" he asked calmly. "It's reasonably common."

"I know, but you'd be surprised what people don't believe. The Ashleys have had this thing in one degree or another as far back as the 1600s when the Jacobean Ashley married a gorgeous girl called Bess Smith, who was half Gypsy. She was burned for witchcraft in the end. I've sometimes wondered if my father had the telepathic gift. We never spoke about it, but I'm pretty sure he had it to some extent. I know once when I was at school and fell out of a tree and broke my leg, he telephoned about ten minutes later to ask if I was all right. And at ten o'clock this morning, on the plane from Madeira, I knew that he died."

Walther said nothing for a while. Then, "I see. But at the end he states that he told someone, presumably meaning that he told him about this important paper, and about this danger to you. If it is so very important, no doubt 'he' will tell you."

I wasn't prepared to meet those kind, clever eyes. I still had part of the message to think about, myself. *I did tell Bryony's . . . Perhaps the boy knows.* It would take a bit of adjustment to come to terms with the fact that my father had known about my secret love. But if he had told my lover, there would be no mystery.

Walther straightened in the big chair. "Well, we shall leave it at that now. Yes? When you have rested, you may find your mind fresher. It is very possible that Mr. Emerson may have the answers already, or whoever of your family comes here for the cremation on Friday. One of them surely will, and will take you home? It may be 'Bryony's cousin,' the one who knows it all."

"So it may. Dr. Gothard, will you tell me something truly?"

"If I can."

"If the driver of that car had brought Daddy straight up to you here, could you have saved him?"

"No. If he had been brought straight in, he might have lived a little longer, but I could not have saved him."

"Not even till I got here?"

"I think not. It was a matter of hours only."

I drew a breath. "If you had said yes, I'd never have slept until the police found the driver who did it. As it is, he ran away out of fear and stupidity, and maybe he's being punished enough already. If the police ever do find him . . ." I paused.

"Yes?" he prompted.

"I don't want to be told who it is. I won't burden myself with a useless hate. Daddy's gone, and I'm here, with a life to live. Those are the facts." I didn't add that Daddy might not be quite gone, not from me, not from such as me.

---

*Ashley Court, 1835*

*The wind moved in the boughs outside. Creepers shifted and tapped against the walls of the pavilion. Since the old man had been ill, the place had been neglected—mercifully, he thought, with a wryness that made the young mouth look soured.*

*He pushed the casement open a fraction, listened. Still nothing, except the rush of the overflow conduit past the maze, and the wind in the beeches. Sudden gusts combed the crests of the yew hedges, as if something were flying past, invisible. A soul on its way home, he thought, and the shudder took him again.*

*At least let us have some light. He shut the window, then drew the heavy curtains across. A candle stood on the writing table. He found a lucifer and lit it. At once the room flowered with light; golden cur-*

141

*tains, rose-wreathed carpet, the bed's rich covering,*
*the glittering sconces on the walls. If he ever came here*
*again, he would light those, too.*


No ONE had come to Bavaria for the cremation. Emory had tele-
phoned from England, not to me but to Walther, to say that
Cousin Howard was still very ill, and that since Francis was on
holiday somewhere in England, James was tied to the Jerez office.
Emory himself could not be free on Friday, but would come to
Ashley as soon as possible. He had no idea where Francis was;
walking somewhere, he thought, in Derbyshire—probably the
Peak District. Presumably the news had not got to him yet. No
doubt he would call me as soon as he came back. Meanwhile, said
Emory, love to Bryony. . . . So much for "Bryony's cousin" who
would tell me what Daddy had meant, and take me home.

I didn't go straight home when I got to England. The first
priority was a visit to Mr. Emerson to find out if he could throw
any light on the jumble of words on Walther's paper.

When I arrived in London I took the train straight to Worcester
and booked in at a small hotel. Next morning I went to see Mr.
Emerson.

He was a youngish man, somewhere in his upper thirties, with
a round, good-tempered face, and hair cut fashionably long. I
liked him, and Daddy, I knew, had trusted him completely. He
did not make the mistake of being too kind. "Well now, Miss
Ashley, you do know that you may call on me to help you in any
way. It will take a fair amount of time to sort out your father's
affairs. None of that need trouble you, as long as you're quite
clear about the way the house and property are left."

I nodded. I had practically been brought up with the terms of
the Ashley Trust, as it was called, which had been designed by
one James Christian Ashley, who had inherited the property in
1850. He was a farsighted man, who had seen, even in the spacious
days of Victoria, that there might come a time when the incumbent
would find a place like Ashley hard to protect and might even
seek to disperse it. This, James Christian was determined to pre-

142

vent. He created a trust whereby, though the Court itself must go outright to the nearest male heir, no part of the estate covered by the trust might be sold unless with the consent in writing of all adult Ashley descendants existing at the time of the proposed disposal. My grandfather James Emory had managed, with the connivance of his brothers and one distant cousin, to sell a couple of outlying farms and some meadowland, and the proceeds had kept the place in good heart until World War II. Since then, apart from the family silver, which had been sold with his cousin's consent, all the articles my father had sold had been things bought since 1850 and consequently not controlled by the trust. If my cousins were in need of funds now, they would find themselves fairly well down to the scrapings.

Mr. Emerson was going on. "Then there is your father's will. He told me you have seen a copy and know all about its contents. It covers everything not included in the entail or embraced by the trust. The most important item is of course the cottage which is now your home. This, with the orchard and the strip of land running along the lake as far as the main road, was purchased after the creation of the trust, and comes, in consequence, outside its terms. It is left to you in its entirety. There may be things that you wish to discuss later, but for the moment, would you like me just to take everything over for you? Settle what bills there are? Perhaps you would like to go through his letters yourself?"

"The personal ones, I think so, please. I'd be glad if you'd deal with any business. Mr. Emerson, has Daddy written to you—recently, I mean?"

"No. Dr. Gothard asked about a letter, too."

"Did he tell you about the paper?"

"Paper? Ah, yes. Of course, he did not tell me what your father had said. This was on the telephone."

"Most of it Dr. Gothard and I couldn't make out at all, but there is one reference to you which we thought you'd be able to clear up for us. I made a copy for you. Here."

He read the paper swiftly, then went through it again slowly. Finally he leaned back in his chair. "It's pretty much nonsense to me, I'm afraid. Except the reference to me. The tenants of the Court have a set of keys, but not a complete one. Certain keys were detached from that set and are in my keeping. I have, for instance, the key to the old muniment chest in the great hall, also the one that opens the locked bookcases in the library."

"*Have* you?" Here was a fragment that might make sense. The locked cases in the library housed William Ashley's collection of Shakespeariana and his own mercifully slim volume of verses, along with the distinctly curious collection made by "Wicked Nick," William's son, the scapegrace Nicholas Ashley. The grilles had been fixed after my father had found Emory and James, at the age of twelve, happily perusing one of Nick's tomes called *Erotica Curiosa*, fortunately in Latin, but with illustrations. Within a few days Nick's additions to the library were all behind bars, along with those of William Ashley's Shakespeare books that my father imagined might be valuable.

"Do you know what's in the muniment chest nowadays?" I said.

"Nothing much. Spare blankets, the old stable books."

I thought for a moment. The rest of the family books were presumably still in the locked cases, and they would go with the house. "Do I need Cousin Howard's permission to go through the library?"

"No."

"Then—" I stopped and sat up. "I've just remembered something. I think Daddy was going through the books in the locked section just before we went to Bavaria. He took one or two of them home to the cottage. Perhaps he found something about the family or the trust that he thought we ought to know."

"It sounds reasonable. I think you're right to take this seriously. Anything that was so much on your father's mind at such a time . . ." He let it hang. "You're going to Ashley now?"

"This afternoon. Mr. Emerson, what's the position about the Court? Am I still allowed access to everything?"

"Certainly. Nothing may be removed or sold, naturally, but it is your home until your father's will is proved and the estate is wound up. That will take quite some time." His eyes twinkled. "The mills of God work like lightning, compared with the law."

"So they say. What about the Underhills?"

"They have a year's lease, which will be up in November. Mr. Underhill offered to move out straight away if it would help you, but I told him that I imagined you and your cousins would wish him to stay put. Things won't be settled for months, and at least it means the Court will have a caretaker. Do you approve?"

"It sounds fine to me."

"Good." He cleared his throat. "Look, I know you want to go back to Ashley as soon as you can, but do you really want to stay at the cottage alone? My wife and I would be delighted if you'd come to us for a few days. It was her suggestion."

"Well, thank you very much. It's terribly good of you both, but honestly, you don't have to worry. I'll be all right, really." I didn't add that I would not be quite alone. I never was.

He waved my thanks aside. "And how do you propose to get out to Ashley? Have you a car?"

"No. I'll take the bus to Ashley Village. There's one that stops at the road end beyond the church."

"And on your way back?"

"I've got a Lambretta—a motor scooter. It's stabled at the farm." I got to my feet and held out my hand. "Thank you for everything, Mr. Emerson. You've been terribly kind. I wonder, would it be all right for you to let me have the keys to the Court? I don't want to go to the house today, but I might tomorrow."

He looked surprised. "Of course. But, surely, you can use your father's keys? The master set has them all."

"I haven't got them. I thought you must have. Do you mean you only have the ones you mentioned?"

"Yes. They were detached from the ring Mr. Underhill has."

I hesitated, obscurely troubled. "If you haven't got the master set, who could he have left them with? One of my cousins?"

"I don't see why," said Mr. Emerson. "How very strange." He frowned over it as he unlocked a drawer and took out a small ring of keys. "You must certainly have these. I'll get in touch with Emory and see if he knows who has the other set."

"But it is all right for me to go in?"

"Miss Ashley, let me insist that the Court is still yours until the estate is handed over." He opened the door for me. The brown eyes behind his trendy spectacles were anxious and kind. "As for the keys, no doubt there will be some perfectly rational explanation," he said.

I got the impression he disliked mystery as much as I did. "No doubt," I agreed, as I took my leave.

Just outside the office there is a pedestrian crossing. The light was red. DON'T WALK. Under it, on the very edge of the pavement, a black cat was sitting, waiting apparently for the light to change to green. As I paused beside him, he glanced up. I said to him, "Can't you reach? Allow me," and pressed the button.

I have a theory that the button never has the least effect on the lights, but at that exact moment the light switched to green. WALK. The cat got straight up and walked across, tail in air. A good-luck cat. "I may need you yet," I told him, and began to follow him onto the crossing.

There was a shriek of brakes. I jumped half out of my skin and stepped back to the pavement. The cat bolted clear across and vanished into a shop doorway. A white E-Type Jaguar clenched its large tyres to the road and stopped dead half a foot from the crossing. The girl who was driving glanced neither at me nor at the fleeing cat. She sat watching the red light with impatience, one hand tapping the wheel, the other pushing back long blonde hair. I had a glimpse of dark eyes shadowed under an inch or so of mink-toned eyelash, and a sallow, small-featured face, which for some reason looked typically American to me. When I had gained the other pavement in the black cat's wake, the lights changed and the E-Type snarled off into the traffic. Something made me glance back. On the other side of the street Mr. Emerson had emerged from his office, complete with bowler and rolled umbrella, presumably on the way to lunch. He, too, was watching the E-Type. Then he noticed me and mouthed something across the roaring flood of cars. I thought he said, "The cat," but he was pointing after the vanished Jaguar. I nodded, smiled, and walked back to my hotel.

---

*Ashley Court, 1835*

*On the writing table, beside the candle, lay his father's books and papers, held down by a glass weight shaped like a peeled orange. The wax light glimmered in the curved segments, and a dozen tiny images mocked him; the fair young man, a slight figure in frilled shirt and pantaloons, standing there, somehow incongruous and lonely against the elegant background of his mother's room.*

*He moved abruptly, striding over to the table, scattering the papers that lay there. He pulled open a drawer. From inside it, his mother's picture smiled up at him. Always, when he had used the pavilion, he had hidden her; or hidden from her. Now he lifted the portrait, and smiling, he set it back in its place on the writing table, facing the room. Facing the bed.*

*His father's papers, those dry, exquisitely penned little verses, lay unheeded on the floor.*

# Part Two

THE big driveway gates at Ashley Court stood, as always, open. I went in, soft-footed on the mossed surface of the avenue, and walked up under the lime trees until I reached the bend. From here one could see the house, its walls of rosy Tudor brick reflected richly in the still glass of the moat. No one was about; no movement anywhere. I stood in the evening shadow, looking at Howard Ashley's home.

For anything so old it was curiously serene. It stood foursquare on its island, an oddly harmonious hotchpotch representing centuries of building. The Norman keep still stood, but the original drawbridge had long ago been replaced by the single span of stone, just wide enough for a car, which now leads through the main gateway and into the small square courtyard. The great door lies opposite, and is Tudor, giving straight onto the big hall with its vast fireplace and blackened beams. The rooms to the right are Tudor, too—the parlour with the priest hole, and the small dark council chamber with its coffered ceiling and coats of arms. To the left of the main gate stands the banqueting hall, a fourteenth-century structure with the mediaeval timbering still intact. I had never known this used; it had been damaged in 1962, when the big storm of mid-September brought the river down in flood and broke the high sluice, which controls the flow to the moat. Before the lower sluice could be opened to relieve the overflow channel and let the water safely into the lake, the cellars and the low-lying floors of the banqueting hall and kitchens were flooded. My father repaired the high sluice and made good the kitchen premises. Money being tight, he left the old hall alone.

Lake was rather too grand a word for the sheet of water which lay below the banked-up moat. I forget when the artificial pool was first dug; to begin with it had been a stewpond for keeping fish and was called The Stew; later it was enlarged and rechristened Mistress Nancy's Pool.

Between moat and pool was a grassed bank which Rob Granger, the gardener, kept cut after a fashion. He kept some sort of order, too, in the walled kitchen garden with its two remaining greenhouses. We sold most of the produce, and this paid Rob's wage and that of the village boy who helped him. There was little else that could be done. The rose garden was impenetrable and the woods beyond the pool had long since engulfed the orchards, with the exception of one stand of apple trees beside the cottage that was now my home.

As I stood there in the deepening dusk, nothing stirred except the two swans, serene on the moat. No light showed in the house. I went quickly up the drive for another fifty yards or so to where the Court's private pathway led to the churchyard.

This had originally been the only way to the church. The lychgate stood there, and beyond it a tunnel of ancient yews. I went through the gate, and suddenly, it seemed, day had altogether gone. The church ahead showed only as a looming shadow.

I didn't mind the dark. I had trodden every centimetre of this path since I could remember. I reached the church porch and, shifting the crematorium's urn carefully into my left hand, groped for the big iron ring of the south door. Smells familiar as childhood met me as I went in. I didn't touch the light switches, but walked slowly up the centre aisle towards the faint glimmer of the east window.

I had come tonight with the urn, instead of in the morning when the vicar expected me, because there was a kind of vigil I wanted to keep first. I wanted to see if here, in the place Ashleys came from and returned to, I could open my mind to whatever message Jonathan Ashley's maimed brain had tried to send me. *Tell Bryony. Tell her. . . . My little Bryony be careful. Danger.*

When I was halfway up the chancel, I paused. There were ways and ways of trying to talk with the dead, and here, I knew suddenly, darkness was wrong, smacking of things which a church should not be asked to house. I would light the sanctuary lights. Feeling somehow absolved, I took the urn up to the altar steps and laid it there. Then I left the chancel and went to the vestry to turn the lights on from there.

This door, too, was unlocked. I pushed it open, fumbled on the wall beside it, found the switch for the sanctuary lights, and pressed. Nothing. I tried the other three on the board, and with each one, nothing.

All this took only a few seconds, but I suppose my mind was preoccupied, so I took in, but failed to register, that the vestry was as airy and full of tree sounds as the churchyard; also, that the papers on the vicar's table were lifting in the light breeze. Even as I noticed them, one or two drifted to the floor. Simultaneously another movement caught my eye, sending the blood out of my heart with a contraction as painful as a blow. The outer door of the vestry stood open, and against the darkness beyond it, another darkness moved. A tall figure, robed. Then the door shut. Only the papers on the floor affirmed the truth of what I had seen. The open door, the vanishing figure, seemed no more than the negative of some dream still printed on the retina as one opens one's eyes from sleep.

I swallowed hard, and willed my heartbeats to slow down again. Any robed figure leaving a church vestry was reasonably likely to be the vicar. And the dead light switches? No doubt Mr. Bryanston thought it safer to turn off the main switch bar at night. And probably, I thought, as I reached for the switch bar, which indeed was up—off—he would come back when he saw the lights go on.

I pressed the bar down, and the whole east end of the church leaped into light. I stood for a moment, listening, but could hear no sound of returning steps. I picked the papers up from the floor

149

and laid them on the table beside a neat pile of books that looked like parish registers. Then I snapped off all the lights except the altar floods, made my way back into the dimness at the west end of the nave, and sat down. Familiar as the blanket of childhood, the place wrapped itself about me.

But in the way I had known it before, in the way I wanted it now, nothing came; nothing but silence. Till, just as I got to my feet, the vestry door opened and a robed figure stood there.

The vicar. As I had thought—the vicar, a prosaic figure in his cassock, with his spectacles glinting in the light. It didn't stop me jumping half out of my skin before I registered who it was and went sheepishly to meet him.

"My dear child! It's you! I understood you were coming in the morning. I saw the light just now when I went into my study. Did I frighten you?"

"You did give me a start. I'm sorry I dragged you out again, Mr. Bryanston. I am staying in Worcester, as I told you, but I— I wanted to bring my father's ashes here, leave them here overnight. Do you mind?"

"Of course not." He was a man comfortably into his middle sixties, with a rounded face and a habit of looking over his spectacles down the arch of his nose. He had been at Ashley as long as I could remember. Fifteen years ago he had buried his wife in the churchyard, and now he asked nothing better from life than what he found at Ashley and his other parishes of One Ash and Hangman's End. Sunday after Sunday he gently delivered an address from notes on suspiciously yellowed pages, and kept the whole parish supplied with seedlings grown in the Court gardens, of which he had the run.

He and my father had got on very well together; they seldom discussed anything more spiritual than chess, but I had heard Daddy say that Mr. Bryanston's faith was the kind of rock on which any Church could be built.

We went into the vestry, and he talked to me now, with an ease quite unlike Mr. Emerson's hesitant kindness, about my father's death. Comfort, you might say, was his profession, but he had a way of offering it as if he really cared, not only about my father, which I knew, but about me.

150

"I'd better go," I said finally. "I'll be back first thing in the morning."

He fished a thin old watch out of a pocket and peered at it. "Dear me, you've just missed a bus. I shouldn't have kept you so long. The next one doesn't go for an hour and a half."

"I'm not catching the bus; my Lambretta's at the farm."

"Ah. Well, take care. If you see Rob, will you tell him that I'll be down in the old orchard tomorrow, not in the greenhouse?"

"Of course. Well, thank you for everything, Vicar. I'll go out by the south door. If you want to put the main switch off again, don't wait for me. I can see quite well."

He looked puzzled. "Main switch? Why should I put it off?"

"I thought you had, just before I got here. You mean it wasn't you who was in the church when I arrived?"

"Certainly not. I haven't been over here since about three o'clock. When was this?"

"About an hour ago, I suppose. I came in and went up to the vestry to put on the altar lights. The main switch was off, and someone was just leaving. I thought it must be you."

"No. It might have been one of the churchwardens, but . . . How very extraordinary. You're sure the main switch *was* off?"

"Certain. And if it wasn't you in the vestry, then whoever was there didn't want to be seen. I've a feeling he threw the switch when he heard me at the door, to give himself time to get away without being recognized. And he was carrying something—I'm quite sure of that."

"What sort of thing?"

"It's hard to say. A box, perhaps, or it could have been a book, about the size of those registers on the table."

"I can't see any reason why one of the wardens should come for them. Those aren't Ashley registers. I had brought them over from One Ash to do a search for some Canadian's forebears. . . . Dear me, it's beginning to look like a mystery, isn't it? I'd better see if anything has been touched. The church safe . . . But surely, no one at Ashley . . ."

He paused to glance at the papers and registers on the table. "Eleven, was it, or twelve? I shall have to check them. But really, there is nothing here of interest to anyone."

He turned finally, with reluctance, to the safe and pulled out a ring of keys. "Well, let us hope not. . . ."

"I suppose you keep the Communion plate in the safe," I said. "Anything else?"

"Only our own registers. And the Communion plate itself is of little value. The one we use now is quite modern; it was your father who suggested that we lodge the old plate in a safer place than this. Did you know that the chalice and paten were Elizabethan, by John Pikenynge, and the alms dish—" The safe door swung open. "Thank God."

I was peering over his shoulder. It certainly looked as if nothing had been touched. The back of the safe was stacked with registers, and some baize-wrapped shapes stood in line in front of these. "Yes, yes, all present and correct," said the vicar, counting. He shut the safe and locked it. "However, this is a lesson to me. I cannot bring myself to lock the church, but I think I must lock the vestry. And I shall do so straight away. There. Perhaps you'll come out this way. . . . Dear me, it's quite dark now, isn't it? Can you see your way to the farm?"

"Yes, thank you. And don't worry about it, Vicar. I'm sure you'll find it was one of the wardens here earlier. If you're in the apple orchard in the morning, I'll see you when I go to the cottage. I'm moving in tomorrow. And I'll give Rob your message."

"Thank you, my dear. God bless you. Good night."

---

*Ashley Court, 1835*

*Seeming a long way off, the church clock chimed the three-quarters. He glanced at the gilt clock on the bed table. It was fast. Five minutes.*

*As he fidgeted about the room, his foot struck one of his father's books, lying on the floor with the papers, where it had fallen. He stooped and began mechanically to collect the scattered things together. The book showed the name "Juliet," glinting in gold. Straightening, he stuffed book and papers in the table drawer and shut it.*

*His father was dead. He was Ashley now, Nicholas Ashley, Esquire, of the Court. Now, he thought, it*

153

*will soon be over and done with. If each of us, in his
own way, can find the courage.*

*But habit made him twitch the curtains closer, to
hide even a glimpse of the candlelight.*

THE buildings of what had once been a fine farm lay about a
hundred and fifty yards beyond the churchyard. Again I made
my way carefully along the pitch-dark tunnel of the yew walk.
The shadows of home reached out for me, comforting me. So, at
the same moment, did my lover. He was here in the cool night,
stronger and closer than at any time since I had left Ashley with
my father. Every shade of feeling came, direct as if spoken, strong
as the scent of the breeze. There was welcome, pleasure, and with
it a kind of apprehension. I paused to identify this, and unbe-
lievingly registered it as guilt.

I had just reached the lych-gate. The darkness here, cast by
the roof, was palpable. I paused, feeling before me for the latch
of the gate. Guilt or shame? From him? My hand, groping in the
dark, touched cloth. For one heart-stopping moment I thought
he was here, that I had touched his sleeve. Then through the
folds I felt the wood of the gate. Some garment had been left
there. My brain identified it even before my fingers felt the ribbed
silky surface. A cassock. The robe I had seen him wearing, flung
down here as he left the churchyard. . . . Guilt and shame indeed.

*Was it you in the church?* I asked the question sharply, but got
no reply. At the same moment I heard, close at hand, steps going
away from me. He must have been standing all this while on the
other side of the wall of yew.

*Lover? Lover!*

He ignored me. The steps quickened. I heard the faint ping of
the wire that crossed a gap in the wall between the churchyard
and the Court gardens. Beyond the gap was a tangle of shrubbery,
and a door into the old high-walled garden. And now, faintly behind the black of the trees, I saw the night slacken into silver.
The moon was rising.

When I reached the gap in the wall, the moon was high enough

154

to send a gleam along the wire. I laid a hand to it; it was humming still. I clambered through into the whippy undergrowth of the shrubbery and plunged forward to the walled garden. The gate in the high wall stood ajar. I ran through and paused at the head of the shallow, slippery steps.

Then I saw him, for the second time that night, still no more than a tall shadow melting into the other shadows. He, too, had paused, standing in the shelter of the far gate. I hesitated. He must know who was pursuing him. If he wanted me, he had only to wait for me. In fact, I realized now, he *had* waited for me. I had been a long time in the church. And, standing as I was in the moonlight, he must see me and know I had followed him.

He was looking, I was certain of it. I stood getting my breath and trying to open my mind to him. But nothing came except that muddled mixture of exhilaration and guilt. Whatever he had been doing in the church, I was with him; I had to be. I sent him all I had of love and need and longing, and got the answer. *Not yet. Trust me. Not yet.* There was a creak as the garden gate shut fast. The latch dropped. I was alone.

I TRUDGED back the way I had come and, regaining the churchyard, went by the normal route to the farm.

The darkness hid the dilapidation of the big farmyard. Barns and sheds lay on the left, and on the other side stood the farmhouse, which had been empty now for years, ever since the land that was not part of the trust had been sold. The farmer who had bought it had not found it worthwhile to repair the house. It was a storehouse now, and hens roosted there. Adjoining it, and in heartening contrast, were the two farm cottages, which still belonged to Ashley. These showed whitewashed walls reflecting the moonlight, and brightly lit windows with gay curtains.

In the cottage nearest to the farmhouse the Hendersons lived. Mr. Henderson, a man well into his sixties, was sexton and gravedigger to Ashley and One Ash; his wife cleaned and mended for the vicar, and for Rob Granger, who lived in the other cottage. The Grangers had lived at the big house until Mr. Granger's death. Then the farm was sold and Rob and his mother moved into the cottage. Mrs. Granger herself had died not long after.

155

As I crossed the yard, Rob opened his door and peered out. "That you, Bryony?"

"Oh, Rob, hullo! Yes, it's me. How did you guess?"

"Well, I reckoned you'd be coming for the bike. I saw you come out of the church. You went after him, did you?"

I stopped dead. "You were there? You saw him?"

"I did. I was down shutting up the greenhouses, you see, and when I came back I heard the dogs barking. Then I saw him, quick as a hare out of the vestry door and behind the yew walk. He stood there the best part of an hour."

"And you didn't ask him what he was doing?"

"I didn't rightly like to, seeing who it was."

There was a pause of seconds. "Well, who was it?"

Something must have come through my voice. He said quickly, "You've no call to worry. It was one of your cousins. I'm not sure which one, but an Ashley; I couldn't mistake that."

"Then why did you stay to watch him?"

"I don't rightly know." He showed no resentment at the rather sharp question. "The way he came running out of the vestry . . . I saw the church lights go on then, for a minute. I guessed that it might be you in the church. Then the main lights went off again, but you didn't come out."

"No," I said. "I—I wanted the dark."

"I guessed that. And I think he did, too. Strange he didn't talk to you. I was sure he was waiting for you."

I said nothing. I was fighting back disappointment so acute that I was afraid he would notice it.

"Come in," said Rob. "No sense standing out in the yard."

I went into the kitchen, where, it was obvious, he had just been about to cook his supper. There was a place set for one at the table, and beside the stove was a pack of sausages and some tomatoes, with a packet of peas defrosting.

"I'm afraid I've come at a bad time."

"You haven't at all. I've got your bike here; it's in the scullery. It'll not take a minute to get it ready. Bryony, why not have a bite of supper with me? There's plenty."

Obviously he wanted his meal before he worked on the bike. "I'd love that. I'll cook while you set another place, shall I?"

156

"O.K. Want some chips with it?"

"Yes, please."

I put the sausages and peas on to cook while Rob took things from cupboards and, neat-handed as a sailor, laid the extra place and sliced some bread and tipped another helping of frozen chips into the frying basket.

There was no question of looking out the best china for Miss Bryony; I had been an intimate of the Granger household all my life. Fish-and-chips straight from the newspaper, and yellow shop cakes with marshmallow cream, had been the tea-at-Mrs. Granger's treat of my childhood. I watched Rob find an extra plate, and I felt the blackness of the yew walk, and the disappointment, recede. Here, with the bright fire and the smell of sausages, was yet another welcome that Ashley was holding out to me. This, too, was home.

Rob glanced up and caught the tail end of the look, but gave no sign that he understood it. He was a tall young man, brown as a gypsy, with black hair, and eyes so dark that it was hard to tell iris from pupil. His slow country voice and his habit of silent pauses masked an intelligence which should have had a better chance to develop. Rob's mother had been the village school-teacher, a gentle, lonely girl. She had married Matt Granger, a handsome lout, who first neglected and then frankly ill-used her and her child. When Matt tumbled, drunk, into the Overflow one night and was drowned, Rob took on his father's job of running the farm with no emotion apparent other than relief. But after a couple of years of struggle, Rob had had to admit defeat. His father had run the farm too deep into debt. My father sold the land and invited Rob to stay on as caretaker and man of all work around the Court. It was something of a surprise to everyone when Rob, who might have done better for himself elsewhere, accepted and stayed.

He came to my elbow, watching as I turned the sausages.

"I'm sorry about your dad."

"Thank you. I brought his ashes home. That's why I came tonight – I wanted to put them in the church."

He had lifted the pan of peas off the stove and was busy draining them. He said nothing.

"Rob—you're sure you couldn't even make a guess?"

He didn't ask what I was referring to. He shook the pan thoughtfully. "If I had to, I'd say it was one of the twins, but they're bad enough to tell apart in daylight."

"Could it have been Francis?"

"I suppose . . . but I'd have thought he was a mite too tall. Why, were you expecting Francis?"

"No. But if it wasn't Francis, it would have to be Emory—"

I stopped. Emory could not be the secret friend with whom I had shared my thoughts since childhood. If it had to be one of those two, it must surely be Francis. . . . Francis the loner, who was nearer my age, and of whom—where one could touch that elusive personality—I was unequivocally fond. But Emory was something else again. I had never had any illusions about Emory—a tough-minded man, determined, self-sufficient. James had a touch of his twin's ruthlessness, but tempered with something less aggressive.

I found myself thinking about James as I had last seen him. An Ashley to the fine bone—tall, with fair hair. The long grey eyes of all the portraits. A way of doing what he wanted, and doing it so charmingly that you overlooked the self-interest and thought he was doing you a favour. Clever, yes; shrewd, yes; but kind, and capable of great generosity.

Rob brought me back from my troubled thoughts, saying, "Why would it have to be?" I must have looked quite blank. "If it was one of the twins, why Emory? In the churchyard."

"Oh. Because James is in Spain, and Emory rang up from England on Wednesday. Rob, you saw him coming out of the vestry. Did you see when he went in?"

"No. When I heard the dogs barking, I took a look around. I saw whoever it was was using a flashlight, so I waited. I thought it might be some of the village boys out for a lark. Then I saw you going onto the porch." He grinned. "Say this for you, Bryony, you don't make more noise than a fox. Remember when I used to take you poaching? . . . Well, I never heard you tonight till you came right up to the church door."

"Then?"

"I'd half a mind to follow you in, in case there was something wrong, but then the flashlight went out and this chap came out of the vestry, sharpish, and I saw it was one of the Ashleys. He didn't run far; stopped by the yew trees and waited. Funny, his bolting away like that when he must have known it was only you. Another queer thing, he had a long coat on or something. Does Emory wear a cloak?"

I hesitated. "Actually, he'd taken a cassock from the church. Don't ask me why. He left it at the lych-gate."

"Funny thing to do. Look, those sausages are done."

"So they are. Oh, Rob, before I forget, the vicar told me to tell you he won't be in the greenhouses tomorrow; he's going down to the old orchard. What are you doing down there?"

"Spraying the trees and tidying up a bit. Things that should have got done this winter past, but there wasn't time. But now, with you back . . . Are you coming to the cottage?"

"I think so, for a bit anyway. I thought I might ask Mrs. Henderson to have the cottage opened up and have things aired for me."

"It's done." He grinned at my look. "The vicar told us you were coming. You can settle in any time you like."

For some absurd reason I felt the tears sting suddenly behind my eyes. Then he said, just behind me, "You've given me too many sausages. Divide them properly."

"I only want two, honestly. Remember the sausage rolls we used to get at Goode's stall?"

"Do I not! Here, then, let's start."

Over the meal we talked easily, he of Ashley Court and of a girl whom he meant to marry before the year was out; I of Madeira and Bavaria and then, irresistibly unloading it all, of the accident, and the puzzle of my father's final message.

"Rob, does the phrase '*William's brook*' mean anything to you?"

"'*William's brook*' . . . never heard of it."

"I wondered if Daddy meant you when he said, '*Perhaps the boy knows.*'" I sighed and pushed my plate away.

Rob got up. "Shall I fix your bike for you now?"

"If you would. I'll wash up while you do it."

"O.K." Then, easily, "Where are you putting your dad's ashes? In the Ashley grave plot?"

He might have been talking about the washing up. I found it oddly comforting. Family talk.

"No, he wanted the open air. So I'll be coming back in the morning, very early, before there's anyone about."

"I'll be about, but I'll not disturb you. If you want breakfast when you've done, I'll be frying up at about seven o'clock. You can go down to the cottage after. Suit you?"

"Suits me."

---

*Ashley Court, 1835*

*Surely she was not often as late as this?*

*The sane part of him insisted that she was. There had been nights when she had been prevented from coming at all, and he had waited all night long in this fret and torment, only to rant and curse at her when, the next night, braving who knew what rough perils from her family and the village see-alls, she came again.*

*He spared a thought for her, hurrying to him through the windy dark, wrapped in her old cloak, the maze key clutched in her hand. "The key to heaven," she had called it.*

*He had had to bite his lips to stop himself saying, "The key to my heart."*

*That had been when he first knew for sure. She was the one.*

FIVE o'clock in the morning. England in May. No wonder they sing about it, I thought, buzzing along on my Lambretta. I had forgotten the light, the sweetness of the air, the newly washed smell of everything. Forgotten, even, the other preoccupation that went with me.

But here he was, crowding me. *Hullo*, I said gaily, without anxiety. *Shall I see you today?*

*I wouldn't be surprised*, said he, and the doors slowly closed between us like a cloud drawing over the sun.

There was no sign of life from the Court. Curtains hung closed

160

over the windows. I took an hour, alone in the great neglected gardens, while the beautiful old house dreamed above its reflection in the still moat. Not mine, I thought; never mine again. All that had vanished, blown away with Jon Ashley's dust. *Hic manet.* Here lies he where he longed to be.

I walked for an hour, but nothing spoke and no one came.

THERE were bacon and eggs for breakfast, and fresh bread baked by Mrs. Henderson. Sunshine poured into the cottage kitchen, and the room was as neat as a ship's galley.

"You do yourself well," I told Rob Granger. "She'll be lucky, your girl. Do I know her, by the way?"

"I doubt it. She used to live near Ashley Village, but her folks moved away. She'll be back soon. Honey?"

"Thanks. Tell her from me that she's on to a good thing."

He grinned and said, "Oh, she knows," and cut a couple of slices off the loaf.

And not just for the cooking, I thought, as I spread honey on the lovely, crusty bread. There was a kind of built-in strength in Rob. His ease of manner with me came from long acquaintance, but it came also from a self-confidence that was part of him, hacked out of a hard life as a fluid line of sculpture is hacked out of stone. Yes, she would be lucky. It was to be hoped, for my cousins' sake, that she would be content to stay at Ashley and not persuade Rob to leave. I said something of the sort.

He made a noncommittal sound, then said, "It'll be strange, with Mr. Howard here. I can't imagine it, somehow. Mind you, everyone in the village is wild to see his wife. I don't know what they think a Spaniard is like."

I laughed. "Actually, she's rather gorgeous, from her photos. But I admit I can't quite see either of them settling here."

"Then it'll be Emory's? Seems funny that James loses it all by about thirty minutes. Must be queer to be a twin."

"Very. But I don't know if James counts it as losing. We all know there's no money here, Rob. Very soon now there'll be a time when no one can keep it."

"Wouldn't you have thought the National Trust would take it on? I mean, a place like this, that historians go wild about?"

161

"I think the National Trust will only take on property that's endowed, and we couldn't manage that."

"You may be thankful yet that it's not your headache."

"Right. It's Mr. Emerson's now, poor man. He'll have to sort out all the legal tangles—what he calls the dead man's hand."

"Dead man's hand? Oh, you mean the trust. Your dad did tell me about it once. You all have to consent before you can sell anything, isn't that it? Well, it maybe makes things a mite safer for you. I mean, they can't sell your cottage over your head."

"They couldn't anyway," I told him. "All the bit they call the cottage strip—the old orchard, and the land along the lake as far as the One Ash road—none of that's included in the trust. It was all Daddy could leave me, but it's mine."

"If they wanted to break the trust and sell the rest, would you consent to it?"

"That would depend. We might have to sell the land to endow the house. I know that Daddy had that on his mind."

Rob straightened in his chair. "Well, this isn't the morning to talk about the future. Once all this—your dad and everything—once it's gone a bit into the background, it'll all settle itself. You've only got to let it take its time."

I nodded, and finished my tea, soothed by his country common sense. Time—there was always time in the country. "Well," I said, "there is something I can do straight away. I can have a look for the paper my father spoke of. I'll have to get into the Court to do that. I don't want to explain myself to the Underhills yet. I suppose you've no idea who has the main house keys?"

"Yes," said Rob. "I have."

As easy as that. "You have?"

He nodded. "Your dad gave them to me before he went to Germany. Didn't you know?"

"Well!" I said with relief. "There's an end to that mystery! You've no idea what mayhem Mr. Emerson and I were picturing!"

While I spoke he pulled open a drawer and fished out a bunch of keys. "Here you are, then. Would you like me to go in with you this morning?"

"No, I don't think so, thanks. I've been thinking, Rob; there'll be tourists going around today, won't there? If I go in on my own, with keys, someone's sure to see me and ask questions. I'll leave the keys with you for now, and go on the tour myself, and just take a look in general. Then later I'll introduce myself to the Underhills. What time's the first tour?"

"Half past ten." He dropped the keys back in the drawer and shut it. No question or comment. There was a sound from the back of the house. "That'll be Mrs. Henderson at the back door now. She'll want a word with you." He smiled and went out.

Mrs. Henderson was small, sixtyish, with greying hair and vivid blue eyes. She worked as efficiently and quickly as she talked.

"Well, now, Miss Bryony, it's nice to see you back again, though I'm sorry about your poor dad. I was just saying to the vicar last week, I said, Mr. Ashley'll be back with us sooner than he thinks, but believe you me, Miss Bryony, I never thought my words would come to pass this way, nor that when I saw you back with us it would be just to pass on yourself. And when I say pass on I just mean that everyone knows now that the Court will go to Mr. Howard, though folk do wonder whether Mr. Howard's wife will take to it here."

While she was talking she had helped me clear the breakfast things and started to wash up. I found the tea towel and wiped, letting the monologue run over me. Sooner or later Mrs. Henderson would stop for breath, and then, adept from long practice, I would pick out the one topic which I might want to pursue.

"I doubt very much if Mr. and Mrs. Howard will come to Ashley," I said. "Have you seen my cousin Emory lately? Or Francis?"

But Mrs. Henderson was just as good as I at fixing on the topics she wanted. "Well, of course if Mr. Howard doesn't come back, then it'll be Mr. Emory and his wife, and a very nice girl she is, and everyone says the same, though a bit young for it—"

"What wife?"

"Not for marriage, I don't mean, because nowadays they're ready for anything before they're turned fifteen."

"*What* wife?"

She had certainly captured my attention at last. She shot me a glance of triumph, turned on the hot tap, and held a jug under it to rinse, taking her time. "Well, not yet, but it's only a matter of time. It's Miss Underhill—Cathy. Didn't Rob say?"

"No. Emory's actually engaged to the Underhill girl?"

"I don't know about engaged, they don't call it that now, do they? They go with someone, or they have a thing going."

"And you really think this is serious?"

"I'd say so." She stopped working and looked at me, the blue eyes quite serious. "You know Mr. Emory, he was always one that went straight for what he wanted. Nice about it, but pity help anything that stood in his way."

Yes, we could do you in and smile with great charm while we did it. The Ashley talent. It had served for several hundred years.

I said, "Is she pretty? Tell me all about her."

She told me, but I wasn't listening. I was thinking about my cousin Emory, that determined and clever man. It was like him, with his hard good sense—the steel-hard Ashley wish for continuity —to marry an asset; and if he was fond of her, the affection and not the fortune was the bonus.

I was also thinking about my lover. Where did this leave us? And why, for heaven's sake, could he not be open with me? I was rapidly having enough of mystery.

*Trust me.* It came suddenly, clear and close.

*Oh, you were reading me, were you? Well, you'll know what I think about you. Where are you?*

*Not far.* It was fading. *Not far.*

*Where, though? Here at Ashley?*

The faintest quiver of amusement came through, mischief, but with a touch of comfort, like a pat on the shoulder.

"Going down to the cottage?" Mrs. Henderson was asking.

"Yes. Rob tells me you've opened it up already. It's marvellous of you, Mrs. Henderson. Can I move straight in?"

"Yes, indeed you can. I put what I thought you'd need, groceries and such, on the kitchen table. And when I pop down to the village this morning, I'll call at the farm and tell them you'll want milk."

I left eventually, overwhelmed with offers of every sort of help under the sun, and made my way down to the cottage. The first thing that struck me was the garden. I had expected the cottage garden to match the outlying parts of the Court gardens for ne-glect, but it was a small marvel of neatness. The two plum trees were pruned and well shaped; the roses around the window had been carefully trimmed, and the plots to either side of the path were hoed and raked and planted within an inch of their lives.

The inside was charming and neat, with pink geraniums in the window and the fresh smell of polish everywhere. The groceries were on the kitchen table. I had only to pay my bill at the hotel, get my things brought over here, and move in.

Which was not a reason to find myself, for the first time since my father's death, crying helplessly, as if there were neither love nor hope left in the world.

---

*Ashley Court, 1835*

*My God, he thought. I've forgotten the list. My father was right to rave at me for a vicious libertine. It had seemed amusing, once, to keep a list of them. And her name on it, too.*

*I'll burn the list. I'll burn the books, too, all of them. She is the last, I promise it. Only let her come tonight.*

Two busloads of tourists were already lining up when I got to the gate of the Court. There was a trestle table set up inside the gatehouse, on the other side of the bridge, and here a young woman sat taking the money. She obviously did not know me. I took my ticket and joined the group in the courtyard. The young woman escorted us into the house and did her best to make the place come to life.

"This is the great hall. It's Tudor, built in Henry the Eighth's time, but there's no record that the King was ever here. . . . Notice the carving on the gallery rail. It's original. But that shield in the centre with the crest was added later, in the nineteenth century, when the family took the motto 'Touch not the cat bot a glove' from their Scottish connection. You can see the motto again carved on the stone shield above the fireplace. It was William Ashley the author who had the old Tudor chimneypiece taken out and this Gothic one put in. It was much admired at the time. This way, please."

It was a comprehensive tour, good value for the money. We saw it all. The Tudor parlour with the priest hole, the council chamber, the dining room with the Queen Anne ceiling; the cellars, the kitchens, the bedrooms, and the gallery; and, at last, the library.

This ran the full length of one wing of the house, a tall room with a heavily corniced ceiling, its walls completely covered with shelves. At intervals shelves stood out from the walls to create bays, each a self-contained room in itself, with a table and heavy chairs of Spanish leather. Here and there stood glass-topped display tables for valuable volumes; and in my childhood there had been on either side of the fireplace a pair of ancient celestial and terrestrial globes. I could remember the firelight on the mellow leather of the books, and being allowed to turn one of the big globes while my father told me about the countries which passed so quickly under my hands.

Now it was a sad ghost of a room, its only beauty that of proportion. It was empty of books except in the locked section, where, behind a gilded grille, two of the three sets of shelves were filled with books in the private collections of Scholar William and of Nicholas Ashley, his son. The guide was saying something about Nick Ashley now, and people were smiling. One or two drifted over to look at the titles behind the grille, and I went with them.

In William's section, Shakespeare predominated. I could see three different copies of *Romeo and Juliet*. Beside them was the volume which explained this interest, a book entitled *A New Romeo to His Juliet*, which contained, I knew, William Ashley's poems to his wife, Julia, whose crest he had scattered so lavishly through the house.

The crest appeared in every other room; it was scrolled over the front gate, carved in the panels of the staircase, even in two of the misericords of the church choir. It was also carved in the pavilion which stood at the centre of the maze. Such devotion was a trifle overpowering. Possibly even to Julia herself it must have been formidable, not to say stifling. After her death at twenty-six William, distracted with grief, had shut himself away with his books and his writing, and had had little, if anything, to do with his son, who was too like the dead Julia.

Our guide was telling the story, under the portrait of Nicholas, aged eighteen, which hung over the chimneypiece.

"He was only seven when his mother died, and he was left alone, one gathers, except for a series of tutors. He grew up wild, and he got wilder. I suppose the story sounds corny now, but it's true, and it did have a really dramatic ending."

It was certainly dramatic, and probably true. What we knew about Wicked Nick's life and death came mainly from the journal of Emma Ashley, the wife of Nick's successor. Emma was almost as wordy as Queen Victoria, and every bit as virtuous. Nicholas himself suffered a good deal in the telling, and the girl—the last of his girls—was allowed to sink into oblivion. But the main facts were there in Emma Ashley's diaries.

Nicholas had adored his gentle mother. Between Emma Ashley's disapproving lines one could read of his affectionate nature, starved, repulsed, bullied, or deferred to by his tutors. What must have started as normal, healthy high spirits changed with mishandling into wildness. Nick Ashley was a few months short of twenty-two when his father fell ill. It was then, with his father safely bedridden, that he began his nightly "orgies" of illicit love.

"There's a tradition," our guide was saying, "that he used to meet his girls in the pavilion in the centre of the maze, though how they found the way in I don't know. There are stories of terrible quarrels about this, because William kept the pavilion sacred to Julia's memory. In any case, Nicholas took it over. There are engravings showing it as he is said to have made it over into a love nest, with a huge bed and a big mirror in the ceiling above it, lots of silk curtains and shaded lamps, but it doesn't seem likely he'd have done that while his father was alive.

"Anyway, when William Ashley died, Nick had been keeping company with a girl from a nearby village, but this was a rash choice, because one of the girl's brothers was the Court gamekeeper. Just one night after William died, this man was out after a poacher. His brother was with him for company, and when they saw their sister coming out of the maze—well, they knew what that meant. They waited outside till Nick Ashley came out, and shot him dead. The brothers weren't ever caught. They took a ship from Bristol and got clear away. The Ashley estate then went to Nick's uncle—William's brother, Charles. It was Charles's wife who wrote the diaries." The girl smiled as she wound up her story. "It's the only tragedy recorded at the Court. Perhaps the sad ghost of Wicked Nick haunts the maze to this day, but nobody meets him, and the family keeps him dark."

Did we? I never remembered feeling anything but sympathy for poor Nick Ashley. The young face in the portrait showed weakness, not wickedness, and a good deal of charm. And already a look of settled unhappiness.

"Now the clock under the portrait is . . ." the guide was saying, and everyone looked obediently at the French ormolu clock. But my attention fixed itself about eighteen inches to the right of the clock, where a small T'ang horse had always stood; it was not there now. Though slightly damaged, it was worth five or six hundred pounds in any market.

The tour party was beginning to leave the library. I lingered to look inside the display tables. Here, too, things were missing. A little oval miniature. A Chinese jade seal carved with a lion.

"Please?" said the guide. I looked up with a start. All the others had gone. "I have to lock up," said the girl.

"I'm so sorry," I said. "Did you say lock up? You mean you lock the rooms behind you as you go?"

"Oh yes. All the rooms are locked except the ones that are being lived in. We open and shut them as we go through."

"The keys you use—who keeps them as a rule?"

She looked faintly surprised, but answered me readily enough. "I give them back to the people who live here. They're tenants; the family's abroad just now."

"Oh. Well, thanks very much," I said, and went thoughtfully out in the wake of the others.

---

*Ashley Court, 1835*

*She was here at last.*

*The light step on the veranda, the hand on the door, the slight figure in the shabby cloak slipping quickly into the room, then shutting the door carefully behind her. The cloak thrown aside, falling across the writing table where, year after year, his father had sat alone, writing those sterile verses to his love.*

*"My love."*

*Her hair, loosened from the hood, fell like rain, straight and dark, but full of rainbow lights from the candle. Outside, as if at a signal, a nightingale began to sing.*

*The room echoed with its song. That damned keeper, he remembered, had threatened to shoot the bird. . . . Damned keeper, indeed. Her brother. My brother's keeper . . . He was getting light-headed.*

*"What are you laughing at, then, love?"*

*"I'll tell you afterward. Here, my sweetest girl, come here to me."*

"Aren't you Miss Ashley?"

The voice, a woman's, and American, brought me out of my thoughts and back to the sunlight of the courtyard, where I now saw a big American car parked. I turned to the woman who had spoken. "Yes, I am. And you must be Mrs. Underhill?"

She was a woman in her middle forties, shortish, and groomed to a high gloss in a flawlessly cut cream suit. "I'm so glad to meet you." She put out a hand. "We're terribly distressed about your father."

She talked on for a little about Daddy, with a gentle concern for me, and seemed pleased when I said I planned to live for a while in the cottage by the lake.

"How did you know me?" I asked her.

"From the portrait in our bedroom."

My parents' room, of course. I said, "Is it so like me? It was painted years ago."

She laughed. "Well, I can see you're not seventeen any more, but you're not that much older, are you?"

"I feel it. I'm twenty-two."

"Look, what are we standing out here for? Come in, Jeff's wild to meet you, I know. He's just flown in from Houston."

As we went into the house, I said, "I was planning to call this afternoon." I laughed rather apologetically. "I've just been around with the guided tour. I was curious to see how they did it."

"Have you really? Well, fancy!" Her eyes danced. "Cathy and I've done it a couple of times. It was a good way to learn all the history, and what a history!" She paused at the door of the small drawing room. "You'll stay to lunch with us, won't you? Now"— as I made the ritual protest—"I won't take no for an answer. We're having a guest already, so it's easy to stretch it." She smiled like someone with a secret that she knew would delight me. "Guess who it is? Your own cousin."

Any delight I felt was tempered with uneasy memories of last night in the churchyard, and with Mrs. Henderson's gossip. "You mean Emory?" I said brightly. "How lovely!" But as Mrs. Underhill gestured me past her into the drawing room, I saw her eyeing me with a slightly wary look. One up for Mrs. Henderson and the village gossip, I thought; it was just such a look as might be given to the about-to-be-dispossessed Miss Ashley, whose ticket back to the Court had been picked up by Miss Underhill.

"Yes," she said. "Emory."

"Well, isn't that nice!" I said. "Thank you, I'd like to stay."

The small drawing room was about thirty feet by eighteen, with three long windows looking out on the terrace above the moat. The water's reflected light moved prettily on the ceiling. They had hardly rearranged the room at all, I saw.

"Let's sit down, shall we?" Mrs. Underhill said. She motioned me to a seat in the corner of the big chesterfield.

"I gather," I said, "that you know my cousin quite well?"

"Yes. He and Cathy—my daughter—met a while back, and they found this connection—that she was staying at Ashley Court. Of course she asked him over. He's a charmer, don't you think?"

"I've always thought so," I agreed. "And so's his twin, James. You've met him? And Francis? No, well, he's abroad a lot." I hesitated fractionally, then hit the ball into the open field. "You know, I suppose, that the Court will belong to Emory's family?"

She looked embarrassed. "He did tell us something about the way things were left, but of course it was all in the future then. It seems you had some ancestor who tied everything up so that it had to be inherited by a man." She smiled at me frankly. "I must say, it seems tough to me. Isn't there anything that can be done?"

She sounded as if she meant it. Some tension that I hardly knew I had been feeling slackened in me.

"I doubt it. That's been built in ever since the place started. The really awkward tying up that the old man did was the trust that stops even the heir from selling any of the unentailed property without the consent of the whole family. Luckily, so far, we haven't fought much over it." I smiled. "And I don't see why we should start now. I expect Emory will do all right; he usually does."

"You don't sound as if you minded one bit."

"I don't believe I do. We've had a good run for our money."

The talk went off then to the comfortable subject of English gardens. Listening with half an ear, I looked around for the T'ang horse, or the jade seal, or anything else that should have been in the locked part of the house. I saw none of them. I knew I would have to tell her about the missing objects, but I wondered how in the world one broached such a subject. Well, I thought, if you have to ask something, then ask.

"Mrs. Underhill, there's something I've been wondering about. I understand that the rooms on the public side of the house are kept locked, and that the tour guide always gives the keys back to you. What happens if you're away from home?"

"They're left with that nice Rob Granger. He keeps an eye on things if we're not here. Why do you ask?"

"It's just . . . Mrs. Underhill, I noticed . . ." I hesitated, then plunged. "One or two things that used to be in the library aren't there. I wondered if you knew—if they'd been moved."

She froze. "Moved? Not that I know of. Valuable things?"

"Well, there's a little Chinese horse, in unglazed earthenware, a sort of biscuit colour, with a mended leg—"

"A Chinese horse? Unglazed—for heaven's sake, you don't mean a T'ang horse?"

She looked so horrified that I realized she probably knew more about the value of Chinese ceramics than I did.

I said hastily, "Yes, a small one. I just noticed it had gone from the mantelpiece in the library. There was a miniature gone from one of the showcases, and a piece of jade gone, too, a seal with a lion on it. You haven't seen them anywhere else, have you?"

171

"No, I have not. Miss Ashley, this is just terrible!"

Her face had lost all its colour. I felt like an executioner. "Look, please don't worry so. Mr. Emerson's probably put them away. I should have asked him first. Please forgive me."

"Well, of course, but—oh, here's Jeff. . . . Jeff, this is Miss Ashley. She's coming back to stay for a piece, in the cottage by the lake. Isn't that wonderful? But right now she's staying to lunch with us. Miss Ashley, this is Jeff, my husband."

We shook hands, and, like her, he said the right things about my father with that enviable American warmth and ease of manner. He was a big man, broad in body, with health kept at concert pitch. He looked to be a rich, clever man, a killer in business hours, and kindness itself in his time off.

Before I could stop her his wife had told him about the missing objects. The pleasant smile vanished and the black brows snapped together. He didn't waste time on apologies; he asked two or three questions, and then said, "The first thing is to call the lawyer. I'll do that now." He glanced at the clock on the mantel. "Cathy went to pick Emory up? They're not back yet?"

"No," said his wife.

He nodded and made for the door, but then turned back to me. "You only noticed things missing from the library?"

"That's right. Though until I missed the T'ang horse, I didn't really look. Mr. Underhill, this is making me feel terrible."

"Would you like to go around now on your own? You might find the things somewhere else. Or you might find more things missing. Either way, the sooner we know, the better."

"Yes, I'd like to. Thank you."

"Fine. Now, Stephanie says you went in with the guide; that means you've no keys of your own?" He crossed to a desk, took a small key from his pocket, unlocked a drawer, and took out the big bunch of house keys. No, I could acquit Mr. Underhill of carelessness. He handed me the keys. "Fix me a martini, please," he said to his wife, and went out.

MY SEARCH, which was fruitless, finished in the big schoolroom of the nursery wing. I don't quite know why I went there, except that the Underhills' swift reaction to my inquiries made me feel

172

as if I had started a full-scale criminal investigation before I was even sure that anything was missing, and I wanted time to think. I glanced at my watch. Just short of twelve thirty. I sat down on the wide window seat.

The sun poured into the shabby room. Beside me on the faded cushion sat three old friends, grubby and grey with much loving: the animal family, Hippo, Pot, and Amos, whose names Francis had chosen. The old dappled rocking horse stood gathering dust; and white-painted shelves still held the beloved storybooks. Below them was the locked cupboard to which, prompted by Leslie Oker, a friend who runs a secondhand bookshop in Ashbury, I had transferred some of the treasures from the open shelves. There was a growing interest, he had told me, in illustrators like Arthur Rackham and Kay Neilsen. Small beer, perhaps, compared with T'ang horses and jade, but there was love to be reckoned with as well.

T'ang horses and jade. Valuable books? Abruptly I crossed to the cupboard and tried the door. It was not locked. With a jerk of sudden apprehension, I pulled the door open.

The books were all there, just as I had left them. As I relaxed, I realized how falsely keyed up I had been. To be valuable they would have to be the deluxe editions, signed by the artist—not the dented and soiled nursery editions we had.

I pulled out *Grimm's Fairy Tales*, and there were the familiar drawings, of the Goosegirl with poor Falada, and of the Princess with the Dragon's head on her lap. . . .

*The Princess and the Dragon!* I swung around and stared up at the empty oblongs, dark on the faded schoolroom wall. Two original Rackhams, given me by a great-aunt, had once hung there; one from Lamb's *Tales from Shakespeare,* the other this illustration from Grimm—*The Princess and the Dragon.* I had locked them away with the books. They were not in the cupboard. And this time I had not miscalculated. They were the real thing, irreplaceable, and worth the kind of money that few people could afford to lose. Certainly not me.

I still remember the rush of anger I felt. I slammed the cupboard door shut, went back to the window, and leaned out. I thought I heard a car, but I made no move. I could not yet face the company. The scent of the garden came floating, sweet and calming as the sunlight on the water below me; a swan slept on her nest, head under wing, her cygnets beside her. The cob floated nearby, in full beauty.

My anger gone now, I closed the window and sat again on the window seat. *Lover?*

*I'm here. What is it?*

I hardly knew I had called him. Our minds had for so long dwelt one with the other that the exchange was as swift and wordless as a glance between intimates across a crowded room. But to describe it, words must serve.

*Things have disappeared. The horse has gone from the library.*

*The what?* For once it came with a catch of puzzlement. *I thought you said the horse has gone from the library.*

*I did.* I sent him as clear an image as I could.

*Oh, that one. Yes. It's gone?*

*That, and other things as well. And now I've found some pictures gone from the schoolroom, valuable ones.*

*And you think they were stolen. He is phoning the lawyer.*

*You knew that? How?*

*From you. You're as open as daylight when you're upset.*

*Am I? Then why didn't you come when I was in the cottage?*

*Because it was time you cried it all out, and that's a thing to do by oneself. But you should have known I was there.*

*I'd have liked you closer.* It was resigned, almost flat.

*Bryony—sweet Bryony.* The patterns came through delicate and warm, like gentle hands touching my cheeks.

*I want you so.* It went out with all the longing of loneliness.

The touch changed, electric now, thrilling as live wire. Then it shut off abruptly, and my cousin stood in the schoolroom doorway.

---

*Ashley Court, 1835*

"*I was afraid you'd missed the way.*"

"*Oh, no, it's easy, now I've got the key.*"

"*I thought you might have said, 'I'd always find the way to you, my lover.'*"

"*So I would, so I would. I didn't have to use the key tonight. I remembered every turning, just as you drew it for me on the map.*"

174

*"There you go again. Well, I shall say it for you.
If you were hidden at the center of the darkest and
most tangled forest in the world, I'd find you."*

"Hullo, Bryony."

"Why, Emory, how lovely!" To my surprise, my voice sounded quite normal. "I could hardly believe it when they said you were coming here to lunch today!"

He smiled. "You're looking wonderful. How are you really?"

"I'm fine—" I stopped short as he came into the room.

He caught my look. "What is it?"

I said, uncertainly, "James? It *is* James, isn't it?"

Meeting the amusement in his eyes, I felt myself colour. I was absurdly at a loss. The only thing certain about this man was that he was one of my cousins. Tall, fine-boned, with fair straight hair and grey eyes, a mouth that was not Ashley—long-lipped, folded at the corners as if it liked to keep secrets, or keep control.

He smiled a familiar sparkle of mischief. "Don't tell me you're slipping, Bryony darling! We never could put one over on you. No, it's Emory. Didn't they tell you I was coming?"

"Yes, they did. . . . Oh, all right, so I'm slipping." I returned the smile. "Well, whichever you are, it's up to me to say welcome to Ashley Court. And of course I mean welcome." I uncurled from the window seat, got to my feet, and held out both hands for his. He took a couple of quick steps forward, and his hands closed around mine. He drew me into his arms and kissed me, a cousin's kiss, on the cheek.

I pulled away sharply. He was laughing, but before I could say anything, he put his hands up in a gesture of surrender.

"All right. I should have known we couldn't fool you."

"Then why did you try, James?" For some reason I was angry.

"For fun," he said lightly, and waited, as if challenging me to say more.

I was silent. It was not just the moment to start explaining that, even had I found it easy to confuse James with Emory, I could not confuse a touch, much less a kiss. The moment he had taken

175

my hands, I had known. Through the dazzle of sunlight I saw his eyes, still smiling and—I was sure—aware.

But he began to talk about my father, and suddenly I couldn't meet his eyes or reply for the thoughts that were crowding out all else. I turned away and sat on the window seat again.

The cool, pleasant voice paused, changed subtly. "Bryony. Try not to be too sad. We'll look after you." Then, as if he were answering something, "It's not time to talk yet, but don't worry, we'll work something out."

The words were gently spoken, but to me they seemed to go ringing on and on. I said something, I'm not sure what, then asked quickly, "How's Cousin Howard?"

He half sat on one of the desks. "Still very ill. Things have been a bit difficult. We felt bad about not getting over for the cremation, but we simply couldn't. I'm sorry."

"I understand. Have you heard from Francis yet?"

"No. He must still be incommunicado in Derbyshire."

"James. Was that you in the vestry last night?"

He straightened, startled. His eyes went momentarily blank; then he said, "Vestry? Why should I have been in the vestry?"

"I've no idea. I went to the church late last night, and I saw someone in the vestry. He was leaving just as I went in. He saw me, but he didn't stay to talk."

"Why would I run away, from you of all people?"

"I don't know. Could it have been Emory?"

"Well, the same applies. Didn't you speak to whoever it was?"

He waited for my reply, his eyes wide and guileless. I knew that look—the I-was-never-even-near-the-orchard look, with the apples literally tumbling out of his pockets. I smiled to myself and turned away. "No. Well, never mind. What's all this about Emory and Cathy Underhill? Have they really got a thing going?"

"I'm not sure. That is, I'm not sure from Twin's side of it."

"Then you are sure from Cathy's?" I asked.

"As far as one can judge, yes."

"You and Emory used not to have secrets from one another."

"We're big boys now."

"Not too big, apparently," I said rather sharply, "to still go in for all that Twin stuff that used to annoy everyone."

"It's convenient," he said, with a slant of the eyebrows that he didn't have to explain. I knew just when it had been convenient; it was when he and Emory were standing in for one another, either for fun or for confusion's sake.

"You mean that you haven't come here today with Emory and Cathy? But that Cathy thinks you are Emory?"

He gave me a sideways glance. "You sound very fierce."

"Well, damn it, why did you do it, James?"

"Oh, nothing deadly. Just that he'd had to stand her up once before, and didn't care to again. And I wanted to see you."

"And do you expect me to back you up?"

"You always did."

"This sounds like the sort of situation one ought not to play about with. If she is serious about him, she might get hurt."

"Why should she get hurt if she doesn't know? She'd be hurt if she knew she'd been stood up again."

"Oh, all right, James," I said resignedly. "You've no right to put me in this position. It's a bit late to tell the truth, so I'll try not to give you away."

"That's my girl." There was nothing in his tone but the offhand approval that there had always been when I helped him. I smiled, and thought how little he'd changed, and how much.

"Penny for them," said my cousin.

"I was just thinking that we might never have been parted at all. It seems like yesterday, you and Emory playing your games."

But he wasn't listening. He was standing now, and looking out of the window over my head. "Did you know one of the beeches had gone?"

"Yes. Rob told me it had to come down after a storm."

"Have you noticed what you can see through the gap?"

I turned. "No. What?"

He nodded downward. "You can see almost all the layout of the maze. You could never see any of that from the house before— Bryony! Why didn't we ever think of it? It's the coat of arms!"

"What is? What are you talking about?"

"The design of the maze," he said impatiently. "The layout. You know that geometric pattern carved on the fireplaces, round old William's 'Touch not the cat' crest? That's it, surely?"

I stared down at the intersecting lines of the maze. "Good heavens, so it is! Well, after all, the maze was very much William Ashley's private place, wasn't it? I always wondered why he put that odd square design behind Julia's badge. He even used it for a bookplate in his own books, I remember that. And talking of books—" I looked up at him. "James, some things from the library seem to have disappeared."

He was still intent on the sunlit maze below. "Ah, yes," he said absently. "The Underhills told me. Underhill had just telephoned Emerson when we got here to see if he knew anything about the stuff. He didn't. It's certainly very odd. Did you find anything else missing?"

"The pictures Great-Aunt Sophie gave me. The ones from there." I pointed to the wall.

"Who on earth would want a couple of nursery pictures?"

"Those nursery pictures are originals, and they're pretty valuable now, though they'd be hard for a thief to sell. James, what can have happened to them?"

He frowned. "Look, Bryony, I can see this is rather worrying, on top of everything else, but try not to fret over it. Can't you just leave it to Twin and me?" He hesitated. "Don't take me wrongly, but now it's really our job. Do you mind?"

"Give me time. I don't know." I began to get up from the window seat. "We'd better go down to lunch, I suppose."

"Bryony." His arm fell lightly across my shoulders. I sat very still. "I've got to talk to you. When can we talk? They said something about your moving into the cottage. Is that true?"

"Yes. I think I'll move in today. I—I'd like to talk to you, James. There's a lot to say. . . . After lunch, perhaps?"

"After lunch I've got to have a chat with Jeff Underhill about the lease of the Court. I'll see you after that. Now I think we'd better go downstairs."

As we left the schoolroom I wondered whether to tell him now about my father's last words to me. Halfway down the great staircase, I stopped by the portrait that hung there—a dark girl, painted rather stiffly, but with beauty showing through even the stylized features of the seventeenth-century society portrait. Bess Ashley, the gypsy girl. She had talked to a lover no one could see, and

179

went to the stake for it. Behind her, almost obscured in the yellowing canvas, was a black cat.

"Jàmes," I said. "Do you ever have dreams?"

"Dreams? Of course. Everyone does. What sort especially?"

"Oh, about the future. People you're going to meet, and then you do meet them. That kind of thing."

There was a little pause. He shot me a look and opened his mouth to reply, but at that moment Mrs. Underhill came to the foot of the stairs. I ran down with an apology, but she brushed it aside and began to say in an undertone, "Do you mind, I wanted to ask you, don't say anything—" Then she stopped short as a girl emerged from a door at the other side of the hall and ran to take James's hand in hers.

"Emory! You've been an age! Where were you both, for heaven's sake? In the middle of the maze?"

It was the girl from the Jaguar. I recognized her straight away, the look of her father somehow translated into long blonde hair and mink lashes. She was taller than her mother, and slim to swooning point in a tight pair of blue jeans and a long loose sweater. She glowed with happiness and well-being, and the glow, it was very obvious, began and ended with my cousin.

"Cathy—" began her mother, but James was already disentangling his fingers and saying, "You haven't met my cousin yet. This is Bryony. Bryony, Cat Underhill."

"Hi, Bryony. I'd have known you anywhere."

She held out a hand and I took it. "That's what your mother said. That portrait must be better than we thought."

"Oh, it's not just that. When you've lived here for a bit you get to know the Ashley face." She glanced up at James again, then added, seriously, to me, "I'm sorry. I should have said before, I'm really sorry about your father."

"Thank you. Didn't I see you in Worcester yesterday? You stopped at a crossing to let me and a black cat over."

"Gosh, sure. At least I remember the cat. I nearly ran him down." She took me by the arm as her mother began to shepherd us towards the drawing room.

"And now I've solved a problem, meeting you like this," I said.

She widened enormous eyes at me. "A problem?"

180

"Yes. I'd just left our lawyer's office. I saw him watching you, too, and I thought he said cat. I couldn't think why, because if he'd meant the black cat, I could see that myself. But now I know. We'd been talking about the Court and your family—so he must have meant you. I just heard my cousin call you Cat. Well, that's one of the mysteries on the way out."

"One of the mysteries?" she asked. "Are there some more?"

"I certainly hope so," said Mrs. Underhill warmly. I glanced at her in surprise, but she hurried on: "All this time in a moated grange and not even the sniff of a ghost or any of the things you might expect! Miss Ashley, we've been longing for you to tell us the secrets about the Court that aren't in the books."

So that was it. She didn't want me to talk about the missing objects in front of her daughter. Fair enough. I laughed. "I'm sorry if it hasn't come up to expectations. There's a secret stair, as a matter of fact. In a way it's a sort of secret inside a secret—it goes down from the priest hole into the wine cellars."

Mr. Underhill came in while I was speaking.

"I was sure all those stories about priests were true," he said genially.

"Would you show us this stairway?" Cathy sounded really eager, if slightly overanxious. "Right away after lunch?"

"I'll be delighted."

"Talking of lunch," said Jeffrey Underhill, "where is it?"

So for the moment mysteries were shelved, and we went in.

Lunch was delicious, a very American affair; plates of salad, cold chicken, cheese, and fruit all served together, with crisp rolls and coffee. Conversation was general, and I thought I could feel Mr. and Mrs. Underhill working to keep it so. But afterwards, back in the drawing room over more coffee, Cathy came straight back to the subject they obviously wanted to avoid.

"When you talked about mysteries, Bryony, what did you mean?"

Jeffrey Underhill's head turned, but I had had time to think. I said smoothly, "It was something that my cousin and I found in the schoolroom. Have you ever been in there?"

"No. Why would I go in the schoolroom? What's the mystery?"

I laughed. "Nothing in the schoolroom. Something outside. We found a new view of the maze from the window."

181

"Oh, the maze!" Cathy's eyes were bright. "If you knew how I'd wondered about that maze! And the elegant little roof you can see. . . . A sort of summerhouse, isn't it? I've walked all around those darned hedges, but I knew if I went in, I'd never get out again. Gosh, I suppose you know the way?"

"Oh, yes. So does my cousin, unless he's forgotten. Have you, Twin?" I caught the glint in James's eye. He knew that I found it impossible to address him as Emory.

"I don't know," he said. "I'd hate to try. But that's what you were going to tell them, wasn't it? We've got a map now."

"A map?" asked Cathy.

The word map set up an echo in my mind. *The cat, it's the cat on the pavement. The map. The letter. In the brook.* I pushed it aside and listened to James explaining.

"Yes, a map. That was the mystery we solved looking down from the schoolroom. One of the old trees on the edge of the lake had to come down after a storm, and now we can see clear through the gap to the maze. From that height the layout can be seen almost completely. And what we saw told us that there are plans everywhere in the house."

The two women looked amazed, but Jeffrey Underhill's brows came together for no more than three seconds; then he said, "The coat of arms. I've wondered about that."

"My, you're quick," said my cousin admiringly. "Yes, it does seem an unlikely design, now one knows, doesn't it?" He nodded towards the carved fireplace. "There, Cat, you see it? That uninspiring pattern surrounding our enigmatic motto. That's a map of the maze."

"Do you mean to tell me," demanded Mrs. Underhill, "that you didn't know this, either of you, till this very morning?"

"We'd no idea," I said. "It's never been possible before to see the maze from above."

"An aerial photograph?" suggested Mr. Underhill. "That could be interesting."

"It's all so overgrown I think it would just look like a huge thicket," I said. "What you really need is a plain geometric map like the one on the coat of arms, and then a machete. Mr. Underhill, there was something—"

He looked up from his coffee cup. "Yes, Miss Ashley?"

"There was something I wanted to ask you. Would I be in any-one's way if I spent a bit of time in the library? I want to go through the locked section. The family books ought to be sorted out . . . if that's all right?"

"Well, of course," said Jeffrey Underhill. "The house is yours, you know that. What about keys? Do you want to keep mine?"

"No, thank you." I fished them out of my handbag. "I can get Rob's set."

"Good. Then there'll be no difficulty about the tours."

He took the keys as Cathy, who was over at the fireplace trac-ing out the design of the maze in the stone, said, " 'Touch not the cat bot a glove.' It's a queer motto. Emory said it was enigmatic. I say it's arrogant. What does it mean? What is this cat they put in the middle of the maze? It looks more like a tiger!"

"It's a Scottish wildcat," James said. "They can't be tamed, even if you take them from their mother while they're still blind and suckling. You'd not touch one of those lightly, glove or no glove."

"Goodness!" exclaimed Mrs. Underhill.

"How does a Scottish wildcat get down here, right in the middle of England?" said Cathy. "And what does 'bot a glove' mean?"

"Without a glove," I said. "The motto belonged—still does, I think—to the Scottish Clan Chattan. One of the Ashleys—William, who died in 1835—married a girl called Julia McCombie, who be-longed to the clan. She was a beautiful girl, and he was wild about her. He altered the whole place for her. The maze was here already; there's an eighteenth-century engraving that shows it newly planted, with a pretty little classical folly in the middle, a sort of imitation Roman temple. William pulled that down and built the pavilion there for Julia. It must have been lovely when it was new. He had it raised high enough so that she could sit inside and have a view right across the hedges of the maze."

"I suppose that's why he put the Scottish cat in the middle of the maze on the coat of arms," said Cathy.

"And he took her family motto as well?" said Mrs. Underhill. "How very romantic. But didn't the rest of the Ashleys mind? Surely they must have had a motto of their own?"

"They did. The odd thing is that it was almost the same. It was

'Touch me who dares,' and the crest was a sort of leopard, so I suppose it seemed natural to poor William to use the coincidence and put his Julia's crest everywhere instead."

"Why 'poor William'?" asked Cathy. "What happened?"

"They didn't have much time," I said. "Julia died soon after the pavilion was finished. He went peculiar then; used to shut himself up there, writing verses to her. There's a little book of them in the closed section of the library, called *A New Romeo to His Juliet*. He had her painted as Juliet. She's the one on the main landing, with a view of the maze behind her."

"And that's my favourite portrait!" Mrs. Underhill said. "How interesting it will be to see the pavilion—"

"Oh, Bryony, yes!" cried Cathy. "Do say you'll take us in."

"Of course. We'll go now, if you like."

Cathy grinned and turned to my cousin. "You're coming, aren't you, Emory?"

"Some other time. Your father and I have some talking to do."

Mrs. Underhill shook her head, too. "I'd love to go, but not right now, if you don't mind. I've things to do. But please don't leave, Miss Ashley, without stopping in again. Get Cat to bring you back later for tea, will you?"

I heard in my head the echo of Dr. Gothard's voice, and thought about *William's brook*, which might or might not be William's book, and *the cat*, which might or might not be Cathy Underhill.


To HAVE a view now from the pavilion, it would have to be built on stilts like a water tower. The yew walls of the maze were eight feet high and so top-heavy as to make the path in places a black-green tunnel. But here and there a thin patch let a probe of sunlight through.

*Lover? Lover, are you with me?*

The only reply was Cathy, bravely treading behind me. "Why did they ever make mazes? Just for fun?"

"This kind, for fun. When this was planted, it was the fashion. But the idea was ancient. Remember the labyrinth in Crete? Legend says it was built for King Minos to hide the Minotaur in."

"That's right, I read a fabulous book about that. The labyrinth was really a storehouse, wasn't it? Do you suppose it was a sort of

184

safe? You know, the treasure in the middle, and if thieves got in, they'd never get out?"

I laughed. "It's an idea. But you were more likely to find a tomb in the middle than a treasure. I read somewhere that a maze was supposed to be the path the dead follow on the way to the world of spirits. Once at the heart of the maze, nothing could touch you again; you'd reached a place outside the world, a place without bearings. They say compasses won't work in a maze."

"For goodness' sake! Are you *sure* you remember the way?"

I laughed at her. "Fairly sure. Here, it's this way."

"But we're heading back to the house! I see the chimneys!"

"I know, but it's right, it is really. You can trace it out tonight on the fireplace."

"If I ever see the fireplace again— Oh!" This as, just in front of us, a patch of sunlight struck green from flowery grass, and, rising from it, the steps of William Ashley's elegant pavilion.

Overgrown with weeds and dilapidated as the place was, it was still charming. It was built of wood, with a steeply pitched roof of shingles gone silver with time. A veranda, edged by a balustrade and sheltered by the overhang of the roof, surrounded it. The panelled front door had a knocker of a leopard's head. To either side of the door stood tall windows with louvered shutters fastened over them. Honeysuckle and clematis and a host of other climbers had ramped up the wooden pillars and were reaching to seal doors and windows. We pushed them aside and mounted the steps.

"'Touch not the cat,'" said Cathy, and reached for the knocker. She rapped sharply at the door. "Just to wake Wicked Ashley up," she said. "Bryony, what's the matter?"

"You made me jump. One's always better not waking things up." Few sounds are so dead as the knocking on the door of an empty house. A goose feather of superstition had brushed my skin.

"I thought you said there weren't any ghosts."

"If there are any, this is where they'll be."

"He's not answering. Anything against me trying the door?"

"No, but it's locked. We can open the shutters on the south side." And in a moment we'd entered through a window, letting light and air into the large, once elegant room. Now all the furnishings were gone except for garden chairs, a table, and a daybed.

"I'm afraid it's rather a dusty end to the romance," I said.

"Is that the table where William wrote his poems?"

"I doubt it. That's late Victorian."

Cathy's eye fixed itself on the one impressive feature which remained. This was the ceiling, made of one huge looking-glass framed in gilt and mounted in an elaborately moulded cornice. Its smeared and flyblown surface was slightly angled, so that the glass caught the sunshine from the window and laid a rhomboid of gritty light across the daybed.

"What a pretty idea, to have a mirror ceiling. Surely that's part of the original building?" she asked.

"It does look old, but I think it was put in by your Wicked Ashley—William and Julia's son, Nicholas. It rather gives one ideas about the ladyloves he brought here, till the brother of the last one shot him. There's a set of rather randy engravings about it, showing the mirror right over where the bed was."

"Oh, for goodness' sake, is that what it was for?" She turned slowly, and her look around the grubby, echoing room was sad. "I don't know why, but the past is always sadder if there's something a bit beautiful about it. And this place must have been beautiful." Cathy's eyes dwelt on me for a moment, with something in them that I couldn't understand, then moved past me. "Oh, look, there's a little something of Julia left here, after all."

On the wall against which presumably Nick Ashley's big bed had once stood was a moulding in plaster, a sort of headboard applied to the wall itself, crowned with the coat of arms.

Cathy walked over to look at it. "The map again. Just to make sure you could get out of the place." She licked a finger and rubbed the grimy plaster. "Someone's marked the way."

I peered up at it. "You're right. I'd never noticed."

"I expect Nick Ashley drew it in so that his girl friends could slink off home and leave him peacefully sleeping." She laughed. "With a good clean up, this could be quite a place still."

I wondered if the gaze she sent around the pavilion was more than idle. My question came straight out of the speculation, but it sounded casual enough. "How long have you known Emory?"

"Not long. We only met last month, but it seems longer."

"And James?"

"I met him soon after, but I've only seen him a couple of times. My, but they're alike, aren't they?"

"Tweedledum and Tweedledee. Could you ever get them mixed up, do you think?"

She laughed. "I hope not. Could you?"

"I don't think so. I never did as a little girl, but that's a long time ago, and we don't meet so often now."

We had gone outside while we talked, and I pulled the window closed and fastened the shutters across. We went down the steps.

"I guess," said Cathy ingenuously, "I could still get them mixed up if they tried to fool me, but they're too nice to do that." She stopped. "Hey, what flower smells like that?"

"Lilies of the valley. Wild, there, under the hedge, see? Let's pick some for your mother." I stooped and pushed the leaves aside, hunting for the bells. She knelt beside me.

"Emory's rather special, isn't he?" I said.

"Special? Bryony, I'm just crazy about him!" She laughed up at me, her eyes brilliant. She meant it, but it came a thought too easily, as if she'd said it before and would again. I found the over-emphasis soothing; it gave her confession the flavour of powder-room gossip. "He's *fabulous*. I'd do just *anything* for him!"

She stopped suddenly and turned away from me. "Bryony. Do you mind?"

"Mind?" Taken by surprise, I sat back on my heels. "Of course I don't. There's no reason why I should."

At that, she faced me again and gave me a clouded, smiling look; some hint of trouble showed itself still. Kneeling there among the flowery grass, with her hair falling over brow and shoulders, she looked younger even than eighteen.

I smiled at her. "Tell me, where's the difference when it comes to being special? Why not James?"

"For one thing, I haven't seen that much of him, and for an-other—" the pale lashes dropped. "He has a girl already."

"How do you know?" I hadn't meant it to come out so sharply. She seemed not to have noticed. "Because he said so."

I bent to add another flower to the spray in my hand. "Did he say who it was?"

"No." She stood up. "Mom'll be wild about these."

"Let's go back by the path along the Overflow," I said.

We came out of the maze into full sunlight, crossed the little bridge, and followed the mossy path along the stream.

"Why do you call it the Overflow?" Cathy asked.

"Because it's just that. It controls the level of the moat. There are the two sluices, the high sluice, on the other side of the house, that lets the water from the river into the moat, and this one, that lets it out into the pool. Originally the Overflow was just a ditch to carry floodwater away, but a few years ago the high sluice broke in a storm, and the lower sluice couldn't cope with the flooding, so parts of the house were damaged. They repaired the high sluice and dug the overflow channel deeper as a precaution."

"Gee, I'd never thought a moat could be dangerous— Oh!"

"What is it?" I asked. She had stopped and was pointing.

Between the moat and the pool was one of the prettiest monuments in the Court gardens, a cascade with a fishing cat. The heavy gate of the lower sluice was usually kept shut, and to either side of this the normal outflow from the moat was channelled to lapse, fall by fall, over a rock water stair to the pool. On one of the rocks just below the sluice gate was a stone cat, its outstretched paw gracefully curved as if to hook a fish.

Or rather, the cat had been there. Now there was nothing but water cascading down the rocks. On the stone where the cat had been, the ugly iron staples stuck out, twisted crooked from the fall of the statue. The cat lay in the basin under the water, with fish tranquilly shuttling across it, under the broken paw.

---

*Ashley Court, 1835*

*They had made love. Now he lay on his back, staring up at the dark square of the ceiling mirror.*

*The candle had burned low. The room smelled of burning wax, and the lavender water she made each summer and used to rinse her hair. He would open the window to let the dawn in, but not yet. Dawn always came too soon.*

*A sound from the door had dragged him from the shallows of reverie. Beside him she slept deeply, like*

*a child. And someone was there, on the veranda.*

*He was alert, instantly up on one elbow. Perhaps something was wrong? His uncle had arrived before he was expected? This little world of peace and love had been broken before its time; the too short night was over.*

*But all was silence. He relaxed again, to see her eyes, darkly shining, watching him. "What is it, love?" she asked.*

*"Nothing. Something waked me. Look, the moon's almost down. No, don't go yet."*

As I had promised, I went back to tea with Cathy, then took myself off to my cottage. Rob had brought my baggage in from Worcester, but before I unpacked I went to the telephone and dialled the number of the secondhand bookshop in Ashbury.

"Is Mr. Oker there, please? Oh, Leslie, this is Bryony Ashley. Yes—a couple of days ago. How are you? Good."

Talking to Leslie had about it something (I imagined) of the ritual of Eastern bargaining, and there was no hurrying him. The impression he fostered, of a genial and impulsive gossip, had stood him in very good stead. In sober fact, Leslie Oker was a knowledgable and wily operator, about as impulsive as a two-toed sloth. The kindness, though, was real.

Thanks to it, the preliminaries today were short. After only three minutes Leslie paused, and then said, "But you didn't ring me up just to tell me you were home, dear. What can I do for you?"

"Well, it's just a quick query. You remember showing me that limited edition of *Rip Van Winkle* last year, the one illustrated by Arthur Rackham? I wondered what sort of price his work was fetching now? I mean the original illustrations."

"Well, it's not exactly my line, but the last one I saw was priced at eight hundred pounds."

"I see. Leslie, if you should come across some mention of Rackham drawings for sale, would you not say anything about this, but just phone me straightaway?"

"Of course. But how very intriguing. I gather one is not allowed to ask why."

"For now, no."

"This *is* exciting," said Leslie comfortably. "Of course, Bryony dear. Count on me."

JAMES came down after supper, just as I was finishing the washing up. He accepted a cup of coffee, then followed me outside to a little seat under a lilac tree that stood near the pool. Dusk was falling, and the orchard trees showed pale and frothy with blossom. The tallest of all, a pear tree, held up its plumes of springtime snow. A thrush was singing in the tree, alone, as freshly and as passionately as if this were the first song in the world. From somewhere in the middle distance, towards the Court, came the sound of someone hammering.

"Rob puts in long hours," said my cousin.

"Maybe he's mending the fishing cat. It's broken, you know."

"Oh? That's a pity. Did you ask him to fix it?"

"No, I've not seen him this evening."

"Well, why should he trouble? The whole place is falling to bits; it'll take more than Rob Granger to stop it."

He spoke without bitterness, but with some special seriousness that made me look searchingly at him. He met my look gravely. His arm came gently around my shoulders, drawing me close.

"Bryony, love, it's time we had a talk, you and I."

I waited, feeling my heartbeat quicken. He cleared his throat. "You may be angry, but if you've any sense you'll hear me out, and in the end, I hope you'll help me." His fingers, cupping my shoulder, tightened a fraction. "You have to be on my side. You know that. It's the way things are."

The thrush stopped singing as suddenly as a turned-off tap.

"I'll start at the beginning. I may as well confess the brutal truth. My father—we—the lot of us are in a jam. We're desperate for ready cash and we have to find it somehow, fast."

This was in no way what I had been expecting. I was startled, and showed it. "But I thought—your family always seemed to be doing so well. What's happened?"

"Everything's happened. All the demands that we could have

191

met if they'd come separately, well, they all seemed to come at once. . . . I told you that my father is not well. He'll probably have to retire. If he does, there's not much guarantee that the Pereiras will go on backing us. Why should they? If we had time—but we haven't."

And now, I was thinking, this has happened. This huge liability, Ashley Court, has fallen on them, too.

"But I thought Juanita had a lot of money of her own. Wouldn't she tide you over? After all, she's Howard's wife."

"Ironically enough, the main part of her money is tied up in a trust. These trusts—" James drew a breath. "So my father asked yours if he could help us."

This time I really was startled. I sat up. "James, you can't be serious! You must have known we were run into the ground."

"Oh, yes, we knew that. But you had Ashley."

"*Ashley?* What on earth use is Ashley? It's the biggest liability this side of the national debt!"

"Yes. But what I'm talking about is the Ashley Trust."

"You mean break the trust? When did you approach Daddy for this?"

"The first time was in November of last year. Your father's answer must have given room to manoeuvre, since my father still seemed to have hopes he would consent."

"The first time? He asked him more than once?"

He nodded. "He wrote again when Cousin Jonathan was in Bad Tölz. He didn't want to press it, but—well, things were getting desperate. That time, though, Cousin Jon said he couldn't even consider it." He was silent for a moment, his head bent. "I can't understand his change of heart. Things have been sold in the past, and no one's argued much about it."

"You're not just talking about things this time, James. I take it you're talking about the place itself. Home."

He gave me a gentle look. "Didn't you know about this?"

"Nothing. Of course if there'd been any question of breaking the trust, he'd have had to bring me in as well. I'd have to consent, too, you know that." I thought for a moment. "So now that Daddy's dead, you come to me. That's what you've been leading up to, isn't it?"

"That is what we want," he said.

A pause. I said abruptly, "Did Daddy give any reason for being so dead set against it?"

"No. He really never mentioned it to you, even indirectly?"

Even as I shook my head, I realized he had. *Trust. Depend. Do what's right.* This was one of the things that had weighed on his mind. Until I knew the rest, I could take no action.

I took refuge in a half-truth. "Of course he spoke about the trust generally, once or twice. I do remember his saying that Cousin Howard didn't seem to have the kind of feeling for Ashley that might bring him back to it. I know he hoped that Emory or you might feel differently. Do you?"

"Are you asking me to speak for Emory?"

"If you can."

"I suppose I can. He doesn't want to keep it."

From beyond the lime trees the church clock tolled the half hour. It sounded remote and serene. "And you?" I asked. "James, I've got to know the truth."

He took his time. When he spoke, at length, his voice was quiet. "I think you know the answer. When we were talking a while ago about the fishing cat, I said the place was rotten, and that's true. You know it is. It's a burden to the living, even if you count keeping it going as homage to the dead." He took a breath like a sigh. "I'm sorry, love, this is the wrong time to talk to you like this, but you asked me. You can't seriously expect us to go on running this—this National Trust reject. If there aren't means to save it, it'll have to go. We've got to face that."

"James, I'm facing it."

Another of those silences. He held me close; his cheek touched my hair. "You will think about it, won't you?"

"Of course I will." The sounds of hammering had stopped. I thought of the fishing cat lying broken under the water and, for some reason, of the pavilion and Cathy's voice asking, "Is that the table where William wrote his poems?"

"Francis," I said suddenly. "How does Francis feel about all this? I thought he loved Ashley."

"He does," said James. "He's a throwback, is Francis. He wouldn't notice if the place fell to pieces round him, as long as

193

he could sit in the maze like William Ashley, making verses— What on earth did I say? You jumped."

"You were reading my thoughts. Do you often do that?"

A pause as long as four quickened heartbeats. Then he said easily, "Twin and I do it with each other as a matter of course. Shades of Bess Ashley, the gypsy, didn't you know?"

"It must save a lot of telephone calls," I said lightly.

He laughed. "It does. As to Francis—I doubt if he'd refuse to help break the trust. We'd have no designs on the house. That's unsaleable. It's the land that would have to go."

"For what?"

"For whatever would bring the most money."

"Building land brings the most."

He answered what I had not said. "Well, and why not? When they build the new motorway across Penny's Flats, we'll be in Birmingham commuter country." He must have felt something in my silence. "Look, Bryony, be realistic."

"I am. Ashley Court hasn't an outlet to Penny's Flats."

His head turned sharply. "Of course it has. That's its whole value. This strip along the pool runs right through the apple orchard to the road."

"Yes, but that's *not* in the Ashley Trust. It's mine."

"Oh, I see." He sounded amused. "Holding out, are you?"

"For the present, yes. I've got to have a home, and I'm planning to stay here . . . well, for a bit," I said, evading it. "James, let's leave it for now, may we?"

"Of course, if you say so. But there was something else. As a matter of fact, I haven't even got to the hard bit yet."

"What hard bit?"

"Well, after your father had refused to consider the trust any further, my father asked Emory and me to do what we could, as quickly as possible. Emory and I agreed to go to Bavaria and talk to your father, but before that, it seemed only sense to—well, to take a look at Ashley itself." He cleared his throat. "We wanted to get into the Court and find out, as a basis for discussion with your father, what there was in the way of quickly disposable assets. Then, by pure chance—it really was pure chance—Emory met Cathy at a party, and she asked him down."

194

"Convenient."

"You sound a bit abrasive. Don't you like her?"

"From what I've seen of her, I like her very much. I'm just not sure that I like her being used by Emory."

"I wouldn't say he was using her." He sounded uncomfortable.

"That had better be true, you know. Jeff Underhill is what they call a tough cookie, and at a guess he adores his daughter. If she's fallen for Emory, Emory'd better reckon it as serious."

"I imagine he does." Somehow, almost unnoticeably, his hand had lifted from my shoulder. "It's the James–Emory thing that gets you, isn't it? You'll have to take my word for it that nothing's happened that Cathy wouldn't mind remembering, even if she ever found out we'd played that game with her—which she won't." He glanced at me again. "Actually, I don't like it any more than you do. . . . There are things I'd rather be doing than escorting an eighteen-year-old who's in love with someone else." One finger touched my shoulder blade, a feather touch. "If you like, love, I'll promise not to do it again."

"That's up to you." The words were indifferent, but I felt myself relaxing. "Go on," I said. "Did you check the disposable assets? Oh, no!" I sat up straight, my hand to my mouth. "The T'ang horse? The jade?"

"I'm afraid so. Bryony, they were ours. I promise you we only took them after your father's death. This last week."

I listened to the tone rather than to the words. I knew it well. James, led into something by Emory. Emory, I knew, was more than capable of playing rough, and James, playing with him, had sometimes suffered for it.

I heard myself asking, in a hard voice quite unlike my own, "Did you have to take the pictures from the schoolroom?"

"I'm sorry. I—they were taken by mistake, only yesterday. As soon as I found out, I said they must go back."

"Yesterday! Who took them, then? Emory wasn't here, was he?"

"No. Cat took them for us."

"*What?*" A whirling pause. "For us? You mean for Emory."

"If you like."

"I do like." My voice was sharp. "It makes a difference."

"For Emory, then. Look, don't worry, you'll get them back."

"I'm not worrying about jade or pictures. I'm thinking about Cathy Underhill. You got that girl to steal for you."

"The things were ours. Aren't you making a bit much of this?"

"Perhaps I am. But not as much as her parents would make of it, I'm sure of that."

"Her parents? You're surely not going to make a thing out of it, are you? Bryony—"

"Wait a minute, James. This takes some getting used to."

I got up abruptly and walked away, across the strip of lawn to the lakeside. There was a low wall there, a length of ancient stonework left to edge the garden. I stood there with my back to my cousin. It was wrong, so wrong. . . . Yet because it was James, I couldn't give way to my first instinctive reaction; because it was James, I must make myself stop and think. . . .

Well, all right, think. *Was* it theft? As soon as the legal formalities allowed, all these things would belong to Howard, and so to his sons. My reaction was an emotional one, nothing more. James knew that and had tried to spare me, raw as I still was from my father's death.

I thought again, briefly, about Rob and the fishing cat. . . . About that, James was right, too; the place, and the life it had represented, was falling to pieces. Why shouldn't my cousins, owners of Ashley, sell the pieces that were theirs?

It came back to the one answer: Cathy. And here I had even less right to judge. I had no idea of the strength of Emory's feeling for her.

I sat down on the wall, still facing the lake, forcing myself to calmness. I thought of the quiet nights filled with my lover's presence. I thought, too, of the strange hesitancy, the impression of guilt and insecurity which now I thought I could understand. It had only begun last night, when I had seen James in the church vestry. Doing what? I could now guess. He must just have picked up the Rackham pictures from their hiding place, somewhere in the church, when he heard someone coming and snatched a cassock from the choirmen's pegs, fled up the nave, and threw the main switch. Whoever came into the church would only see the vanishing cassocked figure and would come to the same conclusion that I had indeed come to.

196

Well, now I knew. And I understood my lover's refusal to come into the open. It was because the affairs of daylight must be settled first. Before anything could be complete between us, we had to settle with the realities of a difficult situation, the hard economics of how and where to live, of Ashley Court and Daddy's will, and the theft of the T'ang horse, the jade seal, and the pictures. The other world, the starlight one, where love was easy because it ran like poetry from mind to mind—that would have to wait. I knew now what he meant by his repeated *Not yet, not yet;* I had to come to terms with what he really was; the outer man, not just that other half of me whom I knew as well as I knew myself. Nor was the outcome certain. It would depend on my handling of this tangled affair, on my finding out what my father had meant. Then, when Ashley was accounted for, my lover and I could come to terms. He could not be sure of me until I had seen and accepted the whole truth about him.

I do not think that at that moment I had any doubts about his identity. A flurry of love, as real as the clematis petals falling on the dim grass . . . I looked at my cousin at last, across the dusk-filled space. He was watching me steadily, patient and intent. Then he smiled and came towards me, and something twisted inside me, like a cord stretched between us that had felt a sudden tug. There seemed no need to speak. There were the Ashley eyes, shadowed in the growing dusk, the casual pose that masked tension. The picture of the real man was blurring, almost as if the imagined picture of my lover was beginning to superimpose itself over the reality of the cousin under the lilac tree. The outlines wouldn't quite fit. Not yet. Not, I suppose, until I had accepted him whole.

"It's all right, James," I said at last. "Please don't worry about this any more. You've a perfect right to do what you think best about the stuff in the house. I suppose we'll have to think what to say to the Underhills, but let's leave it for tonight, shall we?"

"I wasn't worrying," he said, "not really. Blood's thicker than water, whatever that may mean."

His easy assumption of my complicity (why did that hard word occur to me?) took me off-balance. I said nothing.

He must have misinterpreted my silence. Almost before I knew he had moved, he had pulled me into his arms. His mouth found mine, gently at first. "Bryony. Bryony. It's been so long."

I put my hands against my cousin's breast and held myself away from him. "James. But I thought—"

He kissed me again, with growing excitement, stifling what I was trying to say. "You've always known it was me."

"I—yes. I wasn't sure. But—no, wait, please. We've got to get all this business over first."

He persisted for a while, but meeting with no response, let me go gently. "All right. This isn't the time. But don't let's be long about it. I'm so afraid you'll get away from me again."

"I won't do that. Let's go in, shall we, James?" He followed me back into the cottage. "Are you staying at the Court tonight?"

"No. I'll go back to Bristol." That heart-twisting smile again. "I may as well, since you're turning me down."

"For heaven's sake!" I tried for a light tone, but it came out edged. "Did you really expect to stay here?"

"Well, perhaps that would have been pushing it. I'm a patient man." No overtone to suggest that there had ever been any other sort of conversation between us. "I'll telephone Dr. Gothard tonight, to see if there's any news. Have you got his number handy?"

"Yes. I'll write it down for you, shall I?"

I found a pen on the desk, scribbled the number on a used envelope, and handed it to him.

He glanced at it and pocketed it. "Thanks. Oh, where did you find my pen? I've been looking all over for it."

"Yours? Are you sure?"

"Sure I am. Look at the initials. Where'd you find it?"

"In—in the churchyard. Beside the path."

I thought he'd notice my hesitation, but apparently he did not. "Oh. Well, thank you." He kissed me again and went.

I stood for a long time thinking of nothing, my mind closed, a gate slammed shut in sudden panic to keep him out.

Because I was aware of something now that I dared not let him guess at. He and Emory had known more than that my father was ill when they had come to Ashley to check the disposable assets. They had known he was dead.

The pen I had picked up from the desk was the silver ball-point with the initials J.A. that had been among my father's effects in Bad Tölz. I had not recognized it as Daddy's, but there had seemed no doubt that it was his. It had been found, Dr. Gothard had told me, beside his body on that lonely country road.

I don't know how long I stood there, staring, my mind fluttering against a truth so alien and so destructive that I could not, would not, believe it. Heaven knew I did not want to draw the conclusions that followed from it, but they had to be drawn. The first, which seemed now hardly to matter, and which followed from James's easy acceptance of my lie about finding the pen in the churchyard, was that James had in fact been the prowler in the vestry. The second was one that mattered very much indeed. James must have been there, beside my father's body. And he had neither helped the injured man, nor made his presence known.

I could see one further conclusion. James had driven the hit-and-run car that had knocked Daddy down. James had killed my father.

That night, lying wakeful in the little bedroom, I kept my mind guarded against my lover. So strong was my sense of his presence that I could have sworn I saw his very shadow move across the floor. In my grief and loneliness I must have faltered, because I caught it, as clear as a whisper; just my name, insistent and appealing. Then I shut him out again.

NEXT morning, as soon as I could, I went to see the vicar. He was on his knees in the biggest of the greenhouses. The sun was pouring in and the place smelled of warm, newly watered soil and musky tomato leaves.

"Hullo, my dear Bryony. Were you comfortable in the cottage last night?"

"Very, thank you. What are you doing?"

"Tying up the tomatoes. Excellent young plants, aren't they? Tomatoes really are delightful to work with. So easy, and such a big return for such a small investment."

I laughed. "That's too worldly by half, Vicar. You should be drawing morals about it; tall oaks from little acorns grow—"

"So I should. Well, there's a moral in it somewhere, I'm sure. . . . Did you want me for anything special?"

"I wondered if I might talk to you," I said. "Sometime when it's convenient. There's no rush."

His eyes, behind thick glasses, searched my face. "It's always convenient," he said.

"Here and now, then? Can I help with the tomatoes?"

He made no demur, knowing, I suppose, how much easier it is to talk when one's hands are occupied. He started work again, and I moved across the row from him and followed suit. For a moment all was silent, except for the rustling of the tomato leaves and the snip of scissors cutting twine.

"Mr. Bryanston, do you believe in telepathy?"

"I don't query its existence, if that's what you mean. There have been too many instances of it, thoroughly documented; and now I think it is being seriously researched."

"Have you had any experience of it?"

"At first hand, no. At second hand, I am told so. Like everyone else, I had an aunt who had premonitions, at least thirty per cent of which were correct. No, I'm not joking." The fine eyes were gently merry. "I can see that this matters to you. Am I to take it that you yourself have had firsthand experience?"

"Yes. Not just premonitions, either. Messages, conversations even, coming from another mind straight to mine."

"Well," said the vicar, "you are an Ashley, are you not?"

"You *knew?*"

"I know that in your family there's a record of unusual mental powers. Bess Ashley, the 'witch', seems to have done little to deserve that title except to be heard talking to someone who couldn't be seen, and on two occasions conveying information which she claimed had come from her secret friend, and which knowledge could not otherwise be accounted for. Her husband suspected her of taking lovers." He looked up from the tomatoes. "I gather you, too, have a secret friend?"

"Yes," I said, and heard pleading in my voice. "Vicar, please believe me."

"My dear, I do believe you."

"My mind is *not* abnormal—otherwise. But as far back as I can remember, I've been able to talk to this—this person."

"A real person?"

His voice was mild and inquiring, but the question shocked me. "Well, of course. Are you suggesting this is some fantasy thing I made up? It isn't that! It's a real relationship, Vicar!"

"I have conceded that." His voice was sharp, for him. "Dear child, I simply asked if the relationship is with another real and living mind. I gather you don't know who it is?"

"Not yet. But it must be another Ashley, and he must be near. We can talk—communicate—even at quite a distance. When I was in Madeira he told me about Daddy's accident."

"You're sure the news didn't come from your father himself?"

"It couldn't have. We didn't have that sort of communication, just a—well, a feeling for trouble." I stopped, stared. "You mean my father had it, too?"

"To some extent."

I was silent, thinking again about his message: *My little Bryony be careful. Danger. This thing I can feel. . . .*

"Did he know about my secret friend?" I asked.

"He never mentioned it; nor, indeed, did he give any hint that he knew you possessed this gift. His own was, I gathered, much slighter—occasional moments of premonition. They were all, as far as I know, connected with you." The vicar shifted his kneeling pad and addressed himself to the next row of plants. "You say your friend is an Ashley. That narrows the field."

"Yes." Even to myself the syllable sounded dejected. I abandoned the tomatoes and went to perch on a stool. The peace, the sunlight, the warmth, the steady rhythm of the work with the plants slid down like calm over troubled waters. Without any conscious decision, I found myself telling the vicar all about my lover. Not about James or last evening; only the long communication between mind and mind.

When I had finished he said, with his gentle calm, "Well, thank you for telling me. You make it very clear. Now, I take it, something has happened which has worried you and driven you away from him?"

"Yes. I came because I think I know who he is, and I think he's done something very wrong, and I want to know what to do. Normally speaking, I think I'd be able to tell right from wrong myself, but this is different. It's knowing him the way I do—being sure that we are part of one another whether we like it or not. . . . Do you see? Betraying him would be like betraying myself, or even somehow worse."

He straightened up from his task, but did not look at me for so long that I thought he had forgotten my presence. Finally he sighed. "My dear, in a way one might say that the kind of intimacy you've described is like the intimacy of husband and wife; and the law recognizes that. I think—yes, I think that if you do indeed hold the key to someone's inner thoughts, you must not betray them."

"I see," I said. "Yes, that's what I thought."

"If he has done something so wrong, it will come to light without you. But if you see him about to do more harm, you must use this unique relationship to dissuade him. Does this sound daunting, child?"

"A bit. But it seems to be the only thing I can do."

"Bryony, this is not a safe road you are treading."

"I've realized that. That's one reason I had to tell you. Up till now, you see, it's been marvellous . . . being able to talk to him about everything. And it seemed to me that there was nothing but joy for us in the future." I looked down at my hands. "Then, just as I thought I'd found him, I discovered he'd done this really terrible thing that he'd managed to keep secret from me. I only found out by accident."

"You mean you read a thought he didn't want you to read?"

"No, you can't do that. You can close your mind. For instance, he can't know what I'm telling you now. No, I saw something he didn't realize would give him away."

"Then you are not betraying your secret life if you do something about that. There's part of your answer, I believe." He got stiffly to his feet. "But that's not the whole answer, is it? You cannot think of betraying him, yet you cannot live with what he is doing?"

"Yes. Yes, that's it exactly."

"Then, my dear," he said gravely, "you must live without it."

It was the answer I had come to myself, but still it came like a knell. "Without *him?*" I said.

"Yes. You cannot keep as a part of you something that is alien

202

to what you believe, something you know to be wrong, Bryony."

"I know. I've already cut him off, and I feel mutilated. It's like losing half oneself."

"You know, you've given me almost too much to think about. I'm sorry I haven't been more help."

"Oh, you have, you have. You believed me, and that's almost enough in itself. Thank you for that."

"My dear child," he said then, smiling, "you've relieved my mind, too. I said you were treading a dangerous road; I doubt if I need have worried about you. You have a clear head, and you are not afraid to think things through. Was there anything else you wanted to talk about? I see Rob Granger on the other side of the garden. He seems to be coming this way."

I turned to look. Rob was indeed heading towards the greenhouse. I turned back to the vicar and asked quickly, "Did you ever find out what the prowler was doing in the vestry?"

"Yes. What a very strange thing that was! Nothing of value—that is, none of the valuables—had been touched. But something worth much more in its own way, and quite irreplaceable, was missing. One of the registers."

"One of the *registers?* A parish register?" Those at Ashley, I knew, went back to the sixteenth century. But what in the world could James have wanted with a register? "I thought you said the safe had not been opened."

"Oh, not a locked-up Ashley register. One that was placed on the vestry table—from One Ash. Unhappily, it is an old one which is missing, the second volume, 1780 to 1837."

"But surely it won't have been stolen, Vicar. Who would want it? It'll turn up soon."

"Quite, quite. I am not seriously worried," said the vicar, looking very worried indeed. Just then the greenhouse door opened. "Ah, Rob, good morning. Were you looking for me?"

"Good morning, Vicar. Mrs. Henderson said to tell you that a young couple called from Hangman's End about a license."

"Oh, dear," said the vicar, "and I did want to get the plants finished this morning."

"I'll do them," I said. "I'd like to. Good morning, Rob."

"Good morning."

"Are the Underhills at home today?" I asked him.

"They're going out. But Mrs. Underhill said if I saw you to say you were welcome at the house any time. She tried to phone you."

"Thanks, Rob," I said, and turned to the vicar. "I'm going to take a look in the library. I thought I'd go through the family section."

"Yes—well, any time you want me, you know where to find me. Rob, what have you done to your hand?"

"Nothing. Hit it with a hammer, that's all."

"Was that you mending the cat statue at the Overflow last night?" I asked him.

"Not much use wasting time on that kind of thing. The metal's rotten." It was an echo of what my cousin had said, without the bitterness, but with an indifference verging on the surly. "No, I was wedging the lower sluice gates shut. Looked as if they'd been tampered with, but then the whole thing's rotten, anyway."

"Is it safe?"

"Safe enough. The high sluice can take care of anything the river likes to send down."

Rob was at the door, opening it. I got quickly to my feet. "When I go over to the Court, may I take your keys?"

"You know where they're kept. Help yourself." The greenhouse door shut behind him.

"Well, I must go," said the vicar. "If you really will—"

"Finish the tomatoes? Of course I will."

Alone in the greenhouse with the plants, I was content to let my mind stay blank. What slipped into my thoughts, suddenly, was as clear as if it were written up between me and the garden, scrawled on the steamed glass: William Ashley, 1774–1835.

It might be pure chance that a parish record of William Ashley's time had vanished—but also it might not.

---

*Ashley Court, 1835*

*The candle guttered in a pool of wax. Light, cast by the mirror, slid over her. Light o' love, he thought, a beautiful phrase. She is my light of love.*

*"You have the key safely?"*

*"Aye. See? But I'll not need it."*

*"Never be too sure. You know what they say about
a maze?"*

*"No. What, then?"*

*"That a compass won't work there. While we're
here, we're in a world without bearings. Even if you
could see the weather vane, it would be no help. We're
outside the world."*

*"Sounds like we're dead, surely?"*

*"Hush, oh, hush. It just means that once we're
here, at the center, no one can touch us."*

*"Till we go out again."*

*"Even then. Nothing can touch us now."*

No GHOST had ever walked in the Ashley library, but now, as I let
myself quietly into the still, spacious room, it seemed haunted,
probably only by the frail parchment ghosts of the books that
had vanished from the shelves. Somehow, I thought, an empty
library looked worse than an ordinary room that had been stripped
of its furniture. I shut the door behind me, and quietly as a ghost
myself, I walked the length of the room to the locked cases, then
climbed the ladder and unlocked the grille.

William's book . . . ? I might as well start with Scholar Ashley's own verses. I took out *A New Romeo to His Juliet,* sat down
on the top step of the ladder, and opened the book.

There was the bookplate with the maze and the rampant wild-
cat with its grim motto—how touchable had Julia Ashley been?
I wondered briefly—and opposite this the dedicatory letter began:
"To the peerless and beautiful Mistress Julia Ashley, my wife . . ."
Much the usual letter, fulsome and extravagant.

I turned the pages slowly. The work had been privately printed
and very prettily produced. William Ashley could never have
found more than a local immortality, but to me, another Ashley,
the book was fascinating. Many of the verses were about the Court,
and each had, as head- and tailpiece, some small and rather
attractive engraving. There was one of the maze with a detailed
drawing of the pavilion. The poem below it was called *The Maze.*

> *In this fantastickal and Cretan maze*
> *No Theseus to find the centre strays;*
> *This gentler Monster lurked within these Groves*
> *What time the Romans trod their secret ways.*
>
> *No Cretan Bull guards the abode of love,*
> *But where the gentle waters, straying, move,*
> *See! Dionysus' creature here enskied*
> *To greet our 'raptured gaze.*

It was bad verse; so meaningless that, conversely, I thought there must be meaning there. William Ashley's poems were usually transparent as glass. Secret ways, I thought. It was surely only the usual conceit about the Greek myth of Theseus and Ariadne's clue. Then why had he said Romans rather than Greeks? I read on.

Time passed slowly. Finally, the silence of the library oppressing me, I decided to take the book to the cottage, make some lunch, then telephone Dr. Gothard and find out what James had said to him last night. After that I would settle down once more to my reading.

A title in one of the Shakespeare shelves caught my eye, the name *Juliet* in gold on tooled tan leather. The real thing. Any comparison with Scholar Ashley's transports would be unfair in the extreme, but some impulse made me take the volume out. I locked the grille, let myself out of the library, then locked it, too, behind me.

THERE was no delay on the line. Dr. Gothard was at home.

"Bryony? How are you?"

"Fine, thank you, Dr. Gothard. I'm sorry to trouble you again, but there were one or two things I wanted to ask you. I—well, I understand that my cousin James telephoned you last night."

"That is so. He has not been in touch with you about this?"

"I've been out all day. I wondered what news you had for him."

"Ah, I'm afraid there has not been much progress. I told your cousin that the police are still making inquiries. I am sorry that I have nothing more to tell. And yourself? Are you well?"

"Oh, yes, perfectly, thanks. There was one thing I wanted to ask you, though. Do you remember, among Daddy's things that you gave me, a silver ball-point pen?"

"Yes . . . ach, of course! It had his initials on it, yes?"

"That's the one. Where was it found, do you know?"

"Beside him on the road."

"That's definite, is it? It wasn't in his pocket?"

"No. It was found later, when the police went back to search."

"Dr. Gothard, do you remember ever seeing him use it?"

There was a pause. "No. I cannot say that I do. Why?"

"I'm not sure," I said. "Look, something has turned up here. . . . If I sent you a photograph, would you show it to the police and ask if anyone in Bad Tölz remembers seeing such a man?"

"Certainly." I heard the interest quicken his voice. "Why, Bryony? Have you found evidence which points to someone?"

"I don't know. Something happened and it made me wonder. But please don't say anything about this to anybody but the police. I mean, if anyone else should telephone from England—"

"I understand." And now I was sure he did. "Trust me."

"Thank you," I said. "Goodbye."

I cradled the receiver, then came around sharply in my chair at the sound of a step on the flagged path outside.

"Hi, Bryony," said my cousin Emory.

I felt myself go white. He stopped short and said contritely, "Did I frighten you? I thought you heard me coming."

"Not a sound." I forced a smile and got to my feet with a gesture of welcome. "Hullo. It's lovely to see you. Come in."

Emory took my hands and kissed me just as James had done in the schoolroom.

"You know, it's a bit like seeing a ghost," I said apologetically. "I guess I must have stopped being used to you two. And for heaven's sake, he was wearing that same shirt and tie yesterday!"

I was talking perhaps a shade too fast, all the time wondering how much he had heard. Certainly he seemed quite easy and natural, the old charming Emory, and none the worse for what the romantic novelists would have called a hint of steel under it all.

He laughed. "Yes, and you had him taped in two seconds flat. It never did work with you. Well, it's lovely to see you again. But

I wish it could have been a happier homecoming for you, Bryony."

I ushered him into one of the armchairs by the hearth and sat down in the other. Emory leaned back and lit a cigarette.

"James rang Walther Gothard last night," he said.

"Yes, he said he would." I made it sound as noncommittal as I could. How near had Emory been? Had he heard me use Walther's name? Trying a safe tack, I asked, "Had Dr. Gothard anything special to tell him?"

"The usual bromides—police are on the job, and so on."

"Yes, well, I would think that a hit-and-run accident is about the most difficult thing there is to trace, wouldn't you?"

He nodded, inhaling his cigarette deeply, and I found myself sure that he had heard nothing. He looked perfectly normal, calm and unbent. My cousin Emory, who, whatever James had done, must know about it, too.

He was saying gently, "You do realize, Bryony, that we may never know?"

My gaze met his, with, I hoped, exactly the same lack of guile. "I can't agonize about that." I turned, abruptly, to the truth. "All that matters is that my father's dead, and since I can't imagine that anyone would have wanted to kill him deliberately, I don't see that it helps much to run yapping after the fool who caused an accident." I looked straight at him. "Do *you* think it could have been anything but an accident?"

"I? No, of course it couldn't."

I waited, saying nothing, keeping a steady gaze on him; the old interviewer's trick by which you hope to stampede the victim into saying more than he meant. But Emory was not easy to stampede. He only smiled at me as he leaned forward to tap ash from his cigarette. "What has happened to us as a family can't be changed by apportioning whatever guilt there is. Both James and I feel that it's better forgotten."

"I'm sure you do," I said, and saw his gaze flick towards me. I looked away then and peeled off into talk about Madeira and Bad Tölz. It was shocking how quickly I had been able to adapt myself to suspicion. And to deception.

"And what are you going to do now, Bryony?" he asked when I paused. "James seemed to think you wouldn't stay in the cottage."

"How could he?" I said, more sharply than I meant to. "I didn't tell him what I intended to do."

"And here am I," said Emory, with a smile that was as disarming in him as in his brother, "hammering at you within twenty-four hours about your future. And you know why, don't you? Dear sweet Cousin Bryony, have you had time yet to think about breaking that damned trust and letting your poor and dishonest relations have a pound or two to fiddle with?"

I had to laugh. "Well, if you put it like that—"

"I do put it like that. Cards on the table. An Ashley could always be relied on to look after his Ashley self."

"Which," I said smoothly, "is exactly what I'm doing."

A faint line between his brows. "And what does that mean?"

"It means no. I will not break the trust. Not yet."

He flung his cigarette into the hearth. "Bryony—"

I'm not sure what showed in my face, but he bit back what he was going to say and gave me a long, shrewd look—one I didn't relish under the circumstances. I said, rather quickly, "Emory, will you and James just not hound me for a day or two? I'm not saying that I refuse utterly and for ever to break the trust. But good heavens, you haven't even let me talk to Mr. Emerson. Give me a week to think it all out. . . ." I paused, and finished dryly, "Surely you can live for a week on what you got for the T'ang horse and the jade seal?"

"No police, Cousin Bryony?"

"No police. But leave it alone, Cousin Emory, or I might surprise you. And leave Cathy Underhill out of it, or I will surprise you. Now I'm going to make some tea. Will you have some?"

He leaned back in his chair, obviously enjoying the situation. "I'd love some. Thank you."

Yes, I thought, as I went through to the kitchen, that was Emory; not the shadow of regret for anything he might do. That was the Ashley self-sufficiency—and just where, one might ask, did it part company with the criminal mentality? This smiling Emory threw James and his guilt-ridden contrition into very sharp relief. I had been right, I thought. Whatever wrong had been done to Cathy, even more to my father, it must have been Emory who had acted. Not James. Surely the most that James had done

209

had been to hear of it afterwards and feel himself bound to stand by his twin.

And the silver pen with the initials J.A.? There must be an answer even for that. Emory might have borrowed his brother's pen. And James, not having missed it, could have genuinely thought he had dropped it in the churchyard.

When I went back into the sitting room with the tray, my cousin was standing by the table with one of William Ashley's books in his hand. "What's this?" he asked.

"I've been checking through the locked section," I said. "No, not the porn. It's only Shakespeare. I thought it might be interesting to read *Romeo and Juliet* again, alongside William Ashley's attempt to play Romeo."

He turned the volume over and looked at the spine. "*The Tragicall History of Romeus and Juliet.* Hm. It's a poem, not a play. And it's Romeus, not Romeo. Wait a minute, this isn't Shakespeare at all. It's by a chap called Brooke."

"*Brooke?*" It came out in a kind of yelp.

He looked up, surprised. "Yes. Why? Do you know it?"

But I had myself in hand. "No. Sorry, I spilled some hot water. It's nothing. Have a biscuit. You were saying?"

"This isn't the Shakespeare play. It's a poem called *Romeus and Juliet* by Arthur Brooke, and—hey, it's dated 1562!" He sounded excited. "I say, I wonder if this could be Shakespeare's source for his play, or something like that. Surely 1562—that's long before he was writing, isn't it? When did Elizabeth come to the throne?"

That was the kind of thing we knew at Ashley. "Fifteen fifty-eight," I said reluctantly. "It might be, I suppose, but don't start counting chickens till we know a bit more. I'll tell you what, Emory. I'll write, first thing in the morning. I think perhaps someone at the British Museum—"

"Why don't you just telephone someone now? Isn't there someone local—how about what's his name, Leslie Oker, over at Ashbury? He'd have some idea, surely."

"I don't really think—" I began, unwillingly, but he already had the directory in his hand. He pulled the telephone towards him and began to dial. His movements were quick, incisive, excited. At least, I thought, I would be able to read the thing before

210

I had to send it away. Emory could hardly insist on taking it from me. Reading it looked like a long and tedious task, but I would do it if I had to stay up all night. For that this, at last, was William's Brooke, I was quite sure.

Emory was talking rapidly. "Yes, Arthur Brooke, *The Tragicall History of Romeus and Juliet.* Dated 1562. Yes, quite small, about four by eight . . . tan leather with a brown edge to the paper. . . . No, no inscription, no crest. . . . Yes?"

Silence, while the telephone talked and on my cousin's face excitement fought with apprehension. After a few more queries he rang off and turned to me.

"He knows the book. That is, he knows of it; he's never seen a copy. And for a very good reason. There are only three copies of this edition known. One of them's at Cambridge. A second is at Oxford, and I'm not sure about the third. If this is a fourth . . ." A short laugh. "He says he has no idea how valuable it might be, but there's only one thing certain; that it is very valuable indeed. There's a snag, of course, there'd have to be. It may have been rebound. If it has, its value will be diminished—but it would still fetch a lot of money . . . enough to see us through. What's the matter, Bryony? You look as if you hardly cared."

I could not tell him that I was conscious of only one overmastering wish, to have him go, and let me read the book. "Why, of course I'm pleased! It's marvellous! The only thing we mustn't do is rush it, and even if we do send it to Christie's to sell, you know they might take ages. They wait for the right book sale."

"Yes, I understand that. But they could give us some idea of what it might bring. One can borrow on expectation."

"Fair enough," I said. "No, Emory, please—" This as his hand reached for it again. "You'll have to leave this to me. I promise you I'll see about it tomorrow. And then I'm going to ring up Mr. Emerson and see about the trust."

It was blackmail of a kind, and it worked. He hesitated, then, to my great relief, took his leave. He was going back to Bristol, he told me, and yes, he would stop badgering me about the trust. I watched him right out of sight past the orchard; then I went upstairs to hunt for a photograph which Walther could show to the police in Bad Tölz.

211

*He turned his head on the pillow, searching with his cheek for the hollow where her head had lain. The linen was cold now, but still it smelled faintly of her lavender.*

*"Eh"—he said it aloud, in her phrase—"eh, but I love thee."*

*The moon had set, but shadows moved with the breeze as the creepers fretted at the walls. The shutter masking the south window moved, creaking, as if some ghostly hand had pushed it. For a half-dreaming moment he thought he saw her again, kilting her skirts to climb the low sill, standing on tiptoe, laughing, watching herself in the glass.*

*Then the shutter went back with a slam, jarring him full awake. The room was empty.*

IT WAS a good photograph, showing the twins with Rob Granger, fishing for eels on the banks of the pool. The likenesses of both twins were good, even though the photograph was four years old. I wrapped it up and found an envelope to fit it. A commonplace action, but it felt like burning a whole fleet of boats. Then I sat down, resolutely addressed the envelope to Dr. Gothard, and without giving myself time for further thought, set straight out to post it.

The box was half a mile away, where the side road from One Ash, winding past the church, met the main road. I took the shortcut across the farmyard. As I crossed the yard Mrs. Henderson appeared in Rob's doorway, wiping her hands on her apron.

"Miss Bryony! Won't you come along in and take a cup of tea? The kettle's on the boil and I've just made a batch of scones."

My first impulse was to make some excuse. But the smell of the freshly baked scones came meltingly out on the air, along with the scent of woodsmoke and ironing. Details hardly noticed, but adding, together, to something deep out of the past that answered, like an echo to a bell, the distress in me that I had hardly recog-

212

nized yet and had barely begun to suffer. Before I knew I had spoken, I said, "I'd love to."

Rob was inside at the sink, in his shirt sleeves, washing his hands. He greeted me rather shortly, as he had that morning; then his eyes fixed on my face and he straightened, speaking in quite a changed voice. "Is something wrong, then?"

I opened my mouth automatically to deny that anything could be wrong, but instead of the conventional denial, I found myself saying, "Oh, Rob, it's all so awful," and I put a hand to my eyes.

Gently he took my elbow and steered me to the table. "What you need's a cup of tea. Come and sit down."

I don't remember that I ate anything, but I drank the strong, scalding tea and listened to the two of them talking over the commonplaces of the day. They addressed remarks in my direction from time to time, but never anything I had to answer; the talk went around and over me with the instinctive tact of long-standing affection. They were hedging me about with kindness, and I knew why the cottage smells and the sound of Rob's warm country voice had suddenly broken me down. As a little girl I had loved my visits to the Grangers'—tea with shop cakes (which I had thought so much better than anything we had at home) and sardines on toast and tinned fruit and condensed milk, while Mrs. Granger listened to Rob and me boasting about what we had done and dared that day at school in the village. And now the familiar warmth lapped me around, and from somewhere came comfort and calmness.

When tea was done I helped Mrs. Henderson wash the dishes, while Rob spread his account book and papers out on the table and started his figuring. He was surprisingly quick, and long before I had stacked the dishes, he had shut the book and picked up a sheaf of what looked like highly coloured catalogues or holiday brochures. He read them intently, paying no attention to the women around him. It was curiously soothing.

Mrs. Henderson took her leave, and I thanked her for tea. When she'd gone Rob laid the papers down. "Now what's to do? Seems like it might be bad trouble, to upset you like that."

"It might." I sat down at the other side of the table.

It was very different from the recent tête-à-tête with Emory;

213

no tensions, no careful reticences. And different, too, from talking with my cousin James; there, as well, had been the overtones of a difficult affection. But here the dark eyes that watched me steadily were not Ashley eyes, those wary, clever eyes with their cool self-absorption. Rob had nothing to gain, nothing he wanted from me. He was just an old friend, someone who would listen without judgment unless I asked for it, and would answer me then with plain, disinterested common sense. I supposed he loved the Court; I didn't know. But he knew it, and he knew me. Neither fear nor favour . . . He had never feared anything, Rob Granger, and he had no reason to show favour, now that my father was gone, to any of us above the others. Or so I thought.

"Rob," I said, "it's something awful. I oughtn't to tell you, but I've got to tell someone, and there's no one else."

He gave a little nod, as if that was reasonable, and waited.

I swallowed. "I think it was James who knocked Daddy down. I think he was there, in Bad Tölz. They picked up a silver pen with the initials J.A. just where the accident happened. When they gave me Daddy's things I assumed the pen had been his, though I'd never seen it before. And yesterday—yesterday James saw me using it and said it was his."

"Did you tell him where it came from?" Rob asked, in a voice that was sharp for him.

"No. Oh, no. I told him I'd found it in the churchyard night before last."

"Did he accept that?"

"Yes. He didn't even seem surprised."

"Meaning that it was him in the vestry—or at any rate in the churchyard—that night."

"You could say so. I know what he was doing there, too, though it doesn't matter, anyway. Not compared with this."

"What does matter," said Rob bluntly, "is that he shouldn't know you've any call to suspect him of being in Bad Tölz. Wait a minute, though." Rob was frowning. "What was the date your dad was knocked down? The thirtieth of April, wasn't it? Well, James was here then."

I sat up abruptly. "Are you sure?"

"Sure enough. I saw him. He called here to pick up the Under-

214

hill girl. The Underhills said afterwards that it was James. I remember that, because of course I assumed it was Emory, he being the one who's sweet on her."

"So he wasn't ringing for his twin that day? I wonder why?"

I had spoken softly, to myself, but Rob had not only heard, he had got there with almost electronic speed. "So they've been doing that, have they? Can I take it that that wasn't Emory here yesterday, then?"

"No, it was James. It was Emory today, though." I looked at him across the table. "Rob, don't you see? It probably was Emory here that day with Cathy. And James in Bad Tölz."

"Would it matter which of them it was in Bad Tölz," said Rob forcefully, "if he was driving that car?"

I looked down at my hands, which were pressed flat on the table in front of me, covering the letter to Walter Gothard as if to hide it. Then I looked up at him. I knew the longing must be there, naked to view, in my face. I saw him take it in, in one swift look; then he said, in a voice carefully empty of sympathy, "Yes, I see it would. But it doesn't help to go on about it, not till you know a bit more."

It braced me, as it was meant to. "I'm sorry. Throwing it all at you like this. It's your own fault, you know, for being so easy to talk to."

"Maybe because I'm just part of the fittings. I belong in the garden, sort of, along with the trees." He was smiling. "It's all right, you know. You can tell me anything—it's likely enough I'd know it, anyway, with my ear to the ground most days." His face turned solemn again. "Well, you've told me. Never mind why—you don't want it to be James. But you can't leave it at that, you know. Whichever of them it was, even if you don't want to know, you've got to find out. That's true, isn't it?"

"I suppose so. But—"

"And there's something else, Bryony. As far back as I can remember, whatever one twin was in, the other was in just as deep. Are you up to facing that?"

Somehow I wasn't up to facing him. I looked down at my hands again. "I have to, haven't I? You just said so."

"Yes." It was abrupt and uncompromising. I turned to the

215

window. A breeze brushed a scatter of petals off an apple tree, stirring a memory; petals floating from the clematis last night. Last night, when all I had had to worry me was the theft of a few things from the Court. It seemed a lifetime ago.

*Bryony. Bryony, love.*

I must have jumped in my chair. I felt my nerves tighten. Somehow, in that unguarded moment, he had managed to reach me. It came with the breeze, sweet as the summer air; comfort, love, longing as strong as anguish.

*Leave me alone. Do you hear me? You know why.*

*Yes, I know why. Bryony. . . .*

*All right. Did you do it?*

No reply. Just that longing and love, hopeless and receding.

*Did you do it? Were you there when he died?*

No answer. He was gone. And Rob's voice was saying, with that careful lack of warmth, "You don't have to look like that, Bryony. Whoever was driving that car, you surely can't think it was anything but an accident."

"Of course it was an accident! But why not stay and help him? He wasn't dead."

"Would it have saved his life if they had?"

"No. No, Dr. Gothard said not. But one can't help feeling—"

"No, you can't," said Rob, "but you can think as well, and that'll help. Say it was one of your cousins knocked your dad down. O.K. What was he doing in Bad Tölz in the first place?"

"I suppose he must have gone there to see Daddy. About breaking the trust. They need money very badly."

"Who doesn't?" said Rob dryly. "Go on thinking. Your cousin— call him Emory if it makes you feel better—goes to talk your dad into something. Now, since the doctor never saw him, he must have been on his way up when he overtook your dad on the road. Didn't recognize him in the dark, we'll say—"

"*Of course* he didn't recognize him! You couldn't think—"

"Hey, calm down. I said we were taking it as an accident. Well, he knocked him down in the dark, panicked, drove off. It happens. It's human."

"I'd like to accept that. But it doesn't fit, does it? Whichever of them ran Daddy down must have got out of the car to look at him,

216

and if Ja— Emory leaned over him long enough to let that pen drop from his pocket, he must have recognized who it was."

Rob nodded. "He ran away *because* he recognized who it was. Don't you see? Your cousin went there desperate to talk your dad into breaking the trust. Then by accident he knocks your dad down and hurts him—he must have known how badly. Put yourself in his place. If your dad dies, and he of all people is involved, how's it going to look?"

I said nothing. It fitted, all too well. And whichever twin had been there and dropped the pen, the other would have been ready to create an alibi by confusion, in Bristol, at Ashley, or in Spain. This was why neither one had come to the cremation. And Francis . . . The thought came suddenly, unbidden and unwelcome. I slammed the door on that one.

"How long have you been sweet on him?"

Somehow, I wasn't startled. It seemed natural to be asked. The strange thing was that I hesitated. The old, direct country phrase didn't fit what I was feeling; the two-way pull of the affection I felt for my cousin contrasted with the total abandonment to my secret friend. "I—it's hard to say. I suppose always. But . . . in love with him? I just don't know."

Rob's rather sombre look lightened as he smiled. "Well, you've got yourself into a rare muddle, love; and I doubt it helps to have the pair of them taking turns on your doorstep to pressure you." The smile deepened at my look. "I told you I was part of the landscape. You'd be surprised the things I know. It was obvious, anyway. It'll take months to prove your dad's will and get everything sorted out, but if you'd agree to break the trust now, they could borrow on your promise straight away." A silence, broken by the uneven ticking of the clock. Then, "Bryony, would you really want to stay on here?"

"Everyone keeps asking me that, and I keep saying I don't know. But I do know that the cottage strip is the only outlet to Penny's Flats, and the land wouldn't be of much use to a building contractor without access to the main road."

"Aye. So you see how much it matters to them to keep on the sweet side of you. And you see why it matters not to let them make a guess at where you really found that silver pen."

217

I must have been staring. I suppose I knew quite well what he was saying, but something in me could not accept it.

"I'll spell it out," he said. "Your dad talked of danger, didn't he, and told you to be careful? There's no magic about an Ashley that says he couldn't kill, is there?"

"No. . . . But one of my cousins kill my father for gain? No."

"Well, I agree with you. Though we none of us know what a chap's capable of, or even what we might be capable of ourselves." He reached a hand across the table and touched mine gently. "You do what your dad said, and be careful."

In the silence that followed, without looking at him, I turned the envelope over and showed him the address.

"What's in it?"

"A photograph of the twins."

"I see." His voice held satisfaction, and something else I couldn't put a name to. "You mean I've been wasting my breath? You've made your own decision all along?"

"In a way. I might not have mailed it, but I will now."

---

*⟶ Ashley Court, 1835*

*Memories of her stung him, banishing sleep. He could almost hear her voice.*

*"Nick?"*

*"My love?"*

*"You're sure he won't speak? You're sure he won't tell on us?"*

*"Certain. He knows where his duty lies, or, better still, where his meat and drink come from."*

*"But your father? Oh, Nick—"*

*"My father be damned."*

*He had meant it, too. He shut his eyes.*


WHEN I got back to the cottage, Jeffrey Underhill was sitting on the seat in the shadow of the lilac tree. We greeted one another. His manner was as smooth, as pleasant as before, but the Ashley seventh sense saw it as the manner of the chairman preparing

218

to present an adverse report to his board. Cathy. He wants to talk about Cathy. I led him into the cottage.

He settled himself in an armchair, refused tea, and opened the meeting.

"I had to come and talk to you, Miss Ashley. Something my daughter, Cathy, told me has disturbed me very much." The clever dark eyes probed mine for a millisecond; then the brows twitched down as Mr. Underhill registered that I knew what he was about to tell me.

He told me, all the same. It was Cathy's version of the story I had heard from James. Emory—and James passing for him—had persuaded the girl that the contents of the Court were legally theirs, and that Cousin Bryony would not mind a few objects being abstracted for immediate use. Cathy had no idea that the estate must by law be left intact for valuation. So she had taken from the library what Emory wanted, and then, on her own initiative, the Rackham pictures. The church had been used as a cache and a pickup point.

Mr. Underhill told me the whole story, straight and without excuse. He obviously had no idea that the twins had been playing tricks with identity; he referred only to Emory.

Emory picked up the Rackhams at the church, where Cathy had taken them. They had been hidden in the old cupboard, which was blocked from sight by the choirmen's wardrobe. Next day had come my discovery of the theft and my questions.

"My wife and I guessed right away that Cathy might have something to do with it, but naturally we had to talk to Cathy first, before we could say anything to you."

"Of course. But why should you have guessed that?"

The eyes that met mine were those of a deeply troubled man. "Our daughter has had this kind of problem before, Miss Ashley."

I felt my eyes widen. I couldn't think what to say. But he did not wait. He would say what had to be said, and have done.

"It started when she was in high school. We lived in California then, just outside Los Angeles. Cathy is . . ." There was a pause so brief that one hardly registered the effort it hid. "Cathy is a very loving and warmhearted girl, and she follows her impulses without always seeing what they will cost."

I said something that was meant to sound soothing. He smiled appreciatively and went on. "So when my little Cat got into bad company, the next thing we knew she was in the middle of a classic teenage problem. Believe me, she could have ended anywhere. She was in with a wild bunch. They used to steal things—things that didn't matter, but it was stealing for all that. There was this boy she was crazy about, and while that lasted . . . Well, I'll spare you the rest. It took a long time, but she got herself out of it, with God's help and with ours."

He spoke with devastating simplicity. Once again, I could think of nothing to say. But he didn't seem to expect an answer; he was going on. "That was why we decided to live away from home for a few years. When you said there were things missing, we were terribly afraid it was beginning again. So Stephanie and I talked it over most of last night, and then we asked Cathy about it. She told us everything. She'd had it on her mind ever since you came here, and I think she was glad to tell us."

My mind was twisting and turning like some trapped thing. It was worse, far worse, than I had thought. Even this minor affair of the disposable assets had in it the possible springs of tragedy. Yet one more thing for Twin to answer for. . . . I hardly noticed that this time I hadn't specified which twin.

"But Mr. Underhill—this is awful!"

He misunderstood me. "Miss Ashley, I know it's as bad as it can be, but I have to tell you that when Cathy went into all this legal routine about trusts and disposable assets that Emory really owned, we were so relieved that she may have gotten the impression that what she'd done was quite O.K. Which," he added, with uncompromising dryness, "it was not. We owe you an apology, and, Miss Ashley, you have it. I'll get those items back if it takes all I've got."

Coming from Jeffrey Underhill, it was quite an offer. But before I could speak, he said, with another of those probing looks, "You don't seem very surprised by what I have been telling you. You knew how the things were taken."

"Yes. My cousin told me last night."

"And it troubles you a whole lot, I can see that."

"Not too much, really. What I was angry about was that they'd

used Cathy. And if I'd known what you've just told me, I'd have
been angrier still. As for the things themselves, please forget them.
They'll belong in the end to Emory's family, anyway." I remembered something. "Mr. Underhill, did Cathy say anything about
a church register?"

"A what?" He sounded blank.

"One of the parish registers is missing."

"She said nothing about that. I'll ask her. But why should anyone take a thing like that? Is it valuable?"

"Only to local people, one would think. I asked because when
I saw—er, my cousin that night, he was carrying something like
a big book, but it was probably the Rackham pictures."

"Yes, now, those pictures. They're your own, aren't they?"

I nodded. "And unique. If you could get those back, I'd be
terribly grateful. I could put us all in the clear by saying I sent
them for sale myself but thought better of it."

"You're very generous."

Then, as I had half expected, he went on to tell me that he
and his wife had decided to cut short their tenancy of Ashley
Court. They would go to London tomorrow, staying there until
his agents found him a house in Paris. The rent of the Court was
paid for the full term . . . and so on and so forth. Everything but
the real reason for the sudden departure.

When he finished I came straight out into the open with what,
in delicacy, he had not said.

"You're taking Cathy away from Emory."

This time a pause that could be felt. Then, "Yes, I am."

"I think you're perfectly right. But what will Cathy say?"

"That I can't tell." He spoke heavily. "She's been in and out of
love since she was fourteen, so we'll hope this is no more serious.
At this moment the only thought she seems to have in her head is
that we're going to live in Paris, France."

I laughed. "You're a clever man, Mr. Underhill. I doubt if even
Emory can compete with Paris."

He got to his feet, and I followed suit. He looked down at me.
"I find it a great pity that we should leave the Court just when
you come home, Miss Ashley. You are a very lovely girl, and I'm
proud to have met you."

221

I thanked him and saw him to the door and down the path. He paused then and turned his head. His face changed subtly and he cleared his throat. "Why, here's Cathy coming," he said. "I kind of thought she would."

Cathy was coming through the orchard in a frock of some pale summery stuff. She waved, but the halfhearted quality of the gesture gave her away. She was self-conscious and nervous. In other words, she was coming to apologize.

As I waved back I realized that Jeffrey Underhill had melted from my side and was standing over by the pool, making quite a ceremony of lighting a cigar.

"Had to come to tell you I was sorry." Cathy hurried it out in a small, breathless voice, like a child who wants to get it over, and is not sure of the reception.

"You don't have to say any more," I said quickly. I was almost four years older than Cathy, and just at that moment I felt about four hundred.

"I know you only did it because you were fond of Emory." I smiled. "If I told you even half the things my cousins had pressured me into doing . . ."

"Oh, Bryony, you're just sweet, but honestly, you don't fully understand." There were tears in her eyes. "I thought it was all on the level, just a case of getting a few things out for the boys to use. And then I found those pictures upstairs. . . ." She swallowed. "When you started asking about the stuff, I began to think it wasn't O.K. after all . . . and then I found the pictures were your very own. Oh, Bryony, will you ever forgive me?"

"I did, just as soon as they told me about it. Hey, Cathy, don't cry." I took hold of her wrists and gave her a little shake, talking on, reassuring her, being careful not to throw too much blame on Emory, though I got the impression that she was less than starry-eyed about him now. She wouldn't revert to her teenage problem, I was sure, but no thanks to Emory for that. I found myself feeling better about mailing that photograph to Bad Tölz. About James, I refused to think.

Cathy, however, had him on her mind. "You know, James didn't have anything to do with it. Truly he didn't. James is very, very fond of you, and he wouldn't do a thing that would hurt you."

She was watching me with vulnerable eyes. I said, smiling, "I know. And now, what's all this about Paris?"

Her father's cigar was about smoked through before Cathy, talking about Paris, came back to her sparkling norm.

"We're going tomorrow and there's this fabulous party, and we want you to come! Please say you will, Bryony!"

"Well . . ." I was beginning doubtfully, when Mr. Underhill, catching the new tone of his daughter's voice, came back to us.

"Cathy means to London, Miss Ashley. I left her to invite you, but I don't think she's explained. We're giving a party tomorrow night. My wife and I are celebrating our anniversary—it's been planned for quite a while. We'd be honoured if you'd join us."

"It's terribly kind of you, but . . ." I hesitated.

"Please do come," urged Cathy. "It'll make me really feel as if you forgive me for the awful thing I did."

Jeffrey Underhill intervened. "Perhaps Miss Ashley has too much to do here, Cat. Remember, she has only just got home."

"Look," I said warmly, "I'd love to, I really would. I can get the late afternoon train."

At this they both joined in, with such enthusiasm that you would have thought the party was being given solely for me. They would put me up at the Dorchester; they would bring me home again next day; anything, they seemed to be saying, if only I would grace their party by coming. I could hardly tell them what was in my mind; that if my cousins had been invited earlier, then Emory, laying on the charm, would no doubt be there. Well, so would I—to see he kept his distance.

Mr. Underhill scooped Cathy to his side. "Say good night and we'll leave Miss Ashley in peace."

"Good night," I said.

They went together through the apple trees, arms around one another, his head bent to listen, hers raised in excited talk. So that, I thought, was that. Now, back to my own problems.

---

*Ashley Court, 1835*
*He threw back the coverlet and trod lightly across the carpet to the window. Beyond the open shutter the daylight showed an oblong of gray. He pushed the*

*glass wide and leaned out. It was later than he had
thought. Already a thin plume of smoke was rising
from the kitchen chimney.*

*And she—she would be home by now, and they
were safe.*

I HAD had supper and then, by the open window, read for an hour,
and I still only reached line 357 of William's Brooke.

> *"What hap have I," quoth she, "to love my father's foe?*
> *What, am I weary of my weal? What, do I wish my woe?"*

So from Brooke's *Juliet,* dull at best, I found it hardly possible
to take in any meaning, reading, as I was, with my brain running
ahead, looking for something that might be a clue to this other
Ashley maze. But I must. . . . I tried again.

> *But when she should have slept, as wont she was, in bed,*
> *Not half a wink of quiet sleep could harbour in her head,*
> *For lo, an hugy heap of divers thoughts arise . . .*

Sighing, I shut the book. It was impossible to get right through
it tonight, and if I was going to London tomorrow, I would take
it with me, read more on the train, and hand it over to someone
at Christie's to be valued.

I put it down and picked up William Ashley's *New Romeo.*
Again, from the centre of the maze on the bookplate, the wildcat
snarled and clawed. *The map?* Certainly the map. But why?

Well, the poems could not be worse than Brooke's, and at least
they had the merit of being short. I turned to the first one, *The
Catamountain.*

> *What hunter is there who could think to meet*
> *In these low lands the leopard from the sun?*
> *Long hath he lain here, silent 'neath the feet*
> *Indifferent, which all unknowing tread*

> *Across the spotted catamountain's head.*
> *See! By his side the wine-god Bacchus runs,*
> *His basket brimming o'er with lusty grapes . . .*

Bacchus—the Romans again, it seemed. Probably just the usual classical conceit. But no, here was the cat I was looking for.

> *And now in this late age he comes anew,*
> *From Scotia's heights, the catamountain wild,*
> *Brought here by thee, my gentle lady mild.*

A shadow fell over the page. I looked up with a start, but it was only Rob, pausing outside the casement. "I thought you were going to be careful," he said. "Sitting here with the window open, and so deep in a book that you never even heard me."

"Well, but it's early still. I thought you meant tonight."

"I did, mainly. I just came to see that you were all right and properly locked up."

I shut the book and put it away, making rather a play of it, to hide a touch of shame for my cousins' sake.

"All right, I'll close the window. Are you coming in?"

"For a minute, then." I heard a vigorous scrubbing of shoes on the doormat, and he came in rather gingerly. "Muddy feet. I came through the orchard after I'd shut up the greenhouses."

"Would you like a cup of coffee?"

"I wouldn't mind." As I put the kettle on to boil he picked up *Romeus and Juliet.* "What's this?"

"I forgot to tell you. That's what Daddy meant by *William's brook.* It must be. See it? William Ashley's copy of something by a chap called Brooke. It's awfully valuable, apparently."

"Hm." He turned the small volume over. "What was it he said? Something about a paper or letter in it?"

"There's nothing. I've looked. I was reading it to see if there was something in the text that would give me a clue, but it's next to unreadable."

"Looks it." He picked up the *New Romeo.* "This valuable, too?"

"No. That's just William Ashley's own poems. They're not much better than Brooke. Nice pictures, though."

"*What palace then was this?*" read Rob, and went on for a few more lines. In his soft country voice the artificially stilted verses sounded even worse.

He put the book down. "What's all that about, anyway?"

"Heaven knows," I said. "I haven't read that one yet. I got bogged down over Ariadne's clue in *The Maze*."

"Harry Who's clue?"

I laughed, the first real laugh since I had come home. "Oh, Rob! A girl called Ariadne. Greek myths. You know, she gave Theseus the ball of wool to follow out of the maze. To kill the monster, the Minotaur."

"How should I know? We can't all do Greek and Roman at school, can we?" said Rob, unworried.

I gave him his coffee. "Don't come on like the ignorant peasant with me, Rob Granger. You did Greek myths at Ashley School along with me. And we even acted that story out in our own maze. You were the Minotaur."

"Right. I remember. And James came in and killed me." He sat down in the armchair and stretched his long legs in front of him. It was the chair Jeffrey Underhill had sat in, and I could not help a comparison. Rob did not, as the American had done, dominate the room, but somehow his quality of relaxation made itself as strongly felt as the other man's powerful composure. "I never was much of a hand at stories," he went on, "but I was good at sums. I had the better of you there, every time. You used to copy from my book."

"I did not!"

"You did. And who was it told the teacher that a polygon was a dead parrot?"

"Isn't it?" I laughed again. "Oh, Rob, you've made me feel better! Another cup?"

"No, thanks." He set his empty mug down on the hearth beside him. "I saw Mr. Underhill going up through the orchard with Cathy. I suppose they told you they'd be leaving tomorrow?"

"You knew?"

"Well, yes. I'm the caretaker, remember? I was told."

"That wasn't all he came for," I said. I gave him the gist of what had passed. He thought it over for a few moments.

226

"Are you really going to this party in London?"

"I think so. Cathy was very upset, and I think she'd feel that everything was all right if I did go."

"Will your cousins be there?"

"I imagine so, unless Mr. Underhill tells them they're not welcome any more. I wouldn't put it past him."

"Then I'll take you to the train and meet you when you come back," Rob said uncompromisingly. "I don't want James or Emory driving you anywhere."

"Rob, you really can't think that this 'danger' thing of Daddy's could involve Emory or James deliberately harming me?"

"I don't know. When pushed, perhaps? And they are being pushed. Let's not leave it to chance."

"That's pure melodrama."

"Maybe. But to see that they don't is common sense."

"They don't know about the pen and the photograph."

"No, but they know you're no fool."

"Well, all right, I'll be careful. . . . Rob, have you heard anything yet about Francis?"

"Not a thing, but then you know Francis. He never did write letters or behave like anyone else. I remember him saying once that he had his own means of communication."

I looked up. "Did he? What do you suppose he meant?"

He moved an indifferent shoulder. "His poetry, I suppose."

"Yes—I suppose. I wish he'd show up, that's all. I just get a queer feeling that it might solve a thing or two."

He got to his feet. "I'd better be going. I'll take a look, if I may, to see if the back door has a decent bolt. That's something I never checked." He went to inspect the door, then returned. "Seems O.K. You should be safe. Well, good night, Bryony."

"Good night. And thanks for everything, Rob."

He smiled. "For nothing. 'Night."

When he had gone I locked and bolted the door behind him, feeling a fool as I did so. For all that had happened, the men we had been talking about were my own cousins. One of them, in spite of all seeming, might still be my own dear friend. But I bolted the back door, too, and when I went up the narrow stairs I took the Brooke with me, and went to sleep with it under my pillow.

I WOKE WITH THE feeling that I had just come out of a lovely and familiar dream. There had been a beach, a long, long shore of golden sand which stretched as far as the eye could reach. Farther. Ninety miles. . . . Why did I think it was ninety miles long? There were dunes of pale sand, with long reeds blowing in the wind. The ocean poured and poured eternally in from the west. The sky was huge and clean, and the wind full of the sea's salt. Lonely, beautiful, quiet, and safe.

*Safe, safe.* . . . The word echoed in Rob's voice. I remembered it all, then—the book, the locked doors, my cousins.

The moon was bright. I slipped out of bed and went to the window facing on the orchard. The moon was full on the blossoming trees. At the near corner, tallest of them all, the old pear tree lifted its graceful boughs. The bloom was like a cloud, piled shapes of light. It was a tree in a dream.

A shadow moved under it. Someone was standing there.

No, I was wrong. The pear tree's clouded shade was still again, and empty. It had been something conjured up by moonlight and blossom. Lovers' time; Juliet at her window; Romeo under the orchard trees.

But not for me. It was an empty night; I dared not even summon what I had been used to of comfort. No lover to lure back like a bird on a silken thread. If I were to play Juliet at all, it would be Brooke's Juliet, with her torments of indecisive love and her "hugy heap" of very prosaic fears.

I went back to bed. But not to sleep. I thought about James and all the uneasy tangled skein of what had happened.

I could not believe, even with the evidence, that he was guilty. But if he was guilty—not of killing my father, no, that I would never believe. But if it had been an accident, and the rest the result of natural panic afterwards . . . I had said that I would forgive. And if I could extend that charity to strangers, how much more to my cousin?

No, it was simpler than that. Panic after an accident was forgiveable; to use it for profit was not.

But there was nothing I could do until the answer came from Dr. Gothard. I was still on my own. And I must stay that way until the mystery was solved.

It sounded easier than it was. I lay and watched the moon-flung shadow of the pear tree move across the ceiling, and so strong was his insistence that I could have sworn I saw his very shadow move with it. For one weak second I let myself feel him close beside me, so close that—

I sat up like a pulled puppet. It had been so near, so powerful, that I knew he was here in the flesh as well. And I knew where. He was in the orchard, under the pear tree. And whatever he had done, whoever he was, he meant me no harm.

I flung back the bedclothes and reached a coat down from behind the door. I put it on and, barefoot as I was, ran down the stairs and out towards the orchard.

I stopped then. Rob came out from under the pear tree into the moonlight.

I managed to speak, but it came out like a croaking whisper. "What are you doing here? It must be two o'clock."

I thought he hesitated, but his voice sounded quite normal. "I said I'd keep an eye on you, remember? Are you all right?"

"Yes, thank you. But—do you mean to stay here all night?"

"It's a nice night. I was thinking."

"What—what about?"

"As a matter of fact, I was thinking about New Zealand."

"New Zealand?" It was so improbable that I found my voice. "Oh, is that what those brochures in the cottage kitchen were all about?"

"Aye." He hadn't moved. He seemed to be waiting. "That's where I'd like to go when I leave here. Up to the north. I was thinking about the Ninety Mile Beach."

I said shakily, "So was I."

I took another step towards him. Moving quickly, he took hold of me, pulling me tightly against him. As he began to kiss me, the "hugy heap" of trouble melted like snow.

If THE laden arches of pear blossom had suddenly sprung to life like a fountain, tossing a plume of bright water as far as the moon, it would hardly have seemed surprising, so great was the release, the flood of joy that swept through me. Through him, too. We were both perhaps a little mad. We clung and kissed and clung again, wordless. Everything had already been said, everything shared. This was the end of the courtship, and not the beginning. This was how I had thought it would be, this spontaneous meeting, this complete knowing. This was why, when James had kissed me, I had been puzzled and afraid, no longer trusting the bond between myself and my secret friend.

"Rob, oh, Rob." I was shaken by a wave of love so powerful that it seemed to tear me apart to take him in. "How on earth didn't I guess? . . . It was you I ran to when I wanted help or comfort; it was your house that was home."

"Bryony." It came out on a long breath, fierce with relief and the pent-up frustrations of years. "Bryony. . . ."

It was the chill of the soaking grass on my bare feet that made me draw away eventually and say, "Rob, let's go in now."

"Go in?"

"Yes. My feet are like ice."

"The more fool you for not putting your shoes on." His hold on me was relaxed now, affectionate. "High time you did go in. Come along." He picked me up as easily as if I were a sack of meal, and carried me back across the grass to the cottage.

"Actually," I said, "I meant both of us. Won't you stay?"

There was a pause; then he shook his head. "No. I've waited all my life for you, and I reckon I can wait a bit longer. We'll leave all that for its right place."

"Which is?"

"After we're married. Tomorrow night."

"Oh, Rob, be your age. You need a licence, and a special costs twenty-five pounds. And even if you had one, the vicar wouldn't consent to marry us on the spur of the moment."

"Spur of the moment nothing. All our lives. Anyway, I've talked to the vicar. He thinks it's a good thing."

"*Does* he? But he didn't know that I—"

"He's known for a long time how I felt about you, and he let on to me that your dad had said he'd sooner see you wedded to me than anyone else he knew."

"*Daddy* did?"

"So the vicar told me. I think he'd marry us straight away."

"But the licence!"

"I've had a licence burning a hole in my pocket ever since I knew you were coming home," said my lover, and set me down, laughing, on the cottage step.

---

*Ashley Court, 1835*

*Shivering, he dragged his clothes on and flung the fur-lined cloak around himself. His hands were shaking. Defiance ebbed. The hour before daylight was not the time for bravery. This was the hour when men were executed; the hour when they were least resistant. He supposed there was some mercy in it; but for the condemned, as for lovers, dawn always came too soon.*

# Part Three

NEXT morning when I opened the back door I found a milk bottle on the step, and propped against it a package wrapped in brown paper. I knew the neat, slightly over-careful writing. And I guessed what I would find in the package; the brochures about New Zealand. I carried them in and read them with my breakfast.

It already seemed as if the idea of New Zealand had been in my mind for a very long time. I wondered if, unknowing, I had shared Rob's thoughts about it. I accepted the idea of leaving Ashley with a sense of relief, for if this escape from old ties was what my lover had in mind, then by definition so did I. . . .

Now that I knew him, I could see clearly the reasons for his long refusal to reveal himself. Perhaps he would not, even now, have nerved himself to come into the open, had it not been for my father's death. That had left me homeless, without Ashley at my back. It had, so to speak, brought me into Rob's orbit.

So much became clear. The night I had come home, at Ashley church, it had been Rob whose thoughts had come to meet me, and the mixture of exhilaration and nervousness, which I had misconstrued as guilt, was now explained. Rob could never have doubted what we had together, but he might well have doubted the outcome. What he had feared would have been my first reaction to the discovery that my beloved friend was only Rob, the boy from the home farm.

But now here we were, on this bright morning with its dew and its day song. "Tomorrow," he had said, and now tomorrow was today. *Rob, where are you?* The signal was faint, but I got it. He was in the greenhouses.

As I approached I saw him through the glass. He was up on a tall stepladder, mending one of the ventilators. He saw me coming, gave me a smile, and went unhurriedly on with the job. He looked just the same as ever, his movements quite deliberate and relaxed. If I had not been receiving from him a current of excitement something akin to a burst of a thousand volts or so, I would have thought him unmoved.

I went inside. I did not have to ask what the vicar had said; I had known, roughly since breakfast time, that this was really and truly my wedding day. The air was fizzing like champagne. I thought it was time to calm things down into words.

"Thank you for the package. How long have you had this New Zealand dream?"

He gave the ventilator screw a last twist. "Years now. You never knew it, but some folks of mine went out there, way back, and they've done well farming up in the North Island. After Mum died I wrote to New Zealand House in London and asked about emigrating. It seems there's no problem for a farm worker. I wouldn't need a sponsor, either; my folks out there laid a welcome on the mat for me."

"But you didn't go."

"How could I? I was waiting for you." He said it simply.

"I wondered why you stayed. There didn't seem much future for you. Rob, if my father had lived, would you have asked me?"

He began to trickle a few drops of oil onto a rusty joint. "I don't know. I've asked myself that, even though the vicar says I was your dad's choice for you. The way I saw it, it'd have been a queer enough thing, anyway, a man like me and a girl like you, let alone having this link between us as well. . . . That would have taken some explaining, wouldn't it?"

"He'd have understood, because he had something of the same

233

gift." He looked, not surprised, but inquiring. I nodded. "I think that when he was dying he tried to get to me and couldn't, but he had enough of a link with Ashley to get here. And you were here and got the signal and sent it on to me."

"A sort of Telstar. It was a bad night, that." He looked down at me as he pocketed his tools. "I'd been asleep, and I came awake, all very sudden, as if someone had kicked me in the head. It ached like that, too. First of all I thought I must be sickening for something; then after a bit I got there. And I didn't like what I got. Then, as I always did, I began to think of you, and I knew what I was telling you."

"Poor Rob. But you helped. Oh, you did. Rob . . ." I began as he started down the ladder. "Rob, there's something I don't understand. It's been setting me wrong all this time. I thought this seventh sense had to be Ashley. So I never looked beyond my cousins. Where do you fit in?"

He smiled. "Straight down the wrong side of the blanket from donkey's years back. Ellen Makepeace, she was called."

"Ellen Makepeace? That was the girl Nick Ashley was shot for, wasn't it?"

"That's the one. Her brothers shot him. One of them was the Ashley gamekeeper. They got on the next ship to Australia and ended up in New Zealand. A village lad called Granger married Ellen, and they had a baby nearly nine months later. She said it was a Granger baby, and so did he. Our family certainly took it that way. But now you and I know better, don't we? It must have been Nick's baby, and the Ashley thing—this mind talking—came down with it, right to me." He stood over me, smiling.

"I was wondering why I hadn't seen that, either. You've even got the looks. Not what they call the Ashley looks, but you've got Bess Ashley's hair and eyes."

"The gypsy look. Aye." He laughed. "I could see it myself."

"Well, but if you knew, then all the Grangers must have known. Your father and mother—"

"No, why should they? Oh, everyone knew the story about Nick Ashley, of course, but I never heard it told any way except that the Granger boy made an honest woman of Ellen, and it was his own baby. It's a long time ago; why should anyone bother? But

234

then this started, this between you and me. When I was a kid I thought nothing about it, but since I've got older and thought a bit more, that's the only explanation I can see. No one else guessed it, because no one else knew the way you and I can communicate."

His arms went around me, and we closed again, body to body. Two creatures becoming one, lost and oblivious. "As good as last night?" he asked at length.

"Better. Rob—the wedding really can be today?"

"Eleven this morning. It's all arranged."

"It is? Eleven? Isn't that rushing it just a bit?"

"Who was rushing it last night?"

"I didn't mean that way. It's after half past nine now."

"Great jumping beans, so it is, and I haven't fed the hens yet!" He kissed me hurriedly, one for good measure, then released me and picked up the stepladder.

"Go and feed your hens, while I find something to wear for my wedding. See you in church."

MR. AND MRS. Henderson were the witnesses, and Mr. Bryanston, gently beaming, took the service. Rob even produced a ring, which fitted. The church was full of the smell of lilac, and the flowers massed by the chancel steps still had the dew on them. Rob must have picked them at first light.

The vicar flattened a hand on the pages of the register, and Rob signed it. Not "farmer" or "gardener," but "man of all work." I liked that. It sounded proud, somehow, coming from him. When he put the pen in my hand I signed against my own name, "unemployed." I saw him watching over my shoulder, and the corners of his mouth deepened in a smile that did something severely clinical to the base of my spine.

"By the way," said the vicar, "I almost forgot to tell you. The missing register is back, and quite unharmed."

"Which goes without saying"—this, unexpectedly, from Mrs. Henderson—"seeing as where I found it."

"You brought it back?" said the vicar in surprise. "Well, I'm very glad to have it." There was some restraint in his voice. "Though, my dear Mrs. Henderson, I wish you had told me. If you'd wanted to consult it—"

"Me? Why, Vicar, what would I want with those old books?"

"Where did you find it, Mrs. Henderson?" I asked her.

"In your cottage, Miss Bryony. In your dad's room, it was. I found it when I tidied up, ready for you to come home, and I took it home with me, meaning to take it straight to the vicar, but I clean forgot. I thought nothing of it, seeing as I expected Mr. Ashley would have told the vicar he had the book."

"Indeed, now I come to think of it, I believe Mr. Ashley did mention his interest. . . . Why did I *not* think of that? And now perhaps, this morning, on this very happy occasion . . ."

As the vicar trotted competently into the breach, Rob moved past me to the table where *One Ash: 1780–1837* lay, and began to leaf through the pages.

I looked over his shoulder. The pages were all numbered, and they were all there. Rob turned each one, looking, I knew, for some other paper which might have been hidden between the leaves. The letter. My father must have been studying this register just before his illness had banished him to Bad Tölz.

"Nothing there," I said in an undertone.

"Seems not," said Rob. "But look, here's something. A funny sort of coincidence, wouldn't you say?"

His finger pointed to an entry on page 17. It was dated May 12, 1835. The signatories were "Robert Granger, Labourer, of Ashley Parish," and "Ellen Makepeace, Spinster, of One Ash." Signatories is not quite the correct word, for whereas Ellen had signed her name in a writing that was tremulous but correct, against the name of Robert Granger, Labourer, of Ashley Parish, was his mark, a large X.

The vicar, tut-tutting over the coincidence, carried the family register over to the safe to lock it away, then came back beaming.

"And now," he said, "you'll all come over to the vicarage for a glass of sherry, I hope? This Robert Granger didn't give us very much notice, so I'm not at all sure what we can manage in the way of a wedding breakfast, but I imagine—" He threw a nervous glance at Mrs. Henderson.

"No, thanks very much, Vicar," Rob said. "We'd like to come for sherry, but don't trouble yourself further. We've got an errand to do in town. We'll have lunch afterwards."

And so, the formalities completed, the wedding party trooped across the churchyard between the sombre, beautiful yews, to sherry at the vicarage.

SINCE there was now no question of my going to London for Cathy's party, we had decided to take the copy of *Romeus and Juliet* to Leslie Oker for a first opinion. Leslie was not there when we called, so we left the package with his assistant, and then Rob and I were back out on the sunny street.

He slid a hand under my arm. "And now we eat?"

"We certainly do. I'm starving."

"It takes me that way, too. Would you like to go to the Star, or the Olde Talbot, or someplace like that?"

"Not unless you've thought better of that picnic basket I saw on the back seat of the car." I laughed. "Did Mrs. Henderson get it ready for us?"

"She did. Do you mind?"

"I do not. Lovely. I don't want other people yet, just you and me. Where are you taking me?"

"Mystery tour," said Rob, opening the car door. He got in beside me, and we threaded our way through the crowded streets, then turned and headed for the open country.

He took me to a place where a narrow lane crept downhill between high hedges. There at the foot, where a humped bridge crossed the river, was a patch of grass just wide enough to park a car. "And not a square foot for anyone else," said Rob. Beyond the bridge was a steep wooded bank, through which the lane curled up again and out of sight. On the nearer side, cut in a wide green hollow, was a flat pasture as smooth as a lake, through which the river wound, deep and slow. Behind us the pasture rose sharply, seamed with flowering hawthorn and honeycombed by rabbit warrens. A few sheep moved lazily along the hillside, watching us incuriously; no other creature was in sight except the birds that went past on the May breezes.

"The Garden of Eden," I said, surveying it with pleasure.

Rob spread a rug in the sun on the river's bank. "And not an apple tree to be seen. Now, which comes first, love or food?"

"Rob, you've got to be joking! If anyone came—"

"I was joking. If you knew how hungry I was . . . Let's get this lot unpacked. What's she given us? Cold duck, is it? That'll do."

I served the food, while he unearthed the beer. I suppose it was a strange wedding breakfast. I can't remember now all that we talked about. It may be that we didn't talk to begin with, but that our thoughts moved out and mingled as they had before. If we spoke at all, it was about the food, the day, the reactions of people to what Rob persisted in calling our mixed marriage.

"It's plain old-fashioned you are, Rob Granger," I said.

"Maybe. But it's only your sort that say class doesn't matter. Let them go down on the other side of the blanket and see how much it doesn't matter."

"Ellen Makepeace's slip-up? That's a long time ago."

"No, I meant the cottage and castle thing."

"Oh, is that all? Well, my cottage is a good bit smaller than yours now. And we're sharing the same blanket."

"So we are." He handed me his empty plate, then reached for a stalk of grass and began absently to chew it. There was a faint shine on his skin. I shut my mind to him before he read me, and began to pack the debris back into the basket. Once again, irresistibly, I was remembering the patterns of his love that had come to me in the past, the love mixed with doubt, and with something that at times had been hopeless longing. That lover was gone for ever. I could forget the starlight, where love had been easy because it was in the mind, like poetry. This was the real, the daylight man. The man I would live with for the rest of my life.

"If you chew grass you get liver flukes," I said.

"Then I'd be crawling with 'em by now," he said equably, but he threw the stalk away. "Anyway, what you were saying about class, that wasn't the point."

"I know. And I don't say it doesn't exist, but it's nothing to do with money or family. It's habits of mind—ways of thinking."

"Well, if ways of thinking count, then we aren't far apart."

"That's what I keep trying to tell you."

He was silent for a little, relaxing in the sun. "What would you like to do now? What I mean is, how are we going to put the rest of the day in till it's a decent time to go to bed?" The voice sounded sleepy, and it occurred to me that the man of all work

238

who had watched outside my cottage most of the night had probably been up again at five o'clock, going about his jobs.

I touched his hair. "Why don't we just stay here till we feel like going home?"

"Fine, if that's what you'd like. I think this day'll hold up till then. But we'll get storm before night. There's been rain in the hills, and I think it's coming this way. But not yet. . . ." The dark lashes shut. He stretched an arm across and I slid onto it, with my head in the curve of his shoulder.

I think we talked a while longer. Our thoughts moved and mingled, but without the same clarity and force as before. No need now, I thought sleepily, with our bodies touching, and my hair under his cheek. No need.

--------------------------------------◆◇◆-- *Ashley Court, 1835*

*At the door he paused, and looked back at the room. The faint light showed it clearly enough, but he could have shut his eyes and traced, accurately, every flower on the carpet, every line on the plaster maze on the wall.*

*Fletcher would come later and straighten the bed and put all to rights.*

*It would never be the same again, he thought. They had had their time at the still center, in the Wondrous Isles. Now they must submit to the world outside. That they might change one happiness for another did not occur to him. Happiness was not the air he breathed.*

*He shut the door gently behind him, and trod down the slippery steps into the maze.*

WHEN we got back to my cottage we found that Mrs. Henderson had contrived to welcome us in the most substantial way possible. On the sitting-room table was a note. "Supper in oven," it said, and we found an excellent casserole gently bubbling there, with jacket potatoes, hot and soft, beside it on the shelf. The table was laid, and held an apple pie and a generous wedge of cheese.

We had brought a bottle of champagne with us, and we drank this with supper, then washed the dishes together, while outside a thrush sang its heart out in the pear tree.

"Make the most of it, mate," said Rob. "It's going to be a rough night." He caught my look, and grinned. "I was talking to the thrush. I warned you we'd get a storm, didn't I?"

"You did. But it's been such a lovely day."

He cocked his head to one side. "Listen."

I heard it then. Volleys of wind sifting through the orchard trees; blowing and ebbing, then blowing again in gusts.

"This'll fetch down a deal of the apple blossoms," said Rob. I saw him glance at the clock, then reach for his jacket, which he had hung over the back of a chair. "Bryony. . . ." His apologetic look spoke for itself.

"I know," I said. "You've got to go and feed the hens."

I found I had been watching for just that smile. Eleven short hours, and already a glance from him, amused and tender, could do this to me. We forge our own chains.

"Mrs. Henderson did them for me. But I'm afraid I will have to go up to the Court and take a look around. I always do a night-watchman round on the public side, and tonight, with the family gone up to London—"

I clapped a hand to my mouth. "Oh, Rob, I quite forgot! I never rang Cathy up to say I couldn't go to the party!"

"I shouldn't worry. They'll think you missed the train."

"I'll try their flat, but they'll have gone by now, and I don't even know where the party is."

"They may ring up here to find out what happened." Rob hesitated. "Do you mind my leaving you? I'll be gone about an hour, I expect."

I shook my head. "No, go ahead. After I've done the phoning I'm going to have a bath, and I've got a lot of tidying up to do. Heavens, what on earth will I say to them? . . . Would you call yourself an act of God, or what, Rob?"

"I'll leave that to you." He grinned. "Now, as your husband, Bryony Granger, do I rate a latchkey?"

I went to the desk where my father's things still lay and took his key. I held it out to Rob. *Yours now, Ashley.* The familiar name pattern slid through.

*Mine now.*

Our eyes met, and the signals faded abruptly. He took the key delicately, as if he dared not touch me, hesitated briefly, then smiled and went.

As I dialled the Underhills' flat, I reflected that I could do with the hour on my own. It was a little disconcerting to have to stage-manage one's own honeymoon at such short notice.

No reply. I put the receiver back, then ran upstairs to find that Mrs. Henderson, bless her, had been there, too. She had put fresh sheets on the double bed and turned it down, and there were clean towels in the bathroom. I had a bath, hunted out a pretty night-dress, then sat down to brush my hair.

It was barely half an hour since Rob had gone, but already it was full dark. Clouds had come piling up, seemingly from nowhere; and I could hear the growing fret and rush of wind in the orchard branches. Rob had been weather-wise; it would be a rough night.

On that thought, I heard him come in, the soft click of the spring lock almost drowned by a sudden rattle of rain flung against the casement. I pulled on my housecoat, went to the head of the stairs, and leaned over the banister. The room below was in the shadows, but I could see him standing near the door.

"Rob? You've been quick. D'you know, Mrs. Henderson even got the bedroom ready?" I stopped dead. He had turned quickly and looked up. It was not Rob. It was my cousin James.

We stood staring at one another. Damn and damn and damn, I thought. We were to have had tonight, at least, before the world broke in. "James—" I began, and started down the stairway.

Stopped again. The cottage door opened a second time, and Emory came in. He took the bunch of keys James had left in the lock, dropped them in his pocket, and shut the door. As he turned, he saw me. I couldn't see his face, but he stopped still, as if he had been struck.

"Bryony! I thought you were in London!"

"Well, I'm not." I said it slowly, looking from one to the other. "I forgot the party. Silly of me, wasn't it?"

241

"You forgot the party?" James's voice sounded strange. "What do you mean?"

"What I say. You seem to have forgotten it, too."

"Well, not exactly." Emory's ease of manner was a little too good to be true. "Our invitations were cancelled. I suppose we have you to thank for that."

"It's possible. So what brings you here? And how do you happen to have a key?"

"The fact is—" began James, but Emory cut in.

"We thought you'd be in town, so we borrowed Mrs. Henderson's key."

The word borrowed held no touch of irony, but I knew that, had they spoken with Mrs. Henderson, she would have told them about our marriage, and that we would be home tonight. She kept the cottage keys hanging on a nail inside her back door, which, like most doors in the country, was rarely locked.

Emory flashed me a smile, which did not colour his voice. This was the voice of a man thinking quickly. "It's a diabolical liberty, I know, but time pressed. Since you're here, that makes it easier."

"Makes what easier?"

"There was something we wanted rather urgently."

"I see." I pulled the housecoat closer around me, belted it, and began slowly to descend the stairs. I was remembering, as clearly as if it were my lover telling me again, that these two could be dangerous if they were driven to it.

Resolutely I put the thought aside. I concentrated on keeping my mind shut to Rob; if he had received the sudden jagged pattern of fear which had zigzagged across my brain a moment ago, he would come straight here at the run, and an awkward—surely no more than awkward?—scene could easily become nasty. There was still time enough to get rid of them.

I reached the foot of the stairs and said, as easily as I could, "I suppose you came to get the book!" I crossed to the window and drew the curtains. "Put the light on, Emory. That's better. Well, it isn't here. I told you I'd take it to be valued. So, since there aren't any other rare objects to interest you, I suggest—"

"Not even you, seemingly," said James.

"What?" A tiny chill stroked the skin along my arms.

242

"You were expecting Rob Granger," said James. Then, to his brother, "She thought I was Granger. She called down to tell him the bedroom was ready, and came out. Like that."

"Rob Granger?" said Emory. "Well, well, well." Silence for two blood beats, while the eyes of both cousins took me in from head to foot. The hairbrush still in my hand, the scent of the bath; my housecoat parting slightly to show the nightdress underneath.

I crossed to the fireplace, sat down in one of the armchairs, and regarded them both calmly. "Yes, Rob Granger. So now, if you don't mind, I'd rather you went. He'll be coming soon."

James walked slowly forward. He was looking sick. It came to me with surprise that perhaps he had really cared; the scene in the garden had not just been part of the twins' play for the breaking of the trust.

"I'm sorry, James." I said it gently. "What can I say? Only that it took me as much by surprise as anyone. And it's for real. I know now that nothing else was. . . . It was Rob all along."

A muffled exclamation from Emory that sounded almost like a laugh. Then he said impatiently, "Look, Bryony, what's it matter if you're sleeping with Rob Granger? Leave it, Twin. It makes it a whole lot easier."

"Makes what easier?" I demanded. "And I'm not sleeping with Rob Granger, not in the sense you mean. I married him this morning. Now you see why I forgot the party, and why I want to get rid of you."

It was a bombshell, of course. The two of them stood, one to either side of my chair, staring down at me. James was as white as paper now, but Emory wore a look I was unfamiliar with: a pale, hard expression. "Yes," I said steadily, "we're married."

A pause that seemed to last for ever; then James found his voice. "So you're going to stay at Ashley? Here?"

"This is a much nicer cottage," said Emory, "than the one he has in the farmyard."

I gaped up at the pair of them. The conversation seemed to be taking a turn towards sheer irrelevance. Or so one might have thought, if it had not been for those cool Ashley eyes and the impression I got of quick Ashley brains reappraising some situation I hadn't yet grasped.

"No," I said. "We plan to emigrate." I looked at James and tried a smile. "I told you that all I wanted was time to let the future show itself. Now it has, and I'm prepared to break the trust."

James didn't answer. He and Emory were consulting one another in silence across me, as if I weren't there. It was disturbing.

"You can stop worrying, then, Twin," Emory said.

No answer. My sensitive mental antennae picked up some powerful and urgent message that couldn't be spoken. Then Emory smiled down at me.

"You must forgive us for seeming so eager to lose you. Of course that's wonderful news. So, since it's working out so well for everyone, it seems we can offer you congratulations."

Ordinary words, kindly, even; but there was no kindness in his voice—only briskness, with a burnish of flippancy.

James was pursuing something of his own, still with that urgency. "Then you'll sell the cottage strip?"

"Yes," I said slowly. "I don't feel like hedging. We'll not come back to Ashley."

James's face went slack with relief. I had some reappraisal to do, it seemed. Not only did he urgently want the property; he was eager to see me go. Emory pegged it home, saying swiftly, "What splendid news. It really is reprieve, Twin."

"Reprieve?" I queried.

Emory perched on the edge of the table. He seemed relaxed, totally at ease now. "I think you should be told, Cousin dear, that it really was becoming more than ever imperative for us to sell the Court. Our dear stepmother's father finds himself suddenly in need of funds, so he proposes to transfer back to Spain some of the capital he put into the Bristol business."

"I see. And it's tied up, is that it?"

"You could say that." Emory sounded amused. "It's in use elsewhere. We've been repaying the interest in installments, but now they want the principal back. . . . And I'm afraid it isn't there."

Reappraisal was easy after all. "You mean you stole it."

"You have such a way of putting things," said Emory.

I got to my feet. "Well, there doesn't seem to be much more to say, does there? My husband and I"—the phrase was like a shield—"will see Mr. Emerson and let him get on with breaking the trust."

244

I took a breath, trying to control my voice, but it came out edged. "For the present the cottage is still ours, and I should like the keys back. Then I'd like you both to go."

Without a word Emory drew the keys from his pocket and dropped them on the table. I felt curiously numb, though I should have been prepared for the realization that Rob had been only too right: my cousins were more than just self-willed and ruthless; they were criminals. There was no need, now, to hear about the photograph. I knew, as if my father himself had told me, that it had been Emory there on that road. And Emory who had gone (as James) to Jerez, while James had doubled for him here. As before, I crushed the thought aside, in case Rob should catch its echo and react to it. All I wanted now was to be rid of the twins and their dealing for ever.

But even so, when the keys fell from Emory's hand to the table, the sound they made was a knell to the past. Ashley was gone from me, and with it, how much more.

Turning abruptly, I went to the door and opened it. The wind was higher than ever, tempestuous. To my relief the moonlight showed me the path still empty and a light still in the Court. But it showed me something else. The lawn in front of the cottage was underwater as far as the lilac tree. The level of the pool must have risen half a metre.

"It's all right," said Emory behind me. "That's what we meant by reprieve. We'll go now and shut the high sluice."

"Shut the high sluice?" I whirled on him. "What do you mean?"

Behind me the door, caught in a gust of wind, slammed shut. "I told you it's a reprieve," Emory said. "We didn't come all this way to get the book. We came to—well, to hasten your decision to sell the cottage."

No misunderstanding this time. I got the whole picture. "You mean you opened the high sluice deliberately, to flood the place, and on a night like this?"

"We had to take the chance, with you and the Underhills away. The weather was a bonus." A brief laugh. "Well, now you know the lot. We reckoned another bad flood would put paid to the cottage and force your hand. Brutal of us, wasn't it? But needs must, they say. Believe me"—Emory sounded sincere and very charming with it—"we'd have been sorry about the cottage, but you should have more sense than to get sentimental about a gold mine. Tell Rob there's no need to trouble about the water level, we'll go straight to the high sluice now."

"But—" I began, then shut my teeth on it. I wasn't going to tell them that Rob was doing his rounds, would have seen the level of the water. His reaction would be to check straight away on the sluices. He must not run into my cousins on the same errand. If I could get rid of them, I could warn him off.

"You'd better hurry," I said quickly. "The way the pool's risen, it looks as if the Overflow can't carry it all."

"Calm down. We can get the lower sluice open."

"You certainly cannot. It's been wedged shut again, and it's unsafe. Just get the high sluice closed before there's some real damage done."

But as I turned to open the door again, the telephone rang.

---

*Ashley Court, 1835*

*Today . . . Today was not just another day. Today he would have to face them. His father was dead, and he was Ashley. He must find the courage to face them with what he had done. Then, afterward, she would be with him.*

*Something showed pale on the grass near the mouth of the maze. Stooping, he recognized the kerchief of silk he had given her. Wondering how she had come to drop it there, he picked it up and, smiling, held it to his face. The gentle fragrance of lavender brought her near again.*

*Still smiling, he walked out of the maze.*

THE three of us stood as if struck still. Then I made a move. Emory's hand shot out and gripped my wrist.

I was angry now. "It's my phone, Emory. I shan't tell anyone you're here, if you're afraid. But what is there to be afraid of now? Your crime's been called off, hasn't it?" He stepped back.

246

I picked up the telephone. It was Leslie Oker, in full and joyous spate.

"Bryony? My dear, I know it's a dreadful hour, but I've been trying to get you off and on all day. My dear, the book . . ."

It was a loud telephone, Leslie's excitement carrying through almost as if he were in the room. Beside me, Emory made a sharp movement of interest. I started to speak, but Leslie swept on.

"I'm certain that it's genuine. It's been rebound, and that will take something off its value, but it's still very valuable indeed, museum stuff. I wouldn't like to guess at a figure until I've found out a little more. . . ." He talked on, half technical jargon that I hardly took in. Emory's eyes were gleaming, and he mouthed something; I thought it was "How much?" I shook my head as the telephone broadcast what was obviously a question.

"Sorry, Leslie, I didn't catch that. What did you say?"

"I said, when I lifted it, I found something that might be in its way even more interesting. Do you want to hear it now?"

"Hear what? Lifted what?" I asked unguardedly.

"The bookplate. That curious rectangular design with that weird motto of yours, 'Touch not the cat.'"

Something jarred me back to the alert. "Look, Leslie, since Daddy's death, that book and all the family things belong to my cousin Emory. I'll tell him to get in touch with you—"

Emory's hand had come between my mouth and the telephone, covering the mouthpiece. His other hand closed on the receiver, over mine, and lifted it away from me. In midair in front of me, the metallic voice quacked on, all too clear.

"Sorry to hear that, dear, because really, such a *find* . . . Of course, moving the bookplate won't militate against the value of the book at all, since it was put on so much later. In fact, it looked to me as if it had been lifted before, and pasted down again; recently, I'd say. So I felt quite justified in lifting it again. This paper that I found under the bookplate, well, that's of real family interest, I would think. Looks like a mystery to me, Gothic, really, but what fun. Listen."

We listened, all three of us. Whatever Leslie had discovered, I did not see now how I could stop Emory from finding out about it. It was his book, after all.

247

Leslie was explaining. "It looks like a page from a church register. It's numbered seventeen. There are only three entries. One is dated April 15, 1835, and it records the marriage of Nicholas Ashley, Esquire, of Ashley Court, to an Ellen Makepeace."

Not for worlds would I have tried to cut Leslie short now. My mind meshed into gear like a racing engine. The consequences could wait; I had to know. I remembered my father's words: *The paper, it's in William's brook. In the library. . . . The map. The letter.*

"Further down the page," Leslie went on, "someone has written a note. It's signed Charles Ashley. Do you know who he was?"

Emory lowered the receiver to me. I didn't look at him. "He was Nick Ashley's uncle, William Ashley's brother. He succeeded to the Court after Nick Ashley was shot."

"Oh. Well, a note from him. It's rather long, so I'll paraphrase the first bit—he says he bribed the clerk to recopy the page, omitting the Ashley entry, and something about the incumbent—is that the vicar, dear?—being a dependent. Does that make sense?"

"I think so. One Ash was one of the Ashley benefices. A poor relation was often given the benefice. Charles Ashley could have put pressure on him to keep quiet about the wedding. Is that what he says?"

"Could be. He says—shall I read the rest to you?"

"Yes, please."

" 'It is said that the girl goes with child, and should she bear it before the nine months' term is up since my nephew's death, there will be those who, for their own base ends, will rumour it abroad that the child was begotten on her by my nephew before she married her husband. But it is neither right nor fitting that the fruit—if it be so—of so base a connection should take the property from the hands of my own fair family who are sprung from alliance with the highest in the county. Moreover, since the brothers of the said Ellen Makepeace did murder my nephew Nicholas, it were better that the child were born dead than usurp this place with blood upon his head. So, God be my witness, it is not upon my conscience to do what I have done. The girl bears herself lowly, and has avowed publicly that the child is of her own husband. . . .' "

A pause, during which Leslie gave his little laugh. "She would,

248

of course, poor creature. The good squire would probably have
had the baby quietly put down otherwise. Well, Bryony dear? Does
all this mean anything to you?"

I cleared my throat, but even so my voice came out rather unfamiliar. "I think so. Leslie, I'm terribly grateful to you. May I
come over tomorrow? We'll have time to talk about it then."

"Well, of course. This awful hour . . . But I knew you'd like to
know straight away."

"Yes. Thank you for ringing, Leslie. Good night."

The telephone went dead. Emory's hands relaxed, and he stood
back from me. I put the receiver down blindly, and sank, rather
heavily, into the chair beside the table.

"How many more surprises will this night hold?" Emory said.
"This Ellen Makepeace—if she actually had that baby—"

I hadn't looked at them, but James, prompted perhaps by some
stray instinct of the Ashley gift, or more likely by a residuum of
jealousy, got there with frightening speed.

"You can bet your bloody life she did. Makepeaces— One Ash
is full of them, and the Grangers are connected." Then savagely
to me, "That's it, isn't it? Rob Granger—he goes straight back to
this so-called marriage. And you knew it! You knew he was an
Ashley, *and legit.* Why else would you marry a lout like that?"

"Shut up, Twin. Bryony, did you know about this?"

"I knew he was an Ashley, but I didn't know about the marriage.
Neither does he. He told me he was descended from Nick Ashley,
but on the wrong side of the blanket."

"Oh, he knows that much? All his family know, too?"

"Only that the brothers shot Nick for debauching Ellen, and
that she married the Granger lad and had a baby son, but swore
on the Bible it was her husband's, so people accepted it."

"And all the time," said Emory, with a twist to his voice, "she
was telling the exact truth. Charles must fairly have sweated."

I said nothing. I was thinking about Ellen Ashley. Consumed
with pity for that girl, bereft and helpless, swearing on the Scrip-
tures in order to protect her lover's child, and hugging to herself
the comfort that all the time it was the truth.

"Are you trying to pretend," demanded James, "that Rob never
guessed?"

"That his ancestry was legitimate? How could he? The baby was accepted as Robert Granger's. There may have been talk in the family about Nick as Ellen's lover, but as nothing more than that. By the time Rob was born, it was all too long ago, and who cared?"

"But you said he was an Ashley."

"Yes. He knew because—because he has the Ashley gift. Well, so have I. That's why our marriage happened, as it did, so suddenly. I'd meant to tell you about that, anyway."

So I told them then, the merest sketch, and they listened, not very surprised; they were Ashleys, after all.

"You'll tell him all about this, I suppose?" asked James, when I had finished.

"Do you think I *cannot* tell him something that might matter to him like this? He ought to know he's a true Ashley, and that his great-great-grandfather wasn't just a brat fathered on a light-minded girl. That Nick Ashley loved Ellen enough to marry her." I had spoken as hotly as if I were defending Rob himself.

And I knew why Nick and Ellen, just for those fatal few days, had kept their marriage secret. They were trying, like Rob and me, to keep something to themselves for a while, before the world broke in. I moved wearily in my chair.

"Look," I said, "why don't we talk about it tomorrow? With Rob, if you like. As I see it, what we've found out will make no difference, one way or another, to what happens here at Ashley. But if you two don't do something about the high sluice—"

"To hell with the high sluice." It was odd how James seemed to have taken over the scene. "Are you seriously trying to tell us that if you tell Granger all this—this old-time Gothic trash—he won't be tempted to make it public? Claim the Court and everything that goes with it? Stay here with you and play lord of the manor? Someone like that couldn't resist it."

"Rob knows even better than you do what it would mean to have this place unloaded on him," I said, swallowing my fury. "And even if we wanted it, a claim like this would never stand up in a court of law. It wouldn't even be worth trying."

"Your father must have thought it would," said James obstinately. "This is why he refused to break the trust the second time we asked him. He must just have found out about Rob."

"Yes." I spoke with sudden, complete illumination, my father's last words finally clear to me. He had been trying to say: "I did tell Bryanston that she and Rob should marry. Perhaps the boy knows already that he's an Ashley. Tell the boy who he is. This trust; it's his concern now. You can depend on him to do what's right. You have—both of you—my blessing."

I sat up straight, speaking earnestly. "And he was going to tell Rob the truth, as I am. Further than that it's up to him, and I've told you what I think he'll do; cut his losses and go."

Emory stirred. "Leslie Oker saw the paper. You can't tell me he'd keep quiet about a juicy item like that."

"He will if I ask him to. In any case," I said impatiently, "what does it matter who knows, if we don't press anything? Mr. Emerson will do as Rob asks him—and, for pity's sake, can you imagine a courtful of lawyers in the 1970s arguing over an 1837 parish register, and whether or not Bess Ashley really did hand telepathy down the family?"

"All right," said Emory, "so imagine it. Let Oker once start talking and there'll be questions asked about our right to sell the place. And while lawyers make a meal of the Ashley gift, Pereira sues us for twenty thousand pounds."

"We could destroy the paper and square Leslie Oker." This from James; they were at it again.

"He's probably talked already," said Emory.

"Well, but without proof—"

"Any inquiry would mean the kind of delay we can't afford."

"That's true," said James. "Well, what are you going to do?"

"It shouldn't be too difficult," said Emory, "to fix things."

I saw it then, through the weariness and worry, and I knew that Rob had been right. These men were dangerous, even to me and mine. Quick thinking, violent men, who knew how to profit from accidents. . . . I don't think I moved, but James, still on that odd telepathic wavelength, took a swift step towards me. I shut my eyes and reached for Rob. But across the first groping signal I heard James say urgently, "It's true, Twin, she can talk to him. Look at her." Then, in sudden, unbelieving revulsion, "Emory! No!"

Something hit me hard behind the ear, and I went out like a smashed lamp.

*His limbs were stiff, and heavy as if bound with iron. The pain in his chest exploded through his whole body, then died to a slow, unmerciful aching. He moaned, but could hear no sound.*

*He was lying on cold, soaking grass. He must have fainted. He remembered—surely he remembered?— going out of the maze. There had been shadows moving, a rough whisper, then the skin-prickling sound of a fowling piece, cocked. . . .*

*The memory faded, and with it the pain. His head felt light and drowsy, and he had the strangest fancy that he was floating above his own body. Then that, too, faded.*

I HAD a headache, and it was dark. At first I thought the noises were in my head, but as I slowly came fully to myself, I realized that the splashes and the keening gusts of wind were realities, as was the slam of wood on wood that had wakened me.

It took me a little time to discover where I was. I was lying on hard ground strewn with twigs and dead leaves, with the smells of wet earth and rotting wood blown around me strongly on the gusty draughts. Slowly, wooden walls and a kind of roof built themselves out of the near darkness around me, and I saw that I was in an enclosed space, perhaps the size of the cottage sitting room, but with a ceiling so low that I could hardly sit up.

I crawled shakily to a crack in the wall. Peering through it, I saw a thick hedge blocking a square of windy sky and, nearer at hand, the tangles of some thick creeper swinging against the balustrade of a rustic stairway. Everywhere was the sound of trees and water.

I had it then. I was under the pavilion, in the space below the floor. The slamming noise that had roused me was a broken shutter on the veranda above me, swinging in the wind. I groped my way, dazedly, to a little access door, only to discover that it was securely jammed from outside.

I came fully awake then, with all that had happened vividly back in my mind and, with it, all that was due to happen. I remembered quick, incisive instructions from Emory to James, and protests over-ruled. I must have surfaced into consciousness from time to time, enough to catch snatches of the argument. I knew now why James had looked so strained; he had after all cared enough—or been frightened enough—not wanted to see me harmed.

"I tell you, she'll be perfectly safe." That was Emory, impatience held hard on the curb. "I'll put her in the pavilion and lock her in. She'll be above water level there, and out of action long enough for us to get away."

"But she's seen us here, Emory. If anything happens to Granger, our alibis are blown before we start."

"Very well, then"—quick and smooth—"she goes."

"No! Are you crazy? We've got to think of something else—"

"Such as? You can't have it both ways."

A pause, then from James, slowly, "I think we can. I'm willing to bet she'd say nothing about an accident to Rob. . . . All right, so she married him, but it'll never last out the honeymoon, a lout like that. Look, Twin, I mean it. She's never said a word about her father's death, has she? About it's being one of us? . . . And she knows. She cottoned on to that pen of mine that you dropped, I'm certain she did."

"But Cousin Jonathan's death was an accident. She'll know this won't be."

Whether James had agreed with Emory's plan or had simply turned a blind eye, I did not know. But the very fact that I was here proved that, as always, he would go along with whatever Emory suggested. It was easy to guess what that was. They would use the almost aborted plan for flooding the cottage strip. They would leave the high sluice open, letting the swollen river pour into the moat, and when the moat burst its banks and the pool overflowed, flooding everything down through orchard and maze, I would drown. No doubt the access door of my trap was wedged to look as if some floating boughs had been jammed there by the water's force after I had been washed under the pavilion. And Rob? They would improvise an "accident". His body would be found where apparently he had run to rescue me. The two of us, star-crossed lovers, drowned on our wedding night. And all the while the twins, securely alibied, miles away. . . .

There was no flood yet. Straining my ears, I could hear the ripple and rush of the Overflow as it skirted the maze—full, but not yet too full. I might still be in time. Emory must have meant to hit me harder, or perhaps he had not reckoned on the chill, reviving air.

*Rob. Rob.*

I put the call out with all the strength I could muster. It was more difficult than it had ever been. Without quite realizing it then, I switched the signal, using the pattern I had been used to—and which now, ironically, was real.

*Ashley, Ashley, Ashley. . . .*

*Yes?* It was faint, but the wave of relief melted me against the wall like wet paper. He was alive and, from the serenity of his response, unsuspecting and unmolested.

*Bryony?* Serene no longer. He had got the fear pattern. *What is it? What's happened?*

*Danger for you.* It was all I could do to send the warning patterns, without giving him some inkling of my own peril. Some of my fear must have got through in spite of my effort, because his response was violent, a blast of static that splintered the thought waves and sent me back to simple messages of reassurance that took every ounce of control I had: *No. I'm all right. I'm safe. . . .*

I strained to shut out the image of the dark cage that trapped me, and to conjure up instead a picture of the pavilion above. He must have no whisper of my danger, or he might do just as my cousins wished and come running back towards me, past wherever they lay in wait for him.

I began painfully to send those new patterns out to him. My cousins opening the high sluice; the river racing through to fill the moat. The slow flood reaching through the orchard. . . .

The image of the lower sluice slid across the pictures, like a quick shiver of alarm. He knew, even better than I, what would happen if too great a weight of water piled against those rotting gates; or worse, what would happen if anyone tried to move them. He came back at me then, light-edged with relief: *The pavilion, that's where you are?*

I had got it to him, then. He thought I had taken refuge there, safely perched above the encroaching water. *Yes.* I sent it urgently. *I'm safe. But you, Ashley, danger for you.*

I knew he must have got from me the image of the two dark figures lurking in wait somewhere, watching for him. There was a brief flash of a reply, zigzag, as if with interference. *I've got it. I'm on my way. Stay where you are. . . .* It was fading.

*My little Bryony be careful.* It came not with the smooth familiarity of Rob's patterns, but as if straight out of the night.

Then a sound, sharp and distinct, like a shot. From somewhere near the Overflow, at the entrance to the maze.

I hurled myself at the wall of my prison, my hands straining flat against the wood as if nailed there, my face to that crack. *Rob? Rob?* They could not have shot him. It was to have been an accident. Surely I could not have guessed that wrong?

A sound came, shattering thought. A cracking noise, like a door strained to breaking point.

*Ashley?* He had gone, as if a line had fused. I think I was still calling him, on a jagged pattern of terror, when the lower sluice smashed and the flood came.

IT CAME in a tidal wave that tore through the ancient walls of the maze and broke, filthy and swirling, against the pavilion. Then the water found its way in. There was a choking, fighting eternity, in which every second seemed an hour, when the water pounded the gaping walls with terrifying power. The jets shot into my trap from every side to join in a whirlpool which rose rapidly from ankle to crouching thigh, to waist, to breasts. I thrust myself up against the ceiling, arms bent in front of my face to protect mouth and nostrils from the swirling filth. If the pavilion floor were only as solid as it had seemed, it might trap an inch of air for me to breathe until the flood poured past.

The floor above me was not solid. As I pressed hard against it, it lifted like magic into clear air. There was a crash as a square of planking upended itself and fell aside. I pulled myself up onto the pavilion floor, the flood at my heels. I slammed the trapdoor back into place, then jumped on the daybed and craned to look out through the broken window shutter.

What I saw was a waste of moonlit water, broken with black

255

shapes of trees and bushes. There was no maze, no orchard. Visible from moment to moment, as ripples and wind swayed the intervening boughs aside, were the smashed remains of the lower sluice, where the loosened water of the moat plunged down to swell the flooded garden.

I stretched higher, straining to see. And I saw Rob. He was bent half double, wrestling with the wheel of the sluice. For a numbed moment I looked to see my cousins jump at him, but nothing happened. Then I saw that where he stood the ground was dry, and I recognized, with no flicker of disbelief, or even surprise, the high sluice, a full third of a mile away from me, and on the far side of the Court. Across the nearer scene the other came and went, now clear, now fading.

It was something that had never happened before, nor has it again. I can only explain it by suggesting that in that time of near death we were so close that there was more than communication between us; there was identity. I saw with his eyes, but at the same time I saw with my own.

The twins, intending to go back to the high sluice, had left the wheel still in place. Rob wrenched at it and it turned, and the heavy gates surged slowly shut till, with a final suck and swish of water, their flanges met and gripped. He made sure of them, then tugged the wheel off its hub, picked up the flashlight that he had propped on the gate to light the job, and cautiously made his way to the Overflow. Carrying a dangerous freight of branches and stones and pieces of timber, the water was still coming over here, pouring through gaps in the bank of the moat where it had torn its way with frightening power.

Rob floundered down towards the maze, straining his eyes for any movement that might be a man. The maze showed only as a moving flood laced with driftwood and the tracery of hedge tops. He paused for a moment, getting his breath, backing in against a beech bole in deep shadow. He held the heavy flashlight ready in his hand.

*Safe, love?* he asked me.

*Safe.*

At that moment, clearly audible above the noise of the wind and flood, came another crack, like an echo of the first, and with the crack a cry. It came from the lower sluice. Rob ran forward, slipping and stumbling on mud, till he could see the sluice gate. Here, through the smashed gate, the water still poured in a white torrent; but the banks to either side, being heavily reinforced with stone, had held undamaged. Over them, where the double water stair had fed the Overflow, loud slopes of smooth water slid to swell the flood below.

Then Rob saw James, kneeling by the sluice, half in the rushing water, one arm hooked for support across what remained of the gate. In his other hand was an axe.

*Ashley!*

The warning burst in my head, and I saw Rob check momentarily. They were both clear to me now: James, his wet leather jacket gleaming like an otter's, the axe poised and ready; Rob armed only with a flashlight. But my cousin seemed not to have noticed Rob. He was bent low over the rubble of timber below the sluice. Still holding with his left hand, he reached forward and began to hack with what force he could at a spar which, wedged across the channel, held down the mass of wreckage.

Rob shouted something and ran to the edge of the channel. He had seen what lay below the spar, and so had I.

Emory was alive. His head and arms were clear of the rushing water, his hands gripping at the rough stones of the wall; but his shoulders were pinned down by the spar, and his body held under by a tangled mat of weeds and branches. Rob threw himself flat, and reached down to grip Emory's wrists.

James had apparently neither seen him nor heard him shout. But now my cousin looked up sharply. He abandoned the spar he was attacking and got to his feet, axe in hand.

Neither Rob nor I was ever quite clear about what James had meant to do. He was yelling something, and the axe swung high. Then his foot shot from under him on the slimy wood. He lost his footing and fell hard across the spar. The axe flew from his grip. He scrabbled there for a moment, his body down across his brother's; then the water swept him out of sight. At the same moment, the spar, loosened by James's fall, spun away. The clutching hands were torn from the stones, breaking Rob's grip, and suddenly Rob was alone at the sluice.

So much I believe I saw; then there was nothing but the sheen of water and the moon out over it. The trees still roared and the water crept in under the door, meandering across the wooden floor. But its impetus seemed spent. A shallow pool lay in the centre of the room, the last ripple of the flood that had drowned the garden, islanding the pavilion like a ship floating.

What brought me back to myself was the sound, distant but unmistakable, of Emory's car starting. I stiffened. Yes, it was his, and parked, by the sound of it, outside the church gate. I heard the driver—James, surely?—gun the engine twice; then the wheels gained the surface of the road and the sound faded rapidly. My cousins—both, presumably, for neither would have left the place alone—had gone.

There is a gap after that, while I simply sat there on the bed, numbed, waiting for Rob to come. It didn't even occur to me that he might not have remembered the way into the maze, and that I was penned here at the centre, as inaccessible as any Sleeping Beauty.

I suppose I could have guided him through, if I had been able to keep my mind clear. But I didn't try, and he never asked. I felt something move out of the dark like a caress, and knew he was sensing my exhaustion. I got it faintly, very faintly: *Hold up, love. I'm almost with you.*

He was coming. I thought about nothing else. I waited.

Either he had found James's axe or he had been up to the farm for another. I could hear the steady hacking sounds coming gradually nearer as he approached me through the maze. Slowly, but straight. He was slicing his way right through those high walls of yew.

The crashing stopped. I heard the surging splash as he thrust through the last hedge; then he waded across the moonlit water in the clearing and ran up the steps to the door. *Love?*

*Here. The south window, Rob.*

The shutter went back with a slam, and his shadow blacked out the moonlight in the window. He had thought to bring a dry blanket, which he wore wrapped like a burnous around his head and shoulders.

Then he was beside me on the bed, holding me tightly, and

258

somehow, at some point, our soaked clothes came off and we were together under the warm cover, while the terrors and tensions of the night swelled and broke in a fierce explosion of love, and then we lay together, clasped and quiet.

I WOULD not have believed I could have slept like that in all the damp and discomfort of the flooded pavilion. But, between exhaustion and deep happiness, sleep I did, and so did Rob, until the early sun, reaching the window, threw a dazzle of light from the water outside onto the ceiling mirror.

I came awake then, to the warmth of Rob's body along mine. He was lying on his back, eyes wide and wakeful, but with every line of his body relaxed. "Have you been awake long?"

"It doesn't seem like it. I suppose I woke at my usual time. Always do, even on holiday. First time I ever woke like this, though." His arm tightened, and I moved my cheek deeper into the hollow of his shoulder. "Bryony—"

"Mmmm?"

"What did they put the mirror on the ceiling for?"

I gave a little snort of laughter. "It was supposed to be put up there by some loose screw—your ancestor Wicked Nick gets the blame—so he could watch himself in bed with his lady friends."

"But one couldn't."

"But one can," I protested. "And very cozy we look."

"Aye. But then the bed isn't where it ought to be. You can see where that was by the moulding on the wall over there. The way that mirror's angled—if you were lying on the bed, all you'd see was a piece of the floor hereabouts." He tilted his head back, examining it. "And I'm going to move the bed back to its proper place." This as he unwound himself from the blanket, got up, and ran the bed back against the wall.

"Well, then," I said, "poor Nick's been libelled about the mirror as he has about other things."

I said no more. There would be time later to tell him what I had found out about Nick and Ellen, about what had happened in the cottage last night, about my narrow escape from the trap under this very floor. Time to find out what had happened to my cousins. Time for all those things. But for the moment, I would let it go.

We would keep, while we could, our own island world of joy.

Getting back into bed, Rob pulled the blanket up over the pair of us.

When I woke again, Rob was not beside me but fully dressed and kneeling on the floor near the foot of the bed. I slipped out of the blanket and reached for my robe. It was dry. The sun had moved appreciably higher, and now the mirror's light fell, like a spotlight, straight to the boards where the trapdoor lay.

Last night's floodwater had scoured the dust of years from this section of the floor, and there quite distinctly could be seen the sawed edges of the trap with, midway along one edge, what looked like a knothole in the wood. In this Rob had inserted a finger. He gave a heave and the door came up. As he peered over the trap's edge, I opened my mouth to tell him about my experience of last night. But without looking up, he stopped me with an imperative gesture. "Bryony. Look here."

His voice held discovery, and a kind of awe. I moved to his side and lay prone, staring down into my prison of last night.

The force of the flood had swept through, then subsided, leaving the debris piled against the walls and scouring the centre clean. Lighted fiercely from the pavilion above, where the angled mirror threw the sunlight down, was a picture, part of a larger design—the head of a leopard, snarling, with one paw upraised, the claws out and ready. The eyes were huge and brilliant, done in some lustrous shell-like stone which caught and threw back the light; the teeth gleamed white and sharp, and the yellow fur with the black spots, washed clean by the rush of the flood, shone as brightly as on the day the mosaic was laid to make the floor of some Roman's home.

We looked at it for some time in silence. The sunlight shimmered, and the upraised paw stirred. The eyes glared, and the yellow fur ruffled. A young leopard, rousing, as vivid and alive as when, all those centuries ago, some Roman built over this quiet corner between river and hill, and brought his artisans from Italy to make this marvellous picture.

"That's mosaic work, isn't it?" asked Rob. "Looks like part of a floor or something; a big one, too. It must be pretty old."

"I'd guess it was Roman."

"Roman? As old as that?"

"I think so. There were Romans here, a long time ago, and there was a tile kiln not far off. Perhaps when William Ashley cleared the ground for his pavilion, he found this, and so—"

"*The cat, it's the cat on the pavement,*" quoted Rob.

I sat back abruptly as the last piece of the puzzle fell into place. "Of course!" I looked up at the wall above the bed, where the wildcat ramped in the centre of the plaster maze. "That's it, isn't it? The old crest was the leopard, but through time people forgot why. Then poor doting William borrowed Julia's wildcat and her motto, and then, when he found this, he drew the maze around them for a coat of arms. But how do you suppose my father found out about the mosaic?"

"Well, you said he'd been studying William's book. It was all in the poetry, wasn't it? I reckon," said Rob comfortably, "that if you'd taken enough time over the poems, you'd have found it out for yourself. '*What palace then was this?*' Remember?"

"Of course," I said again. I drew a long breath. He was right, it had all been there, carefully riddled down in the little verses; *the leopard from the sun . . . the spotted catamountain.* I lay down again, peering at the exposed mosaic. "No sign of the wine god Bacchus, though. They must have covered him up again and just kept the cat. What d'you bet, Rob, that if we cleared the maze away, we'd find the rest of the villa?"

"You might say I made a start at that last night, hacking my way through to you." He added slowly, "I suppose you couldn't put a value on a thing like this?"

"Not really." I knew what he was thinking; that here was something which could save Ashley—the part of it that I loved—from the bulldozers and make it worth someone's while to clear the gardens and expose this magnificent find for people to see. There were archaeological societies and generous individuals who would preserve what we had found. Whatever the future might bring, it was certain that no builders would be allowed to touch this part of Ashley. The cat had been here long before the Ashleys ever came, and he would outstay them.

Rob got to his feet and pulled me into his arms. "Time we got out of here, I'm afraid. You're getting cold."

262

He put the trapdoor back in place. "Well, and so what do we do about it? Keep quiet, like William?"

I laughed. "The old Scrooge—he seems never to have told a soul. Just hugged it to himself and wrote it into those poems. No wonder he died of a heart seizure when he heard that Nick was using the place as a love nest."

"And Nick got the blame for the mirror, too. Eh, well. . . . And now, the day's got to start. It won't be a good one, but we can face it together. And the mystery's over; we've found out just about all your dad was trying to tell you. All but the last bit."

"I know the last bit, too," I said.

"Well, then?" asked Rob.

I shook my head. "Later . . . after breakfast."

"Breakfast!" He stretched luxuriously, giving me that wide, warm smile of his. "You're dead right; that comes first!"

From the pavilion steps we could see that the water in the clearing below us was now only seven or eight inches deep. It lay still as glass, and under it, like a garden set in crystal, the grass and flowers stood straight, held by the lucid water as perfectly as if it were air. We held hands and walked down the wooden steps, through what was left of the maze, to the wreck of the lower sluice, where the fishing cat, which had tumbled to the mud at the foot of the water stair, bore witness to the rashness of meddling men.

There was debris everywhere, but the swans dipped for fish happily in the pool, and the moat was back in its borders. The old house dreamed above its reflection with nothing but a tidemark to show how high the water had risen last night. On the drive, under the lime trees, stood a rusty-looking Volkswagen. And on the main bridge, gazing around him with a contemplative expression, was my cousin Francis.

The other Ashley. My gentle cousin, the poet. He looked up and saw us approaching. If he noticed anything strange about Rob's crumpled clothes or my bedraggled housecoat and bare feet, his expression gave no hint of it.

"Bryony!" he said, his face lighting. "Rob, nice to see you! What on earth's been going on here? I'd have thought the high sluice would stand a cloudburst."

"It would, if it hadn't been meddled with," said Rob flatly. Then, as my cousin's eyes widened, "Aye, it's more of a mess than you think, Francis. We've a lot to tell you, and it's not good hearing."

For the first time my cousin seemed to notice something odd about our appearance. "All right, then. Tell me."

Rob looked at me and nodded. "It's your story, love."

So I told it, leaving out nothing but the parts of it that were Rob's and my own, and the secret of William's Brooke, which I'd have to tell Rob when we were alone. When I got to last night's scene in my cottage I hesitated, wondering how to gloss over Leslie Oker's telephone call. But I need not have worried. Rob's anger at the scene I was describing blinded him to everything else. To this day I am not sure whether his explosion of rage over Emory's attack on me was in words, or whether it burst straight from his mind into mine with the force of an armour-piercing shell. But by the time he had hold of himself, the tricky part was past.

After I had finished, there was silence. Rob sat down on the parapet of the bridge and drew me to him. I could feel the ebbing shock wave of anger and the surge of protective love. Francis turned away to look down at the water.

We had been lucky, I thought, that the first herald of the daylight world had been the one man who could share its burdens with us. I knew that Rob was, like me, thinking ahead, trying to come to terms with what the night's work meant to our future.

Some of it could be guessed at. Even if Emory eventually recovered (which, from Rob's account of his apparent injuries, seemed unlikely), the twins would never come back to Ashley. With Rob's claim hanging over it, the land was unsaleable and therefore profitless to them. Never again would they be able to threaten me or Rob; I would make sure of that. I would write down the story of the past few days and lodge it, with photostats of the relevant papers, as surety for the future. Further than that, out of mercy for the twins' sick father, we surely need not go?

As for the debts the twins had incurred, William's Brooke, as well as endowing the Court, would take care of those. I could not find it in me to care what happened to James. All I would ever grieve over would be, not the evil man and the weak man who had been here last night, but the two charming and wilful boys who had lived here with us so long ago.

Francis turned back to us. He was grave and rather pale, but otherwise gave no sign of emotion. It was like him that, when he began to speak, it was about my bereavement (which was news to him) and my marriage, not about last night's near tragedy. He was interrupted by the slamming of a car door. Two policemen appeared with the vicar around the bend of the avenue. They paused when they saw us on the bridge, and Mr. Bryanston raised a hand in a gesture conveying both relief and greeting; something, too, of a blessing.

"If we could just tell them the bare outline now, and let Emerson handle the rest?" It was Francis speaking again, rapidly. "What I'm most concerned with is what I'm to tell my father."

"It seems to me"—Rob sounded his old calm, practical self—"that there's no need to add to your dad's troubles by telling him what your brothers were up to. We'll think up some story for him, just as soon as we know where we stand with the law." He paused, glancing at me. "Something else I'd better say. It looks as if this lot's going to land on you. We'd had plans, Bryony and me, to emigrate. But we can't leave you in a mess like this. If you want us to, we'll stay around and help you get things straight. Bryony thinks that, with the discovery we made this morning, the place might even start to pay its way. We'll help you give it a push, mate, and then it's all yours." He slanted another look down at me. "Eh, love?"

"Yes, Rob." I looked around me at the shining water, at the grassy banks and the tops of the orchard trees beyond. Then I looked again at Rob Ashley, the heir to all this. If he chose, when he knew what he did not yet know of the past, to stay here, to push the Court back onto the map in whatever guise—National Trust monument, market garden, farmstead, building site—I would help him do it. If he chose to claim it for himself and stay at Ashley for the rest of our lives, I would do that, too. But if he chose in the end to leave the care of the place to Francis, who loved it . . .

Yes, that would be it. When I had told him everything, I knew that he would still say, with that tranquil expression, and the dark eyes fixed on his own, our own, far horizon, "Francis Ashley, mate, it's all yours."

265

## Interview with Mary Stewart

"You're going to think I'm pixilated if I go on talking like this," said Mary Stewart. "Come on, let's order." Slim and elegant in her smart camel suit, she looked lively, worldly, anything but pixilated. We were about to have lunch in Edinburgh's famous Café Royal, and the waiter's arrival with the menu had interrupted us in a discussion of precognition, telepathy, and other wonders that appear in *Touch Not the Cat.*

Her husband, Frederick Henry Stewart, gave her the book's title. "Touch not the cat bot a glove," she told me, was the motto of his clan, Chattan. Mary Stewart's private life and her phenomenal

*Mary Stewart and Troy*

career have been closely intertwined ever since the summer's day in 1945 when as a young lecturer in English at Durham University she married the lecturer in geology. When she began to write, not long after that, she found that "storytelling came as naturally as leaves to a tree. It was a pity (I told myself) that I had wasted so much time." Success burst upon her with her first novel, *Madam, Will You Talk?* in 1956, and continues to greet every book she produces.

The Stewarts have been from the beginning ardent admirers of each other's work. They love travelling together; whether they are geologists digging or author-historians delving or just two people out for long country rambles, the one observes the world with a scientist's eye, the other with an artist's. "He believes in nothing until it is proved; I believe in everything until it is disproved." In 1974 the eminent professor was knighted for his scientific services to the nation. This award had the effect of turning the eminent writer into Lady Stewart. It changed Mary Stewart's bright, warm, informal self not at all.

After lunch, because I had a couple of hours before plane time, this thoughtful and hospitable lady took me "home to relax". The Stewarts live in a delightful nineteenth-century terrace house which perfectly blends elegance and homeliness. But it was the garden, Mary Stewart's own creation, that took my breath away. Not much more than thirty yards square, it is laid out to suggest unimaginable depths. Strange conifers rise up in unexpected places; orchids twirl and dance in the little greenhouse. This garden reflects the magical side of Mary Stewart, the side that played such a large part in her two most recent books, *The Crystal Cave* and *The Hollow Hills* (both about the magician Merlin and King Arthur of English legend)—and now, of course, in *Touch Not the Cat*.

Mary Stewart tells many strange stories connected with the Arthurian work—how she imagined wells, water mills, burial grounds only to find that they actually existed. Once she envisaged a river curling around the foot of a certain hill. She was disappointed, when visiting the spot, to find the river several hundred yards out of place. Her resident geologist, coming down on the same side as the artist, was able to assure her that the river would originally have run exactly where she had imagined it.

Before I left for London I was introduced to the cats, Blaise and Badger. Two more canny-looking feline characters I have seldom seen. Blaise has an interesting history. His predecessor was a very fine fellow called Troy, whose demise after eighteen years left his owner desolate. Eventually, however, Mary Stewart braced herself to the business of finding a new kitten. She telephoned nearly every pet shop in Edinburgh before one man said he had a kitten that just might do. She checked the name and address and was surprised to find this was where she had bought Troy. She was more surprised to find the new kitten not only sitting in the very cage Troy had sat in, but looking the image of him. At home, her powers of surprise exhausted, she watched with cool detachment as Blaise walked around the house, obviously knowing his way, and finally settled down in Troy's old corner. . . .

Odd things *do* happen, as the author of *Touch Not the Cat* will tell you herself.                                                                —N.D.B.

Illustrated by Don Stivers     Published by Michael Joseph, London

# Vets Might Fly

A condensation of the book by

## JAMES HERRIOT

with extracts from *If Only They Could Talk, It Shouldn't
Happen to a Vet, Let Sleeping Vets Lie,* and *Vet in Harness*

James Herriot, the young vet who practises among the green hills of Yorkshire, is thrown into a totally new environment in the latest of his engaging books. Newly married, he reluctantly leaves Helen and his home in Darrowby for wartime life as a lowly AC2 in the RAF. He describes his service adventures with characteristic humour, but more often his thoughts return nostalgically to his days as a vet and he introduces us to a host of new characters, both animal and human.

James Herriot combines dedication to the care of animals with an unequalled capacity for seeing the comic side of life. His appreciation of the rich rewards of his work, with its triumphs and tragedies, is shared with every reader of this delightful book.

"Full of warmth, wisdom and a real breath of the countryside."—*The Times*

# Chapter One

"Move!" bawled the RAF drill corporal. "Come on, speed it up!" He sprinted effortlessly to the rear of the gasping, panting column of men and urged us on from there.

I was somewhere in the middle, jog-trotting laboriously with the rest and wondering how much longer I could keep going. And as my ribs heaved agonizingly and my leg muscles protested I tried to work out just how many miles we had run.

I had suspected nothing when we lined up outside our billets. We weren't clad in PT kit but in woollen pullovers and regulation slacks, and it seemed unlikely that anything violent was imminent. Also the corporal, a cheerful little cockney, had a kind face and appeared to regard us as his brothers.

"Awright, lads," he cried, smiling over the fifty new airmen. "We're just going to trot round the park, so follow me. Le-eft turn! At the double, qui-ick march! 'Eft-'ight, 'eft-'ight, 'eft-'ight!"

That had been a long, long time ago and we were still reeling through the London streets with never a sign of a park anywhere. The thought hammered in my brain that I had been under the impression that I was fit. A country vet, especially in the Yorkshire Dales, never had the chance to get out of condition; he was always on the move, wrestling with the big animals, walking for miles between the fellside barns; he was hard and tough. That's what I thought.

But now other reflections began to creep in. My few months of married life with Helen before the war came had been so much

271

lotus eating. She was too good a cook and I too faithful a disciple of her art. Just lounging by our bedsitter's fireside was the sweetest of all occupations. I had tried to ignore the disappearance of my abdominal muscles, the sagging of my pectorals, but it was all coming home to me now.

"It's not far now, lads," the corporal chirped from the rear, but he struck no responsive chords in our toiling group. He had said it several times before and we had stopped believing him.

But this time he really meant it. As we turned into yet another street I could see iron railings and trees at the far end. The relief was inexpressible. My legs were beginning to seize up and I would just about have the strength to make it through the gates.

We passed under an arch of branches which still bore a few autumn leaves, and stopped. But the corporal was waving us on. "Come on, lads, round the track!"

He pointed to a broad earthen path which circled the park. We stared at him. He couldn't be serious! A storm of protest broke out. "Aw, no, corp. . . !" "Have a heart corp. . . !"

The smile vanished from the little man's face. "Get movin', I said! Faster, faster . . . one-two, one-two."

As I stumbled forward over the black earth between borders of sooty rhododendrons and tired grass I just couldn't believe it. It was all too sudden. Three days ago I was in Darrowby and half of me was still back there on the green hills, with Helen. Bitter thoughts assailed me. You left a loving, pregnant wife and a happy home to serve king and country and this was how they treated you. It wasn't fair.

My first introduction to the RAF had been at Lord's cricket ground. Masses of forms to fill in, medicals, then the issue of an enormous pile of kit. I was billeted in a block of flats in St. John's Wood—luxurious before the lush fittings had been removed. But they couldn't take away the heavy bathroom ware and one of our blessings was the unlimited hot water that gushed out at a touch.

After that first crowded day I retired to one of those green-tiled sanctuaries and lathered myself with a new bar of a famous toilet soap which Helen had put in my bag. I have never been able to use that soap since. The merest whiff of its scent jerks me back to that first night away from my wife and to the feeling I had then. It was a dull, empty ache which never really went away.

On the second day we were wakened by the hideous 6:00 a.m. clattering of dustbin lids; I hadn't really expected a bugle but I found this noise intolerable. We marched endlessly: lectures, meals, inoculations. I was used to syringes but the very sight of them was too much for many of my friends—especially when the doctor took the blood samples; one look at the dark fluid flowing from their veins and the young men toppled quietly from their chairs, while the orderlies, grinning cheerfully, bore them away.

We ate in a huge dining room at the London Zoo and our meals were made interesting by the chatter of monkeys and the roar of lions in the background. But in between it was march, march, march, with our new boots giving us hell.

And on this third day the whole thing was still a blur. The night before I had dreamed of Darrowby. I was back in old Mr. Dakin's cow byre. The farmer's patient eyes in the long, drooping-moustached face looked down at me from his stooping height.

"It looks as though it's up wi' awd Blossom, then," he said, and rested his hand briefly on the old cow's back. It was an enormous, work-swollen hand. Mr. Dakin's gaunt frame carried little flesh but the grossly thickened fingers bore testimony to a life of toil.

I dried off the needle and dropped it into the metal box where I carried my suture materials, scalpels and blades. "Well, it's up to you of course, Mr. Dakin, but this is the third time I've had to stitch her teats and I'm afraid it's going to keep on happening."

"Aye, it's just the shape she is." The farmer bent and examined the row of knots along the four-inch scar. "By gaw, you wouldn't believe it could mek such a mess—just another cow standin' on it."

"A cow's hoof is sharp," I said. "It's nearly like a knife coming down."

That was the worst of very old cows. Their udders dropped so far that when they lay down in their stalls the vital milk-producing organ was pushed away to one side into the path of the neighbouring animals. If it wasn't Mabel on the right standing on it, it was Buttercup on the other side.

"Aye, well," he said. "Ah reckon t'awd lass doesn't owe me anythin'. Ah remember the night she was born, twelve years ago. She was out of awd Daisy and ah carried her out of this very byre on a sack and the snow was comin' down hard. Sin' then ah wouldn't like to count how many thousand gallons o' milk she's turned out—she's still givin' four a day. Naw, she doesn't owe me a thing."

As if she knew she was the topic of conversation Blossom turned her head and looked at him. She was the classic picture of an ancient bovine; as fleshless as her owner, with jutting pelvic bones, splayed, overgrown feet and, beneath her, the udder drooping forlornly almost to the floor.

She resembled her owner, too, in her quiet, patient demeanour. I had infiltrated her teat with a local anaesthetic before stitching but I don't think she would have moved if I hadn't used any. Stitching teats puts a vet in the ideal position to be kicked, with his head down in front of the hind feet, but there was no danger with Blossom. She had never kicked anybody in her life.

Mr. Dakin blew out his cheeks. "Well, there's nowt else for it. She'll have to go. I'll tell Jack Dodson to pick 'er up for the fat stock market on Thursday. She'll be a bit tough for eatin' but ah reckon she'll make a few steak pies."

He was trying to joke but he was unable to smile as he looked at the old cow. Behind him, beyond the open door, the green hillside ran down to the river and the spring sunshine touched the broad sweep of the shallows with a million dancing lights. A beach of bleached stones gleamed bone-white against the long stretch of grassy bank which rolled up to the pastures lining the valley floor.

I had often felt that this smallholding would be an ideal place to live. I remarked on this once to Mr. Dakin and the old man turned to me with a wry smile.

"Aye, but the view's not very sustainin'," he said.

It happened that I was called back to the farm on the following Thursday to "cleanse" a cow and was in the byre when Dodson the drover called to pick up Blossom. He had collected a group of fat bullocks and cows from other farms and they stood, watched by one of his men, on the road high above.

"Nah then, Mr. Dakin," he cried as he bustled in. "It's easy to see which one you want me to tek."

The farmer went up between the cows and gently rubbed Blossom's forehead. "Aye, this is the one, Jack." He hesitated, then undid the chain round her neck. "Off ye go, awd lass," he murmured, and the old animal turned and made her way placidly from the stall.

"Aye, come on with ye!" shouted the dealer, poking his stick against the cow's rump.

"Doan't hit 'er!" barked Mr. Dakin.

Dodson looked at him in surprise. "Ah never 'it 'em, you know that. Just send 'em on, like."

"Ah knaw, ah knaw, Jack, but you won't need your stick for this 'un. She'll go wherever ye want—allus has done."

Blossom confirmed his words as she ambled through the door and, at a gesture from the farmer, turned along the track.

The old man and I stood watching as the cow made her way unhurriedly up the hill, Jack Dodson in his long khaki smock sauntering behind her. As the path wound behind a clump of sparse trees man and beast disappeared. Mr. Dakin turned to me quickly. "Right, Mr. Herriot, we'll get on wi' our job, then. I'll bring your hot watter."

The farmer was silent as I soaped my arm. If there is one thing more disagreeable than removing the bovine afterbirth it is watching somebody else doing it, and I always try to maintain a conversation as I grope around inside. But this time it was hard work. Mr. Dakin held the cow's tail and blew smoke from his pipe, responding to my sallies on the weather, cricket and the price of milk with a series of grunts.

But at last it was finished. I untied the sack from my middle and pulled my shirt down over my head. The conversation had died and the silence was almost oppressive as we opened the byre door.

Mr. Dakin paused, his hand on the latch. "What's that?" he said.

From somewhere on the hillside I could hear the clip clop of a cow's feet. There were two ways to the farm and the sound came from a narrow track which joined the main road half a mile beyond the other entrance. As we listened Blossom rounded a rocky outcrop, moving at a brisk trot, great udder swinging, eyes fixed purposefully on the open door behind us.

"What the hangment. . . ?" Mr. Dakin burst out, but the old cow brushed past us and marched without hesitation into the stall which she had occupied for all those years. She sniffed inquiringly at the empty hay rack and looked round at her owner.

Heavy boots clattered suddenly outside and Jack Dodson panted his way through the door.

"Oh, you're there, ye awd beggar!" he gasped. "Ah thought I'd lost ye!" He turned to the farmer. "By gaw, I'm sorry, Mr. Dakin. She must 'ave turned off at t'top of your other path. Ah never saw her go."

The farmer shrugged. "It's awright, Jack. It's not your fault."

"That's soon mended anyway." The drover grinned and moved towards Blossom. "Come on, lass, let's have ye out o' there again."

But he halted as Mr. Dakin held an arm in front of him.

There was a long silence as Dodson and I looked in surprise at the farmer. Then, still without speaking, Mr. Dakin moved unhurriedly to the end of the byre and returned with a forkful of hay which he tossed expertly into the rack. This was what Blossom was waiting for. She jerked a mouthful from between the spars and began to chew with quiet satisfaction.

"What's to do, Mr. Dakin?" the drover cried in bewilderment. "They're waiting for me at t'mart!"

The farmer tapped out his pipe on the half door and began to fill it from a battered tin. "Ah'm sorry to waste your time, Jack, but you'll have to go without 'er. Ye'll think I'm daft, but that's how it is. T'awd lass has come 'ome and she's stoppin' 'ome." He directed a look of flat finality at the drover. "Ah'll pay ye for your time, Jack. Put it down on ma bill."

Dodson nodded a couple of times then shuffled from the byre. Mr. Dakin applied a match to his pipe and drew deeply.

"Mr. Herriot," he said, "do you ever feel when summat happened that it was meant to happen?"

"Yes, I do, Mr. Dakin. I often feel that."

"Aye, well, that's how I felt when Blossom came down that hill." He reached out and scratched the root of the cow's tail. "Ah've

276

had an idea. Just came to me when you were tekkin' away that cleansin' and I thowt I was ower late."

"An idea?"

"Aye," the old man nodded. "I can put two or three calves on to 'er instead of milkin' 'er. The old stable is empty—she can live in there where there's nobody to stand on 'er awd tits."

I laughed. "You're right, Mr. Dakin. She'd be safe in the stable and she'd suckle three calves easily. She could pay her way."

"Well, as ah said, it's matterless. After all them years she doesn't owe me a thing." A gentle smile spread over the seamed face. "Main thing is, she's come 'ome."

MY EYES WERE shut most of the time now as I blundered round the park and when I opened them a red mist swirled. But it is incredible what the human frame will stand and at last the iron gates appeared once more under their arch of sooty branches.

"Good lads!" the corporal called out, cheerful as ever. "You're doin' fine. Now we're just going to 'ave a little hoppin' on the spot."

Incredulous wails rose from our demoralized band but the corporal was unabashed.

"Feet together now. Up! Up! Up! That's no good, come on, get some height into it! Up! Up!"

This was the final absurdity. My chest was a flaming cavern of agony. These people were supposed to be making me fit and instead they were doing irreparable damage to my heart and lungs. And as, with the last of my strength, I launched myself into the air it came to me suddenly why I had dreamed about Blossom last night.

I wanted to go home too.

## Chapter Two

There was a lot of shouting in the RAF. The NCO's always seemed to be shouting at me or at somebody else and a lot of them had impressively powerful voices. They reminded me vividly of Len Hampson.

One day I had been on the way to Len's farm and on an impulse I pulled up the car and leaned for a moment on the wheel. It was a hot still day in late summer and this was one of the softer corners of the Dales, sheltered by the enclosing fells. Here, great trees, oak, elm and sycamore in full rich leaf, stood in gentle majesty in the green hollows, their branches quite still in the windless air.

Through the open window drifted the scents of summer; warm grass, clover and the sweetness of hidden flowers. In all the grassy miles around me I could see no movement nor could I hear anything except the fleeting hum of a bee, the distant bleating of a sheep, and from somewhere in the branches high above that most soothing of sounds, the cooing of a wood-pigeon.

Then, although the farm was two fields away, I heard Len Hampson's voice. He wasn't calling the cattle home or anything like that. He was just conversing with his family as he always did in a long tireless shout.

I drove on to the farm and he opened the gate to let me into the yard.

"NOW THEN, MR. HERRIOT," he bawled. "IT'S A GRAND MORNIN'."

The blast of sound drove me back a step but his three sons smiled contentedly. No doubt they were used to it.

I stayed at a safe distance. "You want me to see a pig."

"AYE, A GOOD BACON PIG. GONE RIGHT OFF IT. HASN'T ATE NOWT FOR TWO DAYS."

We went into the pig pen and it was easy to pick out my patient. Most of the big white occupants careered around at the sight of a stranger but one of them stood quietly in a corner.

It isn't often a pig will stand unresisting as you take its temperature but this one never stirred. There was only a slight fever but the animal had the look of doom about it; back slightly arched, unwilling to move, eyes withdrawn and anxious.

I looked up at Len Hampson's red-faced bulk. "Did this start suddenly or gradually?" I asked.

"RIGHT SUDDEN!" In the confined space the full-throated yell was deafening. "HE WERE AS RIGHT AS NINEPENCE ON MONDAY NIGHT AND LIKE THIS ON TUESDAY MORNIN'."

I felt my way over the pig's abdomen. The musculature was tense and boardlike and the abdominal contents were difficult to palpate because of this, but the whole area was tender to the touch.

"I've seen them like this before," I said. "This pig has a ruptured bowel. They do it when they are fighting or jostling each other, especially when they are full after a meal."

"WHAT'S GOIN' TO 'APPEN THEN?"

"Well, the food material has leaked into the abdomen causing peritonitis. I'm afraid the chances of recovery are very small."

He took off his cap, scratched his bald head and replaced the tattered headgear. "GOOD PIG AN' ALL. IS IT 'OPELESS?"

"Yes, I'm afraid it's pretty hopeless. They usually eat very little and just waste away. It would really be best to slaughter him."

"NAY, AH ALLUS LIKE TO 'AVE A GO. ISN'T THERE SUMMAT WE CAN DO? WHERE THERE'S LIFE THERE'S 'OPE THA KNAWS."

I smiled, "I suppose there's always some hope, Mr. Hampson."

"WELL THEN, LET'S GET ON. LET'S TRY!"

"All right." I shrugged. "He's not really in acute pain—more discomfort—so I suppose there's no harm in treating him. I'll leave you a course of powders."

As I pushed my way from the pen I couldn't help noticing the superb sleek condition of the other pigs.

"My word," I said. "These pigs are in grand fettle. I've never seen a better lot. You must feed them well."

It was a mistake. Enthusiasm added many decibels to his volume. "AYE!" he bellowed. "YOU'VE GOT TO GIVE STOCK A BIT O' GOOD STUFF TO MEK 'EM DO RIGHT!"

My head was still ringing when I reached the car and handed over a packet of my faithful sulphonamide powders. They had done great things but I didn't expect much here.

IT WAS STRANGE that I should go straight from the chief shouter of the practice to the chief whisperer. Elijah Wentworth made all his communications *sotto voce*.

I found Mr. Wentworth hosing down his cow byre and he turned and looked at me with his habitual serious expression. He was a

279

tall, thin man, very precise in his speech and ways and though he was a hard-working farmer he didn't look like one. This impression was heightened by his clothes which were more suited to office work than his rough trade.

A fairly new trilby hat sat straight on his head as he came over to me. I was able to examine it thoroughly because he came so close that we were almost touching noses.

He took a quick look around him. "Mr. Herriot," he whispered. "I've got a real bad case." He spoke always as though every pronouncement was of the utmost gravity and secrecy.

"Oh, I'm sorry to hear that. What's the trouble?"

"Fine big bullock, Mr. Herriot. Goin' down fast." He moved in closer till he could murmur directly into my ear. "I suspect TB." He backed away, face drawn.

"That doesn't sound so good," I said. "Where is he?"

The farmer crooked a finger and I followed him into a loose box. The bullock, a Hereford cross that should have weighed about ten hundredweight, was gaunt and emaciated. But I was beginning to develop a clinical sense and it didn't look like TB to me.

"Is he coughing?" I asked.

"No, never coughs, but he's a bit skittered."

I went over the animal carefully. "I think he's got liver fluke, Mr. Wentworth, I'll take a dung sample and have it examined for fluke eggs but I want to treat him right away."

"Liver fluke? Where would he pick that up?"

"Usually from a wet pasture. Where has he been running lately?"

The farmer pointed through the door. "Over yonder. I'll show you."

I walked with him through a couple of gates into a wide flat field lying at the base of the fell. The squelchy feel of the turf and the tufts of bog grass told the whole story.

"This is just the place for it," I said. "As you know, it's a parasite which infests the liver, but during its life cycle it has to pass through a snail and that snail can only live where there is water."

He nodded slowly and solemnly several times then began to look around him and I knew he was going to say something. Again he came very close then scanned the horizon anxiously. In all directions the grassland stretched empty and bare for miles but he still seemed worried he might be overheard.

We were almost cheek to cheek as he breathed the words into my ear. "Ah know who's to blame for this."

"Really? Who is that?"

He made another swift check to ensure that nobody had sprung up through the ground, then: "It's me landlord. Won't do anything for me. Been goin' to drain this field for years but done nowt."

I moved back. "Ah well, I can't help that, Mr. Wentworth. In any case there are other things you can do. You can kill the snails with copper sulphate—I'll tell you about that later—but in the meantime I want to dose your bullock."

I had some hexachlorethane with me in the car and I mixed it in a bottle of water and administered it to the animal. Despite his bulk he offered no resistance as I held his lower jaw and poured the medicine down his throat.

"He's very weak, isn't he?" I said.

The farmer gave me a haggard look. "He is that. I doubt he's a goner."

"Oh don't give up hope, Mr. Wentworth. I know he looks terrible but if it is fluke then the treatment will do a lot for him. Let me know how he goes on."

IT WAS ABOUT a month later, on a market day, and I was strolling among the stalls which packed the cobbles. In front of the entrance to the Drovers' Arms the usual press of farmers stood chatting among themselves, talking business with cattle dealers and corn merchants, while the shouts of the stallholders sounded over everything.

I was particularly fascinated by the man in charge of the sweet stall. He held up a paper bag and stuffed into it handfuls of assorted sweetmeats while he kept up a nonstop brazen-voiced commentary.

"Lovely peppermint drops! Delicious liquorice allsorts! How about some sugar candies! A couple o' bars o' chocolate! Let's 'ave some butterscotch an' all! Chuck in a beautiful slab o' Turkish Delight!" Then holding the bulging bag aloft in triumph, " 'Ere! 'Ere! Who'll give me a tanner for the lot?"

281

Amazing, I thought as I moved on. How did he do it? I was passing the door of the Drovers' when a familiar voice hailed me.

"HEY! MR. HERRIOT!" There was no mistaking Len Hampson. He hove in front of me, red-faced and cheerful. "REMEMBER THAT PIG YE DOCTORED FOR ME?" He had clearly consumed a few market-day beers and his voice was louder than ever.

The packed mass of farmers pricked up their ears. There is nothing so intriguing as the ailments of another farmer's livestock.

"Yes, of course, Mr. Hampson," I replied.

"WELL 'E NEVER DID NO GOOD!" bawled Len.

I could see the farmers' faces lighting up. It is more interesting still when things go wrong.

"Really? Well, I'm sorry."

"NAW 'E DIDN'T. AH'VE NEVER SEEN A PIG GO DOWN AS FAST!"

"Oh, what a pity. But if you recall I rather expected . . ."

"WENT DOWN TO SKIN AND BONE 'E DID!" The great bellow rolled over the market-place drowning the puny cries of the stallholders. In fact the man with the sweets had suspended operations and was listening with as much interest as the others.

I looked around me uneasily. I realized Len wasn't in the least complaining. He was just telling me, but for all that I wished he would stop. "Well, thank you for letting me know," I said. "Now I really must be off . . ."

"AH DON'T KNOW WHAT THEM POWDERS WERE YOU GAVE 'IM."

I cleared my throat. "Actually they were . . ."

"THEY DID 'IM NO BLOODY GOOD ANY ROAD!"

"I see. Well, as I say, I have to run. . . ."

"AH GOT MALLOCK TO KNOCK 'IM ON T'HEAD LAST WEEK."

"Oh dear. . . ."

"WELL, GOOD DAY TO YE, MR. HERRIOT." He turned and walked away, leaving a quivering silence behind him.

With an uncomfortable feeling that I was the centre of attention I was about to retreat hastily when I felt a gentle hand on my arm. I turned and saw Elijah Wentworth.

"Mr. Herriot," he whispered. "About that bullock."

I stared at him, struck by the coincidence. The farmers stared, too, but expectantly.

"Yes. Mr. Wentworth?"

"Well now, I'll tell you." He came very near and breathed into my ear. "It was like a miracle. He began to pick up straight away after you treated him."

I stepped back. "Oh marvellous! But speak up, will you. I can't quite hear you." I looked around hopefully.

He came after me again and put his chin on my shoulder. "Yes, I don't know what you gave 'im but it was wonderful stuff. I could hardly believe it. Every day I looked at 'im he had put on a bit more."

"Great! But do speak a little louder," I said eagerly.

"He's as fat as butter now." The almost inaudible murmur wafted on my cheek. "Ah'm sure he'll get top grade at the auction mart."

I backed away again. "Yes . . . yes . . . what was that you said?"

"I was sure he was dyin', Mr. Herriot, but you saved him by your skill," he said, every word pianissimo, sighed against my face.

The farmers had heard nothing and, their interest evaporating, they began to talk among themselves. Then as the man with the sweets started to fill his bags and shout again Mr. Wentworth moved in and confided softly and secretly into my private ear.

"Mr. Herriot, that was the most brilliant and marvellous cure that I 'ave ever seen."

# Chapter Three

I suppose it had been a little thoughtless of me to allow my scalpel to flash quite so close to Rory O'Hagan's fly buttons.

The incident came back to me as I sat in my room in St. John's Wood reading Black's Veterinary Dictionary. It was a bulky volume to carry around and my RAF friends used to rib me about my "vest pocket edition" but I had resolved to keep reading it in spare moments to remind me of my real life.

I had reached the letter "C" and as the word "Castration" looked up at me from the page I was jerked back to Rory.

I was castrating piglets. The Irish farm worker's young boss was catching the little animals and handing them to Rory who held them upside down, gripped between his thighs. There were several litters to do and I was in a hurry.

"For God's sake, have a care, Mr. Herriot!" Rory gasped at last.

I looked up from my work. "What's wrong, Rory?"

"Watch what you're doin' with that bloody knife! You'll do me a mischief afore you've finished!"

"Aye, be careful, Mr. Herriot," the young farmer cried. "His missus ud never forgive ye." He burst into a loud peal of laughter, and the Irishman grinned sheepishly.

But the momentary inattention was my undoing. It sent my knife-blade slicing across my left forefinger. The razor sharp edge went deep and in an instant the entire neighbourhood seemed flooded with my blood. I thought I would never staunch the flow, and after a long session of self-doctoring from the car boot I finally drove away with my finger swathed in the biggest, clumsiest dressing I had ever seen, a large pad of cotton wool held in place with an enormous length of three-inch bandage.

I left the farm at about five o'clock of a late December day, the light gone early and the stars beginning to show in a frosty sky. I drove slowly, the enormous finger jutting upwards from the wheel. I was within half a mile of Darrowby when a car approached, went past, then I heard a squeal of brakes as it stopped and began to double back. It passed me again, drew into the side and I saw a frantically waving arm. I pulled up and a young man jumped from the driving seat and ran towards me. His voice was breathless, panic-stricken. "Are you the vet?"

"Yes, I am."

"Oh thank God! We're passing through on the way to Manchester and we've been to your surgery . . . they said you were out this way . . . described your car. Please help us!"

"What's the trouble?"

"It's our dog . . . in the back of the car. He's got a ball stuck in his throat. I . . . I think he might be dead."

284

I was out of my seat and running along the road before he had finished. It was a big white saloon and in the darkness of the back seat several little heads were silhouetted against the glass.

I tore open the door and dimly discerned a large dog spread over the knees of four small children. "Oh Daddy, Benny's dead, he's dead!"

"Let's have him out," I gasped.

As the young man pulled on the fore legs I supported the body and we dragged it into the headlights' glare. I saw a huge, beautiful collie in his luxuriant prime, mouth gaping, tongue lolling, eyes staring lifelessly at nothing. He wasn't breathing.

The young father took one look then gripped his head with both hands. "Oh God, oh God . . ." From within the car I heard the quiet sobbing of his wife and the piercing cries from the back. "Benny . . . Benny . . ."

I grabbed the man's shoulder and shouted at him. "What did you say about a ball?"

"It's in his throat . . . I've had my fingers in his mouth for ages but I couldn't move it."

I pushed my hand into the mouth and felt a sphere of hard solid rubber not much bigger than a golf ball, jammed like a cork in the pharynx, effectively blocking the trachea. I scrabbled feverishly at the wet smoothness but there was nothing to get hold of. It took me about three seconds to realize that no human agency would ever get the ball out that way. So I withdrew my hands, braced both thumbs behind the angle of the lower jaw and pushed.

The ball shot forth, bounced on the frosty road and rolled onto the grass verge. I touched the corneal surface of the dog's eye. No reflex. I slumped to my knees, burdened by hopeless regret that I hadn't the chance to do this just a bit sooner. The only function I could perform now was to take the body back to the surgery for disposal. I couldn't allow the family to drive to Manchester with a dead dog. As I passed my hand along the richly coloured coat over the ribs the vast bandaged finger stood out like a symbol of my helplessness.

It was when I was gazing dully at the finger, the heel of my hand resting in an intercostal space, that I felt the faintest flutter.

I jerked upright with a hoarse cry. "His heart's still beating! He's not gone yet!" I began to work on the dog with all I had. And out there on that lonely country road it wasn't much. No stimulant injections, no oxygen cylinders or intratracheal tubes. But I depressed his chest with my palms every three seconds in the old-fashioned way, willing the dog to breathe. Every now and then I blew desperately down the throat or probed between the ribs for that almost imperceptible beat.

I don't know which I noticed first, the slight twitch of an eyelid or the small lift of the ribs which pulled the icy Yorkshire air into his lungs. Maybe they both happened at once but from that moment everything was dreamlike and wonderful. I lost count of time as I sat there while the breathing became deep and regular and the animal began to be aware of his surroundings; and by the time he started to look around him and twitch his tail tentatively I realized suddenly that I was stiff-jointed and almost frozen to the spot. With difficulty I got up and watched as the collie also staggered to his feet. The young father ushered him round to the back where he was received with screams of delight.

The man seemed stunned. Throughout the recovery he had kept muttering, "You just flicked that ball out . . . just flicked it out . . ." And when he turned to me before leaving he appeared to be still in a state of shock.

"I don't . . . I don't know how to thank you," he said huskily. "It's a miracle." He leaned against the car for a second. "And now what is your fee? How much do I owe you?"

I rubbed my chin. I had used no drugs. The only expenditure had been time.

"Five bob," I said. "And never let him play with such a little ball again."

He handed the money over, shook my hand and drove away. His wife, who had never left her place, waved as she left, but my greatest reward was in the last shadowy glimpse of the back seat with little arms twined around the dog, hugging him ecstatically.

Vets often wonder after a patient's recovery just how much credit they might take. Maybe it would have got better without treatment —it happened sometimes; it was difficult to be sure.

But when you know without a shadow of a doubt that, even without doing anything clever, you have pulled an animal back from the brink of death it is a satisfaction which lingers, flowing like balm over the discomforts and frustrations of veterinary practice, making everything right.

Yet, in the case of Benny the whole thing had an unreal quality. I never even glimpsed the faces of those children nor that of their mother huddled in the front seat. Even the dog, in the unnatural glare of the headlights, was a blurred memory.

It seemed the family had the same feeling because a week later I had a pleasant letter from the mother. She apologized for skulking out of the way, she thanked me for saving the life of their beloved dog, and she finished with the regret that she hadn't even asked me my name.

Yes, it had been a strange episode, and not only were those people unaware of my name but I'd like to bet they would fail to recognize me if they saw me again, or I them.

In fact, looking back at the affair, the only thing which stood out was my great white-bound digit which had hovered constantly over the scene. I am sure that is what the family remembered best about me because of the way the mother's letter began.

"Dear Vet with bandaged finger . . ."

## Chapter Four

The fog swirled over the heads of the marching men: a London fog, thick, yellow, metallic on the tongue. I couldn't see the head of the column, only a glimmer of light from the swinging lantern carried by the leader.

This 6.30 a.m. walk to breakfast was just about the worst part of the day, when my morale was low and thoughts of home rose painfully.

We used to have fogs in Darrowby, but they were country fogs, different from this. One morning I drove out on my rounds with the headlights blazing against the curtain ahead, heading up the Dale, climbing steadily. The engine pulled against the rising ground,

288

and then quite suddenly the fog thinned to a shimmering silvery mist and was gone.

And there, above the pall, the sun was dazzling and the long green line of the fells rose before me, thrusting exultantly into a sky of summer blue.

Spellbound, I drove upwards into the bright splendour, staring through the windscreen as though I had never seen it all before: the bronze of the dead bracken spilling down the grassy flanks of the hills, the dark smudges of trees, the grey farmhouses and the endless pattern of walls creeping to the heather above.

I was in a rush as usual but I had to stop. I pulled up in a gateway, and, gulping the sweet air, I gazed about me gratefully at the clean green land where I worked and made my living.

I could have stayed there, wandering round. But reluctantly I got back into the car. I had an appointment to keep, with a horse.

Probably the most dramatic occurrence in the history of veterinary practice was the disappearance of the draught horse. And I was one of those who was there to see it happen. When I first came to Darrowby the tractor had already begun to take over, but tradition dies hard in the agricultural world and there were still a lot of horses around.

I should think in my first two years I treated farm horses nearly every day and though I never was and never will be an equine expert there was a strange thrill in meeting with the age-old conditions whose names rang down almost from mediaeval times. Quittor, fistulous withers, poll evil, thrush, shoulder slip—vets had been wrestling with them for hundreds of years, using very much the same drugs and procedures as myself. Armed with my firing iron and box of blister I plunged determinedly into what had always been the surging mainstream of veterinary life.

In less than three years the stream had dwindled, not exactly to a trickle but certainly to the stage where the final dry-up was in sight. So that then, as I looked at the three-year-old gelding, it occurred to me that this sort of thing wasn't happening as often as it used to. He had a long tear in his flank where he had caught himself on barbed wire and it gaped open whenever he moved. There was no getting away from the fact that it had to be stitched.

The horse was tied by the head in his stall. One of the farm men, a hefty six-footer, took a tight hold of the head collar and leaned back against the manger as I puffed some iodoform into the wound. The horse didn't seem to mind, which was a comfort because he was a massive animal. I threaded my needle with a length of silk, lifted one of the lips of the wound and passed the needle through. This was going to be no trouble, I thought.

But as I was drawing the needle through the flap at the other side the gelding made a convulsive leap and I felt as though a great wind had whistled across the front of my body. Then, strangely, he was standing there against the wooden boards as if nothing had happened.

It is surprising how quickly those great muscular legs can whip out. My needle and silk were nowhere to be seen, the big man at the horse's head was staring at me with wide eyes in a chalk white face, and my gabardine mac looked as if somebody had taken a razor blade and painstakingly cut the material into narrow strips. The great iron-shod hoof had missed my legs by an inch or two, but my mac was a write-off.

I was standing there looking around me in a kind of stupor when I heard a cheerful hail from the doorway.

"Now then, Mr. Herriot, what's he done at you?" Cliff Tyreman, the old horseman, looked me up and down with a mixture of amusement and asperity.

"He's nearly put me in hospital, Cliff," I replied shakily. "About the closest near miss I've ever had. I just felt the wind of it."

"What were you tryin' to do?"

"Stitch that wound, but I'm not going to try any more. I'm off to the surgery to get a chloroform muzzle."

The little man looked shocked. "You don't need no chloroform. I'll haud him and you'll have no trouble."

"I'm sorry, Cliff." I began to put away my suture materials, scissors and powder. "You're a good bloke, I know, but he's had one go at me and he's not getting another chance. I don't want to be lame for the rest of my life."

The horseman's small, wiry frame seemed to bunch into a ball of aggressions. "I've never heard owt as daft in me life." Then he swung round on the big man who was still hanging on to the horse's head. "Come on out o'there, Bob! You're that bloody scared you're upsetting t'oss. Come on out of it and let me have 'im!"

Bob gratefully left the head and moved with care along the side of the horse, passing Cliff on the way. The little man's head didn't reach his shoulders.

Cliff took hold of the head collar and regarded the big animal with the disapproving stare of a schoolmaster at a naughty child. The horse laid back his ears and began to plunge about the stall, but he came to rest quickly as the little man punched him furiously in the ribs.

"Get stood up straight there, ye big bugger. What's the matter with ye?" Again Cliff planted his tiny fist against the swelling barrel of the chest, a puny blow which the animal could scarcely have felt but which reduced him to quivering submission. "Try to kick, would you, eh? I'll bloody fettle you!" He shook the head collar and fixed the horse with a hypnotic stare as he spoke. Then he turned to me. "You can come and do your job, Mr. Herriot, he won't hurt tha."

I looked irresolutely at the huge, lethal animal, dwelling on the frightful power in those enormous shining quarters, on the unyielding flintiness of the feet with their rims of metal. Cliff's voice cut into my musings. "Come on, Mr. Herriot, I tell ye he won't hurt tha."

I re-opened my box and tremblingly threaded another needle. The little man wasn't asking me, he was telling me. I'd have to try again.

I shuffled forwards almost tripping over the tattered hula-hula skirt which dangled in front of me, my shaking hands reaching out once more for the wound. But I needn't have worried. It was just as the little man had said; he didn't hurt me. In fact he never moved. He seemed to be listening attentively to the muttering which Cliff was directing into his face from a few inches' range. I powdered and stitched and clipped as though working on an anatomical specimen. Chloroform couldn't have done it any better.

As I retreated and began to put away my instruments, the monologue at the horse's head changed from a menacing growl to wheedling, teasing chuckle. "You're just a daft old bugger, getting yourself all airigated over nowt. You're a good lad, really, aren't you, a real good lad." Cliff's hand ran caressingly over the horse's neck and the towering animal began to nuzzle his cheek, as completely in his sway as any Labrador puppy.

When he had finished he came slowly from the stall. I pulled a packet of Gold Flake from my pocket. "Cliff, you're a marvel. Will you have a cigarette?"

"It 'ud be like givin' a pig a strawberry," the little man replied, and the rugged little face split into a delighted grin. I looked at that grin—boyish, invincible—and reflected on the phenomenon that was Cliff Tyreman.

When I had first seen him nearly three years before, I had put him down as an unusually fit middle-aged man; but he was in fact nearly seventy. There wasn't much of him but he was formidable; with his long arms swinging, his stumping, pigeon-toed gait and his lowered head, he seemed always to be butting his way through life.

"I didn't expect to see you today," I said. "I heard you had pneumonia."

He shrugged. "Aye, summat of t'sort. First time I've ever been off work since I was a lad."

"And you should be in your bed now, I should say. I could hear you wheezing away when you were at the horse's head."

"Nay, I can't stick that nohow. I'll be right in a day or two." He seized a shovel and began busily clearing away the heap of manure, his breathing loud and stertorous in the silence.

Harland Grange was a large, mainly arable farm and there had been a time when this stable had had a horse standing in every one of the long row of stalls. There had been over twenty but now there were only two, the young horse I had been treating and an ancient grey called Badger.

Cliff had been head horseman and when the revolution came he turned to tractoring and other jobs around the farm with no fuss at all. But he couldn't lose his love of horses; the fellow feeling between working man and working beast which had grown in him since childhood was in his blood for ever.

292

My next visit to the farm was to see a fat bullock with a piece of turnip stuck in his throat, but while I was there, the farmer, Mr. Gilling, asked me to have a look at old Badger.

"I think he's got a touch of colic. Maybe it's just his age, but see what you think. I've sold the three-year-old but I'll still keep the old 'un—he'll be useful for a bit of light carting."

I glanced sideways at the farmer's granite features. He looked the least sentimental of men but I knew why he was keeping the old horse. It was for Cliff.

"Cliff will be pleased, anyway," I said.

Mr. Gilling nodded. "Aye, I never knew such a feller for 'osses. He was never happier than when he was with them." He gave a short laugh. "Do you know, I can remember years ago when he used to fall out with his missus he'd come down to this stable of a night and sit among his 'osses. Just sit here for hours on end looking at 'em."

"And did you have Badger in those days?"

"Aye, we bred him. Cliff helped at his foaling—maybe that's why he was always Cliff's favourite. He always worked Badger himself—year in year out—and he was that proud of 'im that if he had to take him into town for any reason he'd plait ribbons into his mane and hang all his brasses on him first." He shook his head reminiscently. "Anyway, I've got to go out now but Cliff will attend to you."

The little man was waiting for me in the yard. As I came up to him I exclaimed in horror, "Good God, Cliff, what have you been doing to yourself?" His face was a patchwork of cuts and scratches and his nose, almost without skin, jutted from between two black eyes.

He grinned through the wounds, his eyes dancing with merriment. "Came off me bike t'other day. Hit a stone and went right over handlebars, arse over tip." He burst out laughing.

"But damn it, man, haven't you been to a doctor? You're not fit to be out in that state."

"Doctor? Nay, there's no need to bother them fellers. It's nowt much." He fingered a gash on his jaw. "Ah lapped me chin up for a day in a bit o' bandage, but it's right enough now."

293

I shook my head as I followed him into the stable. He went over to the horse. "Can't reckon t'awd feller up," he said. "You'd think there wasn't much ailing him but there's summat."

There were no signs of violent pain but the animal kept transferring his weight from one hind foot to the other as if he did have a little abdominal discomfort. His temperature was normal and he didn't show symptoms of anything else.

I looked at him doubtfully. "Maybe he has a bit of colic. There's nothing else to see, anyway. I'll give him an injection to settle him down."

"Right you are, maister, that's good." Cliff watched me get my syringe out then he looked around him. "Funny seeing only one 'oss standing here. I remember when there was a great row of 'em. By gaw, I were in here at six o'clock every morning feedin' them and gettin' them ready for work and ah'll tell you it was a sight to see us all goin' off ploughing at the start o' the day. Maybe six pairs of 'osses setting off with their harness jinglin' and the ploughmen sittin' sideways on their backs. Like a regular procession it was."

I smiled. "It was an early start, Cliff."

"Aye, by gaw, and a late finish. We'd bring the 'osses home at night and give 'em a light feed and take their harness off, then we'd go and have our own teas and we'd be back 'ere again afterwards, curry-combing and dandy-brushin' all the sweat and dirt off 'em. Then we'd give them a right good stiff feed of chop and oats and hay to set 'em up for the next day."

"There wasn't much left of the evening then, was there?"

"Nay, there wasn't. It was about like work and bed, I reckon, but it never bothered us."

I stepped forward to give Badger the injection, then paused. The old horse had undergone a slight spasm, a barely perceptible stiffening of the muscles, and as I looked at him he cocked his tail for a second then lowered it.

"There's something else here," I said. I rapped him under the chin and as the membrana nictitans flicked across his eye, then slid slowly back, I knew. I paused for a moment. My casual little visit had suddenly become charged with doom. "Cliff," I said. "I'm afraid he's got tetanus."

294

"Lockjaw, you mean?"

"That's right. I'm sorry, but there's no doubt about it. Has he had any wounds lately—especially in his feet?"

"Well, he were dead lame about a fortnight ago and blacksmith let some matter out of his hoof. Made a right big 'ole."

There it was. "It's a pity he didn't get an anti-tetanus shot at the time," I said. I put my hand into the animal's mouth and tried to prise it open but the jaws were clamped tightly together. "I don't suppose he's been able to eat today."

"He had a bit this morning but nowt tonight. What's the lookout for him, Mr. Herriot?"

What indeed? If Cliff had asked me the same question today I would have been just as troubled to give him an answer. The facts are that seventy to eighty per cent of tetanus cases die whatever you do to them. But I didn't want to sound entirely defeatist.

"It's a very serious condition as you know, Cliff, but I'll do all I can. I've got some antitoxin in the car and I'll inject that. And if the spasms get very bad I'll give him a sedative. As long as he can drink there's a chance for him because he'll have to live on fluids—gruel would be fine."

For a few days Badger didn't get any worse and I began to hope. But then he began to deteriorate. A sudden movement or the approach of any person would throw him into a violent spasm so that he would stagger stiff-legged round the box like a big wooden toy, his eyes terrified, saliva drooling from between his fiercely clenched teeth.

One morning just as I was leaving the surgery the phone rang. It was Mr. Gilling. "I'm afraid Badger's flat out on the floor. I doubt it's a bad job, Mr. Herriot. We'll have to put him down, won't we?"

"I'm afraid so."

"There's just one thing. Mallock will be taking him away but old Cliff says he doesn't want Mallock to shoot 'im. Wants you to do it. Will you come?"

I got out the humane killer and drove back to the farm, wondering at the fact that the old man should find the idea of my bullet less repugnant than the knacker man's. Mr. Gilling was waiting in the box and by his side Cliff, shoulders hunched, hands deep in his pockets. He turned to me with a strange smile.

"I was just saying to t'boss how grand t'awd lad used to look when I got 'im up for a show. By gaw, you should have seen him with 'is coat polished and the feathers on his legs scrubbed as white as snow and a big blue ribbon round his tail."

"I can imagine it, Cliff," I said. "Nobody could have looked after him better."

He took his hands from his pockets, crouched by the prostrate animal and for a few minutes stroked the white-flecked neck and pulled at the ears while the old sunken eye looked at him impassively.

He began to speak softly to the old horse but his voice was steady, almost conversational, as though he was chatting to a friend.

"Many's the thousand miles I've walked after you, awd lad, and many's the talk we've had together. But I didn't have to say much to tha, did I? I reckon you knew every move I made, everything I said. Just one little word and you always did what ah wanted you to do." He rose to his feet. "I'll get on with me work now, boss," he said firmly, and strode out of the box.

I waited a while so that he would not hear the bang which signalled the end of Badger, the end of the horses of Harland Grange, and the end of the sweet core of Cliff Tyreman's life.

As I was leaving I saw Cliff again. He was mounting the iron seat of a roaring tractor and I shouted to him above the noise.

"The boss says he's going to get some sheep in and you'll be doing a bit of shepherding. Think you'll enjoy that?"

Cliff's undefeated grin flashed out as he called back to me.

"Aye, I don't mind learnin' summat new. I'm nobbut a lad yet!"

## Chapter Five

My stint in London was nearing its end. Our breaking-in weeks were nearly over and we waited for news of posting to an Initial Training Wing.

The air was thick with rumours. We were going to Aberystwyth in Wales; too far away for me, I wanted the north. Then we were going to Newquay in Cornwall; worse still. I was aware that the impending birth of AC2 Herriot's child did not influence the general war strategy but I still wanted to be as near to Helen as possible at the time.

There were times, too, when I wondered what it was all about. If we weren't being drilled we were being marched to meals, to classes, to talks. Like all the other young men I had imagined that after a few brisk preliminaries I would be sitting in an aeroplane, learning to fly, but it turned out that this was so far in the future that it was hardly mentioned. At ITW we would spend months learning navigation, principles of flight, Morse and many other things.

Still, news of the postings, when they came, blotted out all other feelings. It seemed too good to be true—I was going to Scarborough. I had been there and I knew that it was a beautiful seaside resort, but that wasn't why I was so delighted. It was because it was in Yorkshire.

A few weeks later, as we marched out of the station into the streets of Scarborough, I half closed my eyes and followed the tingle of the crisp tangy air all the way down to my lungs. Even in winter there had been no "feel" to the soft London air.

Mind you, it was cold. Yorkshire is a cold place and I could remember the sensation almost of shock at the start of my first winter in Darrowby.

It was after the first snow and I followed the clanging snow ploughs up the Dale, driving along between high white mounds till I reached old Mr. Stokill's gate. With my fingers on the door handle I looked through the glass at the new world beneath me. The white blanket rolled down the hillside and lapped the outbuildings of the little farm. Beyond, it smoothed out and concealed the stream on the valley floor, turning the whole scene into something unknown and exciting.

But the thrill I felt at the strange beauty was swept away as I got out and the screaming east wind struck me. I was wearing a heavy overcoat but the gust whipped its way right into my bones. I gasped and leaned back against the car while I buttoned the coat up under my chin, then struggled forward to where the gate shook and rattled. I fought it open and went through.

Coming round the corner of the byre I found Mr. Stokill forking muck onto a heap and making a churned brown trail across the whiteness.

"Now then," he muttered along the side of a half-smoked cigarette. He was over seventy but still ran the smallholding single-handed. He told me once that he had worked as a farmhand for six shillings a day for thirty years yet still managed to save enough to buy his own place. Maybe that was why he had never wanted to share it.

Just then the wind tore through the yard, clutching icily at my face, so that I turned involuntarily to one side with an explosive "Aaahh!"

The old farmer looked at me in surprise then glanced around as though he had just noticed the weather. "Aye, blows a bit thin this mornin', lad." Sparks flew from the end of his cigarette as he leaned for a moment on the fork.

He didn't seem to have much protection against the cold. A light khaki smock fluttered over a ragged navy waistcoat, clearly once part of his best suit, and his shirt bore neither collar nor stud. The white stubble on his fleshless jaw was a reproach to my twenty-four years and suddenly I felt an inadequate city-bred softie.

The old man dug his fork into the manure pile and turned towards the buildings. "Ah've got a nice few cases for ye to see today. Fust 'un's in 'ere." He opened a door and I staggered gratefully into warmth. "There's some little pigs in this pen," Mr. Stokill murmured. "Got a bit o' scour. I want you to give 'em a jab wi' your needle."

We had various E coli vaccines which sometimes did a bit of good in these cases and I entered the pen hopefully. But I left in a hurry because the piglets' mother didn't approve of me and came at me open-mouthed, barking explosively. She looked as big as a donkey and when the jaws with the great yellowed teeth brushed my thigh I knew it was time to go.

"We'll have to get her out of there before I can do anything, Mr. Stokill."

298

"Aye, you're right, young man, ah'll shift 'er." He began to shuffle away.

I held up a hand. "No, it's all right, I'll do it." I couldn't let this frail old man go in and maybe get knocked down and savaged.

There was a battered shovel standing against a wall and I seized it as a means of protection.

"Open the door, please," I said. "I'll soon have her out."

Once more inside the pen I held the shovel in front of me and tried to usher the huge sow towards the door. But my efforts were fruitless; she faced me all the time, growling as I circled. When she got the blade of the shovel between her teeth and began to worry it I called a halt.

As I left the pen I saw Mr. Stokill dragging a large dustbin over the cobbles. He entered the pen, and as the sow came at him he allowed her to run her head into the bin. Then he backed her towards the open door. The animal was clearly baffled. Suddenly finding herself in this strange dark place she naturally tried to retreat from it and all the farmer did was guide her.

Before she knew what was happening she was out in the yard. It had taken about twenty seconds. The old man calmly removed the bin and beckoned to me. "Right you are, Mr. Herriot, you can get on now."

Well, I knew what to do next anyway. I would pen the little pigs in a corner with a sheet of corrugated iron and the job would be over in no time.

But their mother's irritation had been communicated to the family. There were sixteen of them hurtling around like little pink racehorses. I spent a long time diving frantically after them, and I might have gone on indefinitely had I not felt a gentle touch on my arm.

"Haud on, young man, haud on." The old farmer looked at me kindly. "If you'll nobbut stop runnin' after 'em they'll settle down."

Slightly breathless, I stood by his side and listened as he addressed the little creatures. "Giss-giss, giss-giss."

The piglets slowed their headlong gallop to a trot, then, as though controlled by telepathy, they all stopped at once, and stood in a group in one corner.

"Giss-giss," said Mr. Stokill approvingly, advancing with the corrugated iron. "Giss-giss."

He unhurriedly placed the length of metal across the corner and jammed his foot against the bottom.

After that the injection of the litter was a matter of a few minutes. Mr. Stokill didn't say, "Well, I'm teaching you a thing or two today, am I not?" There was no hint of triumph or self congratulation in the calm old eyes. All he said was, "I'm keepin' you busy this mornin', young man. I want you to look at a cow now. She's got a pea in her tit."

"Peas" and other obstructions in the teats were very common in the days of hand milking. Some of them were floating milk calculi, others tiny pedunculated tumours, injuries to the teat lining, all sorts of things. It was a whole diverting little field in itself and I approached the cow with interest. —

But I didn't get very near before Mr. Stokill put his hand on my shoulder. "Just a minute, Mr. Herriot, don't touch 'er tit yet or she'll clout ye. She's an awd bitch. Wait a minute till ah rope 'er."

"Oh, right," I said. "But I'll do it."

He hesitated. "Ah reckon I ought to . . ."

"No, no, Mr. Stokill, that's quite unnecessary, I know how to stop a cow kicking," I said primly. "Kindly hand me that rope."

"But . . . she's a bugger . . . kicks like a 'oss. She's a right good milker but . . ."

"Don't worry," I said, smiling. "I'll stop her little games."

I began to unwind the rope. It was good to be able to demonstrate that I did know something about handling animals even though I had been qualified for only a few months. I passed the rope round the animal's body in front of the udder and pulled it tight in a slip knot. Just like they taught us at college. She was a scrawny red shorthorn with a woolly poll and she regarded me with a contemplative eye as I bent down.

"All right, lass," I said soothingly, reaching under her and gently grasping the teat. I squirted a few jets of milk then something blocked the end. Ah yes, there it was, quite large and unattached. I felt sure I could work it through the orifice without any cutting.

I took a firmer grip, squeezed tightly and immediately a cloven foot shot out like a whip lash and smacked me solidly on the knee. It is a particularly painful spot to be kicked and I spent some time hopping round the byre and cursing in a fervent whisper.

The farmer followed me anxiously. "Eh, ah'm sorry, Mr. Herriot, she's a right awd bugger. Better let me . . ."

I held up a hand. "No, Mr. Stokill. I already have her roped. I just didn't tie it tight enough, that's all." I hobbled back to the animal, loosened the knot then retied it, pulling till my eyes popped. When I had finished, her abdomen was lifted high and nipped in like a wasp-waisted Victorian lady of fashion.

"That'll fix you," I grunted, and bent to my work again. A few spurts of milk then the thing was at the teat end again, a pinkish-white object peeping through the orifice. A little extra pressure and I would be able to fish it out with the hypodermic needle I had poised ready. I took a breath and gripped hard.

This time the hoof caught me halfway up the shin bone. She hadn't been able to get so much height into it but it was just as painful. I sat down on a milking stool, rolled up my trouser leg and examined the roll of skin which hung like a diploma at the end of a long graze where the sharp hoof had caught me.

"Now then, you've 'ad enough, young man." Mr. Stokill removed my rope and gazed at me with commiseration. "Ordinary methods don't work with this 'un. I 'ave to milk her and ah knaw."

He fetched a soiled length of plough cord which had obviously seen much service and fastened it round the cow's hock. The other end had a hook which he fitted into a ring on the byre wall. It was just the right length to stretch taut, pulling the leg slightly back.

The old man nodded. "Now try."

With a feeling of fatalism I grasped the teat again. And it was as if the cow knew she was beaten. She never moved as I nipped hard and winkled out the offending obstruction. She couldn't do a thing about it.

"Ah, thank ye, lad," the farmer said. "That's champion. Been bothering me a bit has that. Didn't know what it was." He held up a finger. "One last job for ye. A young heifer with a bit o' stomach trouble, ah think. Saw her last night and she was a bit blown. She's in an outside buildin'."

We went out to where the wind welcomed us with savage glee. As the knife-like blast hit me, I cowered in the lee of the stable. "Where is this heifer?" I gasped.

Mr. Stokill was lighting another cigarette, apparently oblivious of the elements. He clamped the lid on an ancient brass lighter and jerked his thumb. "Across the road. Up there."

I followed his gesture over the buried walls, across the narrow roadway to where the fell rose steeply in a sweep of unbroken white to join the leaden sky. Unbroken, that is, except for a tiny barn, a grey stone speck just visible.

"That barn?" I pointed a shaking finger at the heights. "You mean that building? The heifer's surely not in there!"

"Aye, she is. Ah keep a lot of me young beasts in them spots."

"But . . . but . . ." I was gabbling now. "We'll never get up there! That snow's three feet deep!"

He blew smoke pleasurably from his nostrils. "We will, don't tha worry. Just hang on a second."

He disappeared into the stable and after a few moments I peeped inside. He was saddling a fat brown cob and I stared as he led the little animal out and mounted stiffly.

Looking down at me he waved cheerfully. "Well, let's be goin'. Have you got your stuff?"

Bewilderedly I filled my pockets. A bottle of bloat mixture, a trochar and canula, a packet of gentian and nux vomica. On the other side of the road an opening had been dug and Mr. Stokill rode through. I slithered in his wake, looking up hopelessly at the great smooth wilderness rearing above us.

Mr. Stokill turned in the saddle. "Get haud on t'tail," he said.

"I beg your pardon?"

"Get a haud of 'is tail."

As in a dream I seized the bristly hairs.

"No, both 'ands," the farmer said patiently.

"Like this?"

"That's grand, lad. Now 'ang on."

He clicked his tongue, the cob plodded resolutely forward and so did I.

And it was easy! The whole world fell away beneath us as we

soared upwards, and leaning back and enjoying my walk I watched the little valley unfold along its twisting length until I could see away into the main Dale with the great hills billowing round and white into the dark clouds.

At the barn the farmer dismounted. "All right, young man?"

"All right, Mr. Stokill." As I followed him into the little building I smiled to myself. This old man had once told me that he left school when he was twelve, whereas I had spent most of the twenty-four years of my life in study. Yet when I looked back on the last hour or so I could come to only one conclusion.

He knew a lot more than I did.

## Chapter Six

As I bent over the wash basin in the "ablutions" and went into another violent paroxysm of coughing I had a growing conviction that I was a mere pawn. And I didn't much like being a pawn because the lives of us lowly airmen were ruled by a lot of individuals so exalted that we never knew them.

And so many of their ideas seemed crazy to me.

For instance, who decided that all our bedroom windows should be nailed open throughout a Yorkshire winter so that the mist could swirl straight from the ocean and settle icily on our beds as we slept? The result was an almost 100% incidence of bronchitis in our flight and in the mornings the Grand Hotel, where we were billeted, sounded like a chest sanatorium with a harrowing chorus of barks and wheezes.

The cough seized me again, racking my body, threatening to dislodge my eyeballs. It was a temptation to report sick but I hadn't done it yet. Maybe there was a bit of bravado in my stand, but there were other reasons.

Primarily, I didn't like the look of the sick parade. As I went out to the corridor with my towel round my shoulders a sergeant was reading a list and inflating his lungs at the same time.

"Get on parade, the sick!" he shouted. "C'mon, c'mon, let's be 'avin you!"

From various doors an unhappy group of invalids began to appear, shuffling over the linoleum, each draped with his haversack containing pyjamas, canvas shoes, knife, fork, spoon, etc.

The sergeant unleashed another bellow. "Get into line, there! Come on, you lot, hurry it up, look lively!"

I looked at the young men huddled there, white-faced and trembling. Most of them were coughing and spluttering and one of them clutched his abdomen as though he had a ruptured appendix.

"Parade!" bawled the sergeant. "Parade, atten-shun! Parade, stan-at ease! Atten-shun! Le-eft turn! Qui-ick march! 'Eft-'ight, 'eft-'ight, 'eft-'ight, 'eft-'ight!"

The hapless band trailed wearily off. They had a march of nearly a mile through the rain to the sick quarters in another hotel above the Spa and as I turned into my room it was with renewed resolve to hang on as long as possible.

I seemed a long, long way from my old life, and my mind went back to the warm days of last summer and to the Darrowby garden fête I had been to, pacing graciously with my new wife among the stalls.

It was an annual affair in aid of the NSPCC and it was held on the big lawn behind the Darrowby vicarage with the weathered brick of the old house showing mellow red beyond the trees. The hot June sunshine bathed the typically English scene; the women in their flowered dresses, the men perspiring in their best suits, laughing children running from the tombola to the coconut shy or the ice-cream kiosk.

The curate, Mr. Blenkinsopp, came up to us. "Ah, James," he murmured. "And Helen!" He beamed on us with the benevolence he felt for the entire human race. "How nice to see you here!"

He walked along with us as the scent from the flower beds and the trodden grass rose in the warm air. "You know, James, I was just thinking about you the other day. I was in Rainby—you know I take the service there every second week—and they were telling me they were having great difficulty in finding men for the cricket team. I wondered if you would care to turn out for them."

"Me? Play cricket?" I laughed. "I'm afraid I'm no cricketer."

"Oh, but surely you must have played at some time or other."

"A bit at school, but they go more for tennis in Scotland. And anyway it was a long time ago."

"Oh, well," Mr. Blenkinsopp spread his hands. "It will come back to you easily."

"And another thing—I don't live in Rainby. Doesn't that matter?"

"Not really," the curate replied. "It is such a problem finding eleven players in these tiny villages that they often call on outsiders. Nobody minds."

I stopped my stroll over the grass and turned to Helen. She was giving me an encouraging smile and I began to think, well . . . why not? "All right then, Mr. Blenkinsopp," I said. "You're not getting any bargain but I don't mind having a go."

"Splendid! The next match is on Tuesday evening—against Hedwick. I am playing so I'll pick you up at six o'clock." His face radiated happiness as though I had done him the greatest favour.

"Well, thanks," I replied. "I'll have to fix it with my partner to be off that night, but I'm sure it will be O.K."

The weather was still fine on Tuesday and promptly at six Mr. Blenkinsopp tooted the horn of his little car outside the surgery. Helen had advised me to dress ready for action and she had clearly been right because the curate, too, was resplendent in white flannels and blazer. The three young farmers crammed in the back were, however, wearing open-necked shirts and their ordinary clothes.

"Good afternoon, Mr. Herriot," said the one in the middle, Tom Willis, captain of the Rainby team. He leaned forward, his face set in its usual serious expression. "It's good of you to give up your time, Mr. Herriot. I know you're a busy man but we're allus short o' players at Rainby."

"I'm looking forward to it, Tom, but I'm no cricketer, I'll tell you now."

He gazed at me with gentle disbelief and I had an uncomfortable feeling that everybody had the impression that because I had been to college I was bound to have a blue.

Hedwick was at the top end of Allerdale and we stopped there because we could go no further. This was the head of the Dale, a cluster of cottages, a farm and a pub. A few cars were drawn up by the side of a wall on which leaned a long row of cloth-capped men, a few women and chattering groups of children.

"Ah," said Mr. Blenkinsopp. "A good turn-out of spectators. Hedwick always support their team well. They must have come from all over the Dale."

I looked around in surprise. "Spectators?"

"Yes, of course. They've come to see the match."

Again I gazed about me. "But I can't see the pitch."

"It's there," Tom said. "Just over t'wall."

I leaned across the rough stones and stared in some bewilderment at an undulating field almost knee deep in rough grass among which a cow, some sheep and a few hens wandered contentedly. "Is this it?"

"Aye, that's it. If you stand on t'wall you can see the square."

I did as he said and could just discern a five foot wide strip of bright green cut from the crowding herbage on the only level part of the field. The stumps stood expectantly at either end. A massive oak tree sprouted from somewhere around mid-on.

There was no clubhouse but the home team were seated on a form on the grass near a little metal scoreboard and its pile of hooked number plates.

The rest of our team had arrived, too, and with a pang of alarm I noticed that there was not a single pair of white flannels among them. Only the curate and I were properly attired and the snag was that he could play and I couldn't.

Tom and the home captain tossed a coin. Hedwick won and elected to bat. The umpires, two tousle-haired, sunburnt young fellows in grubby white coats, strolled to the wicket, our team followed and the Hedwick batsmen appeared.

Tom Willis with the air of authority and responsibility which was natural to him began to dispose the field. No doubt convinced that I was a lynx-eyed catcher he stationed me quite close to the bat on the off side, and then, after a grave consultation with Mr. Blenkinsopp he gave him the ball and the game was on.

And Mr. Blenkinsopp was a revelation. He handed his cap to the umpire, retreated about twenty yards into the undergrowth, then turned and, ploughing his way back at ever increasing speed,

306

delivered the ball with remarkable velocity bang on the wicket. The batsman met it respectfully with a dead bat and did the same with the next but then he uncoiled himself and belted the third one high over the fielders onto a steep slope which swept up to a thick wood. As one of our men galloped after it the row of heads above the wall broke into a Babel of noise.

They cheered every hit with raucous yells. And they had plenty to shout about. The Hedwick lads wasted no time on classic strokes; they just gave a great hoick at the ball and when they connected it travelled immense distances. Occasionally they missed and Mr. Blenkinsopp or one of our other bowlers shattered their stumps but the next man started cheerfully where they left off.

It was exhilarating stuff but I was unable to enjoy it. Everything I did proclaimed my ignorance to the knowledgeable people around me. I threw the ball in to the wrong end, I left the ball when I should have chased it and sped after it when I should have stayed in my place. No, there was no doubt about it; here in this cricket-mad corner of a cricket-mad county I was a foreigner.

Five wickets down and the next batsman seemed to be taking a long time to reach the wicket. He was shuffling through the clover like a very old man, trailing his bat wearily behind him, and when he finally arrived at the crease I saw that he was indeed fairly advanced in years. He wore only one pad strapped over baggy grey trousers which came almost up to his armpits and were suspended by braces. A cloth cap surmounted a face shrunken like a sour apple. From one corner of the downturned mouth a cigarette dangled. He took guard and looked at the umpire. "Middle and leg," he grunted.

"Aye, that's about it, Len," the umpire replied.

The old man removed his cigarette, flicked it onto the grass and took up his guard again. His appearance suggested that he might be out first ball, but as the delivery came down he stepped forward and with a scything sweep thumped the ball past the bowler and just a few inches above the rear end of the cow which had wandered into the line of fire. The animal looked round in some surprise as the ball whizzed along its backbone and the old man's crabbed features relaxed into the semblance of a smile.

"By gaw, vitnery," he said, looking over at me, "ah damn near made a bit of work for tha there."

He proved a difficult man to dislodge. But it was the batsman at the other end who was worrying Tom Willis. He had come in first wicket down, a ruddy-faced lad of about nineteen wearing a blue shirt, and he was still there piling on the runs.

At the end of the over, Tom came up to me. "Fancy turning your arm over, Mr. Herriot?" he inquired gravely.

"Huh?"

"Would you like a bowl? A fresh man might just unsettle this feller."

"Well . . . er . . ." I didn't know what to say. The idea of me bowling in a real match was unthinkable. Tom made up my mind by throwing me the ball.

Clasping it in a clammy hand I trotted up to the wicket while the lad in the blue shirt crouched intently over his bat. All the other bowlers had hurled their missiles down at top speed but I knew that if I tried that I would be miles off my target. Accuracy, I decided, must be my watchword and I sent a gentle lob in the direction of the wicket. The batsman, obviously convinced that such a slow ball must be laden with hidden malice, followed its course with deep suspicion and smothered it as soon as it arrived. He did the same with the second but that was enough for him to divine that I wasn't bowling off breaks, leg breaks or googlies but simply little dollies, and he struck the third ball smartly into a sort of small ravine below the spectators' wall.

There was a universal cry of "*Maurice!*" from our team because Maurice Briggs, the Rainby blacksmith, was fielding down there and since he couldn't see the wicket he had to be warned. In due course the ball soared back from the depths, propelled no doubt by Maurice's strong right arm, and I recommenced my attack. The lad in blue thumped my remaining three deliveries effortlessly for six. The first flew straight over the wall and the row of cars into the adjoining field, the next landed in the farmyard and the third climbed in a tremendous arc away above the ravine and I heard it splash into the beck whence it was retrieved with a certain amount of profanity by the invisible Maurice.

308

An old farm man once said to me when describing a moment of embarrassment, "Ah could've got down a mouse 'ole." And I knew just what he meant.

At the end of the over Tom came up to me. "Thank ye, Mr. Herriot, but I'm afraid I'll have to take you off now. This wicket's not suited to your type of bowling—not takin' spin at all." He shook his head in his solemn way.

I nodded thankfully and Tom went on. "Tell ye what, go down and relieve that man in the outfield. We could do wi' a safe pair of hands down there."

I obeyed my skipper's orders and descended to the ravine, and when Maurice had clambered up the small grassy cliff which separated me from the rest of the field I felt strangely alone. It was a dank, garlic-smelling region, perceptibly colder than the land above, and I could see nothing of the pitch, only occasional glimpses of the players' heads. In fact it was difficult to believe I was still taking part in a cricket match but for the spectators. From their position along the wall they had a grandstand view of everything and in fact were looking down at me from short range. They appeared to find me quite interesting, too, making remarks which I couldn't hear but which caused considerable hilarity.

It was a pity about the spectators because it was rather peaceful in the ravine. It took a very big hit to get down there and I was more or less left to ruminate. Occasionally the warning cries would ring out from above and a ball would come bounding over the top. Now and then I clawed my way up the bank and had a look at the progress of the game. The lad in blue was still there.

It was after a long spell of inaction that I heard the frantic yells. "*Jim! James! Mr. Herriot!*" The whole team was giving tongue and, as I learned later, the lad in the blue shirt had made a catchable shot.

But I knew anyway. Nobody but he could have struck the blow which sent that little speck climbing high into the pale evening sky above me; and, as it began with terrifying slowness to fall in my direction, time came to a halt. I was aware of several of my team mates breasting the cliff and watching me breathlessly, of the long row of heads above the wall, and suddenly I was gripped by a

309

cold resolve. I was going to catch this fellow out. He had humiliated me up there but it was my turn now.

The speck was coming down faster now as I stumbled about in the tangled vegetation trying to get into position. Then I was right under the ball, hands cupped, waiting.

It fell, at the end, like a cannon ball on the end of my right thumb, bounded over my shoulder and thumped mournfully on the turf.

A storm of derision broke from the heads, peals of delighted laughter, volleys of candid comment. As I scrabbled for the ball among the herbage I didn't know which was worse—the physical pain, or the mental anguish. After I had finally hurled the thing up the cliff I cradled the throbbing thumb in my other hand and rocked back and forth on my heels, moaning softly.

My team mates returned sadly to their tasks but Tom Willis, I noticed, lingered on, looking down at me. "Hard luck, Mr. Herriot. Very easy to lose t'ball against them trees." He nodded encouragingly then was gone.

I was not troubled further in the innings. We never did get blueshirt out and he had an unbeaten sixty-two at the close. The Hedwick score was a hundred and fifty-four, a very useful total in village cricket.

There was a ten minute interval while our openers strapped on their pads. Tom Willis showed me the batting list he had drawn up and I saw without surprise that I was last man in. "Our team's packed with batting, Mr. Herriot," he said seriously. "I couldn't find a place for you higher up the order."

Mr. Blenkinsopp, preparing to receive the first ball, really looked the part, gay cap pulled well down, college colours bright on the broad V of his sweater. But in this particular situation he had one big disadvantage; he was too good.

All the coaching he had received had been aimed at keeping the ball down. As I watched he stepped out and executed a flawless cover drive. At Headingley the ball would have rattled against the boards for four but here it travelled approximately two and a half feet and a fat lad lifted it carelessly from the dense vegetation and threw it back to the bowler. The next one the curate picked beauti-

310

fully off his toes and flicked it to square leg for what would certainly have been another four anywhere else. This one went for about a yard before the jungle claimed it.

It saddened me to watch him having to resort to swiping tactics. He did manage to get in a few telling blows but was caught on the boundary for twelve.

It was a bad start for Rainby with that large total facing them, and the two Hedwick fast bowlers looked very formidable. But as the match went on I found we had some stalwarts in our ranks. Bert Chapman, the council roadman and an old acquaintance of mine, strode out and began to hoist the ball all over the field. At the other end Maurice Briggs the blacksmith, sleeves rolled high over his mighty biceps, clouted six after six, showing a marked preference for the ravine where there now lurked some hapless member of the other team. I felt for him, whoever it was down there; the sun had gone behind the hills and it must have been desperately gloomy in those humid depths.

And then when Tom came in he showed the true strategical sense of a captain. When Hedwick were batting it had not escaped his notice that they aimed a lot of their shots at a broad patch of particularly impenetrable vegetation, tangled grasses, nettles, thistles and an abundance of un-nameable flora. At every opportunity, therefore, he popped one with the greatest accuracy into the jungle himself.

It was the kind of innings you would expect from him; not spectacular, but thoughtful and methodical. After one well-placed drive he ran seventeen while the fielders clawed at the undergrowth and the yells from the wall took on a frantic note.

And all the time we were creeping nearer to the total. When eight wickets had fallen we had reached a hundred and forty and our batsmen were running whether they hit the ball or not. It was too dark by now to see, in any case.

In the gathering gloom I watched as the batsman swung, there was an eldritch scream from the bowler, and our man was out LBW. It was my turn to bat.

Our score was a hundred and forty-five and as, dry-mouthed, I buckled on my pads, the lines of the poem came back to me. "Ten to make and the last man in." But I had never dreamed that my first innings in an English cricket match would be like this, with the oil lamps of the farms around winking through the darkness.

Pacing my way to the wicket I passed close by the fiercer of the two fast bowlers who eyed me expressionlessly, tossing the ball from one meaty hand to another and whistling softly to himself. As I took guard he began his pounding run up and I braced myself. He had already dropped two of our batsmen in groaning heaps and I realized I had small hope of even seeing the ball.

But I had decided on one thing! I wasn't going to just stand there and take it. I wasn't a cricketer but I was going to try to hit the ball. And as the bowler arrived at full gallop and brought his arm over I stepped out and aimed a violent lunge at where I thought the thing might be. Nothing happened. I heard the smack on the turf and the thud into the wicketkeeper's gloves, that was all.

The same thing happened with the next two deliveries. Great flailing blows which nearly swung me off my feet, but nothing besides the smack and the thud. I was playing a whirlwind innings except that I hadn't managed to make contact so far.

Again the arm came over and again I leapt out. And this time there was a sharp crack. I had got a touch but I had no idea where the ball had gone. I was standing gazing stupidly around me when I heard a bellowed, "*Come on!*" and saw my partner thundering towards me. At the same time I spotted a couple of fielders running after something away down on my left and then the umpire made a signal. I had scored a four.

With the fifth ball I did the same thing and heard another crack, but this time, as I glared wildly about me I saw there was activity somewhere behind me on my right. We ran three and I had made seven.

Then, with the last delivery of the over, my partner's stumps were scattered and the match was lost. By two runs.

"A merry knock, Mr. Herriot," Tom said, as I marched from the arena. "Just for a minute I was beginnin' to think you were goin' to pull it off for us there."

There was a pie and pea supper for both teams in the pub and as I settled down with a frothing pint of beer the thought kept coming back to me. Seven not out! After the humiliations of the evening it was an ultimate respectability. I had not at any time seen the ball during my innings but I had made seven not out. And as I looked around at the roomful of laughing sunburnt men I began to feel good.

Tom sat on one side of me and Mr. Blenkinsopp on the other. The curate smiled as he put down his glass. "Well done indeed, James. Nearly a story-book ending. And you know, I'm quite sure you'd have clinched it if your partner had been able to keep going."

I felt myself blushing. "Well, it's very kind of you, but I was a bit lucky."

"Lucky? Not a bit of it!" said Mr. Blenkinsopp. "You played two beautiful strokes—but I don't know how you did it in the conditions. Don't you agree, Tom?"

Tom sprinkled a little salt on his peas and turned to me. "Ah do agree. And the best bit was how you got 'em up in the air to clear t'long grass. That was clever that was." He conveyed a forkful of pie to his mouth and began to munch stolidly.

I looked at him narrowly. Tom was always serious so there was nothing to be learned from his expression. He was always kind, too, he had been kind all evening.

But I really think he meant it this time.

## Chapter Seven

I had plenty of company for Christmas that year. The Grand Hotel was a massive Victorian pile which dominated Scarborough in turreted splendour from its eminence above the sea, and the big dining room was packed with several hundred airmen. The iron discipline was relaxed to let the Yuletide spirit run free.

It was so different from other Christmasses I had known that it ought to have remained like a beacon in my mind, but I know that my strongest memory of Christmas will always be bound up with a certain little cat at Darrowby.

I first saw her one October afternoon when I was called to see one of Mrs. Ainsworth's dogs. Mrs. Ainsworth was a plumpish, pleasant-faced woman in her forties and the kind of client veterinary surgeons dream of: well off, generous, and the owner of three cosseted basset hounds. It only needed the habitually mournful expressions of one of the dogs to deepen a little and I was summoned round there post haste. Today one of the bassets had raised its paw and scratched its ear a couple of times and that was enough to send its mistress scurrying to the phone in great alarm.

On this visit I saw a furry black creature sitting before the fire.

"I didn't know you had a cat," I said.

The lady smiled. "We haven't. This is Debbie. At least that's what we call her. She's a stray. Comes here two or three times a week and we give her some food. I don't know where she lives but I believe she spends a lot of her time around one of the farms along the road."

"Do you ever get the feeling that she wants to stay with you?"

"No." Mrs. Ainsworth shook her head. "She's a timid little thing. Just creeps in, has some food then flits away. Every now and again she sits by the fire for a few minutes. It's as though she was giving herself a treat. But she doesn't seem to want to let me or anybody into her life."

"Yes . . . I see what you mean." There was no doubt there was something unusual in the attitude of the little animal. She was sitting bolt upright on the thick rug which lay before the fireplace in which the coals glowed and flamed. She made no effort to curl up or wash herself or do anything other than gaze quietly ahead.

I approached her carefully but she leaned away as I stretched out my hand. However, by patient wheedling and soft talk I managed to touch her and gently stroked her cheek with one finger. There was a moment when she responded by putting her head on one side and rubbing back against my hand. But then, as I watched, she turned, crept soundlessly from the room and was gone.

"That's always the way with Debbie." Mrs. Ainsworth laughed. "She never stays more than ten minutes or so, then she's off."

"I wonder where she goes," I murmured half to myself.

Mrs. Ainsworth sighed. "That's something we've never been able to find out," she said.

314

IT MUST HAVE been nearly three months before I next heard from Mrs. Ainsworth and in fact I had begun to wonder at the bassets' long symptomless run when she came on the phone.

It was Christmas morning and she was apologetic. "Mr. Herriot, I'm so sorry to bother you today of all days. I should think you want a rest at Christmas like anybody else." But her natural politeness could not hide the distress in her voice.

"Please don't worry about that," I said. "Which one is it this time?"

"It's not one of the dogs. It's . . . Debbie."

"Debbie? She's at your house now?"

"Yes . . . but there's something wrong. Please come quickly."

Driving through the market-place I thought that Darrowby on Christmas Day was like Dickens come to life; the square with the snow thick on the cobbles and hanging from the eaves of the roofs; the coloured lights of the Christmas trees winking at the windows of the clustering houses, warmly inviting against the cold white bulk of the fells behind.

Mrs. Ainsworth's home was lavishly decorated with tinsel and holly, rows of drinks stood on the sideboard and the rich aroma of turkey and sage and onion stuffing wafted from the kitchen. But her eyes were full of pain as she led me through to the lounge.

Debbie was there all right but this time everything was different. She wasn't sitting upright in her usual position; she was stretched quite motionless and huddled close to her lay a tiny black kitten.

I looked down in bewilderment. "What's happened here?"

"It's the strangest thing," Mrs. Ainsworth replied. "I haven't seen her for several weeks·then she came in about two hours ago—sort of staggered into the kitchen, and she was carrying the kitten in her mouth. She took it through to the lounge and laid it on the rug. Then she lay down like this and she hasn't moved."

I knelt on the rug and passed my hand over Debbie's neck and ribs. She was thinner than ever, her fur dirty and mud-caked. She did not resist as I gently opened her mouth. The tongue and mucous membranes were abnormally pale and the lips ice-cold against my fingers. When I pulled down her eyelid and saw the dead white conjunctiva a knell sounded in my mind.

I palpated the abdomen with a grim certainty as to what I would find and there was no surprise, only a dull sadness as my fingers closed around a hard lobulated mass deep among the viscera. Massive lymphosarcoma. Terminal and hopeless. I straightened up and sat on the rug looking sightlessly into the fireplace, feeling the warmth of the flames on my face.

Mrs. Ainsworth's voice seemed to come from afar. "Is she ill, Mr. Herriot?"

I hesitated. "Yes, I'm afraid so. She has a malignant growth." I stood up. "There's absolutely nothing I can do. I'm sorry."

"Oh!" Her hand went to her mouth. When at last she spoke her voice trembled. "Well, you must put her to sleep immediately. It's the only thing to do. We can't let her suffer."

"Mrs. Ainsworth," I said. "There's no need. She's dying now—in a coma—far beyond suffering."

She turned quickly away from me and was very still as she fought with her emotions. Then she gave up the struggle and dropped on her knees beside Debbie.

"Oh poor little thing!" she sobbed and stroked the cat's head again and again as the tears fell unchecked on the matted fur. "It must have been terrible out there in the cold when she was so desperately ill—I daren't think about it. And having kittens, too—I . . . I wonder how many she did have?"

For a few moments I was silent, feeling her sorrow, so discordant among the bright seasonal colours of this festive room. Then I shrugged. "I don't suppose we'll ever know. Maybe just this one. It happens sometimes. And she brought it to you, didn't she?"

"Yes . . . that's right . . . she did . . ." Mrs. Ainsworth reached out and lifted the bedraggled black morsel.

I bent and put my hand on Debbie's heart. There was no beat. I looked up. "I'm afraid she's gone." I lifted the small feather-light body, wrapped it in a sheet and took it out to the car.

When I came back Mrs. Ainsworth was stroking the kitten. She smoothed her finger along the muddy fur and the tiny mouth opened in a soundless miaow. "I've never had a cat before," Mrs. Ainsworth said.

I smiled. "Well, it looks as though you've got one now."

316

AND SHE CERTAINLY had. That kitten grew rapidly into a sleek handsome cat with a boisterous nature which earned him the name of Buster. In every way he was the opposite to his timid little mother. Not for him the privations of the secret outdoor life; he stalked the rich carpets of the Ainsworth home like a king.

On my visits I watched his development with delight but the occasion which stays in my mind was the following Christmas Day, a year after his arrival.

I was out on my rounds as usual. I can't remember when I haven't had to work on Christmas Day because the animals have never got round to recognizing it as a holiday; but with the passage of the years the vague resentment I used to feel has faded. After all, as I tramped around the hillside barns in the frosty air I was working up a better appetite for my turkey than all the millions lying in bed or slumped by the fire; and this was aided by the innumerable aperitifs I received from the hospitable farmers.

I was on my way home, bathed in a rosy glow. I had consumed several whiskies of the kind Yorkshiremen pour as though it was ginger ale, and I had finished with a glass of old Mrs. Barnshaw's rhubarb wine which had seared its way straight to my toenails.

As I was passing Mrs. Ainsworth's house I heard a cry. "Merry Christmas, Mr. Herriot!" She was letting a visitor out of the front door and she waved at me gaily. "Come in and have a drink to warm you up."

I didn't need warming up but I pulled in to the kerb without hesitation. In the house there was all the festive cheer of last year and the same glorious whiff of sage and onion. But there was not the sorrow; there was Buster.

He was darting up to each of the dogs in turn, ears pricked, eyes blazing with devilment, dabbing a paw at them then streaking away.

Mrs. Ainsworth laughed. "You know, he plagues the life out of them. Gives them no peace."

She was right. To the bassets Buster's arrival was rather like the intrusion of an irreverent outsider into an exclusive London club. For a long time they had led a life of measured grace and unruffled calm. And then came Buster.

317

He was dancing up to the youngest dog, head on one side, goading him. When he started boxing with both paws it was too much even for the basset. He dropped his dignity and rolled over with the cat in a brief wrestling match.

Laughing, Mrs. Ainsworth snatched Buster from his play and held him close to her face as the cat purred and arched himself ecstatically against her cheek.

Looking at him, a picture of health and contentment, my mind went back to his mother. Was it too much to think that that dying little creature with the last of her strength had carried her kitten to the only comfort and warmth she had ever known in the hope that it would be cared for there? Maybe it was.

But it seemed I wasn't the only one with such fancies. Mrs. Ainsworth turned to me and though she was smiling her eyes were wistful. "Debbie would be pleased," she said.

I nodded. "Yes, she would . . . It was just a year ago today she brought him, wasn't it?"

"That's right." She hugged Buster to her again. "The best Christmas present I ever had."

## Chapter Eight

I stared in disbelief at the dial on the weighing machine. Nine stone seven pounds! I had lost two stone since joining the RAF. I was cowering in my usual corner in Boots' chemist's shop in Scarborough where I had developed the habit of a weekly weigh-in to keep a morbid eye on my progressive emaciation. It was incredible —and it wasn't all due to the tough training. Admittedly we were never at rest. It was PT and drill, PT and drill, over and over.

At first I was too busy to see any change in myself. But one morning after a few weeks, when our flight was coming to the end of a five-mile run, we dropped down to a long stretch of empty beach and the sergeant shouted, "Right, sprint to those rocks! Let's see who gets there first!"

We all took off on the last hundred yards dash and I was mildly surprised to find that the first man past the post was myself—and

318

I wasn't really out of breath. I was certainly fit. But there was something wrong—I shouldn't have been as thin as this. Another factor was at work.

In Yorkshire when a man goes into a decline during his wife's pregnancy they giggle behind their hands and say he is "carrying" the baby. I never laugh at these remarks because I am convinced I "carried" my son.

I base this conclusion on a variety of symptoms. It would be an exaggeration to say I suffered from morning sickness but my suspicions were certainly aroused when I began to feel a little queasy in the early part of the day. This was followed by a growing uneasiness as Helen's time drew near and a sensation, despite my physical condition, of being drained and miserable. All doubts were resolved and I knew I had to do something about it.

I had to see Helen. After all, I was in Yorkshire and a bus would take me to her in three hours. The snag was that there was no leave from ITW. They left us in no doubt about that. They said the discipline was as tough as a Guards regiment and the restrictions just as rigid. I would get compassionate leave when the baby was born but I couldn't wait till then. The grim knowledge that any attempt to dodge off unofficially would be like a minor desertion and would be followed by serious consequences, even prison, didn't weigh with me. I had to see Helen.

A study of the timetables revealed that there was a bus at 2:00 p.m. which got to Darrowby at five o'clock, and another leaving Darrowby at six which arrived in Scarborough at nine. Six hours travelling to have one hour with Helen. It was worth it.

At first I couldn't see a way of getting to the bus station at two o'clock in the afternoon because we were never free at that time, but my chance came quite unexpectedly. One Friday lunchtime we learned that there were no more classes that day but we were confined to the Grand till evening. Most of my friends collapsed thankfully onto their beds but I slunk down the long flights of stone stairs and took up a position in the foyer where I could watch the front door.

There was a glass-fronted office on one side of the entrance where the Service Police sat and kept an eye on all departures.

There was only one on duty today and I waited till he turned and moved to the back of the room then I walked quietly past him and out into the square.

That part had been almost too easy and I set off at a brisk pace. All I needed was a little bit of luck and as I pressed on along the empty street it seemed I had found it. Until, that is, I saw two burly Service Policemen strolling towards me.

They would ask me for the pass I didn't have, then they would want to know what I was doing there. This street led to both the bus and railway stations and it wouldn't need a genius to rumble my little game. There was no cover here, no escape, and I wondered idly if there had ever been a veterinary surgeon in the glasshouse. Maybe I was about to set up some kind of a record.

Then behind me I heard the rhythmic tramp of marching feet and the shrill " 'eft-'ight, 'eft-'ight," that usually went with it. I turned and saw a long blue column approaching with a corporal in charge. As they swung past me I looked again at the SPs—they were laughing at some private joke and they hadn't yet seen me. Without thinking I tagged on to the end of the marching men and within a few seconds was past the SPs unnoticed.

With my mind working with the speed of desperation it seemed I would be safest where I was till I could break away in the direction of the bus station. For a while I had a glorious feeling of anonymity. Then the corporal, still shouting, glanced back. He appeared to find something interesting because he shortened his stride till he was marching beside me.

As he looked me up and down I examined him in turn from the corner of my eye. His fierce little eyes glinted from a pallid, skull-like face. It was some time before he spoke.

"Who the hell are you?" he inquired. It was the number one awkward question but I discerned the faintest gleam of hope; he had spoken in the unmistakeable accent of my home town.

"Herriot, corporal. Two flight, four squadron," I replied in my broadest Glasgow.

"Two flight, four. . . ! This is one flight, three squadron. What the hell are ye daein' here?"

Arms swinging high, staring rigidly ahead, I took a deep breath.

Concealment was futile now. "Tryin' to get tae see ma wife, corp. She's havin' a baby soon."

"Get tae see yer wife? Are ye daft or whit?"

"It's no' far, corp. She lives in Darrowby. Three hours in the bus. Ah wid be back tonight."

"Back tonight! Ye want yer heid examinin'!"

"I've got tae go!"

"Eyes front!" he screamed suddenly at the men before us. " 'Eft-'ight, 'eft-'ight!" Then he turned and studied me as though I were an unbelievable phenomenon. He was a typical product of the bad times in Glasgow between the wars. Stunted, undernourished, but as tough and belligerent as a ferret. "D'ye no' ken," he said at length, "That ye get leave when yer wife has the wean?"

"Aye, but ah canna wait that long. Gimme a break, corp. Ah just want tae get to the bus station."

"Jesus! Is that a'?" He quickened his steps to the head of the column. When he returned he surveyed me again. "Whit part o' Glesca are ye frae?"

"Scotstounhill," I replied. "How about you?"

"Govan."

I turned my head slightly. "Rangers supporter, eh?"

He did not change expression, but an eyebrow flickered and I knew I had him.

"Whit a team!" I murmured reverently. "Many's the time I've stood on the terraces at Ibrox."

He said nothing and I began to recite the names of the great Rangers team of the Thirties. "Dawson, Gray, McDonald, Meiklejohn, Simpson, Brown . . ."

His eyes took on a dreamy expression. Then he appeared to shake himself back to normality. " 'Eft-'ight, 'eft-'ight!" he bawled. "C'mon, c'mon, pick it up!" Then he muttered to me from the corner of his mouth. "There's the bus station. When we march past it run like—!"

He took off again, shouting, to the head of the flight. I saw the buses on my left and dived across the road and through the waiting room door. I snatched off my cap and sat trembling among a group of elderly farmers and their wives. Through the window I could see the long lines of blue moving away down the street and I could still hear the shouts of the corporal.

But he didn't turn round and I saw only his receding back, the narrow shoulders squared, the bent legs stepping it out in time with his men. I never saw him again but to this day I wish I could take him to Ibrox and watch the Rangers with him and maybe buy him a pint at one of the Govan pubs. It wouldn't have mattered if he had turned out to be a Celtic supporter because I had the Celtic team on my tongue all ready to trot out, starting with Kennaway, Cook, McGonagle. It was not the only time my profound knowledge of football has stood me in good stead.

Sitting on the bus, it struck me that the whole world changed within a mile or two as we left the town. Back there the war was everywhere, the thousands of uniformed men, the RAF and army vehicles, the almost palpable atmosphere of suspense. And suddenly it all just stopped.

It vanished as the bus trundled westward and the wide sweep of grey-blue sea fell beneath the rising ground behind the town. I looked out on a landscape of untroubled peace. The long moist furrows of the new-turned soil glittered under the pale February sun, contrasting with the gold stubble fields and the grassy pastures where sheep clustered around their feeding troughs. There was no wind and the smoke rose straight from the farm chimneys and the bare branches of the roadside trees were still as they stretched across the cold sky.

Helen was staying in her father's house, on the bus route, well short of Darrowby. As I walked into the kitchen, she turned her head, and the delight on her face was mixed with astonishment; in fact we were both astonished, she because I was so skinny and I because she was so fat. With the baby only two weeks away Helen was very large indeed, but not too large for me to get my arms around her, and we stood there in the middle of the flagged floor clasped together for a long time with neither of us saying much.

She cooked me egg and chips and sat by me while I ate. All my worries melted away as I looked at her. I had been wondering if she was well and there she was, bouncing with energy, shining-eyed, rosy-cheeked and beautiful.

322

The hour winged past and it seemed no time at all before I was back on the top road waiting in the gathering darkness for the Scarborough bus. The journey back was a bit dreary as the blacked-out vehicle bumped and rattled its way through the darkened villages and over the long stretches of anonymous countryside. It was cold, too, but I sat there happily with the memory of Helen wrapped around me like a warm quilt.

The whole day had been a triumph. I had got away by a lucky stroke and there would be no problem getting back into the Grand because one of my pals would be on sentry duty. Closing my eyes in the gloom I could still feel Helen in my arms and I smiled to myself at the memory of her bounding healthiness. She looked marvellous, the egg and chips had tasted wonderful, everything was great.

## Chapter Nine

I suppose once you embark on a life of crime it gets easier all the time. Making a start is the only hard bit.

At any rate, that is how it seemed to me as I sat in the bus, playing hookey again. There had been absolutely no trouble about dodging out of the Grand, the streets of Scarborough had been empty of SPs and nobody had given me a second look as I strolled casually into the bus station.

It was Saturday, February 13th. Helen was expecting our baby this weekend. It could happen any time and I just didn't see how I could sit and do nothing. Nobody would miss me. It was, I told myself, a mere technical offence, and anyway I had no option. Like the first time I just had to see Helen.

And it wouldn't be long now, I thought, as I hurried up to the familiar doorway of her father's home. I went inside and gazed disappointedly at the empty kitchen—somehow I had been sure she would be standing there waiting for me with her arms wide. I shouted her name and her father came through from an inner room.

"You've got a son," he said.

I put my hand on the back of a chair. "What. . . ?"

"You've got a son." He was so calm. "Few minutes ago. Nurse Brown's just been on the phone. Funny you should walk in."

As I leaned on the chair he gave me a keen look. "Would you like a drop of whisky?"

"Whisky? No—why?"

"Well, you've gone a bit white, lad, that's all. Anyway, you'd better have something to eat."

"No, no thanks, I've got to get out there."

He smiled. "There's no hurry, lad. Anyway, they won't want anybody there too soon. Better eat something."

"Sorry, I couldn't. Would you—would you mind if I borrowed your car?"

Greenside Nursing Home sounded impressive but it was in fact Nurse Brown's dwelling house. She was state registered and usually had two or three of the local women in at a time to have their babies.

She opened the door herself and threw up her hands. "Mr. Herriot! It hasn't taken you long! Where did you spring from?" She was a cheerfully dynamic little woman with mischievous eyes.

I smiled sheepishly. "Well, I just happened to drop in on Mr. Alderson and got the news."

"You might have given us time to get the little fellow properly washed," she said. "But never mind, come up and see him. He's a fine baby—nine pounds."

Still in a dreamlike state I followed her up the stairs of the little house into a small bedroom. Helen was there, in the bed, looking flushed.

"Hello," she said.

I went over and kissed her.

"What was it like?" I asked.

"Awful," Helen replied without enthusiasm. Then she nodded towards the cot beside her.

I took my first look at my son. Little Jimmy was brick red in colour and his face had a bloated, dissipated look. As I hung over him he twisted his tiny fists under his chin and appeared to be undergoing some mighty internal struggle. His face swelled and darkened as he contorted his features and stuck his tongue out of the corner of his mouth.

"My God!" I exclaimed.

The nurse looked at me, startled.

"What's the matter?"

"Well, he's a funny looking little thing, isn't he?"

"What!" She stared at me furiously. "Mr. Herriot, how can you say such a thing? He's a beautiful baby!"

I peered into the cot again. Jimmy greeted me with a lop-sided leer, turned purple and blew a few bubbles.

"Are you sure he's all right?" I said.

There was a tired giggle from the bed but Nurse Brown was not amused. "All right? What exactly do you mean?" She drew herself up stiffly.

I shuffled my feet. "Well, er—is there anything wrong with him?"

I thought she was going to strike me. "Anything . . . how dare you! Whatever are you talking about? I've never heard such nonsense!"

She turned towards the bed, but Helen, a weary smile on her face, had closed her eyes.

I drew the enraged little woman to one side. "Look, Nurse, have you by chance got any others on the premises?"

"Any other what?" she asked icily.

"Babies—new babies. I want to compare Jimmy with another one."

There was a long pause as she looked at me as though I was something new and incredible. "Well—there's Mrs. Dewburn in the next room. Little Sidney was born about the same time as Jimmy."

"Can I have a look at him?" I gazed at her appealingly.

She hesitated then a pitying smile crept over her face. "Oh you . . . you . . . just a minute, then."

She went into the other room and I heard a mumble of voices. She reappeared and beckoned to me.

Mrs. Dewburn was the butcher's wife and I knew her well. The face on the pillow was hot and tired like Helen's.

326

"Eee, Mr. Herriot, I didn't expect to see you."

"I'm on—er—leave at the moment, Mrs. Dewburn."

I looked in the cot. Sidney was dark red and bloated, too, and he, also seemed to be wrestling with himself. The inner battle showed in a series of grotesque facial contortions culminating in a toothless snarl.

I stepped back involuntarily. "What a beautiful child," I said.

"Yes, isn't he lovely," said his mother fondly.

"He is indeed, gorgeous." I took another disbelieving glance into the cot. "Well, thank you very much, Mrs. Dewburn. It was kind of you to let me see him."

"Not at all, Mr. Herriot, it's nice of you to take an interest."

Outside the door I took a long breath and wiped my brow. The relief was tremendous. Sidney was even funnier than Jimmy.

When I returned to Helen's room Nurse Brown was sitting on the bed and the two women were clearly laughing at me. And of course, looking back, I must have appeared silly. Sidney Dewburn and my son are now two big, strong, remarkably good-looking young men so my fears were groundless.

The little nurse looked at me quizzically. I think she had forgiven me.

"I suppose you think all your calves and foals are beautiful right from the moment they are born?"

"Well, yes," I replied. "I have to admit it—I think they are."

## Chapter Ten

Do dogs have a sense of humour?

I felt I needed all mine as I stood on guard outside the Grand. It was after midnight with a biting wind swirling across the empty square and wryly I wondered how, after my romantic ideas of training to be a pilot, I came to be defending the Grand Hotel at Scarborough against all comers.

No doubt there was something comic in the situation and I suppose that was what set my mind in the direction of farmer Bailes's dog, Shep.

Mr. Bailes's little place was situated in Highburn Village and to get into the farmyard you had to walk twenty yards or so between the neighbouring house and the five foot wall of the front garden of the farm. In this garden Shep lurked for most of the day.

He was a huge dog, much larger than the average collie. In fact I am convinced he was part Alsatian because he was quite different from the stringy little sheep dogs I mostly saw on my daily round.

As I walked beside the garden wall my mind was already in the byre, just visible at the far end of the yard. One of the Bailes' cows, Rose by name, had begun to grunt and go off her milk. This is the kind of obscure digestive ailment which interferes with a veterinary surgeon's sleep. It is so difficult to diagnose.

Anyway, I was halfway down the alley when an appalling explosion of sound blasted into my right ear. It was Shep.

The wall was just the right height for the dog to make a leap and bark into the ear of the passersby. It was a favourite gambit of his and I had been caught before; but never so successfully as now. My attention had been far away and the dog had timed his jump to a split second so that his bark came at the highest point, his teeth only inches from my face. And his voice befitted his size, a great bull bellow surging out from the depths of his powerful chest and booming from his gaping jaws.

I rose several inches into the air and when I descended, heart thumping, head singing, I glared over the wall. But as usual all I saw was the hairy form bounding away out of sight.

I wasn't in the best of shape therefore to receive bad news and that was what awaited me in the byre. I had only to look at the farmer's face to know that the cow was worse.

"Ah reckon she's got a stoppage," Mr. Bailes muttered gloomily. "She's nobbut passin' little hard bits. It's a proper stoppage, ah tell you."

The entire spectrum of abdominal disorders was lumped as "stoppages" by the older race of farmers. I gritted my teeth and brought in from my car the gastric lavage outfit I loved so well. As I pumped in the two gallons of warm water, rich in formalin and sodium chloride I felt like Napoleon sending in the Old Guard at Waterloo. If this didn't work nothing would.

And yet I didn't feel my usual confidence. There was something different here. I had to do *something* to try to start this cow's insides functioning. I did not like the look of her today: her eyes had begun to retreat into her head—the worst sign of all in bovines —and she had stopped eating.

Next morning I was driving down the village street when I saw Mrs. Bailes coming out of the shop. I drew up and pushed my head out of the window. "How's Rose this morning, Mrs. Bailes?"

She rested her basket on the ground and looked down at me gravely. "Oh, she's bad, Mr. Herriot. Me husband thinks she's goin' down fast. If you want to find him you'll have to go across the field there. He's mendin' the door in that little barn."

Misery enveloped me as I drove over to the gate leading into the field. I left the car in the road and lifted the latch. "Damn! Damn! Damn!" I muttered as I trailed across the green. If this animal died it would be a sickening blow to a small farmer with ten cows and only a few pigs.

And yet, despite it all, I felt peace stealing over me. It was a large field and I could see the barn at the far end as I walked with the tall grass brushing my knees. It was a meadow ready for cutting, the sun was hot and every step brought the fragrance of clover and warm grass rising about me into the crystal freshness of the air.

And there was the silence; it was the most soothing thing of all. I looked drowsily around at the empty green miles sleeping under the sunshine. Nothing stirred, there was no sound.

Then the ground at my feet erupted in an incredible blast of noise. For a dreadful moment the blue sky was obscured by an enormous hairy form and a red mouth went "WAAAHH!" in my face. I staggered back and as I glared wildly I saw Shep disappearing at top speed towards the gate. Concealed right in the middle of the field he had waited till he saw the whites of my eyes before making his assault.

Whether he had been there by accident or had spotted me arriving and slunk into position I shall never know, but the result was certainly the worst fright I have ever had. I live a life which is well larded with scares and alarms but this great dog rising bellowing from that empty landscape was something on its own.

329

I was still trembling when I reached the barn and hardly said a word as Mr. Bailes led me back across the road to the farm and my patient.

The flesh had melted from her and she stared at the wall apathetically from sunken eyes. The doom-laden grunt was louder.

"It's the worst stoppage ah've seen for a bit," said Mr. Bailes. "Ah gave her a dose of some right powerful stuff this mornin' but it's done no good."

I passed a weary hand over my brow. "What was that, Mr. Bailes?" It was always a bad sign when the client started using his own medicine.

The farmer reached to the cluttered windowsill and handed me a bottle. "Doctor Hornibrook's Stomach Elixir. A sovereign remedy for all diseases of cattle." The doctor, in top hat and frock coat, looked confidently out at me from the label. I pulled out the cork and took a sniff, then staggered back with watering eyes. It smelt like pure ammonia but I was in no position to be superior about it.

"That dang grunt!" The farmer hunched his shoulders. "What's cause of it?"

It was no good my saying it sounded like a circumscribed area of peritonitis because I didn't know what was behind it.

I decided to have one last go with the lavage. It was still the strongest weapon in my armoury but this time, even though I added two pounds of black treacle to the mixture, I had no great hopes. The clinical instinct I was beginning to develop told me that something inside this animal was fundamentally awry.

It was not till the following afternoon that I drove into Highburn. I left the car outside the farm and was about to walk between the walls when I paused and stared at a cow in the field on the other side of the road. That cow was Rose. There could be no mistake— she was a fine deep red with a distinctive white mark on her left flank.

I opened the gate and within seconds my cares dropped from me. She was wonderfully improved—in fact she looked like a normal animal. I walked up to her and scratched the root of her tail. She looked round at me as she cropped the grass; her eyes were no longer sunken but bright and full. The grunt had disappeared and her udder hung heavy between her legs. The difference since yesterday was incredible.

As relief and triumph flooded through me I saw Mr. Bailes climbing over the wall from the next field. He would still be mending that barn door.

"Ah, good morning to you, Mr. Bailes," I said expansively as he approached. "Rose looks fine today, doesn't she?"

"Aye, she's a different cow, all right." The farmer took off his cap and wiped his brow. "But ah'll tell you last night she was like dyin'—that pumpin' job hadn't done no good at all."

"What do you mean? It cured her, surely."

"Nay, lad, it were Jim Oakley as cured her."

"Jim Oakley?"

"Aye, Jim was round 'ere. He often comes in of an evenin' and he took one look at the cow and told me to give her a bloody good gallop round t'field."

"What!"

"Aye, that's what he said. He'd seen 'em like that afore and a good gallop put 'em right. So we got Rose out here and did as he said and by gaw it did the trick. She looked better right away."

I drew myself up. "And who is Jim Oakley?"

"He's t'postman, of course. But he used to keep a few beasts years ago. He's a very clever man wi' stock, is Jim."

"No doubt, but I assure you, Mr. Bailes . . ."

The farmer raised a hand. "Say no more, lad. Jim put 'er right and there's no denyin' it."

I had had enough. During the farmer's eulogy I had been distractedly scratching the cow and had soiled my hand in the process. Mustering the remains of my dignity I nodded to Mr. Bailes. "Well, I must be on my way. Do you mind if I go into the house to wash my hands?"

"You go right in," he replied. "T'missus will get you some hot water."

Walking back down the field the cruel injustice of the thing bore down on me increasingly. I wandered as in a dream through the gate and across the road. Before entering the alley between the walls I glanced into the garden. It was empty. Shuffling beside the

331

rough stones I sank deeper into my misery. There was no doubt I had emerged from that episode as a complete Charlie. No matter where I looked I couldn't see a gleam of light.

At the end of the wall, as I was about to turn right towards the door of the farm kitchen, I heard the sudden rattle of a chain then a roaring creature launched itself at me, bayed mightly into my face and was gone.

This time I thought my heart would stop. With my defences at their lowest I was in no state to withstand Shep. I half lay against the wall, the blood thundering in my ears, I had quite forgotten that Mrs. Bailes occasionally chained him in the kennel at the entrance to discourage unwelcome visitors.

Now, I have no time for people who lose their temper with animals, but something snapped in my mind then. I grabbed the chain and began to pull on it frenziedly. That dog which had tortured me was there in that kennel. For once I knew where to get at him and this time I was going to have the matter out with him.

As I hauled inexorably a nose appeared, then a head then all of the big animal hanging limply by his collar. He showed no desire to get up but I was merciless and dragged him inch by inch over the cobbles till he was lying at my feet.

Beside myself with rage, I crouched, shook my fist under his nose and yelled at him. "If you do that to me again I'll knock your bloody head off! Do you hear me, I'll knock your bloody head clean off!"

Shep rolled frightened eyes at me and his tail flickered apologetically between his legs. Finally he rolled on his back where he lay inert with half-closed eyes.

So now I knew. He was a softie. All his ferocious attacks were just a game. I began to calm down but for all that I wanted him to get the message.

"Right, mate," I said in a menacing whisper. "Remember what I've said!" I let go the chain and gave a final shout. "Now get back in there!"

Shep, almost on his knees, tail tucked well in, shot back into his kennel and I turned to the farmhouse to wash my hands.

I WAS SURPRISED, about a month later, to receive another call to one of Mr. Bailes's cows. I felt that after my performance with Rose he would have called on the services of Jim Oakley for any further trouble.

I had no doubt then that I had been unfairly judged but I am wiser now and in retrospect I think I was wrong.

The symptoms displayed by Mr. Bailes's cow were typical of displacement of the abomasum (when the fourth stomach slips round from the right to the left side) and it was a condition that was just not recognized in those days.

At the present time we correct the condition by surgery—pushing the displaced organ back to the right side and tacking it there with sutures. But sometimes a similar result can be obtained by rolling the cow over, so why not by making her run. . . ? I freely admit that I have many times adopted Jim Oakley's precept of a "bloody good gallop", often with spectacular results. To this day I frequently learn things from farmers but that was one time when I learned from a postman.

Anyway, leaving my car outside Mr. Bailes's farm I paused at the end of the alley, waiting. A faint tinkle of metal told me that Shep was lurking there in his kennel but all I saw was the end of a nose which quietly withdrew as I approached. So my outburst had got through to the big dog—he knew I wasn't going to stand any more nonsense from him.

And yet, as I drove away after the visit I didn't feel good about it. A victory over an animal is a hollow one and I had the uncomfortable feeling that I had deprived him of his chief pleasure. After all, though Shep's hobby could result in the occasional heart failure it was his thing and part of him. The thought that I had crushed something out of his life was a disquieting one. I wasn't proud.

So that when, later that summer, I was driving through Highburn, I paused outside the Bailes's farm. The village street, white and dusty, slumbered under the afternoon sun. Nothing moved—except for one small fat man strolling towards the opening between the walls. He was one of the tinkers from a camp outside the village, and he carried an armful of pots and pans.

Fascinated, I watched as the man turned unhurriedly into the opening. As I expected it all happened halfway along. The perfectly timed leap, the momentary pause at the summit then the tremendous "WOOF!" into the unsuspecting ear.

It had its usual effect. I had a brief view of flailing arms and flying pans followed by a prolonged metallic clatter, then the little man reappeared like a projectile, and sped away from me up the street. Considering his physique he showed an astonishing turn of speed, and he did not pause till he disappeared into the shop at the far end of the village.

I don't know why he went in there because he wouldn't find any stronger restorative than ginger pop.

I smiled to myself as I let in the clutch and moved off. I would stop at the shop and tell the little man that he could collect his pans without the slightest fear of being torn limb from limb, but my over-riding emotion was one of relief that I had not cut the sparkle out of the big dog's life.

Shep was still having his fun.

## Chapter Eleven

It must be unusual to feel senile in one's twenties but it was happening to me. There were a few men of my own age among my RAF friends but for the most part I was surrounded by eighteen- and nineteen-year-olds.

These boys used to pull my leg. The fact that I was not merely married but a father put me really in the dotage class. They were all having a marvellous time, chasing the local girls, drinking, going to dances. I often thought that if it had all happened a few years earlier I would have been doing the same.

But it was no good now. Most of me was still back in Darrowby. During the day there was enough pressure to keep my mind occupied, but in the evenings when I was off the leash all I wanted to do was the simple things I had done with Helen; the long games of bezique by the fireside, tense battles on the push-ha'penny board; we even used to throw rings at hooks on a board on the wall. Kid's games after a hard slog round the practice, but even now as I look down the years I know I have never found a better way of living.

Sometimes, however, other pictures floated into my mind. Memories from the very early days in Darrowby. Before the RAF, even before Helen. . . .

Siegfried Farnon and I were at breakfast in his big dining room at Skeldale House. My boss looked up from a letter he was reading.

"James, you remember Stewie Brannan? I've got a letter from him here. He's got six kids now and though he doesn't complain I don't think life is exactly a picnic working in a 'dump like Hensfield. Especially when he knocks a bare living out of it." He pulled thoughtfully at the lobe of his ear. "You know, it would be rather nice if he could have a break. Would you be willing to go there and run his practice for a couple of weeks so that he could take his family on holiday?"

"Certainly. Glad to. But you'll be a bit pushed here on your own, won't you?"

Siegfried waved a hand. "It'll do me good. Anyway it's the quiet time for us. I'll write back today."

Stewie grasped the opportunity eagerly and within a few days I was on the road to Hensfield. Less than two hours after leaving the clean grassy fells and crystal air of Darrowby I saw the forest of factory chimneys sprouting from the brown pall of grime.

This was the industrial West Riding and I drove past mills as dark and satanic as any I had dreamed of, past long rows of dreary houses. Everything was black; houses, mills, trees, even the surrounding hillsides, smeared and soiled from the smoke which drifted across the town from a hundred belching stacks.

Stewie's surgery was right in the heart of it, a gloomy edifice in a terrace of sooty stone. I rang the bell, the door opened, and Stewie stood before me.

He seemed to fill the entrance, his big, good-natured face beaming with delight.

He reached out, grabbed my hand and pulled me through the doorway. "Jim! Great to see you!" He put an arm round my shoulders as we crossed a dark hallway. "It's good of you to help me out like this. The family are thrilled—they're all in the town

335

shopping for the holiday. We've got fixed up in a flat at Blackpool."

We went into a room at the back where a rickety folding table stood on brown linoleum. I saw a sink in one corner, a few shelves with bottles and a white-painted cupboard.

"This is where I see the animals," Stewie said contentedly. He looked at his watch. "Twenty past five—I have a surgery at five thirty. I'll show you round till then."

It didn't take long because there wasn't much to see. I knew there was a more fashionable veterinary firm in Hensfield and that Stewie made his living from the poor people of the town; the whole set-up was an illustration of practice on a shoestring. There didn't seem to be more than one of anything—one straight suture needle, one curved needle, one pair of scissors, one syringe. There was a sparse selection of drugs and an extraordinary array of dispensing bottles and jars. These bottles were of many strange shapes—weird things which I had never seen in a dispensary before.

Stewie seemed to read my thoughts. "It's nothing great, Jim. I haven't a smart practice and I don't make a lot, but we manage to clear the housekeeping and that's the main thing."

The end of the room was cut off by a curtain which my colleague drew to one side. "This is what you might call the waiting room." He smiled as I looked in some surprise at half a dozen wooden chairs arranged round the walls. "No high-powered stuff, Jim, no queues into the street, but we get by."

Some of Stewie's clients were already filing in; two little girls with a black dog, a cloth-capped old man with a terrier on a string, a teenage boy carrying a rabbit in a basket.

"Right," the big man said. "We'll get started." He pulled on a white coat, opened the curtain and said, "First, please."

The girls put their dog on the table. He was a long-tailed mixture of breeds and he stood trembling with fear.

"All right, lad," Stewie murmured. "I'm not going to hurt you." He stroked and patted the quivering head before turning to the girls. "What's the trouble, then?"

"It's 'is leg, 'e's lame," one of them replied.

As if in confirmation the dog raised a foreleg and held it up with a pitiful expression. Stewie engulfed the limb with his great hand

336

and palpated it with the utmost care. And it struck me immediately
—the gentleness of this shambling bear of a man.

"There's nothing broken," he said. "He's just sprained his
shoulder. Try to rest it for a few days and rub this in night and
morning."

He poured some whitish liniment from a Winchester quart into
one of the odd-shaped bottles and handed it over.

One of the little girls held out her hand and unclasped her
fingers to reveal a shilling in her palm.

"Thanks," said Stewie without surprise. "Goodbye."

He saw several other cases; then as he was on his way to the
curtain two grubby urchins appeared through the door carrying a
clothes basket containing a widely varied assortment of glassware.

Stewie bent over the basket, lifting out sauce bottles, pickle jars,
ketchup containers and examining them with the air of a connoisseur. At length he appeared to come to a decision. "Fourpence,"
he said.

"Sixpence," said the urchins in unison.

"Fivepence," grunted Stewie.

"Sixpence," chorused the urchins. There was a hint of triumph
in the cry.

Stewie sighed. "Go on then." He passed over the coin and began
to stack the bottles under the sink.

"I just scrape off the labels and give them a good boil up, Jim.
It's a big saving."

"I see. Yes, of course." The mystery of the strangely shaped
dispensing bottles was resolved.

It was six thirty when the last client came through the curtain.
I had watched Stewie examine each animal, taking his time and
treating their conditions ably within his limited resources. His
charges were all a shilling or two shillings and it was easy to see
why he only just cleared the housekeeping.

One other thing I noticed; the people all seemed to like him. He
had no "front" but he was kind and concerned. I felt there was a
lesson there.

The last arrival was a stout lady with a prim manner and a very
correct manner of speech.

"My dog was bit last week," she announced, "and I'm afraid the wound is goin' antiseptic."

"Ah yes." Stewie nodded gravely. He explored the animal's neck with a gossamer touch. "It's quite nasty, really. He could have an abscess there if we're not careful."

He took a long time over clipping the hair away, swabbing out a deep puncture with peroxide of hydrogen. Then he puffed in some dusting powder, applied a pad of cotton wool and secured it with a bandage. He followed with an anti-staphylococcal injection and finally handed over a sauce bottle filled to the brim with acriflavine solution.

As the lady opened her purse a long inward struggle showed in the occasional twitches of his cheeks and flickering of his eyelids. Finally he squared his shoulders. "That," he said resolutely, "will be three and sixpence."

It was a vast fee by Stewie's standards but probably the minimum in other veterinary establishments and I couldn't see how he could make any profit from the transaction.

After the lady had left a sudden uproar broke out within the house. Stewie gave me a seraphic smile. "That'll be Meg and the kids. Come and meet them."

We went out to the hall and into an incredible hubbub. Children shouted, screamed and laughed, spades and pails clattered, a large ball thumped from wall to wall and above it all a baby bawled relentlessly.

Stewie moved into the mob and extracted a small woman. "This," he murmured with quiet pride, "is my wife." He gazed at her like a small boy admiring a film star.

"How do you do," I said.

Meg Brannan took my hand and smiled. "Oh, Mr. Herriot, it is good of you and Mr. Farnon to help us out like this. We're so looking forward to going away." Any glamour about her existed only in her husband's eye. A ravaged prettiness still remained but her face bore the traces of some tough years. I could imagine her life of mother, housewife, cook, secretary, receptionist and animal nurse.

I shrugged. "Oh, it's a pleasure, Mrs. Brannan. I'm sure I'll enjoy it and I hope you all have a marvellous holiday." I really meant it—she looked as though she needed one.

I was introduced to the children but I never really got them sorted out. Apart from the baby who yelled indefatigably from leather lungs, I think there were three little boys and two little girls but I couldn't be sure—they moved around too quickly.

The only time they were silent was for a brief period at supper when Meg fed them and us from a kind of cauldron of mutton, potatoes and carrots. It was very good, too, and was followed by a vast blancmange with jam on top.

Next morning I saw the family off. Seated at the wheel of a large rust-encrusted Ford V8 Stewie beamed through the cracked side windows with serene contentment. Meg, by his side, managed a harassed smile and at the other windows an assortment of dogs and children fought for a vantage point. As the car moved away a pram, several suitcases and a cot swayed perilously on the roof, the children yelled, the dogs barked, the baby bawled, then they were gone.

As I re-entered the house the unaccustomed silence settled around me and with it came a faint unease. I had to look after this practice for two weeks and in the thinly furnished surgery I just didn't have the tools to tackle any major problem.

But it was easy to comfort myself. From what I had seen this wasn't the sort of place where dramatic things happened. Stewie said he made most of his living by castrating tom cats and I supposed if you threw in a few ear cankers and minor ailments that would be about it.

The morning surgery seemed to confirm this impression: a few nondescript pets with mild conditions, I happily dispensed a series of Bovril bottles and meat-paste jars containing Stewie's limited drug store. I had only one difficulty and that was with the table which kept collapsing when I lifted the animals onto it. It had folding legs held by metal struts underneath and these were apt to disengage at crucial moments causing the patient to slide abruptly to the floor. After a while I got the hang of the thing and kept one leg jammed against the struts throughout the examination.

It was about 10.30 a.m. when I finally parted the curtains and found the waiting room empty. As I locked the door it struck me that I had very little to do till the afternoon surgery. At Darrowby I would have been dashing out to start the long day's driving round the countryside but here almost all the work was done at the practice house.

I was wondering how I would put the time in after the single outside visit on the book when the doorbell rang. Then it rang again followed by a frantic pounding on the wood. I hurried through the curtain and turned the handle. A well-dressed young couple stood on the step. The man held a golden Labrador in his arms; behind them a caravan drawn by a large gleaming car stood by the kerb.

"Are you the vet?" the girl gasped. She was in her twenties, auburn-haired, extremely attractive, but her eyes were terrified.

I nodded. "Yes—yes, I am. What's the trouble?"

"It's our dog." The young man's voice was hoarse, his face deathly pale. "A car hit him."

I stepped forward and as I peered into the crook of the man's arm a freezing wave drove through me. The dog's hind leg was hanging off at the hock. Not fractured but snapped through the joint and dangling from what looked like a mere shred of skin. In the bright morning sunshine the white ends of naked bones glittered with a sickening lustre. When I spoke the voice didn't sound like my own. "Bring him in," I muttered. Clearly I had been wrong when I thought that nothing ever happened here.

I held the waiting room curtains apart as the young man staggered in and placed his burden on the table.

Now I could see the whole thing; the typical signs of a road accident; the dirt driven savagely into the glossy gold of the coat, the multiple abrasions. But that mangled leg wasn't typical. I had never seen anything like it before.

I dragged my eyes round to the girl. "How did it happen?"

"Oh, just in a flash." The tears welled in her eyes. "We are on a caravanning holiday. We had no intention of staying in Hensfield," (I could understand that) "but we stopped for a newspaper, Kim jumped out of the car and that was it."

I looked at the big dog stretched motionless on the table. I

340

reached out a hand and gently ran my fingers over the noble outlines of the head.

"Poor old lad," I murmured and for an instant the beautiful hazel eyes turned to me and the tail thumped briefly against the wood. I began my examination. The abrasions on the skin were trivial. He was shocked but his mucous membranes were pink enough to suggest that there was no internal haemorrhage. He had escaped serious injury except for that terrible leg.

I stared at it intently, appalled by the smooth glistening articular surfaces of the joint. There was something obscene in its exposure in a living animal.

I began a feverish search of the premises, pulling open drawers, cupbards, opening tins and boxes. My heart leaped at each little find; a jar of catgut in spirit, a packet of lint, a sprinkler tin of iodoform, and—treasure trove indeed—a bottle of barbiturate anaesthetic.

Most of all I needed just an ounce or two of sulphanilamide but there I was disappointed. It was when I came upon the box of plaster of Paris bandages that something seemed to click.

At that time the Spanish civil war was still vivid in people's minds. In the chaos of the later stages there had been no proper medicaments to treat the terrible wounds. They had often been encased in plaster and left, in the grim phrase, to "stew in their own juice". Sometimes the results were surprisingly good.

I knew what I was going to do. Gripped by a fierce determination I inserted a needle and slowly injected the anaesthetic. Kim blinked, yawned lazily and went to sleep. I quickly laid out my meagre armoury, then began to shift the dog into a better position. But I had forgotten about the table and as I lifted the hind quarters the whole thing gave way and the dog slithered helplessly towards the floor.

"Catch him!" At my frantic shout the man grabbed the inert form, then I reinserted the struts in their holes and got the wooden surface back on the level.

"Put your leg under there," I gasped, then turned to the girl. "And would you please do the same at the other end. This table mustn't fall over once I get started."

Silently they complied and as I looked at them, each with a leg jammed against the underside, I felt a deep sense of shame. What sort of place did they think this was?

But for a long time after I forgot everything. First I put the joint back in place, slipping the ridges of the tibial-tarsal trochlea into the grooves at the distal end of the tibia as I had done so often in the anatomy lab at college. And I noticed with a flicker of hope that some of the ligaments were still intact and, most important, that a few good blood vessels still ran down to the lower part of the limb.

I never said a word as I cleaned and disinfected the area, and began to stitch. I stitched interminably, pulling together shattered tendons, torn joint capsule and fascia. It was a warm morning and as the sun beat on the surgery window the sweat broke out on my forehead. By the time I had sutured the skin a little river was flowing down my nose and dripping from the tip. Next, more iodoform, then the lint and finally two of the plaster bandages making a firm cast above the hock down over the foot.

I straightened up and faced the young couple. They had never moved from their uncomfortable postures as they held the table upright.

I mopped my brow and drew a long breath. "Well, that's it. I'd be inclined to leave it as it is for a week then wherever you are let a vet have a look at it."

They were silent for a moment then the girl spoke. "I would rather you saw it yourself." The husband nodded agreement.

"Really?" I was amazed. I had thought they would never want to see me or my collapsible table again.

"Yes, of course we would," the man said. "You have taken such pains over him. Whatever happens we are deeply grateful to you, Mr. Brannan."

"Oh, I'm not Mr. Brannan, he's on holiday. I'm his locum, my name is Herriot."

He held out his hand. "Well, thank you again, Mr. Herriot. I am Peter Gillard and this is my wife, Marjorie."

We shook hands and he took the dog in his arms and went out to the car.

342

FOR THE NEXT few days I couldn't keep Kim's leg out of my mind. At times I felt I was crazy trying to salvage a limb that was joined to the dog only by a strip of skin. I had never met anything remotely like it before and in unoccupied moments that hock joint with all its imponderables would float across my vision.

There were plenty of these moments because Stewie's was a restful practice. Apart from the three daily surgeries there was little activity and in particular the uncomfortable pre-breakfast call so common in Darrowby was unknown here.

The Brannans had left the house and me in the care of Mrs. Holroyd, an elderly widow who slouched around in a flowered overall down which ash cascaded from a permanent, dangling cigarette. She wasn't a good riser but she soon had me trained because after a few mornings when I couldn't find her I began to prepare my own breakfast and that was how it stayed.

However, at other times she looked after me very well. She was what you might call a good rough cook and pushed large tasty meals at me regularly with a "There y'are, luv," watching me impassively till I started to eat. The only thing that disturbed me was the long trembling finger of ash which always hung over my food from the cigarette that was part of her.

As I awaited the return of Kim the tension mounted. And even when the seventh day came round I was still in suspense because the Gillards did not appear at the morning surgery. When they failed to show up at the afternoon session I began to conclude that they had had the good sense to return south to a more sophisticated establishment. But at five thirty they were there.

I knew it even before I pulled the curtains apart. The smell of doom was everywhere, filling the premises, and when I went through the curtains it hit me; the sickening stink of putrefaction.

Gangrene. It was the fear which had haunted me all week and now it was realized.

Kim tried to rise when he saw me but I had eyes only for the dangling useless hind limb where my once stone-hard plaster hung in sodden folds. What had I done to this beautiful dog? I had been crazy to try the experiment. A gangrenous leg meant that even amputation might be too late to save his life. Death from septicaemia was likely now and what the hell could I do for him now in this ramshackle surgery?

"Right," I said to Peter Gillard, putting my arms under the chest. "You take the back end and we'll lift him up."

As we hoisted the heavy dog onto the table the flimsy structure disintegrated immediately, but this time the young people were ready for it and thrust their legs under the struts like a well trained team till the surface was level again.

With Kim stretched on his side I fingered the bandage. It usually took time and patience with a special saw to remove a plaster but this was just a stinking pulp. My hand shook as I cut the bandage lengthways with scissors and removed it.

I had steeled myself against the sight of the cold dead limb with its green flesh but though there was pus and serous fluid everywhere the exposed flesh was a surprising, healthy pink. I took the foot in my hand and my heart gave a great bound. It was warm and so was the leg right up to the hock. There was no gangrene.

Feeling suddenly weak I leaned against the table. "I'm sorry about the terrible smell. All the pus and discharge have been decomposing under the bandage for a week but despite the mess it's not as bad as I feared."

"Do you . . . do you think you can save his leg?" Marjorie Gillard's voice trembled.

"I honestly don't know. So much has to happen. But I'd say it was a case of so far so good."

I cleaned the area thoroughly, gave a dusting of iodoform and applied fresh lint and two more plaster bandages.

"You'll feel a lot more comfortable now, Kim," I said, and the big dog flapped his tail against the wood at the sound of his name.

I turned to his owners. "I want him to have another week in plaster, so what would you like to do?"

"Oh, we'll stay around Hensfield," Peter Gillard replied. "We've found a place for our caravan by the river—it's not too bad."

"Very well, till next Saturday, then." I watched Kim walk out, holding his new white cast high and as I went back into the house relief flowed over me in a warm wave. But at the back of my mind the voice of caution sounded. There was still a long way to go.

344

DURING THE second week I had a mildly indecent postcard from Stewie and a view of Blackpool Tower from his wife. The weather was scorching and they were having the best holiday of their lives. I tried to picture them enjoying themselves but I had to wait a few weeks for the evidence—a snap taken by a beach photographer. The whole family were standing in the sea, grinning delightedly into the camera as the wavelets lapped round their ankles. The children brandished buckets and spades, the baby dangled bandy legs towards the water, but it was Stewie who fascinated me. A smile of blissful contentment beamed from beneath a knotted handkerchief, sturdy braces supported baggy flannel trousers rolled decorously calf high. He was the archetype of the British father on holiday.

When I looked into the waiting room on my last day at Hensfield there was only one animal among the odd assortment of chairs. That animal was Kim, golden and beautiful, sitting between his owners! When he saw me he sprang up with swishing tail and laughing mouth.

There was none of the smell which had horrified me before but as I looked at the dog I could sniff something else—the sweet scent of success. Because he was touching the ground with that leg; not putting any weight on it but definitely dotting it down as he capered around me.

I could hardly wait to get started. "Get him on the table," I cried, then began to laugh as the Gillards automatically pushed their legs against the collapsible struts. They knew the drill now.

When I got the plaster off I found a bit of discharge but healthy granulation tissue everywhere. Pink new flesh was binding the shattered joint together, smoothing over and hiding the original mutilation.

"Is his leg safe now?" Marjorie Gillard asked softly.

I looked at her and smiled. "Yes, it is. There's no doubt about it now." I rubbed my hand under the big dog's chin and the tail beat ecstatically on the wood. "He'll probably have a stiff joint but that won't matter, will it?"

I applied the last of Stewie's bandages then we hoisted Kim off the table.

"Well, that's it," I said. "Take him to your own vet in another fortnight. After that I don't think he'll need a bandage at all."

The Gillards left on their journey home and a couple of hours later Stewie and his family returned. The children were very brown; even the baby, still bawling resolutely, had a fine tan. The skin had peeled off Meg's nose but she looked wonderfully relaxed. Stewie, in open necked shirt and with a face like a boiled lobster, seemed to have put on weight.

"That holiday saved our lives, Jim," he said. "I can't thank you enough, and please tell Siegfried how grateful we are. Is everything all right in the practice?"

"Yes, Stewie, it is. I had my ups and downs of course but everything's fine now."

And everything did seem fine as I drove away from the smoke. I watched the houses thin and fall away behind me till the whole world opened out clean and free and I saw the green line of the fells rising over Darrowby.

The following Christmas I had a letter from the Gillards with a packet of snapshots showing a big golden dog clearing a gate, leaping high for a ball. There was hardly any stiffness in the leg, they said; he was perfectly sound.

I suppose we all tend to remember the good things but even now when I think of Hensfield the thing I remember best is Kim.

## Chapter Twelve

"Hey you! Where the 'ell d'you think you're goin'?"

Coming from the RAF Service Police it was a typical mode of address and the man who barked it out wore the usual truculent expression.

"Extra navigation class, corporal," I replied.

"Lemme see your pass!"

He snatched it from my hand, read it and returned it without looking at me. I slunk out into the street feeling like a prisoner on parole.

Not all the SPs were like that but I found most of them lacking in charm. And it brought home to me something which had been slowly dawning on me ever since I joined the Air Force; that I had been spoiled for quite a long time now. Spoiled by the fact that I had always been treated with respect because I was a veterinary surgeon, a member of an honourable profession. And now I was an AC2, on three shillings a day, the lowest form of life in the RAF. The "Hey you!" was a reflection of my status.

Mind you, you have to put up with a certain amount of cheek in most jobs and veterinary practice is no exception. Even now I could recall Ralph Beamish the racehorse trainer's glowering face as he watched me getting out of my car.

"Where's Mr. Farnon?" he grunted.

My toes curled. I had heard that often enough, especially among the horse fraternity around Darrowby. Being an unhorsey vet was a penance at times, especially in a racing stable like this which was an equine shrine. Siegfried, apart altogether from his intuitive skill, was able to talk the horse language. He could discuss effortlessly and at length the breeding and points of his patients; he rode, he hunted, he even looked the part with his long aristocratic face, clipped moustache and lean frame.

The trainers loved him and some, like Beamish, took it as a mortal insult when he failed to come in person to minister to their valuable charges.

I sighed inwardly. "I'm sorry, Mr. Beamish, but he'll be away all day and I thought I'd better come along rather than leave it till tomorrow."

He made no attempt to hide his disgust. "Well, come on, then." He blew out his fat, purpled cheeks, dug his hands deep in his breeches pockets and stumped away towards one of the boxes which bordered the yard.

"He's in there," he muttered. "Came in lame from exercise this morning."

A lad led out a bay gelding and there was no need to trot the animal to diagnose the affected leg; he nodded down on his near fore in an unmistakable way.

"I think he's lame in the shoulder," Beamish said.

I picked up the off fore and cleaned out the frog and sole with a hoof knife; there was no sign of bruising and no sensitivity when I tapped the handle of the knife against the horn.

I felt my way up over the coronet to the fetlock and after some palpation I located a spot which was painful on pressure.

I looked up from my crouching position. "This seems to be the trouble, Mr. Beamish. I think he must have struck into himself with his hind foot just there."

"Where?" The trainer leaned over me and peered down at the leg. "I can't see anything."

"No, the skin isn't broken, but he flinches if you press here."

Beamish grunted. "He'd flinch anywhere if you squeeze him like you're doing."

My hackles began to rise at his tone but I kept my voice calm. "I'm sure that's what it is. I should apply a hot antiphlogistine poultice just above the fetlock and alternate with a cold hose on it twice a day."

"Well, I'm just as sure you're wrong. It's not down there at all. The way that horse carries his leg he's hurt his shoulder." He gestured to the lad. "Harry, see that he gets some heat on that shoulder right away."

If the man had struck me I couldn't have felt worse. I opened my mouth to argue but he was walking away.

"There's another horse I want you to look at," he said. He led the way into a nearby box and pointed to a big brown animal. "Mr. Farnon put a red blister on that leg six months ago. He's been resting in here ever since. He's going sound now—d'you think he's ready to go out?"

I ran my fingers over the length of the flexor tendons. There was no thickening. Then I lifted the foot and as I explored further I found a tender area in the superficial flexor.

I straightened up. "He's still a bit sore," I said. "I think it would be safer to keep him in for a bit longer."

"Can't agree with you," Beamish snapped. He turned to the lad. "Turn him out, Harry."

I stared at him. Was this a deliberate campaign to make me feel small, to rub in the fact that he didn't think much of me? Anyway he was beginning to get under my skin.

"One thing more," Beamish said. "There's a horse through here been coughing. Have a look at him before you go."

We went through a narrow passage into a smaller yard and Harry entered a box and got hold of a horse's head collar. I followed him, fishing out my thermometer.

As I approached the animal's rear end he laid back his ears, whickered and began to caper around. I hesitated then nodded to the lad. "Lift his fore leg while I take his temperature, will you?"

The lad bent down and seized the foot but Beamish broke in. "Don't bother, Harry, there's no need for that. He won't kick. He's quiet as a sheep."

I paused for a moment. I felt I was right but my stock was low in this establishment. I shrugged, lifted the tail and pushed the thermometer into the rectum.

The two hind feet hit me almost simultaneously, the lower hoof landing full on my solar plexus, and I sailed backwards through the door.

Stretched on the concrete of the yard I gasped in a frantic search for breath. At last I struggled painfully into a sitting position. Through the open door I could see Harry hanging on to the horse's head and staring at me with frightened eyes. Mr. Beamish, on the other hand, was anxiously examining the horse's hind feet one after the other. Obviously he was worried lest they might have sustained some damage by coming into contact with my nasty hard ribs.

Slowly I got up. I was shaken but not really hurt. And I suppose it was instinct that had made me hang on to my thermometer; the delicate tube was still in my hand.

My only emotion as I went back into the box was cold rage. "Lift that bloody foot like I told you!" I shouted at the unfortunate Harry.

"Right, sir! Sorry, sir!" He bent, lifted the foot and held it cupped firmly in his hands.

I turned to Beamish to see if he had any observation to make, but the trainer was silent, gazing at the big animal expressionlessly.

This time I took the temperature without incident. I moved to the head and opened the nostril with finger and thumb, revealing a slight discharge.

"He's got a bit of cold," I said. "I'll give him an injection and leave you some sulphonamide—that's what Mr. Farnon uses in these cases." If my final sentence reassured him in any way he gave no sign, watching dead-faced as I injected 10 cc of Prontosil.

Before I left I took a half-pound packet of sulphonamide from the car boot. Mr. Beamish received the medicine unsmilingly and as I opened the car door I felt a gush of relief that the uncomfortable visit was at an end.

I was starting the engine when one of the apprentices panted up to the trainer. "It's Almira, sir. I think she's chokin'!"

"Choking!" Beamish stared at the boy then whipped round to me. "Almira's the best filly I have. You'd better come!"

It wasn't over yet, then. With a feeling of doom I hurried after the squat figure back into the yard where another lad stood by the side of a beautiful filly. And as I saw her a cold hand closed around my heart. So far I had been dealing with trivia but this was very different.

Almira stood immobile, staring ahead with a peculiar intensity. The rise and fall of her ribs was accompanied by a rasping bubbling wheeze and at each intake her nostrils flared wildly. I had never seen a horse breathe like this. And there were other things; saliva drooled from her lips and every few seconds she gave a retching cough.

I turned to the apprentice. "When did this start?"

"Not long ago, sir. I saw her an hour since when I was givin' 'er some hay. There was nowt ailin' her then."

"What the devil's wrong with her?" Beamish exclaimed.

Well, it was a good question and I didn't have a clue to the answer. As I walked round the animal, taking in the trembling limbs and terrified eyes, a jumble of thoughts crowded my brain. I had seen "choking" horses—the dry choke when the gullet becomes impacted with food—but they didn't look like this. I felt my way along the course of the oesophagus and it was perfectly clear. And anyway the respiration was quite different. This filly looked as though she had some obstruction in her airflow. But what. . . ?

"Well, damn it, I'm asking you! What is it?" Mr. Beamish was becoming impatient and I couldn't blame him.

I was aware that I was slightly breathless. "Just a moment while I listen to her lungs."

"Just a moment!" the trainer burst out. "Good God, man, we haven't got many moments! This horse could die!"

He didn't have to tell me. I had seen that ominous trembling of the limbs before and now the filly was beginning to sway a little. Time was running out.

Dry mouthed, I auscultated the chest. I knew there was nothing wrong with her lungs but it gave me a little more time. Even with the stethoscope in my ears I could still hear Beamish's voice.

"It would have to be this one! Sir Eric gave five thousand pounds for her last year. She's the most valuable animal in my stables. Why did this have to happen?"

Groping my way over the ribs, I heartily agreed with him. Why in heaven's name did I have to walk into this nightmare? And with a man like Beamish who had no faith in me.

The filly had begun to reel about, the breathing louder and more stertorous than ever. It was when I was resting my hand on her flank to steady her that I noticed the little swelling under the skin. It was a circular plaque, like a penny pushed under the tissue. And there was another one higher up on the back . . . and another and another. My heart gave a quick double thump . . . so that was it.

"What am I going to tell Sir Eric?" the trainer groaned. "That his filly is dead and the vet didn't know what was wrong with her?"

"I never said I didn't know." I trotted away towards the car. "I do know. She's got urticaria—nettle rash."

"Nettle rash!" He came shambling after me. "But that couldn't cause all this!"

I fumbled among my bottles and drew 5 cc of adrenalin into a syringe and started back. "It's nothing to do with nettles. It's an allergic condition, usually pretty harmless but in a very few cases it causes oedema of the larynx—that's what we've got here."

It was difficult to raise the vein as the filly staggered around, but she came to rest for a few seconds and I dug my thumb into the jugular furrow. As the big vessel came up I thrust in the needle and injected the adrenalin. Then I stepped back and stood by the trainer's side.

352

Neither of us said anything. The spectacle of the toiling animal and the harrowing sound of the breathing absorbed us utterly.

Clearly she was on the verge of suffocation. When she stumbled and almost fell my hand gripped more tightly on the scalpel I had taken from my car along with the adrenalin. I knew only too well that tracheotomy was indicated here but I didn't have a tube with me. If the filly did go off her legs I should have to start cutting into her windpipe anyway but I put the thought away from me. For the moment I had to depend on the adrenalin.

Beamish stretched out a hand in a helpless gesture. "It's hopeless, isn't it?" he whispered.

I shrugged. "There's a small chance. If the injection can reduce the fluid in the larynx in time . . . we'll just have to wait."

He nodded and I could read more than one emotion in his face; not just the dread of breaking the news to the famous owner but also the distress of a horse-lover as he witnessed the plight of the beautiful animal.

At first I thought it was imagination, but it seemed that the breathing was becoming less stertorous. Then I noticed that the salivation was diminishing; she was able to swallow. And from that moment events moved with unbelievable rapidity. The symptoms of allergies appear with dramatic suddenness but mercifully they often disappear as quickly following treatment. Within fifteen minutes the filly looked almost normal. There was still a slight wheeze in her respirations but she was looking around her, quite free from distress.

Beamish, who had been watching like a man in a daze, pulled a handful of hay from a bale and held it out to her. She snatched it eagerly from his hand and began to eat with great relish.

"I can't believe it," the trainer muttered almost to himself. "I've never seen anything work as fast as that injection."

I felt as though I was riding on a pink cloud. Thank God there were moments like this among the traumas of veterinary work; the sudden transition from despair to triumph, from shame to pride.

As I settled in my car seat Beamish put his face to the open window. He was not a man to whom gracious speech came easily and his cheeks, roughened by years of riding on the open moor, twitched as he sought for words. "Mr. Herriot, I've been thinking . . . you don't have to be a horsey man to cure horses, do you?"

I laughed and his expression relaxed. "That's right," I said, and drove away.

## Chapter Thirteen

At last we were ready to march away from Scarborough. In the May sunshine we stood on parade outside the Grand at 7:00 a.m. as we had done throughout the Yorkshire winter, mostly in darkness, often with the icy rain blowing in our faces. But now I felt a pang of regret as I looked over the heads at the wide beautiful bay stretching beneath its cliffs to the far headland, the sand clean-washed and inviting, the great blue expanse of sea shimmering, and over everything the delicious sea-smell of salt and seaweed raising memories of holidays and happy things lost in the war.

"Atten-shun!" Flight Sergeant Blackett's bellow rolled over us as we stiffened in our ranks, every man carrying full kit, our packs braced with cardboard to give the sharp, rectangular look, hair cut short, boots gleaming, buttons shining like gold. Without our knowing, No. 10 ITW had moulded us into a smart, disciplined unit, very different from the shambling, half-baked crew of six months ago. We had all passed our exams and were now Leading Aircraftmen, and as LAC Herriot my wage had rocketed from three shillings to a dizzying seven and threepence a day.

"Right turn!" Again the roar. "By the left qui-ick march!"

Arms high, moving as one, we swung past the front of the Grand for the last time. We were going on a "toughening course", under canvas in the depths of Shropshire.

Black's Veterinary Dictionary dug into my back through the layer of cardboard. It was an unwieldy article but it reminded me of good days, and being away from Darrowby and living a different life I found I was able to stand back and assess certain things objectively. I asked myself many questions. Why, for instance, was my partnership with Siegfried so successful? Even now we still jog along happily after thirty-five years.

This of course doesn't mean that we have never had our differences. Over the years there have been clashes on various points.

One, I recall, was over the new plastic calcium injectors. Their early troubles have now been ironed out but at the beginning I found the things so temperamental that I abandoned them.

My colleague pulled me up about it when he saw me washing out my flutter valve by running the surgery tap through it.

"For God's sake, James, you're not still using that old thing, are you?"

"Yes, I'm afraid I am."

"But haven't you tried the new plastics?"

"Can't get away with them, Siegfried."

"Can't . . . what on earth do you mean?"

I trickled the last drop of water through the tube, rolled it small and slipped it into its case. "Well, the last time I used one the calcium squirted all over the place. And it's messy, sticky stuff. I had great white streaks down my coat."

"But James!" He laughed incredulously. "That's crazy! They're childishly simple to use."

"I believe you," I said. "But you know me. I haven't got a mechanical mind."

"For heaven's sake, you don't need a mechanical mind." He put his hand on my shoulder and his patient look began to creep across his face. "James, James, you must persevere." He raised a finger. "There is another point at issue here, you know."

"What's that?"

"The matter of asepsis. How do you know that length of rubber you have there is clean?"

"Well, I wash it through after use, I use a boiled needle, and . . ."

"But don't you see, my boy, you're only trying to achieve what already exists in the plastic pack. Each one is self-contained and sterilized."

"Oh, I know all about that, but what's the good of it if I can't get the stuff into the cow?" I said querulously.

"Oh, piffle, James!" Siegfried assumed a grave expression. "Look, you're going out now, aren't you, to see that milk fever cow I treated at John Tillot's. I understand it's not up yet."

"That's right."

"Well, as a favour to me, will you give one of the new packs a try?"

I thought for a moment. "All right, Siegfried, I'll have one more go."

When I reached the farm I found the cow comfortably ensconced in a field, in the middle of a rolling yellow ocean of buttercups.

"She's had a few tries to get on 'er feet," the farmer said. "But she can't quite make it."

"Probably just wants another shot." I went to my car which I had driven, rocking and bumping, over the rig and furrow of the field, and took one of the plastic packs from the boot.

Mr. Tillot raised his eyebrows when he saw me coming back. "Is that one o' them new things?"

"Yes, it is, Mr. Tillot, the very latest invention. All completely sterilized."

"Ah don't care what it is, ah don't like it!"

"You don't . . . why not?"

"Ah'll tell ye. Mr. Farnon used one this mornin'. Some of the stuff went in me eye, some went in 'is ear 'ole and the rest went down 'is trousers. Ah don't think t'bloody cow got any!"

THERE WAS another time Siegfried had to take me to task. An old-age pensioner had led a small mongrel dog along the passage on the end of a piece of string. I patted the consulting room table.

"Put him up here, will you?" I said.

The old man bent over slowly, groaning and puffing.

"Wait a minute." I tapped his shoulder. "Let me do it." I hoisted the little animal onto the smooth surface.

"Thank ye, sir." The man straightened up and rubbed his back and leg. "I 'ave arthritis bad and I'm not much good at liftin'. My name's Bailey and I live at t'council houses."

"Right, Mr. Bailey, what's the trouble?"

"It's this cough. He's allus at it. And 'e kind of retches at t'end of it."

"I see. How old is he?"

"He were ten last month."

356

"Yes . . ." I took the temperature and carefully auscultated the chest. As I moved the stethoscope over the ribs Siegfried came in and began to rummage in the cupboard.

"It's a chronic bronchitis, Mr. Bailey," I said. "Many older dogs suffer from it just like old folks."

He laughed. "Aye, ah'm a bit wheezy meself sometimes."

"That's right, but you're not so bad, really, are you?"

"Naw, naw."

"Well, neither is your little dog. I'm going to give him an injection and a course of tablets and it will help him quite a bit. I'm afraid he'll never quite get rid of this cough, but bring him in again if it gets very bad."

He nodded vigorously. "Very good, sir. Thank ye kindly, sir."

As Siegfried banged about in the cupboard I gave the injection and counted out twenty of the new M&B 693 tablets.

The old man gazed at them with interest then put them in his pocket. "Now what do ah owe ye, Mr. Herriot?"

I looked at the ragged tie knotted carefully over the frayed shirt collar, at the threadbare antiquity of the jacket. His trouser knees had been darned but on one side I caught a glimpse of the flesh through the material.

"No, that's all right, Mr. Bailey. There's no charge."

"But . . ."

"Now don't worry about it—it's nothing, really. Just see he gets his tablets regularly."

"I will, sir, and it's very kind of you. I never expected . . ."

"I know you didn't, Mr. Bailey. Goodbye for now and bring him back if he's not a lot better in a few days."

The sound of the old man's footsteps had hardly died away when Siegfried emerged from the cupboard. He brandished a pair of horse tooth forceps in my face. "God, I've been ages hunting these down. I'm sure you deliberately hide things from me, James."

I smiled but made no reply and as I was replacing my syringe on the trolley my colleague spoke again. "James, I don't like to mention this, but aren't you rather rash, doing work for nothing?"

I looked at him in surprise. "He was an old-age pensioner. Pretty hard up I should think."

"Maybe so, but really, you know, you just cannot give your services free."

"Oh but surely occasionally, in a case like this . . ."

"No, James, not even occasionally. It's just not practical. For instance weren't those M&B 693 tablets you were dishing out? Heaven help us, do you know those things are threepence each? It's no good—you must never work without charging."

"But dammit, you're always doing it!" I burst out. "Only last week there was that . . ."

Siegfried held up a restraining hand. "Believe me, my boy, I do understand. You acted from the highest possible motives and I have often been tempted to do the same. But you must be firm. These are hard times and one must be hard to survive. So remember in future—no more Robin Hood stuff, we can't afford it."

I nodded and went on my way somewhat bemusedly, but I soon forgot the incident and would have thought no more about it had I not seen Mr. Bailey about a week later.

His dog was once more on the consulting room table and Siegfried was giving it an injection. I didn't want to interfere so I went back along the passage to the front office and sat down to write in the day book.

As I wrote I heard Siegfried and the old man passing on their way to the front door. They stopped on the steps.

"All right, Mr. Bailey," my colleague said. "I can only tell you the same as Mr. Herriot. I'm afraid he's got that cough for life, but when it gets bad you must come and see us."

"Very good, sir," the old man put his hand in his pocket. "And what is the charge, please?"

"The charge, oh yes . . . the charge . . ." Siegfried cleared his throat a few times, then glanced furtively into the house and spoke in a hoarse whisper. "It's nothing, Mr. Bailey."

"But Mr. Farnon, I can't let ye . . ."

"Shh! Shh!" Siegfried waved a hand agitatedly in the old man's face. "Not a word now! I don't want to hear any more about it."

Having silenced Mr. Bailey he produced a large bag.

"There's about a hundred M&B tablets in here," he said. "He's going to keep needing them so I've given you a good supply."

I could see my colleague had spotted the hole in the trouser knee because he gazed down at it for a long time before putting his hand in his jacket pocket.

"Hang on a minute." He extracted a handful of assorted chattels, and prodded in his palm among scissors, thermometers, pieces of string and bottle openers. Finally his search was rewarded and he pulled out a bank note.

"Here's a quid," he whispered and again nervously shushed the man's attempts to speak.

Mr. Bailey, realizing the futility of argument, pocketed the money. "Well, thank ye, Mr. Farnon. Ah'll take t'missus to Scarborough wi' that."

"Good lad, good lad," muttered Siegfried, still looking around him guiltily. "Now off you go."

The old man solemnly raised his cap and began to shuffle painfully down the street.

"Hey, hold on, there," my colleague called after him. "What's the matter? You're not going very well."

"It's this dang arthritis. Ah go a long way in a long time."

"And you've got to walk all the way to the council houses?" Siegfried rubbed his chin irresolutely. "It's a fair step." He took a last wary peep down the passage then beckoned with his hand. "Look, my car's right here," he whispered. "Just nip in and I'll run you home."

SOME OF OUR disagreements were sharp and short.

I was sitting at the lunch table, rubbing and flexing my elbow. Siegfried, carving enthusiastically at a joint of roast mutton, looked up from his work.

"What's the trouble, James—rheumatism?"

"No, a cow belted me with her horn this morning. Right on the funny bone."

"Oh bad luck. Were you trying to get hold of her nose?"

"No, giving her an injection."

My colleague, transporting a slice of mutton to my plate, paused in mid-air. "Injecting her? Up there?"

"Yes, in the neck."

359

"If I may say so, it's rather a daft place. I always use the rump."

"Is that so?" I helped myself to mashed potatoes. "And what's wrong with the neck?"

"Well, you've illustrated it yourself, haven't you? It's too damn near the horns for a start."

"O.K., well the rump is too damn near the hind feet."

"Oh, come now, James, you know very well a cow very seldom kicks after a rump injection."

"Maybe so, but once is enough."

"And once is enough with a bloody horn, isn't it?"

I made no reply, Siegfried plied the gravy boat over both our plates and we started to eat. But he had hardly swallowed the first mouthful when he returned to the attack.

"Another thing, the rump is so handy. Your way you have to squeeze up between the cows."

"Well, so what?"

"Simply that you get your ribs squashed and your toes stood on, that's all. And besides, the neck is more painful."

"The rump is more subject to contamination," I countered.

"The neck is often thinly muscled," snapped Siegfried. "You haven't got a nice pad there to stick your needle into."

"No, and you haven't got a tail either," I growled.

"Tail? What the hell are you talking about?"

"I'm talking about the bloody tail. It's all right if you have somebody holding it but otherwise it's a menace, lashing about."

Siegfried gave a few rapid chews and swallowed quickly. "Lashing about? What in God's name has that got to do with it?"

"Some cows can whip a syringe out of your hand with their tail. The other day one caught my big fifty cc and smashed it against a wall. Broken glass everywhere."

Siegfried put down his knife and fork. "James, I don't like to speak to you in these terms but I am bound to tell you that you are talking the most unmitigated poppycock."

I gave him a sullen glare. "That's your opinion, is it?"

"It is indeed, James."

"Right."

"Right."

We continued our meal in silence.

But over the next few days my mind kept returning to the conversation. Siegfried has always had a persuasive way with him and the thought kept recurring that there might be a lot in what he said.

It was a week later that I paused, syringe in hand, before pushing between two cows. The animals, divining my intent as they usually did, swung their craggy hind ends together and blocked my way. Yes, by God Siegfried had a point. Why should I fight my way in there when the other end was ready and waiting?

I came to a decision. "Hold the tail, please," I said to the farmer and pushed my needle into the rump.

The cow never moved and as I completed the injection and pulled the needle out I was conscious of a faint sense of shame. That lovely pad of gluteal muscle, the easy availability of the site— my colleague had been dead right and I had been a pig-headed fool. I knew what to do in future.

The farmer laughed as he stepped back across the dung channel. "It's a funny thing how you fellers all have your different ways."

"What do you mean?"

"Well, Mr. Farnon was 'ere yesterday, injecting that cow over there. And 'e had a different system from you. He injected into the neck."

## Chapter Fourteen

I leaned on the handle of my spade, wiped away the sweat which had begun to run into my eyes and gazed around me at the hundreds of men scattered over the dusty green.

We were still on our toughening course. At least that's what they told us it was. I had a private suspicion that they just didn't know what to do with us and that somebody had devised this method of getting us out of the way.

Anyway, we were building a reservoir near a charming little Shropshire town and a whole village of tents had sprung up to house us. Nobody was quite sure about the reservoir but we were supposed to be building *something*. And I couldn't help thinking that things might be a lot worse. The weather was wonderful and it was a treat to be in the open all day. I looked down the slope and away across the sweetly rolling countryside to where low hills rose in the blue distance; it was a gentler landscape than the stark fells and moors I had left behind in Yorkshire but infinitely soothing.

The only snag was the reservoir or whatever it was that we were hacking out of the face of the hill. I could never get really involved with it. So I pricked up my ears when one morning our Flight Sergeant made an announcement.

"Some of the local farmers want help with their harvest," he called out at the early parade. "Are there any volunteers?"

My hand was the first up and after a few moments' hesitation others followed, but none of my particular friends volunteered for the job. When everything had been sorted out I found I had been allotted to a farmer Edwards with three other airmen who were from a different flight and strangers to me.

Mr. Edwards arrived the following day and packed the four of us into a typical big old-fashioned farmer's car. He asked our names but nothing else as though he felt that our station in civilian life was none of his concern. He was about thirty-five with jet black hair above a sunburnt face in which his white teeth and clear blue eyes shone startlingly.

He looked us over with a good-humoured grin. "Well, here we are, lads," he said, as we rolled into his farmyard. "This is where we're going to put you through it."

But I hardly heard him. I was looking around me at the scene which had been part of my life a few months ago. The cobbled yard, the rows of doors leading to cow byre, barn, pigsties and loose boxes. An old man was mucking out the byre and as the rich bovine smell drifted across one of my companions wrinkled his nose. But I inhaled it like perfume.

The farmer led us all into the fields where a reaper-and-binder was at work, leaving the sheaves of corn lying in long golden swathes. "Any of you ever done any stooking?" he asked.

We shook our heads.

"Never mind, you'll soon learn. You come with me, Jim."

362

We spaced ourselves out in the big field, each of my colleagues with an old man while Mr. Edwards took charge of me. It didn't take me long to realize that I had got the tough section.

The farmer grabbed a sheaf in each hand, tucked them under his arms, walked a few steps and planted them on end, resting against each other. I did the same till there were eight sheaves making up a stook. He showed me how to dig the stalks into the ground so that they stood upright and sometimes he gave a nudge with his knee to keep them in the right alignment.

I did my best but often my sheaves would fall over and I had to dart back and replace them. And I noticed with some alarm that Mr. Edwards was going about twice as fast as the two old men and my aching arms and back told me I was in for a testing time.

We went on like that for about two hours; bending, lifting, bending, lifting and shuffling forward without an instant's respite. One of the strongest impressions I had gained when I first came into country practice was that farming was the hardest way of all of making a living and now I was finding out for myself. I was about ready to throw myself down on the stubble when Mrs. Edwards came over the field with her young son and daughter. They carried baskets with the ingredients for our ten o'clock break; crusty apple tart and jugs of cider.

I sank gratefully down and began to drink like a parched traveller in the desert. The cider, from the farmer's own press, was superb. The right thing, it seemed to me, would be to lie here in the sunshine for the rest of the day with about a gallon of this exquisite brew by my side. But Mr. Edwards had other ideas. I was still chewing at the pie crust when he grasped a fresh pair of sheaves.

"Right, lad, must get on," he grunted, and I was back on the treadmill.

With a pause at lunchtime for bread, cheese and more cider we went on at breakneck speed all day. I have always been grateful to the RAF for what they did for my physical wellbeing. After the six months at Scarborough I am certain I didn't carry a surplus pound and I don't think I have ever slipped back. When I arrived in Shropshire I was really fit. But I wasn't as fit as Mr. Edwards.

He was a compact bundle of power. Not very big but with the

wiry durability I remembered in the Yorkshire farmers. He seemed tireless as he moved along the rows, corded brown arms bulging, slightly bowed legs stumping effortlessly.

The sensible thing would have been to tell him straight that I couldn't go at his pace but pride impelled me to keep up with him. I am quite sure he didn't mean to rub it in. Like any other farmer he had a job to do and was anxious to get on with it. At the lunch break he looked at me with some commiseration as I stood there, shirt sticking to my back, mouth hanging open, ribs heaving.

"You're doin' fine, Jim," he said. "I know you city lads ain't used to this kind of work and . . . well . . . it's not a question of strength, it's just knowin' how to do it."

When we drove back to camp that night I could hear my companions groaning in the back of the car. They, too, had suffered, but not as badly as me.

After a few days I did begin to get the knack of the thing and though it still tested me to the utmost I was never on the border of collapse again.

Mr. Edwards noticed the improvement and slapped me playfully on the shoulder. "What did I tell you? It's just knowin' how to do it."

But a new purgatory awaited me when we started to fork the sheaves up onto the cart, rope them there, then throw them higher and higher onto the stack as it grew in size. I realized with a jolt that stooking had been easy.

Mrs. Edwards joined in this part. She stood on the top of the stack with her husband, expertly turning the sheaves towards him while he arranged them as they should be. I had the unskilled job way below, toiling as never before, back breaking, the handle of the fork blistering my palms.

I just couldn't go fast enough and Mr. Edwards had to hop down to help me, grasping a fork and hurling the sheaves up with easy flicks of the wrist.

He looked at me as before and spoke the encouraging words. "You're comin' along grand, Jim. It's just knowin' how to do it."

But there were many compensations. The biggest was being among farming folk again. Mrs. Edwards in her undemonstrative way was obviously anxious to show hospitality to these four rather

364

bewildered city boys far from home, and set us down to a splendid meal every evening. She was dark like her husband with large eyes which joined in her quick smile and a figure which managed to be thin and shapely at the same time. She hadn't much chance to get fat because she never stopped working. When she wasn't outside throwing the corn around like any man she was cooking, baking, cleaning and looking after her children.

Those evening meals were something to look forward to and remember. Steaming rabbit pies with fresh green beans and potatoes from the garden. Bilberry tarts and apple crumble and a massive jug of thick cream to pour ad lib. Home baked bread and cheese.

We revelled in the change from RAF fare. It was said aircrew got the best food in the services and I believed it, but after a while it all began to taste the same. Maybe it was the bulk cooking.

Sitting at the farm table, looking at Mrs. Edwards serving us, at her husband and at the two children, a girl of ten who showed promise of her mother's attractiveness and a sturdy boy of eight, the thought recurred: they were good stock.

It was late one afternoon and I was feeling more of a weakling than ever with Mr. Edwards throwing the sheaves around as though they were weightless while I groaned and strained. The farmer was called away to attend to a calving cow and as he hopped blithely from the stack he patted my shoulder as I leaned on my fork.

"Never mind, Jim," he laughed. "It's just knowin' how to do it."

An hour later we were going into the kitchen for our meal when Mrs. Edwards said, "My husband's still on with that cow. He must be having difficulty with her."

I hesitated in the doorway. "Do you mind if I go and see how he's getting on?"

She smiled. "All right, if you like. I'll keep your food warm for you."

In the byre one of the old men was holding the tail of a big red poll and puffing his pipe placidly. Mr. Edwards, stripped to the waist, had his arm in the cow up to the shoulder. But it was a different Mr. Edwards. His back and chest glistened with sweat, and he panted as he fought his private battle somewhere inside.

365

He turned glazed eyes in my direction. At first he didn't appear to see me in his absorption then recognition dawned.

"'Ullo, Jim," he muttered breathlessly. "I've got a right job on 'ere."

"Sorry to hear that. What's the trouble?"

He began to reply then screwed up his face. "Aaah! The old bitch! She's squeezin' the life out of me arm again! She'll break it afore she's finished!" He paused, head hanging down to recover, then he looked up at me. "The calf's laid wrong, Jim. There's just a tail comin' into the passage and I can't get the hind legs round."

A breech. My favourite presentation but one which always defeated farmers. I couldn't blame them really because they had never had the opportunity to read Franz Benesch's classical work on veterinary obstetrics which explains the mechanics of parturition so lucidly. One phrase has always stuck in my mind: "The necessity for simultaneous application of antagonistic forces."

Benesch points out that in order to correct many malpresentations it is necessary to apply traction and repulsion at the same time, and to do that with one hand in a straining cow is impossible.

As though to endorse my thoughts Mr. Edwards burst out once more. "Dang it, I've missed it again! I keep pushin' the hock away then grabbin' for the foot but the old bitch just shoves it back at me. I've been doing this for an hour now and I'm about knackered."

I never thought I would hear such words from this tough little man but there was no doubt he had suffered. The cow was a massive animal. We didn't see many red polls in Yorkshire but the ones I had met were self-willed and strong as elephants; the idea of pushing against one for an hour made me quail.

Mr. Edwards pulled his arm out and stood for a moment leaning against the hairy rump. The animal was quite unperturbed by the interference of this puny human but the farmer was a picture of exhaustion. He worked his dangling fingers gingerly.

"By God!" he grunted. "She's given me some stick. I've got hardly any feelin' left in this arm."

He didn't have to tell me. I had known that sensation many a time. Even Benesch in the midst of his coldly scientific "malpositions" and "counteracting pressures" so far unbends as to state that

"great demands are made upon the strength of the operator".
Mr. Edwards would agree with him.

The farmer took a long shuddering breath and moved over to the
bucket of hot water on the floor. He washed his arms then turned
back to the cow with something like dread on his face.

"Look," I said. "Please let me help you."

He gave me a pallid smile. "Thanks, Jim, but there's nothin' you
can do. Those legs have got to come round."

"That's what I mean. I can do it."

"What. . . ?"

"With a bit of help from you. Have you got a piece of binder
twine handy?"

"Aye, we've got yards of it, lad, but I'm tellin' you you need
experience for this job. You know nuthin' about . . ."

He stopped because I was already pulling my shirt over my head.
He was too tired to argue in any case. I bent over the bucket and
soaped my arms. Then I held out a hand and Mr. Edwards word-
lessly passed me a length of twine. I soaked it in the water, then
quickly tied a slip knot on one end and inserted my hand into the
cow. Ah yes, there was the tail, so familiar, hanging between the
calf's pelvic bones. I ran my hand along the limb till I reached the
tiny foot. It was a moment's work to push the loop over the fetlock
and tighten it while I passed the free end between the digits of the
cloven foot.

"Hold that," I said, "and pull it steadily when I tell you."

I put my hand on the hock and began to push it away from me.
"Now pull," I said. "But carefully. Don't jerk."

Like a man in a dream he did as I said and within seconds the
foot popped out of the vulva.

"Hell!" said Mr. Edwards.

"Now for the other one," I murmured as I removed the loop.

I repeated the procedure, the farmer, slightly pop-eyed, pulling
on the twine. The second little hoof joined its fellow on the outside
almost immediately.

"Bloody hell!" said Mr. Edwards.

"Right," I said. "Grab a leg and we'll have him out in a couple
of ticks."

We each took a hold and leaned back, but the big cow did the job for us, giving a great heave which deposited the calf wet and wriggling into my arms. I staggered back and dropped with it onto the straw.

"Grand bull calf, Mr. Edwards," I said. "Better give him a rub down."

The farmer shot me an astonished glance then twisted some hay into a wisp and began to dry off the little creature.

"If you ever get stuck with a breech presentation again," I said, "I'll show you what you ought to do. You have to push and pull at the same time and that's where the twine comes in. As you repel the hock with your hand somebody else pulls the feet round, but you'll notice I have the twine between the calf's cleats and that's important. That way it lifts the sharp little foot up and prevents injury to the vaginal wall."

The farmer nodded dumbly and went on with his rubbing. When he had finished he looked up at me in bewilderment and his lips moved soundlessly a few times before he spoke.

"What the . . . how . . . how the heck do you know all that?"

I told him.

There was a long pause then he exploded. "You young bugger! You kept that dark, didn't you?"

"Well . . . you never asked me."

He scratched his head. "Well, I don't want to be nosey with you lads that helps me. Some folks don't like it . . ."

We dried our arms and donned our shirts in silence. Before leaving he looked over at the calf, already making strenuous efforts to rise as its mother licked it.

"He's a lively little beggar," he said. "And we might have lost 'im. I'm right grateful to you." He put an arm round my shoulders. "Anyway, come on, Mister Veterinary Surgeon, and we'll 'ave some supper."

Halfway across the yard he stopped and regarded me ruefully. "You know, I must have looked proper daft to you, fumblin' away inside there for an hour and damn near killin' myself, then you step up and do it in a couple of minutes. I feel as weak as a girl."

"Not in the least, Mr. Edwards," I replied. "It's . . ." I hesitated a moment. "It's not a question of strength, it's just knowing how to do it."

He nodded then became very still and the seconds stretched out as he stared at me. Suddenly his teeth shone as the brown face broke into an ever-widening grin which developed into a great shout of laughter.

"You young devil!" he said. "You really got a bit o' your own back there, didn't you?"

## Chapter Fifteen

There is no doubt that when I looked back at my life in Darrowby I was inclined to bathe the whole thing in a rosy glow, but occasionally the less happy things came to mind. Angus Grier, for instance.

It all began on a morning when I came into our operating room and saw that Siegfried had a patient on the table. He was thoughtfully stroking the head of an elderly and rather woebegone Border terrier.

"James," he said, "I want you to take this dog to Grier."

"Grier?"

"Vet at Brawton. He was treating the case before the owner moved into our district. Stones in the bladder. It needs an immediate operation and I think I'd better let Grier do it. He's a touchy, cantankerous old Scot and I don't want to step on his toes." He lifted the terrier from the table and handed him to me. "The sooner you get there the better. You can see the op and bring the dog back here afterwards. But watch yourself. Don't rub Grier the wrong way or he'll take it out of you somehow."

AT MY FIRST SIGHT of Angus Grier I thought of whisky. Something had to be responsible for the fleshy, mottled cheeks and the pattern of purple veins which chased each other over his prominent nose. He wore a permanently insulted expression.

He didn't waste any charm on me; a nod and a grunt and he grabbed the dog from my arms. The operation was uneventful and as Grier inserted the last stitch he looked up at me. "You'll no' want to take the dog back till he's out of the anaesthetic. I've got a case to visit—you can come with me to pass the time."

We didn't have what you could call a conversation in the car. It was a monologue—complaints of the sissiness of students nowadays, and of wrongs suffered at the hands of wicked clients and greedy colleagues. We drew up in a particularly dirty farmyard and Grier turned to me. "I've got a cow tae cleanse here."

"Right," I said. "Fine." I settled down in my seat and took out my pipe. Grier paused. "Are you no' coming to give me a hand?"

I couldn't understand him. Cleansing of cows is simply the removal of retained afterbirth and is a one-man job.

"Well, there isn't much I can do, is there?" I said. "And my boots and coat are in my car. I'd get messed up for nothing."

I knew immediately that I'd said the wrong thing. He gave me a malevolent glance, and halfway across the yard he stopped and stood for a moment in thought. Then he came back to the car. "I've got something here you can put on. Come in with me—you'll be able to pass me a pessary when I want one."

It sounded nutty to me, but I got out and went around to the back, where Grier was fishing out a large wooden box.

"Here's a calving outfit I got a bit ago. I haven't used it much because I found it a mite heavy, but it'll keep ye grand and clean."

It was a suit of thick, black, shining rubber. I lifted out the jacket; it bristled with zip fasteners and press studs and felt as heavy as lead. The trousers were even weightier. The whole thing was a most imposing creation, obviously designed by somebody who had never seen a cow calve. Anybody wearing it would be pretty well immobilized.

I began to take off my jacket—it was crazy, but I didn't want to offend the man. Grier, heaving and straining, helped me get into the suit. First the gleaming trousers were pulled on and zipped up fore and aft; then it was the turn of the jacket, a wonderful piece of work, fitting tightly around the waist and possessing short sleeves with powerful elastic gripping my biceps. I could hear the zips squeaking into place, the final one being at the back of my neck to close a high stiff collar which held my head in an attitude of supplication, my chin pointing at the sky. For the final touch, Grier produced a black rubber skullcap. I shrank away from the thing, but he insisted. "Stand still a wee minute longer. We might as well do the job right."

When he had finished he stood back admiringly. I must have been a grotesque sight, sheathed from head to foot in gleaming black, my arms sticking out almost at right angles. "Well, come on, it's time we got on wi' the job." He hurried towards the byre; I plodded ponderously after him. Our arrival caused a sensation. There were present the farmer, two cowmen and a little girl. The men's cheerful greeting froze on their lips as my menacing figure paced slowly in. The little girl burst into tears and ran.

"Cleansing" is a dirty, smelly job for the operator and a bore for the onlooker, who may have to stand around for twenty minutes with nothing to see. But this was one time the spectators were not bored. The men never took their eyes away from me as I stood like a suit of armour against the wall. I knew what they were thinking. Just what was going to happen when this formidable unknown went into action? Anybody dressed like that must have some tremendous task ahead of him. The intense pressure of the collar against my larynx kept me out of any conversation and this must have added to the mystery. The little girl had plucked up courage and brought her brothers and sisters to look at me. Screwing my head around painfully, I tried to give them a reassuring smile.

I couldn't say how long I stood there, but Grier at last finished his job and called out, "All right, I'm ready for you now." The atmosphere became suddenly electric. The men straightened up. This was the moment they had been waiting for.

With some difficulty I headed for the tin of pessaries. It was only a few yards away, but it seemed longer as I approached like a robot, head in the air, arms extended stiffly on either side. After a few contortions I bent, I got my hand into the tin, then had to take the paper off the pessary with one hand. The men watched, fascinated. I did a careful about-face and paced back with measured tread. Grier took the pessary and inserted it in the uterus.

I glanced down my nose at the men; their expressions had changed to open disbelief. Surely no man could be wearing that outfit just to hand over a pessary. But when Grier started the complicated business of snapping open the studs and sliding me out of it, they realized the show was over; and fast on the feeling of letdown came amusement.

As I tried to rub some life back into my swollen arms, which had been strangulated by the elastic sleeves, I was surrounded by grinning faces. Pulling together the shreds of my dignity, I put on my jacket and got into the car. Grier stayed to say a few words to the men, but he wasn't holding their attention; it was all on me, huddling in the seat. They couldn't believe I was true.

Back at the surgery the Border terrier raised his head and tried bravely to wag his tail when he saw me. I gathered him up in a blanket and was preparing to leave when I saw Grier through the partly open door of a storeroom. He had the wooden box on a table and he was lifting out the rubber suit, but there was something peculiar about the way he was doing it; his body shook and jerked, the mottled face was strangely contorted and a half-stifled wailing issued from his lips.

I stared in amazement. I would have said it was impossible, yet it was happening right in front of me. There was not a shadow of a doubt—Angus Grier was laughing.

## Chapter Sixteen

A sad, tender nerve twinged as the old lady passed me the cup of tea. She looked just like Miss Stubbs.

One of the local churches was having a social evening to entertain us lonely airmen and as I accepted the cup and sat down I could hardly withdraw my eyes from the lady's face.

Miss Stubbs! I could just see her now. The card dangling above her bed said GOD IS NEAR. But it wasn't like the usual religious text. It didn't have a frame or ornate printing. It was just a strip of cardboard with plain lettering which might have said NO SMOKING or EXIT, and it was looped carelessly over an old gas bracket so that the old lady could look up and read GOD IS NEAR from where she lay.

There wasn't much more Miss Stubbs could see; perhaps a few

feet of privet hedge through the frayed curtains, but mainly it was just the cluttered little room which was her world.

The room was on the ground floor and in the front of the cottage, and as I came up through the wilderness which had once been a garden I could see the dogs watching me from where they stood behind the old lady's bed. And when I knocked, the place erupted with their barking. It was always like this. I had been visiting regularly for over a year and the pattern never changed: the furious barking; then Mrs. Broadwith, who looked after Miss Stubbs, would push all the animals but my patient of the day into the kitchen and I would go in and see Miss Stubbs in her bed with the card hanging over it.

She had been there for a long time and would never get up again. But she never mentioned her illness and pain to me; all her concern was for her three dogs and two cats.

Today it was old Prince and I was worried about him. It was his heart—just about the most spectacular valvular incompetence I had ever heard. He was pleased as ever to see me, his long fringed tail waving gently—that Irish setter tail attached to the bulging black and white body, with shaggy head and upstanding Alsatian ears. Miss Stubbs often used to call him "Mr. Heinz", and though he may not have had fifty-seven varieties in him, Prince's hybrid vigour had stood him in good stead. With a heart like his he should have been dead long ago.

"I thought I'd best give you a ring, Mr. Herriot," Mrs. Broadwith said. "He's been coughing right bad this week and this morning he was a bit staggery. Still eats well, though."

"I bet he does." I ran my hands over the fat on the ribs. "It would take something drastic to put old Prince off his grub."

Miss Stubbs laughed from the bed and the old dog, his mouth wide, eyes dancing, seemed to be joining in the joke. I put my stethoscope over his heart. The beat was a good bit faster than last time; he was on oral digitalis, but it wasn't doing its job. Gloomily I moved the stethoscope over the chest and listened without enthusiasm to the symphony of whistles and squeaks which signalled the workings of Prince's lungs. The old dog stood very erect and proud. He always took it as a tremendous compliment when I

373

examined him and there was no doubt he was enjoying himself now. His was not a painful ailment.

Straightening up, I patted his head and he responded immediately by trying to put his paws on my chest. He didn't quite make it, and even that slight exertion started his ribs heaving and his tongue lolling. I gave him an intramuscular injection of digitalis and another of morphine hydrochloride, which he accepted with apparent pleasure as part of the game.

"I hope that will steady his heart and breathing, Miss Stubbs. You'll find he'll be a bit dopey and that will help, too. I'm going to leave you some more medicine for his bronchitis."

The next stage of the visit began now as Mrs. Broadwith brought in a cup of tea and the rest of the animals were let out of the kitchen. Ben, a Sealyham, and Sally, a cocker spaniel, were closely followed by the cats, Arthur and Susie, who stalked in gracefully and began to rub against my legs.

It was the usual scenario for the many cups of tea I had drunk with Miss Stubbs. "How are you today?" I asked.

"Oh, much better," she said and, as always, changed the subject. She liked to talk about her pets and about the days when her family were alive. She loved to describe the escapades of her brothers, and today she showed me an old photograph of them—three young men in the knee breeches of the 1890s smiled up at me, and the impish humour in their faces came down undimmed over the years.

"My word, they look really bright lads, Miss Stubbs," I said.

"Oh, they were young rips!" She laughed, and for a moment her face was radiant, transfigured by her memories.

Sitting there drinking tea, with the dogs lying beside us and the cats making themselves comfortable on the bed, I felt afraid of the responsibility I had. Except for her memories, the one thing which brought some light into the life of the brave old woman was the transparent devotion of this shaggy bunch, whose eyes were never far from her face. And they were all elderly. A fourth dog, a truly ancient gold Labrador, had died a few months ago. And now I had Prince with his heart; Sally beginning to drink a lot of water, which made me wonder if she was starting with a pyometra; and Ben growing steadily thinner with his nephritis. The cats were better,

374

though Susie was a bit scraggy and I kept up a morbid kneading of her furry abdomen for signs of lymphosarcoma. Arthur, a huge neutered tom, ailed not at all except that his teeth tended to tartar up.

This must have been in Miss Stubbs's mind, because when I had finished my tea she asked me to look at his mouth.

"Yes, there's a bit there. Might as well fix it."

Arthur was a living denial of all those theories that cats are cold-natured, selfish and the rest. His fine eyes, framed in the widest cat's face I have ever seen, looked out on the world with an all-embracing benevolence. His every move was marked by dignity. As I started to scrape his teeth, his chest echoed with a booming purr like a distant outboard motor. I accidentally nicked his gum. He casually raised a massive paw as if to say, Have a care, chum, but his claws were sheathed.

My next visit was less than a month later and was in response to an urgent summons from Mrs. Broadwith—Ben had collapsed. In ten minutes I was threading my way through the front garden with the animals watching from their window.

As I went into the little room I saw Ben lying on his side, very still, by the bed. It wasn't often these nephritis cases went off so suddenly.

"Well, it was quick, Miss Stubbs. I'm sure the old chap didn't suffer at all." My words sounded lame and ineffectual.

The old lady was in full command of herself. No tears as she looked down at her companion of so many years. My idea was to get him out as quickly as possible and I pulled a blanket under him and lifted him up.

"Wait a moment," Miss Stubbs said, and, still with no change of expression, she reached out and touched Ben's head. Then she lay back as I hurried from the room.

In the kitchen I had a whispered conference with Mrs. Broadwith. "I'll run down t'village and get Fred Manners to come and bury him," she said. "Could you stay with the old lady while I'm gone? Talk to her, like, it'll do her good."

I went back and sat down by the bed. "You know, Mr. Herriot," Miss Stubbs said casually, "I'll be the next to go."

"Oh, nonsense! You're feeling a bit low, that's all. We all do when something like this happens." But I was disturbed. I had never heard her even hint at such a thing before.

"I'm not afraid," she said. "There's something better waiting for me. I've never had any doubts." There was silence between us as she lay looking up at the card on the gas bracket.

Then the head on the pillow turned to me again. "I have only one fear." The brave face changed with startling suddenness, as if a mask had dropped, and she grasped my hand. "It's my dogs and cats, Mr. Herriot. I'm afraid I might never see them when I'm gone and it worries me so. You see, I know I'll be reunited with my parents and my brothers, but . . . but . . ."

"Well, why not with your animals?"

"That's just it." For the first time I saw tears on her cheeks. "They say animals have no souls."

"Who says?"

"Oh, I've read it. A lot of religious people believe it."

"Well, I don't." I held her hand firmly. "If having a soul means being able to feel love and loyalty and gratitude, animals are better off than a lot of humans. You've nothing to worry about."

"Oh, I hope you're right. I lie at night thinking about it."

"I know I'm right, Miss Stubbs, and don't you argue with me. They teach us vets all about animals' souls."

She laughed with a return of her old spirit. "I'm sorry. I won't talk about this again. But before you go—I want you to be absolutely honest with me. I know you are very young, but . . . what, truly, are your beliefs? Will my animals go with me?"

"Miss Stubbs," I said, swallowing once or twice. "I'm afraid I'm a bit foggy about all this, but I'm absolutely certain of one thing. Wherever you are going, they are going, too."

She stared at me, but her face was calm again. "Thank you, Mr. Herriot. I know you are being honest with me. That is what you really believe, isn't it?"

"I do," I said. "With all my heart I believe it."

IT WAS NOT MUCH more than a month later that I learned I had seen Miss Stubbs for the last time. I was on my rounds and a farmer happened to mention that her cottage was up for sale.

"But what about Miss Stubbs?" I asked.

"Oh, went off sudden about three weeks ago."

"Mrs. Broadwith isn't staying on in the house, then?"

"Nay, I hear she's staying at t'other end of the village."

"Do you know what's happened to the dogs and cats?"

About dogs and cats he knew nothing. I lost no time in tracking Mrs. Broadwith down. She was settled in a tiny but attractive house, and she answered my knock herself.

"Oh, come in, Mr. Herriot. It's good of you to call." We sat facing each other across a scrubbed table. "It was sad about the old lady. But she just slept away at the finish."

"I'm glad of that. I've only just heard."

Mrs. Broadwith looked around the room. "I was real lucky to get this place—it's just what I've always wanted."

"What's happened to the animals?" I blurted out.

"Oh, they're in t'garden." She got up and opened the door and with a surge of relief I watched my old friends pour in. Arthur was on my knee in a flash, arching himself ecstatically against my arm while his outboard motor roared softly above the barking of the dogs. Prince, wheezy as ever, tail fanning the air, laughed up at me delightedly between barks.

"I couldn't be parted from them," Mrs. Broadwith said. "They'll have a good home with me as long as they live."

I looked at her Yorkshire country face, its grim lines belied by the kindly eyes. "This is wonderful," I said. "But won't you find it just a bit . . . er . . . expensive to feed them?"

"Nay. I 'ave a bit put away."

"Well fine, fine. I'll look in now and then." I rose to go.

"There *is* one thing—before they sell off the things at the cottage, could you get us what's left of your medicines?"

I took the key and drove to the other end of the village. The door creaked open and inside the silence was like a heavy pall. Nothing had been moved. The bed with its rumpled blankets was still there. I picked up half-empty bottles, a jar of ointment, old Ben's tablets— a lot of good they had done him.

I wouldn't be coming here anymore. At the door I paused and read for the last time the card which hung over the empty bed.

# Chapter Seventeen

At last we were on our way to Flying School. It was at Windsor and that didn't seem far on the map, but it was a typical wartime journey of endless stops and changes and interminable waits. It went on all through the night and we took our sleep in snatches. I stole an hour's fitful slumber on the waiting-room table at a tiny nameless station and despite my hard pillowless bed I drifted deliciously back to Darrowby.

I was bumping along the rutted track to Nether Lees farm, hanging on to the jerking steering wheel. I could see the house below me, its faded red tiles showing above the sheltering trees and behind the buildings the hillside rose to the moor.

Up there the trees were stunted and sparse and dotted widely over the steep flanks. Higher still there was only scree and cliff and right at the top, beckoning in the sunshine, I saw the beginning of the moor—smooth, unbroken and bare.

A scar on the broad sweep of green showed where long ago they quarried the stones to build the massive farmhouses and enduring walls which have stood against the unrelenting climate for hundreds of years. Those houses and those endlessly marching walls would still be there when I was gone and forgotten.

Helen was with me in the car. I loved it when she came with me on my rounds, and after the visit to the farm we climbed up the fell-side, panting through the scent of the warm bracken, feeling the old excitement as we neared the summit.

Then we were on the top, facing into the wide free moorland and the clean Yorkshire wind and the cloud shadows racing over the greens and browns. Helen's hand was warm in mine as we wandered among the heather through green islets nibbled to a velvet sward by the sheep.

Helen raised a finger as a curlew's lonely cry sounded across the wild tapestry and the wonder in her eyes shone through the dark flurry of hair blowing across her face.

The gentle shaking at my shoulder pulled me back to wakefulness, to the hiss of steam and the clatter of boots. The table top was hard against my hip and my neck was stiff where it had rested on my pack.

"Train's in, Jim." An airman was looking down at me. "I hated to wake you—you were smiling."

TWO HOURS LATER, unshaven, half asleep, laden with kit, we shuffled into the airfield at Windsor. Sitting in the wooden building we only half listened to the corporal giving us our introductory address. Then suddenly his words struck home.

"There's one other thing," he said. "Remember to wear your identity discs at all times. We had two prangs last week—couple of fellers burned beyond recognition and neither of 'em was wearing his discs. We didn't know who they were." He spread his hands appealingly. "This sort of thing makes a lot of work for us, so remember what I've told you."

In a moment we were all wide awake and listening intently. Probably thinking as I was—that we had only been playing at being airmen up till now.

I looked through the window at the wind sock blowing over the long flat stretch of green, at the scattered aircraft, the fire tender, the huddle of low wooden huts. The playing was over now. This was where everything started.

## James Herriot

An awful lot of publishers in Britain today must be kicking themselves. With all of James Herriot's enchanting books now international best-sellers, it's hard to believe that at the beginning he had the greatest difficulty in getting his first accepted. Although perhaps for a professional vet who had turned to writing for the first time in his middle fifties, it was hardly surprising.

"I became," he says, "a connoisseur of the sickening thud that a rejected manuscript makes when it falls through your letterbox!"

For a time he persevered—partly because both he and his wife were anxious in case the old Yorkshire ways that he records might otherwise be forgotten—but when the manuscript was returned for the umpteenth time he finally decided to put it away in a drawer and forget it.

"I had to give myself ten out of ten for trying," he says, "but obviously I couldn't write, so I'd better stick to vetting."

Luckily for us all his wife still had faith in him. So, entirely at her insistence, he tried again. And again. Until at last his perseverence was rewarded. And the rest, as they say, is history. World-wide success, triumphant tours of America, two hilarious films, delight given to countless millions . . . and all because his wife just wouldn't let him admit defeat. He readily concedes his debt to her. And so must we all.

Not that he hasn't stuck to vetting, though. For him the real magic is still to be found in the beauty of the Yorkshire Dales, in the rugged individuality of the farming people he meets on his rounds, and in the recurring miracle of medicine itself.

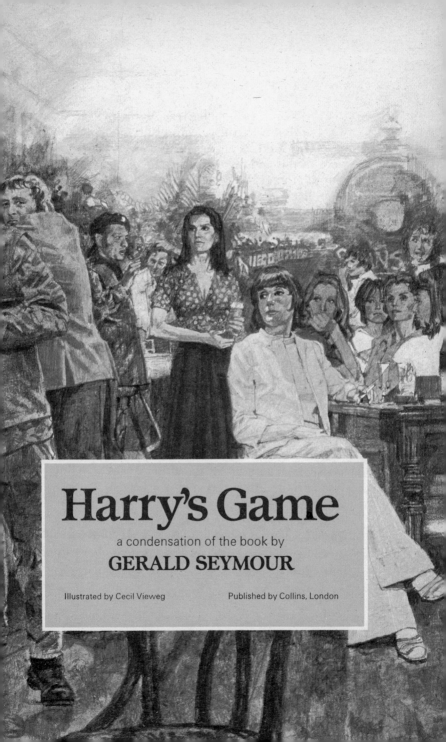

# Harry's Game

a condensation of the book by

**GERALD SEYMOUR**

Illustrated by Cecil Vieweg          Published by Collins, London

"Pawns were expendable. He and the man he was hunting were the queens of his game. The superstars, and secondary only to the kings, who were sacred and inviolate. If, as the queens were moved around the board, the pawns toppled over, then that was the nature of the game. . . ."

Thus Captain Harry Brown reflects on his new job. Specially and speedily trained, he has been sent as an undercover agent to Belfast with instructions to seek out and destroy the IRA gunman who recently assassinated a British minister as he was leaving his Belgravia home.

As the two main protagonists of this gripping story—each a hero to his own side—play their dangerous game in the battle-scarred streets of Belfast, the innocent get caught in the crossfire. For both men, loves and loyalties, old and new, become hopelessly entangled, and Harry comes to realize that the squares on the board—and the figures too—are not so much black and white, as grey.

Stories of Northern Ireland feature daily in our newspapers and on our television sets. Inevitably, among those of us who are far from the battleground, this constant exposure breeds a dull acceptance of the horrifying facts. However, Gerald Seymour's powerful first novel, written from first-hand experience, brings home to us in entirely fresh terms the reality of the tragedy.

# 1

The man was panting slightly, not from the exertion of pushing his way through the shapeless, ungiving mass of the crowd but from the frustration of the delay.

He drove himself out of the knot of people that had formed a defensive wall around the Underground ticket machine, and moved on to the automatic barrier. He inserted his ticket into the machine, and watched it bend upward to admit him.

Now, in the open at last, he cannoned off an elderly man, deep in his paper, making him stumble. As he tried to sidestep his way out of the collision, he knocked into a girl loaded for the launderette, hitting her hard with his left elbow. He saw the look of surprise fill her face, watched as she waited for the mumbled apology and helping hand—the usual etiquette of Oxford Circus Station in the early morning.

He froze the words in his mouth, the discipline of his briefing winning through. He'd been told not to speak en route to the target. Act dumb, rude, anything, but don't let anyone hear the hard, nasal Irish accent of West Belfast.

As he sped from the fracas, leaving the elderly man gasping and the girl to the help of others, he could sense the eyes of the witnesses on him; it was enough of an incident to be remembered.

When he reached the escalator leading to the train for Victoria Station, he was aware of his stupidity back there, conscious that he'd antagonized people who would recognize him, and he felt the

385

slight trembling again in his hands and feet that he'd noticed several times since he'd come across the water. With his right hand, awkwardly and across his body, he gripped the hard rubber escalator rail to steady himself. His left hand, inside the buttons of his raincoat, held tightly onto the barrel of the Kalashnikov automatic rifle he'd strapped to his body before leaving the North London boarding house two hours and twenty minutes earlier.. The barrel and weapon mechanism were little more than twenty inches long, with the shoulder stock of pressed steel folded back alongside it.

He skipped clear of the bottom of the escalator, where the stair drove under the floor, and was carried forward by the crowd onto the platform. They'd timed the frequency of the tube trains; at worst he'd wait less than a minute.

The train blurted its way out of the darkened tunnel, braked, and the doors slid back. As he wormed his way into a seat and the doors closed, he edged his weight off his hip pocket, with the cartridge magazine and its thirty live rounds inside.

It was 8:51 by the cheap watch on his wrist, just visible if he moved the gun towards the coat buttonholes. Five minutes maximum to Victoria, three minutes from the Underground platform to the street, and, taking it gently, seven minutes from there to his target: 9:06 on location. That meant he had two minutes in hand, perhaps three at the most, primarily to assemble the gun and pick his firing position. It was a close schedule now, and he began to tremble again. At the briefing it had been explained that in his favour were his lack of form—never fingerprinted, never photographed—and the fact that no sympathizers' homes in London were being used and no contact was being made with anyone. Keep it tight as an Orangeman's drum, and you'll get away with it. The train jolted into motion.

BY THE START of the nine-o'clock news something approaching order was returning to the cabinet minister's home. Three children already on their way to school, two more still wrestling with overcoats, scarfs, hockey sticks and satchels. The au pair girl in the hall with them. The minister's Afghan hound tangled around their legs.

The minister was alone at the long refectory table in the breakfast room, newspapers spread out where the children's cereal bowls had been, attacking first the editorial columns, then on through the parliamentary reports, and finally to the front-page news. He read quickly, with little outward sign of annoyance or pleasure. After his eighteen months as second man in Belfast, and the attendant publicity, his promotion to the Social Services Ministry and a place in the Cabinet had taken him back out of the public eye. His major speeches in the House of Commons were fully reported, but his monolithic department ticked along, barely feeling his touch at the helm. This morning he wasn't mentioned. He shuffled his papers together and reached for his briefcase under the table; the car would be at the door in three minutes. "Moving off, sweetheart," he called, and made for the hall.

The Afghan was now sitting quietly on the doormat, the children ready, as the minister put on his heavy dark-blue overcoat, gave his wife's offered cheek a kiss and opened the door into Belgrave Square. The Afghan and au pair led the way down the steps, then the children, and after a moment the minister and his wife. To his right he saw the ministry car—the black Austin Princess—turning into Belgrave Square, seventy-five yards away, to pick him up. Across the road a short dark-haired man, slouched against the square's fence, stiffened and moved forward.

The minister's huge voice bellowed after his children, "Have a nice day, darlings, and don't do any damage with those sticks." He was out on the pavement when he saw the rifle come from under the coat of the man across the street.

He had started to shout a warning to his wife when the man fired his first shot. For the minister the street exploded in noise as he felt the sledgehammer blow of the 7.62-millimetre cartridge crashing into his chest. The force spun and felled him, causing the second shot to fly into the hallway, fracturing a mirror.

As the man aimed for his third shot—"Keep steady, aim," he'd been told, "and for Christ's sake be quick"—he heard the screaming. The minister's wife was crawling down the steps to her husband. The man fired two more shots. This time there were no misses, and he watched with detached fascination as the back of the sleek groomed head disintegrated. It was his last sight of the target

387

before the screaming woman flung herself over it, swamping it from his view. He looked to his left and saw the big ministry car stranded, its engine racing, in the middle of the road. To the right on the pavement he saw the children, immobile like statues, with the dog straining at its leash to escape the noise.

Automatically the man flicked the safety catch to On, deflated the catch at the top of the stock, bent the shoulder rest back alongside the barrel and dropped the weapon into the sheath they'd built to be strapped under his coat. Then he ran, jumping out of the way of a woman, into a street leading to Grosvenor Place.

Must get across the road, get a line of traffic between you and them, he told himself. Alongside him now was the high, spiked wall of Buckingham Palace. People moved out of his path. His mind was focused almost exclusively on the road, the traffic, and at what moment he would see a hole in the river of buses and cabs. Get across Buckingham Palace Road and then into the safety and anonymity of the tube station at Victoria. They'd given him a route to Watford. Hard out of breath, he stumbled into the station. His watch showed 9:12.

THE SIRENS of the patrol cars blotted out the screaming of the minister's wife as she lay over the body. They'd been diverted there ninety seconds before with the message: "Man shot in Belgrave Square." The two constables spilled out into the street. George Davies, twenty-two years old and only three years in the Metropolitan Police, was first. He saw the woman, the body of the man under her and the brain tissue on the steps, and stopped in mid-stride as he felt nausea rising into his mouth. Frank Smith, twice his age, screamed, "Don't stop, *move*," ran past him to the huddle on the steps and pulled the minister's wife from her

389

husband's body. "Give him air," he yelled, before he took in the wrecked skull and turned to the pale-faced Davies, ten paces behind him. "Ambulance, reinforcements, tell 'em it's big, and move it fast." When Smith looked again at the minister's wife he recognized her. "It's Mrs. Danby?" he whispered. She nodded. "Your husband?" She nodded again, silent now. The children had edged close to her.

Smith took the scene in. "Get them inside, ma'am." They obeyed, slowly and numbly going through the door and off the street.

Smith lumbered back to the squad car. On the radio he put out a staccato message: "Tango George, in Belgrave Square. Henry Danby has been shot."

THE REPORT of the shooting reached the commissioner's desk at Scotland Yard at 9:25. He was slipping out of his coat after the drive from Epsom when his aide came in with the first flashes. The commissioner read the messages ripped off a teleprinter. He said, "Get me C1, Special Branch and SPG." He went over to his desk, pressed the intercom button, and announced sharply, "Prime Minister, please."

When the orange light flashed on the console the commissioner straightened a little, adjusted his tie, then picked up his phone.

"Good morning, Commissioner," he heard. "What can I do for you?"

The commissioner took it slowly. First reports, much regret, your colleague Henry Danby, dead on arrival in the hospital. Seems on first impression the work of an assassin, very major police activity, but few other details available. When he finished, the voice at the end of the line, in the office overlooking Downing Street and the Foreign Office arch, said, "Nothing else?"

"No, sir. It's early, though."

"You'll shout if you want help—army, air force, intelligence, anything you need?"

There was no reply from the commissioner. The Prime Minister went on. "I'll get out of your hair—call me in half an hour. I'll get one of our people to put it out to the Press Association."

The commissioner smiled to himself bleakly. A press release straight away—the political mind taking stock.

The door opened and the three men he'd summoned came in. They headed critical departments: C1—the élite unit of the Criminal Investigation Department—CID, sometimes called the murder squad; the Special Branch—Scotland Yard's counter-terrorist and surveillance force; and the Special Patrol Group—the specialist unit trained to deal with major incidents. All were commanders, but only the head of the SPG was in uniform.

The commissioner kept his office Spartan, and the commanders collected the armless chairs from the sides of the room and brought them towards the desk. He spoke first to the Special Patrol Group commander and asked him abruptly what was known.

"Not much, sir. The man ran for it in the direction of Victoria. There's a woman on the pavement had a good look at him. Says he's about five eight, thirtyish, and what she calls a pinched sort of face, dark hair. Clothes aren't much good—dark trousers under a biscuit-coloured mackintosh. That's it."

"And the gun?"

"Can't be definite." It was the Special Branch man. "Seems from the woman's description it's an AK-47, usually called a Kalashnikov. The latest version has a folding stock—you could get it into a big briefcase. It's got a noise all of its own, a crack that people who've heard it say is distinctive. We've found four cartridge cases, but no details on them yet."

"And the conclusion?"

"If it is a Kalashnikov, we're not up against an amateur. If they can get one of these things, then they're big and know what they're about."

That struck the chord. All four stayed quiet for a moment. The commissioner lit his first cigarette of the day, two hours ahead of the schedule he'd disciplined himself to after his last medical check, and broke the silence. "He'll have thought out his escape route. It'll be good. Where are we, how do we block him?"

The murder-squad chief took it up. "Usual, sir, at this stage. Ports, ferries, airports, private strips, as soon as we can get men to them. Phone calls ahead to the control towers. I've got as many men as possible concentrated on tube stations, and particularly exit points on the outskirts. . . ."

He trailed away. He'd said enough. The commissioner drummed his desk top with the filter of his cigarette. The others waited, anxious now to get the meeting over and get back to their teams and the reports that were beginning to build.

The commissioner reacted, sensing the mood. "Right, I take it we all accept Danby was a target of the IRA because of his work in Northern Ireland, though God knows, a less controversial minister I never met. Like a bloody willow tree. It's not a nut, because nutters don't get modern commie assault rifles to run round Belgrave Square. So look for a top man, in the IRA. Right? Good luck."

As the door closed on the commanders, the light flashed again on the commissioner's console. When he picked up the phone his secretary told him the Prime Minister had called an emergency Cabinet meeting for 2:30.

THE MAN got off the train at Watford Junction. The detectives he spotted were close to the ticket barrier, not looking down the platform but intent on the passengers. He walked away from the barrier towards the Gents, went into the graffiti-scrawled cubicle and took off the raincoat. He hung it carefully behind a door. He unfastened the shoulder strap, unclipped the magazine from the gun, took off his jacket and put the improvised holster back on. Under his jacket the rifle fitted unseen, close to his armpit. It gave him a stockiness that wasn't his and showed his jacket as a poor fit, but that was all. Trembling again in his fingers, he walked towards the barrier. The CID men had been told the man was in a fawn-brown mackintosh. And they hadn't been told that the Kalashnikov could be folded. They ruled him out even before he handed over his ticket.

He walked away from them, panting quietly, his forehead cold with sweat, waiting for the shout behind him. He walked out of the station to the car park, where the Cortina rented from Avis waited. He stowed the gun under the driver's seat and set off for Heathrow.

In the late-morning traffic the journey took him an hour. He'd anticipated it would, and he found he'd left himself ninety minutes for his flight when he reached the terminal car park. He locked the car, leaving the rifle and its magazine under the seat.

The police were staked out at all corners of the terminal. The man saw the Special Patrol Group men, who he knew were armed. It gave him a chilled feeling in his belly. If they shouted and he ran, would they shoot him? He clenched his fist and walked up to the British Airways ticket desk. "The name is Jones . . . you've a ticket waiting for me. The one o'clock to Amsterdam, BE 467."

The girl behind the counter smiled, nodded, and began to punch the instructions of the flight into her personal reservations computer. The flight was confirmed, and as she made the ticket out, the terminal loudspeakers warned of delays on all flights to Dublin, Cork, Shannon and Belfast. No reason was given.

The man brought out the new British passport supplied him by his unit quartermaster and walked through immigration control.

Two hours later the man strode along the vast pier of Schiphol Airport, Amsterdam, towards the central transit area. If his connections were working he had fifty-eight minutes till the Aer Lingus 727 took off for Dublin. He saw the special airport police with their short-barrelled carbines patrolling the entrance to the pier where the El Al Jumbo was loading, and had noticed the armoured personnel carriers on the aprons. All the precautions of the anti-hijack programme, but nothing to concern him. He went to the Aer Lingus desk, collected the ticket waiting for him and drifted away to the duty-free lounge. For the first time in the day he felt a degree of calm.

## 2

About the same time, in the Cabinet Room of 10 Downing Street, the commissioner delivered his situation report. He picked his words with care, aware that the ministers were shocked and even hostile to what he had to say. There was little comfort for them, until they were told that a new description was being circulated.

"There was a jostling incident at Oxford Circus this morning.

A man barged his way through, nearly knocking people over. Two women independently saw the television news and phoned the Yard. It's the same sort of man they're talking about as we'd already heard of, but a better description. We'll have a photokit by four o'clock—"

He was interrupted by a knock on the door, and the arrival of Frank Scott, the chief constable of the Royal Ulster Constabulary (RUC), and General Sir Jocelyn Fairbairn, the commander-in-chief of British armed forces in Northern Ireland. When they'd sat down, the Prime Minister began.

"We all take it this is an IRA assassination. We don't know for what motive, whether it is the first of several attempts or a one-shot. I want the maximum effort to get the killer—and fast. Every day that these thugs get away with it is a massive plus to them. How it happened that Danby's detective was withdrawn from him so soon after he'd left the Ulster job is a mystery to me. The Home Secretary will report to us tomorrow on that, and also on what is being done to prevent a recurrence of such attacks."

He stopped. The room was silent, disliking the schoolroom lecture. The commissioner wondered for a moment whether to explain that Danby himself had decided to do without the armed guard, ridiculing the detective sergeant's efforts to watch him. He decided to let the Prime Minister hear it from his Home Secretary.

The Prime Minister gestured to the RUC man.

"Well, sir . . . gentlemen," he started in the soft Scots burr of so many of the Ulstermen. He tugged at his jacket and moved his blackthorn cane fractionally across the table. "If he's in Belfast, we'll get him. It's a lot easier to get them to talk these days. The hard men are locked up, the new generation talks. We'll hear about an operation of this scale, and we'll get him."

It was past five and dark outside by the time all of them had had their say. The Prime Minister had just reiterated his demand for action and speed when a private secretary slipped into the room, whispered in the commissioner's ear and ushered him out. Those next to him had heard the word urgent.

When the commissioner came back into the room two minutes later, the Prime Minister saw his face and stopped in mid-sentence.

Everyone's eyes were on the commissioner as he said, "We have some rather bad news. Police officers at Heathrow have discovered a hired car in the terminal car park near building number one. Under the driver's seat was a Kalashnikov rifle, wiped clean of fingerprints. The car park ticket would have given the man time to take a flight to Vienna, Stockholm, Madrid, Rome or Amsterdam. The crew of the British Airways flight to Amsterdam are already back at Heathrow, and one of the stewardesses thinks a man who fits our photokit was a passenger. We are also in touch with Schiphol police, and are wiring the picture, but from the British Airways flight there was ample time to make the connection, which landed in Dublin twenty-five minutes ago, and they are holding all passengers in the baggage reclaim hall."

There was a gasp of relief around the room, then the commissioner went on. "But Dublin reports that those passengers without baggage went through immigration before we notified them."

"Would he have had baggage?" It was the Prime Minister, speaking very quietly.

"I doubt it, sir, but we're trying to establish that with the ticket desk and check-in counter."

"What a foul-up." The Prime Minister was virtually inaudible. "We'll need some results, and soon."

IN THE SUBURBS of Dublin, in the big open-plan newsroom of RTE, the Republic of Ireland's television service, the news editor's phone rang at exactly six o'clock.

"Listen carefully, I'm only going to say this once. This is a spokesman for the military wing of the Provisional IRA. An active service unit of the Provisional IRA today carried out a court-martial execution order on Henry DeLacey Danby, an enemy of the people of Ireland and servant of the British occupation forces in Ireland. During the eighteen months Danby spent in Ireland, one of his duties was responsibility for the concentration camp at Long Kesh. He was repeatedly warned that if the regime of the camp did not change, action would be taken against him. That's it."

The phone clicked off, and the news editor began to read back his shorthand.

395

THE MAN had seen the police convoy racing into the Dublin airport as he'd left, carrying as his sole possessions the Schiphol airport duty-free bag with two hundred cigarettes and a bottle of Scotch. As he'd come through, a young man had stepped forward and asked him if he were Mr. Jones. He'd nodded, nothing more was required of him, and followed the young man out of the new terminal and into the car park. The man had been told he would be met, and reminded that he must not speak at all on the journey, not even on the home trip. The car took the Dundalk road, and then on the stretch between Drogheda and Dundalk turned left and inland towards the hills.

"We'll be away over near Forkhill," muttered the driver.

The man said nothing as the car bumped its way down the side road. After fifteen minutes the driver stopped at a crossroads, where the only building was a corrugated iron-roofed store. He got out and went inside, saying he'd be a minute and had to telephone. The man had started to conjure up images of betrayal and capture, of himself left abandoned near the border and unarmed, when the driver walked back to the car and got in.

"Forkhill's tight, we're going farther down towards the Cullyhanna road. Don't worry, you're home and dry."

The man felt ashamed that the stranger could sense his suspicion and nervousness. As a gesture, he tried to sleep, leaning his head against his safety belt. He stayed in this position till the car suddenly jerked and flung his head hard against the window of the door. He shot forward.

"Don't worry"—again the self-assured approach of the driver. "That was the crater we filled in two years ago. You're in the North now. Home in two hours."

The driver cut back to the east, and on to the north of Newry and the main road to Belfast. The man allowed himself a smile. There was a wide road now, and a good fast one, till the driver pulled up outside Hillsborough and motioned to the duty-free bag.

"Sorry, I don't want that as we come into town. Ditch it."

The man wound down his window and flung the plastic bag into a hedge. The car was moving again. The next sign showed Belfast to be five miles away.

AS SOON AS he returned from London the RUC chief constable put a picked team of detectives on stand-by to wait for information over the heavily publicized Belfast phone numbers by which information is passed anonymously to the police. They waited through the next day, but the call they hoped for never came. There was the usual collection of breathy messages naming people in connection with bombs, shootings, locating the dumping of firearms, but not a word about the Danby killing. In three pubs in the centre of Belfast, British army intelligence officers met their contacts and talked, huddled forward in the little cubicles they favoured. All were to report later to their controller that nothing was known. While they talked, threatening, cajoling, bribing their sources, military police Land-Rovers cruised close by.

The blowing of an intelligence surveillance unit, which kept watch on an IRA base area from the false ceiling of a laundry van, had awakened the operation directors to the need for safeguards. The tortured and mutilated body of a Royal Tank Regiment captain found just three months ago had demonstrated the proba-bility of a security leak close to the heart of the unit, and the public outcry at home at the exposing of soldiers to these out-of-uniform dangers had led to a ministry directive that military personnel were no longer to infiltrate the Catholic community, but instead stay out and cultivate their informers. Funds and the availability of one-way air tickets to Canada were stepped up.

Just before midnight came the first positive information that the killer was back in the city. The duty major in the intelligence section at Lisburn military headquarters, leafing through the situa-tion reports of the evening, read that a patrol of the Life Guards had closed the Hillsborough to Banbridge road while they investi-gated a package at the side of the road. It was cleared after the bomb-disposal expert found that the Schiphol airport duty-free bag contained a carton of cigarettes and a bottle of Scotch. He hurriedly phoned his chief at home and the RUC control centre.

THE MAN was asleep now, in the spare back bedroom of a small terraced house off the Ballymurphy Bull Ring—the "Murph". He'd come at 9:25 that evening from Whiterock, where he had stayed since arriving in Belfast. Around him a safety system was building, with the arrangement that he'd sleep this night till 4:30, then move again to his native Ardoyne district. Only the IRA brigade commander knew the value of the man the precautions were made for—no one else was told, and in the house he was greeted by the family with silence. He made his way through the damp, filthy scullery into the back room, and the family went back to the television.

The man was not known in the Murph and so his name could be kept secret, but not his reason for running—not after the Scotland Yard photokit had been flashed during the late-night news.

The family gathered closely around the set to hear the announcer. High over the fireplace was a carved and painted model of a Thompson machine gun, the present to the family from their eldest son Eamon, held for two years in Long Kesh. Below the gun the family registered no reaction to the picture shown on their screen.

In the small hours Theresa, Eamon's sister, tiptoed her way around the door of the back room. She eased her path over the floorboards, loosened and noisy since the army came to look for her brother. In the darkness she saw the face of the man, out from under his blankets with his arms wrapped around his pillow, like a child holding a favourite doll. She was shivering in the thin nightdress, transparent and reaching barely below her hips. Very gently at first, she shook the shoulder of the man, till he started half out of bed, gripped her wrist, and then pulled her down.

"Who's that?" He said it hard, with fear in his voice.

"It's Theresa." There was silence, just the man's breathing, and still he held her wrist, vicelike. With her free hand she pushed back the bed clothes, and moved alongside him. He was naked and cold.

"You can let go," she said and tried to move closer to him, only to find him backing away till the edge of the single bed stopped him.

"Why did you come?"

"To see you."

"Why did you come?" Again, harsher, louder.

"They showed your picture . . . on the telly . . . on the late news. You had to know, for when they move you on."

398

"There are six men in the city who know I'm here—and you. . . ."

She whispered, "Don't worry yourself, there's no narks here, not in this street, not since the McCoy girl. They shot her."

The hand released her wrist. The man flopped back on the pillow, tension draining out of him. Theresa pressed against his body, but found no response, no acknowledgement of her presence.

"Get out," the man said. "Get out."

Theresa, in her nineteen years, four of them spent on the mill weaving line, had heard and seen enough to say, "Was it that bad . . . London . . . was it—"

There was a stinging blow across the side of her face. His cheap onyx wedding ring gouged the skin below her eye. She was gone, through the door, across the passage to her bed; there she lay, fascinated and horrified at the knowledge she had.

In her half-sleep she heard the whispers and the footsteps on the stairs as the man was taken to his next place of hiding.

AT ALMOST the same time the Saracen armoured cars and Pigs, on dimmed headlights, were moving off from the Belfast police stations, heading out of the sandbagged tin- and chicken-wire fortresses of Andersonstown. Hasting Street and Flax Street and Glenravel Street and Mountpottinger. Inside the armoured cars the troops huddled together, faces blackened with boot polish, laden with gas masks, emergency wound dressings, rubber-bullet guns, truncheons and the medieval plastic see-through shields. In addition they carried with them their high-velocity NATO rifles.

Within a few minutes the convoys had swung off the main roads and were splitting up in the housing developments. Two thousand troops, drawn from six battalions, were sealing off the streets that have the Falls Road as their spinal cord—the Catholic artery out of the west side of the city, and the route to Dublin.

With the dawn came the stones, and the semi-orderliness of the house-to-house searches gave way to the crack of rubber bullets being fired; the streets swirled with CS gas, and always at the end of the narrow line of houses were the kids heaving their fractured paving stones at the military.

For both sides the raid had its achievements. The army and

police had to stir up the pool, get the top men on the other side on the move, perhaps panic one of them into a false step. The street leaders could also claim some benefit from the morning. After the lull of several weeks the army had arrived to kick in the doors, take away the men, break up the rooms, prise out the floorboards. At street level that was valuable currency for the IRA.

IN THE Cabinet Room two days after the shooting, the Prime Minister was showing little patience. He had heard the commissioner say that the boarding house in North London where the man had slept the night before the incident had been searched, but nothing found. As expected, the gun had yielded no fingerprints, and the process of elimination was now being used on the car. Here it was pointed out that the police had to identify the fingerprints of everyone who had handled it the previous six weeks or so before they could begin to come up with a print of the killer's. It would take a long time, said the commissioner, and would involve drivers, Avis staff, garage personnel. He finished by putting the proposition that the killer had no contact in Britain. Reservations for tickets in Dublin, Heathrow and Amsterdam had been made over the phone and were untraceable. He fell back on the theme that the solving of the crime would happen in Belfast.

Frank Scott, the chief constable of the RUC, reported nothing had come in on the Belfast confidential phones, and as yet there had been no whisper on the Special Branch net. "Now we know he's in the city, we'll get him, but it may not be fast." It had been left to him to report the finding of the Amsterdam duty-free bag.

"That's what you said two days ago," snapped the Prime Minister. He drummed his knuckles on the table and invited the opinion of General Fairbairn.

The commander-in-chief of more than fifteen thousand British army men in Northern Ireland expected to be listened to. "The problem, sir, is getting inside the areas the IRA dominate. I would hazard that the motive behind the killing was to get a massive kickback from us at the street level. They want us to hammer them, take house after house to pieces, lock hundreds up, and build a new generation of mini-martyrs. The raids we have been mounting these

400

last thirty-six hours are fair enough as an initial reaction, but if we keep them up, we'll be in danger of reactivating the people who had begun to lose interest in the IRA."

"What about your intelligence men, your men on the inside?"

"We don't go in for that sort of thing so much now, we tend to meet on the outside. After the young captain was murdered three months ago, horrible business . . . we suspended that sort of work."

"Suspended it?" The Prime Minister deliberately accentuated the touch of horror in his voice.

"For around a year there hasn't been the need for intelligence operatives. Now we would have to set up a new unit completely—the men we have there at the moment are too compromised. I don't think in your time scale, Prime Minister, that we can do it."

He said the last dryly, and with only the faintest hint of sarcasm, sufficiently guarded to be just about permissible for a lieutenant-general in the Cabinet Room at 10 Downing Street.

"I want an experienced agent in there as fast as you can make it." The Prime Minister was speaking deliberately, as though for the secretary scribbling in the corner. "A good man. If we've picked the killer up by then, nothing lost; if not . . . I know what you're going to say, General—if he's discovered, I will take the rap. Well?"

The general had heard enough to realize that the interchange of ideas had been over several minutes earlier. This was an instruction by the head of the government.

"For a start, sir, you can get the gentleman making notes over there to take the last page of his book over to the fire and burn it. You can also remind everyone in the room of the small print of the Official Secrets Act. Thank you." The general got up, flushed high in his cheeks, and, followed by the chief constable, who was sharing his RAF plane back to Belfast, left the room.

The Prime Minister waited for the door to close, and the angry footsteps to hasten down the corridor. His eyes ranged up the shining mahogany table, along the line of embarrassed faces, till they locked onto the Minister of Defence.

"Your people have the wherewithal for this sort of thing. Get it set up please, and controlled from this end. If our friend the general doesn't like it, then he won't have to worry himself."

THAT AFTERNOON in a room above a news dealer's shop in Clones, half of the twelve-man Army Council of the Provisional IRA met to consider the London operation. The chief of staff emphasized that now the shooting had taken place, the priority was to keep the man safe. "Every day we keep the man free is a victory. Right? They wanted to pull two battalions out next month; how can they when they can't find one man? At all costs we have to keep their hands off him. He's better dead than in Long Kesh."

# 3

It was getting dark when the RAF Comet took off from Tempelhof Airport, Berlin, with its three passengers. Halfway back and sitting in an aisle seat, Harry still felt bewildered. Two hours earlier he had been called to the army headquarters not too far from the old Nazi Olympic stadium, and instructed he was going to London on urgent military business. He was told he wouldn't need to go home to get his suitcase, that was being done, and no, it would not be suitable for him to phone home, but it would be explained to his wife that he had been called away in a hurry.

Three hours later the plane landed at Northolt and taxied beyond the main reception area to an unmarked square of the landing apron, where a solitary set of steps and civilian Morris 1800 waited. For a captain in transport, it added up to a very remarkable set of circumstances.

THEY'D avoided all checks at Northolt, and Harry hadn't been asked to produce his passport or any travel documents. As soon as he was inside the car the two military policemen who had travelled with him had peeled away. He'd heard the boot bang shut to notify that his suitcase was aboard. Then the car had moved off.

"My name's Davidson." The man beside the driver was talking. "Hope you had a good flight. We've got a bit of a drive now. Perhaps you'd like to sleep for a while."

Harry had nodded, accepted the situation with what grace his position allowed and dozed off.

402

The car had gone fast, south to Dorking and then into the narrow winding side roads under Leith Hill in Surrey. Harry had the back seat to himself, and it was only when the car had swept through the wrought-iron gates of one of those great houses, buried deep among their own woods, that lie hidden in the slopes that he woke. The driveway was rough and in need of repair. Abruptly the rhododendrons gave way to lawns, and the car pulled up at a huge porticoed front door.

"Bit formidable, isn't it? The ministry maintains it's all they could get. Delusions of grandeur. A convent school went broke. Kids all died of exposure, more likely." Davidson opened the door. The suitcase was collected, and they went in.

"We've a long day tomorrow. Lot of talking to do. Let's call it quits, have a good night, and breakfast at seven. O.K.?"

Sandwiches and a thermos of coffee were waiting for Harry when he got to his room.

IT BEGAN in earnest next morning in what must once have been the drawing room, now furnished in the fashion of the Defence Ministry. Heavy tables, sofas with pink flowers all over them and deep army chairs with cloths to prevent greased hair marking the covers.

Davidson was there, and three others.

Harry was not naïve and had realized he was to be briefed for an intelligence mission. It was a little flattering, and welcome after brigade transport. They gave him the armchair to the right of the fireplace.

One man sat behind him by the window; another, not ostentatiously, close to the door. The third sat at a central table, his files spread out on the cloth that covered the polished oak surface. One was of stiff blue cardboard. SECRET had been written across the front in large letters, and underneath were the words: BROWN, HARRY JAMES, CAPT. Four sheets of closely typed paper were inside—Harry's life history and the assessments of his performance by each of his commanding officers. The first page carried the information they had sought when they had begun the search for the officer they wanted.

*Name:* Brown, Harry James
*Current rank:* Captain
*Age:* 34
*Born:* Portadown, NI
*Distinguishing marks and description:* 5' 11" height, medium build, brown hair, blue eyes, no distinguishing marks.
*Service UK:* Catterick, Plymouth, Tidworth, Ministry of Defence.
*Service Overseas:* Cyprus (2nd Lt), Borneo (2nd Lt), Aden (1st Lt), Berlin (Capt).
*Decorations:* Cyprus—Mentioned in despatches. Aden—Military Cross

In the last quarter of the page was the passage that ensured that Harry came into the operation.

*Aden citation:* For three months this officer lived as a native in the Arab quarter of Sheikh Othman, moving inside the community there and supplying most valuable intelligence concerning terrorist operations. As a result of his work, many important arrests were made. This work was extremely dangerous and there was a constant risk of torture and death.

Too right, Harry would have thought, if anyone had let him see the file. Day after day, living with those filthy bastards, watching for movement after curfew, observing the huddles in the coffee shops. And always the terrible fear of discovery, and the pain that would follow. And the know-alls in intelligence back at headquarters who passed discreet little messages—about hanging on just a few more days. They'd seemed surprised when he went up to an army patrol one hot, stinking morning, and introduced himself, and walked out of thirteen weeks of naked terror. And after the nervous breakdown and the days of sick leave, just a metal cross dangling from an inch square of purple and white cloth, all there was to show for it.

Davidson was moving about the room, darting around the furniture. "I don't have to tell you, from your past experience, that everything that is said in this room goes under the Official Secrets

Act. Your name was put forward when we came into the market for a new man for an infiltration job. The work has been demanded by the Prime Minister. Yesterday afternoon he authorized the mission, and I must say frankly it was against, as I understand it, the advice of his closest military advisers. Seems the PM had a brother in special operations thirty years ago who told him how the infiltration of agents into enemy country won the war, and they say he's had a bee about it ever since.

"He wants to put a man into the heart of Provo-land, into the Falls district in Belfast—a man who is quite clean and has no record in that world. He'd be on his own as far as looking after himself is concerned. I think anyone who has thought even a little about it knows that the job the PM has asked us to do is bloody dangerous. Putting it formally, Harry, this is the bit where you either stand up and say 'Not effing likely', and walk out through the door and we'll have you on a flight to Berlin in three hours. Or it's the time when you come in and then stay in."

The man at the table with the files shuffled his papers. Harry was a long way from a rational evaluation of the job, whatever it was they were offering. He was just thinking how large a file they'd got on him when he became aware of the silence in the room.

Harry said, "I'll try it."

"You appreciate, Harry, once you say yes, that's it. That has to be the definitive decision."

Harry was almost impatient with Davidson's caution. "Yes, I said yes. I'll try it."

The atmosphere seemed to change. The man behind Harry coughed. Davidson was on the move again, the file open in his hand.

"We're going to put you into the Falls with the express and only job of listening for any word of the man who shot the minister, Danby, three days ago. Intelligence in Belfast won't handle you, we will. The Special Branch over there won't have heard of you. Why aren't they doing it from Belfast? They haven't got an infiltration set-up any longer that we're happy with. So far, the police and military haven't come up with anything. I don't know whether you will, but the PM's decided we try."

THE TEAM worked Harry hard that first day. Davidson had started by telling him that there could not be a phone call to his wife. "We've told her you've been called away on an urgent posting to Muscat, because of your special Aden knowledge. We have some postcards you can write to her later and we'll get them posted by the RAF."

Then they discussed his cover, and rejected the alternatives in favour of a merchant seaman, home after five years, with his parents dead.

Harry himself supplied most of what they needed. He'd been born a Catholic in one of the little terraces off Obin Street in Portadown. The houses had been replaced by blocks of flats, now daubed with the slogans of revolution. With the destruction of the old buildings, inevitably the people had become dispersed.

Portadown, the Orangemen's town with the ghetto around the long sloping passage of Obin Street, still had vivid memories for Harry. His parents had been killed in a car crash when he was five, and he had stayed with an aunt for twelve years in the Catholic street before joining the army. His childhood in the town gave him adequate knowledge, Davidson decided, for his cover.

For four hours after lunch they quizzed him on Irish affairs, sharpened him on the names of the new political figures. They briefed him particularly on the grievances of the minority.

"You'll want to know what they're beefing about. They're walking encyclopedias on every shot we fired at them."

Papers were spread out in front of him. Fingers reached and pointed at the different essentials for him to take in. Later he was to take many of the papers to his room and read them, into the small hours, till they were second nature.

THE STREET scene in Belfast had reached a new level of violence. In the wake of the Danby killing, army activity had risen sharply, initially in the use of major cordon and search operations, merging into an increase in the number of spot raids on the homes of known republicans on the run. The army activity meant more men were charged with offences, but alongside their appearances in court was an upsurge in street rioting, something that had previously been

406

almost eradicated. The army's posture was sharply criticized by the minority politicians, who accused the troops of venting their frustrations at not being able to find Danby's murderer on innocent Catholic householders.

MEANWHILE, Harry was being prepared for the awesome moment when he would leave the woods of Surrey and fly to Belfast. Davidson had brought him a cassette recorder, complete with four ninety-minute tapes of Belfast accents. They'd been gathered by students from Queen's University who believed they were taking part in a national phonetics study, and had taken their microphones into pubs, launderettes, working men's clubs and supermarkets, wherever there were groups talking in the harsh, cutting accent of Belfast. Night after night Harry listened to the tapes, mouthing over the phrases and trying to lock his speech into the accents he heard.

His walls, almost bare when he had arrived at the big house, were soon covered with aerial photographs of Belfast. For perhaps an hour a day he was left to memorize the photographs, learn the street patterns of the geometric divisions of the artisan cottages that had been allowed to sprawl out from the centre of the city.

From the distance of Germany—where theorists worked out war games in terms of divisions, tank skirmishes, limited nuclear warheads and the possibility of chemical agents being thrown into a critical battle—it had been difficult for Harry to realize why some twenty thousand British soldiers deployed in the province were not able to wind up the Provisional campaign in a matter of months. But when he took in the rabbit warren revealed by the reconnaissance photographs, he began to comprehend the complexity of the problem. Displayed on his walls was a maze of escape routes, ambush positions, and, at strategic crossroads, great towering blocks of flats commanding the approaches to terrorist strongholds.

Davidson fired questions at Harry till he could wheel out at will all the street names they wanted from him—so many of them commemorating the former greatness of British arms: Balkan, Raglan, Alma, Balaclava—their locations and the quickest way to get there. By the second week the knowledge was there and perfection was under way. Davidson felt now that the filing system had worked well, that this man, given the impossible assignment he had, would do as well as any.

At one stage Davidson sent a TV camera and a young officer around to the homes of the eye-witnesses who had been in Belgrave Square, or who had reported the jostling incident in the Underground, in order that they could relive the moments they had been face-to-face with the gunman. For about fifteen minutes the girl with the bag of laundry, the driver of the ministry car and the woman who had stood immobile as the man wove his way past her had spelled out their recollections. They were taken again and again through their experience, milked till their impatience with their questioner grew pointed.

Endlessly the tapes were re-run, and the witnesses' hesitations about hair style, eye colour, nose size, all the details that make each face unique as a fingerprint, were analysed. Davidson made up a chart where all the strong points were listed in green ink, the next category in red, the doubtful points in blue. These were placed against the photokit picture already issued by the Royal Ulster Constabulary and Scotland Yard.

"You have to know him," said Davidson—so often it became like a broken record. "You have to have a sense about him, that when he's on the pavement and you're at the other side you'll have him straight away. It's chemistry, my boy."

Their own photokit of the man was displayed about treble life-size in the rooms where the team worked and on Harry's wall.

By the fifteenth day they were ready to push Harry out into the field. Other than his sleeping time, and those hours he'd worked in his room on the voice tapes and the maps, he'd been allowed to spend little time on his own. That was Davidson's idea—"Don't let him brood on it," he had told the others.

Davidson had wondered whether there ought to be some celebration on Harry's last night, and then decided in favour of a few glasses of beer after their final session, and another early night.

"To be frank, Harry, we all thought they'd have had the killer by now. The word I had last night, however, is that they haven't identified any positive clue yet. In a strange idiotic way, you have a

408

better chance than the military clumping round and the police."

Harry reckoned his chances of seeing the man about minus nil, though he maintained a more public optimism with Davidson. Eventually they wished him luck. A little formal. Harry said nothing, nodded and walked out into the hall and up the stairs to his room. They let him go alone.

TWENTY-FIVE thousand feet up, between the coasts of England and Northern Ireland, Harry had been working things out. The reality of it all had been brutally clear as he had stood in the queue waiting to be searched at the departure gate. Who ever heard of an agent getting his own bags taken apart by his own side? It was painfully clear why his promised Smith & Wesson would have to be picked up at the Belfast main post office.

By the time the Trident was arching over the landfall to the south of Strangford Lough, Harry had decided he was not a little flattered he'd been asked to do the mission. After all, it had been called for by the Prime Minister. In the heat of the plane he thought of his wife, warmth and closeness flooding through him. It was a pity she couldn't share in his pride. For a few minutes, before the aeroplane wheels banged down onto the tarmac, Harry indulged himself, conscious of the softness of the moment. He knew from other times of danger that he could cocoon himself in sentimentality for his family, for Mary and the boys.

He came down the plane steps and hurried past the RAF regiment corporal. The anomaly of going to war in his own country was not lost on him. At the flanks of the terminal building, coils of barbed wire sprawled across the flower beds that had once been sufficient to mark the perimeters of the taxiing area. The viewing gallery where people used to wave to their friends was now fenced with high chicken wire to prevent a bomb being thrown onto the apron; it was out of bounds to civilians, anyway. After getting his bag in the concourse, Harry walked out towards the bus pickup point. Around him was an avenue of white oil drums with heavy planks slung between them—a defence against car bombers moving their lethal loads against the walls of the buildings. He moved by a line of passengers waiting to take the Trident back to London. Only rarely did the faces of the travellers match the brightness of their going-away clothes. Greyness, anxiety, exhaustion.

Harry climbed onto the bus and ensured himself a window seat near the back. By the time the bus was into the top of the Crumlin Road, the man directly behind Harry had taken upon himself the role of guide and raconteur.

"Down there on the right—just round the corner where you can't see—that's where the three Scottish soldiers were murdered . . . the pub . . . the one that's blown up—the one we're passing—they took 'em from there. People used to put flowers, but nothing to see now, except there's no grass in the ditch where they got it. Army dug it all up looking for bullets, and it never grew since. Now on the left, that's where the senator was killed. . . ."

The bus slowed to a crawl. The man behind went on talking. "Now wait for the bumps . . . here we go. See, we're outside a barracks—they all have bumps outside now—stops the Provos belting past and giving the sentry a burst with a Thompson. . . . That's Ardoyne, on the left, where the policeman is. That's a sight for the English, policemen with bulletproof coats and machine guns—"

"Shut up, Joe, nobody wants to know. Just wrap it."

Joe fell silent. Harry watched out of the window, fascinated by the sights. At the traffic lights the driver nudged alongside a Saracen armoured car. Soldiers crouched inside the half-open steel back doors, rifles in hand. On the other side of the crossroads he watched a patrol inching its way through the shopping crowds. On all sides were yards of pale-brown hardboard that had taken the place of glass in the store windows.

At the bus station Harry switched to another single-decker that went high up on the Antrim Road to the north, into residential suburbs. Davidson had given him the name of a boarding house three stops up past the troubled New Lodge junction.

Harry got off the bus at the stop, and spotted the house they had chosen for him, with its seedy "Vacancies" sign. He moved a hundred and fifty yards down the long hill and waited. He watched the front door for twenty-five minutes before a young man came out. Clothes not quite right, walk too long, hair a bit too short.

410

Harry boiled. Stupid bastards. Davidson, you prime bastard. Send me to one of your own bloody places. Nice safe little billet in a nice Protestant area, where you won't find any bloody thing out, but you won't get shot. No, not Davidson, someone in Belfast, having his own back because it isn't his caper. I'm not going through all this to sit on my arse in Proddyland. No way.

He took the next bus back into central Belfast, walked across to the taxi rank and asked to be taken up to mid-Falls. To the driver he said, "I'm working about halfway up, and looking for someone who takes in lodgers. Not too pricey. Yer know anyone?"

The taxi dropped Harry off outside "Delrosa", Mrs. Duncan's boarding house. It didn't take him long to settle into the small room at the back of Mrs. Duncan's two-storey house—about as long as it takes to unpack the contents of a small suitcase and put them into a chest of drawers and a wardrobe. She suggested he wash his hands and come down to the big room where the other guests would gather, first for tea, then to watch television. From his window Harry could see the Falls Road, where army Land-Rovers and Saracens criss-crossed back and forth.

There were six at tea, all eating with concentration. The way to avoid talking, thought Harry. Stuff your face, with just a mutter for the milk or the sugar, or the fresh-cut bread, and you don't have to say anything. No one mentioned the troubled times, but they came into the room with the BBC local television news. Mrs. Duncan came from the kitchen to the doorway, leaning there, arms folded, in her apron. A single shot had killed the first soldier to die in Northern Ireland in three weeks. The pictures showed troops illuminated in doorways and manning roadblocks.

Then the programme changed to an interview in the studio. A Protestant politician and a Catholic politician were arguing over the same ground that they'd been debating on the same channel for several years. Between them was a host, feeding them questions. Before the talk was a minute old, Mrs. Duncan came forward like a battleship under power and turned it off.

"There's enough politics on the street without bringing them into my house. Just words. Won't do that young man any good. Mother of Jesus rest with him."

A youngish man sitting across the table from Harry said, "If they stayed in their barracks, they wouldn't get shot. If they weren't here, there wouldn't be any shooting."

Nobody responded. The young man looked around for someone to argue with. Harry sided with him. "If they were as busy chasing the Prods as us, they'd find things easier for themselves. I've been away a long time, but I can see in the few hours I've been back that nothing's done about those Prods, only us."

With practice Harry would gain the facility to sing the praises of the IRA. But the first time was hard. He excused himself, saying he had been travelling all day, and went to his room.

# 4

It was just after seven when Harry woke. He knew that this was the day he started the hard work of moving on to the inside.

He'd known since his training started that the initial period of infiltration was going to be the difficult part. This was where the expertise and skill he'd acquired in Aden would count. They had chosen him after going over his files, and those of a dozen other men, because they had thought that he of all of them stood the best chance of being able to adapt in those early critical hours in the new environment.

Davidson had struck a chord when he had said, "They seem to have the ability to smell an outsider. Much of it will depend on whether you can look as though you belong. You need confidence. You have to believe that you're not the centre of attention the whole time. The first trick is to get yourself a base. Establish yourself there, and then work outward. Like an upside-down pyramid."

The base was clearly to be the good Mrs. Duncan. She was in the kitchen, washing up the first sitting of breakfast, when Harry came down the stairs.

"Well, it's good to be back, Mrs. Duncan. You miss Ireland when you're away, whatever sort of place it is now. But it can't be easy for you, running a business in these times?"

412

The previous evening he had given his name as Harry McEvoy.

"Well, Mr. McEvoy, they're not the easiest of times, to be sure. What did you say your business was?"

"I've been away, ten years or so, at sea. In the merchant navy. Down in the South Atlantic and Indian Ocean, mainly."

"There's a lot you'll see has changed. Our people have taken a bad time, and now the Protestants hate us as never before. It'll take a long time to sort it out."

"The English don't understand us."

"Of course they don't, Mr. McEvoy." She flipped his egg over expertly, set it on the plate beside the halved tomatoes, the skinned sausage, the mushrooms and the crisp fried bread. "Look at all the ballyhoo when that man of theirs was shot—Danby. You'd think it was the first man who had died since the troubles. Here they are, close to a thousand dead, and all, and one English politician gets killed. . . . You should have seen the searches they did, troops all over. Never found damn all."

"They've not caught a man yet for it?"

"Nor will they. The boys will keep it close. But that's enough talk of politics. If you're back from the sea, what are you going to do now? Have you a job to be away to?"

Before answering, Harry complimented her on the breakfast. He handed her the empty plate. Then he said, "Well, I thought I might try something temporary for a bit while I look round for something permanent."

"There's enough men here would like a job, permanent or not."

"I think I'll walk about a bit this morning. I'll do the bed first . . . an old habit at sea. Tomorrow I'll try round for a job."

MRS. DUNCAN had noticed he'd been away. And a long time at that, she was certain. Something grated on her ear, tuned to three decades of welcoming visitors. She couldn't place what had happened to his accent. Like the sea he talked of, she was aware it came in waves—ebbed in its pitch. Pure Belfast for a few words, or a phrase, then falling off into something that was close to Ulster but softer, without the harshness. She couldn't understand the way he seemed to change his accent so slightly in mid-sentence. If he

413

was away on a boat so long, then he would have lost the Belfast in his voice . . . But then, in contradiction, there were the times when he was pure Belfast. It nagged all morning as she dusted around the house.

THEY DON'T waste time in Belfast lingering over the previous day. By the time Harry was out on the pavements of the Falls Road and walking towards town, there was nothing to show that a large-scale military operation had followed the killing of a young soldier the previous evening. The traffic was on the move, and women with their children in tow were moving down towards the shops. Harry was wearing a pair of old jeans he had brought from Germany and a ragged pullover he'd last worn when painting the white walls around the staircase at home. They were some of the clothes the

officer had collected when he'd called and told Harry's wife that
her husband was on his way to the Middle East.

The clothes were right, and he walked down the road—watched,
but not greatly attracting attention. The time had been noted when
he came out of the side road where Mrs. Duncan had her guest
house, and into the Falls. The youth that saw him from behind
the neat muslin curtain at the corner would remember him when
he came back, and mentally clock him in. There was every reason
why he should be noticed; the only new face to come out of the
road that morning. All Mrs. Duncan's other guests were regulars,
discreetly examined and cleared by the time they'd slept in her
house enough for a pattern to emerge.

Harry had decided to walk this first morning in order to familiarize
himself with his immediate surroundings. "Know your way round,"

they'd said. "It might save your life." He came down past the old Broadway Cinema, where no films had been shown for two years since the fire bomb exploded beside the ticket kiosk, and past the one-time petrol station, where the pumps had long since been flattened. Across the road was the convent school. Children were laughing and shouting in the playground. Harry remembered seeing that same playground on West German television when the newsreader had described the attack by two IRA motor-cyclists on William Staunton. The Catholic magistrate had just dropped his two girls at school and was watching them from his car when he was shot. He had lingered for three months before he died, and then one of the papers had published a poem written by the dead man's twelve-year-old daughter. Harry had read it in the mess, and had not forgotten it.

> *"Don't cry," Mummy said*
> *"They're not real."*
> *But Daddy was*
> *And he's not here.*
>
> *"Don't be bitter," Mummy said*
> *"They've hurt themselves much more."*
> *But they can walk and run*
> *Daddy can't.*
>
> *"Forgive them and forget," Mummy said*
> *But can Daddy know I do?*
> *"Smile for Daddy, kiss him well," Mummy said*
> *But can I ever?*

He was still mouthing the words as the Royal Victoria Hospital loomed up, part modern, part the dark-red brick of old Belfast. Staunton and scores of others had been rushed here, down the curved hill and through the rubber-padded doors of Casualty.

Harry turned left into Grosvenor Road, hurrying his step. Most of the windows on either side of the street showed the scars of the conflict, boarded up, bricked up, sealed to squatters, too dangerous for habitation but remaining available and ideal for the snipers. In

416

the log of the history of the troubles since August 1969 that they'd given Harry to read, the half-mile he was walking down had taken up fifteen entries.

Harry produced a driver's licence made out in the name of McEvoy and the post-office clerk gave him the brown-paper parcel. Harry recognized Davidson's neat copperplate hand on the outside: "Hold for collection". Inside was a .38-calibre Smith & Wesson revolver. Accurate and a man-stopper. One of hundreds of thousands run off in World War II. Untraceable.

That afternoon, with the parcel under his arm, Harry walked back from the centre of the city to the Broadway. He wanted a drink. Could justify it too, on professional grounds. He needed to get the tempo of things.

The "local" was down the street from Mrs. Duncan's corner. Over the last few paces his resolve went haywire, weakened so that he would have dearly loved to walk past the paint-scraped door and regain the security of the little back room he had rented. He checked himself. Breathing hard, and feeling the tightness of fear in his stomach, he pushed the door open and went into the pub. His eyes took a few moments to respond to the darkness within. The talk stopped, and he saw the faces follow him to the counter. He asked for a bottle of Guinness, anxiously projecting his voice, conscious that fear is most easily noticed from speech. Nobody spoke to him as he sipped his drink. The glass was two-thirds empty by the time desultory conversation started up again.

Across the room two young men watched Harry drink. Both were volunteers in E Company of the Third Battalion of the Provisional IRA, Belfast Brigade. They had heard of Harry's cover story. The source, unwittingly, was Mrs. Duncan, who had talked over the clothesline with her neighbour. The neighbour's son, who now stood in the bar watching Harry, had asked his mother to find out from Mrs. Duncan who the new lodger was, where he came from and whether he was staying long.

Mrs. Duncan had told how the new guest had turned up out of the blue, how he hoped to find a job and had already paid three weeks in advance. He was a seaman, the English merchant navy, and had been abroad for many years. But he was from the North, and had come home now. From Portadown he was. "He's been away, all right," she shouted over the fence to her friend. "You can hear it every time he opens his mouth."

The conversation between the two women had been relayed to the son verbatim by his mother. Now he watched and listened, expressionless, as Harry finished his drink. Harry walked quickly back to Delrosa. When he rang the bell, a tall, willowy girl opened the door.

"Hullo, McEvoy's the name. I'm staying here."

She smiled and made way for him, stepping back into the hall. Black hair down to the shoulders, high cheekbones, and dark eyes set deep above them. She stood very straight, breasts angled into the tight sweater before it moulded with her waist and was lost in the wide leather belt threaded through the loops of her jeans.

"I'm Josephine Laverty. Mrs. Duncan said there was someone new. I help her with the cleaning and then the teas."

He looked at her blatantly. "Could you make me one now? A cup of tea?" Hardly adequate, he thought, for an opening chat-up to a beautiful girl.

She walked through into the kitchen, and he followed, catching the cheap scent. "What else do you do?"

"Work at the mill, down the Falls, the big one. I do early shift, then come round and do a bit with Mrs. Duncan."

"There's not much about for people here now, 'cept work, and not enough of that," Harry waded in, "what with the troubles and that. Do you go out much? Do you find much to do?"

"I don't go into town much—there's not much point, really. Go to a film and there'll be a bomb threat and you're cleared out. The Proddys run the centre anyway, so you have to run for dear life to get back into the Falls." She reached into the hip pocket of her jeans for a crumpled handkerchief. She dabbed it against her nose. Harry saw the green embroidered shamrocks in the corners, and fractionally caught the motif in the middle of the square. Crossed black and brown Thompson machine guns.

"That handkerchief," said Harry, "does that mean you follow the boyos?"

"Not bloody likely. They sell them to raise funds for the families

418

of the men that are held in the Kesh. Just try and not buy one. No, I'm not one of those rebels that runs round after the cowboys. When I settle it'll be with a feller with more future than a detention order, I can tell you."

"What sort of evenings do you have now?"

"We have the *caelis*," she said, "not the proper thing they have in the Free State. But there's dancing, and a bit of a band, and a singer and a bar. You've been away, at sea, right? Well, we've got rid of the old songs now . . . 1916 and 1922 are out of the hit parade. We've got 'Men Behind the Wire'—that's internment. 'Bloody Sunday'. 'Provie Birdie'—when the three boys were lifted out of Mountjoy Prison by helicopter . . . and the screws was shouting, 'Shut the gates!' Must have been a laugh. Did you hear about it?"

"I was going through the Middle East. I saw it in the English paper in Beirut."

She was impressed; seemed so anyway. Not that he'd been to an exotic-sounding place like Beirut, but that the fame of Seamus Twomey, Joe O'Hagen and Kevin Mallon had spread that far. Harry weighed her up as gently committed—not out of conviction but out of habit.

"I think I'd like to come to one of your evenings," he said.

"I'll take you. I'll pick you up here, Saturday, round half-past seven. Cheers."

She handed Harry a cup of tea and he took it to his room.

It was just after five in the morning. The man was moving the last few yards to his home. They had checked the streets near his house and given an all-clear on the army patrols.

Ypres Avenue was a little different from the mass of streets that made up the Ardoyne. The World War I battles it was named after gave a clue to its age, and so its state of repair was superior to those streets up in the Falls which took their names from the Crimean War and the Indian Mutiny battles. But no major repairs had been carried out on any considerable scale in the avenue since the day the cottages had been put up to provide dwellings for those working in the mill on the edge of the Ardoyne, where the army now slept.

The houses were joined in groups of four. In between, a narrow passage ran through to the high-walled back-entrance alley that came along behind the tiny yards at the rear.

The blast bombs, nail bombs and petrol bombs of four years of fighting had taken their toll, and several of the houses had been walled up. The bottom eight feet of a wall at the end of the avenue had been whitewashed, the work of housewives at internment time, so that at night, in the near darkness, a soldier's silhouette would stand out all the more clearly and give the boyos a better chance with a rifle.

The army sat heavily on Ardoyne, and the Provos—the Provisional IRA, the militant Catholic group—as they themselves admitted, had had a hard time of it. This was good for the man. A main activist would not be expected to live in an area dominated by the military, where IRA operations had virtually ceased.

Comfort played only a small part in the design of each house. A hall, with a front room off it, led towards a living area with kitchen and scullery two later additions under asbestos roofing. The toilet was in the yard against the far wall in a breeze-block cubicle. Upstairs each house boasted two rooms and a tiny landing. Bathing was in the kitchen. This was Belfast-housing, perfect for the ideological launching of the gunman; perfect, too, as the model ground for him to pursue his work.

The door of the man's house had been recently greased, and made no sound when it swung on its hinges. He slipped inside. The relief was total. He was back.

He moved catlike to the stairs, up three steps, then waited and listened. The house was completely dark and he had found the banister rail by touch. There were the familiar smells of cold tea and cold chips, of the damp that came into the walls. There was no question of using the lights. Any illumination through the sparse curtains would alert the army to the fact that someone in the house was on the move. The man inched his way up the stairs, conscious that no one would have told his wife he was coming home, anxious not to frighten her.

He moved slowly on the landing, pushed open the door of the back room. He made out her hair on the pillow, and beside it the

420

two small shapes, huddled close together for warmth and comfort. In their four years of marriage his wife had borne him twins, both boys, conceived some months before their wedding, and these two daughters. One of the children wriggled and then subsided with the cough. It had just been coming on when he had left home. He watched them a long time, and gradually his wife became aware of his presence. With a half-strangled sob she reached out for her man and pulled him down onto the bed.

"Hullo, my love. I'm back." He mouthed the words pressed hard into the pit of her neck. "I'm home."

She held him very tightly, pulling at him as if some force were working to get him away from her again. "Where've you been?"

"Don't . . . don't . . . I've missed you, I've wanted you."

"No, where've you been?" she persisted. "We thought you were gone—were dead. There was no word, not anything."

"As I told you. I was in the South. Finish, that's it."

"I know now, don't I?" She was lying quite still, rigid and yielding nothing. "It said in the papers that his children were there. And his wife. They saw it all. That the man went on shooting long after he'd gone down. That the children were screaming, that his wife put herself right over him."

She was sitting right up now, and the man's longing for her had gone, sapped from him by her accusation.

She went on, looking not at him but straight in front of her into the darkness. "They said they'd hunt for the man who did it till they found him, then lock him up for the rest of his natural. You stupid, daft bastard."

In his churning mind the replies and counter-attacks flooded through him. But when he spoke, it was without fight. "Someone had to do it. It happened it was me. Danby had it coming. But there's no line on me, and you didn't need to know."

"What a future! The return of the great and famous hero, with half the army after him. We didn't need to know. What sort of statement is that? If they shoot you when they get you, there'll be a bloody song about you. Just right for Saturday nights when they're all drunk. What a hero. You'll want me to teach the kids the words, and all. Is that the future for us?"

She sank back onto the pillow, and holding the nearest of the two children, began to weep, in slight shudders, noiselessly.

He rose from the bed and went down the stairs and into the front room. He groped his way to his armchair by the grate and lowered himself gingerly down into it. Since Danby, all he had wanted was to get back here, to her, to the family. To be safe with them. But she'd clobbered him.

They had never talked about the Provos. She didn't want to know. Wasn't interested. Went and buried herself in the kitchen, played with the children, got out of his way. She accepted, though, that he needed her strength and support when he came home.

He had started like most others as a teenager throwing rocks and abuse in the early days at those wonderful, heaven-sent targets— the British army, with their yellow cards forbidding them to shoot in almost every situation. All the boys in Ypres Avenue threw stones at the soldiers, and it would have been almost impossible to have been uninvolved.

Many of his contemporaries in the street had thrust themselves forward into the IRA. Some were now dead, others in prison. The man had kept apart from them, and been noticed by those older, shadowy figures who ran the movement. He had been marked down as someone out of the ordinary, used sparingly and never with the cannon fodder that carried the bombs into the town shoe shops and supermarkets, or held up the post offices for a few hundred pounds.

He was still slumped in his chair when she came downstairs. She leaned over and kissed him on his forehead.

"We'll have to forget it all," she said. "There's a dance at the club on Saturday. Let's go. We'll have some drinks, forget it ever happened." She kissed him again.

HARRY spent a long time getting himself ready to go out that Saturday night. In the time that he'd been in Belfast he had tried to stop thinking in the terms of an army officer. He attempted to make his first impulses those of any ex-merchant seaman or of the lorry driver that he hoped to become. As he straightened his tie, though, he allowed himself the luxury of thinking that this was a touch different from mess night with the regiment at base camp in Germany.

He'd spent a difficult and nearly unproductive first week. He'd visited a score of firms looking for driver's work, with no success till Friday, when he had come across a scrap merchant on the far side of Andersonstown. There they'd said they might be able to use him, but he should come back on Monday morning. He had been in the pub on the corner several times, but the opening remarks he made to the locals were generally rebutted with noncommittal answers. He felt that the one bright spot was taking Josephine out.

When the doorbell rang shortly after half-past seven, he slipped quickly down to the hall and opened the door. Josephine stood there, breathless. "I'm sorry I'm late. Couldn't get a bus."

"I think all the buses are in the scrap yards up the road, stacks of them there, doubles and singles. Let's go."

IN YPRES AVENUE the man and his wife were making their final preparations to go out. There had been an uneasy understanding between them since their talk in the early hours after his home-coming, and both seemed to accept that the wounds of that night could only be healed by time and silence.

To both of them the evening was something to look forward to, a change from the oppressiveness of the house.

With his wife on his arm, and in her best trouser-suit, the man walked up his street towards the green-painted hut with the corrugated-iron roof that was the social club. He could relax here, among his own. Drain his pints. Talk to people.

BY THE TIME Harry and Josephine arrived at the club, forty-five minutes later, it was nearly full. The girl said she'd find somewhere to sit, and he pushed his way towards the long trestle tables, at the far end from the door, where three men in their shirt sleeves were pouring drinks. Harry forced his way through to the makeshift bar and called for a pint of Guinness and a gin and orange.

As he was struggling back to the table where Josephine was sitting, he saw a man come up to her and gesture towards him. They spoke a few words, and then the man moved away.

"Someone you know?" he said when he sat down.

"It's just they like to know who's who round here."

"What did you tell him?"

"Just who you were, that's all."

Everything was subdued at this stage of the evening, but the effects of the drink and the belting of the four-piece band and their amplified instruments began to have a livening effect. By nine some of the younger couples had piled up the tables and chairs at the far end of the room from the bar, exposing the crude nail-ridden boards. That was the dance floor. The band quickened the tempo. Harry asked the girl if she'd like to dance.

She led the way through the jungle of tables and chairs. Near the floor Harry paused as Josephine slowed and squeezed by a girl in a bright yellow trouser-suit. As Harry's eyes moved to the table where she was sitting, he saw the young man at her side.

There was intuitive, deep-based recognition for a moment. Harry looked at the man, who stared back at him, challenging. Harry moved to the floor. Once more he looked at the man, who still watched him, cold and expressionless—then Harry rejected the suspicion of the likeness. Hair wrong. Face too full. Eyes too close. Mouth was right. That was all. The mouth, nothing else.

Harry's attention was diverted to Josephine, her prettiness and inevitable promise. She was wearing a black skirt, full and flared, so that she had the freedom to swing her hips to the music.

The man, too, had noticed Harry's attention. It had been pronounced enough to make him fidget a little in his chair, but his nerves had calmed when he had seen Harry on the dance floor, no longer interested, now totally involved in the girl he was with.

The man could not dance, had never been taught. He and his wife would sit at the table all evening as a succession of friends and neighbours joined them to talk for a few minutes. Along the wall near the bar was a group of youths, some of them volunteers in the Provisionals, some couriers and some lookouts. These were the expendables of the movement. The teenage girls were gathered around them, attracted by the glamour of the profession of terrorism, hanging on the boys' sneers and boasts. None knew the man except by name. None knew of his involvement.

FIRST THROUGH the door was the big sergeant, a Stirling sub-machine gun in his right hand. He'd hit the door with all the impetus of his two hundred pounds, gathered in a six-foot run. Behind him came a lieutenant, clutching his Browning automatic pistol, and then eight soldiers. They came in fast and fanned out in a protective screen around the officer. Some of the soldiers carried rifles, others the large-barrelled, rubber-bullet guns.

The officer shouted in the general direction of the band, "Wrap it up. I want all the men facing the far wall. Hands right up. Ladies, where you are, please."

From the middle of the dance floor a glass curved its way towards the troops. It hit high on the bridge of a nose creeping under the protective rim of a helmet. Blood was forming from the wound by the time the glass hit the floor. A six-inch rubber bullet, solid, unbending, was fired into the crowd, and there were screams and stampeding away from the troops.

"Come on. No games, please. Let's get it over with."

More soldiers had come through the door. There were perhaps twenty of them in the hall by the time the line of men had formed up, legs wide apart and fingers and palms on the wall high above their heads. Harry was separated from the man by three others. At her table the girl in the yellow trouser-suit sat very still. She was one of the few who weren't barraging the army with obscenities. Her eyes flicked continuously from the troops to her husband. Josephine stood on the dance floor, interested to see what the army made of her merchant-seaman escort.

Six of the soldiers, working in pairs, split up the line against the wall and started to quiz each man. The lieutenant moved among the three groups, checking the procedure.

Private David Jones and Lance-Corporal James Llewellyn were working over the group of men nearest the dance floor. The man and Harry were there. The way the line had formed itself, they would come to the man first. It was very slow. Conscientious, plodding. The man's wife was in agony. Charade, that's all, she was thinking. A game of cat and mouse. They had come for him, and these were the preliminaries, the way they dressed it up. But they'd come for him. They had to know.

The lance-corporal tapped the man's shoulder. "Come on, let's have you." Not unkindly.

The man swung around, bringing his hands down to his sides, fists clenched tight, avoiding the pleading face of his wife. Llewellyn was asking the questions, Jones writing down the answers.

"Name?"

"Billy Downs."

"Age?"

"Twenty-four."

"Address?"

"Forty-one, Ypres Avenue."

Llewellyn paused as Jones struggled with his blunt pencil. The lieutenant walked towards them. He looked hard at the man.

"Billy Downs?"

"That's it."

"We were calling for you a week or so back. Expected to find you home, but you weren't there." He stared into the young man's face.

"I went down to see my mother in the South."

"What's her address?"

"Forty, Dublin Road, Cork."

The lieutenant still searched Downs's face for evasion. "Put him in the truck," he said.

Jones and Llewellyn hustled Downs across the room towards the door. His wife rushed over to him.

"Don't worry, girl, once the Garda have checked with Mam, I'll be home." And he was out into the night to the parked Saracen.

The two soldiers came back to the line. Llewellyn touched Harry's shoulder. "Name?"

"Harry McEvoy."

"Age?"

"Thirty-three."

"Address?"

Jones had had his eyes on his notebook till that moment. When he glanced up to hear the answer, Harry saw an expression of astonishment take hold of him, then change to suspicion, then back to bewilderment. "What are you doing—".

Harry's right foot moved the seven inches to Jones's left ankle.

426

As the private ducked forward, caught off balance by the sudden pain, Harry lurched into him. "Shut your face," he hissed into the soldier's ear. Jones's face came up and met Harry's stare. He saw Harry's head move, a quick shake, left to right.

Llewellyn had been diverted by a commotion at the far end of the hall, where four youths were half carried, half dragged towards the doorway. He was concentrating again now. "Come on—what's the address?"

"Delrosa Guest House, in the Broadway." Harry's eyes were on Jones.

"Bit off course, aren't you?" said Llewellyn.

"My girl's local."

"Which one?"

"In the polka-dot, the dark-haired girl." Harry gazed past Llewellyn, his eyes never leaving Jones.

"Lucky you," said Llewellyn and moved on.

The army had taken ten prisoners when the officer shouted for his men to leave. They went out in single file, the last going backward, with his rifle covering the crowd. As the door closed after him, a hail of empty bottles and glasses cannoned into the woodwork.

A tall man shouted a protest: "Come on, folks, we can do better than that. We're not going to let those swine spoil everything. Let's move it all back and tidy up, and see if we can't get something out of the evening."

It was a good effort on the part of the community leader, but one doomed to failure.

Harry noticed that the girl in yellow was gone before the floor was half cleared. He shifted in his seat. "Come on, let's quit. We don't want to stay for the funeral."

"I'm going to powder my nose, then," Josephine said.

"Looks all right to me. Don't hang about."

She smiled, got up from the table and went out through a side door, where a gaggle of girls had gathered.

It was a cold clear night as Harry, with Josephine on his arm, walked out of the hall and off towards the all-night taxi rank for the drive back to Mrs. Duncan's.

# 5

They'd come into the house on tiptoe, holding their shoes. Both knew the prim well-scrubbed hallway and stairs well enough to estimate where the boards creaked, and where it was safe to put their full weight. Harry held the girl's hand very tight.

In his back room a floorboard had erupted in protest and he had pulled her away from the place near the basin where she was standing, wriggling out of her coat. That was where he had pried up the planks two days earlier to hide his Smith & Wesson revolver.

She slung the coat across his easy chair by the window, and stood waiting for him to move towards her. He felt a tightness streaming through him. Clumsy. Inhibited. He reached out towards the girl, who gazed back at him, those mocking, querying eyes looking as if to challenge or dare him.

"You make me feel . . . a bit like someone who's forgotten most of it," he whispered into her ear.

When it was over, they lay together, silent for a while.

"You've no worries, then?" she said.

"What do you mean? I don't think so."

"You can't do it if you're really worried. Did you know that?"

"Old wives. Where did you hear that?"

"Just what one of the girls said tonight. She said she'd tried to do it with one of the big men, but he was all so tied up he couldn't make it. She was ever so upset."

Harry raised his eyebrows. "Who was this big man?"

"The one they're all looking for. The one that did the politician in London."

Harry was very still now. "Which girl was it?"

"It was Theresa, from Ballymurphy. In the tight pink skirt. Remember? Now come on, the old girl's alarm'll be off in half an hour."

She was out of bed and, minutes later, dressed and making her way quietly down the stairs to the front door. She had refused to let Harry come and see her off, gave him a sisterly kiss on the forehead and was gone.

428

After she had left, Harry lay in his bed, working over in his mind the information she had given him. No problem for the intelligence guys. A girl called Theresa, about eighteen or nineteen, in Bally-murphy. Sleeps around a bit. No problem. Should wrap up the whole thing. He could scarcely believe his luck—getting the big coup so quickly—all falling into his lap—and on a night out, at that.

There was still the worry over being recognized by that stupid, gawping soldier. But Davidson would sort it out. They should have the man within forty-eight hours, and then what the soldier had seen wouldn't matter.

Davidson had told Harry that he would be in his office, up above a paint store in Covent Garden, every day at eight in the morning and stay till ten at night. Harry decided he'd go into town and make the call from one of those anonymous call boxes in the city centre. Now two hours' sleep. He was exhausted.

Across in Germany his wife and the kids would be asleep now. Could she comprehend this tatty, rotten job even if she did know about it? Could she understand the need to kill the man that was hunted? Could she accept what might happen to Harry? I don't know, Harry said to himself: God knows how many years we've been married, and I don't know. She'd be calm enough, but what it would all mean to her, I've not the faintest idea.

That would all sort itself. And when the answers had to be given, then Josephine would be a fantasy, and over.

DOWN near the post office Harry found a bank of empty phone boxes. He took from his pocket a pile of ten-pence pieces and dialled the London number he had memorized in Dorking.

Davidson picked up the receiver. "Four-seven-zero-four-six-eight-one. Can I help you?"

"It's Harry. How are the family?"

"Very well, they liked the postcards, I'm told."

That was the routine they had agreed on. Two sentences of chatter to show the other that he was a free agent and able to talk, and time enough for Davidson to get the drawer of his desk open, switch on the cassette recorder and plug in the lead to the telephone receiver. Then Harry made his report about Theresa.

"Thanks, Harry. We were worried when we didn't hear anything."

"I didn't want to call in till I had something to say."

"But we should know where you're staying."

"I've made it on my own. Quite snug, on the other side of town. Let's leave it that way. I'll call you if anything else shows up."

"We'll do it your way. It's not usual, but O.K. Nothing more?"

"Only tell the people who pick the girl up to go a bit quietly. If you can get her in without a razzamatazz, you should have your man before anyone knows she's gone and can link her to him. Cheers, and good hunting."

Davidson heard the phone click down. The call had lasted one minute and fifty-five seconds.

MINUTES later Harry's message was on a coded teletype machine in the red-brick two-storey building that housed the intelligence unit at army headquarters, Lisburn. It was of sufficient immediate importance for Colonel George Frost to be called from his breakfast. Cursing about amateurs and lack of consultation, he set up an urgent high-level conference. He summoned his own men, the duty operations officer, the police Special Branch people, and the army officer commanding the unit that controlled Ardoyne.

THERESA and her family were at lunch when the army arrived. The armoured troop carriers outside the tiny overgrown front garden, soldiers in fire positions behind the hedge and wall that divided the grass from next door's. Four soldiers went into the house. They called her name, and when she stood up, took her by the arms, the policeman at the back intoning the Special Powers Act. While the rest of the family sat motionless, she was taken out to the armoured car. It was moving before her mother, the first to react, had reached the front door.

An hour or so earlier the ten men taken from the club the previous night had been reinterrogated. One youth, pressed to identify someone who would swear he had been in the club all evening, had unwittingly given Theresa's second name and address.

Billy Downs had been interrogated twice, maintaining quietly

430

that he had been at his mother's in the South. The officers who had questioned him heard the results of the checks in Cork, gave him back his coat, tie and shoes, and told him to go home.

AT THREE THIRTY that afternoon Private Jones was on board a plane back to Heathrow, out of uniform but conspicuous, with his short hair and pressed flannels. He had been told he would be met and taken to Northolt for the first flight to Berlin and a new posting. It had been impressed on him that he was to speak to no one of his encounter in the Ardoyne social club the previous night. The incident was erased.

SEAMUS DUFFRYN, the latest of the intelligence officers of E Company, Third Battalion, Provisional IRA, had made Sunday his main working day. It was the fourth weekend he'd been on the job, with a long list of predecessors in Long Kesh and the Crumlin Road prison.

Duffryn was holding down employment as mate to a lorry driver. It took him out of town several days a week. Being out of circulation, he reckoned, would extend his chances of remaining undetected longer than the mean average of nine weeks that most company-level officers lasted. He encouraged those with information for him to leave it at his house during the week, where his mother would put it in a plastic laundry bag under the grate of the made-up but unlit front-room fire. There was a fair chance if the military came that they would stop short of scattering the old lady's fuel to the four winds in an off-the-cuff search.

Now, on Sunday afternoon, his mother sat at the back of the house with her radio while Duffryn took over the front-room table and, under the fading coloured print of the Madonna and Child, laid out the messages that had been sent to him. The daylight had nearly exhausted itself by the time he came to the report on the stranger called Harry McEvoy who was said to be looking for a job and getting long-term rates at Delrosa with Mrs. Duncan. Something had been noticed about his accent as not right.

It was enough to cause Duffryn anxiety, and it took him half an hour to make out a painstaking report for his superiors, setting down all the information he had available. The responsibility would rest higher up the chain of command as to whether or not further action was taken. He would keep up surveillance.

INTERROGATION was an art of which Howard Rennie had made himself a master. The detective inspector of the RUC's Special Branch was a big man who knew the various techniques: the bully, the friend, the quiet business-like man—all the approaches that softened the different types of people who sat at the bare table opposite him. The first session with the girl had been a gentle one, polite and paternal. It had taken him nowhere. Before they went into the police station's interview room for the second time Rennie had explained his new tactics to the officer from army intelligence. The girl was tired now, dazed by the surroundings and the lights, and hungry, having defiantly refused the sandwiches they brought her. Rennie would attack, and the Englishman capitalize on it.

"We'll start at the beginning again, right? You were at the dance last night. What were you wearing?"

"My pink skirt."

They'd got that far before. The army captain said nothing as he sat behind the girl. A policewoman was also in the interview room, taking no part in the questioning.

"Your home in Ballymurphy . . . it's a hideout?"

"No."

"We know it is. We know the boyos stay there."

"Why ask me, then?" she shouted back.

"How often is it used?"

"Not often."

"How many times in the last month? Ten times?"

"No, nothing like that."

"Five times, would that be right?"

"Not as often as that."

"How about just once, Theresa?" It was the officer behind her who spoke. Soft voice, English. She sat motionless on the wooden chair, hands clenched together round the soaked handkerchief from the cuff in her blouse. "I think we know one man came."

"We know one man came." The big Special Branch man took

432

over again. "Say three weeks ago, for a night or so. Yes or no?"

She said nothing.

"Look, girl, one man and we know he was there."

Her eyes stayed on her hands. The light was very bright, the tiredness was ebbing over her, swallowing her into itself.

"You agreed with us that people came, right? Not as many as five, that was agreed. Now, understand this, we say that one man came about three weeks ago. One of the big men. He slept in the house, yes or no? Look at me, now."

Her head came up slowly to look at the policeman directly in front of her. Rennie kept talking. It was about to happen, he could sense it. The poor girl had damn all left to offer. One more shove and it would all roll out.

"You don't think we'd send out all those troops just for one girl if we don't have it cast-iron why we want to talk to her. Now the man. Yes or no?"

"Yes." It was barely audible, her lips framing the word with a fractional fluttering of the chin. The army man behind her could not hear the answer, it was so softly spoken.

"Say it again," Rennie said. Rub it in, make the girl hear herself squealing. Keep up the momentum.

"Yes."

The detective's face lost some of its hostility. He leaned forward on the table. "What was his name?"

She laughed. Too loud, hysterically. "You trying to get me done in? I couldn't anyway, I don't know it."

"We want his name." The crisis of the interrogation.

"I don't know his name. He just came and went."

"He was in your house, and you didn't know his name? Don't you know anything about him? Come on, Theresa, better than that."

"I don't know. I tell you I don't . . . that's honest to God. He was gone before morning. We didn't see him again. We weren't told anything. There was no need for us to know his name."

Behind the girl, and out of her sight, the army officer put up his hand for Rennie to hold his questions a moment. His voice was mellow, more reasonable and understanding to the exhausted girl in the chair four feet in front of him.

433

"But your father, Theresa, he'd know that man's name. We don't want to bring him in. We know all about what happened that night in this man's room. We'd have to mention it. How would your dad stand up to all this, at his age? Then there's your brother. It's many a month he's been in Long Kesh . . . it would go well for him."

"You have to believe me. He never said his name. It's because he wasn't known that he came, don't you see that? Dad doesn't know who he was. None of us did."

"You know why we want him?" the detective chimed in. He pulled a photokit picture of the man from a brown envelope and flipped it across the table to the girl. She looked at it briefly and nodded. Then she pushed it back to him.

"You know what he did?"

"I know."

"Well, what was his name? We want his name."

"So help me, Mother of Jesus, he never said his name."

"Take her down," the inspector said to the policewoman. The two men went out of the interview room and away towards the station's cells. He went on, "Damn it. I thought we had her, but I have a horrible feeling she's telling the truth. Come on. Let's get a nap for a bit, and then one last bash at her."

AFTER THEY had gone Theresa sat a long time in her cell. The policewoman had left her. Her position was very clear. When the man was arrested and charged and all Ballymurphy knew she had spent two days in the station being questioned . . . what would they say? Who would believe her when she denied she had ever known his name?

She went back again over all she could remember of what she had said to the copper, the one who shouted in the front. Nothing, she'd said nothing that helped them. But how had they learned of the night? She had told a few girls. Would they betray her?

She had heard what the IRA did to informers. All Ballymurphy knew. It was part of the folklore all over the city where the Provos operated—the vengeance of the young men against their own people who betrayed them. There'd been a girl, left at a lamp post. Tarred and feathered, they'd called it. Black paint and the feathers from a stinking old eiderdown. Hair cut off. She'd talked to a soldier. Not loved him, not cuddled or kissed him, just talked to him, standing with him outside the barracks in the shadows. Provo justice. They killed girls, she knew that, and men who they reckoned were informers.

It was very easy to imagine. A kangaroo court in a locked storage garage. Young men with dark glasses at a table. Hurricane lamp for illumination. Arms tied behind her. Shouting her innocence— and who listens? Pulled from the garage, and the sweet smelliness of the hood going over her head, and bundled into a car for the drive to the dumping ground and the single shot.

She wanted to scream, but in her terror she had no voice. She quivered on the bed, silhouetted against the light biscuit-coloured regulation blanket with the barred-over light bulb shining down on her. She knew the men would come again to talk to her. They would ask her if she had ever seen the man on any other occasion. They would ask that over and over again, however many times she maintained she'd not set eyes on him since the night at her house. They would go on asking that question till they had their answer. They would know when she was lying, especially the quiet one behind her, the Englishman. She was tired, so tired, and slipping away. Could she keep up her denials? Before morning they would know about the dance, how the man had been there with his wife. They had taken him away. So why did they still need the name? Confusion swayed and tossed through the girl. They had taken him, but they didn't know him. Perhaps they had not made the connection, and then what she might say in her exhaustion would weave the net around him. Betray him, and then she would wear the brand. Tout. Informer.

She looked around the brick and tile walls of the cell till she came to the heavy metal bar attached to the window that moved backward and forward a distance of two inches to allow ventilation. As it was winter and the window tight shut, the bar protruded from the fitting. She estimated that if she stood on her bed and stretched up, she could reach the bar. Very deliberately she sat up on the edge of the bed and began to peel down the thick warm tights she was wearing.

COLONEL FROST of intelligence headquarters was awakened at home by the duty officer. The message was simply that he should be in headquarters, and that "all hell is about to break loose." By the time he reached the building, there was a report from the police station, signed by his own man, who had been present at the interrogation.

Theresa . . . was interrogated twice while in police custody in the presence of myself, Detective Inspector Howard Rennie and Police-woman Gwen Myerscough. During questioning she identified the photokit picture of a man wanted in connection with the Danby killing as a man who had stayed in her father's house around three weeks ago. After the second session of questions she was returned to her cell. She was found later hanging by her stockings in the cell, and was dead by the time medical attention reached her.

Fairclough, Arthur. Capt.,
Intelligence Corps

No marks for style, thought Frost, as he read it through. "Where's Fairclough?" he snapped at the duty officer.

"Should be here in about ten minutes, sir." Then the sparks will come, thought the duty officer. Poor old Fairclough.

The colonel went to his filing cabinet and unlocked the top drawer, pulling out a dog-eared book that listed the home telephone numbers of senior staff at the Ministry of Defence, military and civilian. He found the number of the Permanent Under Secretary for whom Davidson worked, and dialled it.

"My name's Frost. Army intelligence in Lisburn. It's a hell of an hour, but something has come up which you should be aware of. Sounds a bit of a foul-up to me, and I wouldn't care to be in your man's shoes when the opposition finds out about it. . . ."

HARRY heard about the girl, with the rest of the province, on the early-morning radio news bulletin. He felt numb. No more playing about. No more kindergarten. These were the powers of the forces at work. A simple, ordinary, decent girl. Harry remembered her. Across the far side of the club, in with the boyos near the bar.

436

Rolling a little. Too much gin, and not enough chips to soak it up.

He was responsible for the agony of the girl, before she slung whatever it was underneath her chin and swung off into the void. Had she even been questioned by then he wondered? Had she been able to say anything? Or was it all a lot of boasting?

They all listen to those bulletins, Harry reflected, every last one of them, catching up on the night's disasters, funding themselves with conversation for the day. Josephine would be no different. She'd hear it, and she'd put it together. What then?

Harry would have to wait to find out. She wasn't doing teas this week, had a different shift at work. He'd have to wait till the weekend and their next date. Have to sit it out, Harry boy.

He went down the staircase, across the hall and out to the street. He would chase the job at the scrap merchant's and try to get a bit of permanence into his life. He heard Mrs. Duncan calling after him about his breakfast, ignored her as she kept on, and turned left towards Andersonstown. As he walked he set out the position, making a chessboard of his job in his mind. Pawns, that's where Theresa rated, and pawns were expendable. Bishops and knights hurt more, but they could also be lost. He and the man he was hunting were the queens of his game. The superstars, and secondary only to the kings, who were sacred and inviolate. If, as the queens were moved around the board, the pawns toppled over, then that was the nature of the game. There was no time to lament the loss of pawns.

It had been different in Aden. There had been no involvement there. Nothing personal. A clear enemy—all that was on the board was black or white, but definite. Now all the squares were grey, and the figures, too. Even the two queens. There would be a problem for an outsider in picking one set of pieces from another.

# 6

Within four hours of the first broadcast of Theresa's death, a soldier had been killed and heavy rioting had broken out in the Ballymurphy and New Barnsley housing developments.

In the Falls and Springfield roads, youths had hijacked buses and set fire to them in the middle of the street. After that the army moved in. Armoured cars and Land-Rovers were pelted with milk bottles and rocks. At one building site the Saracens had crashed into and scattered a barricade of oil drums crazily across the street. A lone youth, at the controls of a brilliant yellow bulldozer, charged back defiantly. The troops, who had been advancing behind the cover of the armoured cars, fell back as the mechanical dinosaur accelerated down a slight hill towards them. A few feet from the impact the youth jumped clear, leaving his runaway machine to collide head on with the toadlike Saracens. Acting in strange concert for things so large, they edged it against a wall, where it spent its force revving in demented futility.

The stoning went on a long time. Unit commanders reported to army intelligence headquarters at Lisburn a genuine anger among people. There were rumours, they said, that the girl in the police station had been tortured to a degree that she could stand no more, and that she had then killed herself. Theresa's parents had been on television, maintaining that their daughter had never belonged to any Republican organization. They described graphically how she had been taken from the lunch table the previous day. The army press desk received scores of calls, and stalled by saying this was a police matter, that the girl had died in a police station. At police headquarters the harassed man on the receiving end told reporters that an investigation was still going on.

Both at army headquarters and within the secretariat that administered the Secretary of State's office at Stormont Castle in Belfast there was a realization that something better by way of explanation was going to have to come out before the day was over.

FACED with crises, the Prime Minister had a well-tried formula to fall back upon. Identify the problem. Focus all attention on it. Solve it, and then leave it alone.

From the backroom office overlooking the Downing Street gardens, insipid in the November light, he called the army commander in Lisburn. Without any interruption he listened to a rundown of the morning's events, and made no comment either when the general launched into the background of the girl's arrest.

"Is this the first we've had from our chap?"

"First that I've heard of."

"And it was good stuff. Something we hadn't had before?"

"The information was factual. It didn't take us as far as we'd hoped it might at first."

"Seems we set a bit of a trap, and it's rather missed its target. Could be difficult, if he were to be identified in this context. Problem now is at what stage to get him out."

"It's not so easy, Prime Minister. It seems faintly ridiculous to me, but I'm told his controllers don't know where he is. He calls in, they don't call him. You appreciate that he's not being controlled from here. Your instructions were interpreted very strictly on this point." The sarcasm bit down the line.

The Prime Minister banged the phone down, then flipped the console button on his desk and asked abruptly for the Secretary of State in Stormont Castle. After forty-one years in politics he could see the storm clouds gathering long in advance. The time had come to pull in sail and close down the hatches. The combination of an agent working under the Prime Minister's orders and a teenage girl hanging herself in a cell were better ingredients than most for a major political scandal. He must start to plan his defensive lines. In the event of catastrophe, no acknowledgment of the agent and a denial of all knowledge of the mission. . . .

The Secretary of State was on the line. The Prime Minister wasted no time on pleasantries. "I've been hearing about the troubles today, and the girl. Difficult situation. I think we need to be a lot more positive. I suggest you say something like this—that the girl was a known associate of the man we are hunting in connection with the killing of Danby. By the by, his memorial service is at St. Paul's this week. You'll be there, I hope. It'll all be in the public gaze again. We'll be all right if we play a bit bold and attack. Worst thing we can do is to get on the defensive."

The linking of the killing of the British cabinet minister with the death of the teenager in the Falls Road police station was splashed across the last edition of the *Belfast Telegraph* and extensively reported on television and radio news. The few men in intelligence who knew of Harry's existence were uncertain what effect the disclosure would have on the agent's work and safety. They acknowledged an immediate lifting of the pressure on army public relations for more information concerning the circumstances of the death. Harry was not the only man in the city with pawns on the chessboard.

THE SCRAP MERCHANT would put Harry on his payroll. He'd obviously liked the look of him. He said he had a brother at sea, and asked Harry if he could start there and then. There was not a word about National Insurance cards or stamps, and twenty pounds a week was offered as pay. Harry was told he'd need to spend a month or so in the yard to see the way the place was run. There was to be expansion, more lorries. When they came, if it all worked out, there would be a driving job and more money.

On his first morning Harry prowled around the mountains of burned and rusted cars. The scrap merchant walked around with him. "It's an ill wind. Scrap men, builders, glaziers . . . we're all minting it. Shouldn't say so, but that's how it is. The military men dump the cars that have been burned, up there on the open ground. We send a truck up and pull them down here. Not formal, you know. Just an understanding. They want them off the street and know if they put them there, I'll shift them. We'll have a few more today, and all."

He looked up at Harry and smiled. Small, chirpy, long silk scarf around his neck, choker style, hat flat on his head. They're all the same, thought Harry, likable rogues.

Later he introduced Harry to the six other men in the yard, and they shook hands formally. He was accepted. And each day he was watched by Seamus Duffryn's volunteers, from Delrosa to the yard and back again.

DOWNS was in the kitchen swilling his face in the sink, Monday morning wash, when his wife came in white-faced, shutting the door behind her on the noise of the playing children.

"It's just been on the radio, about you. About a girl. The girl who killed herself."

440

"What do you mean? What about me?"

"This girl from the Murph, it says she was linked with the man that did the London killing."

"What was her name?"

"Theresa something. I didn't catch it."

"Well, I don't know her."

"It said she was being questioned about him because she was a known associate."

"Well, I don't know her, and that's the truth."

"You're lying. Who was she?"

"She was just a kid who brought me some food."

"Just brought some food, did she? And on the strength of that they brought her in and questioned her?"

"Leave it," he snapped at her. He wanted escape.

"Just tell me what the little bitch meant to you."

"She was nothing. Must have blabbed her mouth off. Squealed."

"How did she know who you were?"

She shouted the last question at him. She would have taken it back once the words were out and had crumpled against him. The noise and aggression slewed out of him. Beseeching. Pleading. Don't make me answer. The found-out child and the hollow victory.

"I'm sorry," she said. "Just forget it."

She turned away, back towards the door into the living room, where the children were fighting.

"I'll tell you what happened. . . ." She shook her head, but he went on. "This is once and for all, never ask again. If I'd wanted her, I couldn't have done anything about it. I was so screwed up. She asked if it was me in London. I hit her. Across the face. She went back to her room. I've only seen her once since then. She was at the club on Saturday night. I suppose she saw me."

He walked across to his wife and put his arms around her. The children were crying now, and the pitch was growing. He pulled her head against his shoulder. She was pliant against him.

Downs went on, "That's when she must have talked. Going home after the dance. Must have said that she knew the man that had been in London. Then some rat squealed. A spy, right there at one of our dances. That's what must have happened."

"Forget it. We have to forget all these things. There's nothing left otherwise."

She controlled her grief and clung to him. Nothing would be different, nothing in his way of life would change. He needed her now, to recharge him. When the dose was enough, he would go back into his own vicious, lonely world. Of which she was no part.

It was acknowledged at the highest levels of the IRA's Belfast brigade command that the campaign was at a crucial stage, the impetus of the struggle consistently harder to maintain. The leadership detected a weariness among the people on whom they relied so greatly for the success of their attacks. Money was harder to collect for the families of those imprisoned, doors generally left unlocked for the gunman or blast bomber to escape through were now bolted, and the confidential phones at police headquarters where the informers left their anonymous messages were kept busy with tip-offs that could only come from the Catholic heartland.

It was the brigade commander who made the decision to call Billy Downs out from Ardoyne.

Early in the week they had passed the death sentence on Inspector Howard Rennie of the RUC's Special Branch. The decision to eliminate the detective had been taken after an IRA company intelligence officer reported on the licence plates and models of the police cars that had left the police station after the death of the girl in her cell. His car had been recognized. A priority was put on his death, and it was reckoned important enough to risk the exposure of one of the movement's top cards.

Billy Downs was given a dossier to read, but not to keep. The caller who came to his house late on Friday night, after the wife and children had gone upstairs, was to bring it away with him when Downs had done his reading. His wife came down the stairs to see who the visitor was, paled at the sight of the long-haired youth in jeans and heavy quilted parka who returned her stare and then turned away without speaking to her. She went back upstairs and drifted into sleep, tossing through an immediate nightmare. She saw her man cut down by a burst of bullets, grotesque soldiers standing over him. Life throbbing away in the gutter. Feet pushing and manoeuvring him. When she reached across to see if he had come upstairs, she found only the emptiness of the sheets beside her. Back in her half-sleep she witnessed over and over again the firing of those perpetual rifles and the agony of her man. And then exhaustion took her beyond the stage of dreams and into deep sleep.

THAT Saturday morning Seamus Duffryn met his battalion intelligence officer for the first time. Duffryn had originally intended that his message should go by hand, but the nagging worry about this man, Harry McEvoy, had led to the direct meeting risky as it was.

They met in a pub in the heart of the ravaged area around the Lower Falls Road. Taking their pints of beer with them, they went to a corner table and spoke with their heads huddled together. Duffryn told the battalion man of the stranger who had come to the guest house farther up the Falls. About this strange accent that was noted when he first came, but which his latest reports said was not so pronounced. The battalion officer looked at him, intrigued, and the junior man explained the apparent lapses in speech. Duffryn wanted a decision. Either the man should be cleared or there would have to be authorization for more surveillance, with its problems of manpower.

"You never know with these things," said the man from battalion. "The accent could mean he's a man put in to infiltrate us. It could be nothing. It counts against him that his accent is improving. Would do, wouldn't it? With each day he spends here, it would improve. From now on, no more following him. Let him ride on his own a bit. I want it taken gently, very gently, you see? Just log him in and out of the guest house."

DAVIDSON had had a bad week. He admitted it to the young man who was drafted in to share the office with him. The fiasco of the girl had started it off. The Permanent Under Secretary had been on him as well, laying the smoke screen that would be used if the operation went aground. There had been silence from Harry himself after his first call. Davidson and the aide sat in the office reading papers, making coffee, devouring take-out fish and chips, take-out Indian, take-out Chinese.

When Harry did call, on Saturday morning, the effect was electric. Davidson started up from his easy chair, pitching it sideways, tipping a coffee beaker off his desk as he lunged for the telephone.

"Hello, is that four-seven-zero-four-six-eight-one?"

"Harry?"

"How are the family?"

"Very well. They liked the postcards, I'm told."

Davidson was on his knees, his head level with the drawer where the recording apparatus was kept. He pulled up the lead and plugged it into the telephone's body. The cassette was rolling. "Anything for us?"

"Nothing, old chap. No, I'm just digging in a bit."

"We're worried about you in the wake of that girl. We must have some regular way to get in touch with you. This may suit you, but it's ridiculous for us."

"It's the way I'm happiest, I've been bitten, remember, on the first house, and it's the way I want it to be. More of a problem is that I don't see where the next break is going to come from. I was very lucky last time, and it can't be on a plate like that again."

"Perhaps it is time you should come out. Like this weekend. I don't want you hanging about wasting time. Look, Harry, we know it's bloody difficult in there, but you've given the military and security people a lead—"

The phone clicked dead in his hand before the dial tone purred back at him. Despairingly he flicked the receiver buttons. The call was over.

Damn it. Played it wrong. Unsettled him. Just when he needs lifting. Should have made it an order, not a suggestion.

Davidson thought of Harry walking back up the Falls, past the wreckage and the troops, the legacy of the week-long street fighting he had been the spark to. Keep your head down, Harry boy.

HARRY had not been aware of the watchers before they were called off, and therefore had no idea that he had in fact thrown off a trail on both occasions that he had telephoned Davidson. Now, as he walked back from the city centre with his wage packet in his

444

hip pocket, he felt safe in the knowledge that there seemed to be no sign of suspicion towards him from the men he was working with. Furthermore, he had a hired car booked for the afternoon for his date with Josephine.

THAT SATURDAY lunchtime, in the restaurant of the big hotel on the outskirts of the city, a British brigadier and a chief superintendent were out of uniform and mildly celebrating the promotion and transfer of the army officer from his post in Belfast to a new appointment in Germany. Both knew from their own intelligence-gathering agencies of the sending of Harry and the Prime Minister's directive—it had come in a terse, brief message from the commander-in-chief's headquarters. During the serving of the food neither had spoken of it, as the waiters hovered around them. But with the coffee cups full, and the brandy glasses topped up, the subject was inevitably fielded.

"That fellow the PM launched," muttered the brigadier. "No word, I'm told, since Sunday, and Frost in intelligence is still leaping about. Called it a bloody insult. See his point."

The recorded music was loud in the dining room, and both men needed to speak firmly to hear each other above the canned violin strings. The policeman spoke. "I think Frost's got a case. So have we for that matter"—in midchord and without warning, the music had stopped—"to put a special operator in on the ground without telling—" Dramatically conscious of the way his voice had carried in the sudden moment of silence, he cut himself short.

Awkwardly the two men waited for the half-minute or so that it took the restaurant staff to get things working properly; then the talking began again.

The eighteen-year-old waiter serving the next table had clearly heard the second half of the sentence. He repeated the words to himself as he went around the table: "special operator in on the ground without telling". Then he hurried to the kitchen, scribbling the words in large spidery writing on the back of his order pad.

He went off duty at 3:30, and seventy-five minutes later the message of what he had overheard, and its context, was on its way to the intelligence officer of the Provisionals' Third Battalion.

# 7

Josephine was waiting for Harry at the junction of Grosvenor and the Falls when he pulled up in the hired Cortina. Tall in the brittle sunlight, her black hair blown around her face, and shivering in the mock-sheepskin coat over the sweaters and jeans he'd told her to wear.

"Come on, get that door open. I'm frozen out here." A bit distant, perhaps too offhand, but not the clamouring alarm bells Harry had steeled himself to face.

He was laughing as he reached across the passenger seat and unlocked the door. She came inside, a bundle of coat and cold air, stealing the warmth he had built up in the car.

"All right then, sunshine?" He leaned over to kiss her, but she turned her head away presenting her cheek for a brotherly peck.

"Enough of that. Where are we going?" She straightened up, and began to fasten her seat belt.

"You said you wanted some country. Where do you suggest?"

"Let's off to the Sperrins. About an hour down the Derry road. You've seen the slogans on the Proddy walls before the troubles started, 'We will not exchange the blue skies of Ulster for the grey mists of the Republic.' Well, the blue skies are over the Sperrins."

"Well, if it's O.K. for the Prods, it'll do for us Micks."

"I was brought up down there. My dad had a bit of land. It's a hard living down there. It's yourself and that's all to do the work. We cut peat and had some cows and sheep. There was no gas, no electricity, no water when I was born. He's dead, now, the old man, and my mam came to Belfast."

"Were you involved with the politics? Was the old man?"

"Not at all. Not a flicker. Most of the farmers round were Prods, and I couldn't walk out with the Prod boys. But that's years back now. There was no politics down there, just bloody hard work."

He drove slowly out of town. Josephine slept. "Just follow the Derry road and wake me up when we get to the top of the Glenshane," she'd said.

The road slipped economically through the countryside. Rain

gathered on the windshield. It was the first time Harry had seen the fields and hedgerows, farms and cottages, since he came in on the airport bus. It was near impossible to believe that this was a country ravaged by what some called civil war.

As he came to the hills that divided the Protestant farmlands of the Ulster hinterland from Catholic Dungiven and Londonderry, Harry spotted a damp, out-of-season picnic site on his right, and pulled into the parking area. There was a sign marking the pass and its altitude, a thousand feet above sea level. He stopped and shook Josephine's shoulder.

"Not so much of the blue skies and the promised land here. Looks more like its going to tip down," he said.

"Doesn't matter. Come on, Mr. McEvoy, we're going to do some walking and talking. Walking first. Up there." She pointed far out to the right of the road where Glenshane's squat summit merged towards the dark clouds.

"It's a hell of a way," he said, pulling on a heavy parka.

"Won't do you any harm. Come on."

She led the way, up a path of sorts made by peat cutters at first and then carried on by the rabbits and the sheep. The wind picked up and surged against them. Josephine had pushed her arm through the crook of his elbow and walked in step half a pace behind him, using him part as shelter and part as battering ram as they forced their way into the near gale. High above, a buzzard with an awesome dignity allowed itself to be carried on the thrusts and flows of the currents. The wind stung Harry's face, pulling his hair back over his ears and slashing at his nose and eyes.

"I haven't been anywhere in a wind like this in years," he shouted across the few inches that separated them.

' No reply. Just the wind hitting and buffeting against him.

"I said I haven't been in a wind like this in years. It's marvellous."

She rose on her toes, so that her mouth was in under his ear. "Wasn't it like this at sea, sometimes? Weren't there any gales and things all those years you were at sea?"

The cutting edge of it chopped into him. "That was different. Sea wind is not like this."

Poor. Stupid. Not convincing. He flashed a look down to where

447

her head nestled into his coat. He looked into her eyes, and saw what he expected. Quizzical, half confused, half amused; she had spotted it. The inconsistency that he'd known the moment he'd repeated it. Phrase by phrase he went over it in his mind, seeking to undo the mistake. The second time he'd said it, that was when she would have been sure.

There were no more words as they went on to the summit.

A few yards beyond the cairn of stones that marked the hilltop, the rain running down over the years had sliced out a gully. They slid down into it, pushing against the sandy earth till they were at last sheltered.

For a long time she stayed buried in his coat, pressed against his chest with only her black tossed hair for him to see. He felt the warmth from her seeping through the layers of clothes. For Harry it was a moment of beauty and isolation and complete tenderness with the girl. She broke it suddenly.

"You slipped up a bit there, Harry boy. Didn't you? Not what I'd have expected from you."

Her face was still away from his. He said nothing.

"A bit mixed up then, weren't you, Harry? Your story was, anyway. Merchant seaman who was never in a storm like they have in the Sperrins? A bit of a slip-up, Harry."

She'd relaxed in her voice now. Easy. In her stride. "Harry . . ." And she twisted under him to turn into his face and look at him. Big eyes, mocking and piercing at the same time, and staring at him. "I'm saying you made something of a slip-up there. Harry, it's a great bloody lie you're living. Right?"

He willed her now to let it go. Don't take it to the brink where explanation or action is necessary.

"It's a bad place, this, for strangers these days, Harry. It will be rather worse if the boyos find your story isn't quite so pat as it should be. We're not all stupid here, you know. I'm not stupid. It didn't take the world to put eight and eight together after Saturday night, or ten and ten, or whatever you thought too much for an 'eejit' Mick girl. It wasn't much I said to you. Just a little bit of chat. But there's half the British army round the wee girl's house for Sunday lunch. What did they find to talk to her about? Do you

448

know, Harry? It was enough for the poor girl to hang herself, God rest her."

The eyes that drove into him were still bright and relaxed, looking for his reaction. As he listened she grew in strength and boldness. "There had to be something odd about you. Obvious. No family. But you come right back into the centre of Belfast. And you've no friends. No one who knows you. People might have gone to a quiet place on the outskirts if they just wanted to come back and work. The voice also worried me, till Theresa died. I thought about it and worked it out then. The accent's good now. You're quite Belfast, but you didn't use to be. So I don't reckon your chances, Harry, not when the Provos get a hold of you. There is some who can talk their way out of it, but I don't reckon you've a chance. Not unless you run."

Harry knew he should kill her. He looked fascinated at the soft skin, and the delicate line that searched down on either side of the little mound in her throat, saw the suspicion of a vein beneath the gentle surface. The endless strands of black hair were playing across her face, encircling her mouth, taken past her eyes . . . but there was no fear there, no expectation of death.

Harry had heard it said once that to kill in close combat you had to act instinctively, there were no second chances, the will to cause death evaporates quickly and does not come again except to the psychopath. He looked out onto the moorlands where the spears of sunlight played down from the cloud gaps.

She was tall, but she wouldn't be able to fight him off. He could kill her now. While she yapped on. It would be a long time before they found her. Could be the spring. But he had hesitated, and the moment was gone.

"If I went to the bookies," she went on, "I'd say you were a real slow horse. I'd say not to put any money on you reaching the finish. Well, don't just sit there. Say something, Harry."

"There's not much to say, is there? What would you like to hear me say? If you go off to Portadown and see people there, they'll tell you who I am. Yes, I've been away a long time. That's why the accent was strange. I'm acclimatized. The girl—I can't explain that. How could I? I've no idea about it."

449

There was no conviction, and he communicated it to her.

"Rubbish," she said. She smiled at him and turned away to put her head back into the roughness of his coat. "That won't do, Harry. You're not a good enough liar."

"Let it go, then. Forget it, drop it." Pathetic. Was that all he had to say to the girl?

"Who are you, Harry? What did you come here for? When you touted on young Theresa, it was after I mentioned the man that did the killing in London. Is that why you're here? You're not just run-of-the-mill intelligence. There's more than that, I hope. I'd want to think my feller was a wee bit special. What's the handle? The Man who Tracked the Most Wanted Man in Britain?" She snorted with amusement. "But seriously, Harry, is that what you

are?" She gave him time now. He was not ready. As an afterthought she said, "You don't have to worry, you know. I won't split on you. It's the national characteristic—the Ulster Catholics, we don't inform. But they don't take well to spies here, Harry. If they find you, God help you."

Harry started to move. "There's not very much to say. What do you expect me to say? Confess . . . dramatic revelations? Shout you down? Strangle you? What the hell do you want me to say?"

He got up out of the ditch and moved towards the summit of the hill, where rain lashed him and the wind fought him in crude rushes that caused him to give ground. He'd gone a hundred and fifty yards from her when she caught him and thrust her arm into his. They went together down the hill, hurrying along the worn-out

451

path. They ran the last few yards to the car. She stood shaking by the door as he looked for the keys. It was raining hard now, and once they were inside he switched on the motor and the heater. The water ran down the windows in wide streams, and they were as cocooned and private as they had been on the hill.

"What are you going to do if you find him?" she said.

"Are we serious now, or sparring still?"

"Serious now. Really serious. What will you do?"

"I'll kill him. He's not for capturing. We pretend he is, but he's dead if we get close enough to him."

"Is that what you came for? Because a man kills a politico in England, then they send for you? That minister was—wait for it, I'm working it out—yes, he was a tenth of one per cent of all the people that have died here. He wasn't mourned here, you know. Always on the box telling us how well he was doing flushing out the gunmen from off our backs. Why was he so special? They didn't send the big team over when they shot the senator in Strabane. So why have you come this time?"

"They put the glove down, didn't they? That's what shooting Danby was about. They killed him as a test of strength. We have to get the man and the team that did it. Either we do, or they've won. That's the game."

"And where does little Theresa fit into this? You're here to avenge a death. There's been one more already. How many more people get hurt, getting in the way, to make it still worth while for you?"

"Quite a lot."

"So, even in death, some count for more than others."

"Right."

She shifted the ground and softened the attack. "What sort of fellow is he, this man you're looking for?"

"I don't know much about him. I've an idea what he looks like, but I don't know his name."

"Do you know what it was made Theresa talk about him?"

"Course I don't know. How could I."

"I mean, she wouldn't just bring a thing like that out of the blue, now would she? She said to me that the man that did the London

452

killing was at that dance. He was there with his wife. That's how it all started. Then she went into her own bit. That was to back her story up. She didn't know anything else."

"That's the truth, Josephine?"

"She didn't have to die like that. All she knew was what I said. I doubt she even knew the man's name." She had started to shout again. "You might as well have killed her yourself, Harry. You came here with the bloody games you play. And a wee girl dies who had nothing to do with it. There's enough innocent people killed here without strangers coming and putting their fingers in."

She crumpled then. Sobbing rhythmically and noiselessly.

Harry was deciding what he should do on his return to Belfast. His ego was rumpled by the way the girl had broken through him. His ego was of less importance, though, than the news she had just given him. The man he searched for had been at the *caeli* the previous weekend.

She shook herself, trying to shrug away her misery. "Come on, let's go have a couple of hot tods. You can't stop for the dead. Not in Ulster. Like they say, it all goes on." She leaned over and kissed him lightly on the cheek. Then she began to adjust her face, working with deftness from her little pouch that came out of her bag.

When she had finished she said, "Don't worry, hero boy, I won't tell the big bad Provies about you. But if you've ever taken advice, I'm telling you, don't hang about. Or whatever medal you're after will have to go in the box with you."

They stopped at a pub, then drove back to the city. They spoke hardly a word all the way, and Harry dropped her off where he had met her on the corner of Grosvenor and the Falls.

"When will I see you again?" he said as she climbed out of the car. The traffic was hustling them.

"Next week, at Mrs. Duncan's. You'll see me there."

"And we'll go out somewhere? Have a drink?"

"Perhaps."

She knew so much more than she had wanted to, or was equipped to handle. She darted out of the car, and without a wave disappeared into the Clonard side streets.

BILLY DOWNS decided to go for Inspector Rennie the next day, Sunday. The reports that were available from investigators suggested that the detective made a habit of going to the police interrogation centre on Sunday afternoons. He stayed a few hours and reached his home, a bungalow in Dunmurry, down a cul-de-sac, around seven in the evening. Downs discussed none of this with his wife, but as his preoccupation with the killing grew, they moved about their house, two strangers under the same roof. Life was carried on with a series of gestures and monosyllabic phrases.

A BRANDY in his hand, Colonel Frost was sitting on his own in a corner of the mess at Lisburn, mulling over the magazines of weekly comment with which he prided himself he kept abreast. The mess waiter came over and hesitated beside the chair.

"Excuse me, sir. There's a reporter from *The Times* on the phone. Says he needs to speak to you. Says it's urgent."

Frost nodded and followed the waiter to the phone cubicle. "Hello, Frost here. What can I do for you?"

He listened without interruption as the reporter read to him a story that was being prepared. The Provisional IRA had tipped off one of their favoured reporters in Belfast that they believed the British had infiltrated a new secret agent into the city on a mission so sensitive that only the commander-in-chief, General Fairbairn, had been told of it. The Provos were claiming that the operation had caused great anger at British army headquarters. On Monday the story would appear in Dublin papers as well as British ones, and the IRA would call for special vigilance from the people to seek out the spy.

"I'm not expecting you to comment, Colonel. This is a private call, just to let you know what's going on. Good night."

The colonel flicked the phone's buttons up and down till the operator came on the line.

"Evening. Frost here. General Fairbairn, at home, please." When he was connected, he told the general he needed to see him immediately.

The general and Frost talked for an hour. They agreed to get on to the Ministry of Defence and demand Harry's immediate

454

recall, before the awkward business became necessary of dragging him out of some hedgerow with an IRA bullet in the back of his head.

ACROSS the city in Mrs. Duncan's boarding house Harry was asleep. He had been somewhat unnerved by the brutality with which his cover had been stripped aside by the girl. On his return he had lifted the carpets and floorboards at the place where the revolver was hidden. The Smith & Wesson, with its six chambers loaded, was now wrapped in a towel under his pillow.

Harry was up early again that Sunday morning, and out of the house well before eight to make his way down to the city centre and the phone that he could use to talk to Davidson. This time he took the revolver with him, in his coat pocket, its shape shielded by the covering parka. There were no eyes on him after he left Delrosa; the orders of the IRA battalion intelligence officer were being strictly obeyed.

He dialled Davidson's number. After several desultory clicks he heard it ringing at the other end. It was answered.

"It's Harry here. How are the family?"

Davidson was in early, too, and hoping for the call. "Very well, they liked the postcards."

"I've got a bit of a problem. My cover's been blown by this girl, the one that helped me with the business I gave you last week." Pause. "She knows what I am. Not who I am but what we're here for. I want you to take her out of the scene for the duration. You can do that, can't you? She tells me that the man we want was at the same dance that we were. I half thought I remembered him. But the face wasn't quite right on the photokit. If it's the man, then the army pulled him in, but that looked routine. He had a woman with him, presumably his wife, in a yellow trouser-suit. Have you got all that?"

"I've got it on tape, Harry. Anything else?"

"Hell, what more do you want? If you don't wrap it up on what I've just given you, then it'll be a very long time."

"You're all right yourself, are you, Harry? No one following you about, no awkward questioning?"

455

"No, there's nothing like that," Harry said. "I'm working in a scrap yard in Andersonstown, incidentally, and being paid well. Cheers, maestro."

"'Bye, Harry. Take care, and listen to the news. As soon as you hear we've got him, head on up to the airport, fast."

Harry put the phone down and hurried out into the cold and the long walk back up the Falls. He was concerned that they should get the girl out, and fast, before her involvement became too great for her to extricate herself . . . before she followed the other girl he'd brought into the game.

But things did not move fast that Sunday.

TWENTY MINUTES after Harry had rung off, Davidson called the Permanent Under Secretary of Defence at his home. He caught the civil servant on the point of going to early morning service.

"Keep your news for a moment," snapped the official. "I've had calls in the night. The general has been on, and that man of his, Frost of intelligence. Bloody misnomer, that. They want our fellow out. They think he's blown."

Davidson bit at his tongue. He heard at the end of the line the call for the rest of the civil servant's family to go on to church.

"There's been some sort of leak. The papers have got a story from the opposition that they know a big man has been put in. There's panic stations over there. Anyway, the order is get the chap out or the general says he'll go to the PM. I suppose you haven't an idea where we could go and just take hold of him?"

"All I have is that he works in a scrap merchant's in Andersonstown. Nothing more."

"That won't do us much good till Monday morning."

"He's done well again, our chap. The man we want was actually at the dance where Harry was the other night. The military had him, and—"

"Look, for God's sake, Davidson, I'm at home. I'm going to church. There's no point feeding me that sort of material over the phone. Talk to Frost direct. He'll be in his office, prancing about. He's having a bloody field day, Sunday and all. But if this Harry man should call again, get him out. That now is an instruction."

Davidson had always had to admit that he enjoyed the complicated paraphernalia of introducing the agent into the operations theatre. There had been the months with the undercover Greeks and Turks in Cyprus and three years in Singapore. But those men he had sent into the field were all foreigners with whom he had had a very loose involvement. With Harry it had become quite different. The danger that he now knew his agent to be facing numbed Davidson to an almost shameful degree.

Davidson had a growing feeling of nausea when he remembered how Harry had been brought to Dorking and told, "The Prime Minister personally authorized the setting up of the team, and we've chosen you as the most suitable man." What chance did he have of side-stepping that little lot?

Other operations had gone wrong before, Davidson recalled. But if they lost Harry, then the ramifications would be huge, and public. The roundup of scapegoats would be spectacular. Davidson had no doubt of that. The Permanent Under Secretary would have faded from the picture by then, and the old hack would be left holding the baby.

He called Frost. At the other end of the line the serving colonel in intelligence left the London-based civilian with no illusions as to what he thought of armchair administrators organizing undercover work without consultation or know-how. Davidson, resigned, let it blaze over him. Between the interruptions he read over the transcript of Harry's message. He ended on a high note.

"He did pretty well with the first lot of stuff we gave you. We were disappointed that it didn't come to much. You should have it sewn up this time, don't you think, old boy?"

Frost didn't rise to the bait. It was not the day for telephone brawling. That would come after this merry little show was wrapped up and in mothballs—what was left of it. He called the Springfield Road police to request the locating and picking up of the girl, Josephine Laverty of Clonard, and then turned his attention to the matter of the man having been in, and presumably out of, military hands on Saturday night one week back. Cool bastard he must be, appraised the colonel. In between calls he cancelled his planned nine holes of golf.

457

THAT SAME MORNING Seamus Duffryn was summoned to a house in Beachmount and ordered by the battalion intelligence officer to resume close surveillance on McEvoy. Duffryn was told a squad was going out in the afternoon to find a friend of McEvoy's, the girl who had been out with him. Josephine Laverty from Clonard.

A few hundred yards away, in Springfield Road, the British army unit that had been asked to find the girl was puzzled that it had no record of her or her mother living in the area. There was no reason why they should have, as the house was in the name of Josephine's uncle, Michael O'Leary. A little after three o'clock the unit reported in that it had been unable to locate the girl. By then a critical amount of the available time had run out.

IT TOOK more than two hours from the time Frost called the army headquarters dominating Ardoyne to the moment Billy Downs was identified. The lieutenant who had led the raid on the *caeli* was in Norfolk on weekend leave. The sergeant, the next senior man out, recalled that he had busied himself near the door on security, but he was able to name the six soldiers who had carried out the questioning. Private Jones was now in Berlin, but Lance-Corporal James Llewellyn was picked up by a Saracen from a foot patrol on the far side of the battalion area.

Llewellyn stared at the photokit issued in London that had been brought up from the guard room. "It's Downs, if it's any of them. His woman was there, in yellow."

With the name, they attacked the filing system and, in the afternoon, they called Frost back. "We think we've located the man you want. He's Billy Downs. Ypres Avenue, wife and kids. Very quiet, from what we've seen of him. Unemployed. His story stuck after the Garda ran a check on the alibi he gave us to account for an absence from the area. There was no other reason to hold him. Perhaps you'll let us know what you want done. We've a platoon on immediate call. We can see pretty much down that street—I've an observation post in the roof of a mill, right up the top."

Frost growled back into the phone, "I'd be interested in knowing if Mr. Downs is currently at home."

"Wait one." As he held on, Frost could hear the distant sounds of the unit operations room as they called up the roof post on a field telephone. "Not quite so hot, I'm afraid. We think Downs left his home around twenty-five minutes ago. That's fifteen-oh-five hours precisely. No reason to think he won't be back in a bit."

"I'd like it watched," said Frost, "but don't move in yet. Call me as soon as you see him."

DOWNS was being driven up the Lisburn Road at the time that the observation post in the mill overlooking Ypres Avenue was warned to look out for him. The car had been hijacked in the Falls thirty-five minutes earlier.

Half a mile from Rennie's house in Dunmurry, the teenage driver stopped the car in a small belt of woods, unlocked the boot and handed over an Armalite rifle. Downs checked the firing mechanism. He was passed two magazines and fitted one into the slot under the belly of the gun. He activated a bullet up into the breach. The volunteer at the wheel watched fascinated as finally Downs released the catch on the stock, folded the weapon, thus reducing its length by eleven inches.

Downs pushed the rifle, now less than two and a half feet in length, into the hidden pocket of his coat. "I don't know how long I'll be," he said. "For God's sake, don't suddenly clear off. Stick here till midnight."

They were the only words Downs spoke before he disappeared into the growing darkness to walk towards Rennie's house.

THE REGULAR Sunday-afternoon visit to the police interrogation centre was no longer a source of controversy between Rennie and his wife. It had been at first, with accusations of "putting the family into second place", but the increasing depression of the security situation in the province had caused her to relent.

Over the last four years Janet Rennie had become used to the problems of being a policeman's wife. A familiar sight now was the shoulder holster slung over the bedside chair when he came to bed. At night all mortise locks on all the doors were turned with a formal ritual of order, lest one should be forgotten, and the detective's personal firearm lay in the half-opened drawer of the bedside table. Promotion and transfer to Belfast had been hard at first. The frequency of the police funerals they attended, along with the general level of danger in the city, had intimidated her. But out of the fear had come a fierce-rooted hatred of the IRA enemy. Her husband was often out late, seldom in before eight or nine, but she felt pride for his work, and shared something of his commitment.

The girls, Margaret and Fiona, six and four, were in the bright, warm living room of the bungalow, kneeling together on the sheep-skin rug in front of the fire, watching the television when the door bell rang.

"Mama! Mama! Front doorbell!" Margaret shouted to her mother at the back, too absorbed to drag herself away from the set.

Janet Rennie was making sandwiches for tea, her mind taken by fish-paste fillings and the neatness of the arrangement of the little bread triangles. They had become a treat, these Sunday teas. With annoyance she wondered who it could be. She wiped her hands on the cloth hanging beside the sink and went to the front door. As her hand reached for the Yale lock that was always on, she noticed that the chain had been left off by the children when they returned from play. She should have fastened the chain before she opened the door. But she ignored the rules her husband had laid down and pulled the door back.

"Excuse me, is it Mrs. Rennie?"

She looked at the shortish man standing there on her doorstep, hands in his coat pockets, an open smile on his face, dark hair nicely parted. "Yes, that's right."

Very quietly he said, "Put your hands behind your head, and don't shout. I know the kids are here."

She watched helplessly as he drew out the ugly squat Armalite. Holding it in one hand, with the stock still folded, he prodded her with the barrel back into the hallway. She felt strange, detached from what was happening, as if it were a scenario. He came across the carpet towards her, flicking the door closed with his heel. It clattered as it swung to, the lock engaging behind him.

"Who is it, Mama?" From behind the closed door of the living room Fiona called out.

"We'll go in there now and wait for that husband of yours."

The narrow barrel of the Armalite dug into her flesh just above the hip as he pushed past her to the door and opened it. She was half into the room before Fiona turned, words part out of her mouth but frozen when she saw the man with the rifle. Even to a child three months short of her fifth birthday, the message was brilliantly obvious. The girl rose up on her knees, her face clouding from astonishment to terror. As if in slow motion, her elder sister registered the new mood. Wide-eyed, she saw first her sister's face, then her mother standing hunched, as if bowed down by some great weight, and behind her Downs with the small shiny rifle.

Too frightened to scream, the children remained stock-still till their mother reached them, gathered them to her, and took them to the sofa.

The three of them held tightly to each other as Downs eased himself into Rennie's chair on the other side of the room. From there he was directly facing the family, who were huddled in the corner of the sofa as far as possible from him. He also had a clear view of the door into the room, and of the window beyond it at the far end of the living room. It was there that he expected the first sign of Rennie's return, the headlights of the policeman's car.

"We'll leave the TV on, missus. Any moves, anything clever, and you'll be dead, the lot of you. Don't think, Mrs. Rennie, that you're the only one at risk. That would be getting it very wrong. If I shoot you, I do the kids as well."

Billy Downs let the effect of his words sink in.

"We're just going to wait," he said.

# 8

Smiling broadly, the leader and oldest of the four men sent to question Josephine Laverty suggested that old Mrs. Laverty might care to go into the kitchen and take herself a good long cup of tea.

They took Josephine up to her bedroom, far from the mother's ears. One of the younger men drew the curtains against the frail shafts of sunlight, and took up his position by the window. Another

461

stood at the door. The third stood behind the chair and cursorily suggested Josephine should sit. The older man they called Frank, and he was treated with respect and with caution.

The girl was poorly equipped to handle an interrogation. Frank's opening question was harmless enough, and he was as astonished as the other three men in the room at the way she collapsed.

"This fellow McEvoy. Who is he?"

Her head went down to her lap and she buried her cheeks and her eyes and ears in the palms of her hands.

"Who is he?" Frank was insistent. "Where does he come from?"

"You know who he is. Why come to me for it?" .

Frank paced up and down, short steps, continually twisting towards the girl, moving back and forth between the window and the door, skirting the single bed.

"I want you to tell me." Like a stoat with a rabbit, he dominated the cringing girl. "I want it from you. D'ye hear?"

Josephine shook her head, partly from the convulsion of her collapse, and reeled away from him as he swung his clenched fist backhanded across her face.

"I'm getting impatient, girl."

She straightened up, steadying herself as she prepared the words. "He's with the British, isn't he? You knew that. He's looking for the man that killed the London politico. He said when he found him he'd exterminate him."

She stopped. Below she could hear her mother about the kitchen, picking things up and putting them down. Josephine saw the enormity of what she had said. She'd told Harry, hadn't she, that his truth was safe with her. One backhander and she spilled it all.

Frank stared intently at her. "He was sent in to infiltrate us? A British agent!"

"You knew? You knew, didn't you? You wouldn't have come if you hadn't known."

The room was near-dark now. Josephine could barely make out the men in the room—only the one silhouetted at the window by the early streetlight. Her mother called up for tea for her visitors. No one answered. The old lady lingered at the bottom of the stairs waiting for the reply, then went back to the kitchen, accepting and perhaps understanding the situation and unable to intervene.

The girl wavered one last time in her loyalties. Upbringing, traditions, community—all came down heavily on the scales and balanced there against the laugh and bed of Harry. But there was Theresa, with the tossing feet and the tightening stocking and the obscenity of death in the police cell, and that wiped Harry from the slate. She spoke again.

"He was the one that shopped the girl that hung herself. She said she'd been with the man that did the London killing. Harry tipped the army about it."

The volunteers said nothing, their imagination stretched by what the girl said. Frank spoke. "Was he close to the man he was looking for? Did he know his name? Just how much did he know?"

"He thought he knew what the man looked like, but not his name."

"And you, how did you spot this highly trained British assassin, little girl?"

"I spotted him because of a silly thing. You have to believe me, but we were on the Sperrins yesterday. He said he'd been in the merchant navy and sailed all over, but the gale on the mountain seemed to shake him a bit. I said to him it wasn't very good if he'd been to sea as much as he said. Then he didn't hide it any more. He seemed to want to talk about it."

Clever, thought Frank. "Is he armed?"

"I don't know. I never saw a gun. I've told you all I know. That's God's truth."

"There's one little problem for you, Miss Josephine." Frank's voice had a cutting edge to it now. "You haven't explained to me yet how this British agent came to hear about Theresa and what she was saying about the London man. You may need a bit of time for that, you treacherous whore."

He came very close to her now. She could smell the tobacco and beer on his breath. "Just work it out," he said. "Then tell the lads, because they'll be waiting for an answer. To us you're nothing, dirt, scum. You've shopped one of your own . . . a wee girl who hanged herself rather than talk to the bloody British. You betrayed her. You've just betrayed your lover boy as well. But then, when these lads have finished with you, you'll be thinking twice before you go with another Britisher."

Frank turned away and walked to the door. He said to the man who was standing there, "It's just a lesson this time, Jamie. Nothing permanent. Something just for her to remember, to think about for a long time. And, little girl, if you've half an inch of sense in your double-dealing painted head, you'll not mention what's happened here tonight, nor what's going to."

He went out of the room and down the steep staircase. The three younger men followed him fifteen minutes later. They left Josephine doubled up on the bed wheezing for air, fighting the pain and willing it away. Her clothes lay scattered where the men had ripped them off her. She'd thought they were going to rape her, but instead they simply beat her.

Her breath came back, and after that the long, deep aching of the muscles and, mingled with it, the agony of the betrayal. Betrayal of Theresa. Betrayal of Harry. Frank would have gone straight to the house to find him. He'd be taken, tortured and shot. Her reasoning made any thought of warning Harry irrelevant. They would have him already, but did she want to warn him? One night with him, and what had he done? Lifted her bedroom tattle from pillow confidence to military intelligence. Let him rot with it.

When her mother came up the stairs late in the evening, she was still doubled up, holding her stomach, and cold now on her skin. The old lady helped the girl into her nightdress and into bed. She spent some minutes picking up the clothes from the floor.

FRANK did not go straight to Delrosa. He had ridden up to Andersonstown on his bicycle in search of his battalion commander. It was arranged that later that night he would be taken to the brigade commander. Frank knew his name, but had never met him.

FROM HIS HOME the Permanent Under Secretary had authorized the sending of a photograph of Harry to Belfast. It had originally shown him in uniform, but that had been painted out. The next morning, Monday, copies were to be issued to troops who would raid the various Andersonstown scrap merchants.

464

THE BIG TELEVISION in the Rennies' living room droned on, its Sunday message of hope, charity, goodwill and universal kindness expounded by ranks of singers and earnest balding parsons. The family sat quite still on the sofa watching the man with the Armalite rifle.

The pictures claimed no part of Janet Rennie's attention as she stared, minute after minute, at the man, but for long moments the children's concentration was taken by the images on the screen before being jerked to the nightmare facing them across the carpet. They held fast to their mother, waiting to see what would happen, what she would do.

In the first twenty minutes that Downs had been in the room, Fiona, who traded on her ability to charm, had attempted to win the stranger with a smile. He looked right through her, grin and all. She'd then subsided against her mother.

Margaret understood that the gun on Downs's lap was to kill her father. Her sister, twenty months younger, was unable to finish off the equation and so was left in a limbo of expectancy, aware only of an incomprehensible awfulness.

He'll be a hard one, Janet Rennie had decided. One of the big men sent in for a killing like this. She saw the wedding ring on his finger. Would have his own kids at home. But he'd still shoot hers. She felt the fingers of her daughters gripping through her blouse. But she kept her head straight, and her gaze fastened on Downs, searching him for weakness. If he were nervous or under great strain, then she would notice the fidgeting of the hands or the reflection of perspiration on the stock or barrel of the gun. But there was no response to her stare, only the indifference of the professional. Like a man come to give an estimate on the plumbing, or the life insurance, she thought. None of the tensions she would have expected on display.

He held the gun lightly, his left hand halfway along the shaft. Just after he had sat down, the man had eased the safety catch off with his right index finger, which now lay spanning the half-moon of the trigger guard.

Thirty minutes or so before she thought her husband might be arriving home she decided to talk. "We have no quarrel with you.

You've none with us. We've done nothing to you. If you go now, you'll be clean away." That was her start. Poor, she told herself, it wouldn't divert a flea.

He looked back with amused detachment.

"If you go through with this, they'll get you. They always get them now. It's a fact. You'll be in the Kesh for the rest of your life. Is that what you want?"

"Save it, Mrs. Rennie. Save it and listen to the hymns."

She persisted. "It'll get you nowhere. It's the Provisionals, isn't it? You're beaten. One more cruel killing, senseless. It won't do any good."

"Shut up." He said it quietly. "Just shut up and sit still."

She spoke again. "It'll soon be over. All your big men are gone. There'll have to be a cease-fire soon." Keep it calm, talk as an equal with something on your side. There's nothing to counter-

balance that rifle, but you have to make believe he doesn't hold everything.

"We're not beaten. We've more men than we can handle. There'll be no cease-fire. Not while there are pigs like your man running round free and live."

The children beside her started up at the way the crouched stranger spoke of their father. Janet Rennie was an intelligent woman, hardened by her country upbringing. She watched the hands change position on the weapon. From resting against the gun, they were now gripping it. For the first time in nearly two hours she believed she stood a chance.

"There's no future for you boys. Your best men are all locked up. The people are sick and tired of you. Even in your own ratholes they've had enough of you—"

"You don't know a thing about what goes on. Not a thing. What do you know of the support we have? All you see is what's on the television. You don't know what life is like in the Falls, with

467

murderers like your husband to beat the muck out of boys and girls. We're doing people a service when we kill swine like that husband of yours."

"My husband never killed anyone." She said it as a statement of fact. Safe.

"He told you that, did he?" Very precise, low, and hissing the words out. "Pity you never asked him what sort of chat he had with the wee girl what hanged herself in the cells at Springfield."

She had built herself towards the climax. The rebuttal caught her hard, draining her. She remembered reading about the girl, though it had not been mentioned at home. His hands. Concentrate on the hands. The left knuckle was white on the barrel, blood drained out from around the bones.

"You're nothing, are you? That's all you're fit for. Sitting in people's homes with guns, guarding women and wee bairns. You're a rat, a creeping, disease-ridden little rat. Is that what the great movement is about? Killing people in their homes?"

Her voice was battering it out now, watching the anger rise first in his neck and spreading through the lower jaw, tension, veins hardening and protruding. Safe. What can the gun do now that would not rouse the neighbours who lived just a few feet from her own bungalow?

"You've made it all out wrong, Mrs. Rennie. Whatever your man says, you don't kill the Provos just by locking a few up. We are of the people. The people are with us. You've lost, you are the losers. Your way of life, God-given superiority, is over and finished, not us. We're winning."

He was shouting, half rising out of the flower-covered seat of the chair. The rifle was now only in the right hand. His left arm was waving above his head. She saw the hint in his eye that he no longer dominated the situation.

The hate between the two was total. His fury was fanned by the calmness she showed in face of his Armalite, and the way she had made him shout and the speed with which he had lost his control. Her loathing for the Republicans, bred into her from the cradle, gave her strength. With something near detachment she weighed the pluses and minuses of rushing him there and then. There was

468

no possibility that she could succeed. She felt the children's grip on her arms. If she surged suddenly across the room, she would carry them like two anchors halfway with her.

WHEN RENNIE turned into the cul-de-sac he noted immediately that the garage interior light was not switched on. He stopped his car forty yards from the bottom of the road and turned off his engine and lights. The bungalow seemed quite normal. But no light in the garage. For months now it had been a set routine that an hour or so before he was expected Janet would go into the kitchen and switch on the garage light.

The detective sat for some minutes in the car, watching. There was no light upstairs. Usually, Fiona would be having her bath by now. That was another cautionary factor.

He eased out of the car, pushing the door to but not engaging the lock, and reached for the Walther PPK in his shoulder holster. He had loaded and checked it before starting his drive home, but he again looked to see that the safety catch was in the On position. On the balls of his feet he went towards the front gate. The gate was wrought iron. It rattled and needed a lifting, forcing movement to open it. Rennie instead went through a gap in the hedge. The walk up to the front door was gravel, and he kept to the grass. Though light showed from a gap between the hall window curtains, it was not enough for him to see through.

Rennie came off the grass and stepped onto the tiled step of the doorway. The Walther was in his right hand, as with the left he found his Yale key and inserted it gently into the opening. For a fraction he felt sheepish at the stupidity of tiptoeing across his own front lawn. Had the neighbours seen? The door opened, just enough to get him inside. To the living room door. It was open an inch or so. As the sound of the choir's lusty singing tailed away he heard his wife speak. "Great hero, aren't you? With your bloody rifle. Need it to make a man of you. . . ."

The voice, shrill and aggressive, was enough to deaden the sound Rennie made as he leaned into the door, and the man in his chair was aware of nothing till the door started swinging on its hinges towards him.

469

His body stiffened as he fought for concentration; he had been distracted by the argument across the room. He was still raising his rifle into the fire position when Rennie came in, low and fast, hitting the carpet and rolling in one continuous action towards the heavy armchair between the fireplace and the window.

The movement was too fast for Billy Downs, who fired three times into the space by the door before checking to realize that the policeman was no longer there. He struggled up from the deep, soft armchair, flooded with panic that he had fired and missed.

The metallic click of Rennie's safety catch, and the single shot that howled by his ear and into the French windows behind, located the target.

Rennie's momentum had carried him on till he cannoned into the solid bulk of the big chair. He was on his right side, wedged between the wall and the chair. He twisted his head, seeing for the first time with agonizing clarity the man, his wife and the children, as he struggled to swivel his body around.

The rifle was against Downs's shoulder now, eye down the barrel, poised to fire. Wait for it, copper.

Rennie was screaming, "No, no. Keep away."

As soon as Fiona saw her father come through the door, she fled from the sofa across the middle of the room towards him.

It was the moment that the man had chosen to fire. His vision was blocked fractionally by the checkered dress and the long golden hair. He hesitated.

He saw the child with pinpoint clarity, as sharp as the muted, stunned children in London as he fired at their father. Not part of the war. Couldn't destroy her. Rennie was struggling to pull the child under him to protect her, and when he'd done so, he would be free to fire himself. Downs knew that. It had no effect. Not shoot a child, no way he could do it. If his wife knew he'd slaughtered a small one. . . . He saw the slight body fade under the shape of the detective, and the other man's firing arm come up to aim.

Behind the man were the French windows. He spun and dived at one of the glass panels. The light framework of wood and the glass squares gave way. Rennie, the child spread-eagled under him, emptied the revolver in the direction of the window.

470

It was the fifth or sixth shot that caught Downs in the muscle of the left arm, just above the elbow. The impact heaved him forward and across the patio towards the well-cut back lawn. The pain was searing hot as Downs ran. At the bottom of the lawn he crooked the rifle under his injured arm, and with his right, levered himself over the garden fence and into a lane.

Struggling for breath, he ran down the lane and across a field to the road where the car was parked. As with the fox discovered at work in the chicken coop who flees empty-handed, the sense of survival dominated. Then, as he neared the car, came the knowledge that if he had fired he might have hit the child, but he would have killed the policeman, that was a certainty. He had hesitated, and through his hesitation, his target was alive. It was weakness, and he had thought himself above that.

The young driver was asleep when he felt his shoulder shaken violently and saw the frantic face of the man.

"Come on. Get the thing moving."

"Aren't you going to do something about that—" The youth pointed to the still-assembled Armalite, but cut off when he saw the blood on the arm that was holding the rifle.

"Just get moving. Mind your own business and drive."

The boy surged the car forward and out onto the road in the direction of Andersonstown.

"Did it go O.K.?" he asked.

THE BELFAST brigade staff met in a back bedroom of a semi-detached house in the centre of the conglomeration of avenues, crescents, walks and terraces that make up the huge housing estate of Andersonstown. It was very different country from the Falls and Ardoyne. Landscaped roads, and flanking them a jigsaw of neat red brick homes. Ostensibly the war had not come here with the same force as in the older battlegrounds closer to the city centre, but such an impression would be false. This was the Provo redoubt, where the brigade officers and top bomb-makers had their hideouts, where the master snipers lay up between operations, where five thousand people voted for a Provisional supporter in a Westminster election.

The brigade commanders were key figures in Northern Ireland. Their capture called for rounds of celebration drinks in the mess of the army unit concerned, and articles in the national press maintaining that the Provos were about to fold up. But within a week of any commander's being carried off to Long Kesh, another young man would move forward to take over. During their reign in office, however short, they would set the tone of the administration. One would favour car bombs, another would limit attacks to military and police targets, or direct operations towards spectaculars such as big fires, major shoot-outs and prison escapes.

Each left his imprint on the situation, and all went into the mythology of the movement. Their names were well known to the troops, but their faces were blurs taken for the most part from out-of-date photographs. One had ordered his wife to destroy all family pictures that included him, and given all his briefings from behind curtains and drapes, so that under the rigours of cross-examinations his lieutenants would not be able to give an accurate description of him.

To a portion of the community their names provoked unchecked admiration, while to those less well disposed they sowed an atmosphere of fear. That there were a few touts prepared to risk the automatic hooding and assassination was a constant surprise to the army intelligence officers. Money was mostly the reason that men would whisper a message from a telephone booth. It was seldom because of the wish to rid the community of the Provisionals. Men who felt that way kept their peace and went about their lives.

Because the brigade commander and his principal lieutenants could never be totally certain of the loyalty of the people in Andersonstown, they delayed their meeting till almost midnight and staggered their arrivals at the house. None was armed. All were of sufficient importance to face sentences of up to a dozen years if caught in possession of a firearm. If arrested without a proveable criminal offence against them, they could only be detained in the Kesh, with the constant likelihood of amnesties.

There were six men in the room when the meeting started. The brigade commander sat on the bed with two others, and one more stood. Frank, who had interrogated Josephine Laverty, and Seamus

472

Duffryn were on the wooden chairs that, apart from the bed and the chest, represented the only furniture in the room. The present commander brought a small transistor radio from the pocket of his dark parka. The crucial listening times of the day for him were 7:50 a.m., the 12:55 lunchtime summary and then five to midnight. Each day the BBC's Northern Ireland news listed with minute detail the successes and failures of his men. Shootings, hijackings, blast bombs, arms finds, stone-throwing incidents—all were listed and chronicled for him. The lead story that night was of the shooting at a policeman's house in Dunmurry.

The men in the room listened, absorbed, to the firm English accent of the announcer:

"It seems that Mr. Rennie's younger daughter ran into the field of fire of the terrorist, who then stopped shooting and ran from the house. Mr. Rennie told detectives that when the girl moved he thought she was going to be killed, as the gunman was on the point of firing at him. The family are said to be suffering from shock and are staying the night with friends.

"In the Shantallow district of Londonderry a blast bomb slightly wounded—"

The commander had switched off the set. "That's not like Downs. Not like him to lose his nerve." He pondered on the decision he was about to take as the other men waited for him. He alone knew of the link between Danby in London and the man Downs.

"Well, no matter for the moment. What about the man the Brits have put in? What do we have?"

"I think it's watertight." Frank had taken the cue and come in. "The girl he was going with has spilled it all. The Englishman told her he was sent over to get the man that shot Danby in London. The name he's using is Harry McEvoy. I doubt if it's real or—"

"Of course it isn't. Doesn't matter, that. They must be a bit touched over there, if they send a man on his own, to find us just like that."

Seamus Duffryn spoke. "But it all fits with what you told us had come in from the hotel. About the army man and the RUC. The

473

bit about them putting a man in and then not telling the brass."

The brigade commander looked at Seamus. "You had a line on the man first, right? Through his accent? Where is he now?"

"He's at the guest house. The front and back are watched, and the lads have been told that if he goes out, he's to be tailed."

"And the girl you've talked to, won't she warn him?"

"She won't do anything," Frank said.

The commander lit his fourth cigarette in less than half an hour. "I think we would like to talk to him for a bit first, before we hood him. Does he work?"

"In a scrap yard. He leaves to walk there about eight."

"Take him with a car when he's walking, and get him up the Whiterock, into the Crescent."

For Frank and Duffryn it seemed the end of their part in the evening. They rose, but were waved down by the commander.

"Where's Downs now?"

The brigade quartermaster said, "The message came through just before I left to come here. The wound he got, it's a light one, in the arm, but he hasn't gone home yet. The quack who is fixing him up wants to keep an eye on him for the next few hours."

The brigade commander talked to no one in particular. "What do they say when a driver's been in a crash? Send him straight back out. Downs can go on this one. His nerve wasn't too good last night. He'll want to retrieve himself a bit. Get him here in an hour." It amused him: the fox turning back on the hound.

Frank and Duffryn went out through the back of the house to where a car was parked. Frank would drive on to the doctor and drop Seamus near his home.

Seamus was frightened for the first time since he had become involved with the movement. He'd been present three months earlier at an interrogation. A kid from up in Lenadoon. The charge was that he had betrayed colleagues in the movement to the military. The muffled screaming of the youth was still in his ears. They'd burned his stomach with cigarette ends while he was strapped in a chair, with a blanket folded over his head to deaden the noise. The hood had gone on, and at the moment they shot him, the kid was still screaming. Seamus had become involved that

474

night, and would become involved again tomorrow. That kid was a nothing from Lenadoon. If McEvoy was British army, how would he take it? Seamus wondered.

He would find out by tomorrow night. He hurried on his way through the darkness to his home and his mother.

AFTER he'd made his phone call to London, Harry had spent the rest of the day in his room. He had not gone down to Sunday high tea, and to Mrs. Duncan's inquiries only replied that he thought he had something of a chill coming on. He was going to have an early night, he shouted through the door. She had wanted to bring him a hot drink, but he managed to persuade her that there was no need.

He wanted to be alone, shutting out the perpetual tension of moving in company and living the falsehood that had been planned for him. He'd heard all the radio broadcasts, searching for the formula announcement that would end it all. Arrest. . . . Man wanted for questioning. . . . London murder. . . . Tip-off. There had been nothing.

He had steeled himself to what he would do if he heard of the capture of the man. He'd be out of the front door, with no farewells or packing or luggage, straight down to the Broadway barracks, and in through the front door. But without the news he couldn't end it. He had to stay, finish the job. No arrest, no return.

But where was the bloody army? Why wasn't it all wrapped up? Harry's frustration mounted, welling up against his reason and his training. The girl, that was where it had gone wrong. Lovely face, lovely girl, but that was where it all loused up. Gossip, and she won't keep her mouth shut any more than the rest of them. Like she talked about Theresa, so she'll talk about me. A lonely man in a back room bed-sitter. He brooded away the hours. He'd put faith down on the line of a girl whose address he didn't even know.

When he finally went to bed he turned his mind to his wife and the children. With difficulty he re-created them and home on the NATO base. The chasm between their environment and Harry's was too difficult for him to bridge. He was too tired, too exhausted.

IN THEIR EYRIE under the roof of the mill, high above Ardoyne, two soldiers looked down on Ypres Avenue. There were no street lights, old casualties of the conflict, but they watched the front door of number 41 from the image intensifier, a sophisticated visual aid that washed everything with a greenish haze and enabled them to see the doorway with great clarity. Hourly they whispered the same message into their field telephone: no one had used the front door of the house. When this was reported to Colonel Frost, he authorized the unit to move in and search at 5:30 a.m.

THE DOCTOR had cleaned Downs's wound. He'd found that a small portion of flesh had been ripped clear, close by the smallpox vaccination scar. There was an entry and exit wound, almost together, and after he had cleaned them the doctor put a light lint dressing over the pale numbed skin.

"If you look after it, you'll be O.K. Go put yourself in the easy chair out the back, and get a rest."

The doctor had been on the fringes of the movement since the start of the violence. Once every fortnight or so he would hear the gravel flick once, twice, against his bedroom window, and in his dressing gown he would open the door to a casualty too sensitive to face ordinary hospital treatment. He had made his attitude clear, that there was no point in their bringing men to him who were already close to death. Take them to the Royal Victoria Hospital, he'd said. If their wounds were that bad, they'd be out of it for months anyway, so better for them to get top medical treatment or the best hospital than the hand-to-mouth service he could provide. He was able to remove bullets, clean minor gunshot wounds and prevent sepsis getting in.

Downs was very white, and still in the chair, when he heard the faint knock on the door down the corridor at the front of the house. There was a whispered dispute in the hall. Then two men pushed their way past the doctor and into the room.

There was a tall man, in jeans and a roll-neck sweater. "The chief's waiting in Andytown. Wants to see you straight away."

The doctor remonstrated, "Look at the state he's in. You can see that for yourself. He should rest. He's in shock."

"No chance. We'll see you get a look at him tomorrow. Right now we have to go. Come on."

This last was to Downs. He looked backward and forward from the messenger to the doctor, willing the doctor to be more insistent. But the doctor avoided the pleading in Downs's eyes. The tall man and his colleague took hold of Downs under his armpits and gently but decisively lifted him towards the door.

From the high wall-cabinet in the back room the doctor took down a brown pill bottle. "You may need these to pull him up a bit," he said. "Not more than a couple at a time. They'll help him for a few hours, then it's doubly important that he rests."

They always said they'd come back, but few did. If they needed further treatment, they headed south, where they could lie up more easily away from the daily tensions of the perpetual hunt by the military. The doctor watched them carry the man to the car and ease him into the back.

The drive between the doctor's house and the meeting place in Andersonstown took twenty minutes. They helped the wounded man out of the car and in through the back entrance. Irritably he shrugged them off once he was inside.

Only the brigade commander had remained behind to see him.

"How are you, Billy? Have they fixed you up all right?"

"Not much more than a graze. It's bandaged up now and the doc says it's clean."

"I heard a bit about it on the radio. Said his brat got in the way and you didn't fire. Is that right?"

"It's not as simple as that." Oh, no, not an inquest at this time of night. "I fired once and missed, then when I had a clear shot at him the kid came right across. I couldn't see him, so I didn't fire."

The brigade commander was smoking, in front of him a glass ashtray filled with filtered ends and grey powder. "If you'd just fired, child and all . . . you would have got him, yes?"

"Is that what they said on the radio?" Downs was peeved by the reception. "Is that what Rennie is saying, on the radio? If I had fired through the kid, then I would have killed him?"

Who did this bastard think he was, thought Downs. When did he go out with an Armalite? Get out on the streets, know the terrible noise of action, feel a nine-millimetre slug hit you. Then come quizzing me. Anger rose in him, but not sufficient for him to shout. That would be mutiny.

"I don't know what Rennie is saying," said the commander. "The radio said the child was in the way and that you didn't fire. That's all. There's no criticism of you."

"There shouldn't be. Rennie moved well."

"One or two people, who don't know the facts as we do, might feel, if they had only half the story, that Billy Downs had gone soft. These people, they might recall that when we shot Sean Russell, of the UDR, in New Barnsley, that he had his kids draped all over him. Two of them were wounded, but Russell was still shot dead. The order had been to shoot him. Now we all know that it wouldn't be fair to put your escapade tonight in the same category. And we know that your nerve is as good as ever. Don't we, Billy?"

"You know I'm not soft," said Downs. "My nerve hasn't gone. We're not fighting five-year-olds. Are you saying that I should have fired straight through the girl?"

"Don't get ratty, Billy. It's just we have to be careful that people who don't know the circumstances might think that." The voice droned on, repetition of failure dragging itself through Downs. He had to sleep, to rest, to escape from this room with this nagging man.

"We know it's not true, Billy. We know there was a good reason for you not to shoot. We know you couldn't see the target. But that's enough of that. Nobody will have a leg to stand on by tomorrow night. Right, Billy? We have a little job tomorrow, and by the time that's done, they'll be silenced."

Downs looked away, broken by the twisting of the screw.

"I'm the only one of brigade group that knows about London," the commander continued. "We've kept it tight for your protection. It's worked pretty well . . . up to now. There's a difficulty come up. The Brits have put a man in to find you. Lodging down in Broadway."

He let it sink in, watched the colour return to the man's face, watched the fear come back to his eyes.

"His job is to find you. Perhaps to kill you, perhaps to take you in, or just tell them where to go. Tomorrow we're going to lift this

478

fellow, and we'll talk to him, then we'll hood him. That's where you come in. You'll shoot him, like you shot Danby, like you should have shot Rennie."

Downs felt faint now, exhausted by the sarcasm of the top man.

"When it's over we'll send you down to Donegal. Sleep it all off, and get fit again. Tonight you'll stay here in Andytown. They'll pick you up at six fifteen. They'll have the guns when they meet you. This will sort it out, I think. Be just the right answer to those who say that Billy Downs has gone soft."

He wanted out, and this was the chance. The way to do it properly, not so as you were looking over your shoulder for half a lifetime, and running. One more day, one more job. Then out. Leave it to the cowboys. The heroes who didn't hold their fire, who shot wee kids.

# 9

The long Sunday night was coming to its close when B Company swarmed into Ypres Avenue. The column of armoured cars had split up some hundreds of yards from the street, and guided by coordinated radio messages, had arrived at each end of the row of bleak terraced houses simultaneously. The first troops out sprinted down the back alleys behind the houses, taking up positions every fifteen yards or so along the debris-strewn pathways. From the tops of Land-Rovers searchlights played across the fronts of the houses as the noise in the street brought the upstairs lights flickering on.

The major who commanded the company had received only a short briefing. He had been told the man they were looking for was named Billy Downs, the address of his house, and that he was expected to search several houses. The major was thirty-three years old, on his fourth tour to Northern Ireland, and on his last visit had witnessed the killing of four of his men in a culvert bomb explosion. Unlike some of his brother officers who respected the expertise of the opposition, he felt only consuming contempt.

What Downs was wanted for he hadn't been told. He'd only guessed when they unpinned the picture from the guardroom wall and gave it to him. It was the photokit that had gone up after the London shooting and remained at the top of the soldiers' priority list.

The soldiers banged on the door of number 41 with their rifle butts. The few who had seen the picture of the man they wanted were hanging on the moment of anticipation, wondering who would come and open the door.

From upstairs came the noise of crying, steadily increasing to screaming pitch as the children woke. Downs's wife came to the door, thin and frail in her cotton dressing gown. The troops pushed past her, huge in their boots and helmets and flak jackets. They raced up the stairs, equipment catching and bouncing off the banisters. A lieutenant and two sergeants. The officer, his Browning pistol cocked and fastened to his body by a lanyard, swung his left shoulder into the front-bedroom door and bullocked his way to the window. The man behind switched on the light, covering the bed with his automatic rifle.

Two faces peered back at the intruders. Saucer-eyed, mouths open, and motionless. The troops patted the bodies of the children and pressed down into the bedclothes around them. They looked under the bed and in the wardrobe. There were no other hiding places in the room.

The lieutenant went to the top of the stairs and shouted down. "Not here, sir."

"Wait there, I'll come up."

The major came in and looked slowly round the room.

"Right, not here now. But he has been, or she's dirty round the house. There, his pants, shirt, socks."

By the window was a crumpled pile of dirty clothes.

"Get her up here," said the major. "And get the floorboard chaps. May still be in the house. If he's about, I want him found."

She came into the room, her two youngest children hanging like monkeys over her shoulders, thumbs in mouths. Like their mother they were white-faced, and shivering in the cold.

"We wonder where we might find your husband, Mrs. Downs."

"He's not here. You've poked your bloody noses in, and you can see that. Now get out of here."

480

"His clothes are here, Mrs. Downs. I wouldn't expect a nice girl like you to leave his dirty pants lying on the floor."

"Don't be clever with me," she snarled back at him. "He's not here, now get your soldiers out."

"The problem, Mrs. Downs, is that we think your husband could still be here. That would be the explanation for his clothes. I'm afraid we're going to have to search around a bit. We'll cause as little disruption as possible."

"Big heroes, aren't you, when you have your tanks and guns."

A soldier with a crowbar mouthed an apology as he came past her. He flipped up a corner of the threadbare carpet and with a rending scrape pulled up the boards at the end of the room. In four separate places he took the planks up, before disappearing to his hips down the hole he had made. The major and the soldiers waited above for him to emerge with his torch for the last time and announce with an air of professional disappointment that the floor space was clear. Using ladders, they went up into the attic, shaking the beams above the major and the man's wife, and swinging the light fixture.

"Nothing up there either, sir."

The ground floor was of stone and tile, so that stayed put, while the expert banged on the walls with his hammer in search of cavities. The coal bunker out in the yard was cleared out.

"It's clean, sir."

That was the cue for her to return to the attack.

"Are you through now? All these men and one little house, and one wee girl with her kids—"

"You know why we want him?" The major lashed out. "We'll go on till we get him, even if we have to rip this house to pieces each week. Doesn't he tell you where he's going at night? Doesn't he tell you what he did last month? Try asking him one day."

He strode out, followed by his search team. It was three minutes after six o'clock. Failure and frustration—that was how the majority of these raids ended, but he'd never lost his temper before, as he'd done with the woman in number 41. He comforted himself on two points: that it needed saying, and that the intelligence officer who had tagged along hadn't heard it.

481

ONCE THE ARMY had gone, a clutch of neighbours moved into the house to gather around the woman and commiserate on the damage left behind and to help in the clearing up. Those that came noted how subdued she was. That was not the usual way. The familiar reaction was to greet the going of the soldiers with a hail of insults and obscenities at their backs. But not this woman.

When the friends had left her to get their own families ready for work or school or just dressed and fed, the words of the officer returned to ring in her ears. Quietly she padded about the house, her children in a crocodile procession behind her, checking to see which of her few possessions were damaged or tarnished or moved.

This was the confirmation. This was what she had feared. Ever since his first night back home after London, she had been waiting. So much wind, this confidence he had. Like a rat he was, waiting in a barn with the door shut for the farmer to come in the morning with his gun and his dogs. The big, fresh-faced officer, with his suspicion of a moustache and posh accent, who hated her, he had laid down the future, had mirrored her nightmares. They would come, and come again for her man, and keep on till they found him.

Last night he had not slept beside her. On the radio she heard the early news. A policeman shot at . . . an intruder hit . . . in the middle evening. Whoever had been involved should have been home now. Her man was usually home by now. Around the passage and stairs and landing of the house she thought of her man. Wounded, maimed, alone in the dawn of the city.

With the efficiency of tribal tom-toms word passed over the sprawling urban conglomeration that the terraced houses in Ypres Avenue had been raided. Less than half an hour after the major had walked out the front door of number 41, Billy Downs would hear of it. Brigade staff of the IRA had decided that he should know. They felt it could only enhance his motivation for the job he had at hand.

HARRY'S ALARM CLOCK dragged him from the comfort of his dreaming, and woke him to the blackness of his room. His dreams had been of home, wife and children, holidays in timber forest chalets, fishing out in the cool before the sun came up, trout barbecued for breakfast. With consciousness came the knowledge of another Monday morning. He thought back to the day that he had left the house at Dorking, with the view of the hills and vegetable garden. "Must have been out of my mind," he muttered to the emptiness of the room.

In Aden, good old Aden, it had been so much more simple, British lives at stake, the justification of everything, with the enemy clearly defined. The Red Cross man from Switzerland, in his little white suit, even with a big bright cross on his hat so they wouldn't throw a grenade at him from a rooftop, had come to visit the unit once. He'd said to the colonel something like, "One man's terrorist is another man's freedom fighter." The colonel hadn't liked that. Pretty heady stuff, they all thought in the mess. Such rubbish. Terrorists they were then, Arab terrorists at that.

But here, who was the enemy? Why was the man the enemy? Did you have to know why to take his life?

In spite of the fact that Harry came originally from the country town an hour or so's drive from Belfast, the army's mould had been the real influence, over-reaching his childhood. Like his brother officers, he was still perplexed at the staying power of the opposition. But here he parted company. To the others they were the enemy, to Harry they were still the opposition. You could kill them if it was necessary, or if that was demanded for operational reasons, but they remained the opposition.

What made such men prepared to risk their lives on the streets when they took on the power of a British army infantry section? What led them to sacrifice most of the creature comforts of life to go on the run?

It didn't involve Harry. The man he was searching for was a killer. He was a challenge. Harry could focus on that.

"A cup of tea, Mr. McEvoy?" Mrs. Duncan at the door cut short his thoughts. "What would you be wanting for breakfast? There's the lot, if you can manage it. Sausages, bacon, tomatoes, eggs, and I've some soda bread. . . ."

"Just toast and coffee, thanks."

"That won't get you far. It's a raw day, right enough."

"Nothing more, thank you, Mrs. Duncan. Really, that's all I want. I'll be right down."

"Please yourself, then. Bathroom's clear. Coffee's made, and remember to wrap up well, with your cold."

After he'd shaved, there was not much to the dressing. Sweater, faded jeans, his socks and boots and his parka. He took the face towel from the bathroom, brought it back into his room and laid it on the bed. About two feet by one and a half, it was bigger than the one the Smith & Wesson was already wrapped in, and he changed them over, putting the revolver in the new towel.

He needed a towel to disguise the outline of the weapon when it sat in the deep pocket of his parka on the way to work. But he didn't need a clean towel. That's the army for you, he thought, everything clean on a Monday morning.

He breezed into the kitchen. "Morning, Mrs. Duncan, all right then?"

"Little enough to complain about. You're sure about the toast and coffee?" Disappointment clouded her face when he nodded. "Anything on the news, then?"

"Just the usual. A policeman up Dunmurry way chased a man out of his house and shot him. That's his version, anyway."

Harry laughed. "They haven't caught the London man?"

"Well, Mr. McEvoy, if they have, they didn't say so, which means they haven't. They'd be trumpeting it if they had."

Harry had banked a lot on the man being in custody. It was twenty-one hours after the call to London, to Davidson. Couldn't be that difficult to pick the man up. They must have him, but they weren't saying yet, had to be that way. The explanation was facile, but enough to tide him over his breakfast.

On Monday mornings he was the only guest. Tonight, at teatime, the travellers and others would be back in the front room.

"Will Josephine be in this afternoon?" He sounded casual, matter of fact.

"Should be, Mr. McEvoy. You wanted to see her?"

Shrewd old goat, thought Harry. Beautiful throw-away, real after-thought. "I'd said I'd lend her a book," he lied gracefully.

"She'll be here when you get back. Your sandwiches are there on the sideboard. Some coffee in the flask. I put a boiled egg in, too, and an apple."

"Very naughty, Mrs. Duncan, you'll make me into an elephant."

She liked the banter and was still laughing with him as he walked into the hall and to the front door.

"You've got enough clothes on, then? We don't want you with a worse cold."

"Don't fuss, Mrs. Duncan."

EARLY that Monday morning in the Covent Garden office, Davidson was scanning the first London editions of the papers. Both *The Times* and *The Guardian* carried reports from Northern Ireland that the Provisional IRA was claiming that British intelligence had launched a special agent into the Catholic areas, and that people in those areas had been warned to be especially vigilant. Both the writers emphasized that, whether true or false, the claim would have the effect of further reducing the minimal trust between the people of the minority areas and the security forces. There was much other news competing for space, and the Belfast copy was not prominently displayed, but to Davidson it presented a shattering blow. For a moment he comforted himself that Harry might see the report and do a bunk on his own. No, scrap men don't take *The Times* or *The Guardian*, that wouldn't match the cover.

He dialled Lisburn military headquarters direct, and asked for Frost. The intelligence colonel was already in his office.

"Morning, Colonel. I take it there's been no positive news or you would have called me."

"Right, Mr. Davidson." Had to rub in the "mister", didn't he? "There is no news. We did Downs's home, and the report an hour ago said he wasn't there, but had been a few hours earlier. There's an off chance he's in trouble. A man of his description attacked a policeman's home late yesterday and botched it up. The policeman thinks he hit him with a single revolver shot as he was escaping. As for your man, well, we're taking out the Andersonstown scrap merchants in about forty minutes."

"Thank you very much, Colonel."

"That's all right, Mr. Davidson. I'm sure we'll never have the opportunity again of providing a similar service to your organization."

Davidson put the phone down. "Stupid, pompous man. Does he think I'm having a picnic at this end?"

THE POSTCARD was lying on the mat, colour side down, when Mary Brown responded to the flap of the letterbox in the front door.

"There's a card from Daddy, darlings," she called into the back of the house, where the boys were having breakfast.

"Not a letter, Mum?" her elder boy shouted back.

"No, just a card. You know how awful your father is about letters."

There was a market scene on the card. Men in *kaffiyehs* staring blankly from the gold market that stood in the middle distance.

"Hope to see you all soon. Still very hot, and not much to do. Love you all, Harry." That was all there was on the card, written in Harry's large hand.

THE PRIME MINISTER liked to start the day with his papers, a cup of tea and the first radio news bulletin. He waded through the politics, diplomatic, economic, pausing longer on the gossip columns than he would have wanted others to know, and through sport, where he delayed no longer than it took him to turn the pages. The pace was enormous, nothing read twice unless it had major impact.

The frown began deep between the overbearing bushiness of the eyebrows. The degree of concentration extended. The mixture written on his stubbly face was of puzzlement and anger.

*The Times* had put it on page two, and not given it much. Eight paragraphs. The length of the copy had relatively little importance to the Prime Minister. The content flabbergasted him. A British agent had been identified by the Provisional IRA, and the ghetto areas had been alerted to be on their guard against him.

He considered calling the Ministry of Defence or Fairbairn in Lisburn, and then dismissed it. Protocol up the spout if he did. If they were to be dropped in a monumental mess, then the Secretary of State should do some of the lifting, and take a bit of the weight.

486

Time to play things straight down the middle, the Prime Minister reflected.

With a surge he swept the bedclothes from him. He never had been able to make a telephone call lying on his side. He slung the dressing gown over his shoulders and sat on the edge of the single bed which he had occupied since his wife died, and picked up the telephone.

"Morning; Jennifer, first of the day." Always something friendly to the girls on the switchboard, worked wonders with them. "Secretary of State for Northern Ireland. Quick as you can, there's a good girl."

He sat for two and a half minutes, reading other papers but unable to turn his full attention to them, till the telephone buzzed in its console.

"Morning, Prime Minister."

"I won't keep you long. I wondered how thoroughly you'd read your *Times* this morning. Provisionals claiming they've identified an agent of ours, warning the population."

"I haven't seen it, I'm afraid."

The Prime Minister said, "We're a little anxious at this end that it could be the fellow we sent over, after Danby was killed. Could be difficult if they nabbed him and he talked."

"Trifle awkward, no doubt about that. Well, we'll get the people who run him to move him out right away. That's the simple answer."

"The problem lies right there," said the Prime Minister. "It's a bit incredible, but the chaps controlling him in London cannot contact him. Seems he just calls in when he has something to say."

The Secretary of State sounded surprised. "Bit unusual that, isn't it? Bit unique. And what do we do? Sorry, I'll rephrase that one. What do you want done about it?"

"I'm just letting you know. There's not very much we can do about it beyond the obvious. Stand by to catch the cradle."

"If it comes, it'll be from a fair altitude." The Secretary of State paused, as if to let it sink home. "I'm glad it wasn't down to me, this one. Still, I'll keep a weather eye out for the storm clouds. Goodbye, Prime Minister."

487

JOSEPHINE LAVERTY was late, and hurried in a frantic mixture of a run and a walk down the Falls to the mill where she worked. She couldn't go fast, as the pain from her beating still bit into her ribs. She, too, had heard the early radio news, half expecting in an uninvolved sort of way to hear that Harry McEvoy had been found face down, hooded and dead. It had surprised her that there was no mention of him. This morning she had wondered for a wild moment whether to go and see if he was still at Delrosa, but there was no will-power, and the emotion he had created was now drained from her.

Perhaps she would go to Mrs. Duncan's tonight to help with the teas. Perhaps not. But that could be a later decision. There was now an irrelevance about Harry McEvoy. The pillow eavesdropper who had a girl killed. Forget him.

WITH THEIR photographs of Harry, the troops raided the five scrap yards in Andersonstown. No one in the operation had been told why they were to pick up the smiling man in the picture who wore his hair shorter than their more general customers. The orders were that if the man was found, he was to be taken straight to battalion headquarters and handed over.

At the scrap yards the employees who had arrived before the troops stood sullenly against the walls of the huts, hands above their heads, as they were searched and then matched with the photograph. At the yard where Harry in fact worked, the little man who was in charge reckoned Harry must be important, and determined to say nothing. He confirmed that he employed a man called Harry McEvoy, that was all.

"Where does he live?" the lieutenant who led the raid asked.

"Don't know. He never said."

"What about his stamps, his insurance?"

The little man looked embarrassed. The answer was clear.

The lieutenant was new to Northern Ireland. The man opposite him seemed of substance, a cut above the yobbos. Out of earshot of the others, the officer said, "Look, we need this man rather badly."

"Well, you'll have to wait for him, won't you?"

But time was ticking on its way, and as the soldiers crouched behind the wrecked cars and buses and waited, there was no sign of the face in the photograph. Even the little man became worried by Harry's non-arrival. The soldiers radioed in, hung about a few more minutes, then drove back, empty-handed, to Fort Monagh.

# 10

The ambush was in position.

It was a proven, brutally simple piece of organization. A stolen Ford Escort was parked sixty yards up from Delrosa just before the junction with the Falls Road. Harry would walk along on the opposite side of the pavement and turn into the main road. He would be watched by three men who had placed themselves behind the lace curtains of the house in front of which the car was parked. With Harry safely around the corner, the men could come out of the house, start up the car and cruise up from behind to surprise him. The three in the room, standing back from the lace curtains, were Downs, Frank, and Seamus Duffryn. All were at this stage without their guns, but in the Escort's glove compartment was a Luger, and underneath the driver's seat a folded-down Armalite, loaded and cocked.

To both Frank and Duffryn this was a novel situation. They had never been entrusted with a mission of such importance, and the tension they felt was reflected in the frequency with which both of them came forward and tugged at the flimsiness of the curtain to view the other side of the road. They talked quietly in staccato style to each other, avoiding the eyes and attention of Downs, who stayed at the back behind them. Neither Frank nor Duffryn knew the third man's name, only vaguely his reputation as a marksman. Both looked to him for leadership, but he buried himself away from them, not communicating the confidence and expertise they were seeking.

Since he had been told of the operation Downs had had little to say. He burned up his anger and frustration inside himself. The pain of his injury told on him, too, and though that was slightly

489

compensated for by the tablets he had taken, he felt weak and disorganized. He wore a loose overall sweater, with his left arm in a sling underneath, the sleeve hanging free at his side. He knew he was not fit enough for a firefight, but for a pick-up and at close range he'd see it through. He would sit in the front with Duffryn driving, and Frank in the back with the Englishman for the short ride to Whiterock.

Frank said, "He's late now. He can't be much longer."

"How long do we wait after he's round the corner?" Duffryn asked.

"Hardly at all," said Frank. "Just a few yards. We want to pick him on the bend near the cemetery."

"Hope the stupid car starts." Duffryn giggled weakly, and looked at Downs. "You done this sort of thing before?"

Duffryn saw the pale, pinched, hating face. Sensed the quality of his anger and hostility.

"Yes," said Downs.

"It works like they plan it, does it?"

"Sometimes. Other times it doesn't."

"The thing that worries me—" like a tap, drip, drip, drip, thought Downs as Duffryn chattered on "—is if they have a tank going by as we jump him. Who knows what we do then?"

He said the last to himself, as the anxiety built up in him about the calibre of the morose and injured man on whom he and Frank were depending for success. Just as Duffryn put it out of his mind, Frank stiffened and edged forward again towards the window.

"He's coming. Here comes the Englishman."

Duffryn pushed his friend to the side to see for himself. The tall figure in the distance closed the wicket gate of Delrosa behind him. Looks as if he owns the place, thought Duffryn.

"Keep back from the window, you stupid bastards," the man behind them hissed.

Harry was stepping out, aware of his slow start to the morning, and conscious that whatever speed he walked to the yard, he would still be late. The combination of Mrs. Duncan's chatter and her insistence on the fresh coffee that percolated interminably had delayed him. He came up the familiar pavement fast, with his

490

sandwiches and flask in the bag bouncing on his shoulder and the weight of the wrapped revolver thudding against his right hip.

He saw the car, one of several parked on the other side of the road. It was small, neat and well kept, but slightly different, something strange . . . the kerbside doors ajar. Daft idiot, who leaves doors open in his car down the Falls? People didn't leave car doors open around here.

Harry moved on past the car and up to the junction of the side street and the Falls. He checked his left wrist to see how far behind the morning schedule he was, and realized with a suppressed oath that he had left his watch behind. Where? Not in his room, not at breakfast. In the bathroom after shaving. He was around the corner into the Falls. Blast it. He wavered. Only a hundred yards back to the guest house to get it. It's a naked feeling without a watch. Harry swung on his heel and walked back towards Delrosa.

As he turned the corner, Duffryn was beside the driver's door. Frank was already in the back seat, and the last man out of the house was halfway between the front door and the car.

For a moment all four men froze.

Harry, mind racing like a flywheel, tried to put a situation and background to the familiarity of the face in front of him. Where? Where did that face come from?

It was fractional, the lapse of doubt before the image slotted. The dance, the woman in yellow, the army crashing in, and as the concentration lasted, so the face confronting him across the street dissolved into the detail of the photokit picture. Perhaps it was the strain Downs had been under, or the pain from the wound, but the features at last resembled those that various witnesses had seen.

The first movement. Harry reached into his parka pocket, thrust deep with both hands to pull out the pistol. He dragged at the sharp white towelling and ripped it from the blackness of the gun, tearing a ladder of bright cotton on the foresight. Thirty feet away, Duffryn flung himself face down behind the car. Frank jack-knifed his body over the head rest on the front passenger seat to open the glove compartment where the Luger lay. Downs ducked towards the floor of the car, where his Armalite was resting.

Aimed shots, Harry boy. Don't blaze. Aim and you'll hit them.

491

He shrugged the duffel bag from his shoulder onto the paving stones, and, legs squat and apart, brought the revolver up to the aim position. Knees slightly bent, body weight forward, both arms extended and coming together with the gun at eye level. The classic killing position. Squeeze, don't jerk the trigger. The thumb of the right hand fumbled forward, rested on the safety catch in the On position and eased it forward.

In the big V of the arms, reaching to the barrel of the revolver, was the contorted shape of Frank, still stretching for the Luger. As the man lurched back into the rear seat with the gun in his hand, Harry steadied and fired his first shot. The left rear window disintegrated, and Frank jolted as the bullet hit him in the throat. Bewilderment was spread over his face as he subsided onto the back seat with a rivulet of crimson flooding down onto the collar of his shirt. Not in itself a fatal shot, but it would become one if Frank did not get immediate hospital treatment.

Harry stood stock-still, looking for the next target. Show yourselves. Who shoots next? Steady, Harry boy. You're like a big lamp post up there, right in the open. Get some cover.

Harry knelt on the pavement. "Come out with your hands above your heads. Any attempt to escape and I'll shoot." Good control, Harry, dominate them.

Downs whispered to Duffryn as they huddled on the reverse side of the car. "Make a run down the hill. He'll not hit you with a handgun. But for God's sake, run—and now!" He shoved Duffryn out into the open, away from the car, and shouted after him, "Run, you little idiot, and weave. . . ."

Duffryn, in deep terror, bolted from the cover down towards Delrosa. As he shifted direction from right to left, the effect was to slow him down and make him the easier target. Harry fired four times. He heard Duffryn sob out as he ran, pleading, merging with his shout as the third shot caught him between the shoulder blades. Duffryn cannoned forward into the lamp post, spread-eagled against it for a few seconds, and then slid down to become a shapeless mass at its base.

The moment that Duffryn had run, Downs eased open the front door of the Escort, forced himself into the driver's seat and started the engine. The car started rolling in the direction of the Falls.

Harry swung the revolver around, tracking his attention away from the fallen young man to the moving car. He saw Downs's head low over the wheel before it swung lower still, below the dashboard. That was the moment he fired. The bullet struck the angle of the roof of the car, exited and thudded into the wall of the house opposite. Count your shots, they always drilled that. He had done so, and he was out, chamber empty. Three more cartridges in the lunch bag, down at the bottom below the plastic food box. Frantically he broke the gun and pushed the used cases out, so that they clattered on the pavement. He slid in the three replacements, copper-plated ends and grey snub-nosed tips.

Downs was out in the traffic of the Falls. As a reflex, Harry ran after him, revolver in hand. He saw cars shy away from him as though he had some plague and could kill by contact. His man was edging away when Harry spotted a Cortina Estate, crawling with the others and unwilling to come past him. Harry ran to the passenger door. It was unlocked. He shouted at the driver. "This is loaded. You're to follow that white Escort. About nine cars in front. For your own safety don't mess me about. I'm army."

Donal McKeogh, aged twenty-seven, a plastics salesman, gave a mechanical, numbed response. The car trickled forward.

Harry saw the Escort drawing away. "Don't mess me," he screamed again at the face a few inches away, and to reinforce the effect of his intentions, fired a single shot through the roof of the car. McKeogh surged forward.

Two bullets remained in the Smith & Wesson.

IT HAD taken Billy Downs little time to work out where he was going. The failure to kill the Englishman dictated the decision. He was going home. To his wife. To his children. To Ypres Avenue. Away from the guns, and the firing, and the blood. His logic, will-power and control were drained from him. No emotion, no sensitivity left. Even the slight bubbling coughs of Frank in the back seat could not disturb him.

Driving was hard. He had to stretch his left arm to the gear handle, and even the movement from second to third aggravated the injury. A bad pain that dug at him, then went, but came again with renewed force, chewing at his strength and resolve. He mapped out a route for himself to Carlisle Circus. Could park there. It was a walk to Ardoyne then, and the car and Frank would be close to the Mater, their own people's hospital.

It was nine minutes to the Circus where the Crumlin and the Antrim roads come together. He drove onto a parking space and stopped. He looked behind and into the back. Frank was very white, with much of his blood pooled beside his face on the plastic seat cover. In his eyes was just enough light to signal recognition.

"Don't worry, Frank. You're close to the Mater. You'll be there in five minutes. I'm going now, and you'll be safe."

Frank could say nothing.

Downs left the engine running and the door open as he ran away from the car, to ensure that someone would look inside. The broken back window would clinch it. The Armalite was still under the driver's seat, and the Luger lay beneath Frank's body. He ran up the Crumlin, Mater Hospital on his right, huge and red and cleansed, giving way to the prison. High walls, coils of barbed wire, stone sentry towers and, dominating all, the great gatehouse. Downs ran past the soldiers on duty. None spared him a glance.

The sprint gave way to a jog, then to little more than a stumble as he neared the safety of Ardoyne at the top of the long hill. The weight of his legs seemed to pin him back as he forced his feet forward. His breath came in great sobs as he reached the corrugated fence that divided Shankhill from Ardoyne.

IN THE RACE across the city McKeogh had several times fallen back in the traffic stream, losing sight completely of the white Escort before spotting it again far to the front, manoeuvring among the lorries and vans and cars. Then Harry screamed and threatened McKeogh, and the salesman would speed up. As they came out of the centre of town and reached Carlisle Circus, the Escort was gone. Four major routes come together there, including the Crumlin leading up to Ardoyne and the Antrim Road running up to the nearer, equally hard-line, New Lodge. New Lodge offered the quicker refuge, and Harry aimed his arm that way, as McKeogh swung around the Circus and then up the wide road. They drove a mile, and fast, up beyond the scorched entrance to the ghetto, before Harry indicated they should turn back.

"Try the Crumlin, it has to be that way."

"If he went up the Crumlin, he'll be out of the city by now, halfway to the airport," said McKeogh.

"Just drive and close your attention on that," Harry snapped back. He knew he would be lucky now to find him again. Neither saw the Escort still parked among the other cars on Carlisle Circus, and they turned up the long haul of the Crumlin. Harry was forward in his seat now, peering right and left as McKeogh swept up the road. At the top he shouted. The exultation of a master of hounds throwing off the frustration of a lost quarry. "There he is, at the tin wall."

McKeogh slowed the car in against the near pavement. "Who is he?"

Harry looked at him and bolted from the car. He ran across the road and through the gap in the silver corrugated fence. Downs had a start of less than a hundred yards.

FEVERISH in the torment of her uncertainty, Billy Downs's wife had sent two of her children to the community infant-care centre, and dumped the others with her neighbours. In her threadbare green coat, and with her bag and purse, she had taken herself to the shops at the top of Ardoyne. The screw had been well twisted on her exhausted nerves.

The news programme less than two hours earlier had carried reports of the gunman who hesitated, the intervention of the child, and the wounding of the gunman at the policeman's house. There had been a trail of blood, the report said.

Men from the community association would come in later in the day to help repair the boards pulled up at dawn by the army, but for now the debris and confusion in the house coupled with the danger to her husband threatened to defeat her. But the single factor that weighed most with her was the knowledge that the military knew of her husband, had identified him, and that their life together was effectively over. If he had survived last night, then he would be on the run and go underground, otherwise the future held only the prospect of years in the Kesh or the Crumlin.

And for what? That a cabinet minister should die in London, or a policeman in Dunmurry, was not the fuel that fired her. Her conviction was of far too low a grade to sustain her in her present misery.

Her purse had been full from the social security last Thursday. Now most of it was spent, with only enough for the basics of bread and milk bolstered by sausages and baked beans. At the shops as she queued, many eyes were on her. Word had passed that the army had raided her house, that they were looking for her man.

She glared back at them, embarrassing the lookers enough to deflect their eyes. She paid for her food, pecking in her purse for the money, and swung out of the door and back to Ypres Avenue.

WHEN SHE TURNED into the narrow long street, the observation post in the roof of the old mill spotted her. The soldiers came and went by the back stairs, and where the boards were too rotten, hauled themselves up by rope ladder. Once in position, they put a heavy padlock on the door behind them, locking themselves in the roughly fashioned cubicle, constructed out of sandbags, blankets and sacking. To see down the avenue they lay on their stomachs with their heads forward into the angle of the roof, with a missing tile providing the vantage point. The two men in the post did twelve hours there at a stretch, and would rotate in the position with three other teams, familiarizing themselves enough with the street so that they would know each man and woman and child who lived there. The comings and goings were logged, then sifted each evening by their battalion's intelligence officer. It was a process repeated in scores of streets in the Catholic areas of Belfast.

Lance-Corporal David Burns and Private George Smith had been in the mill since six that morning. Burns, face intent behind powerful German binoculars, called out the details on the slight woman walking towards him. "The bird from forty-one. Must have been shopping. Looks a bit rough. Didn't find her husband, did they?"

He squirmed closer to the aperture, pressing the glasses against his eyebrows. "Hey, Smithie, behind her. I think he's coming.

Right up the top there. Sort of running. That is her old man, isn't it?"

Smith took over the hole. "I'm not sure, not at this stage," he said. "We'll be definite when he gets down the road a bit. Is he a shoot-on-sight, or what?"

"Don't know. I'm sure it's him. Get HQ. Looks like he's run a bloody marathon. Knackered, he is."

IT WAS the pounding of his feet that first broke through her pre-occupations. She turned and stopped still at the sight.

Downs was struggling to run now, head rolling from side to side and the rhythm of his arm movements lost. The stitch in his right side bit into the stomach wall. His legs flailed forward over the last few paces to her, uncoordinated and wild. His face was pale, the skin glistening with sweat. But it was the eyes that held her. Their desperation, loneliness and dependence.

She put down her shopping bag on the paving, careful that it should not topple over, and held out her arms for her man. He fell against her, stumbling, and she reeled with the sudden weight. There were words, but she could not understand them as they buried themselves in the shoulder of her coat. Far distant, on the top street corner, a knot of women had gathered.

"They came for you, you know, this morning."

"I know."

"They searched all over, and they said they'd come again." He nodded, numbed and shocked by the pain of the running and the throbbing in his arm. "They know. They're not so daft as you said."

"I was told." The speaking was a little easier now. The air was there, coming more naturally. "That stupid copper . . ."

She felt him wince and tear away his left arm. "Last night it was you? I heard it on the radio. Is that where he hit you?" He nodded. "Has it been looked at? Have you seen a doctor?" Again he nodded.

"Where are you going now? What are you going to do?"

"I'm going home. I just want to go home."

"But they came this morning for you," she screamed, her voice hysterical. "They'll be back as soon as you walk through the door."

497

He wasn't listening. "They put a man in, just to find me." He said it with wonder, as if surprised that the enemy would classify him as of such importance that they would take a step so great. "There's no point in running now. I'm finished with it. It's over."

"You mean that? It's not just because you're hurt? We can get you away from here, the boys will shift you."

"It's definite," he said. He was very tired now and needing to sit down. He picked up her shopping bag with his right hand, and

draped the injured left arm over the small woman's shoulder. They began to walk by the terraced doors and the chipped and daubed red brick of the street towards their house.

The moment the two had created for each other was broken by the footsteps behind. Instinctively both knew the noise of pursuit.

The women on the corner were silent as Harry ran by them down the gentle incline towards where the man and his wife were walking away from him. He held the revolver close to him. He pulled up twenty feet short of the pair, who swung around to face him.

"Don't move. If you do, I'll shoot." Harry barked the instructions. The harshness of his tone and its assurance surprised him. He felt almost detached from the orders he was shouting.

"Put the bag down and begin to walk towards me, and slowly. Your hands on your head. The woman—she stays where she is."

Be strong. Don't mess about with him. Keep the gun on him, so it's only got to come straight up to fire, and the catch off. Two bullets only. One up the spout, and the other in the next chamber, that's all.

Harry studied him hard. Dirty, cowed and frightened—is that the terrorist? Is that all he is?

"Start walking now, and remember—keep it very cool, or I shoot. What's your name?"

"Billy Downs. You're the Englishman they sent for me? The one that had the girl killed?" The fight for survival was returning, steadily and surely. "You won't get out of here, you know. Not with me on the end of your pistol, you won't."

He looked past Harry and seemed to nod his head into the middle distance. It was cleverly done. Good try, Billy boy. But you're with the professionals now, lad. A squaddie might have turned and given you the third of a second you needed to jump him. Not Harry. Pivot around. Get your back to the wall. Keep going till you feel the brickwork.

Faced with troops in uniform, Downs would probably have submitted without a struggle. But not this way. No surrender to a single hack sent from London to kill him, watched by his wife and in his own road. For a year it would be talked about—the day when a lone Englishman came into Ardoyne and shot down meek little Billy Downs. The day the boy's nerve went.

He was formidable, this Englishman, in his old jeans and dark parka. He had not been reared through the anguish of the troubles, and it showed in the freshness of his features. But he was hard. They'd trained him and sent him from London for this moment, and Downs knew his life rested on his capacity to read the expressionless mouth. When he made his break, all would depend on how well the Englishman could shoot, and when he fired, on how straight. Downs made his assessment—he'll fire, but fire late, and he'll miss. He turned himself now from the waist only, and very slowly, towards his wife. He was close to her, much closer than Harry, and with his face in profile he mouthed, from the far side of his lips, the one word."

"Scream."

It came from deep down. A fierce noise from so small a woman. Harry jerked from his preoccupation with Downs as his eyes searched for the source of the noise.

Downs pushed his wife violently towards Harry and started for the freedom of the open street down the hill. His first two strides took him to the edge of the pavement. A flood of adrenalin . . . anticipating the shot, head down, shoulders crouched. This was the moment. Either he fires now or I make it, three, four more paces, then the range and accuracy of the revolver is stretched. His eyes half closed, he saw nothing in front of him as his left foot hit hard on the steep edge of the pavement. For his heel there was support, for his sole there was nothing, only the gap between the flagstones and the gutter eight inches below. His weight was all there as he catapulted forward.

He hit the rough gravel of the road on his left arm, right where the flesh had been twice torn open by Rennie's bullet. With his right arm he clawed at the road, trying to push himself up and away from Harry, who was coming to him, revolver outstretched.

Harry saw the hand scruffing under the body. If the man had a gun, that was where it would be, down by the waist, where the hand was fumbling now. It wasn't a difficult decision. He raised the revolver so that the line went down from his right eye, down his right arm to the V of the back sight and along the black barrel to the sharp foresight, and then onto the man's upper chest. He held the aim just long enough for his hand to steady, then squeezed the trigger gently. The noise was not great, and the revolver gave only a slight kick. Downs's body began to twitch, giving way to spasmodic convulsions. The blood found its own pathway from the side of his mouth out onto the greyness of the road.

There was no need for the second bullet.

"Why did you shoot him? He had no gun." She was moving towards Downs, looking at Harry as she spoke. "You didn't have to shoot. You could have run after him, and caught him. You know he was hit last night. He wasn't much opposition, you Britisher bastard."

She knelt down beside her husband, her stocking dragging on the harsh surface of the road. He lay on his side, and she could not cradle him as she would have wanted. Both her hands touched his face, unmarked in death, fingering his nose and ears and eyes.

Harry felt no part of the scene; but something was demanded of him, and painstakingly he began to explain. "He knew the rules.

501

He knew the game he was playing. He came to London and murdered the cabinet minister. In cold blood. Shot him down in front of his house. It was a challenge to us. He must have known we had to get him—you must have known that. It was a test of will. We couldn't afford to lose."

Harry had wondered how this moment would be. How he would feel if the man were dead, destroyed. There was no hatred, no loathing for the slight body that lay on the grit of the street. There was no elation, either, that his world and his system had beaten that of the young man who they had told him was the enemy. All the training, all the fear, all the agony, directed to killing this awkward, shapeless nonentity. And now nothingness. He pushed the revolver down into his parka pocket, looked again at the wife as she bent over her lifeless man, and began his walk up the hill out of Ardoyne.

HIGH IN THE hidden observation post both soldiers had heard the single shot. It was Smith who was at the aperture, giving a continuous description of events to the lance-corporal, who relayed the messages back to headquarters over the radio telephone.

From the telephone set Burns called, "What about the other bloke, they want to know, what's he look like?"

"Civvies, anorak and jeans. Scruffy-looking. I can get him, can't I, Dave? He just shot Downs. Waving a gun about and all that, it's enough." Smith was manoeuvring his rifle into position. The old Lee Enfield with the big telescopic sight, the sniper's weapon.

"I've a good line on him from here. No problem." Smith was talking to himself, whispering into the butt of the rifle. He drew back the bolt action and settled himself. He was a long time aiming, wanting to be certain. The firing echoed around under the roof of the mill.

"Did you get him?" urged Burns from the back of the observation post.

"A real peach."

Harry staggered, and then swayed backward, before thudding against the front wall of a house. His arms were pressed across the middle of his chest. Then he toppled over onto the pavement.

THE SOLDIERS looked over the two bodies, made the decision that they were beyond medical help and left them where they had fallen. Both Billy Downs and Harry were in that awkward, sacklike form that the soldiers recognized as death. Downs lay a few feet from the kerb out in the road. His wife stood now, beside him, with some of the other women of the road who had come to her after Harry was shot. Harry was propped against the wall, his face still showing great astonishment and shock.

Several men had come from the houses and stood in clumps at the doorways, unspeaking, unsmiling, unshocked, leaving the business of comforting and abusing to their women.

In their shawls and head scarfs they shouted at the officer with the platoon. "He's one of yours. That dead one over there."

"He's a rotten Englishman."

"Shot a man without a gun."

"Killed an unarmed man in front of his wife, and he never in trouble before."

The crescendo gathered around the young man. In a few moments his company commander and his battalion commander would be there, and he would be spared, but till then he would take the brunt of their fury. Faced with the accusation that Harry was one of theirs, the soldiers looked curiously at the body of the big man. They knew a certain amount about army undercover operations, but to the men in uniform it was a different and basically distasteful world.

In exasperation the lieutenant shouted above the babble. "Well, if you say the chap who shot Downs is one of ours, who shot him then?" He phrased it clumsily, expecting no answer.

The chorus came back, "The Provos got him. One shot. From the bottom of the street."

The far end of the street was deserted, dominated by the massive wall of the old mill. The lieutenant looked up at the roof, and winced. "Like hell," he said.

"IT'S just as we found it, as you requested," they told Frost when he arrived. "The chap by the wall shoots Downs, and then is shot himself. I'm not a hundred per cent sure where the second shot came from. Indications are that it's the OP, up in the mill roof. But I haven't spoken to my men there yet."

There was no reaction on Frost's face. His eyes travelled around the street, taking in the faces and the scene. He walked from one body to another, his bodyguards hovering at each shoulder. He recognized Harry from the photograph that had been sent the previous night from England. It should never have worked. But it had succeeded, and now right at the end was all loused up. Poor devil.

He paused at Downs's body, looking into the profile of the face and running a mental check against the picture they'd issued. Lucky to have spotted him from that, the colonel thought, not really good enough, something to be learned from that.

"It's not for general release," he said to the local unit commander, "but you'll hear about it soon enough anyway. The Prime Minister ordered a special chap put in with the sole job of finding Danby's killer. Downs was the gunman. By something of a miracle, and a quite unaccountable amount of good luck, the agent tracked him down and shot him dead. That's not a generous assessment, but that's how I evaluate it. I think your OP has just killed the Prime Minister's man."

Frost stopped there, let it sink, then went on: "We'll deflect it as much as we can, but if I were you, I'd leave it to HQ in Lisburn to make the statements. It may be some consolation to you that I was one of the many who didn't know about it either."

The other man considered. There was nothing to say, nothing that would help the prone figure by the wall. Business-like and brisk as always, he said to Frost, "Is there any reason for us not to clean this lot up now? Our photographer has done his stuff."

"No reason at all. Get it out of the way before the press and cameras start showing up."

THE PRESS STATEMENT from Lisburn took something more than two hours to prepare. It was the result of a series of compromises.

> Billy Downs, a known IRA gunman, was shot dead at 0910 hours
> in Ypres Avenue, where he lived. He was involved in an exchange
> of shots with a member of the security forces, an officer engaged in

plainclothes surveillance duties. The officer, who will not be named till his next of kin have been informed, was hit by a single shot in the chest and died before medical treatment reached him. Downs was high on the army's wanted list in Northern Ireland, and was also wanted in London for questioning by detectives investigating the murder of Mr. Henry Danby.

The main thing was to keep it short, pack it with information and deflect the press away from the sensitive bit.

A solitary journalist moved towards the delicate area that first day, but without knowing it, and was easily put off. "Then this man Downs was carrying a gun?" he asked the duty press officer.

"Obviously, old man, it says in our statement that there was an exchange of shots. Have to be armed, wouldn't he?"

There were no other questions to be asked. Among the resident reporters that night, interest was warm but not exceptional, and the treatment of the story was straight and factual.

# 11

The Prime Minister learned the news at lunchtime. As he read the message that the aide gave him, his attentive smile switched to a frown of public concern, studied by the bankers around the table with him at 10 Downing Street. They looked for a clue as to the information that had been important enough to interrupt their discussions on the floating pound, albeit the end of the discussions. The Prime Minister was anxious to satisfy their anticipation.

"Just on a final note, gentlemen." He refolded the typewritten sheet. "You will all be reading it in the papers tomorrow, but you might be interested to hear we have killed the man who assassinated Henry Danby. He was shot in Belfast this morning after being hunted down as part of a special investigation that was launched from this building a few hours after our colleague was murdered."

There was a murmur of applause around the table.

"But you will be sorry to hear, as I am, that the man we sent to find this terrorist was himself killed in the shooting exchange. He'd been operating undercover there for some weeks, and carried out a difficult task extremely successfully. The whole concept of this operation really goes back to the last war—my family was involved in special operations, you know. I had a devil of a job getting the military and police to agree to it. But it just shows, you sometimes need a fresh approach to these things. Perhaps we should get that general over there, who always seems to be wanting more troops, to have a try at banking and running a budget!"

There was general and polite laughter.

Later in the day he called the Under Secretary at the Ministry of Defence to express his appreciation of the way the operation had been handled. "It'll get a good show in the papers, I trust," said the Prime Minister. "We ought to blow our own trumpets a bit."

"I don't think there will be too much of that, sir," the civil servant replied decisively. "The Ministry of Defence have put out a short statement only. I think the feeling is that undercover is bad news in Ulster, and they're playing it rather low key."

"As you like. Though I sometimes feel we don't give ourselves the pat on the back we deserve. One more thing. The man we sent over there, I'd like a medal for him now it's over. What sort of chap was he, by the way?"

"I'll see to that. He already had a Military Cross from Aden. We could make it a bar to that, but perhaps that's a bit on the short side. I personally would favour the OBE. You asked what sort of chap. Pretty straightforward, not too bright. Dedicated, conscientious, and a lot of guts. He was the right man."

The Prime Minister thanked him and rang off. He hurried from his study to the limousine waiting outside the front door of the official residence. He was late for the House.

THE TWO MEMBERS of the army council of the Provisional IRA, the top planning wing of the military side of the movement, who had been asked to report on the practicality and desirability of further assassinations in the political arena, particularly the plan involving the British Prime Minister, delivered their assessment at the first meeting of all members after the Ardoyne shoot-out.

They advised against the continuation of attacks on the style of the Danby assassination. It had, they said, been disastrous for fund-raising in the United States: the picture of Mrs. Danby and her children at the funeral had been flashed across the Atlantic and coast-to-coast by the wire syndication services. The Provisionals' supporters in the States reported that if there were a repeat or a stepping-up of the tactics, the results could prove fatal. And money was always a key factor for the movement.

The chief of staff summed up that in the foreseeable future they would not consider a repetition of the Danby attack, but he finished: "I still defend the attack we carried out against Danby. He was a straight, legitimate target, and it was well carried out. They acknowledge that on their side, too. There's been no trumpeting even though they've shot our lad."

LITTLE OF the credit for the killing of Billy Downs landed on Davidson's desk.

Frost put in a long and detailed complaint about the amount of work the independent, and for so many days unidentified, agent had meant for the security services. He logged the man-hours involved in the search for Harry at the scrap yards, and described them as wasteful and unprofessional.

The Under Secretary at the Ministry of Defence, who had a copy of the document forwarded to him, read it over the phone to Davidson. The response was predictably angry.

"He forgets that our man got the fellow, not all their troops and police and Special Branch," Davidson roared into the receiver. "The fact is we were set a mission, and carried it out, with success. Is that cause for an inquest?"

Davidson had not been told how Harry had died. That was to be kept very close in London. "Need to know" was being applied with rigour. The Under Secretary decided that if the PM wasn't on the list, then Davidson ranked no greater priority.

"Of course the mission was a success, but it's put a great strain on interservice and interdepartment cooperation. The feeling here is that a similar operation would not be mounted again. That means, I regret, that the team we set up to direct our man will have

507

to be dismantled." There was no change in his voice as he delivered the hammer blow. "I did have hopes at one stage that if this went off without a hitch, we might have had something a bit more regular going through Dorking. But that's not to be."

Davidson could recognize the shut-out. The shouting was over. He asked, "And what now? What happens to me?"

"It's recognized here, Davidson, that in fact you did very well on this one, particularly in the preparation of our man. You must not take all that Frost says too seriously. You've a great deal of experience to offer, and the feeling is that there's a good opening abroad for you."

Here it comes, the old payoff, reckoned Davidson. What would they have for him, sewing blankets in the Aleutians?

"I won't beat about the bush. Hong Kong wants a man who can advise them on the posture they should be in. Now don't say anything hasty, the terms are first class. You'd get more than I'm getting. Good allowances, good accommodation, and pretty much of a free hand. Don't give me an answer now, but sleep on it and call me in the morning. Cheers." The conversation was over.

Davidson ranged around the office, fumbling at his papers. He aimed a kick at the desk. It took around an hour to find the will to exert some order to the anger of his feelings. The documents and maps of the operation filled two briefcases, the rest was government property, some other man could clear that up.

He made a call to his wife. Didn't speak much, just said he'd be home early, that he had some news, they would be going out for a meal. Then he locked up. He'd thought about Harry considerably since the shooting, and by the time he had reached his commuter train, his rage had subsided and he brooded in a corner over the evening paper, about the young man who had died in Belfast . . . sent across the water with all that damn-fool optimism coursing through him.

FOR DAYS Mrs. Duncan talked of little more than the strange events that preceded the death of her favourite lodger. That the man who shared her bathroom, her front room and occasionally her kitchen, who had lived in her best back bedroom, should have

508

turned out to be an English agent was rather too much for her to serve out in a single session of conversation. Her neighbours came several times to hear the full saga, culminating in an eyewitness description of the final shoot-out beyond the front garden gate.

She was to remain unaware of her full role in the death of Harry and of Billy Downs. She never discovered that it was her chatter over the back fence about the strange accent of the man who lived under her roof that had started the process that led, nearly directly, to the gunfire in the street. She told those who came to listen that the thing she found the strangest was the authority with which Harry was holding the gun as he shot down Duffryn against the lamp-post. The cold methodical power with which that quiet man executed the youngster had shaken her more than any of the other horrors of five years of living in the Falls.

The army had come midmorning and backed a Saracen right up to the gate. They had searched Harry's room slowly and carefully, and when they left, it was with all Harry's possessions slung together into big plastic bags.

Later that same day Josephine arrived to help with the teas. It was a wasted visit, as the guests had cried off. There were no takers for the lodging used by British intelligence. Instead, Josephine was told the events of the day. She listened without comment, and sat on a straight chair in the kitchen, sipping her tea and smoking a cigarette. She was another who would never learn her full part in the affair. She went home that night believing her information alone had led the Provisionals to Harry. In the months ahead she was to remain at home in the evenings with her mother, shutting out the memories of the few hours she had spent with Harry, of how he had betrayed her, and of how she had betrayed him.

BILLY DOWNS'S funeral was a bigger day than any in his young life. Eight men from Ypres Avenue took the tricolour-draped coffin on their shoulders. Grim, set faces, they marched up the Falls Road at the head of a crowd estimated at around three thousand. Behind them came the display of force, youths and girls in semi-uniform, polished Sam Brownes, shouted commands and tramping of feet.

At the bleak, over-ornate gates of Milltown Cemetery, faces in the crowd were recorded by the Asahi cameras of the military from behind the sandbags on the top of the walls of the Andersonstown bus station. Inside the cemetery the chief of staff of the movement, who arrived and departed unseen by those who were hunting him, delivered the graveside oration. They played "The Last Post" while small children in their best clothes skipped among the stones that marked the last resting place of other heroes of the cause.

With the passing of weeks and months, the adulation and estimation in which Billy Downs was held increased. They named a club after him and wove his picture into a big, wide banner that could be carried high in the marches the Provisionals organized.

The songs followed, sung with the nasal lament in the bars of Andersonstown and Ardoyne. They helped to cement the legend that in Ulster solidifies so quickly. The brave soldier had been gunned down by the British killer squads while his woman and bairns were around him.

His wife lived on in Ypres Avenue. She was asked several times to take part in anniversary marches organized by various factions of the Republican movement, but always declined. The invitations would eventually dry up, and with them the weekly cash supplied by the Provisionals. New horrors would overtake the Ardoyne community, and soon she would no longer be pointed out, stared at.

THEY BURIED Harry Brown in a village close to where his wife's parents lived. By army standards it was a conventional funeral. An honour party, a staccato volley over the grave, a short address from an army chaplain. In the event, it was not much different from the funeral accorded to Billy Downs. Smaller, less stylized, less sentimental, but with all the same ingredients. There were few civilians present, mostly soldiers in uniform, and upright as the bugler played the same final haunting farewell.

There was a wreath from the Prime Minister, and Davidson was there. He was one of the few not in khaki. He didn't introduce himself to Harry's widow, and stayed very much at the back, unknown to the family and to the brother officers who had come over from Germany. When he left the graveside, it was to complete his arrangements for the transfer on loan to Hong Kong authorities.

## Gerald Seymour
### by Stuart Wavell

"I wanted to belt people with a sledge-hammer and say the problem hasn't gone away, you can't ignore it."

Gerald Seymour has the build to do a bit of damage, but the intense face—so well-known on television—beams when he talks about the literary form his sledgehammer finally took. *Harry's Game* has highlighted the Northern Ireland problem with devastating effect.

His achievement is especially remarkable in that this is the first piece of fiction he has written since his schooldays. (He received the highest mark ever given for an A-level essay, which he presented as a short story.) Yet, from the time he went to university, the closest he came to serious writing was scribbling TV commentaries in the backs of cars.

His parentage explains a lot, however. His father, William Kean Seymour, was a distinguished poet and novelist and his mother, Rosalind Wade, is the author of more than thirty novels. Furthermore, he himself has become something of an expert on terrorism and insurgency. He got off to a dramatic start at ITN with his coverage of The Great Train Robbery—just eight days after joining as a graduate trainee. There followed five weeks in Cyprus, a year in Singapore covering Vietnam and the Pakistan-India war, then Aden.

He spotted Harry Brown there in 1967 and filed him away. "We were in a sandbagged place on top of a hill. One of the squaddies pointed down to a chap in Arab clothes who was hammering packing boards into the shape of a little hut on the edge of a shanty town. He said, 'You see that guy? He's SAS.' I wished I hadn't been told. I was afraid I might get terribly drunk one night and repeat it in a loud voice."

He has been out in Northern Ireland since the violence flared in 1969, and was there on Bloody Sunday. "You're dealing with a different sort of person now," he says, "younger and harder. It is something the English don't comprehend."

After *Harry's Game*, they might.